Nicole James

Nicole Jacquelyn

L. Wilder

Avelyn Paige

Peace,
Bink

XO
Sapphire
Knight

Mary Martel

Enjoy the ride!
♥ Chelsea
Camaron

Maria Lisa
♥ de Mora

Nina
Levine
xx

XOXO
Laramie
Briscoe

Ryan
Michele

Love, Loyalty and MAYHEM MC

AN ANTHOLOGY

Sicko by Amo Jones
Swagger & Sass by USA Today Best Selling Author Autumn Jones Lake
Voodoo Vows by International Best Selling Author Avelyn Paige
The Arrangement by Bink Cummings
Breathe for It by USA Today Best Selling Author Chelsea Camaron
Snow White & The Biker by Glenna Maynard
Unkillable by Kristen Hope Mazzola
Gus by New York Times Best Selling Author L. Wilder
At Your Service by USA Today Best Selling Author Laramie Briscoe
Ride Deep by New York Times Best Selling Author Laura Kaye
Creed & Mia by USA Today Best Selling Author M. Robinson
No Man's Land by MariaLisa deMora
Killing Time by Mary Martel
Mama by Nicole Jacquelyn
My Brother's Old Lady by Nicole James
Heart & Soul by USA Today Best Selling Author Nina Levine
Bound by Chance by Ryan Michele
Blaze by International Best Selling Author Sapphire Knight
Prelude to Salvation by USA Today Best Selling Author Terri Anne Browning
Forever Lo by USA Today Best Selling Author Winter Travers

1st Edition; July 16, 2019

IBSN: 9780998128061

PROLOGUE

Dear Readers,

Thank you for purchasing Love, Loyalty and Mayhem. We are so appreciative for your support. All proceeds from LLMA will be going to Bikers Against Bullies USA.

Who are they? (From their website)

We Fight Bullying in Communities Across the Nation

Who we are: Bikers Against Bullies USA (BAB USA) is a national not-for-profit organization created by bikers to raise awareness and empower the community to fight the terrible effects of bullying on young people through education, community outreach and fundraising.

Mission Statement: BAB USA is a not-for-profit group created by bikers -- but not limited to bikers -- that is committed to creating awareness and educating both children and adults on the benefits of living in a society of respect for each other combined with self empowerment. We strive to create a society in which our mutual respect will create a new role model for others, and through our actions enable others to have the confidence to emulate this behavior and reiterate its positive message to others.

Our children deserve to be safe, to be empowered and to live their lives without fear.

100% of funds raised by **BAB USA** at any event are be used to fund child-oriented charities.

https://www.bikersagainstbulliesusa.com/

SICKO BY AMO JONES

PROLOGUE

He was my foster brother.

He swore to protect me.

He failed.

They all failed.

I'm an open box of passé photographs, snapped in chaste daylight, but filtered in sepia. I'm the past that he tried to forget, and he was the future I needed. When he left six years ago, I screamed for him every night. But then it all stopped. My screams were suddenly muffled by cruelty, and further coaxed by pain.

But he has come back. He's not the cute big brother I had a furtive crush on, or the bad boy, rich brat that I hated to love.

He's the ruthless vice president of Wolf Pack MC, and he doesn't answer to Royce Kane anymore.

He answers to Sicko.

CHAPTER 1

THEY SAY IF YOU STRUGGLE TO SLEEP AT NIGHT, THAT SOMEONE IS THINKING OF you. Like an anchor, tugging on your soul to keep it in this world, as opposed to losing yourself in (basically), purgatory. Isn't that what a dream state is? Purgatory for your head and the messed-up shit that happens inside of it? The place your demons meet with your sanity, and they fight about who will win. Will it be your nightmares or the actuality of peace? I like to think of my life as purgatory, where every day I struggle with both sides. The good, the bad, and the demons I can't get rid of. Unfortunately.

Sloan, my best-friend of too many years, drops down on the chair opposite me at our favorite coffee shop in the heart of San Francisco, right near The Market. After graduating high school a few weeks ago, it's safe to say that we're both hanging on the edge of our seat to start college.

For Sloan, it's to get out of San Francisco.

For me, it's to escape my house.

"Are we going out this weekend?" Sloan asks, hiding her beautiful face behind a curtain of red hair. "You know, one last hurrah before we have plenty more hurrahs." Her logic doesn't make sense since we already spend a lot of time partying. Sloan was the most popular girl at Edgewood Academy. I did okay, but half of the reason why was because she was my best friend, and the other half, was, well—him.

"Yes," I answer quickly. "I need a distraction this weekend." It's Friday night, and that's not the reason why I need a distraction. It's the date that this Friday is. That today is.

Her hand comes to mine. "I'm sorry. How long has it been now?" The waiter comes to our table.

"Six years," I murmur, my eyes going to the waiter. "Can I get a caramel latte, please."

Sloan orders hers before looking back at me. "Shall we change the subject?"

I nod. "Yes. About this weekend..."

Sloan starts yapping off about what she wants us to do and how we should go about it. I'm not surprised to hear that Matty, one of our close friends, was having a party. He's the son of the senator, and a royal pain in my ass at times. We continue through our plans as I sip on two lattes, a bowl of chili fries, and a chocolate cake. When it's time for both of us to head home, I kiss her goodbye and make my way out to my car.

I pull my little BMW hatchback up the driveway of my home. *Home.* The large white pillars hold the old school plantation mansion up delicately. The manicured grass springs up to life and the scatter of vibrant flowers give the otherwise plain style multi-million-dollar property life.

I sigh, reaching for my handbag and crawling out of my car. I can't wait to not be here. *Here.*

"Jade? Is that you?" Mom asks as I slam the front door closed. I was hoping to slip in discretely, but I'm shit out of luck.

I drop my bags near the front door, removing my scarf.

When I amble into the kitchen, I catch mom with wooden spoon in her fragile hand, stirring through a couple of large bowls. Her blonde hair is cut razor sharp and hanging around her jaw. "Will you be home for dinner tonight?"

"Um." My eyes fall to my toes. Bright blue nails. I like blue, it reminds me of the ocean. Of tranquility and the sound of angry waves crashing against the acquiescent damp sand. "I guess."

The Kanes. I was adopted into this family with open arms. For the most part, it was always okay. Great, actually. They had money. They offered me a warm home and food in my hungry belly. I counted myself lucky. I was well cultured on how adverse some foster children had it. *Should we really compare our lives to the unfortunate occurrences of others? Has the human race really hit rock bottom?*

"Great!" Mom interrupts my coiled thoughts, smiling at me. "Because Royce will be home tonight for the weekend."

I freeze, my hands stilling over my water bottle. *She didn't just say what you thought she did, Jade. Your brain is in purgatory again.* "What?" My tone is loud, the syllables sharp enough to slice whoever says *that* name again. I shake off my instant thoughts and bring my eyes back to hers. "He's coming home?!" I swallow long gulps of water to stop from my panic illustrating over my face. *No. No. No.*

"It's his birthday, Jade. I thought you would remember. He's your brother. Yes, he's coming home. I'm just" —tears fall down her cheeks— "so happy, Jade. I thought. He was gone."

So did I. My brother who left me. *He fucking left me.* Abandoned me just like everyone else. *He was no better.* I squash the memories that begin to rise to the surface of my brain. I'm not feeling very nostalgic.

"I haven't seen him in so long," is all I manage to say, unable to process what's happening right now.

Mom nods her head, going back to stirring. Cake. Vanilla, no doubt. Royce's favorite. "I know. It's been six years, so we want to welcome him home with open arms. God, Jade." She turns to face me, tears filling her eyes. "I'm so happy that he's coming home."

I want to be happy too, if he wasn't such a piece of shit for leaving. I was six years old when I was fostered into the Kane family. They took me in as their own, and even Royce pulled me in and treated me like I was his real-life sibling. He was my everything. Being five years older than me, I already looked up to him like a god. He took care of me every single day that I was in this house. When he got his license and Mom bought him his first car—a fucking GTO—I rolled to school with him. He was the most popular guy in school. Every boy worshipped him, and every girl wanted him. I didn't do either of those things. I just needed him. But he left me. Alone. In this house. I hate him.

I drag my sad mood back upstairs, wishing I could fast forward this day. Or rewind back to when I was born and just *not* be born.

As soon as I reach my bedroom door, I swing it open and fall onto my bed. The feathers inside my blanket curve around my petite body as my long brown hair sprawls out around my head. *I'm going to see Royce tonight.* I don't want to see Royce tonight. I wanted him for so long, cried for him every night until the tears stung the corners of my eyes and my lips cracked from dehydration. Now that I know he's coming home tonight, I don't want him. I'm angry at him. It's like all those six years did nothing to ease my anger. Time only bathed it, kept it under control.

I sigh, pulling out my phone and flicking through my playlist. I hit an old school Guns and Roses song and slip into my bathroom, needing to scrub the day away from my skin.

Black. It's my favorite color. Not because it's slimming—I don't need to look slimmer. But because it's the color you can wear when you don't need to put in any effort at all. Like right now. I don't want to put in any effort even though mom will no doubt be wearing Prada. The prodigal son returns. I squeeze on a pair of tight black skinny jeans and a black shirt. It's thin straps cling to my frail collarbones. I always wear makeup. I love everything about makeup and how you can artfully apply it to pull off a different look. But tonight, I only rub on some CC cream and light mascara, piling my long hair into a high ponytail. I just want this over with.

My phone starts vibrating on my bedside table and I pick it up, answering. "What's up?"

"Okay, I need to ask you a question..." Sloan purrs.

I hesitate. "Sure?"

"What happened between you and Matty?"

I still, my eyebrows furrowing. Matty and I were nothing, but I also know that Sloan has been pining after him since around when Royce left. Matty is also attending UCLA with us, so it's no surprise that she's still asking about him. "Nothing that you're thinking of. Why?" Fresh out of high school, about to move to LA, and she's still asking about Matty. "If you want him, he's yours. Honestly, we didn't go far..."

Sloan sighs. "Okay. I guess. It's just we all know he has always had a crush on you."

I roll my eyes, leaning my phone on my shoulder.

She continues. "Wanna go get loaded fries?"

"Um, I sort of can't." I catch my movement in the mirror, realization once again crashing into me like a cold bucket of water.

"Why?"

I hear the deep growl of a loud engine—*is that a fucking motorbike?* "Will talk later." The rumble is low, reverberating around my room like a pounding symphony.

"Jade!" my mom yells out from the kitchen. "Downstairs."

I quickly shove on my Ugg boots and give myself one more once over before pushing my phone into my back pocket and making my way downstairs. I can see a gathering around the front door as I come down, but I don't look up until the last minute.

"Sorry I'm—" I pause.

There, standing in front of me, is Royce Kane.

When my eyes meet his, my heart slows in my chest. The hate is still there, the anger and pain, but now there's something else happening. Something I'm not ready to acknowledge yet. His ice blue eyes. Colder than the Atlantic Ocean, but hotter than the pits of Hell. His dark unruly hair looks like his hands have brushed through it one too many times, and his big, lean body towers over everyone in the room—including the room itself. He has tattoos all over what skin I can see. Royce Kane doesn't just look like a bad boy. Royce Kane looks like a bad man... he's not the spoiled rich boy, playing every girl at school. He's—different. His sharp jaw is clean shaven, illustrating every cut line of his perfectly constructed face. His straight nose and soft plump lips. Shit. Double fucking shit. He's even fucking hotter than he was when he was young.

He's in loose faded jeans, military boots, and a black shirt. But there's something over top of his shirt that catches my eye. Well, two things actually…

The embroidered patch that's sewn into his left pec. *Wolf Pack MC Motorcycle Club.*

And second, I'm pretty sure, Royce Kane hates me.

My eyes glass over, before going back to his. This time his scowl is matched with a dark grin that spreads over his swollen lips. "Well, didn't you grow up…"

CHAPTER 2

ROYCE

I'M NOT GONNA LIE, SEEING HER SQUIRM UNDER MY PRESENCE IS SOMEWHAT fascinating. She was my fucking world the day she walked her sad, little soul into our house. I mean, I wanted a brother, but Jade wasn't half as bad as what I thought having a little sister would be like. She hated Barbie dolls and preferred Transformer trucks. Not much else I could complain about.

"Monkey," I smirk, throwing out her nickname. I was almost certain I loved the little shit when she was growing up. Now I can't. I won't.

She flinches. I didn't miss the scan she did as soon as her pretty little eyes landed on me. Then I watched as the blood drained from her face when she read my patch on my left pec.

"Great!" Mom says, clapping her hands. "Dinner is ready. Royce, please tell me you haven't joined a motorcycle gang..."

I follow behind her as my father hushes her already smart mouth and Jade steps slightly behind me.

When our parents are out of earshot, I grin, turning my head slightly. "What's the matter, Monkey, didn't miss me?"

Her eyes come to mine, and I see the defiance that flashes over them briefly before it's gone. "Never."

I chuckle, turning to face her. Just before we turn into the kitchen, I slam my hands against the wall, caging her in. I run the tip of my nose over her cheek and inhale her sweet, innocent flesh. She's like a breath of fresh air after being face down in club girl pussy. Only her air is fucking laced with poison. "You should be scared, Monkey. You're not safe from me anymore." My eyes drop down her little body, taking in the soft curves that stretch out over her otherwise delicate stature.

"You two!" Dad calls from the dining room. "What's taking so long?"

Tense bastard.

I let her go, knowing full well no one can see us. Fucking hate my rich ass parents and their rich ass house.

"You might be right, Royce." She squares her shoulders and looks me deep in the eye. "But I'm not the same girl you left behind. I have teeth now." Then she shoves past me.

Before I can grab her and slam her little ass back up against the wall, my phone vibrates in my pocket. I don't bother to tell the old man that I'll be in in a second, because he knows I'll be in in a second.

"What?"

"Ah," Phat mutters. "Did I catch you at a bad time?" There's shuffling in the background. "Sorry, Sicko, it's just Lion told me that I can call you about—" Phat, our new prospect, stammers on the other side of the phone.

I attempt to count to fucking ten, because my therapist says it'll help. My therapist also calls me daddy and lets me fuck her over her counter every Friday night before her after-work drinks.

"What is it?" I snap. "You know I'm away, so this better be a fucking emergency."

"Oh, it is. Sorry."

"Stop saying fucking sorry."

"Oh, right, ah, so, Arrow has been shot and we're wondering what we should do."

My jaw tenses. "Is it a fatal wound?"

There's more shuffling and then Lion's old ass voice comes through. Lion is our club president. How he got that name is a long fucking sorry, Mine is Sicko, and that's also… a long fucking story.

"Can always count on my VP to put the fear of God into the prospects," Lion chuckles down the phone.

"Maybe we need to reevaluate who we are letting drag their feet through our clubhouse then."

"I think Phat is a good one. You've just got to be nice."

"I'm never nice. You know this."

He chuckles again, and I can just imagine the cigar hanging from between his lips.

"Is it fatal?" I ask again, sighing.

"It's not. How are the parents?"

"Same, same. I'll be back tomorrow morning." I hang up my phone and make my way back into the kitchen, pulling out a chair opposite Jade.

Her eyes cut to mine, but she picks up her glass of water and empties it in one go.

"Son, how have you been?" my father asks beside me, cutting into his steak. We lose ourselves in conversation about normal ass shit that I used to be into. I feel bad, I fucking do. I felt bad the day I walked away from them both with the intention of never returning. That boy with an attitude problem was rather fucking dramatic. But until recently, I've found myself having to drag my ass back to this house for the very reason I fucking left.

Her.

"Royce," my mom mutters, patting her mouth after her meal and placing it daintily onto the table. "Please tell me you haven't joined a motorcycle club."

Dad silences beside me.

My eyes find Jade, who isn't watching me smugly, she's more bored. She doesn't want to be here anymore than I do.

"I have. Been there for six years now, Ma."

"Where is there, and why, Royce?"

I toss my napkin onto my plate. "LA. Not too far from you." My eyes cut to Jade's. "But far enough."

"Aren't you going to say something, Jade?" My mother grasps at Jade. "You two were always so close…"

Jade chokes on her water. It was no secret how close Jade and I were. Everyone called Jade my pet. She was always hanging off my arm, wanting to do everything with me and the boys, and she was the only one who was allowed. Pissed a lot of bitches off, the fact that they couldn't ride with us, but my little foster sister could, but they dealt with it. Jade would make my birthday cakes every year too, her and Mom in the kitchen getting messy while Dad was always late home from work.

"I have nothing to say," Jade mutters. "Actually, can I be excused?" Mom flicks her wrist, agreeing and Jade shuffles out of the dining room, my eyes never straying from her. When she jogs up the stairs, I watch as her ass bounces with each step.

I bite my lip and grin.

"Travis?" My mom points at my old man.

He looks at me and I look at him and all of that awkward bullshit that happens anytime someone is in trouble.

"Mom? I'm twenty-fucking-three years old. I don't need you stressing. I survived on my own, with my brothers, for six years."

"That's beyond the point, Royce! I thought you were dead in a ditch somewhere in Mission District! You have—" Her tears start coming and it's the first time I look at her. Really fucking look at her. She's aged drastically since I left. Wearing her hair short, wrapped around her jaw. Wrinkles line the curves around her eyes, but we all know she gets injections on her forehead.

"Sorry, Ma...wasn't the plan."

"So what happened?" Mom asks, finally bringing her eyes to me.

"I can't talk about that with you."

She sighs, standing and clearing the table. "Well, I hope you at least visit more often."

I stand with her, my eyes going to my old man who is watching me carefully. "Been a very empty house without you, boy..." Dad, on the other hand, looks good for his age. But then, he always fucking did.

I punch his arm. "How much are you benching?"

He shakes his head and laughs. "More than you." I go into the kitchen and help Mom with the dishes.

"Where's Louise?" I ask, wondering where the maid is. She always walked her old ass around our house doing all the shit my mom was supposed to be doing instead of shopping with her friends.

Mom sighs, putting dish after dish into the washer. "I let her go not long after you left. I didn't want to make the same mistakes I did with you with Jade too."

Her eyes go out to the front of the house where the garage is built to the side. "She kept your car, you know?" Mom whispers. "She screamed for you every night for the first year, waking up in a sweat. Then it just stopped. Like she gave up."

My lips pinch together. Wish I could say I gave a fuck, but I didn't. I felt for the young Monkey, not the one that's sitting her pert little ass upstairs now.

"Yeah, well, shit changed..."

Mom brings her hands up to my cheeks. "Don't be a stranger. That's an order."

"Sure thing, Ma."

After helping Mom clean up, I say goodbye to them both and then head out to my bike. Swinging my leg over my Dyna Glide, I kick start her to life and listen as she rumbles underneath me. Putting a cigarette into my mouth, Jade's bedroom light catches the corner of my eye. The only light that's on, on that level. I blow out a cloud of smoke.

One day soon, your ass will be sitting in my clubhouse, and it won't be by choice.

CHAPTER 3

JADE

"Hurry up, Monkey. Get in the car or you're going to be late," Royce yells from inside his flashy, loud car.

I quickly butter my toast and slap some jelly on top, biting down and rushing out. I slam the front door closed and take the steps down fast.

"Aye, aye, aye! You know the rules!" He points to my toast.

"I'm hungry!" I whine.

Royce rolls his eyes. "Just this once." It's just this once every morning, but that's just Royce. He pulls out of the driveway, turning the music up. I dance in my seat when we start driving down the street I recognize as Bethany's. Bethany, as in Royce's bitchy girlfriend who secretly hates me.

I go to take my seat belt off to get in the back, but Royce stops me, hitting the music down and parking up the curb of her driveway. "Hell naw, Monkey sits shotgun."

And she's about to hate me even more.

I smile at him and we wait for Bethany to come out. When she finally walks her long, skinny legs down, her eyes cut to me and turn to slits. Great.

"I'll drop you off and pick you up from school at the same time."

"Where are you going?" I ask, batting my lashes at him.

"Nowhere for you to worry about."

Bethany slides into the backseat. "Morning! Morning, Jade!" She's so fucking fake.

I smile at her as Royce drives me to school. He pulls up, opens my door and kisses me on top of my head. "Have a good day, Monkey. See you later."

I didn't see him later. I watched as his car disappeared down the road and went about my day. It wasn't until later that night when I finally got home when my mom was crying and my dad was seething, pacing back and forth in the living room. I suspected he blamed me for Royce leaving.

One year after that day, it was proven I was right.

"Are you happy we're done?" Sloan mutters, pushing her sunglasses over her eyes as she floats on top of the water, courtesy of our inflatable unicorn. We had plans to go out tonight, but I squashed them after Royce's appearance. He has thrown me off balance.

"Of school? It's been almost three months." I kick my legs into the water to get farther away from the edge. "But yes."

She removes her glasses, her eyes coming up to the big house behind me. "This place gives me the creeps."

I shrug. "You're not alone. Shall we go get food? I just can't wait to get the fuck to college."

"I seriously just can't wait to get the fuck out of San Francisco."

I laugh, squirting her with water. "It's not that bad..."

But she's right. I can't wait either.

CHAPTER 4

JADE

"Come on, Jade!" my mom yells from downstairs. "We're going to be late if we don't get on the road right now. It's a long drive."

Why. Why did my mom want to drive to UCLA instead of put me on a plane? Why must she be so difficult.

"Coming!" I holler, throwing my backpack over my shoulder. I take one last look around my bedroom. The dark purple walls faded somewhat, and the bed unmade. I won't miss it at all.

I open my car door and glare at her. "You do know I'm totally capable of driving myself? It's why you bought me the car…"

She waves me off, putting her seatbelt on in the passenger seat. "Nonsense. I get to fly home. It works perfectly."

The drive was long. So freaking long we ended up stopping for a night to break the trip in half. There was a pile-up on the highway which only delayed our time even more, but it's Sunday and I am here.

I slam the door closed and smile at Mom.

"I'm so proud of you, sweetheart," she whispers, her eyes never falling from mine. I love my mom. She's everything everyone would ever ask for in one, but she isn't perfect. No parent is, only mine failed me a little harder.

"Thanks, Mom. I wa—"

I hear a loud rumble of bikes behind me, but I don't turn. There's no point. It won't be him and bikers obviously go to college too.

The bikes pull up right beside my car and my mom's face pales before she grins.

"Royce?"

My mouth snaps closed, still refusing to turn and face the music.

"I wasn't expecting you—all of you..."

"Hey, Ma, thought I'd come see my little sister off on her first day. You know, catching up on those years..."

I finally turn to face him, but I'm momentarily thrown by how many bikers there are behind him, as well as an older man on the bike beside him. They're all wearing the same leather cuts.

"Thanks, Royce, but it really wasn't needed..."

Royce grins, putting a smoke into his mouth, his head tilting to the side as he watches people pile into the school. "Naw, Monkey, it *really* was..."

I sigh, because I truthfully can't be fucked arguing with him right now. "Well, thanks..." My eyes flick to all the guys. "You can leave now."

He removes his helmet, dropping his cigarette to the ground and putting it out. "I'm walking you up."

"Royce," Mom says. "A word?"

"Not right now, Ma. I told you that I'll come see you next weekend. I'm just here to make sure Jade gets settled in."

I lick my lips, rolling my eyes. "Fine." I throw my backpack into his chest. "You can carry this."

After we grab my dorm details from the snobby girl in the main foyer, we make our way up the stairs and until we find my room. Royce's friends obviously all wanted to stay downstairs. Bar one. His name is Gypsy and he has to be around the same age as me, or in between me and Royce. After his obvious perving of every girl, it was made clear exactly why he was here.

"Sicko, your sister is cute."

I turn to face them both, my eyes cutting to Gypsy. Just when I'm about to cuss him out and tell him to go fuck himself, I look at him for the first time today. Young, light brown floppy hair, and a cheeky smile. He's the boy next door in a leather motorcycle vest. I can imagine he would *get* more attention than he would *give*.

"Thanks," I grumble, turning back to my door and pushing my key in.

"We made sure that you have your own room..." Mom says, pointing to the double bed.

"How?" I ask, surprised.

Mom shrugs. "Your father made sure."

My heart sinks. "Oh."

"Hey," Royce's hand comes to my chin, tilting my face up to his. "I'll come check on you every weekend."

"Royce?" I murmur, even though his grip is so tight it's making my lips push out.

"What?" he asks, his eyes searching mine.

"Really not necessary. I have Sloan here too, and Matty. I don't need you petting me here like you did at home."

He laughs, stepping away and winking. "You ain't seen nothing yet."

Then his eyes go to Mom. "I'll look after her."

Mom nods, pulling me in for one last hug. "Okay. I better head to the airport. I planned to spend the day with you but all that traffic delaying us."

"It's okay, Mom. I love you," I whisper, squeezing her roughly.

"Love you too."

When I told my parents that I'd be studying political science, I half expected them to doubt me. A lot. But they didn't. I have always wanted to be involved in politics, while not being in the front of the show. More behind the scenes, organizing everything and making sure people are doing as they're told. Political consultation is where I'd like to be, so today is day one of a very long road ahead.

Mom leaves and I'm in the room alone with Royce and Gypsy.

"Roy, I'm serious. You don't need to be here."

He flops down onto my bed, leaning back onto his elbows. "Ah, but I do."

"Why?" I ask, opening box one of six. "Why do you care?"

He seems to think over my words, his eyes scanning me up and down. "Because you're in my city now, so it's only fair. But here's the deal…"

I laugh. "I'm not making a deal with you, Royce."

"Oh, you will…" he smirks. "So here's the deal. I'll let you party with Sloan but not Mathew. If you don't oblige, I'll drag you to the clubhouse and cage you."

I freeze. "Clubhouse, you mean…"

My lack of education in the biker category obviously makes him happy, because his smirk deepens as he jack-knifes up from the bed. "Think you know what that means. Another thing. You are not—" he pauses, moving his face in front of mine when I get distracted from unpacking. "—Under any circumstances to put that tight little ass on another man's bike."

"Fine," I give up, tossing my makeup bag onto my bed. "Is that all? Because I'd really like to relax and unpack." He can't tell me who to hang out with. He won't know and right now, I'm too tired to argue about Matty.

"No." He snatches my phone from my bed and punches in his number. "That's my number." He drops it back onto the bed. "Use it." Then he walks out like a fucking earthquake, leaving rubble in its wake.

I won't be using his number.

It took me a couple hours to settle into my room before I got batshit bored and called Sloan.

"Hey!" she breathes into the phone. "Are you here? Matty doesn't arrive until next week and I'm bored!"

"Yes!" I give her my dorm details and then wait for her to come up. I still haven't told her about Royce. I don't really want to. One, because she had a massive crush on him when we were kids and two, I don't know what it is that Royce is actually doing back in my life. It's almost too good to be true. I can't trust him the way I used to. He's not the same boy anymore. Now, he feels calculated. Like a snake in the grass, waiting to take his bite, only there's no fucking antidote.

There's a knock on the door, pulling me out of my Royce induced thoughts and I swing it open to Sloan and another girl. She has dark hair and slanted eyes, I'm guessing some sort of Chinese background. But I could be wrong, so I won't make that assumption out loud.

"Yay!" Sloan pulls me in for a hug. I let her, even though she and I both know how much I hate my personal bubble being violated. "Wow, your dorm is so much nicer than mine!"

"Yeah, I wish I had a bunk buddy though."

"Speaking of," Sloan announces, gesturing to the girl beside her. "This is mine! Jade, this is Nellie, Nellie, this is Jade."

Nellie nudges her head at me. I take in her appearance. Bright purple hair on the ends of dark roots and a very eccentric style of dress. Striped thigh-high socks, short leather miniskirt, and a strapless top, squashing her tits to the high heavens.

"Hi..."

"So," Sloan slumps onto my bed. "How did the drive with your mom go?"

"Ah," I answer. "Fine, but then Royce showed up and it—"

"—Wait!" Sloan stands abruptly from my bed. "Royce is back?"

"Who's Royce?" Nellie asks from behind me.

"Um," I answer her quickly, but before I can get a word in, Sloan has her palms pressed to my cheeks, yanking my attention back to her.

"Tell me everything."

I whack her hand away. "Nothing to tell. He came home last weekend for his birthday and told us that he had been with a motorcycle club for the past six years."

"Oh my god..." Sloan drools, her mouth wide open. "Is he hotter than he was when we were younger?"

"What? I'm not answering that. He's my *brother.*"

"—*Foster* brother."

"Sounds like I need to meet him," Nellie smirks, sitting on my bed. I don't mention that I barely know her and that she most definitely should not be sitting on my bed, but I want to. "What club is he with?" Nellie further asks.

"What? Ah, I don't remember." Because I don't, and also, I don't want to tell them any more than I already have. Not that I care if they find him hot, just that I don't want to be talking about him right now.

"Can we change the subject?" I mutter, piling my long hair up into a high ponytail. "Like food. Where can we get food?"

We find a small diner off campus. It's the typical greasy-spoon diner, with gloss red leather seats, checked floors and tired waiters. I slip into the booth and scan over the menu.

"So what else has Royce been doing?" Sloan asks. I ignore her. I can't do the song and dance to Royce's tune today—or ever. When the waiter comes to our table, I smile up to her, thankful for the distraction. "I'll have the double cheeseburger with extra bacon, please."

"Fine," Sloan groans. "But we are going out this weekend. Right, Nellie?"

Nellie nods. "Yep. There's a spot I go to every weekend. We'll pick Jade up."

I dive into my burger, ignoring their talks of what boys is what in the school. To say that I'm not interested is probably an understatement. My sex life isn't one worth mentioning, so I zone out and dig into my fries.

"Do you know where your classes are on Monday, Jade?" Nellie asks around her straw.

"I think so," I pop another fry in my mouth. Out of the corner of my eye, I see the door open, but I don't pay it any attention. "I mean, I have the school map and all of my class numbers, so I'm guessing they won't be hard to find."

I look to Sloan, whose eyes are over Nellie's shoulder and on the new group who just sauntered in. I lean over to see who she is looking at.

"Sloan…" I nudge her. My friend is blatant when it comes to what she wants. The entire back section of the diner is now occupied with red and grey varsity jackets. Of course Sloan would sniff out the school's football team like a dog in heat.

"Yes?" She bats her eyelashes at me, and when I look back at the group, I find a couple of them already watching us. Well, probably Sloan more than me. She's the beautiful red-haired bombshell with great tits, and I'm the basic brunette with great tits.

Chuckling, I shake my head. "You are terrible." I lazily scan the group, when one guy catches my eye who is watching me carefully. His scruffy blond hair looks like ash has been smudged into it and his dark eyes tug me in. He has tanned skin, broad shoulders and the face structure of a GQ model.

He's really, really attractive. No, actually, he's hot as fucking sin, and I'd gladly kneel at church on Sunday for devouring that.

"—Jade!" Now it's Sloan's turn to demand my attention.

"Hmm?" Sloan looks between me and the guy, and then smirks.

"Ah, I see. Well, don't stop your eye fuck on my account..."

Nellie looks over her shoulder, finally figuring out what we're staring at. I notice she visibly stills, her face falling before she turns back to face me. "I wouldn't even try."

"Wasn't going to."

Finishing up with our food, we all stand and make our way to the door. The whole time, (all of a few steps), I can feel eyes on us. It's Sloan. She does this and it drives me fucking insane. I hate going anywhere with her. Like a magnet, I turn toward them in passing, but my eyes find Ash Blond again and my heart speeds up in my chest. No smile, no frown, he's simply observing me. I don't know if it's intimidating or turning me on, I settle for the first because there's no way he could be turning me on. The cold air hits across my face as we reach outside, treading down the stairs and making our way to Nellie's beat up Honda. It's a small little hatchback that looks like maybe fourteen years ago, it would have been worth something. I said to take my car, but Nellie insisted on hers.

"So my mom and dad are one of those gross parents who have been together for like, way too long..." Nellie murmurs. "It's actually so disturbing because they still make-out at breakfast."

"Le sigh..." Sloan murmurs, pulling open the passenger door and pushing the seat forward for me to slip into the back. "I want that one day."

"Well," Nellie mutters, clipping her belt on and starting the car—after a misfire. "You won't get that from any of the guys in there..."

"You don't like them much, huh?" I ask. I meant it as a joke, but as soon as it leaves my mouth, I feel the snark in my tone.

"No," Nellie confirms, taking us onto the highway. "I don't."

Maybe I'll ask her another time why.

Sunday, I spend the day gathering all of my books that I'll need for Monday, which includes but is not limited to meal prepping. I love a good takeout, or munch sessions with potato chips and chocolate, but my body can only survive on meat, vegetables, and carbs. Yes, I said carbs. Carbs are life and give me life. I'm climbing into bed at the end of the day when my phone lights up on the bedside table. I reach for it aimlessly, knowing it will be Sloan. She's probably drunk.

"Hello?"

"Jade..."

Dread fills my body. "Yes, sir?"

"...I need you. Meet me downstairs now."

"Sir, I can't. I ha—"

"—Now."

"Okay," I whisper, my voice dropping to a deathly level. I clutch the phone to my chest and lay there for a few seconds. I don't want to do this. *I thought I would be free.* Free to live my life. How stupid could I be? He's always made it very clear that I never will be free. I'll always be indebted to him and I'll always have to make myself available to him.

I fling the blanket off my body and tiptoe around my room like I would at home. I'm frightened that he can hear me, because knowing he's right downstairs awaiting in his fancy Porsche is enough to put fear into me. I quickly slip on some tight sweatpants and tank before throwing on a hoodie and zipping up.

Breathe in, and out. *You've done this thousands of times, Jade. Pull it together.* I push my phone and dorm key into my pocket and make my way downstairs. I didn't want to start my college year like this. I didn't.

It takes me one second to find his car idling near the curb. I walk straight for it and open the passenger door before sliding into the soft, warm leather. "Hello, sir."

"Jade," Travis growls, turning to face me.

I lick my lips. "I wasn't expecting you here. Mom said that you had business to attend..."

His hand comes to my cheek, his thumb caressing across my lip where he tugs on it gently. "I was. But now I'm here. I can't have my big girl start her college year without a big bang."

I clear my throat but vomit almost surfaces, so I swallow down roughly. I'm used to this. It has happened to me every single day twelve months after Royce left me. I figured he started it because he was angry with me. He blamed me for Royce leaving. But somewhere in those six years, it shifted. It turned into something more without being more on my part. I got used to it. The first time it happened, he snuck into my room. I remember the time because my clock flashed brightly on my bedside table. 3:05am. I hate 3:05am now. He didn't speak at first. His hand caressed my thigh from beneath my covers, his cold Rolex watch igniting goosebumps all over my flesh. He fucked me that night. Forced himself inside of me in one thrust. I yelped, but his hand slammed over my mouth to stop any more noise. I was shocked. I didn't know what to do. I was thirteen years old, and up until that night, Travis Kane was my father, not just some hot shot CEO who had a handsome son and ran a whole bunch of charity galas.

Dark. Colored dots dance around the room as pain ripples between my thighs. My stomach flips upside down, threatening to spill over the edges. He doesn't speak. I feel his damp cock press in and out of me, like a knife twisting and turning through my walls. Tears pour out of my eyes, but he still doesn't stop. Finally, after speeding up, he slows down and I feel his cock pulsing inside of me. He leans up, extracting himself from me and bends down between my thighs, kissing the blood that's no doubt seeping out of my most private, and now exposed and violated area.

"I'm going to teach you so many things, Jade. You'll learn to love it eventually. Crave it. You'll learn to submit to me whenever I come calling. Clean yourself up, Monkey. You're my zoo creature now."

I flinch, but I know better than to pull away from his touch. The second time he raped me, I tried to pull away from him. I had half of a swollen face after that day.

"Spend the night with me and I'll drop you off here early in the morning. I have a hotel—sound proof walls," he grins and then pulls us out of the parking lot. I look out the window and watch as young people laugh with their friends. They have no idea how lucky they are. I have so much more shame to come.

The hotel is nice, but of course it is. Penthouse, rich red colors and glass windows that overlook Hollywood Boulevard.

Travis hands me a glass of alcohol, loosening his tie. His blue eyes meet mine, so blue. So much like Royce. *Royce.* Pain slams into me at the thought of him. I shoot back the rest of the liquid, ignoring the burn that settles in the back of my throat.

"Thank you," I whisper once my voice is stable.

"On your knees."

I obey, sinking to the floor.

"Remove your clothes." He tosses his tie across the room, removing his belt. He slaps the belt across the palms of his hands a few times and then his eyes come to mine. "You like Royce, don't you?"

"Wh—" *slap.* Pain vibrates over my right cheek and I hit the ground, my palms spread out.

"I said you like Royce, don't you? Because you're such a dirty little slut with a tight little cunt."

Warm fluid fills my mouth. "Please," I plead. "It's my first day tomorrow."

"You're right." Travis grins, shooting back the rest of his drink and turning back around to face me. "Get up and bend over. I'm going to fuck you and hurt you until the sun comes up. Next time you think of batting those pretty eyelashes toward Royce, I'm going to rip them out."

I stand and comply, my fingers latching around my ankles.

The first slap hits me hard and fast, the belt buckle biting my hip. A scream erupts out of me, my eyes rolling back.

I wish I wasn't born. Unworthy of love. Always unworthy of love.

The next morning, I'm standing in the hot shower as the water trickles over my aching body. Everything between my hips and my upper thighs is severely bruised, and every time I move, my vagina feels like it's going to fall out. I'm so swollen that even when I walk, everything south rubs against my upper thighs. My face stings too, and I already know that I'm going to have to spend a good hour this morning hiding the bruise on my cheek. Well, attempt to, even though it's not going to do shit for the swelling. I hit the faucet off and quickly wrap a towel around me as I make my way back to my dorm—in fast time. I knew that that was why Travis had made sure I was alone. So no one could ask questions on where I was ducking out to during the night, and no one to question my bruises. I shiver, and as soon as I'm back in my room, I slam my door closed and squeeze my towel.

Day one of college. I make my way to my makeup bag and get started. This routine is natural for me. Conceal the abuse, fake a smile. If only I could conceal the turmoil that's effervescing in my soul.

CHAPTER 5

JADE

THE FIRST WEEK OF COLLEGE WENT FAST. I FOUND THAT MY CLASSES WERE pretty easy to get to. It's Friday now and I'm dreading getting ready to go out to whatever it is Nellie has us planned on going to. I don't hear from Travis all week, thankfully, but my face still looks bad and my ass and thighs ache every time I walk. The bruising has turned to a dark purple, and not just on my legs and hips, but on my face too now. We're riding in Nellie's car to another side of LA when Sloan hands me a flask.

I take it and sip on it before handing it back. I'm not a big drinker, but I'm feeling bruised tonight, and I'm not just talking about the physical ones. My soul is a gaping wound, and alcohol just so happens to be the band-aid. I rub my hands up and down my black skinny jeans that are cut at the knees. If I was smarter, I would have opted for something that is easy to slide up and over my ass.

"So, are you going to tell us where we're going?" I say, zipping my puffer jacket farther up.

"It's a surprise." Nellie's eyes come to mine in the rear-view mirror. A few seconds pass between us before she focuses back on the road. *Weird.*

"Hey, Jade, you know those varsity players we saw at the diner last week?" Sloan turns in her seat to look at me.

"Yeah?"

"Well, one of them has been asking about you."

I freeze. "What? How do you know?"

Sloan flashes her phone in front of my face. "Because I'm fucking his best friend, also known as the linebacker."

I roll my eyes. "You didn't take long."

SWAGGER & SASS BY AUTUMN JONES LAKE

A Lost Kings MC short story

CHAPTER 1

ROOSTER

Bikers party with the fire of nonconformity all the time. Rebellion. Mayhem. That's kind of our thing. While I enjoy living outside the box of civilized society as much as any biker, even I can't see a damsel in distress and turn my back.

Both the upstate and downstate New York charters of the Lost Kings MC took the long ride down to San Antonio. We met up with two clubs we're friendly with on the way, and are all staying at a ranch outside the city.

The older brothers—ones tied down with old ladies and kids—including my club president, are somewhere behind us. Sparky, Jigsaw, and I pulled ahead of the happy family pack to explore. We're charging down the narrow concrete path of the Riverwalk along the San Antonio River when I stop and hold out my arms, blocking my biker brothers, Jigsaw and Sparky from taking another step. "What the fuck's that guy doing?"

Sparky may be high-as-fuck, but he zeroes in on the scene in front of us fast. "Damn. Girl's dress is see-through."

Okay, maybe he didn't grasp the problem.

Yeah, Texas sun is no joke. Every inch of the girl's curvy figure is visible under the thin white dress. That's not what stopped me. Grade A tits and ass are pretty much available to me whenever I want 'em.

"He has her move back another inch, she's going in the water," Jigsaw says, nailing the issue.

Straight ahead and to the right, one of the walkways over the river is empty, except for some douchewaffle with a digital camera and the girl.

"Arch your back!" he calls out.

The girl hesitates and glances over her shoulder, giving me a glimpse of sun-touched cheeks and rose-red lips. "I can't swim." Nervous laughter follows her words.

Her companion rolls his eyes. "You're fine." He waves his hand in the air. "Besides, it's like twenty feet deep."

"What an asshole," I mutter.

"Actually," Sparky says. "It's probably only two to four feet deep here."

As the last word leaves his mouth, the girl lets out a short yelp and tumbles backwards off the concrete bridge. Her brief scream is cut off by a loud splash.

"Shit." I push past Jiggy and Sparky, moving closer to the water. My gaze snaps to the guy peering over the edge. Isn't he going to go in after his girl?

"Brad!" she screams and flails her arms, gasping. "Help!"

"Come on, babe, it's like two feet deep. Just walk to the edge." He points to the side we're standing on and laughs.

What an asshole.

Up ahead, a pair of bicycle cops seem to have taken notice of the situation.

Either it's deeper than the creep realizes, or the girl's too scared to listen. She keeps flailing and yelling in the water.

"That water's filthy. She's gonna catch beaver fever," Sparky says.

"I'm catching beaver fever right here. You can see her nipples through her wet dress," Jigsaw says.

"You're an asshole." I shrug off my cut and slap it against his chest. "Hold that." I smack Sparky's arm. "Don't let that douchebag get away. I want to have a word with him."

"Rooster, you fuckin' nuts?" Jigsaw says.

I'm already jumping into the river to go after the girl, so I ignore the question.

The water only comes up to my waist. Smells like shit and fuel oil. I reach the girl in a few quick strides. Poor thing's still thrashing and sputtering. It's cute, really.

"Calm down." I slip my arms under her and lift her in the air. "I gotcha, darlin'."

"What the? Oh!" She wraps her arms around my neck and buries her face against my chest, making it easier to carry her to the side where my brothers are waiting and laughing their fool asses off.

"Help me, dick," I snap at Jigsaw.

He gives me a what-the-fuck look and holds out a hand to the scared girl. She ignores him and tightens her hold on me. "Sweetheart, I gotta get us out of the water." I don't like the way the cops are eyeing me. I swear to fuck if one of 'em gives me a ticket, they're gettin' a throat-punch in return.

Hesitantly she touches her toes to the sidewalk and Jigsaw helps her stand. I haul myself out of the water, shaking hell only knows what kind of filth off me. My water-logged jeans and boots cling in an especially uncomfortable way in the humid summer air.

"What's your name, sweetheart?" I ask.

"Shelby. Thank you," she whispers in a sweet southern drawl that perks my dick right up. Don't often hear twang like that in upstate New York.

Her scared eyes peek up at me and widen. Three six-foot-plus bikers crowding her would be too much for anyone. "Back off," I mutter to Sparky and Jigsaw.

"Shelby! You okay?" the photographer yells.

The asshole already earned a beating from me for letting the girl fall in the water and doing nothing to help her. But when he pushes Jigsaw out of the way to get to the girl, he's risking death.

"Excuse you," Jigsaw says in the same tone of voice a serial killer might say, "Your liver will taste good with red wine and potatoes."

He didn't get the road name Jigsaw by accident.

As scary as Jigsaw can be, this is my show. That's my girl. I fished her out of the water, I get to keep her. At least for a little while. Bumping Jigsaw out of the way, I step up to this Brad asshole.

"Now's the time for you to disappear." My voice is full of cold menace meant to scare the piss out of him.

He cowers and looks around me, reaching for the girl.

Hell fucking no. "You don't listen very well, Brad."

"Got a hearing problem?" Sparky asks.

I chuckle, but it's more hollow and evil than humorous.

"Shelby, come on," Brad whispers as if I'm not standing right in front of him.

Rooster laughs.

The scarred biker is fixin' to launch himself at the cops when Rooster turns his head. "Don't, Jiggy."

"Jiggy?" I mutter.

"Jigsaw." The biker who gave me his shirt points to his friend then touches his own chest. "Sparky."

"Interesting names."

He grins at me then turns toward the cops. "Why you hassling us? This dickweed practically threw the young lady in the river. We were helping her out."

"Yeah, right." One of the cops turns and stares at me. "Shelby? Shelby Morgan?"

"Shit," I mutter.

"You famous, sweetheart?" Jigsaw asks.

The cop holds out his hand like he's calling over a reluctant cat. "Miss. Step over here, please."

I glance up at Sparky and Jigsaw. "I'm fine where I am."

The cop frowns at me.

His partner handcuffs Rooster, so now I have to do something. I can't let him get arrested for helping me. "Please don't. He really did rescue me." I turn on what I've been told is my sweet, southern charm. "I can't swim, and I was terrified." I fire a glare at Brad. "My *boyfriend* watched and laughed. My *ex*-boyfriend," I correct. "He saved me." I nod to Rooster.

"Miss Shelby, the water is only four feet deep here," the cop says, smirking at me like he thinks I'm an utter nitwit.

"I realize that *now,* officer," I answer as respectfully as I can. "But in the moment, it was scary."

He glances down at Rooster and then at his partner. "All right. Get him up."

"What's going on?" A low, commanding voice asks from behind us. I turn and yet another biker wearing the same patches these guys have is staring at us. The beautiful brunette at his side takes a step back as he drills Sparky and Jigsaw with a stare. "What did I tell you?"

My gaze skips to the patch over his heart. *President.*

"Uh-oh. Are you in trouble?" I whisper to Sparky.

Sparky snorts. Jigsaw laughs. "No."

"Keep your boys in line while you're in town, Prez," the first officer says with a nasty sneer.

The president ignores the attitude and nods. "I'll handle it."

The cops write out a few tickets. Two for Brad, one for Rooster, and one for *me.*

"I didn't go in the water on purpose!" I shout. I don't have fifty bucks let alone five hundred to pay the fine.

The cop who recognized me shrugs apologetically. "Explain to the judge. He'll probably let it go."

Like I have time for that shit.

"You still gonna be at the Tipsy Saddle Friday night?" he asks me.

"That's why we were taking the photos." If he shows up after writing me a ticket, I'm dumping a pitcher of beer in his dang lap.

This has been the worst day.

Except for Rooster.

"Dumb bitch," Brad sneers.

"Kiss my go-to-hell!" I shoot back.

Brad hurls a few more insults at me, and the cops threaten to arrest him before he finally goes away.

"You sure you're all right, Miss Shelby?" The cop asks me, throwing plenty of stink-eye at the bikers now surrounding me.

"I'm fine."

The cops take off on their bicycles, leaving me with the pack of bikers.

The biker president's patient face slips into something more disciplinary as he zeroes in on Rooster. "What'd I tell you?"

"Z, the girl went in the water. What was I supposed to do, let her drown?"

Z turns his laser blue eyes my way and smiles down at me, dimples flashing. How does this terrifying looking man actually have dimples? "You all right?"

"Yes." It takes effort to meet his commanding stare. "Rooster really did come rescue me."

He nods once. The woman at his side tugs on his hand and whispers something in his ear. "You got this?" he asks Rooster.

Rooster confirms it with a chin lift, and the pack of bikers continues along the river walk. A few hassle Rooster as they pass, but mercifully most of them ignore me.

Rooster's gaze bounces from Sparky to Jigsaw and finally lands on me. "You need a ride, Shelby?" he asks.

"Actually, yes." Oh, shit. "My purse is in Brad's truck." Hot tears threaten to rain down my cheeks. Brad's probably long gone. He'll probably toss my purse out the window.

"Let's go get it. Where'd he park?" Rooster asks.

Jigsaw's already cracking his knuckles, apparently looking forward to the confrontation.

"You can't."

His beard is softer than I expected and tickles my chin. When I laugh, he deepens our kiss.

"That didn't take long," someone says behind us.

Rooster groans and sets me down. Keeping an arm around me, he turns to glare at Jigsaw.

I'd be embarrassed, but I really just want to keep kissing Rooster.

Jigsaw's gaze darts between Rooster and me. Asking him some silent question? Rooster gives him a subtle head shake and tightens his hold on me. Jigsaw lifts his hands as if he's surrendering.

What's up with that?

"Sparky, I need to give you back your shirt." I grasp the hem to lift it up even though I'm probably still see-through. Rooster stops me.

"I'll get it later," Sparky says with a good-natured smile. He slips on his helmet and holds out his hands, palms up. "We going or what?" he asks Jigsaw.

"Yeah." Jigsaw slaps Rooster's chest twice. "Z wants us at the table no later than six."

"Got it," Rooster growls.

"I have to work at five," I say.

"Nice meeting you, Shelby." Jigsaw grabs his helmet and nods.

The rumble from their bikes is deafening. I can't imagine what it must sound like when all three of them are fired up. Jigsaw takes off first and Sparky follows. Rooster watches them until they turn the corner. The aggressive roar of the bikes can be heard long after they're out of sight.

My gaze strays from the direction the bikers went to find Rooster watching me intently. "What are you doing until five?"

I tug my sticky, damp dress away from my skin. "Well, I'd like to shower and change."

The corners of his mouth quirk. "I can help you with that."

Oh, wow. I might be in over my head here.

CHAPTER 3

ROOSTER

SHELBY'S EITHER GETTING SUNBURNED OR SHE'S SHY. SHE DIDN'T KISS LIKE A shy girl. But the offer to soap her up leaves her flustered.

My bad. We just met. She's not some random club girl. Offering to shower with her less than an hour after meeting might have been a bit much.

"Where are we going?" I ask.

Must not have scared her too bad. She gives me the address and enough directions to find her place. "It's about seventeen minutes—"

"Seventeen, huh? That's real specific."

She blushes and unleashes that pretty smile again. "Off 1-10 West. I hope it's not out of your way."

"Not at all. We're staying at a ranch off 291."

"There are a bunch of them."

Ranch probably paints the wrong picture. It's more the compound of a club we're friendly with down here. Four different clubs have taken up residence on the six hundred acre ranch this week. Hanging out. Partying. Conducting business. Strengthening alliances. Most of the officers, including me, have rooms inside the massive clubhouse. Everyone else was either bunking in a tent on the property or wherever they found room. Every night's been a party. I'd like to bring Shelby back with me. It should be calm during the day. But she's also an unpatched woman walking into a clubhouse that's housing a lot of different bikers.

"I've noticed." I reach over and grab my helmet, handing it to her. "Lot of open spaces."

"Bet you don't see that in New York."

"I'm a good hour or two above the city. We have lots of rural areas. It's just flatter here."

"We have mountains."

I chuckle. "Those are hills."

She laughs, not offended.

"Where's your helmet?"

"I'll be fine." I study her long dress and sandals. "I'm more worried about you riding in that dress and open shoes."

"I'll be okay." She glances at the bike and winces. "I think."

"I'll go easy."

Must not have scared her off too bad. She eagerly climbs on behind me and wraps her arms around my middle. Feels good having her soft, warm little body hugging mine. Been a while since anyone's been back there.

"Hang on."

The sunglasses I slipped on keep most of the dust and road dirt out of my eyes. Don't do a whole lot to keep bugs from smacking into my cheeks. I take it easy through the city and open it up a bit more on the highway. Shelby's a good passenger. Moves when I move but otherwise, she's pretty still.

For some absurd reason, I'm jealous that she might have done this with another guy.

Her place is easy enough to find. A modest home on a postage-stamp sized piece of property. Modest might have been too generous. As I pull into the narrow, cracked driveway, I notice the yellow exterior could use a fresh coat of paint. Someone tried to cheer the place up by painting the trim a bright green. Can't say it's an improvement. Not that I'm judging. I mean, for fuck's sake I live in a clubhouse with a bunch of bikers back home. More like a girl as sweet and pretty as Shelby should live in nicer surroundings.

Shelby braces herself on my shoulders to hop off and hands me the helmet. She's fidgety as all hell now. "It's no ranch." She waves her hand at the house. "I live with my mom."

Something about that makes me sadder.

"She home?"

"No." She stares at me for a minute then tugs on the T-shirt she's wearing. "Do you want to come in? I should probably give this to you so you can give it to Sparky. I feel so bad he had to ride without his shirt."

"He'll be fine." Actually, he's probably fried to a crisp right about now. Fucker almost never leaves the basement. This is more sun than his pasty skin has seen in a couple years. But the more my club's been mixing with our upstate charter, the better I've gotten to know Sparky. It doesn't surprise me he'd give a girl the shirt off his back. Even if he knows damn well, he has no chance of bagging her.

And while Shelby looks damn fine in my club's colors, I can't say I care for her wearing another man's shirt. Even if it belongs to a brother and was for an emergency.

Her fidgeting only increases as we approach the front door. She slips a key out of her purse and steps inside. A wave of heat rolls over us, and she rushes to crank the knobs on an old window unit. It does little to cool the place off. I stop to unlace my soggy boots and leave them by the front door.

"Do you want lemonade? Iced tea?"

"Sure."

"Which one?"

"Whatever you're having."

She hesitates and glances over her shoulder. "Uh, I was going to take a shower."

I step closer and curl my hand over her hip. "Have some tea with me first."

"Okay." She turns and I follow her the short distance into the kitchen.

There's a small round table with four off-white chairs. I nod to the impressive line of baskets nailed along the top of the wall like some country version of crown molding. "You collect 'em?"

"No. My mom does." She grabs glasses, setting them on the counter with a *thunk* then moves to the refrigerator. "You want half-and-half?

"What's that?" I can't really think with her bending over in front of me.

"Half lemonade, half tea."

"Sure. I'm pretty easy to please, Shelby."

"Ugh." She sets the two pitchers on the counter and whips off her shirt.

Now I really almost lose my frickin' mind. But no, she's not getting naked for me. There's a washing machine in the kitchen and she tosses the shirt in. "Do you want me to do yours?" she offers.

The corners of my mouth twitch. "Then I'll be shirtless."

"I was—"

I slip off my cut and drape it on the back of one of the chairs. "I'm just messing with you, Shelby."

I toss her the shirt, and she catches it mid-air. My jeans are what really need the wash. As if she heard the thought, her gaze drops to my crotch, but she doesn't offer.

Pulling one of the chairs all the way out, I turn it so I can watch her. After the laundry's started, she brings over the glasses, setting one on the table in front of me. Before she moves away, I place my hands on her hips and turn her to face me. "Thanks."

"It's the least I can do after what you did for me today. You and your friends."

"You looked terrified. I couldn't leave you."

She ducks her head. "I feel so silly now."

"Don't." I pull her closer so she's standing between my legs, then sit upright, placing my hand at the back of her head, drawing her down for a kiss. Haven't stopped thinking about getting my mouth on hers again.

She tastes like sugar and lemons.

A soft moan drags out of her throat and she staggers closer.

I bring my hands to her hips again, slowly sliding her dress up and encouraging her to straddle my lap, so I can keep kissing her. Fuck if she doesn't slide right into my lap like she was made for me. She presses her hot center right up against my already stiff-as-fuck cock and I groan.

Abruptly, she pulls back. "I'm not having sex with you."

Huh. First time a girl has ever said *that* to me. "I'm just having fun kissing you right now, Shelby."

Fuck me, that's actually true.

CHAPTER 4

SHELBY

It's not that I don't *want* to have sex with Rooster. Honestly, I'm close to sliding my panties to the side, unzipping his jeans and having my way with him. Whatever he's packing behind that fly seems like it will hit the spot.

But I just broke up with my boyfriend not even two hours ago. Somehow sleeping with someone else so soon seems wrong.

Although, it's not like I need to worry about what Rooster thinks of me. He lives over a thousand miles away. No matter how much I like him, this can't be anything more than a fling.

Wait, I *am* supposed to visit New York later this summer.

Don't be an idiot. Whether or not I sleep with him, I highly doubt Rooster will even remember who I am two months from now.

All my warring thoughts ebb away as he tangles one of his big hands in my hair and pulls me down for more soft, slow kisses. "You're thinking too much, Shelby. Just be here with me."

His rough words send a shiver of desire down my spine. I cup his cheeks and throw myself into the kiss. He groans in appreciation and his hand slides down to cup my butt, pushing me against him. The straps of my dress and bra slide down my left shoulder and a few seconds later, Rooster traces the bare skin with his mouth. His beard tickling and igniting my skin at the same time.

He slips his finger under the other straps and whisper-soft drags them down.

"Shelby," he whispers before kissing my neck and down my chest.

He palms one of my breasts, gently kneading. I'm hyper-aware of the

CHAPTER 5

ROOSTER

"Oh my God!" Shelby's laughter seems to drive her fear and uncertainty away. "Does that line ever really work for you?"

"Don't know. Never used it before."

She tilts her head like she thinks I'm full of shit. But it's not a lie. I've had girls ask *me* if they could ride the beard. I've never had to offer. Shelby's all sorts of fun.

It's awkward as fuck in the tiny space, but I pull her close enough to finally get my mouth on her pussy. She's smooth and bare everywhere. Shame, I was hoping for blonde curls to match her hair, but I'm not complaining.

I hike one of her legs up and hold her so she doesn't slip. Using my thumbs, I part her swollen lips and swipe my tongue through her wetness. Above me she gasps and moans the second I taste her. "Hang on," I warn her.

She digs her hands into my hair, and I put my whole mouth on her, slowly licking up her center until I find her little clit.

"Oh my God," she gasps and her knees buckle. "Rooster."

A few seconds of focused attention has her quivering and moaning so loud. My cock's screaming to get inside her, but I can be a patient man when I need to be. I want her to come hard before I impale her.

I'm also getting a vicious cramp in my neck from the awkward position. Shower sex in a space this small is bullshit. Her hips jerk and I encourage her to grind her hot pussy against my face. Fuck, she tastes amazing. I want her juices coating my face before I'm done with her.

Keeping one hand on her hip, I give her ass a slap and she cries out, grinding into me even harder. I keep licking and sucking until she jerks away. Breathing hard and shaking, she stares down at me.

"I've never…oh my God. Thank you."

That's what I'm talking about.

"I need a lot more of you, Shelby," I warn her as I pick myself up off the floor.

She presses her hands against my chest and slides her fingers over my skin. "Do you want to go in my bedroom?"

More than I want to breathe.

Before I have a chance to answer her or shut off the water, there's a whoosh and a blast of cooler air hits us.

"Shelby?" a high-pitched voice calls out.

The fuck?

"Oh my, oh my," Shelby starts chanting.

"Shelby? Why is there a motorcycle in the driveway?" The voice is coming closer. There's no way the woman—who I assume is Shelby's mom—can't see me. My head sticks out above the top of the shower. Something, Shelby seems to realize as she urges me to duck down.

"Too late for that, sweetheart," I whisper, thoroughly amused at the situation.

"Shelby? Oh my God!" her mom screeches as she must finally realize her daughter isn't alone. "Are you okay?"

"I'm fine, Mom." Shelby's voice is barely more than a squeak.

The door slams shut.

Shelby slaps her hands over her face. "I'm so sorry," she mutters.

I almost say, "not the first time something like that's happened," but it feels shitty for some reason. Instead, I pry her hands away from her face. "You're twenty-two. Never had a guy over before?"

"No, I have. Just not…nothing like this ever. Oh my God. I'm so sorry."

"Stop apologizing. It's not a big deal." I glance over my shoulder. "Unless she's going for a shotgun or something." This is Texas after all.

Finally, she laughs. "No shotgun."

The water starts to cool. Whether we've exhausted the hot water tank or it's the mom's way of forcing us out of the shower, I'm not sure. Either way, it does nothing to cure my raging hard-on.

"Rooster," she whispers, wrapping her fingers around my dick. "I wanted to take care of you."

I suck in a quick hit of air. Her little fingers feel amazing. "Keep stroking, baby."

She gives me a wicked smile, then drops to her knees. Guess she forgot her mom's right outside. Not that I'm complaining.

Her soft, wet tongue flicks against the underside of my cock. "Oh, fuck. This won't take long."

She peeks up at me and presses a finger to her lips. "Shhh."

"I'll do my—"

My words are lost as she swoops in and wraps her lips around my cock, sliding down as far as she can. She curls her hand around what she can't fit in her mouth and gives a nice counter-twist. "Fuck," I groan.

Bracing one hand on the wall and the other on the back of her head, I pump my hips a few times. I'm so erratic and out of control, she ends up placing her hands on my hips and letting me have my way with her mouth.

"Shelby, fuck. That's it." At the last minute I yank my dick out of her mouth and shoot cum all over her wet tits.

"Thank you," she whispers.

It wasn't politeness that stopped me from shooting down her throat. It was the desire to see my cum painting her beautiful body. But I'm thoroughly spent, so I just nod and brush my knuckles against her cheek. "You okay?"

She nods and I help her stand, turning her to face the water so I can reluctantly clean her off.

Washing turns to groping and a few seconds later, I'm pinching her little nipples and turning her head so I can kiss her again. She grinds her ass into my half-hard cock, and I groan. I haven't had enough of her yet.

"Shelby!" someone bangs on the bathroom door. Right. Forgot about the scandalized mom out there.

"Shoot." Shelby pulls away and slams the water off. "I'm so sorry," she whispers to me.

"It's okay.

We climb out and she tosses a towel at me. Fuck, I forgot she took my clothes and washed them.

Shelby seems to have the same thought. Her lips twist with remorse. "I'm so sorry. I probably have a pair of gym shorts or something…"

"I'm fine." Got nothing to hide. I mean, it's not like her mom didn't just hear her daughter giving me head. Might as well go for full-throttle awkward and parade around the house in a towel that barely hides my balls.

Thankfully, the mom's not waiting outside the bathroom door for us.

Something awful occurs to me and I grasp Shelby's arm, stopping her in her tracks. "You *are* twenty-two, right?"

She lets out a soft laugh. "Yes." She points to the right. "My bedroom, if you'd rather wait there."

I'm not going to wait in there like a pussy, but I do follow her in while she gets dressed. The gym shorts she has for me must have belonged to a high school boyfriend because they wouldn't fit my arm, let alone my anywhere else.

"Sorry," she says again. "I'll get your stuff in the dryer."

"Hey." I stop her and push her wet, tangled hair off her shoulder. "Stop apologizing." I search her face. "You embarrassed to introduce me to your mom?"

"No. God, Rooster. Not at all."

"Good."

She slips into this short, loose black dress. I almost lose my damn mind when she slips a tiny black thong underneath.

Still wearing the towel, I follow her into the kitchen where an older, plumper, just-as-pretty version of Shelby paces back and forth. "Oh my God! Shelby are you okay!?"

"I'm fine."

The woman's gaze lands on me then returns to her daughter.

Shelby's cheeks turn pink. "This is my friend, Rooster."

"Rooster?"

I hold out my hand. "Nice to meet you, Mrs. Morgan."

The lady narrows her eyes and quickly shakes my hand.

"I thought you left with Brad this morning," she asks Shelby. By the tone she uses to say Brad's name, I'm guessing she's not a fan.

"I did." Shelby rests her hips against the counter and feeling protective, I place my hands on her shoulders. "He wanted to take these stupid photos at the Riverwalk. I fell in the water."

"Oh, baby," her mom coos. "You can't swim."

"I know." Shelby shrugs. "Brad thought it was hysterical. But I was scared to death." She turns and nods at me. "Rooster jumped in the water and carried me out."

Mom's suspicious hawk eyes are softer when they land on me again. "You did?"

I shrug. "She sounded terrified. I couldn't leave her in there."

"Well, thank you." Her lips quirk as she pulls Shelby against her for a hug. "You could've thanked him with dinner, you know?"

"Mom," Shelby protests. "We were all gross from the river water."

Her mom laughs and releases Shelby. "Sure, honey." Her gaze skips to my towel and she raises an eyebrow at me.

"Your daughter took my clothes hostage, Mrs. Morgan."

"You can call me Lynn." She gestures at the washing machine. "I think it's done. Better get his stuff in the dryer if you want to get to work on time, Shelbs."

Shelby drags herself away from both of us and busies herself pulling stuff out of the washer and plopping it into the dryer.

"That bike yours?" Lynn asks.

"Yup."

"Got New York plates."

"Yeah, I'm visiting the area."

"Uh-huh." Suspicious mom returns. She nods at my leather cut still draped over one of the dining room chairs. "Your whole MC down here?"

"Yeah, we're friendly with the local club. It's all good."

She breathes out a sigh of relief. "Okay, I just don't want her…"

"No one will bother her, Lynn."

The fear drains out of her eyes. She tilts her head and studies me. "You're nicer than I'd expect."

Meaning she's had some bad run-ins with bikers. "I have my moments." I wink at her. "And a weakness for pretty ladies."

Flirting seems to work. She opens the refrigerator and offers to feed me. Shelby's jaw drops. Maybe Lynn's not usually so polite to Shelby's boyfriends, but in Brad's case, I kind of don't blame the woman.

Shelby fusses with setting the table and pouring tea while her mother fixes lunch. As Shelby backs away, I reach out and grab her hand. "Hey, you okay?"

Her nervous eyes meet mine. "I'm sorry I'm basically holding you hostage here."

I laugh and lean in to kiss her forehead. "Baby, if I wanted to go, I'd go. Pants or not."

She chuckles and some of the tension seems to drain out of her. "Okay."

Her mother sets out heaping portions of chicken fried steak, mashed potatoes, and green beans. Shit, I think I'm in love with this family.

"Leftovers from the diner," Lynn says almost as an apology.

"Looks great to me. Thank you." It's been an eventful day and I'm starving.

"Shelby?" Lynn's voice is low as if she's hoping I won't notice. But we're all in pretty tight quarters. Even so, I keep my face focused on my plate.

"You and Brad?" she prompts her daughter.

"O-V-E-R." Shelby sighs. "He was such a jackass."

"Boy was born on third and always thought he hit a triple," Lynn mutters. Damn, I like this lady. "Dickless wonder too."

Now I see where Shelby gets her sass from.

Shelby snorts. "We got the photos, though. Rooster saved the SD card for me."

"Good." They're both quiet and I look up to see them sharing some sort of silent communication. Shelby shrugs and shakes her head.

As we're finishing up, my phone buzzes. I flick the screen and check the texts from Jiggy. "Damn," I mutter.

"Do you have to go? One of your friends said you were meeting…are you late?"

"Nah, it's okay." Actually, that's not true. Z needs me at this meeting and after everything he's done to keep our charter together and the faith he's put in me, I don't want to disappoint him. Shelby seems to sense my inner conflict and leans over to yank open the dryer door.

"Your stuff's almost finished."

"Thanks."

She hands me the bundle of clothes and I head to her bedroom to change.

CHAPTER 6

SHELBY

"IT TAKES AN AWFULLY CONFIDENT MAN TO EAT A MEAL IN A TOWEL IN A stranger's house," my mother says when I return to the kitchen.

I laugh and shrug. "I guess."

"You seem to like him."

"I do." I shrug again not quite comfortable discussing this with my mother when Rooster's in the other room.

"Fine looking man too." Her gaze darts to the hallway.

"Hands off, Mom."

She laughs and starts clearing the table. "Don't worry, sweetheart. I still like my men more seasoned."

Rooster's plenty seasoned. I swear my legs are still jelly from the orgasm he gave me before. I'd never come so hard in my life.

"Are you going to invite him to—"

"Hell, no. He's only here for a few days. He doesn't want to go to some hillbilly bar—"

"Shelby." She sighs and shakes her head. "Baby, you're so talented. How much more do you need to accomplish before you believe it?"

I raise my hands and sweep my gaze over our tiny rental house. "Getting us out of here would help."

"That's not your job, honey."

Shit, I didn't mean to make my mother feel bad. She's been struggling to provide for both of us since my dad walked out more than a decade ago. She's sacrificed a lot to help me achieve my dreams. "You've done enough. It's time for me to take care of you, Mom."

She wraps me up in a comforting hug. "You're doin' fine and I have faith in you."

"Thanks."

The floor creaks as Rooster enters the kitchen. "I'm sorry, Shelby. I really do need to go. Do you need a ride to work or anything?"

"No, my Mom will take me."

My mother—meddler that she is—elbows me but I ignore it. "I'll walk you out, though."

He stops by the door to lace up his boots and I admire his long, dexterous hands. He'd be a great piano player. "Do you play any instruments?" I blurt out.

He doesn't even blink at the out-of-nowhere question. "Nope. No musical talent whatsoever."

"Hmm. Shame. You have great hands."

One corner of his mouth twitches and he pulls me closer. "Didn't get to put them on you enough to satisfy me."

"Oh no?"

"No."

We stare at each other for a few minutes. "Come outside with me."

When we reach his bike, he leans against the seat and pulls me between his legs. "When can I see you again?"

Surprised and maybe a little suspicious, I don't answer right away. "How long are you here?"

"A week or so, but I can rearrange some things."

Rearrange them, how? "Don't you have a job back in New York?"

There's that sexy half-smile again. "Yeah, but it's a make-up-my-own hours sort of situation."

"Oh."

"This trip is part business too."

"Oh," I say again. Apparently, words are too complicated.

"You working tonight?"

"Until midnight."

"At the Tipsy Saddle?"

Surprised he remembered, I blink before answering. "Ah, no. That's uh, my side job."

"What's your main job?"

"Waitressing. Same place my mom works."

"You get to eat chicken fried steak like that every night?" he teases.

I poke my stomach. "Hell, no. I have enough padding."

He rolls his eyes. "Your perfect body is forever burned in my mind, Shelby."

I lean in and run my fingers over his stomach. "Same here."

He makes this sexy growly noise and leans in to kiss me. When he pulls back, he searches my face for a few seconds. "That cell phone in your bedroom yours?"

"Uh, yeah. Why?"

"I got your number. And you've got mine. We're having a big party this weekend. I'd like you to come if you're interested."

"Yeah. Sure."

"Don't get too excited. It'll be outdoors."

"That's okay."

He leans in and kisses my forehead. "I'm free later tonight if you want to call me when you get off work."

"Okay," I whisper.

Watching him go leaves an ache inside I've never quite felt before.

CHAPTER 7

ROOSTER

"LOOK WHO DECIDED TO SHOW UP!" JIGSAW CALLS OUT AS SOON AS HE sees me.

"Shut up, dick," I grumble, not wanting him to draw attention to my late arrival.

"Bro, Blaise pushed the meeting back. You're good."

"Why didn't you tell me?" I could've spent more time with Shelby if I wasn't so worried about missing this meeting.

"I just found out." He lifts his chin. "Z's waiting for you, though."

"Fucking great." I turn and Z is indeed outside. But he's busy with his old lady and his kid, so I don't think he's real worried about my whereabouts.

There's a scraping noise behind me and someone tackles me from behind. By the size and chokehold, I assume it's Murphy. "Don't make me break your ass in front of your wifey and daughter," I warn him.

"Heard you played hero this morning." He releases me and slaps my back a few times.

I roll my eyes at Jigsaw. "Can't you keep your mouth shut?"

"Wasn't me. Sparky told everyone."

Whatever. It's impossible to be pissed at our stoner brother. "I got his shirt. Where is he?"

"You fuck her?" Jigsaw asks.

"Shut up," I grumble.

"Sounds like a no." Murphy laughs.

I flip him off. "Don't you have your own girl to worry about?"

"I'm not the one who asked. Don't really care where you stick your dick."

Jigsaw slaps Murphy's arm. "She was hot. Had nice round little titties—"

"Shut the fuck up," I snap.

Murphy rolls his eyes at Jiggy. "Why you gotta be a dick?"

"Oh, sorry. You marrying her or something?" Jigsaw asks without a note of remorse in his voice.

"No, asshole. I did invite her up Saturday, though."

"Why? There's going to be so much free pussy—"

"Worry about your own dick, would ya?"

"She up for a spitroast?"

"You looking to die today?"

"Brother must be tired of his guts being on the inside," Murphy says.

Jigsaw grins. "Jealous, ginger?"

"Nope. I got all I need right over there." He nods at his fiancée who's busy playing with her daughter and Z's son while talking to Z's old lady.

"Upstate's going to infect our charter with monogamy, brother," Jigsaw says. "It's up to us to stop the spread of that disease."

"For fuck's sake," Murphy mutters. "You and Ravage really need to hang out more."

"You act like I'm patching her and taking her back to New York with me." Although, now that the words are out of my mouth, I can't shake the idea of having her back home with me out of my head.

"She got any hot sisters you can bring Saturday?" Jigsaw asks.

"I don't think so. She lives with her mom."

"Her mom hot?"

"Jesus Christ."

"What? Age ain't nothin' but a number, bro. I don't discriminate."

"Tell me, is your ass jealous of the shit that comes out of your mouth?" Murphy asks.

I snort and give him a fist-bump before answering Jiggy's question. "Yeah, she could be Shelby's older sister."

"Bring her."

"Yeah, I'll put that at the top of my list."

"Cock-a-doodle-doo!" someone yells out right before something soft hits me in the back of the head.

"What the fuck?" I bend down and pick up the bundle of koozies Ravage tossed my way. They're neon pink and have three symbols printed on the front: an eye, a heart, and a rooster. "The fuck is this?"

"I love cock," Ravage answers, rolling his eyes. "For the party."

I vaguely remember talking about this with him before we left New

York. At the time it seemed like a funny idea. Hand them out to chicks, then go up and tell them my name's Rooster. Something stupid like that. I was probably high when Ravage brought it up.

Ravage snatches the package out of my hands. "Ingrate. More for me."

"If we weren't in the middle of fucking nowhere," Murphy mutters, "Heidi and I would've stayed at a hotel."

Ravage shoves Murphy to the side. "Fuck you, bro. You got a nice cushy room in the fancy part of the ranch."

"It's Dad alley down there," Jigsaw says. "Nothing but our fallen, castrated brothers. We don't want to be anywhere near there."

Murphy clasps his hands under his beard prayer style. "Please say that to Rock's face and let me know how it works out for you."

Ravage taps his chin. "Our prez is likely to gut a motherfucker for even *looking* at his wife."

"She's quite MILF-y, so I get it," Jigsaw says.

"Bro, you need to go rub one out before we sit down?" I slap Jigsaw's chest. "You seem awfully one-track minded today."

"Nah, Josie sucked me dry when we got back."

"Way too much info."

Ravage scowls at me as if he'd planned to ask for details.

"You fuck Shelby or not?" Jigsaw asks.

"None of your business."

"You did, didn't you? Was she a firecracker?"

"Shut up."

Murphy shakes his head in disgust. "I'll see you at the table."

Ravage watches Murphy talk to Lilly for a minute, then drag Heidi into the house. "Teller's been bitching all day that their room is right next to his." He laughs. "Should be an eventful afternoon."

"Christ, I feel like I walked into a fucking soap opera this afternoon," I grumble.

"Lost Kings MC: Road Trip Season." Ravage spreads his arms out wide. "It's awesome."

Chuckling, I slap his shoulder and make my way over to Z.

"Hey, hero." He grins at me. "Everything go okay?"

"Eh, got a ticket from the cops."

"Get the girl home all right?"

My mouth curves up. "Yeah, she's nice. Thinking of having her up on Saturday."

He nods and searches the grounds. "Keep an eye on her. We got a lot of out-of-town bikers here we don't know. Couple different clubs."

"I will," I promise. "I heard Blaise pushed back the meeting?"

"Yeah, he had something going on. Dante's supposed to call everyone when they're ready."

Only the officers of each club would be sitting down at the big meeting. Then each club will discuss the details of what went down. More efficient. First time we've ever done this. It'll be good for all four organizations if we can make it work.

Give us easy passage and alliances throughout a huge portion of the country. All of us want it to go smoothly.

When we all finally sit down, it's clear Lost Kings have the best operation. Yeah, I'm biased, but we do. Upstate has their weed operation. They run that shit tight. Sparky's the genius behind their grow-op. Downstate, we have our porn studio that brings in the majority of our cash. Some other side-ventures too, but they have nothing to do with this meeting.

Iron Bulls MC runs narcotics and probably guns down to Mexico. Devil Demons MC runs narcotics into Canada. Savage Dragons MC—I'm not really clear what the fuck they do. But they're a close ally of the Iron Bulls and one of them owns this ranch, so that's how they ended up here. While Lost Kings have no interest in the heavier end of the criminal spectrum, we *do* want to keep relationships with these clubs running smoothly. Sparky's been helping the Iron Bulls set up their own grow operation and he goes into a lengthy lecture about strains and growing techniques that puts most of us to sleep.

My treasurer, Hustler, lays out some details about the porn proposal we put together. We held some stuff back, naturally. Kings first and all that. Iron Bulls have some connections to talent in California that we want, and we work out a deal on that.

Once business finishes, it's time to party.

And I'm wondering if there's any way Shelby can get off work a little early.

CHAPTER 8

SHELBY

I'M FEELING LIKE TEN MILES OF BAD ROAD WHEN I CLOCK IN AT THE DINER. A steady stream of customers comes and goes all night. Even so, my shift seems to drag on and on.

Rooster: You never told me where you work?

Me: Is your meeting over already?

I shove my phone back in my apron pocket and finish placing the giant five-pound cinnamon roll on a plate before carrying it over to one of my tables.

After another lap around the room, refilling coffees and clearing empty plates, I finally have a second to text Rooster back.

Me: Auntie Eclair's diner.

It's too far out of his way to worry about seeing him tonight.

Two hours later, I realize my assumption was dead wrong. The parking lot vibrates with the rumble of dozens of motorcycles. Okay, dozens might be stretching it, but there are a lot of them pulling up.

Customers glance out the windows and cast nervous glances around.

Rooster walks in the door first and smiles as soon as he sees me.

I recognize Jigsaw and Sparky from earlier but at least ten more don't-fuck-with-me type of men wearing leather vests crowd in behind them.

"Hey." I rush over and greet Rooster. "Give me a second to put enough tables together for you."

"We can do it." He nods to an empty section in the back of the diner. "That okay?"

"Perfect."

He pats my shoulder and stalks past me. Jigsaw nods as he passes. "Evening, Shelby."

Sparky stops in front of me. "Tell me there are more of those cinnamon buns."

"Yup. Got at least a dozen fresh ones in the back."

"Bring *all* of them to us."

"They're like fifteen dollars apiece."

He smirks as if he's insulted. "Coffee too," he adds before following his brothers.

The rest of the guys nod at me as they go by. I'm too flustered to bother reading their patches and learning their names. I do notice that not all of them belong to the same club as Rooster. They all seem friendly and familiar with each other. *That's a good sign, right?*

My manager steps out and assesses the room. "Friends of yours?"

"Sort of. Well one of them is."

"Make sure it stays civil."

Yeah, because a bunch of beefy bikers give a damn what I have to say about anything. "Of course."

Positive Sparky was kidding, I only bring two of the cinnamon buns to the table. He makes sad puppy eyes at me. "Where's the rest of them?"

"Are you sure?"

He glances at them again. "Box up the rest, we'll take 'em home."

One of his brothers slaps his shoulder. "Wrath will kill you if you bring all that sugar back."

Sparky shrugs. "We're on vacation."

One of the other bikers pipes up, "I wouldn't need sugar either if I was married to a sweet piece of ass like his wife."

Sparky shoots a glare down the table.

I rest my hand on Rooster's shoulder. "Couple pots of coffee for the table?"

"That'd be perfect."

"Thanks, darlin'," someone else calls out.

It takes forever to get everyone their coffee, water, and other drinks. I'm praying no one wants any real food because the kitchen is almost shut down. But they seem content with the cinnamon buns and coffee.

About a quarter to midnight, Rooster and Jigsaw get up and do a lap around the restaurant, eying my straggling customers in an unfriendly way.

"You trying to slash my tips in half tonight?" I whisper when he stops by the counter.

"We'll take care of you, sweetheart."

"I don't need charity, Rooster."

"You've earned every penny taking care of a big party like ours tight at the last minute."

He says it in a sweet way that doesn't make me feel like he looks down on me for being a waitress. "Thanks."

He leans his elbows on the counter. "You need a ride home?"

The low rumble of his voice suggests he has more than dropping me off at home in mind. "I have my mom's car." If I'd known he was stopping in, I would've walked the seven miles here. "But she's out tonight if you want to come over and watch a movie or something." A movie sounds safe. I mean, I can't openly invite him over for sex, right?

"I have to be up early for my other job," I add. Technically, it's a rehearsal, but I don't know how to say that without inviting questions I'm not ready to answer.

His mouth turns down as if he's disappointed. "You work two jobs?"

Maybe he's more concerned about how hard I have to hustle. "Sort of. More when I can." I shrug. "I try to help out my mom."

"I get that." He places his warm hands over mine, drawing them closer. "Sure you're not too tired? You've had an exciting day."

Exhaustion tugs at me, but I grab his beard and give it a gentle tug. "You did offer me a ride earlier."

His sensual lips curl into a panty-dropping smile. "I sure did, sugar."

CHAPTER 9

ROOSTER

I'M RAPIDLY BECOMING ADDICTED TO THIS GIRL.

How could I not? She's sweet as hell. Sassy sometimes. Shy other times. A whole bunch of contradictions I really enjoy.

"Let me guess, you're not coming back to the clubhouse with us tonight," Jigsaw says when I take my place at the table again.

"Fuck off." I'm really not in the mood to be ribbed by my brothers anymore tonight. I'd wanted to be here earlier, but it'd been like herding turtles to get these guys on the road.

"You know there's plenty of ass back at the clubhouse, right?" Hammer asks. He's a member of the Savage Dragons MC. If I'd known he was going to be so obnoxious, I wouldn't have invited him along on this four-club-bonding activity Z suggested.

Shelby returns to the table with four huge white pastry boxes and sets them in front of Sparky. "That's everything I've got back there."

"Cool. Thanks, Shelbs."

"How're you planning to get those back?" Ravage asks.

"We can each take one."

The guys at the end of the table rumble with laughter. "I'll call a prospect down," Blaise offers.

I let them deal with the logistics of getting Sparky's munchies home and go find Shelby.

IT SEEMS like hours later until she's finally able to leave. Poor girl's dead on her feet. "I'll follow you home. You sure you're up for company?"

"Yes. Unless you don't want to..."

"I want to."

She nods but before I let her slip into her car, I pull her to me and slam my mouth over hers. She gasps and wraps her arms around my neck, going up on her tiptoes to get closer to me. Pushing her back against her car, I lift her so she's at the perfect height. My hands slip under her dress, gripping her ass.

"I'm wide awake now," she whispers.

"Good."

I set her down and hold her door open, shutting it only after she's safely tucked inside. She quickly rolls the window down. "You remember where it is in case we get separated?"

"I'll be right on your ass, don't worry."

She reaches out and takes my hand for a brief second. "Okay."

The ride to her house has to be the longest fifteen minutes of my life.

While she invited me over under the pretense of watching a movie, I never give her the chance to flick on the television.

Once we're inside, I pin her to the front door, lifting her the way I'd done in the parking lot. "You sure your mom won't walk in on us again?"

"Ninety-five percent sure."

"Good enough for me."

"Rooster?"

"Yeah?" I slide her purse off her shoulder and drop it on the bench next to the door. After taking one more taste of her lips, I carry her to the bedroom.

"Uh, remember I said I didn't want to have sex earlier?"

I stop cold right outside her bedroom door. "Uh-huh."

Her fingers twist in my hair. "Well, I, uh, kinda changed my mind."

"Jesus, woman. You trying to give me a heart attack?"

She giggles and starts unbuttoning the top of her dress. I set her down and close her bedroom door. Thank fuck there's a lock, because I flick that too. "Just in case."

She laughs some more and tosses her dress in the direction of an overflowing hamper. "Sorry for the mess."

"I couldn't give a fuck. I'm only interested in you, Shelby." My hungry eyes sweep over every exposed inch of her. Really digging the sexy black lace bra that gives me a glimpse of her sweet pink nipples. "God damn, you're sexy."

"Thank you." She curls her index finger, calling me to the bed. It's a double bed. Small, but doable. Fuck, I think I'd fuck her on the floor right about now if that was my only option.

She slides my cut off and gently places it on her desk. I like the way she knows to treat it with care and not just toss it aside.

"Come here." I cup her cheeks with my hands and lean down to take her lips. Her eager little hands slide up under my shirt, pushing it up. "Eager much?" I tease, taking it off and tossing it on the desk.

"Yes. I've been turned on all afternoon. I thought I was going to explode when you swaggered into the diner tonight."

Shit, there's something really sweet about that. No games or coy hesitation. But she's not overly aggressive like a club girl on the prowl either.

Her hands skim around the waistband of my jeans and I work the belt loose.

"Rooster?"

"Yeah?"

"What's your name? Your real name," she clarifies.

"Who says it's not Rooster?"

She glances at the bed. "I just—"

I get it. She doesn't want to sleep with someone whose name she doesn't know. Can't remember the last girl I was with who gave a shit about stuff like that. "Logan. Logan Randall."

"Logan. I like that."

Stripped down to my boxer briefs now, I stretch out on her bed. "Come get your ride, little girl." She laughs. "There's nothing little about me."

"Next to me there is. Now get up here." I sit up and grab her hand, dragging her onto the bed. She kneels next to me and traces her fingers down my chest.

"Are you sure?"

"About wanting that pretty pussy of yours in my face? Fuck yeah, I am."

She chuckles again. Really love the sound of her laugh.

I hook my fingers in her little black panties. "Take these off for me."

She wiggles out of them and also stops to unhook her bra.

"Fuck." I scrub my hand over my face. "How are you even hotter than I remembered?"

Instead of answering, she grips my cock through my shorts. "I'm wondering if I imagined how big this monster really is."

"Go ahead and verify."

She works my briefs down my legs and my cock springs up, excited to see her again.

"Rooster," she whispers, using both hands to stroke up and down my shaft. Leaning over, she takes me in her mouth and my hips jerk.

"Fuck." My fingers tangle in her hair. This wasn't quite how I saw things going, but I'm certainly not complaining.

She keeps up the sweet torture until I'm ready to blow.

"Stop. Stop. Get up here."

CHAPTER 10

SHELBY

I swipe my hand over my lips. "You taste good." Maybe that's a weird thing to say, but I can't help it. Rooster doesn't seem to mind.

The intensity in his eyes ratchets up another notch. "Climb on up here."

The pleasure he'd given me earlier was so intense, that I'm almost scared. Not scared enough to turn him down. Just enough to make my heart beat faster.

He guides me up over his chest. Flexing his sinfully sculpted arms, he lifts me until I'm hovering over his face. "That's it. Come to me," he encourages.

The first touch of his tongue against my flesh is a jolt of electricity to my system. "Uh," I gasp, my hips jerking forward.

He hums an encouraging noise and I brace my hands against the wall.

After that, it's game on. He's completely focused on licking, kissing, and tasting every inch of me. Not just my core. He stops to take soft nibbles and licks of my inner thighs, my mound. No portion of me is left untouched. All my nerve endings fire up, leaving me trembling and close to orgasming again.

"Rooster." My voice comes out with a desperate, breathy urgency.

He makes some encouraging noises that sound like *come*. Maybe I'm too wound up from today, but my orgasm remains just out of reach no matter how much pressure he applies to my clit, Finally, he slips two fingers inside me and I shudder with relief. He keeps sucking at my clit while I grind myself against his face. His beard tickles my thighs, adding to the flood of sensations.

"Rooster, I'm—" The rest of my words are lost to crying and moaning in relief. "Oh my God," I mutter over and over.

"Shelby," he rasps, voice raw with desperation. "Need you on my dick, sugar."

"God yes." I shimmy down his body, eager for more, then stop. "Do you have condoms?"

He lifts up and I admire the flex and ripple of his stomach muscles. "Jeans."

"Good, I don't think the ones I have will fit you."

He falls back on the bed laughing as I snag the jeans and yank the little foil squares out of his pocket. I hand one to him and he flips me on my back. After rolling the condom on, he kisses his way up my body, stopping to lick and nibble spots that make me writhe under him. Finally, he straddles my hips.

I'm so wet and eager, I shamelessly spread my legs wide. Doesn't stop him from teasing me by dragging his cock up and down my slit a few times.

"Logan, please."

A shift of his hips lines us up perfectly. With agonizing slowness, he sinks inside. We fit together so right. A tight fit. But perfect. We both groan and his lips meet mine. His hips keep rolling at that teasing, slow pace designed to drive me wild.

Heat races over every exposed inch of my skin. He twines his fingers with mine and pulls my arms over my head. With one hand he pins my wrists to the bed. He clutches my hip with his free hand and drives into me harder.

I've never experienced anything like this before. There's the amazing physical connection. But something else bubbles below all our amazing chemistry.

My nerve endings tingle and sizzle. I'm close to going off again. He accelerates, hooking his arm behind my knee. "Fuck me back, Shelby," he whispers against my lips.

I buck against his thrusts and gasp at the swelling pleasure.

"That's a girl. Harder," he encourages.

He rams into me with such force, I'm sure I'll splinter apart. At the last second, he captures my gaze. The steady eye contact pushes me over the edge. He groans and thrusts harder, letting out a stream of beautiful curses as he explodes inside me.

He keeps moving and groaning and finally slows his frantic movements. He drops his forehead to my chest and places a kiss between my breasts.

"You're unreal, Shelby," he murmurs.

Carefully, he holds the base of the condom and slips free. "Give me a second."

Too content to speak, I watch him go. After a minute, I jump up and use the bathroom. He's returning from the kitchen with a glass of water when I open the door.

"I was worried you left."

He scowls. "Not fucking likely." He stays rooted to the spot, his gaze roaming over my nude body.

"You're more beautiful than I deserve."

I take the water and sip slowly before answering. "I doubt that."

"You all right with me staying?" He follows me back to my room.

I scoot to the side of the bed against the wall to make room for him. "I'll be offended if you don't."

He snaps off the light and stretches out next to me. "Come here."

Our breaths mingle together and within seconds I'm out cold.

CHAPTER 11

ROOSTER

STEADY THUMPS AND SHOUTS PULL ME FROM SLEEP. SHELBY'S SOFT, WARM naked body is still sprawled out against me. I allow my hands to wander over her curves for a few seconds before noticing the ruckus outside again.

What the fuck?

Afraid whoever it is will wake her, I reach down and snatch up my jeans.

"Rooster?" Her morning rough voice is sexy-as-fuck and I'm ready to pin her down and fuck her speechless again.

"I think someone's at your door."

She wrinkles her nose and glances at the clock. "Shoot, I never set my alarm. I'm late."

She's squirrelly about telling me where she's working tonight. Maybe she's a stripper and she's embarrassed? But I don't get that vibe from her. Plus, she doesn't seem to own anything with glitter or sequins on it.

Tipsy Saddle. Isn't that where one of the cops said she'd be tonight? Sounds like a bar. Maybe she's a topless waitress? Certainly, has the tits for the job.

Guys would be tripping over themselves to get at her.

Fuck, the idea of beating guys off her heats my blood.

The pounding on the front door starts up again. I stalk out to the living room and yank open the door.

The douchebag I didn't punch nearly enough yesterday, Brad, is on the other side. He recoils the second he sees me.

"Where's Shelby?"

"Not your concern."

"Brad?" Shelby yells. "What are you doing here?"

"You fucking slut! Took me two months to pry open your legs but you're fucking this guy—"

I cut off his insults by wrapping a hand around his neck, choking off his air supply. "Say one more word to her and I'll snap your motherfucking head off. We clear?"

He nods once and gasps. His hands claw at my arm, but I'm not done.

"You two are *over*. You stop by, call her, do anything to bother her ever again, I'll fucking end you."

His head moves a millimeter or two. I'm grasping too tight for him to nod properly. "Yes," he gasps.

"Good." I throw him to the ground, and he crab crawls away a few feet before standing.

His lips part to throw more nasty words at Shelby and I'm right up in his face again. "Do it and I'll beat you to death on her front lawn."

Finally, he holds his hands up in surrender. "I'm going."

I wait and watch him leave before going back inside.

"Thank you," Shelby whispers. "I'm sorry."

"What are you sorry for? He's the asshole."

She shrugs.

"You need a ride?"

"No. I called and let them know I'm running late. Come inside so I can make you breakfast." She leans up and kisses my cheek. "I at least owe you some eggs after all those magnificent orgasms you gave me."

"Magnificent, huh?" I slam the door behind us and follow her into the kitchen.

CHAPTER 12

SHELBY

"I'M SO SORRY!" I YELP AS I HURRY INSIDE THE BACK DOOR OF THE TIPSY Saddle.

Trent's waiting right inside and scowls at me. "You're never late. Everything okay?"

"Broke up with Brad."

"'Bout time. He ain't worth two cents, Shelby. Never was good enough for ya."

Yeah, the few times I'd brought Brad to rehearsal, he'd managed to alienate every member of my back up band. Even Trent who's the most laid-back person ever.

"You all right?"

I blush and duck my head. "I kind of met someone. It's a long story."

"Tell me later. The guys are getting restless."

I hurry to the stage and check my equipment. Trent has everything ready and rarin' to go. "Thank you."

"No problem." He picks up his guitar and lifts his chin.

I don't need to look at the list. I know it by heart.

After rehearsal, my manager stops by to discuss tour plans. I still can't believe I have an actual manager. But Greg's been helpful to me over the last month.

For the rest of the day, I help get the bar ready to open. My mother stops by and takes me out to lunch.

"I'm guessing you had a sleepover?" she asks.

"What makes you say that?"

"The condom wrappers in your room."

"Mom! Jesus. Really?"

She snickers and sips her drink. "I hope it was Rooster and not Brad."

"Yes, it was Rooster. Brad and I are done."

"Good. That boy was all hat and no cattle."

I snort at her description of Brad.

"Rooster looks like he's *all* cattle," she adds.

"Why are you so happy about me having a fling with a guy who's leaving town in a couple of weeks?"

"Because now isn't the time for you to be tied down. You've got a big tour and all sorts of opportunities opening up. But that doesn't mean you shouldn't have some fun. Just be careful."

Sure, my mom's own dreams were ruined when she got pregnant with me. I get it, even if the reminder stings. "Is he going to come watch you tonight?"

"No, I didn't even tell him."

"What? Why not?"

I shrug, not sure I can put it into words. It was nice being with someone who didn't know anything about the last year of my life. Clearly, Rooster didn't consume a lot of reality television. Just the kind of person I needed in my life right now.

CHAPTER 13

ROOSTER

Fuck, that's good.

The double shot of tequila had been served to me between two giant tits. The bartender seemed to serve everyone that way, so I wasn't special. Although she'd made it clear she'd be more than willing to sneak in the back and suck me off if I wanted.

Normally, I'd be jamming my cock down her throat a few minutes after that type of offer. Tonight, the only woman on my mind is one particular tiny blonde. One I've been searching for ever since we arrived.

Murphy and his old lady, Heidi tagged along tonight. Doubt they'll stay long, but I appreciated the company. Heidi's a smart, thoughtful old lady. Grew up around the club since her brother's the treasurer of our upstate charter. Loyal as fuck to the club, even though she's barely twenty-one. Can't blame Murphy one bit for claiming her ass as soon as he could.

Jigsaw, Ravage, and Sparky also rode with us. They're busy prowling the bar in search of non-clubwhore pussy. I should've set Jiggy loose on the bartender who can't seem to grasp that I'm not interested.

The lights blink and go down, plunging the bar into darkness.

Murphy elbows me. "Guess they actually use that stage."

There'd been some sign about "live music" tonight. Heidi had shown more interest in it than any of us. I turn around with the barest amount of interest, still irritated I haven't seen Shelby yet.

A spotlight shines down on the stage. Four figures saunter out and fiddle with instruments.

The crowd gasps and rushes forward. Over the small pack of fans, familiar blonde curls bounce into view.

Shelby?

"How y'all doing tonight!?" she shouts at the crowd.

I sit up to take a better look. She's wearing an innocent enough flowered dress with brown suede cowboy boots covered in long fringe. Underneath the pounds of makeup and big hair, I recognize my Shelby.

"Oh!" Heidi bounces up and down. "The sign outside the door said one of the winners of *Redneck Roadhouse Star* is performing live tonight. That must be her."

I turn and stare at her. "Redneck *what*?"

She shrugs. "Some reality country music star-finding show. I only watched it once or twice."

Shelby's some kind of reality television star? A singer?

Reality television, hell television in general, isn't something I waste my time with. If she's so famous, why's she slinging cinnamon rolls at that cheap diner?

The music starts up. Same kind of twangy shit that's been assaulting my ears since we invaded Texas. Not that country music isn't popular in New York, but down here it seems to be a religion.

Then Shelby opens her mouth and the voice of an angel floats out. Corny as fuck? Maybe. I don't exactly know how else to describe what I'm hearing.

All her shyness seems to evaporate onstage. She vibrates with the bold sass I've witnessed a few times. Big voice, big personality on stage. Fucking beautiful.

Most days I'd rather shoot myself than listen to country music, but I could listen to Shelby caress that microphone all damn night.

Why didn't she tell me?

Because you're just a fuck.

I know I'd made it clear I wasn't sticking around for long, but I thought we connected enough for her to tell me she's kind of a big deal.

Christ, it's been what, forty-eight hours and I've turned into a whiny pussy over this chick? I should be thrilled she's only interested in me as a dick to ride and nothing more.

During one part of the performance, the guitarist leans up against her, and they share some sort of look while singing a duet. Maybe it's all an act, but the dude seems to be in love with her. Is it for the crowd? Are they involved?

Does it matter? Maybe not, but it sure annoys the shit out of me.

The place fills up with more and more people. Doesn't seem to be any sort of security keeping things in check. I keep my eye on the door in case Brad decides to show his face.

Jigsaw leans up against me and slaps my back. "Isn't that your girl?"

"Yup."

"You didn't tell us she was famous."

"I didn't know," I grumble.

"She's good."

"Yeah." Shelby fascinates me on several different levels. I've never met a woman quite like her.

The band goes through several more songs before the lights go out again. People crowd the edge of the stage waiting for Shelby to sign stuff or take photos with them. I sit back and watch as she interacts with the crowd. Her fans, I guess.

Damn. It shouldn't surprise me, but she's sweet and patient with everyone who comes up to her.

Finally, she's free and she heads straight for the bar. As soon as she sees me, she slows her steps. Her eyes widen. Her jaw drops.

"Rooster? What're you doing here?" The hesitation vanishes and she grins wide, running over and flinging her arms around my neck. I catch her and lean down to kiss her.

"You're something else." I press my forehead to hers and lower my voice. "Why didn't you say something?"

She shrugs and signals the bartender to bring her some water.

"Shelby?" I prod.

"Can we talk about it later? I have to do another set." She swoops in and kisses my cheek. "I'm real happy to see ya, though."

I turn and introduce her to Heidi and Murphy. "Sparky and Ravage are around here somewhere." I point to Jigsaw. "You remember this clown."

"Hi, Jigsaw."

Heidi gushes over Shelby's performance and the two girls seem to hit it off. Murphy glances at me and shrugs. While she's invested in her conversation with Heidi, Shelby's butt rests against my thigh, her fingers laced with mine. Like the pervy fucker I am, I spend some time enjoying the view down the front of her dress.

The guitar player makes his way over and throws a dark scowl at Shelby when he notices her ass in my lap.

"Shelby? Who are your friends?" he asks without acknowledging me.

Murphy's mouth twists in an *are-we-killing-this-disrespectful-punk* sort of way. I give him a subtle head shake. Not yet.

"Oh! Trent. This is my friend, Rooster."

Friend. Huh.

I'm busy mulling over how I feel about *friend* while she introduces Murphy and Heidi. When there's a lull in the conversation, I squeeze her hip and brush my lips against her ear. "I think I'm a lil' more than your friend, sugar."

She leans back and gives me a sultry look before whispering in my ear. "Did you want me to introduce you as my fuck-buddy?"

"No," I growl.

She pulls back and turns to stare at me.

"Never mind." I flash a smile at her. "I'm just messing with you. You're a pretty damn good singer." Fuck, that's inadequate.

"Thanks. It's been a crazy year. I play some of my own, original stuff during the next set."

"None of that was yours?"

"No, silly." She scrunches up her nose. "You don't listen to country, do you?"

"Not if I can help it."

Not insulted, she laughs and slaps my chest.

Fuck, I want her under me again tonight.

CHAPTER 14

SHELBY

Dang. Rooster has me rattled right down to my bones.

Never in a million years did I expect him to remember what the cops said and come find me here tonight.

The sexy, confident way he was leaning back on the bar with both elbows, facing me left me breathless. Then it sunk in, he came here to see *me.* Specifically, for me. He didn't drop in to a random bar for a drink and run into me accidentally. He wanted to see me again.

I end up rubbing up against him like a horny little kitten, wondering if it will be totally detrimental to my career if I take him in the storage room and…

"Shelby, let's go!" Trent shouts.

"Are you staying?" I ask Rooster.

"Wouldn't miss it."

He gives me a quick kiss for luck and a gentle shove into the crowd.

Knowing he's out there watching—with his friends no less—leaves me jittery. Trent nudges my arm as I step on stage.

"You okay?" he mouths.

"I'm fine."

"That your new boyfriend?"

"Sort of."

He grunts and turns around, giving me his back.

Whatever.

The lights go down and the music kicks in. Everything else seems to melt away and it's just me and the music for the next thirty minutes. This is where I'm happiest. Doesn't matter that it's a dumpy little bar in Texas.

Or a huge stage in front of a television audience. The throb of the music lights me up inside and I thrive on sharing beautiful words with the strangers filling the bar.

Even as a little girl, music touched me emotionally in a way simple words never could. Music has always given me a way to express the things I shouldn't say but couldn't keep quiet about.

As silly as it sounds *Redneck Roadhouse Star* had been a dream come true. It had been a complete eye-opener and left me cynical at times too. But I poured those disappointments and hurts into my music, giving it a jaded quality it lacked before the show.

Every cloud has a glitter lining.

Sure, lots of people mocked me on the online gossip sites. Everyone thought I was dimmer than a dying light bulb. People commented and criticized my weight so many times I still couldn't eat food in public for fear of an unflattering photo showing up somewhere.

All the scrutiny eased up a little once I came home. I hadn't made it to the end of the show, or won the big prize, but I'd gotten enough attention to win an opening spot on a major tour. I planned to make the best of it. Ride it out as long as I can and pray like hell I make it to the top.

People seemed to assume I was rolling in money, but the show barely replaced the wages I lost from leaving my job for so long. I wouldn't make any money until I started touring and even then, it would be pennies at first.

We finished *Big Lies.* It was probably my favorite of the new songs I'd written since I came home.

"Good job!" Trent shouted as the lights died down.

"It was a good one, right?" I laughed and hugged him, allowing him to give me a quick spin around the stage.

People rushed up and pushed to get closer to the stage. The simple barrier the club used to keep some space between the floor and the stage wasn't strong enough to keep them back.

"Shelby! I love you!" A kid close to my age shouted. He shoved something in my face, and I backed away so quick, I tripped, landing hard on my ass. Maybe they didn't know I was on the floor or maybe they didn't care, but the crowd kept coming, A sea of boots and jeans threatened to drown me. Or stomp me to death.

I pushed and shoved, trying to right myself, but kept getting knocked right back down.

The guy who'd startled me bent down, to help me. But, instead of helping, he runs his hands up my bare legs and under my dress.

"Get off me!" I pull back and kick him square in the chest with both boots. "Fucker."

Suddenly, the crowd parts. The guy who touched me is airborne. He lands on a nearby table with a crash.

"Motherfucker!"

I recognize that rage-filled, growly voice.

"Rooster!"

He peers down and plucks me off the ground. "You okay?"

"I'm fine." I wrap my arms around his neck and cling to him. Now that I know I'm safe, the fear evaporates but leaves my entire body shaking.

And I have no doubt I'm safe. Murphy and Jigsaw are busy throwing punches at a couple of frat boys who kept trying to take pictures up my dress during the show. Sparky and another biker wearing the same patches as Rooster's are shoving people out of Rooster's way.

Heidi's sitting cross-legged on top of the bar, holding what I'm pretty sure is a ballpeen hammer in her hands. She grins when she sees me but stays put. Rooster sets me on the bar next to her.

"You all right?" He shouts.

"Yeah." My mouth twists. "Shit. My mic is on stage. It's actually mine. Not the bar's. It cost me a fortune."

"I'll get it." His gaze swings to Heidi. "Stay with Heidi."

"Okay." I tug his hand before he returns to the mayhem of the crowded bar. "Thank you."

"You got it. Stay here," he reminds me.

Heidi wraps an arm around my shoulders. "You're amazing! Your voice is beautiful." She reaches behind her and hands me a bottle of water. "Bet you're parched."

"Yeah." I take a long swallow before capping it and setting it next to me.

"Girl, this is wild," Heidi says. "Happen every night?"

"Not this bad." I glance at the hammer in her hands. "Planning to do some remodeling?"

She gives me a sly grin. "Murphy set me on the bar, gave me the hammer, and told me to stay put. Anyone who bothers me is getting bopped on the head." She taps the air with the hammer to demonstrate.

"Aren't you tougher than a pine knot," I mutter impressed that none of this seems to ruffle her feathers. And that her boyfriend apparently doesn't leave home without a hammer to use as a weapon in case they encounter a little mayhem.

"He wanted to stay with me." Heidi waves her hands at the stage. "But I'm fine. Looked like you needed the help."

"Yeah." I glance around for our bartender, Sherry, but she's nowhere to be found. "Shit, Sherry's probably calling the cops."

Heidi gracefully stands on top of the bar and whistles an ear-splitting sound to get Murphy's attention. She makes a few hand signals that must be code for "Cops!" and he taps Jigsaw's shoulder. The five bikers slowly back out of the chaos and find us at the bar.

Sherry finally reappears.

With a shotgun in her hands.

She aims at the ceiling and fires. A deafening blast that quiets everyone. Chunks of wood spray down over the center of the bar.

Rooster slips his arm around me. "Where was she ten minutes ago?" he mutters.

I can't help it. Maybe it's the fear or adrenaline, but I press my palms against his face and yank him down for a kiss.

"Thank you," I whisper against his lips.

"Thank me later when I get you out of here before the cops show up." He pulls back a few inches. "You're trouble, little darlin'."

He's teasing, but I melt against him anyway. In his arms, I know I'm safe.

He eyes Sherry who's still holding the shotgun. "I think she's got it under control." He turns to his brothers. "Let's go."

CHAPTER 15

ROOSTER

WHAT A NIGHT.

But I got what I came for.

My girl on the back of my bike headed toward the clubhouse.

After the shitshow at the Tipsy Saddle, I figured surrounded by dozens of bikers is where she'd be safest tonight. Not that I'll let her wander far from my sight.

We stopped at her house to drop off her mom's car and she ran in to pack a bag, leaving a note for her mom.

I turn up the long, dirt driveway and pass the iron gates into the main property. People are everywhere. Drunk and stumbling. Doing hell knows what in the woods. I back the bike into one of the spots reserved for our club and shut it down.

Murphy and Heidi are already here and wave to us from their spot by the fire. They'd headed back here right after leaving the Tipsy Saddle.

"Oh! Heidi has a leather vest like yours," Shelby says. She hesitates and studies the patches a little closer. "Property of Murphy? What the—"

"It's club tradition," I cut her off before she says something that will sour this whole night. "An honor. Means as much if not more than that ring on her finger. Heidi's proud to wear her patch and it lets everyone here know who she belongs to."

She seems to take a second to digest my words. "I guess when you put it that way, it's kind of romantic." She glances down at her jeans, T-shirt, and boots. "Am I okay here?"

"You're with me, babe." I sling my arm over her shoulders and steer her toward the fire.

She stops and raises her eyebrows. "You don't want to…"

So, she assumed I only brought her here to fuck her. "You mind hanging out for a bit?"

"No, not at all."

I lean down and kiss her neck, tease her earlobe with my tongue. "Sugar, don't you worry. I'm plannin' to ride you hard until the sun comes up."

"That right?"

"Fuck yeah. First, I want to introduce you to a few of my brothers." I laugh when I see who's joined the crowd tonight. "What dragged you out here, Wrath?"

He points his bottle of beer at Murphy. "He did."

The beautiful blonde tucked close to Wrath's side laughs. "Heidi said you were bringing Shelby Morgan back with you and I wanted to say hi."

I pull Shelby forward and introduce her to Trinity. Heidi joins them and they pepper Shelby with questions about her time on that show.

I shrug and snag a spot on the blanket next to Murphy. "Teller come down?"

"Nah, he's watching Alexa for us. Watching Grace too." He glances around. "Rock and Hope were down here but they disappeared into the woods a couple minutes ago."

That doesn't exactly surprise me.

Planning to disappear with Shelby soon myself.

Except, I kind of like her hanging out with the old ladies from my club. Doesn't seem like she has a lot of fun in her life. Works damn hard.

Eventually, I pull her into my lap, and she rests her head on my shoulder.

I brush her hair off her face and run my fingers through it. "Tired?"

"Little bit."

"Had a long day."

She picks up her head and gives me a sexy smile. "And not much sleep."

"You play there every week?"

"I used to. A producer from *Roadhouse* saw me and asked me to audition for the show."

"How long you been singing?"

She tips her head back and stares at the stars for a few minutes. Texas hill country nights have been gorgeous. The heat fades as the sun sets and the scent of wildflowers still clings to the cooler air. Perfect night for stargazing, but all I can look at is Shelby.

"Long as I can remember," she finally answers.

"Your voice is beautiful."

"You don't even like country music."

"I like *your* music."

She turns and shifts in my lap. "Thank you for saying that."

"Sugar, one thing you should know about me, I don't say shit I don't mean."

"I see that about you, Logan." She shifts again, straddling my lap, knees hugging my hips.

"Like it when you say my name."

She leans in and kisses my cheek and over to my ear. Sinks her teeth into my earlobe sending zaps of electricity down my spine. "Thank you for coming to see me tonight."

I run my hands up and down her legs. "Really wish I hadn't let you change out of that sexy dress."

Her hot breath skims over my cheek. "What would you do right now?"

Keeping my hands on her ass, I sit forward, pressing her against my erection. "I'd stroke that pretty little clit of yours until you were wet and begging for my cock."

Her eyes sparkle with desire, but I'm not done talking to her yet. I groan and can't believe I'm going to steer this conversation away from getting my dick inside her. "So, tell me, you were on this show. What happened?"

She tilts her head as if she's surprised I care more about information than fucking. Can't blame her, I'm surprised myself.

"Well, I didn't *win,* but I made it far enough for a jump start."

"Like?"

"I have a few singles up for digital download now. A tour coming up with Dawson Roads."

"Now, *that* name I recognize."

She laughs and loops her arms around my neck. "Why doesn't that surprise me?"

"When's that happening?"

"In a couple weeks. That's why I'm doing rehearsals every morning. Playing when I can." She bites her bottom lip. "There are a few dates of the tour in New York."

Damn, why does my heart pound even faster when she says that? I pull her closer and brush my lips against hers. "That so?"

She nods slowly.

"Think I can still get tickets?"

Her eyes widen. "You'd want to?"

"Fuck yeah. Why are you so surprised?"

She shrugs and looks away. "I'm not dumb, Rooster. A year or two from now, you probably won't remember my name."

I move my hand to the back of her head and pull her close. "You have no idea how wrong you are. I'll never forget you, Shelby."

"I won't forget you either. You've rescued me twice now."

"Happy to do it." I rub my thumb over her cheek. "I'm gonna need front row tickets and a backstage pass."

She reaches down and squeezes my cock through my jeans. "You'll always have an all-access pass, Logan."

If you'd like to know more about the Lost Kings MC...

The first book in the series, Slow Burn, is free at all retailers!

Connect with Autumn Jones Lake

Facebook: http://pxlme.me/4d522cC2

BookBub: http://pxlme.me/JBR2zsUo

Goodreads: http://pxlme.me/7-M0ukmA

Instagram: http://pxlme.me/uenoX87z

Book & Main Bites: https://pxlme.me/XnYQCkbM

Newsletter: http://eepurl.com/gqihoP

Website: http://www.autumnjoneslake.com

VOODOO VOWS

A HEAVEN'S REJECTS MC SERIES NOVELLA

AVELYN PAIGE

CHAPTER 1

VOODOO

"ARE YOU SURE ABOUT THIS?" PRESLEY'S SMOOTH, SULTRY VOICE CALLS OUT from the closet of our bedroom.

"The answer hasn't changed, babe. It's still a yes."

She sashays from the doorframe with a few articles of clothing, filling her arms. One of the tops, spills to the ground, and Presley grimaces at it. I take a few steps towards her, bend down, and retrieve it, tossing it onto the bed. "Thanks," she mutters, as she passes me.

I quietly observe, as she flits and flutters from one end of our room to the other, stuffing more random shit into her suitcase, like we're taking a month-long trip versus just a few days. I know all about the stigma of women overpacking, but this? *Total overkill.* My girl is nervous, and despite the fact that she's been trying to hide it, she's failing hard. Like George Clooney, as Batman level failure, and don't even get me started on the piss poor casting.

Presley bends over, and the pencil skirt, she wore to meet with one of her clients, stretches tight over her ass, and I let out a groan, as I bite my knuckle. Kim Kardashian has absolutely nothing on my girl because she has perfect curves in all the right places. I'm pretty positive Meghan Trainor's hit song *"All About That Bass"* was written with my girl's ass in mind. She's so out of my league that it's not even funny. I'm dating up, that's for damn sure.

With the start of her new practice and an onslaught of legitimate work coming in at a steady pace for the club's security business, our time together has been scarce, unless you count her coming into my office and falling asleep on the couch, while I work. It's not exactly my idea of spending quality time together. That terminology is reserved for more sexy things, like fucking Presley's sweet pussy, until I can't think straight, followed by a homemade meal, and then some video games. Now, that's what I call quality time. My girl, good sex, good food, and then decimating some thirteen-year-old boy, who fancies himself a big-time gamer. *Best. Day. Ever.*

"You going to take the kitchen sink, too?" I tease, as she flips me the bird.

The padawan is becoming a master Jedi. Don't get me wrong, Presley is definitely a Sanders through and through. She's judgmental, quick to temper, and most of all demanding. All those endearing qualities of her older brother and my club president are wrapped up inside her sexy as fuck package, but the smartass peeking out? Yeah, that's all my doing. A development that I take great pride in.

Raze, her brother, is often at the ass end of her snarky sarcasm, and he isn't so impressed. Now, if I can only get her to agree to binge watch all the Marvel movies in order in one sitting. She keeps saying no, but she'll cave soon. That or I'll lull her into submission with some killer sex and a belly full of her favorite restaurant food. Southern charm and the gift of sexual persuasion are definitely on my side to get me the win. Even if I have to get all the Infinity Stones and snap her reluctance away. And maybe snap her brother too, sparing me from those glares of his, but I'd bring him back. *Maybe.*

Presley tosses another article of clothing on top of the mountain on our bed, smothering her suitcase even more. I can almost hear the imaginary cries of her bag, begging to be freed under the weight of it all.

With her back turned to me, I quietly sneak up behind her.

"Babe, I get that your nervous," I say, sliding my arm around her waist. "But, this?" I motion to her bag. "You don't need all of this or any clothes at all for that matter. At least, not in my opinion."

"Right. Like you would even let me parade around New Orleans in the nude."

"Touché," I agree. The thought of any man seeing her the way I do makes me Hulk level angry. I'd only scratch the surface of how far I would go for her, when she was kidnapped. If I had to lay down my life for her, I would. No questions asked. Her life is way more valuable than mine. End of story.

Her head leans over onto my shoulder, as she lets out a sigh. "I know, but this is your family, Beau. I want to make a good impression."

I'm not like most of my other brothers, who keep their real names out of the public eye in our clubhouse. Maybe it's a status thing, but to me, my nickname isn't anything more than a fitting moniker. If Presley wants to shout it off the rooftops, and then announce my real name to the world, so be it. I owe that much to her, since our relationship didn't exactly start off on the best of terms. I mean, I did catfish her, but it was for the good of my club brother, and I did come clean. It was just before she got kidnapped by a mob boss, but that's neither here nor there. All that matters is that she's here with me, reconciled with our rocky past, and ready to take on the future by my side, as the Hermione to my Ron. She is the brains, and I'm the charm with a particular Liam Neeson set of skills.

"It'll be fine," I reassure her, as her body slacks against mine, leaning harder into me. "We'll get there. I'll give you New Orleans grand tour. Beignets at Café Du Monde, plantation tour, all the seafood you can eat, and meeting my sister."

"See!" She exclaims. "All of that sounds good, except the last part."

"I've met your family, and your brother broke my nose. I think you kind of owe me this one, babe."

She scrunches up her face at the mention of how her brother reacted, when he found out about the relationship I had built with his sister, under his roof and nose. We are solid now, but my Prez took his dear sweet fucking time getting used to it. You save the club from going down for past discretions and from the mob, and the guy still doesn't give you a free pass for dating his sister. *Bastard.* He should have given me a medal. Even Han Solo got one for saving the galaxy in *A New Hope*. Presley would have been my own personal Princess Leia. I could have had my medal, and then celebratory zero gravity space sex. *Hell yeah! Now, that's my kind of party.*

"What if she doesn't like me?" She asks nervously. "She's your only family."

"That's not true. I have you and the club." I pause, considering my next words carefully. "She'll like you. Trust me."

With Presley being a therapist, sometimes it makes it a bit harder to reason with her. She never takes anything at face value, and she's always looking for the internal driver for any rashly made decision. When a problem arises, she sits and stews, as I do over computer code, to find the root cause. *No matter how long it takes.* She's good with human brains, and I'm good with computers. It's both a blessing and a curse. It's also a pain in the ass, if you ask me, but it's how our brains are hardwired, and we are perfect for each other.

"Why don't I take your mind off of it?"

She pivots sharply on her heels, pulling away and waggling a finger at me. "Don't even try to distract me with some new video game. I'm all gamed out, after the sixty-hour marathon of Red Dead Redemption Two."

"Hey! Don't knock Red Dead. You loved it."

"Loved it like a hole in the head."

Presley pushes off on her heels, heading back towards the bed and her unpacked suitcase. She sighs, as she stares down at it again. I'm sure she's probably wishing it would pack itself. I creep up behind her, wrapping my arms around her waist and rest my chin on her shoulder.

"Stop worrying," I say, as I plant a kiss against her neck, and she shivers under the touch of my lips. "Stop thinking so hard about an easy solution. Don't pack anything."

"What are you doing?" She quietly questions.

"Distracting you." My right hand slides from her waist up her flat stomach, cupping one of her breasts. My thumb brushes over the thin t-shirt, covering her nipple, while I kiss a trail down her neck. "Is it working?" I murmur against her flesh. Presley spins in my arms, her body pressed flush against me, as her hands pull my lips against hers in a greedy kiss. My hardening cock presses tightly against my fly in response to her approval of my proposal.

Operation Distraction is a go.

"The plane leaves in a couple of hours. You aren't packed either."

"And?" I say between kisses. "We can take a later flight. That's the beauty of air travel. There's more than one plane going to a destination."

I back us up to the bed, pushing her ass against the bed frame, and her suitcase goes sliding to the floor. She breaks away from me to peer down at it. "Want me to get that for you?" She takes a few glances between me and her toppled suitcase and shrugs, before going straight for my belt buckle, pulling it free and tossing it on the bed behind her. "I'll take that as a no."

"You wanted me distracted. You got it. Now, get your pants off and fuck me, before I remember that I have zero time to finish packing."

"Yes, ma'am." I grin, unzipping my fly, and then shoving my jeans off my hips and to the floor, kicking them off. Presley slides her fingers under her skirt, while my hand strokes my hardening cock, giving him a few good luck pumps. *All systems primed and ready for a pre-flight fuck.* This isn't about romance. It's about blowing off some pre-flight steam and making her relax.

We have a solo vacation awaiting us. No jobs to worry about. No meddling club president slash brother trying to kill me regularly. We have absolutely no cares in the world, and we both need this. More so with Hero being in and out the last few months with Dani's third pregnancy. My club brother has a severe problem on his hands with three girls at home and a fourth on the way. My suggestion that maybe they should start trying some butt stuff, or even him getting snipped lead to a one-way ticket to a cold cock in the face. He acts like he hates me, but he really does love me. *I think.*

I watch intently, as she drags her black panties down her ample thighs. If there is a man upstairs, then he made this woman just to tempt me into signing away my soul to the devil. *Bring it on. I'll give the devil a run for his money.* Presley could ask me to hack the biggest bank in the world, and I'd do it for her. She is my kryptonite and the air in my lungs. Without her, I don't make sense.

"Am I doing this solo, Beau, or are you going to participate? Either way, the clock's ticking." She points to an imaginary watch on her wrist, as she taps it. My smartass girl entirely on display. She hikes her skirt farther up her hips, giving me a damn good show, as she leans back on her elbows with a come and get me smile.

"Wasn't this my idea?" I remind her with a cocked eyebrow, but I don't budge an inch towards her, despite my cock protesting. You just have to say no sometimes, when the brain below the belt wants to supersede the one up top. She wants to play, and I'll give her that. "Stop stealing my thunder."

"Stop arguing with me, and just give me what I want," she commands with a roll of her eyes. "Only you would argue over ownership of the initiation of getting laid."

"Meh, it's who I am. Frustrating and yours. Gotta love me." I shrug with indifference, and she rewards me with a growl of audible frustration.

"I do, but I question my sanity sometimes." And then she smiles that sexy smile of hers, that never fails to set my world on fire.

"I do too, babe." I look myself up and down, motioning with my hands. "You said yes to this."

Presley smiles up at me, shaking her head with a laugh. "Don't remind me. Now, can we get back to the task at hand?"

"You mean your packing?" I tease, knowing damn well that the second the chastise left my mouth, she's probably going to slug me. Thankfully, her brother skipped her self-defense lesson this week. She glares up at me in a way that wipes the smile right off my face. "Asshole."

"That's my name. Don't wear it out, babe. Now, where were we?"

Presley reaches out with a foot, locking it behind one of my thighs, pulling me closer to her. "I think you were about to fuck me, but at this point, I'm not really sure. Wild tangent and all."

"I'll show you the wildest of tangents, babe."

Shoving myself forward against the bed, I lean over her beautiful body, while my hand slips between her legs. Her slick pussy slides under my touch, when I find her sweetness.

"Been thinking about this, haven't you?"

"Yes," she sighs, and her breathy voice is thick with arousal. Two of my fingers slip easily inside of her, as her body clenches around me. *So respon-*

sive already. It really has been too long. Positioning my thumb on her clit, I continue plunging my fingers deep inside of her, crooking on as I pull, and her hips buck upwards, as I do. Most men don't take enough time to learn their partner's bodies, but I did. My brain is like a Rolodex on just the ways she likes to be touched, kissed, and fucked. A lack of passion in the bedroom has never been a problem for our relationship. *Finding time on the other hand is.*

My free hand cradles her neck, when my mouth connects again with hers. Kissing Presley is something that even the best mommy porn writer couldn't describe. Her full lips dancing upon mine weave a story of passion, need, and intensity, and it would take an entire dictionary of words to express this feeling. I'm far from a sappy romantic, but for her, I'd be anything she asked just to be able to kiss her like this again.

I adjust, as I feel one of her hands sliding between us, grasping my cock. The feeling of her smooth skin sends a hiss spiraling out of me, as she blindly positions me at her apex, begging me to shove inside of her tight fucking pussy and claim her again. I push my way inside and still, taking in the feeling of her sheathed around me for the first time in a few weeks. I missed this more than I can put into words. Well, coherent words anyway. I move slightly, and she moans. Her reaction gives me all the cues I need to realize that moments like this have been too far apart and in between with us lately.

"It's going to be fast and quick, babe," I warn her. "Been craving you like an In N' Out double-double animal style at three o'clock in the morning. Not sure I can hold back."

"I'm going to ignore the fact that you just compared our sex life with a burger. We'll discuss that later," she declares with a fake scowl plastered on her face.

"As long as that discussion involves you naked, doing your therapist thing, on the tiny little couch, then maybe, I'll let you really poke around in my head and rattle the cobwebs a bit."

"God, you're weird."

"God has nothing to do with my weird, babe."

Maybe she's right, and I am fucking weird. What else is new? I'm funny, and she's hot. Really, the only thing that I care about is how long I can hold onto her without weirding her away.

"Shall we?" I ask, directing her back to the fact that my cock has been throbbing inside of her for the better part of two minutes without a single thrust to shut him the fuck up. And shall we, we did with enough time to spare to shower, pack, and hit the road. It may not have been my best performance, but the encore I have planned for later on the plane, will more than make up for it. *Wild tangents and all.*

CHAPTER 2

PRESLEY

"WOULD YOU STOP IT," I GRUMBLE A WARNING TO BEAU, AND HIS HUMMING of that stupid "Just Had Sex" song by The Lonely Island. It's bad enough that he joyfully mentioned our pre-flight activities to the TSA agent, checking our IDs at the security checkpoint, but this? Absolutely ridiculous, but my warning only makes him hum louder. "You do realize that it's my client who has the all-access passes to Comic-Con, right? No lines, and front row reserved seating to every panel. So, keep it up, and I'll sell those passes to the highest bidder."

"You wouldn't," he fake gasps with his hand clamped over his heart. If there's one thing he cherishes more than me, it's Comic-Con weekend. Most people consider Christmas or Easter their biggest religious holidays of the year, but for Beau, it's definitely Comic-Con. The second that last year's convention was over, he was already planning for the next one. I just had the unfortunate opportunity to be his plus one this year. It's not that I don't like some of the more recent movies like Marvel or Star Wars. I just don't obsess over them like he does. I sure as hell don't plan on dressing up as a character. He on the other hand already custom ordered a Deadpool costume from a well-known cosplayer costumer. How much that cost is one thing I really don't think I'd like to know.

"Keep testing me, and you'll find out, Beau." And, I mean it. His unhealthy obsession with all things that are for teenage boys I can live with. It's who he is, but underneath all that, he is nothing like any other man in my life. He's strong, self-sacrificing, and most importantly, loyal to anyone he loves. After he nearly gave up everything to protect my brother's club and myself, I knew that everything that had happened between us in the past meant absolutely nothing. Beauregard Martin is a good man. Just a weird one, but he's my weird.

"The Sanders' in you is showing. Your brother would be so proud."

"You know, your obsession with my brother is really starting to worry me. Maybe you should talk to someone about it," I snark back.

"Good thing my super-hot girlfriend happens to run her own practice." He says, leaning over the arm of our seat on the plane, planting a kiss on my cheek. "Just don't tell her about us. She might get jealous."

For the millionth time today, I roll my eyes. I'm very confident that I could be the world record holder for most eye rolls, since meeting Beau. He has that effect on people. Me, my brother, and every single member of the Heaven's Rejects MC. Just another one of his unique gifts.

The flight attendant comes through, offering each of us a beverage menu. I snatch it quickly, and Beau shoots me a slight look of confusion. Meeting his sister and her family unnerves me. I've faced a mob family, kidnapping, being on the run, and so much more in the last year, but meeting his sister terrifies me. I've racked my brain so many times between patients. My emotional connection to taking the next step in our relationship isn't a surprise. We practically live with my brother and his family, so it's only natural for him to want me to meet his. So, why do I find his sister so intimidating? Outside of his weekly Facetime call with his nephew, I really only know what he's told me. Bits and pieces of a patchwork past, and one not unlike my own.

"Take it easy on the booze," he half chuckles. "You will feel it way more up here than you would on the ground."

The flight attendant returns, and I order two glasses of Merlot, while Beau opts for a beer. The second they hit my hands, I down them quickly, and Beau stops mid chug, eyeing me carefully. "I'm fine," I reassure him. "I know my limits."

"Your lying needs work, babe. You might convince that screaming kid back in coach, but not me." He jerks his head back to the cries of the tiny baby that had passed us earlier. "We have an hour, before we land, so you talk, and I'll listen. What else do we have to do to kill the time?"

"I really don't want to talk, Beau." My deflection fails. After nearly a year together, he has finally learned just about every trick I have in my playbook save one, but tagging in my brother is and always will be the last resort. It's hard enough watching Mikey and Beau go toe to toe about our relationship, especially living under the same roof. I didn't get to experience the protective big brother stick back in high school because dating was the last thing on my mind at the time. Unfortunately, that teenage milestone in my life is coming back to bite me in the ass now.

"I'm going to need you to elaborate more on that. Don't think that's how therapy works, and I don't have Jedi mind trick powers or truth serum. You're going to have to do this the old-fashioned way." He mimes the turning of a sign with his hands. "Dr. Martin is now in," he mutters in a fake accent. "Tell me all of your problems."

I chuckle to myself only to get a look of sheer seriousness in return.

"Well, I have this really weird boyfriend who has dolls in his room." The surprise on Beau's face is absolutely priceless. What did he think I would say? I'm not about to reveal all my deepest and darkest secrets right here on a plane full of strangers.

"Not what I meant," he chastises me with a stern voice. "And they aren't dolls. They're action figures, and our nest egg for the future."

"So, we'll be living at the clubhouse for the rest of our lives then?" I tease back.

He growls and mumbles under his breath inaudibly. How does it feel now to be the frustrating one in the relationship? I reach over and grasp his hand, "I was just kidding, you know." He peers back skeptically.

"You can apologize to them, when we get home."

"Not happening."

"Fine, then the only way to get out of this is by telling me the truth. What scares you so much about my sister? And be honest this time. She's my family, but you're my girl. One doesn't work without the other."

Should I tell him? Would this help relieve the pressure I've been feeling being back home? I take a deep breath, and just put it all out there on the table. "Your sister intimidates me." The relief of my revelation doesn't do a damn thing to ease my nerves. So much for the truth setting you free.

"Go on," he mutters, pretending to write down notes. Watching him mimic what he thinks really goes on in a therapist's office, makes me laugh and cringe all at the same time. For Beau, television is like reading Wikipedia. If he sees it in a show, it has to be real.

"Remy grew up in her father's MC just like me. She broke out on her own."

"Not exactly at her own choosing, Presley. Remember that."

"I know, but she lived a life outside of the club for a few years. Again, just like me. I think my brain looks at all the information that I have about Remy, and it sees an alternative path for myself. I didn't want the MC life. Not in the slightest, but here I am. Dating a man in my father's old club, and back to square one."

The admittance of what's really bothering me stings once it's out. He loves his club. Just like my brother. It's their home, and for me, it's a constant reminder of how different my life could have been had my dad not been killed. I could have just as easily been in Remy's shoes. Riding on the back of my ol' man's bike or leading a women's auxiliary club of my own. Dad made no bones that he had plans for me, when it came to my future. I would live the MC life whether I wanted to or not. As a woman in an MC, I held no power. Not in the way my father ran his club, when I was growing up, but then he died, and an entire world of possibilities opened for me.

The fact that I had found myself back inside the walls of the Heaven's Rejects' clubhouse was purely by chance and circumstance. I came to them at a hour of desperate need and fell in love with Beau. The club would and always will be a source of painful memories for me no matter how much Mikey has changed it for the better.

"It isn't back to square one. You and my sister are completely different people with a similar past. The club life suits her. Just like your brother was suited for his role as president. It doesn't have to mean that it's what suits you. I've told you before, and I'll tell you again. If giving up the club is what you want, then I'll do it. Nothing is more important to me than you."

"I would never ask you do to that. The club is a part of you." And I mean it. Him leaving the club would be just like me leaving my patients behind. It's inside of us, and imbedded in our very soul. Ripping it away would take a piece of it with us.

"Just like it is for my sister."

I slump back into my seat, realizing that Beau is right. My association of his sister and my life isn't fair. We're different people, and I'm mentally short-changing building a relationship with her based on my own issues, when it comes to the MC life. All this anxiety that I've been feeling, since he asked me to go, isn't about her. It isn't about us a couple. It's not about the duality and ironic nature of our life together. *It's about me.* My fears and my hesitations.

Owning my truth and dealing with the pain behind my past, comes hurtling forward, and hot tears begin to stream down my face. Beau reaches over, threading his fingers through mine, and squeezes my hand gently.

"Your life is yours to mold it to whatever you want it to be."

His words hit fast and hard inside my belly, and they're like a sucker punch to the gut. He's right. I know he is. Beau has been nothing but up front with me about his allegiance to the Heaven's Rejects and where I stand with it, since we decided to try this thing again. While our relationship had been based on a series of unfortunately necessary, at the time, lies and illusions, what we have now isn't. We are honest and upfront with each other. Sometimes, very brutally so, but it has made us stronger than ever. Now, here I am doubting this all over again. His club and my birthright rescued me, when they could have left me there to rot as a prisoner, but they didn't. They brought me home to him and to my brother. The family I never wanted, but yet truly needed. A pang of shameful regret hits harder than the realization gut punch.

"What movie is that from?" I question, trying to lighten the mood, as a dark cloud of guilt swirls inside of me.

"None. That one is a Beau special." He pretends to brush off his shoulders, but it's more like brushing his obsessive pop culture ego. "All-original, babe. Just like me."

"And there's the man that I know."

"And love," he adds with a smile. "Feel better now?"

"Much. I needed that."

"Good," he says. "As payment for services rendered, meet me in the bathroom in five minutes. I've got a box on my bucket list that needs checking."

"In your dreams, flyboy."

"I don't need to dream, babe. My dream is sitting right here next to me, and she's about to make another one come true."

He starts to unbuckle his seatbelt, but I reach over and stop him. I point up and direct his attention to the fasten seatbelt sign illuminated above us. He cocks a sly smile, "Do you think that will stop me?"

"I know it won't," I chuckle. "By all means, try it and see what happens, when you have to explain to the flight attendant why the rules don't apply to you."

"I make the rules, babe."

"I think TSA might trump you on this one, Beau, but I'll make you a deal. You do it, and I'll send the video back to my brother, when they haul you off the plane for not complying."

He is the one who rolls his eyes this time, while I laugh. "You know, I like it much better, when that snark isn't directed at me."

"Whose fault is that again?" I ponder with exaggerated fake curiosity. He knows precisely who is to blame. *Him.* I might be a Sanders, but this new side of me is all of his doings. You can only live so long with the most sarcastic person on the planet and not pick up a few new tricks.

"Keep reminding me," he teases. "You may have gotten away this time, Presley, but remember, there's another flight home to go. We're checking that box. One way or another."

CHAPTER 3

VOODOO

THE DAMP AND THICK SOUTHERN SUMMER AIR SMACKS BOTH OF US IN THE FACE, like a wet blanket, the second we step off the plane. Presley scrunches up her face, when she looks back at me. Living in the south is an acquired taste. As much as I love my life in southern California now, this place will always be my home. Weather flaws and all. It's the price you have to pay for such good damn cooking and nightlife.

We walk a little farther and finally find our carousal to collect our luggage, as Presley and I both check our phones instinctually. I see only one message from Ratchet. A meme reminder of Raze's threat of Presley's safety on our trip. I fire back a middle finger emoji, satisfied that the reply is suitable enough for him, and that the message will be relayed back to the Prez. Like anything will happen to my girl here. I mean, this is Louisiana. Family protects family, and my sister's club has the protection game in spades with a bounty hunter in its ranks. I stow away my phone and continue to wait for our bags to appear. I begin to hum the Jeopardy theme song, but Presley elbows me hard to make me quit. *Fun murderer.*

"Kentucky was bad, but this," she says with a lift of her hand in the air. "This is one thousand times worse. How does anyone live down here?" Presley asks, as she stows her phone away, when the carousel begins to buzz, and bags start to appear.

"Why do you think drinkin' is one of our favorite pastimes, sugar? Got to do something to forget about the fact we're meltin' the second we step outside?" A strange voice answers back. A voice that I haven't heard in person for way too damn long. I spin, only to be hit head-on with a blur of dark hair, belonging to my sister. I lift her up in my arms, while she squeezes my neck tightly.

"Welcome home, BoBo," she greets me in a teasing tone, as Presley shoots me a smile. She mouths back my nickname, and I raise my middle finger against my sister's back. There's not a lot of things in this world that make me cringe. I mean, hello, I've watched an exhaustive amount of D-rated movies and surfed the darkest portions of the web underground, but Remy's nickname for me is still one of my least favorite things to be called. But I'll never tell her that. You don't do that to family, despite how much I really hate it.

I sit her back down, but her grip doesn't release from my neck. "Good to be home, Remy, but you're kind of choking the life out of me, Cher. Where's Beaux?" She finally relents, taking me in, as she steps back, and I do the same. Seeing Remy in person, is nothing like seeing her on the other side of my laptop. A lingering pang of guilt sucker punches me in the gut. I've missed this. She's grown a few inches taller, and her face is far more hardened than I had expected to see. Life hasn't been easy for her, after her old man died, and it hurt being so far away from her and my former step-mom, especially since they didn't have to take me in, when I found myself homeless after my biological parents died. The guilt of not being able to pay either of them back will always be one of my biggest regrets in life.

"He's with mama." She says, releasing me, but then takes notice of Presley. My girl reaches out her hand politely to greet her, but Remy pulls her into a hug. Presley's beautiful eyes grow wide with surprise. I shrug back, watching the two most important women in my life embracing, like this isn't the first time they're meeting each other. This is a Kodak Moment kind of special. "You're family, sugar. We don't shake hands," Remy's full southern voice drawls. "We hug."

The hug lingers longer than Presley is comfortable with, and like the man in shining armor that I am, I swoop in to help her. "Remy," I mutter, while breaking her free of her grasp on my girl. She finally takes notice of the obvious discomfort on Presley's face and backs away. "I'm a hugger. What can I say?" She shrugs, like it's no big deal.

Remy idly chats away, filling me in about what my step-mom has in store for us on our short trip, as we continue waiting on our luggage. When I called Remy to tell her I was really coming home, she had insisted that she was going to meet us here. It took a lot of convincing and promises to go to a family dinner first thing to even get her to relent on the fact that we would be staying in the Quarter at a hotel. I love my family, but this is our vacation. Being cooped up with Remy, my nephew, and her club sister roommate didn't really scream holiday to me.

Presley looks as if she's a deer in headlights with the long list of activities and family functions that Remy rattles off. While my step-sister has definitely grown up, the bossiness I remember from my brief stay with them sure hasn't changed a bit. No wonder her club is doing so well under her presidency.

Our bags finally rotate around on the carousel, and I snatch them, before having to play chase the bag. One suitcase for me and two for her, I might add. I lost the great luggage battle of two thousand nineteen, when I suggested only one bag. A rare defeat on my nearly spotless record.

"Ready to go to family dinner?" Remy asks with a smile. "Mama and Aunt Kitty have been cooking for days. I hope y'all are hungry."

"Family dinner?" Presley asks, and I cringe. I probably should have mentioned that to her, before we landed. "We aren't going straight to the hotel first?"

"It'll be fine," I reassure her with a kiss to her temple. "Just my step-mom, aunt, and nephew. Nothing big."

Remy pauses and slowly pivots on her heels with guilt clear across her face. "About that..." she trails off. "Mom may have invited the club over, and a couple of the neighbors."

"Remy," I warn her.

"Sorry, but you know Mom. When you come home, it's a production. Be happy I talked her out of the parade. She had a Krewe on call. She has to show off her city slicker big shot step-son, when he brings home a girl for the first time." Presley takes an instant interest in the only part of her revelation. She knew that I wasn't really that big into dating. Not until her. Why would that be a surprise to know that she's the first woman I've brought home to meet the family?

"Ex-stepson," I correct her.

"Knock that shit off. Ex nothing. You're family, BoBo, and it's our southern duty to parade you and your girl around for all of the family to see."

"We'll see about that."

"Try and tell Mama differently."

Remy had a very valid point. My former step-mom was a force to be reckoned with. When my parents died, I had no one to call family. Ameline Laveau wouldn't have it. No sooner had my father's funeral ended, did I find her packing up my things and moving me straight into their house. Remy's dad, Rene, was upfront with his disapproval about the son of his woman's ex-husband living under their roof, but Ameline fought him tooth and nail every single time he tried to kick me out. She was all I had, and she protected me like my real mother never did. I'll always be grateful for her opening her home up to me.

"Fine," I relent. "But after dinner, we're going to the hotel. Do we have a deal?"

"Deal," Remy says, as she leads us to a black SUV parked in the short-term terminal parking. I grab Presley's bags and load them into the back along with mine. Presley tries to slide into the back seat, but I stop her, insisting she ride shotgun. Seeing New Orleans for the first time, will be far better in the front seat. Remy starts up the car and drives us towards her Aunt Kitty's, where Ameline lives with her. I watch Presley closely from the backseat. Her eyes are wide, as we pass the Superdome. Sports are definitely not her forte, but even she was admiring the dome for all its splendor. After Hurricane Katrina, the Superdome housed so many displaced families. Remy's family and her father's business were spared from the worst of it, but so many others weren't. Even now, years later, the scars from Katrina are still clear as day in the lower ninth ward and also near the Quarter, where the closest thing we have to a world trade center now stands boarded up and abandoned.

"What's that?" Presley asks, pointing out of the window to the sugar refinery on the north side of the Mississippi River. Remy tells her, providing way too much information for such a simple question.

"I see how you two are related," Presley remarks.

"It's a southern thing, sugar. You can't live here without knowing the history. It's a requirement."

A short while later, Remy pulls up to Kitty's house, parking on the street in front of it. I hop out of the car and open Presley's door, and she steps out with a smile and pauses, taking in the sights around her. Rows of shotgun and creole cottage style houses line the narrow street along with half a dozen bikes, flanking either side of Remy's car. Her club no doubt did indeed come for dinner. Presley's fingers interlace through mine, when she grabs my hand.

"Ready?"

"No turning back now," she nervously remarks.

A heavenly breeze of creole spices fills the air, making my stomach groan. Damn, I missed this place, and apparently, so did my stomach. Remy leads us up to the steps to Kitty's modest cottage through a large, black iron fence into the courtyard filled with newspaper covered tables and chairs lined up in three sections. A large stockpot steams under the heat of the fire below it in the left corner near a table, overflowing with colorful pots and plates. *Hot damn.* If what I think is in that pot, then this is definitely the way to be welcomed back home. Please, please, please let it be a crawfish boil.

Remy disappears into the house, leaving Presley and I alone outside. Taking the opportunity to check my suspicions, I drag Presley over with me to the simmering pot. Steam wafts off of it, bringing one of the best damn smells to a guy from the south. I take a peek over my shoulder, before grabbing a pot holder and going for the handle. The second the lid moves away I smile. Bingo. Crawfish Boil.

Presley peeks over my shoulder and down at the meal. "What is that?" Grabbing a spoon from the table beside the pot, I dip it inside, scooping up two crawfish. No harm in sampling the meal. Quality control tests and all that. But before I can whisk away my pilfered bounty, a wood spoon smacks the ladle from right out of my hand and onto the ground with the crawfish in tow.

"Ain't nobody taste testin' this food, until we say grace. You know the rules." Presley starts to open her mouth, likely to start apologizing for my behavior, but I jump in, before my former step-mom starts in on me again.

"Hi Ameline," I backpedal. "Nice to see you, too." The years have been kind to her. Her dark hair is slightly lighter with a few sprigs of gray, popping from the knot at the top of her head, but nothing else has changed much.

"Did you lose those manners I taught you out in California, Beauregard Lee Martin?" Full name. Ouch. She moves me out of the way and stirs the boil, teasing me at my failure to sample the goods. I spy Remy leaning against the doorframe of the house with a satisfied smirk on her face. After all these years, she's still a snitch. Ameline places the spoon onto the table and turns back to us.

"You going to introduce me to your friend?" She asks, wiping her hand on the towel hanging from her apron. "Or did you forget how to do that, too?"

"Mama, cut the shit," Remy calls from the porch. "Stop trying to scare Presley off."

"You watch your mouth, baby girl. You know I don't like you cussin'. It ain't ladylike."

Remy shoves off from the front porch and joins us. "That ship sailed a long time ago, Mama." Ameline mumbles under her breath. I barely catch what she's saying, but I'm almost positive I heard a 'wash your mouth out with soap' in there somewhere. That is something that I would pay to see. At least, five bucks anyway for Ameline to give Remy a country ass whopping with a bar of lye soap.

"Ameline, I'd like you to meet, Presley," I interject to diffuse the situation and to save that pot of boil from going to waste. I place my hand on the small of her back and gently nudge her forward. Presley stretches out her hand to my step-mom, and Ameline eyes it, before taking it, giving her a firm shake.

"It's nice to see you didn't bring home some stick thin blonde bimbo," Ameline remarks.

"Jesus, Mama," Remy swears. "Not all people from California are what you see on television."

Ameline raps Remy on the hand with her wooden spoon. How she grabbed it that fast that even I didn't notice is one of the motherly wonders of the world. "What did I say about swearing?" It takes everything I have not to laugh out loud, as I watch Remy nurse her hand, and Ameline heads back into the house without another word.

"Well, that went well," Presley remarks with a slight edge of sadness in her voice. I tug on her, pulling her into me and engulfing her in my arms, trying to ease her nerves. I want to pull her aside and reassure her that Remy was right, but before I can, a steady stream of women start coming out of the house with plates and bowls of food in their arms. Remy jogs up to the porch and grabs one from her mom's hand. The tables fill quickly with enough food to feed an army, and once everyone is back outside, Kitty emerges. She mutters a quick grace, before the feeding frenzy begins. Being the guests of honor, Presley and I push to the front of the line. Presley eyes each item carefully, asking questions as we go down the path. Satisfied with her selections, we find an open table and are soon joined by Remy and a couple of her club sisters.

"Forgive my mama," Remy chimes in, as she sits down. "Ever since my daddy died, it takes her a little while to warm up to people, especially someone who comes from the MC life. Give her time, and she'll figure out you're one of the good ones."

Presley nods. I already filled her in about Remy's past history with her father's MC, and how she and Ameline were thrown out of the club, before Rene's body was even cold. She has lived a rough life and being cautious about a newcomer comes with that territory. Thankfully, Remy hadn't fallen in line with the same mindset. She took the cards that she was dealt and built an empire around her. She thrived in it. Much like I did. Being in an MC, wasn't exactly where I saw myself, when a job offer came from Raze's security firm. I was a kid fresh out of college with nothing holding me back, so I took what was offered to me and ran with it. I was happy. Just like Remy. I only hope that Ameline will find her happiness to someday.

We fall into casual conservation easily. Remy talks about the new things her club has lined up, and the business they'd purchased over the years, until she turns her sights back on Presley with a million and one questions of her own. Presley takes them with ease and makes me smile, while I watch her open up to Remy. Just as we are about finished eating, my nephew comes stumbling out of the house, lazily rubbing the sleep from his eyes. It's not until the last step that he spies me.

"Uncle Beau!" He screams, running towards me, and barreling into me like a ton of bricks.

"Hey B," I smile, squeezing him tightly back. He releases me and instantly notices Presley beside me. Beaux shoves away from me and goes directly towards her, giving her a hug even more prominent than mine. The damn kid is named after me, and I'm chopped liver next to her. Figures, but I can't fault him for that. I'd have done the same thing, if I were in his shoes.

Presley gives her first genuine smile, since we got here. Leave it to my nephew to bring that out in her. "How did you get her? She's pretty," he remarks, as he shoves me down to sit between us.

"Well B, let me tell you a little story. Once upon a time, there was a man who decided to stalk a woman online for a friend," I start, before both Remy and Presley stop me from continuing the story. That's okay. I'll just save it for another time, like bedtime, when Remy isn't watching.

CHAPTER 4

PRESLEY

I WAKE UP, FINDING BEAU'S PLACE NEXT TO MINE IN THE BED EMPTY.

After our meal with his family last night, I barely remember Remy driving us back to our hotel or passing out in the softest bed I've ever slept in. The whirlwind of our flight and the very crazy dinner was exhausting. Both physically and mentally. My trepidations about Remy weren't justified, but his former step-mom is a completely different story. There is something there, and a calling to dig deeper. Maybe it's the therapist in me, but she has piqued a nagging interest inside of me. I just can't act on it. Ameline is not a patient, and I can't overstep my bounds approaching her. Not when her approval means so much to Beau. I'll find a way to prove myself to her, even if it kills me.

"Good morning, beautiful," Beau's voice calls out from the open balcony door of our hotel, as he leans against the frame with only a pair of pajama pants riding low on his hips. His lean body on full display. "Ready for breakfast?" I lick my lips at the sight of him, and he takes an instant notice, as a wicked idea pops into my head. One way too corrupt for me. Screwing around on that balcony in the light of day will definitely have to be stowed on the back burner. Getting a public lewdness charge is not on my vacation checklist. Not now, or not ever. Slowly walking towards me, he exaggerates his steps. Beau pauses just at the edge, leaning down to kiss me quickly, brushing his finger across my lips, as he steps back. "I don't know what you're thinking about, but whatever it is, I think I like it." "Come back to bed and find out."

He rips the covers off of me, and I scrunch up my face in pretend anger at him. So much for spending the day in bed. Sleeping in is one of those guilty pleasures I never seem to get anymore, and while I had hopes that would be the case while we are on vacation, it seems I'm very, very wrong. *Damnit.*

"As much as I would like to do whatever that deliciously dirty mind of yours has thought up, Presley, we have a city explore. So, get your ass up, and go get ready. New Orleans is waiting."

I could protest, and I know I could change his mind about leaving the hotel, but that's not why we are here. And on the flip side, a little sight-seeing might just be the trick to distract me from the Ameline problem. Beau plops another kiss on my cheek, before he starts towards the attached bathroom in our room.

"And where do you think you're going?"

"Shower."

"But I thought maybe we could shower together." He immediately stops dead in his tracks. *Got him.* He pivots on his heels and grins back at me, as he roughly rubs his hand across his face, while I giggle at his frustration. If I know him as well as I think I do, then he and his own internal committee are trying to think of a way that we can both get what we want. "Well?"

"Quit tempting me, woman. Go eat, before I change my mind."

"Fine," I sigh, slipping from the bed and returning the favor from his teasing this morning with a more significant than usual sway of my hips. I peer over my shoulder and notice him biting his knuckle, before disappearing into the bathroom. Can't say I didn't try. Stepping out on the balcony, the warm and humid air wraps around me, and the table in front of me is filled with breakfast cakes and coffee. It's the breakfast of champions.

I pick a cake covered in powdered sugar and pop it into my mouth, and a cloud of powder puffs out in front of me, when I chew. It's absolutely delicious with its warm and gooey center. I finger the handle of the coffee and bring it to my lips. It's a heavenly scent, if I ever smelled one. The first sip is very surprising. Slightly spicier than regular coffee, but still good. I lean against the railing, while I take another sip, taking in my surroundings. Old, tall buildings surround our balcony, and I spot the belfry of the cathedral a few blocks away from our hotel. The city is quieter than I expected this time of morning, but by the time I finish my coffee, a few people are beginning to trickle down the streets below.

"How'd you like it?' Beau asks from behind me, toweling off his hair from just inside the door. "Good, right?"

"It is. Chicory?" I ask, and he nods back his affirmation. "Not bad. Little different, but I can see why you like it so much."

"Tastes like home." He takes the cup from my hand and sits it down on the table beside him. Beau tugs me forward into his warm body, and the fresh scent of his woodsy body wash fills my nostrils. "Thank you for coming with me."

"This is your home. Of course, I wanted to see it."

"About that," he smiles down at me. "Better go get ready. Our first tour starts in an hour. I promised an abbreviated adventure of what this city has to offer, didn't I? We have a plantation tour and swamp ride awaiting us." He releases me with a slight reluctance to his grasp. "I'm going to head downstairs and make a couple of calls. Raze left me a voicemail. Might have an update for getting Slider out early."

Slider, the club's oldest prospect, traded himself for Beau, when Ginny and I were being hunted. Every second he's in that prison for Beau's crimes, it haunts him. He has worked tediously to figure out how to reduce the sentence. Slider doesn't deserve to be there, and if anyone can make it happen, it's Beau and my brother. It's just taking longer than either of them had anticipated.

Beau slips from the room, and I make quick work of a hot shower and getting dressed. Being this warm already, I grab a pair of jean shorts and a pink tank top, and I don't even bother drying my hair. The second the humidity peaks it's going to be a frizzy wreck anyway, so I just twist it up into a wet bun.

My phone dings on the nightstand with a time warning from Beau, so I fire back a sass-filled response. A year together, and he still thinks pushing will make me move faster. Maybe slower. Grabbing my purse and tossing on the flip flops I wore on the plane, I exit our room and head downstairs. I find Beau typing away furiously on his phone without any notice of my presence.

"Good news?" I ask.

"Lawyer got a meeting with the Feds set-up. Should know something in a few days." I know he's not satisfied with the outcome. He wants him free, and every day he's still there, eats at him. Ratchet's disdain for the fact that his sister was whisked back into protective custody, is making it even worse. The Zezza empire had done its toll on us all. The sooner both Slider and Ginny are back under the club's roof, the better it will be for us all.

Beau pockets his phone, when a bus pulls up to the front of our hotel. The bright red letters on the side gives it away as our ride. With his hand on my back, he leads me to the bus. A few more people from our hotel join us, and we take off for our first destination. The Louisiana countryside is not what I had pictured. The wide-open spaces are a stark contrast to the crowded city with sprawling estates, antebellum homes, and the large dams on the side of the Mississippi River, making you nearly feel like you are going back in time. We pass various plantations, until we arrive at our destination. The Whitney Plantation. This spot was my only request for our trip. Many of the plantations in the south focus on the families, and their lives there. The Whitney's story comes from the other side of our country's brutal and inhumane past from the perspective of the slaves.

The stories our tour guide tells are emotional. Stories of pain, suffering, and for some, death. Listening to their stories, seeing their living conditions, and walking the grounds where so many before us were enslaved humbles me. Reading about our history is one thing, but walking where they walked is the exact opposite. While my heart is filled with sadness by the time our tour is over, I'm glad we came. We load onto the bus, heading towards our next stop a swamp, and Beau's choice for our activities for today. Why he wants to ride on a boat in alligator infested waters is beyond me, but a deal is a deal.

The swamp tour is a bit more fun than I want to admit. Watching our boat driver, Captain Dan, and his animated stories about local lore, and his vampire friend, Miss Vicky, brings a smile back to my face. Even more so, when he pulls a baby alligator out of a cooler near the wheel and lets anyone who is brave enough hold him. Beau, of course, takes it upon himself to not only take a gator selfie, but to kiss the animal on the nose, while shoving his phone into my hands for another picture. The couple sitting behind us also make sure to photobomb it.

After leaving the tour and arriving back at our hotel, we head towards the French Quarter, walking hand in hand in the oldest part of the city, before popping into a local restaurant for dinner. The food, the music, and the drinks are a perfect end to a perfect day.

CHAPTER 5

VOODOO

Our last day in New Orleans, comes far too quickly. Had the potential break in Slider's case not have come up, I would have opted to talk to Presley about staying a couple of extra days. There's so much more here I want to show her, but at least for this trip, we can't swing it. With just one day left, I have a few things that I need to do. Things that I've been dreading for a very long time. I waited until dinner last night to drop them on Presley, but true to herself, she was far more understanding than I expected her to be. It's not every day that your boyfriend takes you on a date to a romantic restaurant and drops the bomb on you that he wants to go see his dead parents in the cemetery. She took my request all in stride. Subtly really isn't my thing, and damn, am I glad that Presley already buckled up into the crazy train that is my life.

The gravel of the walking paths into the cemetery crunch under our feet, as we slowly walk hand in hand towards a place that I haven't visited, since Dad was buried next to Mom. I was man enough to admit that it hurt being an orphan. Yeah, I had Ameline and Remy to lean on in the family department, but it isn't the same.

I lead Presley down a row, until we finally find them. A fresh bouquet of flowers lies neatly in front of their crypt. Remy's doing no doubt.

We stand in silence for a few moments, while I try to find the right words to say, but nothing comes out. Not a damn word. It would take two hands and then some to count the number of times I've cursed their names for leaving me to fend for myself. The drunk driver wasn't their fault. I know that, but the pain of having to grow up without them, despite how shitty their parenting skills were, wasn't easy.

Presley stands next to me, stroking my back in comforting circles, until I can't take it anymore. We exit the cemetery just as a band enters with a horse-drawn casket being pulled behind them.

"It's okay to miss them, Beau," Presley says, when we finally get far enough away from the cemetery, where the swirling coil of pain and anger inside of me dissipates. Her timing is too perfect to be a coincidence. No wonder her patients love her.

"I know. Thank you for going with me."

"Where you go, I go." I can tell she means every single word too. Presley's convictions are stronger than anyone else's I know. Even stronger than her demanding brother.

"So glad you said that," I interject to change gears. "Remy's shop isn't far from here, and I want to pop in on her, before we leave."

"I'd like to see it." Her voice is confident in her answer.

"Really?" I question with a slight edge of confusion. "No hesitations?"

"Not a one."

I can't help myself, when my next question comes barreling out at warp speed. "What changed?"

"Our talk, and texting with Remy."

"When did you get her number?"

"At the dinner the other night. We've been talking."

"About… "I trail off. "Me?"

"Narcissist much?" She teases. "About everything really. Club life. Being on the outside. All of it. Remy's really given me the perspective I was missing."

"As long as it helps you," I declare, pulling her against me. "Just don't go sharing secrets about me. She doesn't need any more blackmail than she already has."

"Too late," she grins. "I know all about your crush on Betty White, and your obsession with the Golden Girls, when you were a kid. Are you planning on dressing up as Blanche soon for Halloween? I want to make sure that I have my camera ready."

"I'm going to kill her," I growl, but even I have to admit that Remy's effect on her has been a positive one. I just have to figure out how exactly to keep the blackmail material at a minimum. Remy knows too much to be providing Presley with historical tidbits to share with the rest of the club. Hero and Ratchet don't need anything else to help out their comedic cause against me.

Presley regals me with all of the things that Remy has told her about me, while we walk towards her shop. For each of her transgressions, revenge will be coming back two-fold. Beaux is the perfect age to embarrass the hell out of his mom with a few well-timed outbursts of randomness. Wonder how she would like it, when he announces all about her balloon collection that actually turned out to be condoms? I doubt even Ameline knows about that one. Payback will undoubtedly be a bitch, if she keeps it up.

Finding her shop hadn't been the hard part. Maneuvering around the film crew for one of those naval crime shows just a few blocks away from the French Market, on the other hand, is a different story. It took four attempts of alleys and re-routes, before we finally make it. The dark blue flashing sign with the figure of Papa Midnight himself contrasted starkly against the white shiplap siding on the outside of the building. We walk through one of the open bay doors and find Remy cussing up a storm with a wrench in hand.

"Don't let Ameline hear you talking like that," I warn her, as Remy clutches the wrench tightly in her fist. "Easy, killer. I was just fucking joking."

"Language!" I hear Ameline's voice call out from the second floor.

"How in the hell did she hear that all the way up there?" I groan, pointing to the railing of the second floor, where I spot her standing. "Is she a bat?"

"I'm pretty sure the second you push a kid of out your body you get superhuman hearing."

I immediately grimace, "I did not need that visual."

"You're welcome," Remy grins back in a reply. "You hear to see her?"

"Which one? The bike or your mama?"

"The what?" Presley interjects. "What bike?"

"The one that he's had me working on for the last year. Oh shit... I wasn't supposed to tell her was I." One damn sentence, is all that it takes for my step-sister to reveal one of my ulterior motives for our trip here. Family, of course, being the biggest of them, but the other was coming to see the progress on my present to Presley.

"Way to ruin the surprise, Remy." I scold her. "Show her."

"Follow me." Remy tosses the wrench in her hand into the open toolbox with a clang that echoes throughout the entire shop. Not a single person turns their head or takes notice. Odd, but knowing Remy's temper, a few wrenches flying around probably isn't a random act of aggression. Not when you really piss her off. She leads us back to a separate space and flicks on the light. Her gift is now entirely on display. It's unfinished, but not precisely unrecognizable either.

"Is that for me?" Presley questions with a wavering and unsure tone.

"It is. A present from me and your brother. An olive branch for if and when you made your decision about the club."

She looks back at me confused at first, but I watch closely, as she inches her way towards her gift. A nineteen twenty-nine Indian Scout. Her fingers trace against the worn metal tank, as she takes it all in.

"Your dad bought it for you. Raze found it, when he was cleaning out one of the club's old barns. Your mom confirmed it."

Presley doesn't say a single word, as she continues to look over it carefully.

I just want to start rattling off the historical significance to this bike. It's the same model that Bessie Springfield rode back in the early nineteen thirties, or that finding one intact is like finding a needle in the world's biggest haystack. These bikes aren't just rare. They are non-existent. But it will be lost on her right now. Maybe later, when all of this has really sunk it.

A tear rolls down her face, and she tries to hide it quickly, but another just shows up right after it, until she can't stop them from falling. They ping on the exposed metal of the bike below her, and I go to her, embracing her, as she sobs against my shoulder.

"I don't understand. Why would my dad buy this for me? I was ten, when he died."

"Your brother doesn't know either, but she's yours."

"I don't even know how to ride," she admits.

"I can teach you," Remy offers.

"Really?" Presley answers, lifting her beautiful face from my now tear-stained shirt.

"We're family, aren't we?"

CHAPTER 6

PRESLEY

WITH PROMISES OF REMY VISITING US WITH BEAUX AND A RETURN TRIP IN THE future, we board our plane for home. Leaving New Orleans is harder than I ever imagined. It may have only been a few short days, but a piece of my heart will always belong there. I just wish that I had a chance to talk more with Ameline, but I have faith that our relationship will soften with each trip we make back. At least, I hope it's that way.

That city and Beau's sister gave me the closure and the hope that I needed to move forward in our new life. Every ounce of hatred I have for my father still lingers below the surface, but spending time with Remy, has helped me to understand that every club, even one with bloodstained pasts like the Heaven's Rejects, are worthy of redemption. I just have to give them a chance. Beau belongs there under the Rejects' colors, and so do I. It will take some time to work through the lingering effects of my sordid childhood, but knowing just how fantastic the future can be, will be worth every single tear. The debt that I owe to both Remy and Beau can't be priced.

Although, I do have a good idea of where to start with repaying him.

"I'll be right back," I mention, while unbuckling my seatbelt and sliding past Beau in the aisle seat. I can feel his eyes on my ass with every step that I take towards the front lavatory of the plane. Thankfully, it's unoccupied. Pulling the latch, I slide inside, locking it behind me. The lights flicker on, drawing my attention to the mirror to my left.

The reflection shining back at me isn't the one I saw, when we left for New Orleans. Long gone, is the part of me who hated the club. I hated what my father had done to our family. Hated the blood coursing through my veins, and how that blood drove my brother to stay in the club life. For too long, hate has inspired me, but that ends now. Spending time away with Beau and his family, gave me hope. Hope, that I desperately needed about the club and my life with Beau could co-exist. And Remy gave that to me, like a present under the Christmas tree. Neatly wrapped with love and acceptance. This trip is only the beginning to a significant relationship between the two of us. Remy and I have way too much in common not to keep in touch. Plus, she promised me, before I left, that anytime I need blackmail ammo against her brother that she is my go-to girl.

Pulling my phone from my pocket, I press my finger to the home button, unlocking it and firing off a quick message to Beau. Mere seconds tick by, before a knock raps on the door. I take a deep breath and open it, as Beau slides inside, locking it again. A sigh of relief exits me, knowing that I didn't just open the door for some stranger, who wanted to use the bathroom for its intended purposes, and not for what we are about to do.

"Babe, you okay?" He asks with a wild flash of curiosity. I shift to lean against the tiny sink, trying my best to look casually sexy, all the while my adrenaline and anxiety are hitting off the chart levels. Embracing every single moment in my life, is starting here and now. No more hiding. No more trying to be above what I really am. I'm a biker's old lady, and I'm a therapist. Crazy is my life, and it's high time that I accept it and start to live that way.

"Fine," I smile. "I was thinking…" I start, praying that my nerves aren't as apparent as I think they are to Beau. He'd never go through with this, if he knew I was freaking the fuck out on the inside.

"That I just paraded to the front of the plane with the occupied sign on over the entrance?" He isn't the least bit annoyed. Knowing Beau, he was probably humming that fucking Akon song all the way up the aisle and getting high fives from all the men, as he passed them. Subtle, he is not.

I shrug with a smile, "Oops?" Playing hard to get isn't really in my wheelhouse, but I have to admit, torturing him is a little fun. I might have to do this more often. Just not on a plane full of people. The fact that there is a group of elderly men seated not ten feet away from this door sends my nerves spiraling into overdrive, but that is the old me. This is the first step in finding out who I really am with the duality in my life. It's time I embrace the crazy and the unknown in my life with both hands.

"Oops, my ass, babe. You and me," he says pointing between us," in this room means something. Hopefully, it's the something I mentioned on the way out here."

"Possibly," I answer coyly. "Maybe I just wanted to see you." Beau cocks his brow.

"We doing this, or will I be telling our grandkids someday the story about how Pappy had to walk through a crowded plane with a woody?"

Did he just call an erection a woody? Lord help me, he's reverting back to his teenage years. Not like that's anything new. He just didn't outwardly and verbally express that to me regularly. The video games and action figures are a different story. Just more reasons why I love this man. Weirdness and all.

"Grandkids, really?"

"This goes the way I'm thinking. We'll have loads."

"Let's just start with one of our own first, and then see how that goes."

"Fair enough, but you can't resist this." He tries to show off his best assets, but bumps into absolutely everything in the tight space, including me. "Need a better runway."

The plane shudders, when it hits an air pocket. Beau falls against the door with a thud, and we both freeze, praying that no one heard that. We wait a few minutes, and no one knocks on the door, but the plane dips again.

"If this keeps up, then we don't have much time, before they force us back to our seats. Decision time. Go or no go?" He asks hopefully.

"Wouldn't have asked you to come here, if I wasn't."

"Alright then," he affirms, going for his belt.

"Wait," I tell him, before he gets his fly unzipped, and he freezes.

"Changed your mind already?"

"No, but how in the hell are we going to do this? We're packed in here." I scan around the tiny space. It's not like this room has a pull-out bed or a slide out for more room. We barely have enough room to breathe let alone try to screw around quietly.

"Baby, your lack of faith saddens me. I've been thinking about this, since the minute I booked the flight. I extensively researched this."

"You mean, you've watched movies."

"Correct. Just trust me."

Beau goes back for his fly. He pushes his jeans down to just below his hips, before he turns his attention back to me, standing there unsure of where to even start.

"Turn around," he orders. I shift, pressing my front against the sink, as Beau's lips press against my neck. "Relax." His hand slips under the waistband of my shorts, and I freeze momentarily, while my brain battles with my body. Experiencing something like this is so outside of my comfort zone, but I want to test my boundaries. Giving this to Beau, means something to him, and this is my first chance to break away from common sense and just feel.

He presses me hard against his body. His hardening cock tight against my ass.

"Ahh," I moan uncontrollably, when his teeth gently graze against where my neck and shoulder meet. It's one of those instant turn-on spots that he has spent the last year trying to memorize. It felt almost scientific at first, but Beau's determination to learn my body, showed me just how much he was in with this relationship. He is an all or nothing type of guy. Head first no matter what the situation is, and I envy him for that lack of fear.

The nervousness begins to fade away to a driving want and need. Then the need begins to turn into a raw emotional pull to take this opportunity by the proverbial balls and give into everything that scares me. His finger slips inside of my panties gently touching the wetness between my legs, before he slides two fingers inside of me with a quick thrust. He leans in close. His warm breath prickling against my skin. "See not so scary, is it?" He comments with a low, lustful tone. "Block out the world, Presley. It's just us here."

"And all one hundred and forty-five passengers on board."

"Not helping," he chastises me. "Block it out. Feel me. Feel what I'm doing to your body."

How can I not feel it? Every time Beau walks into a room, my body ignites. He's the match, and I'm the flame. My body burns and aches for him. Every single touch feels like his fingers are pure fire, flicking at my surface. I need to feel the burn again. Now, before my courage burns away, and the self-doubt kicks back in.

His hand dances against my flesh, brushing against my clit and sending shockwaves of arousal cascading all over my body. Heavy footsteps stop outside of the locked door. We both pause, and I pray that someone doesn't come busting in, while Beau's hand is down my pants.

His breath hitches, when the footsteps move away.

"We don't have much time," I remind him. "They'll be back soon."

"As much as I would like to drag this out, until we land, you're right. Damnit."

Beau pulls away from me, giving me just enough space to slip my shorts and panties from my hips, as his large hands help me. I step out of them, spinning to face him and pull him into a kiss. He cups the back of my head, deepening it, and I let out a moan in his mouth, when his tongue invades mine. God bless the genes that can make this man kiss. It's like every single one of them is his way of staking a further claim on my body and my heart without placing a single mark on my lips.

"Ass on the sink," he commands. "Only way this is going to happen without one of us falling through the door." I give him a questioning look.

"Movies," he reminds me. While I would generally take this opportunity to argue with him, his logic seems sound enough to me. We also don't have time to take it up with the morality committee that is my brain regularly. Sometimes being so full of common sense is a pain in the ass, especially when your man is staring at you waiting for the meeting to adjourn, like Beau is right now.

"Sorry," I mutter, pivoting again and pushing my ass against the microscopic counter.

"I love your mind, babe, but…" he trails off.

"Shut it off, I know. I know."

Beau reaches down and kisses me again, and with it, taking away every ounce of inhibition inside of me. This trip is what I needed, but this moment between us is what we needed, even if it is in an airplane bathroom with an audience likely listening in.

"Ready?" He whispers against my lips.

I break the contact between us, pushing myself up on the sink. It's cold steel biting into my flesh. Beau steps forward and presses his erection against my core. He kisses me again, before shoving himself inside of me, and he hisses to my moan. His entire length pushes inside of me, as the plane jerks with turbulence. My hairs brace against the sides of the wall, as he stills inside of me. We wait only for a second, before he pulls back and plunges inside of me again.

"Fuck," he growls, when his pace quickens. "Presley you have no idea how you fucking feel, when you're wrapped around me."

"Tell me," I encourage him. "How do I make you feel?"

"Like I'm a sinner getting a second chance to reach heaven," he mutters. I wrap my hands around his neck, and his hands grip my ass tightly, lifting me from the counter. He nudges me roughly, as he tries to get the right support not to drop me. Beau sinks himself back inside of me deeper and deeper, until there's nothing left between us. I know that I'll be sore later, but I just don't care anymore. Soreness. Getting caught. The fact this is a bathroom. None of it matters.

Planting my hands on the edge of the counter, I arch my back, deepening his thrust. My core nearing combustion from both the sensation of our two bodies joined and the excitement of being caught.

"Gives a whole new meaning to if the plane is a-rockin'," he starts, but I shift a hand from the wall and press a finger to his lips. "Don't think about finishing that." He murmurs against my finger in protest, but a shift of my hips brings him back to reality.

A soft rap comes at the door, and we both look at each other wild-eyed, but he doesn't stop. He pushes and pulls, until the cusp of my orgasm breaks free, rippling over like a flooded lake breaking the dam. I bite down into his shoulder to mask the moan I so desperately want to scream out, and to shout to the world.

Beau finds his release a few minutes after me, and we fall back onto the counter. Chests heaving, and smiles beaming from our faces.

"Welcome to the mile-high club, babe," he jokes. I try not to laugh, but once the giggles leave my lips, I can't help it. Beau joins in, until a cabin notification dings, and the captain's low voice fills the air.

"Ladies and Gentlemen, air traffic control is diverting us to Las Vegas due to adverse weather conditions in the area. All flights going into the LA area have been canceled." A collective of groans echo outside. "It might get a little bumpy, so we will be putting on the fasten seatbelt sign. We ask that all passengers return to their seats."

We both panic, re-dressing in a hurry, when a sudden realization hits me. It isn't going to take a rocket scientist to figure out that there's only one bathroom and two people coming from it. *Fuck. My. Life.* Why did I think this was a good idea? I need one of those time machines from that Dr. Who show that Beau watches to teleport myself back in time and kick my ass for this.

"Can we just stay in here?" I squeak out. "I'm not going out there."

"Babe, I hate to tell you, but if we don't, they'll come in after us. Pretty sure the guy a few rows back is an air marshal."

"Why didn't you tell me there's an air marshal on the plane?"

"Didn't seem relevant at the time."

Beau slips out of the door, before I can stop him. Thanks jackass, for leaving me to face the music alone. If he had waited, I could have at least hidden behind him. *This was your idea, dummy.* Albeit a bad one in hindsight.

I crack open the door and peer out. A few of the men he passes whistle and give him a congratulatory high five, including one of the elderly men in the front row. My face flushes even more. The men on our flight clearly think our mile-high club status is great, whereas the few women I can see are sneering a disgusted hole through him. I can only imagine the kind of looks that I'll be getting. I take one last look in the mirror, straighten my clothes, and suck in a deep breath, before exiting. The cabin erupts into cheers and claps the second I'm visible at the front of the plane. I can feel the face of the sun flush illuminating my face, as I stalk back to our row with my eyes plastered to the ground. If I don't make eye contact, then they can't see me, right? Wrong. So wrong. I can feel every single set of eyes locked onto me with each and every step that I take. *Every. Single. One.*

I finally reach our seats and plop into it, completely rattled. Beau notices me fumbling with the seat belt, and helps me click it into the correct position.

"Relax," he whispers. "Happens all the time. You're like a local celebrity now. Bet someone is going to tweet about us later."

"Are you serious?" I gasp.

"Babe, it's fine. Besides, we're going to Vegas. The voyeur capital of the country. We'll be fine."

"Fine my ass." He chuckles beside me. This is not the time to laugh, and here he is just yucking it up, like I just told the world's funniest joke.

"Yes, your ass is fine, but what does that have to do with this?"

"Are you trying to distract me again?"

"Marry me," he blurts out, and the world stills around me. Did he? Did he really just propose to me like that? Right now, after the bathroom? My brain nearly explodes from the puzzle. "Committee meeting over yet?" Beau leans over the seat, takes my hand in his, and grins at me. "Yes, I asked you to marry me. We're landing in Vegas. Why not?"

"I can think of a thousand reasons why we shouldn't get married. Namely, my brother."

"Fuck him," he laughs. "And fuck your thousand reasons. I love you, and you love me, right?"

"Of course, I do."

"Then why not? You want a big wedding? Fine. We can do that too, but I want this. Have since we first met online. Is the committee okay with that?" I elbow him hard, but I am considering his side of this. Both of our families are complicated. They live on the other sides of the country, coordinating would be a nightmare. I know that getting two clubs together is hard enough, but I don't even know the red tape that would have to be discussed. Maybe Beau has a point. Even if it isn't my dream wedding, I could have this and that all at the same time.

"You know what. You're right. Why not?"

"That a yes?" He questions.

"Yes." Beau reaches across from me and kisses me hard. "Next question. Leia or Amidala?"

"Come again?"

"Who do you want to dress as, so I can match. Princess Leia or Queen Amidala. Though slave girl Leia would be good, too."

"Explain…" I state almost regretting to agree to this without first having asked all of his terms. I knew there had to be a catch.

"That's the best part. There's a new Star Wars theme wedding chapel that just opened up. You're gonna look so sexy dressed up, babe."

For better or worse, and in sickness and in a galaxy far, far away, right?

Lord help me.

. . .

Loved Voodoo Vows? Check out the rest of the series: HERE: http://bit.ly/2HS0PZw

---

Want to learn more about Avelyn?
Facebook: http://bit.ly/2MP9tHD
Website: http://bit.ly/2Pedqrd
Twitter: http://bit.ly/2OEBdPU
Instagram: http://bit.ly/2Pdtbyz
Bookbub: http://bit.ly/2KQ8avl
Newsletter: http://bit.ly/2Mp9zc2

THE ARRANGEMENT BY BINK CUMMINGS

SACRED SINNERS MC- MOTHER CHAPTER

CHAPTER 1

Seated at my best friend's kitchen island, half with it at this time of the morning, I double knock on the granite countertop. Jade's got the coffee brewing and bagels toasting in the toaster. This is our weekday ritual and has been for the better part of a decade.

Ya see Jade, my heavily tatted, curvalicious bestie, moved in next door eleven years ago with a toddler on her hip and little money to her name. We bonded on account of my social nature and single momdom. By social nature, I mean batshit crazy. Just ask my twenty-two-year-old son Josh, he'll give ya the colorful version of his mother's eccentricities. I'm a wild one, with wild hair and wild clothes, to go with my equally wild personality. Did ya catch all that?

Padding on sleepy feet to the fridge, Jade grabs an armful of flavored creamers from the door for me to choose from as her half-dressed teenager lifts his chin in greeting before joining me at the island.

"Mornin', Hunter." I smile at his tousled bed head. Bet mine doesn't fare any better at this hour. There's no use in getting dolled up before noon unless my fuck buddy slept over. Then, I might consider taming this curly mane and brush my teeth. A threadbare pair of tie-dyed cotton shorts and a fluorescent pink spaghetti tank with built-in bra will have to do, for now.

"Mornin', Loretta," Hunter parrots, rubbing the sleep from his eyes.

"Josh gettin' you today?" I ask.

He nods the affirmative.

"You gonna work at the garage?" By garage, I'm talking about the Sacred Sinner's automotive shop. My son's a patched member of their motorcycle club, known as White Boy. Dumb as hell nickname if ya ask me, but he likes it. Hunter hangs with them a lot, learning the ins and outs of engines and whatnot. It keeps him outta trouble, which gives Jade peace of mind when she works odd hours as a tattoo artist.

Creamers are spread before us along with two silly printed coffee mugs filled with the drink of gods. Hunter takes his and I mine, as Jade smears our bagels with the ushe, then slides the plates over. I pour a healthy amount of Almond Joy into my cup. Hunter opts for the pumpkin spice. I'm tempted to give him shit about being a basic bitch, but think better of it. He ain't a morning person, and I don't wanna poke the teenage bear this early. Maybe later.

Leaning her round badonkadonk against the counter, Jade takes a sip of her black coffee waiting on us to dig in. She's doing that stupid keto diet to lose weight. I give her a week and she'll be back to her normal self. Dunno why she's gotta lose pounds anyhow. Her thickness suits her, just as my size three suits me. What I wouldn't give to have beach ball tits like hers, though. Lucky bitch.

"You gonna keep staring at my chest, or you gonna eat?" Jade arches an amused brow.

I roll my eyes. It ain't my fault she's got a low-cut tank on and her nips are hard as diamonds. Can't blame a woman for appreciating another's assets.

"Fuck off," I tease, and Hunter snickers.

"What are you getting yourself into tonight?" Jade asks.

"I gotta work." I'm a bartender at a local watering hole. The weekends, including Friday nights, are our busiest. Lots of tips to be made.

"Then Blimp?" Jade smothers a smart-ass smirk and tucks a stray piece of onyx hair behind her ear. Hooker.

Hunter chokes on his food. I slap his back to dislodge it before I take a bite of onion bagel smeared with butter and cream cheese. Because I want the nosy bitch to wait it out, I chew slowly. She snorts, knowing damn well I'm stalling. Blimp's an older brother in my son's motorcycle club and has been a friend for years. And by friend, I'm talking with benefits. Bow-chicka-wow-wow. We don't feel the need to define whatever it is we've been doing since before Jade moved in. We have fun. Neither of us are relationship material. Not really.

After Josh's piece of shit father ran out when he was two, I gave up on all that rose-colored romancey crap. Now that I'm in my forties, I don't have time for games. Fucking and a little cuddling is all this crazy broad needs. Blimp supplies that in spades. No use in complicating something that doesn't need complicating. We fuck, do our thing and enjoy ourselves — end of story. Jade doesn't see it that way, though, and has been giving me hell about our arrangement for, well... ten goddamn years. This, coming from a chick who hasn't dated a soul in the same amount of time. Pretty sure her pussy has cobwebs. Damn thing needs a dusting.

Once I finish half my bagel and half my coffee, I give up the goods, "Blimp said he'd drop by the bar at some point tonight."

Jade's eyes round in surprise. "No club?"

"No. I'm closing and he's leaving Sunday on a run for however long. Don't wanna waste time." A.K.A. I wanna fuck right after work. When I'm not working the weekends, I go to the Sacred Sinner compound to fool around. We've been known to put on quite the show in the common room of their clubhouse on party nights. Blimp's a fan of public displays of indecency and I'm a more than willing participant. Exhibitionism is hot. You should try it sometime. If that's not your thing, maybe you can watch Blimp and I go at it instead. Voyeurism can be sexy. In our case, you have to be down with a thick, long-bearded, mature biker who smells like maryjane, leather, and cologne. Who also rocks the cock of a thoroughbred stallion. His cum tastes like granny smith apples. True story, from my lips to God's ears. You're welcome to taste it anytime. I don't mind sharing.

Hunter finishes his bagel before I'm done and shuffles back into his bedroom to get dressed. Once he's out of earshot, I speak freely. There's no need to scar the kid before he's gotten his dick wet. We try to keep the sex talk to a minimum around him. Not that there's always gotta be sex talk. I'm not *that* much of a hussy.

Jade refills our cups and retakes her spot against the cupboards, ankles crossed.

"You wanna drop by the bar tonight?" I prompt. She'll say no. She always says no. This one's a lightweight. Bet an infant could hold liquor better than this girl.

Jade shakes her head, half a grin surfacing. "You know I gotta work, too."

"Only 'til ten."

"Ten?" She gives me a droll, *think twice bitch* look. "It's the first Friday of the month and there's no club party."

Right. Duh. The brothers get ink into the wee hours of the morning. Her back will kill her tomorrow.

"Who's on the books?" I'm nosy.

Her head cocks to the side. "Who do ya think?"

I take a sip of my coffee, lip grazing the rim. "How the fuck should I know?"

"Think long and hard about the brother who's been turning his entire body into a suit of ink."

"Viper." That fucker's on a mission. The green hair and multiple piercings ain't enough. He's moved onto ink as far as the eye can see. Quality ink, since Jade's been working it. Freehand, at that. He lets her go wild. No stencil. No preconceived thoughts. Just her and the machine. She's our very own sexy, big-titted, born again tattoo wizard.

She scratches a patch of colorful ink on her forearm. "Exactly. Viper. I'm the one who's gotta endure his eight-hour sessions. Tonight, we're working the neck. I'm gonna bring tears to his eyes."

Hell yeah, she will.

I salute my mug , smiling. "Make the bitch cry. Post that shit on YouTube."

"You know I won't do that."

She's the nice one of this duo. I'm always tryin' to corrupt her. Life is too short to stroll through it like it's some boring, snooze fest. This lady needs to live a little. Get some dick. Any dick. Christ, I'd be over-the-moon if she used the sparkly dildo I gave her for her birthday to tickle her sleepy kitten. It's collecting dust in her bedside drawer. I checked. 'Cause boundaries don't exist here. Well, mine don't.

"It's a shame I'm workin'. 'Cause I would post a vid of him cryin'. Of his dick. Of his ass." I groan, picturing that biteable rump in my mind. "Have you seen that fine ass?"

She chuckles. "I know you would. And yes, I have."

The front door opens and slams shut without so much as a knock. There's only one person who'd welcome themselves into this humble abode without a proper invitation—my son. Like mother, like offspring.

Jade watches him enter her remodeled kitchen before I do and nods a hello.

"Beautiful," he greets, blowing her a sugary kiss that she catches midair and smacks to her juicy booty.

Josh snorts his approval. I roll my eyes so far back they might get stuck. You think I'm weird? These two… They're… I dunno what they are. Friends? Besties? Which doesn't work; she's my BFF. I claimed her when he was still in elementary school. No take backs.

My beautiful boy dressed in torn jeans, his Sacred Sinner cut, and a tight Harley t-shirt takes Hunter's vacated stool, then kisses my cheek as Jade sets his mug of black tar in front of him. Mr. I'm-The-Greatest has a special cup. The only mug in the house dedicated to one drinker. He bought it for Jade around Christmas when he was sixteen. It says *I'm not crazy. I just love cock… a lot.* There's a picture of a rooster beneath the plain black lettering. Now she makes him drink from it every time he's here. It gives her some sort of sick satisfaction. My son, he'll do just about anything to make her happy. He's a good man. I'm a proud mama.

"You workin' at the shop with Hunter today?" I nudge his shoulder with mine.

Josh combs fingers through his blond, windblown hair, an elbow resting on the counter. "No. Deke's gonna be there. We're prepping for a run. All hands on deck."

Guess that works. Deke's a decent brother. Better than some.

For the next however long we lapse into comfortable banter as Josh waits for Hunter to get his butt in gear. It's summertime, we're lucky the teen's up before lunch. If it weren't for the gearhead in him, he wouldn't be. Jade's got a fine kid on her hands. Just as I got mine, who's now grown and living on the Sacred Sinner compound in a clubhouse bedroom. It ain't nothing to write home about, but he's a biker through and through. Doesn't take much to make him happy. Some mothers might be put-off by the lifestyle he's leading. Me, not so much. I've been a club whore since before I was legal. Bangin' men in their leather cuts has always been my thing. It takes a special kind of woman to embrace sluthood. Just slap my ass and call me Whore. I'm ready for the ride and always prepared for the wet slide.

CHAPTER 2

BLIMP

Booted feet flat on the ground, straddlin' my Harley outside Clove's Bar, I take a long hit from my blunt. The smooth smoke fills my lungs as my eyes slide closed in high bliss. Enjoyin' myself, my head tips back and I hold in the quality stuff for the count of five before blowing it to the heavens. A set of nearby footsteps refocuses my surroundings. Two regulars lift their hands in greeting as they pull open a metal door to enter the bar. I jerk my chin in acknowledgment, knowin' not a person around will give a fuck I light up in the parking lot before I see my girl. Truth, nobody in this town cares. And if they do, they don't say shit. The patch on my back is a deterrent for opinionated dumbfucks, unless they're lookin' for a fist to the face. I'm a chill guy 99% of the time. I don't do drama. You want to drink, then drink. You wanna smoke, then smoke. You wanna fuck, then fuck. That's on you. I'm too damn old to give a rat's scrawny ass about your life choices. We on the same page? I sure hope so.

Not lettin' my weed to go to waste, I snuff out the blunt and return it to my inner pocket just as my phone vibrates with an incoming text. It vibrates a second time when I retrieve it from my jeans pocket.

Shoulda guessed... It's Viper spouting off in our group text. First, there's a selfie of his new neck ink. It looks badass, but swollen as fuck. Jade's got her purple gun next to his Adam's apple, doin' what she does best. Below, is a ridiculous message I'm sure will have all the brothers salivating to see. 'Cept me.

You gotta stop by. Jade's tits are practically in my face. If it wouldn't fuck up my neck, I'd motorboat those juicy melons. You're missing out brothers.

The chorus of raunchy replies flood in. If I were in the mood to joke, I would. But I've got better things to do than carry on about a woman's jugs. Especially Loretta's best friend. I respect them both enough not to participate.

Turning my phone off, I put it away, comb my beard with my fingers to look presentable and dismount my bike with an old man grunt. Making sure I'm not showin' off my gut, I double check my shirt placement and belt before I stroll into Clover's to see my favorite gal.

Three steps in the door and I've got a biker groupie hangin' from my neck. This chick is smashed and old enough to be my kid. Not that I discriminate against age. I'll fuck twentysomethings. I'm no saint. But I don't fuck drunk biker groupies outside the Sacred Sinner's compound. That's cause for drama I don't have time for.

"Heyyy." She rubs her perky tits against my stomach, batting a set of green eyes up at me with the prettiest cock suckin' lips painted in shiny gloss. She's gorgeous, I'll give her that. Red hair and curves for days. My dick ain't picky. But… like I said, she's drunk, and I don't do drunk bitches. Maybe if I was twenty again, I'd consider it. Fifties give ya a whole new perspective. Clingy groupies, I'll pass.

I politely detach her arms from around my neck and take a step back. "Sorry, sweetheart."

Her bottom lip juts into a pout.

"Court-*ney*," her less-than-pretty friend scolds as she stomps over, gives me a dirty look, and drags Courtney away by the hand. I get it. Biker dick is foreign dick. You see a patch and you wanna go for a ride. We live it all the time. It doesn't hurt I'm a regular when Loretta's workin'. People see me and think I'm down to pound. When the brothers come along for some fun, they are. Where else do ya think they pick up new club whores? They're recruited from here, with Loretta's expert help. If it weren't for her, Dixie wouldn't have met my club brother Brew.

Staying away from the flirty redhead and her gang of friends, I lumber to my seat at the far end of the bar. This place ain't much more than beer posters, fluorescent signs, dingy black walls, a couple of pool tables, and a large wrap around bar with stools covered in cracked, black vinyl doctored with duct tape. Not the classiest place, but the liquor's cheap, clientele's varied, and the music is classic rock all night, all the time. Clove's is the only bar in thirty miles you'll never get stuck listening to that wannabe trash millennials love. Anything after 95' is pure junk. You don't have to agree with me. Not my problem you don't have good taste in music; different strokes and all that PC horseshit.

No sooner does my ass kiss the stool, does the foxy Loretta have a pint of lager ready for me to sip. I pull out my wallet and slap a fifty on the bar as payment and tip. Happy to see me, a smile breaks across that angelic face. Then she reaches across the bar and tugs on my beard in hello. No words are necessary. I'm happy to sit and watch her work all night. That ass is hypnotizing in skin-tight leopard print leggings, like Peg Bundy wore in Married with Children. The top she's got on ain't much different, either. It's black and hangs off one shoulder, then dips down to show off a classy amount of cleavage. Bet the tips are rollin' in tonight. They damn well better be with her lookin' like that. Though, I'm glad to see she didn't go for heels and has on the pair of black flats I bought her years ago. Man, what's it been? Four years? Five? Time flies when you've been screwin' the same gal for twenty years.

Not giving a damn about who's here, I perch an elbow on the bar and sip my beer in private. It's a dark, smooth blend, just how I like.

Some suit wearin', pretty boy down the way catcalls Loretta as she passes him to fill a different order. She turns and flips him off with a smile. He throws his head back and laughs along with his friends. I slap another fifty down to get her to serve me again, before him. The dick notices and does the same with a defiant chin lift. Game on, douchebag. I add another fifty. He slaps down the same, plus a fiver. Callin' his bluff, I toss out a hundred like it ain't no thing. 'Cause it ain't. I've owned the same gun and ammo shop goin' on twenty years. It's done me well. That, and I live with my brothers on our Sacred Sinner compound. No cost of living. His jaw clenches as that clean-shaven face turns a healthy shade of tomato red. I wink, then smirk, knowin' I'm about to win whatever's goin' down.

Nothing happens for a good bit as his friends lean into some frat boy huddle tryin' to figure out how to best the old biker down the bar. Little do they know, the woman they're objectifyin' I plan to fuck in a few short hours. Not that it matters, when I can get Loretta a fat stack of cash to take home tonight.

When the dark-haired goddess that rocks my world finishes fillin' a dozen or more orders, she saunters back my way to top me off. Before she makes it, the douches have convened and wallets open. They compile what cash they've got to add to the stack. There's a good four hundred maybe five there. Not bad.

"Hey, sweetheart." Pretty Boy whistles, shoving the money out for her to collect.

Loretta spins their way. "Can I help you?" Those long lashes flutter with enough flirtation to make half the bar hard as a rock.

Blondie Boy winks at me like he's won before addressing her. "If you can get us a round of top-shelf cognac next, this would be in it for ya." Cash is lined along the edge closest to my gal, who takes the stack and pockets it without a second thought. *Good girl.*

The men high-five as she fills their orders with an extra pep in her step.

Each of the four glasses are set in front of the douchebags before she walks to my end of the bar, reaches out, grabs a fistful of my beard, yanks me out of my seat and halfway across the fuckin' thing to lay a soul burning kiss on my lips. And I let her. Damn, do I let her.

Our tongues meet like old friends, tangling across the wooden top as my stomach digs into the side. I swallow Loretta's needy little moans until the fox is left panting, and I'm so hard I could pound a dozen nails into concrete.

When she pulls away and wipes her mouth with the back of her hand, I do my best to conceal the spike in my pants. A smug, grateful smile consumes my face as I retake my seat.

"There's more where that came from." She fans herself, smiling all sweet and bashful when I know she's anything but.

"I'd hope so." I down the rest of my beer, not givin' a damn who saw our little show.

"I've missed your…" Those sparkling eyes flick to where I'm hiding an erection.

I cover it with my hand, knowin' she can't see it. "Oh, yeah? It's only been ten days." We try to get together a handful of times a month. With all that's been goin' on at the club, things haven't worked in our favor.

"A week too long." She grabs my empty glass and saunters that sexy ass away to refill it. Yet, the money I left still sits on the counter, untouched. I should've guessed she wouldn't take more than the fifty. She never does, no matter how much I try to give her. Beautiful, stubborn woman. Guess I'll pay her in other ways tonight. Orgasm currency sounds mighty fuckin' fine.

I check the glowing Miller Lite clock above the register.

Only two hours and twelve minutes 'til I get to make good on our monthly arrangement. It's about damn time. I missed my gal.

CHAPTER 3

LORETTA

Brick digs into my palms as they press against the wall outside the bar, in the alleyway after my shift. Animal print leggings and panties cuff around my knees. I push my ass back to give Blimp the perfect angle to stick that fat cock into my cunt. I'm wet for him. Have been all night. That stunt he pulled with the businessmen has me hotter than a firecracker. I need him here and now. We can't wait. It's been too long.

A rough hand clamps over my hip as Blimp's tip glides through my folds, teasing me, smearing his pre-cum around.

"Please," I whine, rotating my ass for more friction.

Blunt fingers sink into my flesh, deep enough to bruise. I relish every second. Hungry for whatever he's willing to give, my eyelids flutter in submission as I let him take control. A cool breeze swirls through the alley, arousing goosebumps. I shiver.

"Say it," Blimp commands.

"Please."

He swats my ass. "No. No. No, naughty slut. Say it."

Oh, how I've missed you, baby. That dirty talk. That dick.

Knowing what he seeks, I give Blimp what he wants. "I need your fat cock."

Rewarding my words, he slides in the smallest bit. "Need it. Eh?"

"Yes," I moan, not caring who hears.

Blimp knocks my feet apart, forcing me to widen my stance. The leggings roll down to my ankles, baring my legs. "What else you gotta say?" he prompts.

What else does he want? What more can I say? Can't he see I'm at his mercy? That I always will be?

When I don't reply quick enough, a sharp sting radiates across my backside as his hand brands flesh. I cry out. Not from pain, but desire. Frustration. I don't like to wait. This is the sexiest form of torture. Watching him sitting at my bar, drinking my drinks just so he can see me has always been a turn on. He knows it. I know it. It's our hottest form of foreplay. One neither of us will admit to, but a game we both play to have moments like this.

Growing impatient, Blimp prompts a second time. "Well?"

Saying what must be said, I express my innermost feelings. "I missed you." More than any woman should.

Gentle, almost reverent, fingertips brush my hip bone, swirling designs there as Blimp's cock remains motionless, hovering inside my pussy. "What'd you miss?" His voice is low and jagged.

"Your dick."

An inch glides in, stretching my walls around its immense girth.

"What else?"

"That mouth."

Another inch has my toes curling in my shoes. Sweat beads on my brow as he touches that special spot, sending sparks of pleasure straight to my nipples. They harden, stabbing the lace of my bra. A rush of air bursts from my lungs and my stomach quakes, as he grants me mercy giving a second inch. We're halfway there.

"And?" Blimp grits. Resuming his hold on my hip with one hand, he releases his dick with the other to gain complete control.

"You." *I missed you so much.*

"That's right, my sweet, sweet, slut, you missed me." With that Blimp slams home, giving me the full eight inches to the hilt, knocking my world askew. I pitch forward, taking the brunt of his power, but Blimp's got me, as he always does.

Using me as his fuck toy, he pistons his thickness in and out of my hole relentlessly, not giving me a chance to work for it. To beg. To do anything more than go along for the brutal, erotic ride.

"That's it, slut. Take it." He lands another smack, and my walls convulse around his shaft. I almost come.

He unleashes another, knowing the right buttons to push.

And it works.

Closing my eyes, I throw my head back and scream into the night as starbursts of colors explode behind my lids. I shudder, knees giving out. But there's Blimp, anchoring my smaller body to his larger, much softer and cuddlier form. His beard tickles the back of my neck as he pulls out and…

"Fuck!" Blimp jerks away as blinding police lights fill the alleyway. An officer exits his car.

I stand here dumbfounded, watching him approach with my shoulder resting against the building, bottoms around my ankles. I squint to make the man out, trying my damndest to see if this is a joke, or if we're caught with our pants down.

When I glance at Blimp, he's grinding his jaw, nostrils flaring, clothes back in place. Unlike me, who still has orgasm brain. It's a thing. I promise. One night with Blimp and you'd understand. It'll make you forget your own name. Or the fact you're flashing the popo your hoo-ha. Oh well, in for a penny, in for a pound. I let it ride.

The young blond officer stops a safe distance away as he eyes Blimp. Noticing the leather cut, he pulls his gun. Rookie. This punk is out patrolling on a Friday night in our town by himself, and he has the balls to draw his weapon because of a Sacred Sinner. Big's gonna have a field day with this. So is this boy's chief, Wanda, when I tell her about it.

"Get back in your car, son. Leave us be," Blimp warns, both arms down at his sides, fists flexing and unflexing in anger.

The officer raises his gun and aims it at Blimp's chest.

Dumbshit.

Not fazed in the least, my favorite guy looks at me. "Sweetheart, get yourself together, please."

Right. Clothes.

Sighing, I push off the wall to do as I'm told. Which is boring, but whatever. It's obvious the newcomer doesn't know the score, or he'd have apologized and left. Trust me when I say this isn't the first, nor will it be the last time, Blimp and I have gotten caught having naughty fun outdoors. Thing is, we won't do it with kids around and adults are smart enough to turn a blind eye.

"Identification, sir," the rookie addresses Blimp, who then slaps the patch on his chest that displays his name.

The police officer repeats himself. "Identification, sir."

Rolling my eyes, I rest my back against the building, hoping this game will be over soon so we can get back to fucking. Maybe not here, but somewhere. His tongue will be on my clit by night's end.

Not one to fight authority in my presence, Blimp produces his wallet without argument and hands over his ID. The cop radios it in over the com on his shoulder. The person who responds is laughing their ass off when they reply. I press my lips together to keep from joining them. The rookie's face turns beet red as he holsters his weapon, but…

Oh, this little dickhead is not pulling out the cuffs.

"Turn around, sir. Place your hands behind your back."

Blimp arches his brow at me, almost amused. Almost.

"Sure thing." Blimp complies. I have to cover my mouth to keep from losing it. This is too damn funny. If I hadn't left my phone in the bar, I'd take a picture to send to Jade. She'd love this. So would my son.

"Ma'am." The officer addresses me after he has Blimp locked down.

"Yes?"

"Can you please follow behind? I'm taking you in, as well. Don't run or I will have to chase you."

This keeps getting better and better. We're headed for the slammer.

I cock my head to the side. "Can you tell me what you're arresting us for?"

"I think that'd be obvious, ma'am. You and Mr. Blimp were illegally exposing yourselves."

The poor thing can't even say it aloud. How old is this kid? Josh's age?

I play along because this'll make for a damn good story. "Right. So, you're arresting us for having sex behind a bar?"

"That is correct, ma'am. Now please come along, or I'll have to cuff you, too."

It's Blimp's turn to press his lips together to keep from busting a gut. He knows all too well how much I love cuffs. The real ones. None of those toy gadgets.

I nod in compliance. "Yes, officer."

Satisfied with my docile response, I stroll ahead of them to the rear of the patrol car. Still holding onto Blimp's bicep, the officer opens the back door and folds my fuckbuddy in first before giving me a chance to enter. Once we're locked inside, I look at Blimp, he looks at me, we lean in, give the other a quick kiss, then smother whatever laugher we want to unleash until we reach the station, which isn't more than a five-minute trip.

CHAPTER 4

BLIMP

Seated on a bench in the middle of our small-town police station, Loretta's knee bounces beside mine. The second Officer Shitstain brought us in, the place has been buzzing like bees. Even at the early hour, eyes flash our way in concern. They know what's up. If they're smart, they do. It's common sense 'round these parts.

They're lucky word hasn't reached Big or Gunz, yet. I give it another twenty minutes before my prez busts through that front door and causes a scene nobody will soon forget. If Loretta hadn't been with me, Officer Shitstain woulda learned the hard way we don't take kindly to guns bein' aimed at our chest. But I'm not about to get my favorite gal cuffed on account of me bein' a biker. So, I'll play along to this pathetic charade 'til it no longer suits me.

Elbows restin' on her knees, Loretta shakes that pretty head. "What's takin' so damn long?" she hisses under breath.

I knock my knee into hers in support, since my hands are still incapacitated. "Babe, it's early in the mornin'. We might be here a while, 'til someone shows up to scold that stupid kid." I get rules are rules and laws are laws, but we weren't hurtin' anybody and were keepin' to ourselves. He ruined that. Didn't even give me time to bust a nut in that sweet, sweet, wet cunt. The only hole I go bare in. Do you know what that does to a man? To his dick? Condom fuckin' works and all, but bareback is a whole different world of pleasure. Seein' as though I've only ever done it with Loretta, I'm pissed. That slit looks mighty sexy with cum dripping from it.

"My son is gonna lose his mind."

She's not wrong. White Boy respects his mama. Would kill for her... die for her, as would I.

"So is my prez." Let's pray Big doesn't try to send a message by doin' something rash. Since he and his old lady have settled down, he's been better, more even-keeled. Though, you can't take the outlaw outta a biker any more than you can take the bite from a dog.

Loretta sits up and looks at me, eyes wide. "Oh shit. Big. I didn't even think about him."

"Let this be a lesson to the new blood 'round here. Better they learn it with us than pickin' somebody else up. Can you imagine what'd happen if Bink got arrested?"

The flash of horror that crosses her face says it all. You arrest Bink, you die a slow and painful death. No questions asked.

"Guess it's a good thing I'm a club whore and not someone's old lady," she remarks, which couldn't be further from the truth. The cop saw her pussy. My slut's pussy. Oh, you bet there will be hell to pay when she's not around. Club biz doesn't go down with bitches present. Never has, never will. Not if I can help it.

I lean over and peck my gal's cheek to calm her britches. "It's gonna—" The rest of my words fade away as a familiar, brass-balled voice causes chaos in the station.

"Who in here arrested Loretta and Blimp?!" Wanda growls, and everybody pauses. The ballbuster has that effect. She might be a woman, but she runs this place, and not a person here would question why. The feisty redhead's presence says it all.

"Moranis did, ma'am," a female employee explains. I can't see much, not even Wanda. This bench doesn't give us much of a view; apart from two windows, two doors, and a whole lotta dingy white walls.

"Release them now," she orders.

I smirk and so does Loretta as we exchange a knowing look. Wanda is a far better outcome than Big. Her clout in this place has a helluva lot more staying power than his.

"But... Captain." It's Moranis A.K.A. Officer Shitstain.

Loretta's nose wrinkles in distaste upon hearing his voice.

Wanda scoffs, having none of his back talk. "I don't want to hear it. Not now. Not tomorrow. Not in a month. When I get woken in the middle of the night with this shit, Moranis, I am not a happy woman. I've ordered you, and every single officer under my command to never arrest a Sacred Sinner without my permission. And when I say you don't arrest a Sacred Sinner, you don't arrest a Sacred Sinner. Are we clear?"

"But they were—" Oh, little boy wants to argue with the boss. This won't go well for him. Even I don't fuck with the authority in my club. You respect leadership. Damn kid needs to learn his place.

"Did I ask what they were doing? Does it look like I give a damn? 'Cause I don't. Release them at once, or you're out on your ass."

"Yes, Captain. Sorry, Captain." The idiot scurries into the room, headed straight for me, to unlock my cuffs. Wanda's right on his tail, standing in the door frame; her face bright red, jaw set. She glances at Loretta, then me. That's when she notices Officer Shitstain unlocking my wrists from behind my back. If I thought she was angry before, nothing covers the fury boiling in her veins now.

"What else did he do?" she grits, eyeing Loretta for an explanation.

My gal rubs both palms up and down the tops of her thighs. "Pulled his weapon."

The hands trying to unfasten me shake like a leaf. The man knows he's in deep with the stunt he pulled tonight. If we were causing mayhem in town, I'd understand the arrest. But we're too old for all that.

"Was Blimp confrontational?" Wanda takes a step closer, wearing civilian clothes, her red hair in a messy bun on the top of her head. She's a looker: full hips, perky tits, lush ass, and a mouth made for clit sucking.

Loretta shakes her head. "No."

"Then what?"

One wrist is set free. I pull it onto my lap.

"Blimp explained he should walk away. He didn't listen and aimed his gun instead. Then cuffed him after."

"Aimed his gun?" Wanda's eyebrows hike into her hairline.

"Yes."

The Captain peers over her shoulder at the man hovering outside the room. The tat on his arm is all I can see at this angle and all I need to know. "You heard her account. Write the report and check his body cam footage."

"There is none." Officer Marik clarifies. He's one of the good ones on the force. All the brothers, even prez, likes him. He's fair and only steps in when necessary.

Their boss spins around to address the situation. "Excuse me?"

"We've tried to pull footage twice. His cam was off. All we could pull from is the dash cam."

"And?" she presses.

"Loretta's story matches what I observed."

Fuck yeah, it does.

"And Moranis' account?" Wanda prompts, foot tapping the ground in agitation.

"Says Blimp was hostile and refused to leave."

"So, you're saying Officer Moranis disobeyed direct orders, left his body cam off, and lied?"

Marik confirms what we all know to be true. "Yes. It would appear that way, Captain."

Moranis breaks into a soft sob, unable to get the final cuff loose. Knowing this needs to get handled sooner rather than later, Marik strides in and takes over my release as Wanda waves her insubordinate officer from the room with the jerk of her chin.

"Thanks," I tell Marik, as I massage my wrists that'll have bruises on them by tomorrow.

Holding the cuffs in one hand, the buff cop stands in front of us, head shaking. "No thanks needed. This shouldn't have happened in the first place. I already reached out to Big. He knows Cap is handling it. I don't see Moranis makin' it past tonight."

"It's probably for the best he's gone before Big… ya know." Loses his temper and makes Moranis disappear. It's bound to happen with the kid's reckless behavior. In most cities, they'd applaud him for bringing a biker in. Not here. Transferring him to some place better suited for his type of patrolling is smarter for us all. I don't want the boy to get dead on our account. He's too young to die from stupidity.

Marik nods once, then ambles to the door. "Yep… Well, y'all have a good night."

"Thanks, Marik. You, too." Loretta waves goodbye.

"Later," I call to his back before turning to my gal. "You ready to blow this popsicle stand, beautiful?"

Smiling like I handed her a million dollars, Loretta leans in for a hug, which I am more than happy to give. 'Cause I'm a greedy bastard, I pull the fox onto my lap for a quick cuddle. Her nose nuzzles my shoulder as she strokes my beard. "Time with you is never boring."

"Back atcha, babe." I caress the side of her breast and she chuckles.

"We can't do that here. Let me talk to Wanda. See if she can give us a ride back to my place."

"That all you want her for?" I tease, searching for her nipple through the outside of her shirt. It pebbles on contact, so I do what any red-blooded man would do and roll it between my fingers to get her wet. Hell, my dick is already back to full mast. He's determined to paint the inside of Loretta's cunt white tonight. Picasso ain't got nothin' on him.

Groaning into my shoulder, my gal lets me play however I wish.

Now let's go get our fuck on before I take her right on this bench.

CHAPTER 5

LORETTA

Arms cuffed to my slatted headboard, head thrown back, my spine arches off the bed, heels digging into the mattress as I come, and come, and fucking come.

"Wanda!" I howl, jerking my restraints as she sucks my clit with abandon. Her hands keep my hips from bucking.

"Suck harder." Blimp shoves the back of Wanda's head, forcing her to latch onto my pussy, as he fucks her face down, ass up. The sound of skin slapping skin and her moans vibrating against my sensitive nerves has my body shaking uncontrollably.

She does as she's told, and I gasp, eyes squeezing shut, tears leaking from the corners.

"That's it. Eat her sweet cunt. She tastes good. Doesn't she?"

Wanda groans in agreement, never giving my clit a moment's reprieve. It goes on and on, pleasure sparking through my entire body. Unintelligible words babble from my lips as I lose all sense of reality, my brain too focused on her mouth, the strong scent of sex that hangs in the air, and Blimp, the man who never fails to rock my world.

Wanda's whimpery moans intensify as he takes her to the precipice. When she's ready to let go, he grips a fistful of her hair and wrenches that sinful mouth from my core to make her look at me. "Tell her you're about to come on my dick."

Wanda's wrecked, saturated lips form a beautiful 'O' as her channel sucks wetly around his monster dick, making me want to see the show firsthand—how he slams between those puffy, rose colored folds — the ones I've licked and sucked on hundreds of times before.

"Tell her," he growls as I look on with hooded eyes, my chest rising and falling with laden breaths. I've never been more turned on in my life... At least, not since the last time we were together like this.

"He's gonna... oh fuck... make me... Comeee... Ohhh... Ngh... Fuuuck." Wanda's face screws into the sexiest blissed-out grimace as Blimp takes her there, slamming into her so violently she can barely stay on her hands, tits jiggling beneath her. It's quite a sight to behold, one I never tire of.

A broken wail of ecstasy pours from those lips as she dives down the well of no return, emerald eyes tipping into the back of her skull. As always, Blimp doesn't stop. Showing no mercy, he fucks Wanda until she loses her voice; upper body collapsing, cheek meeting my pussy. Still exerting his control, Blimp grabs the base of Wanda's neck and presses her face against my sex. Nose on mound, lips on clit.

"Lick," he commands.

She whines.

"I said lick."

That tongue tries to get to work, but the poor woman is too fucked out to accomplish much. Her breath bathes my folds in heavy pants as she flicks my sensitive bud the tiniest bit. If I had the use of my hands, I'd brush my fingers through her mangled hair and maybe cuddle her after such an intense climax. An intimacy Blimp will never give her. Their sex doesn't work that way.

His pumps grow lazy as he finishes wringing her body dry. When he's sure she's through, he pulls out, and like the dominant man he is, pushes her off me. Wanda's boneless form spreads out beside me on the queen bed as Blimp tears off the condom and tosses it onto the floor. Then he crawls forward on those thick thighs, pushes both of my legs up, and enters me without warning, driving to the hilt.

"Blimp!" I screech, doing my best to accommodate such girth all at once.

He folds me in half, knees to shoulders, toes touching the headboard. "Love this pussy, slut." His brash words achieve their desired effect, turning me into a wanton, pussy dripping mess.

"Yes," I cry out.

"Love this cunt so fuckin' much. Gonna make a mess in you." That glorious slab of cock jackhammers me as Blimp's neck tightens in pleasure. Sweat drips off his forehead, those tattooed pecs flexing with each stroke.

"Yes." I whimper, tightening my sex around him.

"Say it."

"Please."

"Please what, whore?"

I fucking love it when he calls me that.

"Come inside me." That's what he wants to hear. It's part of the endless game we play. I'll tell him whatever he wants as long as he doesn't stop performing tricks on my g-spot like a big, burly magician.

"You want my cum?" He smiles wickedly.

Always. Always. Always.

I lick my lips, wanting his on mine. "Please. Yes."

"That's what I thought." That's all it takes for Blimp's jaw to set, then he's there, pumping hot jets of cum into my center, filling me, fucking it deep. Low, animalistic growls of satisfaction rumble in that thick chest as he empties himself fully.

My legs are eventually released. I wrap them around his middle as his chest comes to rest on top of mine, our lips brushing.

"I think I made a mess," he chuckles the sexiest, laziest sound that makes me smile, spreading warmth through my center. This is the best part of Blimp; the soft, sweet, yet dominant part—when he's sated and cuddly.

Wanda rolls over, sliding up beside us. I turn to meet her lips with mine for a sensual kiss. Our tongues glide in unison, making my pussy clench with need. She tastes of me, of beauty, and sex. I love men, but sleeping with a woman is a unique feel you can't get anywhere else. Wanda's my favorite female lay. Her pussy is smooth and tastes like heaven. That body is to die for.

Joining in on the intimacy, Blimp peppers kisses along my cheek and down my throat until he glides far enough to reach my nipples, where he suckles a stiff peak into his mouth. I cry into Wanda's kiss. She swallows it down with greedy noises of her own.

Blimp's cock slips free. Cum drips out but is pushed back inside as he thrusts two thick fingers into me, going straight for that special spot he knows drives me mad. And it works. Playing my body like a fiddle, Blimp owns my tits as he finger fucks me to the tempo of his suckling. I grip the slats of the bed, thrusting my hips for more connection. He chuckles around my flesh as Wanda takes this opportunity to trail a hand down my side and over my hip to my clit, where she rubs me off.

"I… I…"

"No complaints, slut. You're gonna take it." Blimp orders as he releases my nipple to kiss my cheek. Then grabs a fistful of Wanda's mane and brings it to my bare breast. Taking orders like a champ, she takes his spot and resumes the torture on my tits that leaves me squirming.

Blimp climbs off the bed, and when he returns, his hard shaft is coated in lube. My eyes widen as he knocks Wanda's hand from my clit and places a pillow under my ass before he pushes my legs up. That's when I realize what he's about to do.

"Blimp?" My voice waivers in concern.

"You love this." Kneeling, he massages his cockhead against my exposed asshole, smearing around lube and the cum that's dripped there.

I shake my head. "It's too much." When we have anal sex, I lose my mind. It's not a joke. I... I can't take it. Not tonight. Not when Wanda's here. The only time he's done this with her around, I... I couldn't remember my name. I couldn't walk. I couldn't do a damn thing but scream, because it's never just sex. It's more. And the more part is what I can't handle.

"No. It's not. Sluts take dicks in their ass. You're my slut, aren't you?"

Why does he have to pull that card? Of course, I'm his. Of course, I want him. Of course, I'm willing to be used.

"Yes," I whimper.

Blimp slaps my hole with his mushroom tip. "Then beg me to fuck your ass."

"I..." This won't end well.

He tweaks my clit with his fingers, sending a glorious shock of pain from toes to nose. "Beg. Me." His nostrils flare as if he's growing impatient... as if he can't wait to be inside me.

My stomach quivers. "Blimp... please."

"Please what?" The wet tip pokes my back door.

I gasp and swallow hard to find my voice. "Fuck my ass."

"That's my girl... Now bear down and let my dick inside your tight little hole, baby. Gonna make this feel so good."

Shaking in part fear, part excitement, I do as I'm told. It stings at first, but Wanda's mouth on my nipple dulls the pain, focusing my mind elsewhere. By the time he's seated to the hilt, I'm panting, toes curling so tight they ache.

Then my maestro does what I knew he'd do. One pump into my hole has my eyes slamming shut as those sensitive walls are lit on fire. Two fingers reinsert into my cum soaked cunt. Wanda's thumb finds my clit again. Taking things to the final step, the one I'm most worried about, Blimp pushes down on my lower stomach as those digits curve inside. That's all it takes. The pressure consumes me with a level of ecstasy few will find... A freefall over the cliff of the great unknown, into a shallow pool of rhapsody below- where Sin and Pleasure frolic in the shimmery indigo waters. There's no use in fighting. Not now. So, I let it take me.

The world falls away as my biker plunders my asshole in time with those talented fingers. Violent waves of pleasure tremble in my veins as Blimp coerces my body to do his bidding. And it does. It always does.

"Gonna make you come."

Dynamite explodes from my pussy as he presses down on my stomach, forcing me to squirt my climax. Neck elongating, every muscle contracts as I scream through it, unable to hold back as I shower him in lady cum.

"Hell yeah, baby." He keeps going, applying more pressure until my world goes dark, and every part of me is ripped asunder. I splash him in my essence, again and again, howling my pleasure, but he doesn't stop. Never stops.

At some point, Wanda releases my nipple with a pop, but I'm too far gone to care.

"Again, my beautiful slut. Give it to me." That cock buries deep, fingers too, as I unwillingly do as I'm told. Giving him the cum he desires, my asshole clamps down on his shaft, my entire form shuddering until it shatters into a million euphoric pieces.

A wet finger slides across my tongue mid-moan. It tastes of her. Wrapping my lips around the salty digit, I suck Wanda's flavor with vigor.

"Give her another hit," Blimp orders.

Wanda pulls that finger from my hungry mouth only to insert another with more of her essence, thus beginning a new game. Every time I give Blimp what he wants, Wanda rewards me with taste after taste until I'm begging for her to sit on my face for an endless supply.

"More, please." I lick my lips, savoring every drop.

"You think you deserve her wet cunt?" Blimp rubs my clit, giving it a second of attention.

I shiver, praying he doesn't stop touching there. "Yes."

"Why?"

"'Cause I'm being a good slut." So good. So, so, so good. I've come for him as much as he wanted.

Blimp chuckles fondly. "Oh yeah?"

"Yes."

"You gonna be a good enough slut to beg me to cum in your asshole, too? I think it's jealous of your pussy."

"Yes. It's jealous," I blurt. I want it. All of it. Everywhere.

"Jealous of what?" Blimp's dick pumps in and out of my asshole in lazy, perfect strokes.

"My pussy."

"Does your pretty hole want a drink of my cum?"

Dear God, yes!

"Please, give it a drink. *Pleeeaase.* Give it to my hole. It's jealous. It wants you," I blather on not caring how slurred or whiny my words sound.

Because Blimp is the most amazing man ever, he drags my body down the bed to elongate my arms so Wanda can straddle my face without hurting me. Warm, sopping wet folds descend upon my lips, smearing them in tangy juices. The pure scent of woman invades my nostrils as I lick through soft pillows to feast on her center, tonguing that well-used entrance. Wanda threads her fingers through my hair, holding me to her core, feeding me like I want to be fed. I revel in her as Blimp lets me enjoy the treat without interruption. Moaning as she moans, her essence floods my face. I drink it down, thirsty for more.

"Lore, God, I… your mouth," Wanda rasps, rocking her hips. Wisps of her curly red hair tickle my nose.

I sense Blimp move before fingers are removed from my center, as is his dick. The bed dips, then his mouth covers my center as I devour Wanda's. We indulge in bodies and sounds, in desires and flavors. I come, she comes. Rejoicing in her body's ability to have multiples, I lave that fat, hard clit until she quakes above me with one last climax.

When she's through, Wanda climbs off my face and leans down to clean up the mess she's made there. I let her do as she wishes before we end our adventure in a sensual kiss. Palming my breast a final time, her body half on mine, heat on heat, our heavy breaths mingle in shared passion. This is why I love being with her, the special brand of intimacy you can't get with a man. The softness of her breast touching my side. The tang of pussy on her lips.

"Thank you," Wanda whispers as she pulls away wearing a lopsided smile and hooded eyes that speak of happy times.

As the redhead climbs her sexy ass off the bed she nods goodbye to Blimp, who returns the gesture in kind before resuming our previous position, dick in hole, fingers in pussy. With our extra gone, we spend the rest of the evening coming together until I can barely keep my eyes open and we're coated in sweat.

Blimp's spent cock deflates, slipping from my asshole. "It's time to shower, sweetheart."

Incapable of forming words, I nod, at least I think I do. Floating high on carnal satiation, my body's nothing more than a lump of overcooked noodles. I need sleep. Hours of it. Weeks. I don't care as long as I don't have to move a muscle.

Tending to me, Blimp uncuffs me from the bed and massages my wrists before the big, burly biker carries me from the bedroom into my bathroom shower stall, which is running with hot water already. Too tired to care, I rest my head on his shoulder, legs around his thick waist, as Blimp washes me under the soothing spray.

"It's okay, babe, I've got ya. Just relax."

I peck his neck, dragging lips over damp flesh. "I think you broke me."

"You'll be sore tomorrow. But it'll be okay." He kisses my shoulder. The sweetness does funny things to my insides.

"We're old. We're both gonna hurt." Pain killers will be our best friends. They always are after a night like tonight.

He laughs, light and carefree. "This is true, but I wouldn't have it any other way."

I squeeze him a little tighter. "You're a sex fiend."

Using the shampoo pump to gather a dollop, Blimp's giant hand then massages the soap into my curly mess of hair, careful not to get any in my face. "No, I'm a fiend for you."

Whatever. Crazy man. "You only say that after you come inside me."

He shrugs before rinsing the soap from my locks. "Well, yeah, I love that shit. But it's not why I'm sayin' it. I'm thinkin' when I get back from this run we need to handle this old lady business."

Huh?

Playing like I don't know what he's talking about, 'cause I don't, I keep it light. "What old lady business? You got another bitch I don't know about?" I know he doesn't. Blimp is forthcoming about all his exploits. If he screws a whore on Sunday, you can bet by Monday morning I've heard the entire play-by-play down to if she spits or swallows. Have I forgotten to mention that when he bangs other bitches he forces them to drink his spunk? Yep. That's a thing. Fucking and dick sucking until he spills down their throat. The gentleman in him allows them to spit after he's unloaded, but he refuses to pull out. Blimp loves painting a woman's insides with cum—takes pride in it. I find it hot when I watch him do it with other women. Most of them can't get enough.

Blimp kisses my shoulder a second time. "No. I'm thinkin' we're good together. Maybe we should… ya know."

"No, sexy, I don't know," I lie, worried I'm reading into crap I shouldn't be. "My brain is fucked out of my head. There's nothin' left. That's what happens when you force me to come like that." Which is true. Mostly.

He nips the cap of my shoulder playfully. "I like when ya squirt."

Like it? If I'd let him do it every time, he would. He loves it. Probably too much.

"I know ya do, but it makes a huge mess. And I can't stand for like five hours afterward." Also, true.

"Worth it, though. You know I'll handle the sheets and all that shit before we get some sleep."

"I do know that." He's the kindest man after a wild sex session. Always has been. Even when we were in our prime, he was considerate.

The older he's gotten, the more it shows. I love that about him. It's a huge reason why I've been with him all these years.

Using the wall to brace himself, Blimp lowers us to the shower floor. My legs stay wrapped around him as his stretch out. That naughty cock twitches as it cuddles up to its favorite partner. "Sweetheart, look at me for a minute."

I do, but keep my arms draped around his neck. My droopy, sleep deprived eyes meet his equally tired ones as water drips from his beard down his front. "Yes?"

Blimp brushes the apple of my cheek with his thumb. "Let's not lie to ourselves."

"O-kay?" My stomach somersaults in trepidation.

Blimp's face softens to the cuddly bear version of the man I adore. "I love you. You love me. We've loved each other a long damn time even if we don't say it… Been through a lot together. Seen a lot together. Done a lot together. Yeah?"

Holy. Shit.

Tongue tied, I nod like an idiot.

"Don't ya think it's about time you're my old lady and my slut? Things won't change. I'm still gonna bang who I want. You're still gonna do what you want. But we're gettin' a little too old to dance around this any longer. Wouldn't you agree?"

Where is this coming from?

"I… I don't know." And I don't. I can honestly say I've never considered this an option before. We do us. It works. End of story.

Blimp's lip twitches as if he's trying hard not to laugh at the befuddled expression written across my face. "Have I been readin' shit wrong for years?"

Um… I guess not. "No."

"Then there's love here, true?" he tests.

Am I dreaming? Did I fall asleep after that last orgasm? 'Cause we've never talked like this before. Not about feelings and stuff.

"Yes…I love you." I'm apprehensive. He's the only man I've ever loved. Apart from Jade, Blimp is my best friend, my lover, and the person I trust most in this world.

He drops a quick kiss to my upper lip before carrying on. I'm too shocked to do more than stare as water cascades down my spine. "And I love the hell outta you. So, I wanna put a property patch on that back."

A property patch like Bink? Like Pixie? And Debbie and… all the Sacred Sisters? Fuck.

"Umm… Do I gotta wear a cut?" Like them.

Blimp massages those mitts up and down my biceps before gliding them up my shoulders to my throat, where he curves his fingers around it in a dominant display of ownership. "Yes. You gotta wear one." His thumbs stroke the underside of my jaw.

I swallow against the pressure. "Then nobody will ever touch me again."

His brows furrow. "Why?"

"'Cause men won't touch another man's old lady." That's the way of the biker world.

"They will if I say they can. Your pussy has been mine for years. Sharin' it has never been an issue before. It won't be an issue if we do this," Blimp assures, and I believe him.

If things won't change… then maybe.

"Can I think about it?"

"No." Blimp's forehead wrinkles in confusion, like he wasn't expecting me to want time to consider things. Those all-seeing eyes trace my face, trying to read me before he drops the next bomb. "I already told Gunz to order a cut in your size."

This man… this insane, beautiful man. Ugh.

"You're joking." I heave a sigh.

He shakes his head. "No, sweetheart, I'm not. I'm plannin' on growin' old with you one way or another. Might as well make the shit official."

What was he thinking? Grow old with me? Since when? I mean… I kind of always knew we would. But not formally.

Not sure what to do with these revelations, I yank on his beard as I pretend my insides aren't going haywire with the news. "You're a jerk."

That stupid lip twitches. "Yep. But I'm your jerk."

"Fine…" I roll my eyes dramatically as I keep a tight hold on his beard for leverage. "I guess I agree to this. But the minute this goes south, and you piss me off, I'm burning that motherfucker in a bye-bye Blimp bonfire and never speaking to you again."

A bright smile surfaces that has my heart beating extra fast. "Or… I'll fuck you 'til you forget why you were mad at me in the first place, just like I've done for the past two decades."

Damn jerk, always knowing the right thing to say.

"Ugh. I hate you sometimes." To show him just how much, I yank those lips close enough to skim mine. His beard tickles my chin.

"Love you, too, babe," he whispers there before slamming our mouths together to seal our fate. And what a fate it is. With him by my side, our life will never be boring. Bring on the cut. I'm Blimp's old lady now and a club slut forevermore.

The End.

Want more Bink Books?
Grab MC Chronicles Vol 1 for FREE for a limited time!

-Follow Bink Cummings on-
Instagram: https://www.instagram.com/binkcummings/
Facebook: https://www.facebook.com/binkcummings/
Newsletter: https://landing.mailerlite.com/webforms/landing/f9a7l6

BREATHE FOR IT

Hellions Ride On Series

Written By
USA Today Bestselling Author
Chelsea Camaron

INTRODUCTION

Breathe for It

Life rarely gives us a second chance at love. These two find it in this passion-fueled ride.

Crunch

I don't know where it all went so wrong. I was born a Hellion. I breathe for the club life, but at every turn I put it all at risk.

I am Rhett "Crunch" Oleander.

I am still finding my way since losing the one person who meant the most.

Jennissey

Once upon a time I believed everyone had this good inside of them. Now, I see the darkness in every single person.

I am Jennissey Rose Rivera.

Family over everything, even if it kills me inside every single day.

She's the only taste of Heaven he's ever had. When given a second chance, he's refusing to let go. The question is will she walk away again or hang on for the ride?

Content warning:

This book contains mature content not suitable for those under the age of 18.

Content involves strong language and sexual situations. All parties portrayed in sexual situations are over the age of 18. All characters are a work of fiction.

This is not meant to be an exact depiction of life in a motorcycle club, but rather a work of fiction meant to entertain.

CHAPTER 1

CRUNCH

"KISS ME," I WHISPER.

Immediately, she rolls to her tip toes and presses her lips to mine. The same spark that hit me the very first time I put my lips to hers rushes through me again. It's crazy the way she makes me feel.

"Oleander," Coach Orr says sternly, "break it up."

Jennissey pushes away and immediately I want her lips connected to mine once again. I let out a low groan in frustration.

High school sucks.

I'm so ready to be done with this place. Life is in front of us and I'm ready to take on the world.

Taking her hand in mine, I lace our fingers together as we walk to class. Mrs. Davey gives the same soft sigh she does every day when we walk in together.

"Good morning, Rhett, Jenni, hope you're ready to learn!"

I swear to fuck this woman thinks it's her job to be fucking sunshine or something. Mrs. Davey is four-feet-eleven, brown hair she always wears pinned back in a bun, round rimmed glasses, and a Hufflepuff pin always attached to every dress she wears. She is a self-proclaimed super nerd and proud of her Harry Potter obsession.

Me, I've never read the books. Mom forced a family night where I watched one of the movies. Only one, I couldn't stomach another. My older brother, Red, he watched all the movies with mom; but me, I dealt with the single one my dad said we had to sit through, and that was it. If my dad hadn't forced the issue I wouldn't have watched it then.

Truthfully, I'm not Red. He's the golden child.

Four boys.

I guess Mom needs one of us to be the good one, and it just happens to be him.

Kenneth "Red" Oleander is the example and takes his role as first born serious. He does what they ask, when they ask, and never gets in trouble. In fact, he's prospecting for the club now and will easily earn his rockers and final patch at twenty-one. I have no doubts in his ability to be the perfect son and stepping into his place in the brotherhood that is the Hellions MC.

I'm the second-born and considered the problem child to most. My gramps, Rhett "Danza" Perchton, believes I choose to be difficult because I have the soul of a gypsy. I don't disagree. But I also don't find myself to be difficult, rather I like to question authority. What gives anyone the power or the right to tell me what to do? I am a man with a mind of my own.

Sometimes small town life doesn't work for everyone. Haywood's Landing, North Carolina is nothing more than some sign on a road off Highway 58. There is no challenge to life here, not when you're born a Haywood's Landing Hellion.

Danza, he's an original. The only one left here now. Two of the four are in plots in the local cemetery. Since Roundman passed away and Tripp took the gavel, Gramps has made it his mission to be involved with our lives—more specifically my life, rather than spend his time all up in club business. When I was little, I begged my mom and dad to leave me with Gramps and Grams. Even when my brother's were sick or just wanted to go home, I didn't.

Gramps and I spent hours in his garage working on his cars. When I turned fourteen, he bought me a busted up 1968 Chevy Impala SS with the original 427 motor. She's a beast. Elvira is what he christened her name. It took three years for her to be the beauty she is today. Every inch has been worked over by Gramps and me.

The car building process has taught me so much. Mostly patience, but also if you want something, you have to work for it.

Blood, sweat, and motherfucking tears.

Gramps gets me like no one else. I'm the kind of guy that has to learn the hard way. Like my car, when shit didn't fit, she didn't run. I couldn't rush the process, I couldn't rig it, I had to do the job right the first time.

Except right now Gramps and Grams aren't all that happy with me. My parents, well, they're downright livid.

My brothers … depends on which one you ask as to what they think.

Red says I've lost my way. Which honestly I find fucking hilarious. How can I lose my way when I didn't have a clue where I'm headed in the first damn place? *Riddle me that one, joker!*

Sure, Red expects me to fall in line with him. Graduate, go to college, work at the shop, and patch to the club. He thinks its simple. And for him, it is. I just don't know if Haywood's Landing is the place for me forever.

Pretty Boy, that's Kellum, he's the other middle child with me. He is angry at the world, not just me, so it's hard to say why he's hell bent on getting in my shit more than usual. Every time my name is called, he just gives a huff and an annoyed look my way. What does he know anyway?

Tommy Boy, he's the baby and my best friend. He doesn't give me shit about shit. In fact, it doesn't matter what I do, Tommy Boy takes my back.

Isn't that what the Hellions preach? Isn't that the core of their brotherhood, acceptance?

I'm eighteen-years-old, I'm failing my senior year, and everyone has an opinion about what I need to do with my life.

When I was younger, I couldn't wait to feel the weight of that leather cut hit my shoulders. Now, well, I feel like the I am fond of the idea of fitting in my family mold more than I like the reality of it.

Maybe I need to experience more in life than what Haywood's Landing has to offer. Maybe I don't.

I don't have all the answers right this second, but what I do know is I got a damn good woman in Jennissey Rose Rivera and I'm not letting her go.

CHAPTER 2

JENNISSEY

I HOLD THE PEN IN MY HAND. I'M SHAKING.

"Jenni, this is your future. It's waiting and it's yours for the taking," my recruiter says happily.

"After basic training, if my sister wants and a judge allows it, she can move with me, right?"

The recruiter nods sitting behind the large desk in their Cracker Jack Naval uniform. "We even have base legal who can guide you free of charge. The benefits are abundant."

"Jami, will she be able to reach me if she needs to?"

To this, my recruiter shakes his head. Petty Officer Second Class Decker explains, "I told you, Rivera, during basic training you can call home during designated times. In the event of an emergency, she can have a Red Cross message relayed to you. At which point your command will guide you through the next steps."

I blow out a breath trying to push myself to do this. Jami can make it eight weeks without me. Get through this time and I'll make the next plan when I have more information. This is a career, not some dead-end job. This is my out. This is about our future.

Scribbling my name on the forms it's all a blur as Petty Officer Decker tells me about my upcoming trip to Raleigh for my physical. Today is step one of the rest of my life.

Now, I have to figure out how to tell Rhett I'm leaving Haywood's Landing.

***

"You okay?" Rhett asks as we sit in his car at our spot. With the weather being mild this spring, we have the windows down and the car turned off so it's a quiet night in the woods. We're in a camping spot in the Croatan Forest, but it's secluded.

"Yeah, babe," I lie.

The weight of what is coming is heavy on my shoulders. I signed the papers. I leave for Raleigh in a week. When I'm there, I will officially swear in and I will be issued my orders to leave for basic training in the United States Navy. I don't want to leave Rhett. He's everything to me, but it's not about me.

My little sister, Jamison Violet Rivera, is depending on me to get us both out of here and away from *him*. I shake my head trying to shake off the thoughts of home.

"Talk to me, Jenni."

His voice is soft, comforting. I relax. "You think we'll make it, Rhett?"

He gives me this smirk half-smile that somehow tells me everything is right in the world. Rhett is tall, built, and gorgeous. I'm only five feet, three inches, so it doesn't take much to be taller than me, but he is just under six feet tall. He is built like a tank, which is funny since that's what everyone calls his dad, who is truly built like a tank. He has this strawberry blonde hair that he wears short and spikey. With his chiseled jaw, he's more than handsome, he's hot!

Leaning over, he cups my chin with his thumb and first finger. "Baby, ain't no one got a love like ours. Know we're young and people think they know shit to tell us this won't last, but man I am, there ain't a woman I'll ever love the way I love you, Jennissey Rose. One day, I'm gonna give you my ring, my last name, and my babies."

I melt.

The world around us slips away as I lean over and press my lips to his.

My hands roam, his hands roam. I moan as my body seeks more contact. He slides over the bench seat to get closer. We continue to make-out. As the gear shift in the floorboard gets bumped, he effortlessly lifts me up and slides under me so I'm straddling him in the passenger seat.

Passion consumes me. I grind against him. My summer sundress sliding up over my thighs and my silk panties dampen against the hardness of him in his jeans.

Rhett rubs his hands up and down my thighs encouraging me to keep moving. Our tongues tangle as I run my hands through his hair. His hands slide up my thighs, grabbing my ass and spreading my cheeks. My body is on fire.

The friction continues to build. I rock with need, desire, and love.

Reaching down, I find the hem of his t-shirt. Rhett and I have made-out many times before and I want to be skin-to-skin against him. Breaking the kiss to pull off his shirt, I kiss his neck. He begins to move the straps of my dress down off my shoulders as I lick, nip, and suck on the sweet spot of his neck behind his ear.

He lets out a groan as he finds I'm not wearing a bra and my c-cup boobs are exposed for him. I continue grinding against him as he twists his neck away from me so he can put his mouth on my nipple. Rhett cups my right breast, tweaking my nipple, while he sucks on my left and I feel the heat shoot right to my core.

The confines of the car are forcing us to maintain this position, but I need more. I'm ready to explode.

Alternating between sides, he continues to feast on my boobs as his hands cup my ass and his fingertips tease my opening with every slide I make.

He blows against my sensitive skin of my nipple and I cry out. "Rhett, I need you."

Slowly, I feel his finger slide my panties over before he moves inside me. My muscles tighten around the digit as my body comes alive.

"Wet for me," he says with a gravelly rasp to his voice.

"Yes," I moan.

"You want more?" He asks as he continues to slowly glide his finger in and out of me. When he adds the second finger to stretch me, I am lost. I'm almost ready to explode.

"Rhett, I need more. Please," I beg.

His fingers slide out and I immediately stop moving in a whimper.

Opening my eyes, I lock them to him. "Never gone this far, baby. Not gonna lie, I wanna have this with you, but I wanna know you're ready, Jenni."

And just like that I fall more in love with the man under me. "I'm ready, Rhett."

"Thank fuck, because my balls are gonna bust."

I bite my bottom lip trying not to laugh. He shifts me back just enough for him to unbuckle and unzip his pants. Lifting us both up, he slides his pants and boxers down. I move enough for him to continue pushing them down. As soon as he settles back into his spot, he reaches over to the dash to grab his wallet and retrieve a condom.

Feeling a little self-conscious, I reach down taking his dick in my hands. At first I'm not sure what to do. Sure, I have jacked him off, but this moment is so much more than exploring. Then as if instinct takes over, I find myself eagerly working him up as I think about the pleasure he's given me time and again in this car. As I stroke him, I watch as his abs tighten making a clearly defined six pack. His groans encourage me to keep my pass.

Slowly, I kiss and lick my way down his waist where I find myself scooting off his lap and settling onto the floorboard. Thank goodness I'm small. While the space is tight, it's manageable. With his large erection in front of me, I begin to wonder how he will fit inside of me. Thinking we need lubrication, I start by licking his shaft and working my way up to the head. Using my hand, I gently massage his balls.

"Thank fuck for muscle cars that have room," he mutters as he holds my head gently in both hands and I continue to suck his dick.

Concentrating on my teeth, I go up and down gently sucking trying to take more of him with every breath. As he grips the door handle and squirms under me I know I'm getting him as worked up as he gets me.

"Baby, you want more than what you've already had from me, you better stop and let me get inside you."

Releasing him with a pop, it's a split second before I find him rolling the condom down himself and scooping me up.

"Take off your panties, baby," he commands and I obey.

As he lines our bodies up, I lock my eyes to his.

Inch by inch he fills me. Tears threaten to fall as I feel so full. It's not painful but it's uncomfortable as my body adjusts to him.

"I love you, Jennissey Rose Rivera, and there isn't a thing I wouldn't do for you."

Feeling the need to move, I slowly work up and then back down. "There is no one who has accepted me for who I am the way you have. There is no one I will ever love more than I love you, Rhett Rebel Oleander."

We begin to move in sync slowly. The confines keeping us close as my body heats. My inner muscles takeover and begin to milk and grip him. I'm close to exploding. Rhett reaches between us and presses his thumb to my clit.

Time stops.

I can't breathe.

My vision blurs as my body trembles and I can't stop the way I cry out.

He feels deeper and thicker as his pace becomes wild. What feels like aftershocks roll through my body in waves as he keeps working himself in and out of me before he stills and releases a soft groan.

We both work to recover as I feel him pulse inside of me.

"That was incredible," he whispers as he takes a few deep breaths.

"Wow," is all I manage to say as he reaches over and grabs the door handle.

"Gonna have to climb out, baby. Gotta clean up."

I nod and after he gets the door open, I slide off of him immediately feeling empty. Looking between us the hints of pink on the condom show him the gift we just shared. I fix my dress straps and lean over to get my panties off the floorboard. Rhett climbs out of the car and moves to the trunk.

Before I have time to get my panties on, he's looking at me. "Let me clean you."

I give him a nod as he opens the trunk, tosses the condom, cleans himself, rights his boxers and jeans. Then he comes back to me with a roll of paper towels.

"This might be a little rough, sorry baby."

I can only let out a half laugh as I find myself a little embarrassed.

He goes about wiping me before he helps me get my panties back on. As he stands he presses his lips softly to mine and for this moment everything is right in my world.

For that reason alone, I don't tell him about my plans. At least not tonight.

CHAPTER 3

CRUNCH

Two Weeks Later

"ARE YOU FUCKING SHITTING ME?" I ASK NOT HIDING MY ANGER.

"Calm down," Jennissey begs. "This is what's best."

"You went and made all these decisions about the future and not one of them includes me!"

Her face pales and I see my words are a direct hit. "Rhett, I have to do this. I can't afford to go to college and nothing is here for me in Haywood's Landing." Her words cut me to the very core.

I pace the space of my room in front of her. "Nothing's here for you! What about me?"

"This isn't about you, Rhett. Look, it's just eight weeks of basic training. While I'm in school I can talk on the phone, you can come see me. When I get my orders, we can start our life there."

I can't think straight.

"What if this isn't the life I want, Jenni?"

Tears build and quickly fall down her face. "This is what I need to do, Rhett, and you might not understand it, but I need you to do it with me. I love you, but I have no future here. The Navy is my future for me and for Jami."

She blows out a breath. I can't wrap my head around this. She's leaving me. Right after graduation. Jennissey will be gone.

"Rhett, I need you to calm down and I need you to promise me you'll take care of Jami."

I throw my hands up. "You just tell me you're leaving me and you're worried about your sister! What the fuck, Jenni! What. The. Fuck!"

"Jamison needs support while I'm gone and you're the only person I trust." Her eyes lock onto mine. "Please," she whispers.

"Fine," I mutter unable to deny this woman anything. "I'll take care of Jami while you do what you need to." That doesn't mean I'm going to be here waiting on her when she gets back. I love her, but she's the one walking away, not me.

"When I get settled, I want you both to come be with me."

I shrug my shoulders not sure how to take any of this.

I've never had someone leave me before and the pain I have right now I'm not sure I can find a cure for.

Six Weeks Later

THE TRAILER IS BUSTED UP. This is not good.

I managed to graduate four weeks ago ... barely. It doesn't matter though, I got the damn piece of paper. While I should be riding this high that things are falling into place, I can't.

I can't because a piece of me is in the Great Lakes at Basic Training for the United States Navy. I can't relax because all I can think about is her. I can't sleep because all I can do is wonder what comes next. I can't do a damn thing because too much of me is tied to too much of her.

Surprisingly, the Hellions gave me my cut on graduation day too. I'm officially prospecting for the club. It's good since I'm nursing the pain of losing Jenni and all the bullshit jobs are a nice distraction.

She really left me.

The woman I love joined the Navy and thought this was a good idea for our relationship. She's called from boot camp and the fool I am answers every fucking call. I feel like some desperate housewife just waiting. It's ridiculous.

I need to cut her loose. We're never going to work. Not after she made this decision without me. Red, of course in his mighty wisdom, says she's young and is doing what she needs to for a future. He supports Jenni's decision. My mom, my dad, fuck my whole family think it's honorable for her to serve our country.

I think it's bullshit she left me and that's all I care about—She. Left. Me.

Being a prospect means shit jobs, but it also means resources. Since I gave Jenni my word I would keep an eye on Jamison, her sister, I have people who check in with me on her movements. Jennissey whose parents pronounce her name Hennessey and Jamison were named after their father's favorite alcohol. Her mom thought it would be cute to have them as Jenni and Jami even if her father refuses to call her Jenni. I used to ask questions about her family, but after she kept avoiding the conversations or bringing me home, I dropped the subject. Maybe I should have pushed harder. It's too late now. The only thing I can do for the woman I love is watch over her little sister.

Which is why I'm at this trailer that has seen better days. Every single window is busted out and half the metal on the outside is gone exposing the insulation. There are a couple of cars out front so I know there are people here with her. Walking in, I find her on a couch with a far-away look in her eyes.

"Jamison, let's go," I order as everyone here seems to ignore me, all of them blitzed out of their minds.

"Oh Rhett, you came to join the party," she smiles and I can see she's high. Anger builds inside me along with a helpless feeling I don't like. The needle on the floor let's me know she's been shooting up.

"Party's over," I tell her as I move closer.

She shifts and I watch in horror as she picks up a spoon from the floor. Stupidly, I stand in place as she drops some white rocks to the spoon before lighting a lighter under the metal and heating the substance.

"What are you doing?" I roar as the guy closer to her takes a needle and draws back the syringe to fill the liquid from the spoon into the needle. This can't be happening. I stand in place simply stunned at the scene in front of me. The guy moves closer.

"No!" I yell as I lunge towards her.

The guy grabs the spoon as she takes the needle. "Rhett, I need this. Without Jennissey, I'm lost. I need it. Don't you understand this is medicine and it takes away the pain."

Just as she extends her arm to find a vein, I grab the needle and jab it in my own arm not thinking. I have to protect her at all costs. I can't let her do this. I have to keep Jami safe for Jenni. It's all for the love of Jennissey.

A needle to my vein.

It should have been a bullet to my brain.

The End ...Until the next ride!

You made it to the end!

. . .

I HOPE you enjoyed *Breathe for It...*! I know this is a bit of a tease, but I promise Crunch and Jennissey will share their entire story in the full length version of *Breathe for It*, coming November 25.

New to the Hellions MC well, check out One Ride (Hellions Ride Series 1) for free through all major eBook retailers.

Don't want to miss a single release or update to my schedule? Sign up for my newsletter here! I promise I won't spam you. I send out a monthly update on my release schedule and a quarterly Steals and Deals email full of bargain books waiting to fill your library.

Thank you for giving my book the honor of your time and a place on your shelf. I truly love writing and sharing every story with you.

ABOUT THE AUTHOR

USA TODAY BESTSELLING author Chelsea Camaron is a small town Carolina girl with a big imagination. She's a wife and mom, chasing her dreams. She writes contemporary romance, romantic suspense, and romance thrillers. She loves to write about blue-collar men who have real problems with a fictional twist. From mechanics, bikers, oil riggers, smokejumpers, bar owners, and beyond she loves a strong hero who works hard and plays harder.

Connect with Chelsea

WEBSITE: http://www.authorchelseacamaron.com

FACEBOOK: http://bit.ly/2ptgaYE

TWITTER: http://bit.ly/2psqNuT

INSTAGRAM: http://bit.ly/2DK0nHW

NEWSLETTER: http://www.subscribepage.com/z4k8f4

BOOKBUB: http://bit.ly/2BLVVvd

SNOW WHITE & THE BIKER
BY GLENNA MAYNARD

A Dark Fairytale
Original Seven MC

PREFACE

Once upon a time, a man loved a woman. He treated her as his queen, and she gave her king a princess. Hair as dark as night. Lips as red as blood. They named her Sybil White. Their princess was the apple of their eye but like in all fairytales there was a villain who was jealous of their love—she sought to destroy their happily ever after and all they held dear. One by one she watched them fall until all that was left was unsuspecting Sybil.

"Mirror, mirror watch them fall.
Mirror, mirror burn them all.
Mirror, mirror kill Sybil White.
Kill them. Kill them all."

CHAPTER 1

DIEGO

ROLLING UP TO THE CLUBHOUSE DISAPPOINTMENT FILLS ME. WRATH'S BACK. My bastard of a stepfather and my Prez. His black and red chopper is parked in his usual spot. I was hoping the asshole was still on his run. Once a month he travels to various businesses to collect protection fees. The owners hand over a percentage of their earnings to the Original Seven MC. The motorcycle club I'm a prospect for. The club my father used to be the president of until Wrath killed him and took the club and my mother as his own.

One day I will end him and deliver his head to my mother.

Parking my bike, I light up a cigarette and debate going inside. I really don't want to see his ugly mug, but it isn't like I have much of a choice. As I walk through the door Freak gives me a chin lift. I start for the bar when I hear, "Prospect," boom from across the room.

That didn't take long. I cross the room in five strides. With my cigarette hanging from my bottom lip, I run a hand through my dark hair and mutter, "What?"

Fucking Wrath is sunk down in the worn leather cushions of a couch in the back of the bar getting his nuts sucked by one of the Frisco twins and he's knuckle deep fisting the other bitch's pussy. The sight is nothing new, but it repulses me that when he's through, he'll go home to my mother where she'll have dinner on the table and not a hair out of place. Pretending to be the perfect old lady while praying for his death or her own.

It isn't for lack of trying on her part. She's attempted to take her life so many times now that I would only be surprised if she succeeded.

"Got a job for you. Do this right and I'll personally patch you in."

"What's the catch?" With him there is always a big but tacked on at the end. I take a hard drag of my Winston light and flick my ashes on twin one's backside. She doesn't even notice. The whore is too busy slobbing on Wrath's dick like it's coated in gold. Both these stupid cunts think one day he'll take them both as his old ladies. They come as a package deal. I find their relationship to be sick but the whole thing is none of my business.

Twin two starts to moan as she rides his hand. He brings his slick fist up to his mouth and licks his fingers, and I refrain from making a disgusted face. Every brother in here just about has used the twins like cum buckets. I'd be afraid my fingers would fall off if I touched either of their snatches.

Wrath's eyes roll back in his head, and he shoots his load all over twin one's tits. "Go on. Clean up." He shoves them away and tucks his dick back in his jeans. "Got a file on my desk needs tending to. You do what is needed and that O Seven patch is yours."

Prick knows that all I have wanted since my old man died was to wear his patch.

Flicking my cigarette to the ground I snuff it out with the toe of my worn boot. Giving him a nod, I go to his office. The office that once belonged to my father, Emanuel "Killshot" Diaz, son of Hector "Wildman" Diaz a founder of the Original Seven. My father was too good for this life, too trusting of snakes like Wrath.

Plopping down in his chair, I pick up the folder. It's a hit job and no more complicated than the normal one bullet and done. Mulling over the file there isn't much to go on. Sybil also known as Sybi is a twenty-year-old college student who stands to inherit her father's fashion empire on her twenty-first birthday. It's my job to make sure that doesn't happen. Her stepmother paid handsomely for my dear old stepfather to take her out, but he's retiring from the killing business, and I am next in line to earn my cut.

It's simple really. Kill the girl and earn my patch or let her live and end up in her place—six feet under. I don't plan on dying anytime soon.

Fingering her photograph, it seems a shame to end such a beautiful life.

Lips as red as blood. Hair as dark as night. *Sweet Sybil White I'm going to cut out your heart and keep it in a jar as my trophy.* After I push the old man out and claim his seat at the head of the table that is. A grim smile crosses my face at the thought.

CHAPTER 2

CONSUELA

Earlier that same day

I've always hated places like this. Biker bars are simply gross, so beneath a woman like me. However, I need to be here. I'm searching for a man by the name of Wrath. I was told by my source that this was the place to find him.

When I step inside the filthy watering hole, the music cuts off and all eyes are on me as they should be. I'm a woman who captures the attention of every man I meet. I have been featured on the list of the world's most beautiful models every year for the past fifteen years. I've always been number one. Well...one year I was number two, but nature took care of that. It was such a tragedy when Martina White passed away from complications during childbirth leaving her husband heartbroken and ripe for the picking. Richard should've been mine from the start.

I met him first.

Martina and I were roommates when we first started in the fashion industry. She never would've met Richard had I not introduced them. They never would have married.

That's in the past now. Once Martina and her son passed away, Richard found his way to me. We could have been happy, had it not been for his and Martina's brat, Sybil.

That child hated me from day one. Richard coddled the girl too much. He always gave her what she wanted. He'd cancel our plans to tend to her every whim. I had everything planned. I'd get rid of the brat and Richard would finally be all mine.

Things didn't go as planned and Richard died in her place.

Richard's Will left everything to Sybil. She'll inherit his fortune and his company upon her twenty-first birthday. She's an insolent child who knows nothing about running a high-end fashion line. I thought I had a hold on her, but I should've kept a tighter lock and key on her. With her 21st birthday approaching it's imperative I end her, before I have to hand over what should be mine.

I'm told this miscreant, Wrath, is my best hope. He's ruthless, discreet, and for hire. He's perfect.

The bartender looks me over with his greasy smile practically oozing calories. "You lost?" he says with a grunt.

Saddling up to the bar I put forth my most dazzling smile. "I'm looking for Wrath."

"Get out," the man barks at me, and I nearly jump straight out of my Manolo Blahniks.

I came prepared for such a cold reception such as this. Sliding a few hundreds across the bar, I say once more, "I'm here to see Wrath."

The slimeball pockets the cash and says, "Take a seat, back booth. He'll arrive soon."

With my shoulders back and my head high, I parade through the crowd of vagrants to the seat the bartender pointed out.

Wrath

Pulling up outside of Hell's Gate, a bar on the freeway not far from the airport, the parking lot is full of motorcycles just like mine...all except for one car. You don't see many Cadillacs here. You won't find a man who drives a car like that here unless he's here on business or lost.

I've been on the road for weeks. There's only two things on my mind. A cold drink and pussy. However, you won't find good pussy here. That can wait. My thirst can't.

Grabbing a stool, I toss a twenty on the bar top and Raider opens me a longneck bottle of Budweiser.

"You got company. Back booth."

I raise my beer, taking a hard swig with a grunt.

The back booth is occupied by a woman who is too damn classy to be here. She must own that Cadillac. Probably a rich bitch looking to off her unsuspecting husband. She's not the first, and I'm damn sure she won't be the last.

Too damn fancy to be looking for the likes of me.

Her well manicured fingers tap against the hardwood of the table. Her blonde hair is pinned neatly to her head. That won't last long around here.

I won't be the one to ruin her hair or smudge her lipstick though. She's a bit too old and plastic for my taste. I prefer a natural woman who doesn't have to try so damn hard. Her eyes are cold, like damn glaciers that would cut a man in two.

I'm not just any man though. I didn't earn my name or rank by being a cowering pussy.

No, my road has been paved with blood.

The blood of weaker and lesser men.

Low lives.

Scum.

I make the world shine a bit brighter by taking them out.

"You Wrath?" My name comes out as though it tastes bitter on her tongue.

"Depends on who's asking."

"I have a proposition for you." She hands me a piece of paper.

Glancing at the number, I smile.

She doesn't waste any time. I can appreciate a woman who knows how to get down to business.

Taking a seat, I lean in across the table. "Start talking. I charge by the minute."

She clears her throat. "I have a person I need you to dispose of."

"Send the information and the payment to this address." I slide a card across the table.

"I'll pay when I have proof," she sneers.

"No money no job, lady. Don't jerk me around. I'm the best at what I do, you wouldn't be here if you didn't already know that. Cash only."

She nods.

"Now, get the fuck outta here."

She scoffs but marches her happy stuck up ass out the door.

Now to see about that pussy.

CHAPTER 3

DIEGO

DAY TWO WATCHING SYBIL WHITE. THE GIRL IS BORING AS FUCK FOR A college student who is also a rich bitch. Yesterday she attended three classes then spent four hours in the library before hitting the campus cafeteria to eat dinner alone. After that she returned to her apartment. I found the routine a bit pathetic but normal aside from the fact that she doesn't seem to have friends. I have only observed her speaking with who appeared to be her professors. I sat outside of her apartment for two hours before she turned off the lights and went to bed. I went home after that and returned early this morning.

I thought chicks travelled in packs and never go to the bathroom alone. Grabbing her will be a piece of cake. From the looks of things no one will miss her when I kill her. I'll be doing her a favor. Lighting up a cigarette, I wait for her to leave her apartment. She lives alone according to her file. Today will be much of the same, except while she is in class, I will be casing her apartment. Making my plans for her to meet her end. I watch as she double checks the lock. She proceeds to the mailbox and sticks an envelope in the out box. Today she is dressed differently though. She's wearing a fucking costume. Like the fairytale princess, Snow White. She's wearing a dress that is blue on the top half and yellow on the bottom. She even has short black hair like the character. *What the hell is she doing dressed like that? Why the hell do I find it sexy and imagine her going down on her knees and sucking my dick while wearing it?*

I adjust my dick in my pants and try to think of anything but her lips wrapped around me. Breaking into her apartment can wait. Curiosity has gotten the best of me. I watch from a distance as she tosses her purse into the passenger seat of her yellow Volkswagen Beetle. Her choice in car is also surprising. I thought girls like her drove Mercedes or something fancy and expensive. A smile crosses her face as she rolls the window down. Rock music blares from the speakers. My lips lift into a smirk. She is nothing like I expected. Nothing at all.

I hang back by a few cars and follow her to the public library. There's a sign out front that says today is story hour with a princess. Parked across the street I observe mothers escorting their toddlers inside. In her car Sybil touches up her makeup. I go ahead into the library to find a spot to watch her without being obvious. In the children's section there's a multicolored puzzle rug. The kids are already taking their seats sitting cross-legged on the floor. In the center of the room is a chair that resembles a throne. Sybil enters the room and takes her designated seat. An older woman hands her a book and she has the full attention of the children. The way they are looking at her you'd think she was the real deal and filled with magic. They are in awe of her and right now I have to admit part of me is too. She speaks softly to them as she reads, taking her time to pause and show them the pictures on the pages and changing her voice to match how the character might sound. It's sweet. So damn sweet it makes my teeth ache.

Having seen enough, I shove off from my spot before she notices me and head back to her apartment. Her lock is easy enough to pick. All it takes is a bobby pin. Quietly, I enter the apartment and hope she doesn't have a dog. The air conditioner and the refrigerator both are humming but other than that the place is relatively quiet. Sybil lives in a one-bedroom unit. The living room is basic. A white loveseat, a yellow wide back chair, and a glass coffee table make up the furnishings aside from a bookcase. She doesn't have a TV. Who the hell doesn't have a television in their living room? The kitchen is nothing special, but I check out her fridge and cabinets. She doesn't have a lot of food. Milk, cereal, bread, bananas, and a small container of ice cream. Maybe she is a minimalist.

Her bathroom is small and contains the usual girly stuff one would expect to find. Hair products, face wash, tampons, and toothpaste. I move on to her bedroom. I haven't found any personal effects. No pictures or whatnots. I don't even think the girl owns a vibrator. There is a small flat screen television. Inside her nightstand drawer is the remote control, a pad of paper that looks as though it has never been used, and one of those black silk eye masks. Her closet is full of dark clothing. She owns a lot of blue jeans and dark blue tops. Must be her favorite color other than yellow.

On day four I have come to realize that Sybil White may just be the sweetest creature on earth, and I don't know if I will have it in me to kill her when the time comes. She intrigues and confounds me. Every day she volunteers for some new charity. First it was reading to children at the library, then it was taking food to the local animal shelter and volunteering at an adoption fair for the animals. The next day she visited an old folk's home and played board and card games with them. I watched her sit with an elderly man for forty minutes and help him work a puzzle.

She's fucking perfect and pure. How could anyone want to see her dead?

Why would anyone hire someone to kill something so sweet and innocent?

Why would I agree to carry the act of her murder out?

Why does anyone do anything?

Greed.

Lust.

Envy.

Revenge.

Those are the usual but not Sybil. She seems to do good deeds because she simply wants to. I've never met anyone like her in my life. None of it matters. At the end of the day, I have a job to complete. It's none of my business why her stepmother wants her out of the way. Though I am sure it is purely greed. My reason is purely selfish. I have a vendetta to settle with Wrath. I will put him to the ground if it is the last thing I do. Sybil just happens to be a steppingstone in getting there. I can't allow myself to care about her or see her as a person. She's a means to an end.

Nothing more.

CHAPTER 4

SYBIL

Squinting from under the brim of my hat, I smile as my favorite person approaches.

"Like an apple from a tree I picked you, muñequita," Sofia singsongs as she hands me a crate from the wagon. Sofia was my late paternal grandmother's childhood friend and my godmother. She's always called me her little doll. I'm not so little now though. My twenty-first birthday is approaching.

I take the wooden crate, and Jose hops down and collects the three I've filled. "Buenos Dias, Sybi," he says with a toothy grin.

One would think with my heritage and four years of language lessons my Spanish would be better, but it hasn't improved in the least. "Good morning, Jose," I return.

Jose doesn't speak a lick of English, but he smiles at me anyway. I come here to Sofia's family farm when I need to get away. It's been four years since my father died and ten since my mother passed away. Sofia has always been a constant in my life. Always looking out for me despite my evil step-monster trying to keep her away.

"What are you doing here? You should be out doing things young folk do. Not here sweating. Your skin is going to burn," Sofia chastises me. I have my mother's dark hair, but I inherited my father's fair skin.

"I have plans," I lie coolly, while trying to come up with something to do.

"Come on. You can help me start the pies for the festival." I hook my arm through hers and start back toward the house. The Apple Festival is an annual event that Sofia lives for. She loves baking apple goods and she is phenomenal at it too.

Back at the house Sofia's grandchildren run through the house playing tag while the dogs chase them. Her ranch style household is in constant motion. Family coming in and out. This is what I wish I had experienced growing up.

Once my mother passed away and my father married Consuela my home tuned from bright and cheery to cold and dreary. The moment I turned eighteen I moved out, eager to get away from her. So harsh and controlling. She didn't want me having friends or leaving the house. Though things have been better since I left for college. I rarely go home. Only showing my face when I am needed to make an appearance for Sybi Kids, my father's children's couture line. He started out as a cotton logo t-shirt manufacture. Sybi Kids was my mother's dream and he made it come true.

When I turn twenty-one, I will inherit the company—my legacy.

Jesus, Sofia's youngest son brings a basket of the apples in and places it on the counter. I start washing and he hands the apples off to his mother to peel. "That band you like is playing at Rocky's Bar tonight."

I shove his shoulder. "No way. Get out."

"Way." He bumps his shoulder against mine. Jesus is a few years older than me and like the big brother I always wanted growing up. I think Sofia has always hoped for there to be something more between us, but I just don't see him in a romantic way. Not that he isn't attractive with his obsidian eyes and dimples. "Thought maybe we could check it out."

"Sure. Sounds fun."

"You two should go out to a nice dinner and movie. You don't belong in that trash bar," Sofia complains.

I smile at her and Jesus shakes his head. "You worry too much, Mamá."

Later that night I ride to the bar with Jesus hoping he doesn't think this is a date. We pull up to the Rusty Bucket known for its fights and loud music. The neon sign flickers overhead and there is a line outside the door. Morbid Duplicity rarely does smaller venues these days as their popularity has grown. They started out locally in a garage and playing the festivals and fairs. Now they are going on tour with some bigger names.

Jesus grabs my hand as a fight breaks out in line and pulls me back against his chest. "Stay close." His days old stubble rubs against the shell of my ear, and I step forward, dropping his hand. The bouncers have already tossed the brawlers out of the line.

I wipe my palm on the pant leg of my dark skinny jeans. His hand was sweaty. "I'm fine." Shooting him a smile over my shoulder, I move up with the line now that the bouncers have restored order to the group. I have my ID ready. Too bad I'm not old enough to drink. I get the yellow wristband that implies I can't be served alcohol, but Jesus will sneak me something I am sure once the lights go down and the music starts.

Inside it's loud and smoky as we navigate the large, tight crowd hoping to find a seat.

"I'm going to grab a beer. You want anything?"

"Nah. I'm good. I'm going to go to the bathroom. Meet you near the stage in ten?" I'm too nervous to drink just yet though it would probably calm my nerves.

He gives me a wink and flashes his dimples at me.

I make my way to the narrow hall that houses the bathrooms and groan internally when I see the line. I really don't need to go, but I am getting a vibe from Jesus that implies that he does indeed think this could be a date. I don't know how to feel about it honestly, but I don't want to hurt him or give him the wrong idea. I won't lead him on. Maybe his mother has been putting ideas in his head. Jesus would make any woman a great boyfriend. I adore his friendship but that is all we will ever be —friends.

I know I spend a lot of time there on the weekends at their farm. Maybe I spend too much time there giving them the impression that I am interested. I frown to myself and am bumped roughly from behind, knocking me to my knees. A drink spills down my back, and I hear some guy muttering, "Shit. I'm sorry. Are you okay?" A tattooed hand waves past my face and extends to help me up.

Taking his offered hand, I look up to see a gorgeous pair of blue eyes trained on me. "I'll live." He pulls me to my feet, and I bump foreheads with the guy. "Shit," I hiss.

"Damn. I'm not making a good impression, am I?" he rubs his forehead as I hold my palm to mine. I'm glad I don't wear much makeup, or I would look like hell right now.

I laugh. "Not really."

"Can I buy you a drink to make up for it?" He rolls his bottom lip inward, sucking his lip ring and rolling it outward. He's cute. Dark hair frames his face and he runs a hand through it, pushing it behind his ears. "I'm Diego."

"Sybil," I tell him, losing my place in line.

"Sybil. I like that." He gives me another smile and warmth flutters in my lower belly.

"Thanks."

"I didn't mean to knock you down and spill my beer on you. I was trying to get through and tripped over some bi—broad's shoe."

I shrug. "Accidents happen."

He nods his head back toward the bar. "You want to get that drink?"

I hold my wrist up to show him that they won't serve me.

"Don't worry about it. I come here all the time." He takes my hand again, cuts the yellow band off my wrist with a pocketknife, and shoves it in his pocket.

I smirk at him. "Souvenir?"

"Something like that." His lips curve into a smile and the curious side of me wonders if he is a good kisser with that lip piercing. "Come on." He takes my hand in his once more, and I look down at them joined together. The contrast between my pale skin and his dark ink is startling. I try to read what his knuckles say, but I can't with the way he is leading me through the throngs of people that are packed together like sardines. We make it to the bar with him standing behind me, caging me in. The musky scent of his cologne wraps around me, intoxicating me.

Glancing down I study his tattoo sleeves that leave no slither of skin un-inked. I can't tell what they all are but make out a huge number seven with the word original attached to it.

"Whatchu' drinkin'?" His lips move along the shell of my ear, and a shiver courses up and down my spine at the proximity.

"Um, I'll take a beer."

"Two Heinekens." He moves one arm and holds up two fingers as he tosses a twenty on the bar. "Thanks man." He pops the cap off one with the bottle opener at the end of the bar and hands it to me.

With his hand on my waist he guides me to a table that magically becomes empty with the snap of his fingers. Part of me misses his touch when he removes his hand and pulls out a chair for me. "What? You some kind of royalty around here?" I tease, arching a brow.

"Something like that." He takes a hard drink, and I study him. His jawline is smooth, but I wouldn't say he has a baby face. His head cocks to the side. "That your boyfriend or brother over there giving me the evil eye."

Oh shit. I completely forgot about Jesus. I'm such a bitch. In my defense I was distracted by this intriguing guy. My eyes widen, and I turn my head to the direction he's looking off to and chuckling. Jesus' eyes meet mine, and I can feel the disappointment radiating from him. "No. He's just a friend. We grew up together. I feel like an ass. I completely forgot I was supposed to meet him by the stage." I don't know why I am explaining myself. I suppose it is the guilt swimming like a shark ready to attack in the pit of my stomach. I wave Jesus over and he stalks toward us with an angry but hurt scowl on his face.

"Do you mind?"

"Not at all." I can tell this guy—Diego is amused by the situation.

I don't find it all that funny and when Jesus shoots me a fake smile as he takes up an empty seat, I feel even worse. I'm a crummy friend.

CHAPTER 5

DIEGO

TALK ABOUT LUCK. WHEN I CAME OUT TO FUCK AROUND TONIGHT, I WASN'T expecting to run into my mark. But it seems fate is smiling down on me. When I bumped into a chick on my way to the bathroom, I wasn't expecting it to be Sybil. She's even more beautiful in person. Meeting her here tonight however changes my plans. So does the fucker sitting next to her that can't keep his eyes off her. I need to find a way to get rid of him. He needs a distraction. Someone to get his focus off Sybil. He is a complication I wasn't counting on, but no matter. I scan the room looking for a familiar face. Bingo. Taty, pronounced Tauty is here. *Perfect.* Discreetly under the cloak of the table as the lights go down for the show, I shoot her a text.

D- Got a dude at my table get him gone.

I watch her as she gets the message and shove my phone in my pocket. She smirks at me and fingers the straw in her drink as she approaches our table. "Hey there, D. Who's your friend?" She runs her black nail polish coated fingernails down his arm.

Sybil speaks up. "His name is Jesus."

"Well hey there, Jesus. I'm Taty. Mind if I join you. I'm feeling incredibly religious tonight," she coos, and he rolls his eyes. Taty is the opposite of Sybil. Bleach blonde hair, freckles on her nose, grey eyes, and tattoos.

Sybil smiles at me, and I scoot our chairs closer together. "So Jesus and Taty can see the stage better," I explain and squeeze the top of her thigh.

I watch her take a drink of her beer unable to look away. She's fucking stunning. It will be a pity when I snuff the light in her eyes out. I don't want to think about that right now. Not yet. I came here tonight for two things. To listen to some damn good music and get laid. I can tell that cocksucker she came with is irritated. She may have arrived with him, but I guarantee by the end of the night I'll be the one to drive her home.

I can't grab her tonight, but soon, very soon she will meet her demise.

Rocky takes to the stage and taps the mic, the loud feedback noise pierces the room. Loud voices lower into whispered murmurs, and the drummer for Morbid Duplicity takes his seat. "Are you ready to get your rock on?" he holds the mic out for dramatic effect and the crowd shouts, "yes," back at him. "I am happy to present to you Morbid Duplicity." He rushes from the stage and the rest of band makes their entrance.

"How's everyone doing tonight?" The crowd yells back, howling and whistling.

The music starts, and Sybil is dancing in her seat. My fingers graze the small sliver of skin exposed along her lower, back and I smile when I notice a tattoo on her hip. It's a small black heart. Dainty just like her.

I finish my beer and ask her to go out on the floor with me before that Jesus dude can. I'm not much of a dancer but for tonight I can pretend.

Sybil's hips move to the music and her ass grinds over my crotch as the lead singer belts out the lyrics. "Close your eyes. Let my voice carry you away. I'm gonna take you to dreamland." The girl can move that's for damn sure, and I wouldn't mind taking her home for the night. Let her wrap them red lips around the head of my dick and suck me off. Bet she's never had a big cock in her mouth before. According to her file she's never had a boyfriend. Maybe I'll find out if she's a virgin before I kill her. The thought of taking her life has my chest squeezing tight. I suck in a breath and push away the dark thought and enjoy the way her tight little body is pressing against mine.

An elbow hits me in the side, and I look over to see Jesus and Taty next to us. *Great.* I underestimated this asshole's commitment to seeing this through. Normally I'd beat the fuck out of a punk like him, but I don't want to scare Sybil off. I want her to trust me. I need her to trust me.

"Let's get another drink," I suggest, gripping her upper arms, skimming the shell of her ear with my teeth just enough to get a reaction out of her. I feel her shiver under my touch.

"I'll come with you," Jesus calls out over the music, inserting himself into our conversation. This motherfucker is getting on my nerves. I wasn't talking to him.

"What do you want? We'll get it." I try my damnedest not to give him my signature fuck off glare.

"I don't want Sybi to miss any of the show," he presses and moves toward me. *Cockblocking bastard.*

"Right." I turn my attention back on her. "I'll be right back."

She smiles and nods. I give Taty a side eye glance and she moves in and starts chatting up Sybil. *Good girl.*

We get closer to the bar and he grabs my arm. I jerk my arm back. He doesn't know me like that to be putting his fucking hands on me. I've beat the fuck out of fuckers for less. "I know what you're trying to do. I just want you to know it isn't going to work. Sybil is still young but the day she's ready I'm going to marry her."

I snort. He has no chance in hell of that happening. I only just met them and even I can see how wrong they are together. She's got a hidden desire that burns for something more. Something I could give her if only I didn't have to kill her. "You're so off base, man. I'm just here to have a good time."

"She won't fuck you if that's what you're after." His brows are furrowed, and his lips turned down. He doesn't believe his own words.

"You mean she won't fuck you." I laugh with a shake of my head and step up to order my beer. This asshole has the balls to shove me from behind. I slowly turn around and he's waiting for me to hit him. He'd love for me to throw a punch and piss Sybil off. "Look. I don't want to see you hurt. I get that you've been sniffing at her ass for years waiting for the perfect chance. Maybe you thought tonight would be the night to test the water. You'd bring her to see her favorite band and at the end of the night you'd get a little kiss in. And if you were lucky, she'd let you cop a feel. You're a good dude so I'm going to be straight with you. You're right. I'm going to fuck your girl. She'll scratch her nails down my back and scream out my name and then we'll never see each other again. Hell, she might get pregnant and then there you'll be waiting in the wings ready to swoop in and be her white knight. But there is something you fail to understand. Something I knew from the moment I saw her. She doesn't need a white horse she wants the dark stallion."

I turn my back on him and grab my beer, knowing he will swing at me once the shock of my words settle in. He hates me only because he knows I speak the truth. He hates me because deep down he knows she's no innocent Snow White. There is something behind her eyes. Something dark and needy. A craving that sings to me like a little bird. A sparrow whose feathers I will pluck one by one.

I take a sip of my beer, smiling to myself as I count to three. On what would be four, I block Jesus' attack with my left forearm. Guys like him are so damn predictable, it is almost comical.

Turning around I smirk at him. "Gonna have to try harder than that."

"What the?" I hear him mutter as Sybil rushes toward us.

"What the hell are you doing?" She smacks at him and directs her attention my way. "I'm so sorry. He's normally not like this."

"It's no big deal." I shrug. "Why don't we go finish the show, and afterward I will introduce you to the band."

"*Seriously*?" The way her eyes light up I know who is going to drive her home.

"Whatever. Sybi, I'm leaving. You can stay here with this douche who only wants to get in your pants, or you can come home with me."

"I'm staying," she whispers, not meeting his eyes.

Sorry fuck. I bet he will cry on the way home then crawl into bed and jack off while he thinks about what an idiot he is and how Sybil will come crawling back to him once I throw her away. He'd be right except when I am done playing with her, she'll be dead, and he'll take the fall.

CHAPTER 6

SYBIL

Whoa. This sexy stranger—Diego wasn't lying. We are currently hanging backstage with Morbid Duplicity. I'm utterly speechless. Never in a million years would I have dreamed of this. Diego's fingers dig into my hips burning with possession, and I find the act cute. He's rough and reeks of trouble, but I like the dangerous glint in his eyes when he looks at me like he could devour me.

The lead singer, Lennox Hardin, gets the message loud and clear. I'm off limits. He shakes my hand and gives me an autograph on a bar napkin. I feel like a bumbling idiot and mumble a tense, "Thank you." He winks at me and shakes Diego's hand. They slap palms then bump fists.

"Nice to meet you, Sybil. You ever ditch this asshole and want a good time he knows where to find me."

My mouth opens and closes quickly.

"Ha. Funny," Diego quips. "You ready to get out of here?" Those rough fingers skirt along my waist.

"Yeah. Okay." I graze my bottom lip with my teeth. I never do things like this—go off with random guys at bars, but there is something about Diego that has me wanting to get to know him outside of the club scene. Guilt over how things transpired between Jesus and me tonight eats at me, but I push the negative thoughts away. I deserve a good time.

Taking my hand in his, he leads me out the back door of the club. The door slams shut, and Diego turns into me, pushing me against the cold metal. Hot, needy, raw, hungry, and tasting of beer his mouth claims mine in a stolen kiss. I've never been kissed like this before. With such want. I feel desired as warmth pools in my lower belly. I've kissed plenty of guys at parties and on dates but never quite this intense. Sucking my bottom lip between his teeth he gives the plump skin a tug and I moan. Thrusting his tongue between the part of my mouth, Diego maintains complete control, dominating me. I feel the metal of his piercing pressing into my lip and suck it into my mouth, nipping at him with my teeth.

His hand moves up my side and I break away, needing to catch my breath. My head swims and my pulse is racing. I feel dizzy with excitement. My mouth curves into a sated pout. "That was unexpected but nice," I tell him in a breathless whisper.

"Nice?" He quirks at brow at me and chuckles. "I can do better than nice." Curling a finger through the belt loop of my low-cut jeans Diego jerks my body into his. The man smirks, closing the distance between our mouths again.

I'd like to say that I'm drunk, but I've not had that much to drink. Fisting my fingers in his hair, I deepen the kiss, moving my tongue in tandem with his. Our bodies press together as he backs me into the door again, his lips fused to mine. We're a flurry of teeth, tongues, lips, and fingers. Taking and giving pleasure.

Someone trying to exit through the back breaks the moment. Diego licks his bottom lip then wipes it with his thumb. "Come on, pretty girl. Let's get out of here." He leads me around the side of the building to the parking lot where his motorcycle awaits. A thrill shoots through me like an electric current zapping every nerve in my body. Reaching into the saddle bag he pulls out a leather jacket. "Don't want you getting cold."

I push my arms through the sleeves, inhaling the scent of the well-worn leather as I hug it to my body. I get on after him, putting my feet on the pegs, and wrapping my arms around his waist. I bury my face in the back of his shoulder, getting a good whiff of his earthy scented cologne. He smells all manly—like sex and danger. The bike rumbles beneath me and I hold on tight.

As we leave the parking lot, I spot Jesus waiting for me by his truck. I close my eyes like a coward when he throws his hands up and calls out my name. "Sybil?!"

I can feel Diego's stomach move as he chuckles.

"Wait," I call out as guilt consumes me.

Diego stops on the side of the road.

"I'm sorry." I throw a leg over the side of the bike and get off. I take off his leather jacket and hand it back to him with regret coursing through my veins. I don't want to part like this, but I feel I owe it to Jesus to ride home with him. He did bring me here tonight, and I completely blew him off for a guy I don't even know.

Diego lifts his shoulder. "Can I get your number?"

"Yeah. Totally." We quickly exchange digits and he roars off on his motorcycle. I turn back and cross the road to where Jesus is waiting in the parking lot.

He pushes his shoulder length hair back into a low ponytail.

"Jesus, listen…" I start but don't know what to say really.

"Don't, Sybil. I don't get you." He shakes his head and gets in the truck slamming the driver's side door shut.

Letting out a sigh, I climb into the passenger side and lay my head back on the bench seat.

He pulls out of the parking lot a little too fast, but I keep quiet. I know he's hurt and angry. A bad combination.

The ride back to my car is quiet, awkward, and downright tense. He parks the truck next to my car, and I take out my keys. Maybe in a few days he will have cooled down. We can talk and he'll see that a romantic relationship between us would never work. I love him to death. Just not in the way he wants me to.

Jesus follows me out of the truck and stops next to my car. He leans against the driver's side door, keeping me from getting in my car and leaving. "Just tell me why him?"

I shrug and offer him a weak smile. "I can't answer that. It's like asking why the sky is blue or why leaves are green, or birds sing. You'll always be my best friend. *Always*. But I don't see you the way that you see me. I'm sorry if I ever gave you the impression we could be something more. I never wanted to hurt you."

He nods his head and offers me a sad smile that doesn't reach his eyes. His arms wrap around me in a tight embrace and he kisses the top of my head. I breathe in his familiar scent of sandalwood and vanilla. A smell that has always made me feel safe. Looking up at him I hope that this means we will be okay. I try to pull back. "I should go."

Not letting me go, Jesus holds me tighter and gazes into my eyes with a weird expression on his face. "I've always wanted you. I get it. You're still young and need to experience life a little more but in time I know you'll come to see that we're meant to be."

"Jesus." I shake my head.

He silences me by bringing his mouth down on mine. It's a sloppy kiss that feels all wrong. Like I am kissing my brother. He doesn't make me feel alive in the way that Diego did when he kissed me. Pushing my hands against his chest, I try to break away. Jesus ignores my signal and kisses me harder, trying to force his tongue into my mouth. I bite his bottom lip and smack his cheek, scratching him with my car key.

His head whips to the side, his hand moving to his jaw. "What the hell, Sybi?"

"I'm sorry. You wouldn't stop. I will never want you in that way. Now please move so I can leave."

Tears form in his eyes, and I hate the pain I see laced there, but there is nothing I can do to change how I feel.

Those obsidian eyes narrow on me and his nostrils widen as he breathes harder, clenching a fist at his side. "You feel nothing for me?" His hurt is turning to anger, and I take a step back.

"No," I whisper.

His fist connects with the roof of my car and then he kicks the door, leaving a dent in the side. I flinch afraid of his temper. I have never seen him behave this way. It scares me. With one last look at me he swallows his pride and storms off into the night.

I let out a ragged breath and climb into my car. With my head on the steering wheel I take a few minutes to mourn the loss of my friend. I don't know how we can come back from this. If I hadn't smacked him would he have stopped, or would he have pushed things further?

CHAPTER 7

SYBIL

It's been one day since my fight with Jesus. One day since I had the best kiss of my life with Diego. He sent me a text message that night asking if I made it home okay. I guess he was worried about leaving me with Jesus. I didn't tell him what happened. I feel partly to blame. And I get the feeling that Diego is the kind of guy who would go kick his ass just because he can. I don't want Jesus hurt anymore than he already is. I haven't spoken to him and don't plan to anytime soon. I think we both could use some space after everything.

I have been texting back and forth with Diego. He makes me smile and laugh.

D- Good morning, beautiful. What's your day looking like? I'd like to see you again.

S- Busy. Lots of laundry and reading to catch up on for school.

D- You really gonna turn down all this for some chores?

Attached to his text is a picture of him laying back in his bed. The sheet is covering most of his body leaving me to imagine what's underneath. I am still in bed myself and decide to have a little fun with him too. I snap a photo of myself using my selfie stick only I tease him more than he did me. I pull the sheet down and lay on my side, showing off my bare hip where I have a small tattoo of a black heart. I hit send and wait.

D- Damn, girl. You don't play fair.

I don't reply right away. I need to get in the shower and get my day started. I want to let him sweat a little bit. I can't have him thinking I'm easy. I have known his type before. The kind who loves the thrill of the chase. I have dodged getting involved with guys like that in the past but there is something about Diego that has me thinking for him I would make an exception.

I move through my day, getting caught up with my laundry and my final assignment for my business class. It's my last assignment. Once I hit send on my business plan that's it. I will be graduating. Then I will inherit my father's company and deicide if I want to take my rightful place as CEO or leave it to Heath to continue to run in my place. He's done a great job. The there is Consuela, my step-monster to deal with. She's been a thorn in my side since my father married her.

I can't wait to see the look on her face when I toss her out on her ass and take back everything my parents built together. The family home. The charities. It will all be mine in a few weeks' time.

It's getting late and I still haven't responded to Diego. Speaking of the devil, a new text comes through from him.

D- Going for a ride. My bike would look a lot better with you on it.

Instead of a text back, I dial him. I want to hear his voice.

"Lo," his gritty voice picks up on the third ring.

"Pick me up outside of Imperial Apartments in thirty." I don't wait for him to respond I end the call before I lose my nerve and back out. Then I shut it off and toss it on the coffee table. I'll grab it on my way out.

Rushing to my bathroom, I wash my face and brush my teeth. I look down at my shorts and dash to my bedroom closet to grab a pair of jeans and a cute top.

With five minutes to spare I walk out to the front of the building and wait. The loud roar of a motorcycle coming down the street sends goosebumps up and down my arms. I'm not nervous. I'm excited to see Diego again. He rolls to a stop on the street in front of me. God, he looks good. Dangerous and so sexy. Dressed in dark jeans, a white tee, and leather jacket, he's such a bad boy with his tattoos and piercings. He shrugs his jacket off and hands it to me without a word.

I accept the well-worn leather, and inhale his scent, getting on the bike behind him as I did the other night.

I'm being impulsive but it feels good. The bike veers onto the highway and my hair whips around my face violently. I must be crazy. This guy could be a serial killer for all I know, but I am tired of always playing it safe. When I first went away to college the media loved to follow my every move because Consuela never wanted me in the public eye. I guess they were fascinated by me because of my parents and my father's wealth. There was a blog dedicated to my outfit choices. The whole thing was ridiculous. Eventually when I proved that I was boring and never did anything newsworthy they left me alone and my stepmother loosened her leash.

We travel for what seems like an hour, turning off on a gravel road that winds up the side of a mountain and back down the other side. Diego brings the motorcycle to a stop in a clearing that houses a cabin. "You live all the way out here?" I question as I follow him onto the porch.

"Naw, it's more of a weekend getaway fishing cabin. Was my old man's favorite spot." He shuffles around in the dark and unlocks the door.

My pulse spikes, the hair on my arms stands at attention as realization hits me. I'm alone at remote location with a guy I know absolutely nothing about. It is either crazy or really dumb. I let out a breath and walk through the doorway. Diego flips the light switch on revealing a cozy setting.

The back of the couch is covered with a patchwork quilt. A stone fireplace takes up the center of the living room. To the left is a small kitchen and two the left is two doors that I assume lead to the bedroom and bathroom. I take off his leather jacket and sling it over the back of a chair.

I stand in the center of the room soaking it all in. Over the fireplace is one single photo frame. I cross the room and take the wooden frame between my hands. My lips curve into a smile. There's a young guy appearing to be in his twenties standing in front of a Harley Davidson motorcycle wearing a leather vest. I recognize the O7 I noticed tattooed on Diego's neck in almost the same exact spot. The man has a little boy on his shoulders. "Is that you and your dad?'

"The one and only Killshot." He grins with a haunted expression in his eyes and takes the frame from me, placing it back on the mantle.

"Killshot?" My brow moves into an arch. "What do they call you?"

Diego stares deeply into my eyes, and I feel like I can't breathe from the intensity I find in his darkened gaze. "They call me Diablo." He winks.

"Are you a devil?"

"You have no idea, sweetness." His wicked tongue darts out and licks his lip piercing.

"Are you a bad guy? You a member of that motorcycle club you father rode with?"

"The less questions you ask about that side of my life, the better." Diego caresses my cheek with his finger, trailing a path of fire down my neck.

"Why'd you bring me here?"

"Why'd you come?" Not waiting for my reply, he kisses the corner of my mouth. "I bet you're a good girl in need of an adventure. I bet you always do what you're told like a good little princessa. You need a bad guy like me to dirty you up. Show you how rough boys do it."

"I bet you always get your way," I whisper then pull away before he kisses me again.

His jaw ticks. "I don't play games. When I see something I want. I take it." His large hand wraps around the back of my head. "You gonna deny me of that mouth?"

CHAPTER 8

DIEGO

SYBIL SMIRKS AT ME. "THOUGHT YOU WERE A BAD BOY. DON'T BAD BOYS TAKE what they want?"

I suck in a deep breath. She's playing with fire and has no idea how badly she's going to burn. I could kill her now and be done with the whole fucking thing. One bullet between the eyes and I get what I want. The O7 patch that was once sewn on the back of my father's cut. I'm going to kill Wrath and claim that president's patch. I'm going to bleed the bastard out. Make him suffer an excruciating death.

There's just one problem. Her. Sybil White. I've only just met her and she's already under my skin. She has no idea the dirty things I want to do to her. The thoughts I have of taking her into the bedroom—tying her up to the bed and making her submit to me. Marking every inch of her pale skin with my mouth and fingers. I want to see her pale skin ripe with my teeth marks and my fingerprints. I want to possess her body in every way imaginable.

I'm completely fucked.

How am I going to end her life when all I want right now is to claim her? I've heard other brothers in the club talking about what they call the boom. The moment you know when you've met the woman you want to make your old lady. The woman you want to wear your brand and birth your children. I always thought they were full of shit. I've felt many a thing when fucking someone but here with her… no—the moment I kissed her outside that damn shithole club, I felt it. I was hit with the goddamn boom, and I don't know what to do about it. That's a lie too. I think I fell for her the moment she walked out of her apartment wearing that stupid costume—Snow White. She's a goodie goodie. Too good for a bastard like me, but I want her anyway.

"Just kill the girl and I'll patch you in myself," the bastard's voice echoes in my thoughts.

"Diego? Everything okay?"

I blink. "Never better. Why don't we sit, and you can tell me about yourself?"

Confusion colors her face. "You want to talk?"

No. I want to get you completely naked and spread out beneath me. "Come on." I lace my fingers with hers, feeling an electric shock jolt through me as our skin connects. Sinking down on the old worn leather couch, I bring Sybil down with me. A giggle escapes her. It's a musical sound. One I want to hear her make over and over again. Only I'm not supposed to be thinking about making her mine. I'm supposed to end her life. Her all too trusting gaze meets mine full of such hope, I have to break away.

Desire burns between us, but I don't dare to kiss her again or I will be completely lost to her.

"What do you do for fun?"

"I don't really get a lot of time to myself. I do a lot of charity work. My father was big into giving back, and it is something that always stuck with me. I volunteer at the local animal clinic, do story hour at the library, and I visit nursing homes and take care baskets to the patients there. So many of them have been dumped there and forgotten. Bringing them the smallest everyday things like lotion or a book means the world to them."

"Takes a special person to care so much for others."

"I don't know if I do it because I want to or because I want to keep honoring my father's memory. It was something we always did together."

"What about you, Diego. What do you do besides get tattoos or ride your motorcycle?"

I laugh. "Stalk pretty women like you." I make it sound like a joke but if she only knew I had been stalking her. Tracking her every move…going through her things…she'd hate me.

I change the subject. I want to know everything about her. "Tell me something that no one knows about you."

Sybil offers me a weak smile. There's this far off look in her eyes that I don't like. It's full of sadness. "I think that my stepmother is wicked. I think she is an evil witch who killed my parents and one day she'll succeed in killing me too."

My eyes widen. I was expecting her to tell me she doesn't recycle or some dumb bullshit like that. I wasn't expecting her to know that her life is in danger and yet she came here with me anyway.

"I know how crazy that must sound to you because you don't know her or what she is capable of." Nervous laughter flutters from her belly.

How would she react if I told her that I was hired to kill her? Would she scream? Faint perhaps? Beg me not to do it…beg me to get it over with. "Why would she kill them and want you dead?"

"Why does anyone do anything? Greed," she says the word in a low whisper.

Greed indeed.

"Tell me something about you?"

If she only knew my deep dark secret. "I'm going to kill my stepfather to avenge my father."

"Seems we have more in common than you know. I plan to kill my stepmother unless she gets to me first." Her tone is serious as she looks me straight in the eyes full of conviction.

I nearly choke on my beer as I spit it out onto the floor. It takes me a minute to regain my wits. "No offense, sweet thing, but you don't strike me as the killing kind."

"No, but you do." She smiles mischievously at me. I attempt to mask my surprise and wonder if she's smarter than I thought. Does she know who I am and what I am supposed to do? I swallow hard and stare into her eyes trying to read her thoughts. "I didn't put it together until a minute ago. A biker was seen fleeing the scene after my father was gunned down. You're a biker. Maybe Consuela hired you to kill me too."

"What if she did? Maybe I brought you here to kill you." I grip her jaw and pull her head toward mine. "You ready to die?" I brush my lips over hers.

Her tongue presses between my lips tasting of danger and desire. The thought of dying turns her on. She's more fucked in the head than I am.

Sybil pulls back. "We could kill them together. Your stepfather and my stepmother."

Her gaze meets mine and she's serious. I knew I saw a darkness in her, but I hadn't realized how deep that darkness flows. "You think you got what it takes?"

"Do you?" Her breath falls against my lips, hot and needy. I pull her to my lap, her knees moving to either side to straddle me.

I smirk and wrap a hand around her throat, pressing my thumb where her clavicle meets her breastbone. "I could squeeze the air from your lungs till you begged me to either stop or kill you."

Sybil rolls her hips, and I press my thumb harder.

"Does that turn you on?" I grit and rake my teeth along her jaw. A gasp leaves the part of her lips before I claim her mouth again. "What about your boy—the one at the club…he know he'll never satisfy you?"

"I think deep down but he doesn't want to accept it."

I grab her between the legs. "You ever give him a taste?"

Her hips move and she rubs against my hand. "What do you think?"

"I think I'm going to carry you to bed, then I'm going to fuck your brains out, and tomorrow we will decide how we are going to commit double homicide and not get caught."

"I like that," she mutters, sealing our fate with a kiss.

CHAPTER 9

SYBIL

DIEGO MOVES TO STAND WITH MY LEGS WRAPPED AROUND HIS WAIST AND MY arms cradled around his neck. His firm hands support my butt as he carries me to the bedroom.

He curses under his breath as he jiggles the door handle. I bite the shell of his ear feeling like my true self. Diego doesn't make the dark thoughts I keep hidden seem so crazy. I've never felt more drawn to anyone in my life. It's wild because we hardly know one another, but I feel I have known him my whole life. Like I could tell him anything.

The door swings open and he flicks on the light. I glance over my shoulder at the large bed with a wooden head and footboard that appears to be made of natural wood. The rails that go across the top of the bed look like curved branches. It's beautiful. Diego drops me to the bed and smiles at me as he runs a hand through his dark hair. Behind the bed is a full window with a view of a lake and a full moon that looks like it sits on the water's edge.

"Turn off the light," I demand and pull my top over my head. I fling it at him, and he grins wider. The light flicks off and he closes the door. Tugging on his lip ring with his teeth he stalks toward me, kicking his boots off, and removing his clothing along the way. His chest is covered in tattoos just as his arms are. A grim reaper covers the left side of his torso. On the boney knuckles of the hand holding a scythe is a ring adorned with an O7 on it. The bed dips under Diego's weight as he sits on the opposite side of the bed.

We gaze at each other knowing that once we cross this line there is no going back. I'm about to give him the one part of me that has never been shared with another soul. He crawls across the bed like a predator. Resting his head on my shoulder he tells me, "Take these off." Snaking an arm around my waist he unbuttons my jeans.

I should be nervous…maybe even a little scared but I'm not. Going up on my feet I stand with my back to him and shove the tight denim down my legs. I'm left standing in my undergarments. Blue lace triangles cover my intimate zones. Places no one has truly touched me skin to skin.

"Turn around. Let me look at what's *mine*." The way he says the word with such raw possession sends a shiver coursing down my spine and to my toes. His fingers skim along the curve of my bottom. I feel his lips kiss the dimple at the small of my back and pepper up my spine. I turn into him, stepping between his thick thighs and smirking at his blue boxer briefs that match my lace in color. Those skillful lips press against my stomach as his hands grip my hips, his fingers biting into my bones. "You have the skin of a porcelain doll," he murmurs between kisses working his way up my torso. I move to straddle his lap, feeling the heat of his growing erection pressing at my center. I stare into his blue eyes wanting to disappear in them. To get lost between the sheets with him and forget who I am for a while. A girl with a target on her back and a price on her head. A girl who wishes for death but fears it.

I've been saving myself for the right person, but no one knows how I truly fear for the day Consuela will have me murdered like the rest of my family. I'm tired of being afraid and hiding away being a good girl who never does anything wrong or takes chances. I'm ready to live my life for me. I want to be with Diego, and I meant it when I said I want him to help me take that bitch out.

Moving up my sides and around my back he unhooks my bra and returns my attention to the present. The straps slide down my arms with ease. I drop my bra to his lap. Diego flings it across the room and stares at me. "You're beautiful. I don't think I've ever seen anything more pretty than you in this moment."

My cheeks bloom a soft shade of red. "I bet you say that to all the girls."

He smirks. "Maybe but I never meant it till now." I gasp as he kisses my breast, sucking my nipple into his mouth. He caresses the taut skin with his tongue, repeating the action with the other. I squirm against the bulge in his boxer briefs, loving the sensation the friction creates.

I feel beautiful with the way he looks at me and the way he touches me. Maybe it is only lust, but I feel a deeper connection one of belonging and understanding. I push him back by the shoulder, covering his body with mine. Chest to chest. Skin to skin. I suck on his neck, marking his inked skin with my teeth. My body is aching for him to take what he wants. There's something about the idea of being taken by force that turns me on.

Sitting up, I circle my hips, rubbing against him. "Do you want me, Diablo?" I grin, fingering the nickname tatted over his right pec.

His hips thrust, his erection pressing against me. Wetness pools between my thighs as he repeats the motion over and over again. Those crystal blues never leave mine. My lips part as a wave of pleasure washes over me. I'm drowning in him. Hooking his fingers along the crotch of my lace bottoms he smiles. "You're soaked." Leaning up he claims my mouth as his finger glides through my silken heat. "Do you taste as sweet as you look?" Bringing his finger to his mouth he sucks on the long thick digit. Closing his eyes, he lets out an, "Mhmm," sound.

Rolling me to my back, Diego takes control, pinning my arms over my head with one hand while the other works on removing my panties. "You're fucking perfect."

I kick at my left ankle with my right foot, freeing myself of the lace. Diego eases his boxers down, and I know this is it. He's going to fuck me. The dangerous biker continues to gaze down at my body with hungry eyes. Moonlight glows through the window setting an eerie yet romantic scene.

"You gonna keep staring at me like that or are you going to fuck me?"

"My princessa has a dirty mouth." He looms over me, spreading my thighs wider, settling between them. I feel the head of his cock pressing against my entrance. "Damn, baby, you're tight." I grimace as he pushes inside me and stops. My body is burning and stretching like a rubber band that is ready to snap. Diego lets out a guttural groan. His body trembles against mine. "*Fuck me.* Are you a virgin, Sybil?"

I bite my bottom lip and give him a nod.

"And you're giving this to me?"

I arch my back and flex my hips sending him deeper.

"I don't deserve you, but I want you anyway." Drawing back out he comes back harder than before. Diego breaks through my hymen and the pain is almost unbearable. A tear trickles down my cheek and he bends his head down to kiss it away. "It'll start to feel good. I promise."

And he's right. It does feel good. Moving his hips, Diego starts thrusting at a leisurely pace, giving me time to adjust to the intrusion. The more he moves the better it feels as his thick cock slides in and out of my heat. Digging my nails into his back I urge him to go faster. Pressure is building in my lower abdomen. My toes curl into the mattress beneath me as he rubs his finger over my clit in sync with his relentless thrusts.

"Oh," I let out in a whisper, my eyes rolling back in my head as a tremble quakes through my body.

"That's it, Princessa, cum on this cock."

I smile up at Diego and his lips come down on mine kissing me with possession.

"Are you on birth control?"

I tilt my head to the side and shake it slightly.

Diego's forehead rests against mine.

"Fuck it. Doesn't matter." He kisses me hard and deep, thrusting his tongue into my mouth as his dick plunges deeper inside me. Our hips rub as he hammers me against the mattress. Diego doesn't stop until I feel him twitching inside me and warmth runs down my thighs.

**

Coming to, I move to stretch my arms over my head but can't. My eyes pop open, and I thrash against the restraints keeping me tied to the bed. Panic seizes me and pain shoots through my chest. My heart is in my throat as I look around the room. The night before becomes a distant memory as I scream. "Diego?!" Even my ankles are secured to the footboard. My body is stiff, and my wrists feel numb.

The bedroom door swings open and he leans against the frame wearing a smirk, watching me with amusement dancing in his eyes. He peels a slice from the juicy red apple in his hand with a pocketknife. I hear the fruit crunch between his teeth as he chews.

I pull with my arms again, hoping this is some sort of prank. "Diego, please. What's the meaning of this?" I croak. Betrayal burns through my veins. I gave him my virginity. I trusted him with secrets I've never told a soul.

"Last night when you said that I was hired to kill you…you were right." He pops another slice of the apple into his mouth. My head swims with dizziness and he crosses the room as I try to make sense of it all. "I need you to trust me, Princessa." His traitorous lips press down on my forehead. Tears threaten to fall when a needle stabs me in the neck.

"Diego," I whisper his name and my world fades to black dying with my unshed tears.

To be continued…

About the Author.

Glenna Maynard is a Kentucky native with a passion for romance best known for her bestselling saga The Black Rebel Riders' MC series. When she isn't arguing with the voices in her head or drinking reader tears, she enjoys watching classic TV shows with her two children and longtime leading man.

Website: https://www.glennamaynard.com/ Facebook: https://www.facebook.com/AuthorGlennaMaynard/ Twitter: https://twitter.com/gchellewrites Instagram: https://www.instagram.com/gchellewrites/

UNKILLABLE BY KRISTEN HOPE MAZZOLA

An Unacceptables MC Standalone

CHAPTER 1

Blood dripped from the tip of the knife. It tapped and splattered on the wood flooring as I bellowed out a rumbling growl.

The air was chillingly still.

My breathing was level and soft as I stared down at the lifeless body at my feet.

Another day.

Another casualty.

Another enemy vanquished.

The Renegade Kings were about to be warned.

Throwing their signature King of Swords tarot card down on top of the corpse, the message was sent. Now we would wait for them to come to us. We were ready. The war hadn't been started by the Unacceptables, but we would finish it. One battle was won, but there were surely more to come.

I never killed anyone who didn't deserve it. I wasn't a bloodthirsty murderer like some would think, but once I had a target, there was no saving that poor soul. This last one was no different than the rest—a poor excuse for a human being, complete scum of the earth. He was a rapist who'd attacked the old lady of one of my club members one night outside a roadhouse bar.

I would never forget that call or the aftermath of what that sociopath did to Katherine.

"Maccon." Reese's voice shot through the speaker, breaking sharply as soon as I picked up my phone in the middle of the night.

"Yeah?" I coughed, rolling out of bed.

"It's Katherine. Something terrible has happened. Get here."

My VP wasn't one to send up alert flags without cause. The tremble in his voice was enough to send daggers into my heart. Something was seriously wrong.

I hung up the phone, kissed my sleeping wife, and drove like a bat out of hell for the few miles to Reese's house.

Walking in without knocking, horror overtook me.

Reese was sitting on the floor with his wife bloodied and hysterical in his arms. Her body was covered in cuts and bruises, her clothes torn and stained.

"What the fuck happened?" I roared, rushing toward the couple.

"Katherine had just finished up her shift at the Red Crow when a guy grabbed her out back. I should have been there. Honey, I am so sorry." Reese's face was blood red as he tried to comfort his wife.

"We'll fix this, but you need to get her to the hospital." I pulled both of them up to their feet, whisking Katherine into my arms. "I'll drive."

We rushed for Reese's pickup where it was parked out front.

"Have you called Jett?" I asked, putting Katherine in the back seat with Reese.

"No!" she wailed. "He can't see me like this."

Reese tried to reason with his wife. "Baby, we need to tell your brother."

"Jett will do something stupid. Promise me you'll handle this, Maccon."

I looked back at her through the rearview mirror as I sped to the closest emergency room. "I promise."

IT WAS a promise I was glad to fulfill. Katherine was right; her husband and brother were both too emotional to deal with the problem objectively. Either one of them would have ambushed the douchebag in a crowded bar or on the street. I was more patient, more methodical.

The Renegade Kings had never been on our radar before. They kept to themselves and so did we. Now though, with the tides turning, a peaceful rivalry had twisted into two armies of adversaries who would stop at nothing to protect their clubs and families.

I walked out of the isolated cabin hideout into the muggy Arkansas air. With every stomp of my boots down the front steps, the weight of the situation lifted. I had done my job well.

"IT'S DONE," I stated, sitting at the head of the Unacceptables' war room table.

"Was he alone?" Reese, my number two, dripped with bloodlust as he eyed me. Katherine was still shaken up from what the villain had done, and I knew Reese would stop at nothing to make every member of the Renegade Kings pay for one member's sins.

"He was," I confirmed. "Foolish mistake."

Reese's hands fisted as his jaw clenched. "That it was," he growled.

"What do we do next?" Jett glanced over at me, scowling. He was my right hand and one of the best men I knew, but he also was a wild card we had to watch out for. A slight twitch came to his eye, and I knew he wouldn't sit idle for long. Without a clear path, he'd take matters into his own hands. It wasn't just our brotherhood he needed to protect; Katherine was his little sister and the only true family he had left.

"We wait and let the other charters know what is going on here. We might need some backup depending on what their next move is, but we'll be ready." I looked across the table to my old man as he nodded, and I breathed a sigh of relief. His approval meant everything to me.

The president's flash wasn't something I felt ready for, but it was my cross to bear. Once my father had decided to step down in his old age, the seat was my birthright to fill.

"How can you agree with this, Hawk? How can we just sit on our hands and wait?" Jett slammed his fist onto the worn mahogany. "All of those fuckers need to pay for what happened to my little sister!"

"My son is right and you know it," my old man seethed as he stood. "The piece of shit who hurt Katherine has been taken care of. Our end of the bargain has been fulfilled. Those assholes know who we are and what we are capable of. They know where to find us if they want to. We stay on alert and let them come to us. We have to be smart about this. We can't afford to have mass casualties from hasty stupidity." Hawk's low voice thundered into my men as they all nodded in agreement.

I wasn't an idiot. I knew the guys thought I wasn't ready to hold the gavel, and it was my responsibility to prove to them I was worthy of being their leader.

"Aye, boss." Jett glared at me. "I'm with you, brother."

That was all I needed to hear.

I slapped Reese on the shoulder. "Go home and take care of your girl. It's been a long couple of days for all of us."

Once the meeting adjourned, I pulled out my cellphone. There was one call I needed to make on my own.

As I stared down at the contact lighting up the screen, my father approached.

"You good, son?" he asked, standing over me with a concerned look only a father could give.

"Yeah, Pop. It's time for the Butcher to come home." Furrowing my brow, I looked my old man in the eye.

He sucked in a long drag from his cigarette before responding. "I think you're right."

I waited for my father to join the rest of the guys in the lounge room before making the call.

"Yeah?" a guff voice answered.

"Ravage?" I choked out.

"Maccon? Is everything all right?" Rave's voice was low.

"We may have just started a war, and we need you back out this way as soon as possible."

"Abel and I will leave first thing in the morning. See you soon, kid."

"Thanks, brother."

Ravage Hellock was as fearless as they came and the president of the Vilas chapter of our organization. Between him and his stepson, Abel, we would be able to handle anything the Renegade Kings threw at us.

CHAPTER 2

"ALLIE?" I CALLED UP THE STAIRS AS I FINALLY WALKED INTO MY HOME.

Like an angel glowing in the moonlight, my wife glided into view in her white nightgown. Her long blonde hair framed her tired, smiling face.

"It's about time you came home," she teased as I rushed up the steps and gathered her in my arms.

"I'm sorry I'm so late, sweetheart. The meeting took longer than I anticipated." *Meeting*—a horrible front that didn't fool my girl.

As she looked up at me with her stormy green eyes, her hand landed on my cheek. "Is everything all right?"

She could see right through me every damn time.

"It is now," I told her, sighing as she relaxed into my arms. Running my hand over her stomach, I felt a subtle kick from our baby girl.

"She's been restless tonight. I think she's been waiting for her daddy to come home." The sweetest grin popped on Allie's face as I melted from her words.

"Don't worry, princess," I whispered to Allie's belly. "Daddy is home."

Allie ran her thumb over my swelling cheek below a blackening eye. I could see it all over her face—she was proud of me.

Grabbing my hand, Allie pulled me down the stairs. "Time to talk all this out or you'll never get a wink of sleep tonight and you know it, Mr. Allred."

"You're always right, Mrs. Allred." I followed my very pregnant wife to the kitchen—I knew better than to argue with her.

Grabbing the bottle of Jameson from the top of the fridge and a glass for me, she sat at the table like she did every time I came home like I just had.

I watched her yawn and couldn't help but feel selfish for keeping her up.

"It's late, darlin'. You really should be sleeping," I tried to protest.

"It's one drink, Maccon." She pointed to the chair across the table, pursing her adorable strawberry lips.

I pulled the chair out. "As you wish," I relented.

She poured my drink and slid it over to me before getting up to grab the first aid kit out of the cupboard.

"Give me that hand," she demanded. As she tended to my busted knuckles, she muttered, "Out with it. Today wasn't just any ol' day."

"Remember the shit that happened with Katherine a few weeks ago?"

She nodded as her smile twisted into a hateful glare.

"He was part of the Renegade Kings."

My wife's hands flew up to cover her mouth. "Does that mean…?"

My old lady wasn't naïve to the life we lived, and I didn't hide anything from her. She was my backbone and the heart of my club.

"Everything is going to be fine. I took care of that son of a bitch. He'll never attack another woman or breathe another breath," I reassured her before chugging down the contents of my glass.

"We're in danger, aren't we?" Her voice was even and calm.

"You know I will protect you and our little girl. Nothing is going to happen to either of you." I took her hand. "I promise."

"I know that, Maccon. I love you." Her fingertips softly traced the skull and bones tattooed on my forearm.

"And I love you." I shoved away from the table and scooped my wife into my arms in one swift motion. "Now, let's get you to bed. You're sleeping for two, after all."

Flinging her arms around my neck, she kissed me quickly. "Who would have thought Prince Charming wore leather and his steed was a Harley?"

"All of those fairytale books got it wrong, babe."

"That they did."

I tucked Allie close into my side, and she rested her head in the crook of my shoulder as I rubbed her stomach.

"What are we going to call this little bundle of joy?" I asked. We had been going back and forth for months, never being able to settle on a name.

"How about McKenzie?" She batted her eyelashes at me, hopeful.

"Nope." I had vetoed that name from the get-go.

"Fine," she pouted. "What about Emerson?"

There it was, the perfect name for our precious baby. "I love it."

Her face lit up. "Really?"

"Really, really. Now it's time for you to get some rest so Emerson can grow big and strong." I brushed my lips over my sleepy wife's forehead.

"Good night, handsome," she murmured as she yawned.

"Good night, my love."

CHAPTER 3

WALKING INTO THE CLUBHOUSE THE NEXT AFTERNOON, I WAS GREETED WITH A sight for sore eyes.

"Maccon!" Abel yelled as he stood up from his seat at the bar. "It's good to see you again, brother."

I gave him a quick hug. "It's been too long."

"It's been too quiet. About time y'all saw some action in your neck of the woods for a change." Rave grunted as he walked up to us with a shit-eating grin plastered on his face, his axe in its sheath and strapped to his back. Ravage was a menacing man in and of himself, but add in his weapon of choice and he was downright scary. That axe had seen more blood than most could even fathom. I guess you don't get the nickname the Butcher for nothing.

"How are you guys doing? How are Crickett and Raine?"

"We're all good for the most part out in Vilas. Nothing too exciting to report," Ravage answered.

Abel puffed his chest out with pride before adding, "Crickett is amazing, and Raine is a fifteen-year-old girl. I swear, all my graying hair is from dealing with a teenage daughter."

"I don't envy you in the slightest."

"You have a little one on the way, I hear," Rave said, congratulating me.

"She'll be here in a little under two months. Allie is going to be so happy to see the two of you. She's already started cooking a feast for all of us tonight."

"I'll never pass up a free meal, especially when your wife is the one cooking. Please tell me she is making her fried chicken." Abel licked his lips dramatically.

"She made me get her seven chickens this morning before I could come over here. I hope it's enough," I responded with a chuckle.

"Enough for Abel alone," Rave badgered as he poured himself a shot of whiskey.

"He's not wrong." Abel smiled with a shrug as my father walked in behind me.

"Gents, you made good time." My dad greeted both of them quickly before joining Ravage in taking shots.

"Got on our bikes right after Maccon called. It seemed important." Rave slammed his shot glass down and poured another round for all four of us.

"Maybe we should go in and talk." I glanced around the lounge room of our clubhouse. There were too many cut sluts and low-level guys hanging around to speak openly.

"Sounds good." Abel grabbed the bottle and his glass then followed me into the war room.

After we all took seats around the table with our skull and bones burned into the wood, I began to recap the last few weeks' events. Abel and Rave sat there with fire building in their eyes as they listened to what all had happened.

"At least you took care of the damn asshole. Good for you." Abel raised his glass to me before taking the shot.

"Do you know what we're actually dealing with? How big is their organization?" Ravage looked from my father to me.

"They're about two-thirds the size of this charter. They mostly handle deals, minor shit. Honestly, I don't think they're really the out-for-vengeance types. It gets messy when crank and shit is involved. They have a lot of heat on them from that alone to add in bloodshed," I answered.

My father leaned back in his chair, lighting a cowboy killer. "That's what worries me," he muttered, letting out a large puff of smoke.

"Me too. We don't know what they are capable of if you haven't seen it before." Abel looked over to my father with respect and admiration.

"How are Jett and Reese handling all of this?" Rave asked quickly.

I shrugged. "The best we could hope for. Jett hasn't gone on a killing spree yet. I consider that a win for that crazy son of a bitch."

My father laughed. "Ain't that the damn truth."

"So what do y'all want us to do? How can we help?" Abel looked like he was ready to go on a witch hunt.

"I just wanted you here for backup while we see what their play is going to be. I need the best guys here protecting this family. That's why I called y'all in on this." I wasn't shy about admitting we needed help. Our club was getting older and we weren't having luck with our newest recruits. I didn't trust any of the young blood enough yet.

"We'll stay as long as you need us to." Rave looked me dead in the eye. "Anything you need. We've got your back, Pres." The little wink he shot me was priceless. Ravage was like an uncle to me, and it had been hard with him so far away for so many years. It was for the best and I knew it, but it was good to have him home for a change.

"Is it time to go eat?" Abel smiled up at me before slamming his last shot.

"I think it is." I clambered to my feet. "Thanks again for making the trip."

"Don't mention it. It's what family does for each other. You'd do the same thing for us." Rave clapped me on the back.

We all walked back out into the main room.

"Let me just call Allie and make sure she's ready for all of us to descend on the house."

I walked out front, lighting a cigarette before dialing my wife.

"Hey, handsome," she cooed into the phone.

"Hey babe. Are you ready for us?"

"I am just getting back from the store now. I needed to get more potatoes. Come on home. We miss you."

The sound of her voice coursed through me. She was my bright light in a life filled with darkness.

"We're heading your way now then."

IT ONLY TOOK a few minutes to round up the guys and give the green light to the others that would be joining us. In a pack of screaming hogs, fifteen of us pulled into my gravel driveway.

Allie rushed out the front door to greet us. Just as she got to the first step, my house erupted into a ball of flames, sending all of us cascading to the ground.

Searing pain shot through me as I tried to scramble to my feet to no avail. The overwhelming sound of ringing crashed into my ears as I crawled to my wife. The heat from the roaring flames was overpowering once I got close enough to Allie.

Her body was sprawled out on the front lawn, motionless.

Rolling her over, I screamed for her to wake up.

Abel appeared at my side. "Is she alive?"

I could barely hear his words as I pulled Allie's body into my arms.

Everything was a blur. Everything was spinning. My body was screaming.

I didn't snap back into focus until I was running next to her as her gurney was wheeled into the emergency room.

"You have to save her," I bawled as doctors and nurses rushed over to us.

"Sir, we need to get her stabilized and into labor and delivery," a nurse stated, pulling me away from Allie's side. "We need to check you out, too."

"I can't leave her," I cried. "She has to be all right."

"She's in good hands." The nurse tried to comfort me, but there was no way that was going to work. I watched my whole world get rolled away from me, and there was nothing I could do about it. My heart was breaking as I fell to my knees right there.

Rave's strong hands gripped me, yanking me back up. "You have to stay strong right now."

His face was bloody and torn from the blast.

"I can't." I could feel my heart breaking into a million pieces.

"You don't have a choice, son." Glaring at me, he shook me hard. "You have to be a president, husband, and father all at the same time right now. You can do this. Let the nurse check you out then go wait for your wife and that precious baby girl of yours. Show your men that you can be strong."

I felt my knees getting weak again. "I don't know how to do this."

Rave quickly steadied me, shaking me hard. "Do you know why you have the reputation of being unkillable, Maccon?"

I shook my head.

"Because you fucking are," he continued. "It's not that you're immortal. We're all going to meet our maker someday. It's because through all of the shit you've had to do, all the crap you've waded through – your spirit has never died. You're fierce and determined. You need to remember that."

I sucked in a sharp breath. "Thank you, Rave."

I didn't know if I believed him but his words sunk in deep. I had to suck it up and be the leader all of my men needed and my wife deserved. I was about the become a father. The first moments of my daughter's life weren't going to be while I was weak and falling apart.

I straightened up, clapped Rave on the back and walked to the waiting area just outside of my wife's room.

SITTING in the waiting room with all of my brothers around me was torture.

Finally, a doctor came out of Allie's room. I scrambled to my feet as he walked up to me with a tiny baby wrapped in a pink blanket.

"Mr. Allred?" the doctor asked as I nodded feverishly. "I'd like for you to meet your daughter."

I took the sleeping baby into my arms as tears streamed down my face. "Hello, Emerson," I cooed as I kissed her soft forehead. Looking back to the doctor, I could barely get the words out. "How's Allie?"

His gaze darted away from me briefly and I knew it was over.

"I am so sorry, Mr. Allred." The doctor put his hand on my shoulder. "Would you like to say goodbye?"

My brothers stood behind me as I took the hardest steps I'd ever had to take.

With my daughter clutched in my arms, I made my way to the bedside where my wife lay still. She didn't even look like herself. Her body was limp, her skin ashen, and her gorgeous lips had lost their pink glow.

"You did so good," I whispered as I stood rocking my little girl. "Emerson is so beautiful and strong just like you."

Standing there, I sobbed.

"I don't know how to do this without you, but I will find a way. I will be the best father I can be and I will never let Emerson forget who you are. I love you so much and I am going to miss you every day."

My blood boiled. Allie was innocent in all of this. She deserved to be a mother, to watch her daughter grow up. We had been robbed of so much.

I didn't want to leave Allie's side, but I knew it was time. As I walked back out to the waiting room, all my brothers gathered around me, meeting the newest member of our family.

"Maccon," a familiar singsong voice called to me.

Turning, I saw the sorrowful face of my sister as she ran to me. "I came as fast as I could."

"Thank you for coming, Piper. Want to meet your niece?"

My sister took Emerson from my arms as she started crying. "She's beautiful."

A nurse came up to us while we were fawning over our little miracle. "I am so sorry, but we need to take her into the newborn intensive care unit."

As the nurse took my daughter, my heart was crushed again. "Is she all right?"

The nurse gave me a sympathetic smile. "We have to be careful with premature babies, but she's a strong one. She's going to be fine, will probably only stay with us for a few days. It's just a precaution, that's all."

"Will you go with her?" I asked Piper.

Giving me a quick hug, she sighed. "Of course, big brother."

"I'm so sorry, son." My father pulled me into his arms. "It's your call. What do you want to do?"

I took a step back, straightening up as I looked at all of the guys huddled around. "We're going to make them pay for all of this, for Katherine and Allie. We're going to destroy them."

Reese put his hand on my shoulder. "Aye, brother. They have no idea who they messed with."

CHAPTER 4

After three sleepless nights at the hospital, I finally got the all-clear to take Emerson home. It should have been the happiest day of my life, but I was empty. The one person I wanted by my side couldn't be there.

"You sit in the back with her. I'll drive." Piper grabbed my keys out of my hand before I could protest.

"Thanks." I clicked Emerson's car seat into the back of my pickup and climbed in beside her.

I couldn't take my eyes off of my fussing daughter as she took her first car ride. I tried everything to soothe her and failed miserably.

"Allie would have known just how to keep her calm," I muttered to myself.

Piper glanced at me in the rearview mirror. "Hey, bro?"

"Yeah?"

"I've been thinking—Dad has a spare room in the back of the house. Why don't I move in with you to help the two of you with Emerson? I've been trying to figure out a way to leave my job at the Quick Stop anyway, and it seems like you could use another set of hands right now. It's been a long time since Dad dealt with a newborn, and I bet you've never changed a diaper in your damn life."

I didn't know what to say. I hadn't thought about what I was going to do once Emerson was home. Piper was right—we needed help.

"You're right about the diaper thing. and I think that is a perfect idea," I responded in a high-pitched, goo-goo voice as I stroked Emerson's cheek.

"Would you like it if Auntie Piper lived with us? Cry if you think it's a good idea."

Emerson wailed, taking the screeching to a whole new level.

"We're in," I added while laughing.

"Fantastic." Piper chortled as she pulled into the driveway of my father's house. "Home sweet home."

It wasn't home, but it would have to do while I was figuring out how to rebuild mine. It broke my heart that the nursery Allie had painstakingly put together for our little girl had gone up in flames, but those things could be replaced. I just didn't know if I was going to be able to do it as well as she had the first time around.

Just as I was getting Emerson out of the truck, my phone started ringing. Handing the car seat over to Piper, I picked up.

"Hello?"

"Church. Now," my father barked into the phone.

"I'm just getting Emerson home," I complained.

"You need to get here now."

I wasn't going to argue, sure this meant they finally had a lead. "Yeah, okay. Be right there."

"Let me guess," Piper started as she popped out her hip to rest the carrier on. "Dad just snapped his fingers and you're going running."

I kissed her on the cheek. "Don't start. You know what this is about."

"Give 'em hell." She tossed me a quick smile. "We'll be fine."

"You know where the formula and everything is right?" I asked, diving into the front seat of my Chevy.

"I helped you organize it all yesterday. We're fine. Be safe."

"Thanks, Piper. I'll be back as soon as I can."

I BURST into the room where my men were already surrounding the table waiting for me.

"Did you find them?" I barked, taking my seat.

I gripped the gavel as Abel cleared his throat. "For drug dealers, these dudes weren't easy to find, at least their higher-ups weren't, but I think I pinned down their main safe house last night."

"What are we waiting for?" I could feel my heart beating out of my chest as the thirst for revenge consumed my entire body. It tingled and coursed as flashes of Allie's lifeless body assaulted my mind.

"For you," my father admitted. "This is your fight, son. We weren't going to take it from you."

"We're prepared to hit them like they did to you. I have enough C4 to turn that place into a damn Fourth of July fireworks show." Reese was scary when it came to how good he was with explosives, but that wasn't going to be our play. They needed to suffer. Blowing them up would be too quick and painless for them.

"Do we know who their president is?" My blood was boiling with every word.

Rave nodded, pulling out photos of two men. "Darren Paterson. His number two is Elijah Clark." Rave pointed to each snapshot in turn, showing me who my next targets were going to be.

"That's who we have to go after."

"They're never in the same place at the same time. Surprisingly, I saw Darren last night, and he was never alone. No sign of Elijah, though," Abel explained.

Jett jumped to his feet. "I say we take out as many as we can. No sense in just sitting here when we know where a lot of them are hiding out."

"Sit your jumpy ass down and shut up," Hawk howled at Jett.

Doing as he was told, Jett huffed back into his seat.

"Get me Darren and take him to the woods," I instructed Abel and Rave. "I'll meet you there with a surprise for our guest of honor. Jett, Reese, you're with me. The rest of you, we're in lockdown. Dad, I need you to go get Piper and Emerson. Bring them here. I don't want them to be alone right now."

"You got it, son." My old man stood. "You heard the man. Let's get to it."

CHAPTER 5

It didn't take long for us to make it out to the cabin we had tucked away in the woods. The crickets were chirping under a cloudless, star-cloaked sky as we got out of my truck.

"What's the plan, brother?" Reese asked, following me around the back of the house.

I popped open the shed door. "Fight fire with fire." Grabbing the fine-tipped soldering iron off of the shelf, I grinned at my number two. "It's poetic, isn't it?" I chuckled before grabbing a few boxes of ammunition for his revolver off of the shelf. "Can't be too careful."

"You always were the brains of the operation," he remarked before we headed back up to the front porch of the cabin. "Now we wait."

After a pack of smokes and a fifth of Jack Daniels, Abel and Ravage finally joined us. Pulling up in a blacked-out van, they hopped out quickly.

"We have a present for you," Abel hollered up to us.

"About damn time. I was beginning to think y'all weren't going to pull this off." I made my way down the steps to join them.

"We'd never let you down, brother," Rave stated as he opened the back doors. The hogtied man inside screamed through his gag at the top of his lungs.

"Shut up." I spit in his face as Reese and Jett pulled him out of the back.

"Basement?" Reese looked up at me.

"Yep." I felt like a damn kid on Christmas. It was the weirdest feeling in the world. The excitement of the torture I was about to inflict on the man responsible for Allie's death was all-consuming.

We dragged him into the dimly lit, plastic-covered basement and tied him to a chair in the middle of the room.

"Take his shoes off," I demanded, plugging in my tool.

I let the soldering iron heat up to its maximum nine-hundred degrees and began with the bottom of his right foot. Abel and Jett held his leg steady while Reese held his shoulders down.

Darren tried to thrash as wails of pain leapt from his chest.

"This is nothing compared to what you did to my wife," I screamed, setting the instrument down for a second. "Other foot," I barked.

Abel and Jett shifted, pulling his leg up. Darren tried to knee Abel in the face, barely missing him.

"Not today, fuckface," Abel growled, pulling his Glock 26 from its ankle holster. Firing off one round into Darren's knee, Abel shot me a sinister sneer.

"You picked the wrong motherfuckers to mess with," Rave bellowed from behind me as he watched the show while chain-smoking.

Once both of the bottoms of Darren's feet were medium rare, I cut open his shirt. Darren's head nodded from side to side, barely able to stay awake through the pain.

"Wakey, wakey," I snickered as I splashed water in his face.

His eyes shot open as he screamed out. "Please," he muttered over and over. "Please don't."

"It's too late for that. If you wanted mercy, you shouldn't have blown up my house and killed my pregnant wife." I smiled with my face an inch away from his. "Don't worry, it'll all be over soon."

His chest was covered in the Renegade King's reaper. That was about to change.

Taking the soldering iron, I slowly branded Allie's name over the intricate artwork. I watched as the black-inked skin bubbled up under each letter. Tears started to stream down my face as the E was finished.

The smell of burnt flesh overtook the small space as I stared at the blubbering sack of shit in front of me, and the high that had consumed me faded. No retaliation would bring Allie back. No amount of bloodshed would soothe my aching soul.

Demons crashed inside of me as I dropped to my knees. I wasn't ashamed. Grief was part of life, and if I couldn't break down in front of my men and show them I was human, how could I be a true leader? I was only one man—one man with a broken heart and a duty to my family and brotherhood.

Jett pulled me to my feet. "It's done, brother. Go back to your daughter. We'll finish up here."

Taking out my Kimber Micro Crimson Carry, I shot Darren in the temple.

"Now it's done." I exhaled before turning for the stairs. "The lye is in the shed. Y'all know what to do."

Rave walked up to me, resting his hand on my shoulder. "We got this, brother. Get outta here. You have a little one waiting for you."

PULLING Emerson out of her crib, I went and sat on the couch in the lounge. Everyone was asleep in the back bedrooms and scattered around on the floor in sleeping bags. My entire family was under one roof, and that scared the shit out of me. Even with guards posted around the entire place, I knew I would never rest easy again. There was too much to lose now that Emerson was in the world.

Staring down at her sweet face as she slept, I cooed to my daughter, "Daddy got the bad guy, sweetheart. I promise I will always protect you."

Daggers shot through me. How could I promise her that when I hadn't been able to protect her mother? How was I going to be able to raise her on my own?

"Maccon?" Piper trotted into the room.

"What're you doing up?" I whispered to her as she took a seat next to me.

"I went to check on the baby and she wasn't in the crib. I nearly had a panic attack." She rested her head on my shoulder. "How was your night?"

I leaned my head against hers. "Better now that I'm here with my girls."

"She looks so peaceful in your arms."

"I think she's definitely going to be a daddy's girl," I teased.

"There's no doubt about that one." Piper yawned against me.

"Go back to bed. I'm going to sit up with her for a while."

"All right. Get some rest. You've been going nonstop and you're no good to anyone running on an empty tank."

"Yes ma'am."

She stuck her tongue out at me before hopping up from the couch. "Love ya."

"Love you too, punk."

CHAPTER 6

A little over ten years later

I CRACKED MY BACK AS I GOT OUT OF BED. WITH THE RENEGADE KINGS completely underground since the night we took out their leader, life had slowed down to a normal pace for us. We had lost a few good men over the years, all in the name of war. Ravage and Abel had both been taken. They were missed and their loss was felt on a daily basis, but the world kept turning anyway.

Staring at my weathered face and grayed beard in the mirror over my dresser, I hardly recognized myself. It had taken a while to make my rebuilt house feel like a home, but Emerson and Piper both helped exponentially.

I could smell bacon and coffee wafting up from the kitchen as I made my way down the stairs.

"Daddy," Emerson cheered as she popped up from her seat at the table.

"Morning, princess," I muttered before kissing the top of her head. "Are you excited for your first day of school?"

She bounced in her chair. "Yep."

"I can't believe she is starting fifth grade this year. Where has the time gone?" Piper handed me a cup of black coffee and a plate full of eggs and bacon.

"Bless you." I smiled at her, joining my family for breakfast. "Are you going into the shop today?"

Piper nodded with bacon rolling around in her mouth. "Right after I drop this little one off for her first day. I'll see you there."

Emerson wiggled away from her aunt as Piper tousled her hair a bit.

"Now my hair is going to be all messed up," Emerson complained.

"I'll help you fix it. Go grab your brush." I beamed at my daughter as she darted for her room in a flash.

"She's so grown up," Piper remarked.

"Tell me about it." I rolled my eyes. "She's going to be a handful here shortly."

"She already is," Piper baited with a toothy grin. "She takes after her mother."

My sister was right. I saw more and more of Allie in our daughter every day.

Emerson thrust my brush into my hands. "Here, Daddy."

I pulled my little girl into my lap, brushing her hair into pigtails, just the way she liked it. "There you go, sweetheart. Now you're all ready for your last first day of elementary school." The words caught in the back of my throat. She was growing up too fast.

"Grab your bag, Em. We gotta go. You can't be late on your first day." Piper placed the dirty dishes from our breakfast into the sink.

"Love you, Daddy." Emerson threw her arms around my neck, making me melt on the spot.

"Have the best day ever, princess."

AFTER A LONG DAY of selling discount auto parts and dealing with paperwork, I was finally in my happy place—tucking Emerson in for the night.

"Story time," she sang out, shoving a worn copy of *The Lion, The Witch and The Wardrobe* into my hands.

"That it is, princess. Now get all situated." I helped her climb into her bed next to me so she could cuddle up as I read from her favorite book.

Pulling out the bookmark at the beginning of chapter two, I started reading the familiar words. "'Good evening,' said Lucy. But the Faun was so busy picking up its parcels that at first it did not reply. When it had finished it made her a little bow."

I paused for a split second to take in the moment. There was nothing better than being there with her in simple moments like that.

When chapter two was finished, I put the bookmark back in and kissed Emerson on her forehead. "Sleep well, princess."

"Good night, Daddy," she muttered while rubbing her sleepy eyes.

Joining Piper on the couch, I let out a sigh. "I think I need to head out for a drink."

"I think you deserve one," she replied. "It's about time you did something for yourself for a change."

My sister eyed me as I deflated. My life was my family. I worked, I took care of Emerson, I ran my club, rinse and repeat—that was all she wrote.

"It's really not that bad, is it?"

"You need to get laid, big brother." Hearing my sister tell me to get my dick wet was the strangest thing in the world.

"Don't be gross."

She shrugged. "Just stating facts, man. It's been over ten years, and I feel like you're turning into a priest or something."

It wasn't like I didn't have a conquest or two from time to time, but I kept them as far away from my family life as possible. I didn't want someone else messing up the wonderful dynamic we had together. It was too risky.

"Far from it, sis." I grabbed my cut and keys before turning to Piper. "Thank you, though. Sometimes I need a little push."

"You don't have to tell me, Maccon. Now get goin'." She shooed me away as I walked out the door.

CHAPTER 7

Bellying up to the bar at the Red Crow, I ordered a bottle of Coors Light and a shot of Jameson. It had been so long since I drank alone at a bar, I didn't really know what to do. The people-watching was prime that night with drunkards hollering at each other over rounds of pool, couples line-dancing their hearts out, and swarms of barflies trying to outdrink each other.

It didn't take long for a gorgeous brunette at the far end of the bar to catch my eye. Just as I mustered up enough courage to walk over to her, a guy took a seat next to her.

The blacked-out tattoo on his forearm wasn't lost on me as I tried to place his somewhat familiar face. The brunette seemed to know him, and I chalked it up to bad timing.

There will be other women to talk to. I tried to reassure myself, but I couldn't stop glancing over at her delicate features as she laughed and carried on with her guy.

Suddenly, her face twisted and his hand gripped around her wrist. He pulled her to her feet as she slapped him across the face.

I scrambled over to their side. "I think the lady has made it very clear that you're no longer welcome here," I growled in a low tone.

"Fuck you," the douchebag snarled at me. "I think my old lady here just needs to know her place."

I stepped in between them. "Don't make me say it again."

He threw his hands into the air. "You're not worth it, slut. He can have you."

The asshole spit at my feet before turning to walk away.

He backed down easily. What a pussy.

"Thanks," the gorgeous brunette huffed as she sank back onto her chair.

"You all right?" I asked, taking the empty stool next to her.

"Yeah, just an old boyfriend who needs to stay an ex. I don't know why I even entertained the thought of being around him tonight." She nudged the lime in her drink with a straw.

"Old habits die hard," I responded, holding out my hand for her to take. "I'm Maccon."

"Kinsley," she replied, taking my hand. "Thank you."

"No problem. What're you drinkin'?" I pointed to her glass, which was almost empty.

"Jameson and ginger," she replied.

I called over to the bartender, ordering us a round.

"So what brings a white knight like you into this seedy bar?" she asked with a little giggle.

"Just needed to get out of the house for a little bit. It's been a while," I admitted.

"I can understand that. It was a very long Monday for me too."

We made small talk while finishing our drinks. It was nice to just shoot the shit with someone who wasn't in my club, a ten-year-old, or my sister.

"Do you wanna get outta here?" I boldly asked as I slammed the bottom of my beer.

"Actually, I do." She jumped up from her seat. "Lead the way. That dick-hole Elijah was my ride, so I hope you're driving."

The name clicked in my head and I saw red. All I wanted to do was rush into the parking lot and beat that motherfucker to death, but I cooled my temper and forced myself to focus on the beautiful girl I had just rescued. "Yes ma'am. I'd be happy to."

I escorted Kinsley to my motorcycle, which was parked on the side of the bar.

As I started to get onto my bike, she grabbed my arm. "Hey," she muttered before crushing her lips to mine.

I pulled her into me, gripping her hips as our lips danced together. It had been far too long since I had been kissed passionately, and I hadn't realized how much I missed it.

"Give me directions as I drive?" I asked, subtly telling her we weren't going back to my place.

She nodded before climbing onto my bike behind me.

Once we walked into her house, desire took over completely.

I pressed her up against the wall next to her front door, pulling her leg up onto my hip, and she lightly nipped at my neck as I growled in her ear. As I kissed from her collarbone to her chin, she slowly rubbed my growing erection over my tightening jeans. I rumbled into her neck, feeling my need grow with every second.

"God, it's been too long," I huffed quickly as she started to undo my belt.

I reached up under her loose tank top and her bra, tugging on her nipples gently.

A low moan escaped from her lips as she breathlessly said, "That feels so damn good."

She grabbed my hand, leading me back to her bedroom. Going straight for her bed, she stripped down to her bra and panties.

I groaned as I watched her slowly undress from the other side of the bed where I was following suit. "You're so damn hot."

I couldn't believe my eyes. From her delicate features to her soft breasts, all the way down to her toned thighs—she was magnificent.

She got on her knees on the bed, staring right at me, slowly starting to massage her breasts over the black lace, playing with her nipples. My dick twitched as I took in the show in front of me.

"You like that?" she asked as a coy smile spread on her lips.

I nodded.

"And this?" She ran her middle finger under her panties, slowly biting her lower lip out of sheer pleasure.

A low rumble came from the back of my throat. "Fuck. Come here," I demanded, grabbing her hips. I helped her off of the bed then pushed her down onto her knees.

She took my length into her mouth instantly, forcing it all the way into the back of her throat like a champ.

"*Fuck*. You're so good at that," I moaned as she sucked and licked my growing cock. My fingers curled into her long hair, pulling her head back. "Look at me. The. Whole. Time." I thrust in hard, making her gag, but she never broke eye contact.

Her mouth felt so good.

I was fucking addicted it.

I plunged harder and deeper into her mouth until tears formed in the corners of her eyes, making her mascara run. Just as my dick started to throb, I released my grip on her hair.

"Get on the bed, on your knees, and put your hands behind your back."

She did exactly what I told her to do without question. Sliding my belt out of its loops and freeing it from my jeans, I wrapped the leather around her wrists.

"Like that?" I asked sharply, not really caring what her answer was unless she was about to freak out on me.

"I love it, actually," she responded, giving me the green light.

"Your ass is perfect." I rolled my fingers over her soft skin as she purred.

"Take it then." She looked over her shoulder with a close-lipped smile. "I like it."

I pressed my tattooed chest against her back, letting my cock slide between her cheeks snuggly. "Are you sure?"

"You can have whatever you want," she moaned, letting her head roll back.

Quickly, I spun her around and shoved her head down next to my dick. "Get it nice and wet. We don't want to go in dry, now do we?"

She spit and sucked until I was more than lubed enough to enter her. I forced her back into position, her perfect ass high in the air. Gripping her sides, I slowly slid into her as she gasped, and she moaned as I pulled out.

"How was that?" My husky voice was coated in lustful desire.

"Fucking amazing," she groaned into the comforter.

"How about this?" Forcefully, I thrust deeper into her. Pulling out, I spit onto her, rolling the head of my cock around on her back door teasingly.

"More," she cried.

Without warning, I thrust into her over and over as her cries of pleasure cheered me on.

"Fuck. Your dick is unbelievable." She sighed as I slowly pulled out before releasing her wrists from my belt and tossing it onto the floor.

"Now I need your pussy." I rolled her over, getting on my knees in front of her. I flattened my tongue over her pulsing clit as her knees started to shake.

"Holy shit," she cried out as I licked and teased her sensitive skin.

"You like that?" I asked between laps.

Her entire body shook. "So much."

Her sweet nectar filled my mouth as I felt her climax starting to build. When I shoved two fingers into her, her walls collapsed around them. She screamed out as all of her muscles tensed from sheer euphoria.

"You're incredible. Where have you been all my life?" She panted, pulling me on top of her.

"I was just about to say something very similar."

Reaching up into her nightstand drawer, I pulled a condom wrapper out. I rolled the rubber on, shifting to make her get on top of me.

As she rode my dick, I was mesmerized by her tits bouncing in my face. I could barely contain myself. Her pussy was so tight, her hips bucked perfectly, and her body was incredible.

"You're going to make me cum," I bellowed, pulling her hips down onto me.

"Cum for me, Maccon," she cried out, picking up her pace.

My cock throbbed as my entire body was overtaken with blazing pleasure. She collapsed on top of me, slowly catching her breath.

"Fuck, Kinsley. That was..." My head hit the pillow as she crawled into my arms.

"Yeah, amazing. I agree." She slipped under the covers and we quickly drifted off into a post-sex coma.

CHAPTER 8

The next morning, I lay awake with Kinsley fast asleep, her head on my shoulder. All I could think about was the fact that her ex-boyfriend was the elusive number two I had looked for all those years ago. We had assumed all of the Renegade Kings had left town, but apparently they were just good at laying low.

As she started to stir, I pulled away from her. "Good morning," I muttered before kissing her forehead.

"You stayed," she muttered with a sleepy smile.

"Was I not supposed to?" I asked as I got up to get dressed.

"I'm glad you did. Most guys don't." Her face twisted into a grimace.

Leaning down, I kissed her one more time. "I'm not like most guys, but I do need to get home before my daughter wakes up."

"He's a dad," she teased.

"That I am."

"I like that. Kids are my whole world. I'm a teacher."

I smiled down at her. "Perfect."

I pulled a receipt out of my pocket, scribbling my number before putting it on the nightstand. "I hope I can see you again."

"I'll probably be at the Red Crow tonight, if you're interested." She grinned up at me, pulling her tank top over her bare chest.

"It's a date."

Sitting at my desk in the auto parts store, I couldn't get Kinsley out of my head. I hadn't felt that way about a woman since meeting Allie, and it scared the ever-loving shit out of me.

"Knock, knock." Piper waltz into my office, plopping down on the chair in front of me.

"So?" She was grinning at me with wide eyes.

"It was a good night," I admitted, barely able to contain the smirk that took over quickly.

"Fantastic. What's her name?"

"Kinsley," I replied.

"That's cute. What is she, twenty?" Piper teased.

"Thirty-one," I replied.

"Robbing the cradle, old man." Piper snickered.

"Forty-eight isn't too much older, is it?"

Great, now I feel like a perv.

"I'm just jerking you around, bro. Good for you."

"Is Reese here yet?"

She nodded. "Nice way to change the subject."

"Can you send him in here? Please and thank you."

"Don't forget about the parent-teacher thing tonight at Em's school. You have to make it to one before she leaves that place."

"I promise I will be there with bells on."

Piper stuck her tongue out at me—her normal bratty move—before leaving to get my VP.

"You needed to see me?" Reese walked in quickly.

"Shut the door," I growled before lighting a cigarette and throwing him the pack.

"What's going on?"

I took in a deep breath. "I found Elijah last night at the Red Crow."

His eyes grew ten times as he took in a long drag. "No fucking way."

"I think it was him anyway. I met his ex-girlfriend last night. He had blacked-out ink and everything. It has to be him." I paused for a moment before continuing. "I'm meeting her there tonight. I need you and Jett to wait in the parking lot just in case he shows up."

"Shouldn't we bring this to the club?" Reese worked his jaw, waiting for my response.

"We should, but there isn't time, and I don't really give a fuck about procedure right now. What if we lose him again?"

"I couldn't agree more, and I am on it." The fire that lit in the back of Reese's eyes was contagious. The second part of my revenge was finally going to play out.

Even though I knew it wasn't going to fix anything, I would sleep better at night knowing there was one less scumbag out there in the world.

"Today is going to be a good day."

"That it is, brother. That it is."

Reese left the office and I leaned back in my chair, thinking about all the fucked-up things I was going to do to Elijah. He had been living on borrowed time for the last decade, and I was going to make that very clear to him as soon as I got my hands on him.

CHAPTER 9

"Daddy, come on," Emerson whined, pulling me into her classroom. "I want you to meet my teacher."

With Piper in tow, we made our way into the tiny, brightly decorated space, and I stopped dead in my tracks.

Kinsley locked eyes with me from the other side of the room where she was talking with a husband and wife.

"Excuse me." She didn't break eye contact with me as she ducked away from the parents. "Maccon? Are you stalking me?" she whispered teasingly as she crossed her arms over her chest.

"No. Emerson is my daughter." I pulled my kid into my side, feeling completely awkward.

"Hi, Miss Rogers." Emerson wiggled her fingers at her teacher.

"Hey, Emerson. Thanks for bringing your parents here tonight." Kinsley looked from me to Piper, and I was mortified.

Piper cleared her throat. "Parent," she corrected. "I'm the aunt, Piper."

I could see the relief wash over Kinsley as she shook my sister's hand.

"I think I saw you dropping Emerson off this morning." Kinsley was blushing as she stared at me while talking to Piper.

"That would be me."

"Aunt Piper, let me show you my cubby." Emerson dragged Piper away, leaving Kinsley and me standing awkwardly in the middle of the classroom with parents fluttering around with their excited kids.

"I should probably get back to it." Kinsley rubbed her sides nervously.

"See you after at the Red Crow?"

"I definitely need a drink after this. I'll see you there."

"Going back out to see your hot little teacher?" Piper pestered me while cleaning up from dinner.

"As a matter of fact, I am." I pulled on my leather and dug in my pocket for the keys to my Harley. Tossing them into the bowl on the counter, I swapped them out for my truck keys. I didn't want Elijah to recognize my bike from the night before and get spooked. I wasn't going to take any chances.

"Don't wait up for me, sis." I pecked her on the cheek.

"I wasn't planning on it."

Sitting right where she had been the night before, Kinsley was waiting for me.

"Fancy meeting you here." I kissed her cheek before sitting down.

"Hey there, handsome." She smiled over her shoulder at me. "That was some surprise tonight."

"You're telling me." I still wasn't over the embarrassment of banging my kid's teacher.

"It's not weird for you, is it?" she asked with a frown.

I took a swig from my freshly opened beer bottle. "Not if it isn't for you."

"I like that answer. Don't expect special treatment for Emerson, though. There's no amount of amazing oral in the world that will get me to play favorites."

I pulled her into me. "Oh come on, there has to be some amount of amazing oral that would earn a little bit of special treatment," I whispered in her ear. "I'll take you into the bathroom right now and show you just how amazing it can be."

She moaned a little as her head fell onto my shoulder. "All right, there might be an amount, but I am telling you, it's not going to be easy."

"I like a challenge." My phone buzzed in my pocket. "Sorry, I have to check this," I muttered to Kinsley.

"Have at it."

I opened the message from Reese: **We're in place. We'll let you know.**

Me: Perfect.

"Now where were we?" I smirked at Kinsley as she sipped from her drink.

"I think we were discussing you licking my clit again," she breathily whispered into my ear.

"I can't wait to taste you again," I admitted.

Just as she was about to respond, I saw Elijah walk out the back door.

"I'll be right back." I leapt to my feet, holding a finger up to Kinsley. "Hold that thought."

She stared at me as I followed him out.

Whistling for Reese and Jett, I looked right at my enemy as he whipped out his dick to piss in the parking lot next to his bike.

With Reese and Jett trotting over to me, I rushed up behind the fucker, punching him in the shoulder.

"Hey man, remember me?" I yelled as he stumbled forward, frantically trying to put his cock away.

Reese grabbed his arm, spinning him around.

"Oh shit," Elijah stammered as he tried to make a break for it.

"Not so fast." Jett stopped him, showing him the baseball bat in his hand.

"I didn't do anything. You can have Kinsley. I didn't even talk to her tonight." He was shaking.

"I'm not here because of Kinsley. I'm here because you murdered my wife and almost killed my daughter ten years ago. Ring a fucking bell?" I was seething as Reese and Jett held the arms of the squirming coward.

"It wasn't me. I didn't make that call," he whined. "I swear. I left the club right after that happened. I didn't sign up to be a woman killer. You gotta believe me."

"Maccon? What the hell is going on?" Kinsley was thundering toward us.

"You need to go back inside." I grabbed her arm. "Please, Kinsley. I need to take care of something."

"He's not worth it. I'm not worth it. What are you thinking?" she yelled in my face, ripping her arm out of my grasp.

"This has nothing to do with you. He helped kill my wife." The words felt bitter as I admitted them to her.

"He did wh-what?" she stammered, taking a step back. "You did what?" she screamed at her ex.

"I didn't mean to. I thought I was just blowing up an empty house. No one was home when we put the shit in the crawlspace." He was blubbering as snot started to pour from his nose.

"What do you want to do, boss?" Reese asked.

I looked into Kinsley's eyes. For some reason I didn't want anything to do with my revenge anymore, and a part of me believed the sniveling fucktard.

She put her hand on my shoulder as her eyes pleaded with me.

"Let him go," I ordered, and Reese and Jett instantly released their grip. Taking a step toward Elijah, I glared at him. "Show me."

He blinked at me. "What?"

"Show me you're actually out of the Renegade Kings. I need to see the covered ink."

Ripping his shirt up over his head, he tossed it on his bike. He turned slowly with his arms stretched out. All of his tattoos were blackened blobs.

"I wasn't lying. There hasn't been a day I haven't thought about what happened that night," he murmured, his head hanging. "I am so fucking sorry, man."

Watching him fall apart in front of me was enough. I was done. I needed to move on.

"Get the fuck out of my sight. I never want to see you around here again, and you better never contact my girl."

He dragged his keys out and got on his bike right away. "I fucking swear, man, you'll never see me again."

We stood in the parking lot, making sure he actually rode away.

Pulling Kinsley into my arms, I looked down at her. "I'm sorry for this."

She kissed my cheek. "If my wife had been brutally murdered, I probably would have done a lot worse."

"Does that mean you'll go out with me again?" I shot her a crooked smile.

"Let's see..." She tapped a finger onto her lips for a few seconds. "A handsome, single dad with a heart of gold who also happens to be badass biker wants to date me? I think I could handle that."

Reese and Jett both made cooing noises behind us.

"Shut the fuck up. Don't ruin the damn moment," I growled at them.

Throwing their hands in the air, they each took a couple of steps back.

"I'm really glad I met you, Kinsley Rogers." I picked her up into my arms, twirling her around in the gravel lot.

As she giggled, she beamed down at me. "That feeling is very much mutual."

THE END...FOR now.

Catch up with Kristen Hope Mazola
Website: http://www.kristenhopemazzola.com
Newsletter: http://www.kristenhopemazzola.com/mailing-list.html
Bookbub: https://www.bookbub.com/profile/kristen-hope-mazzola

Gus

SATAN'S FURY MC- MEMPHIS

NYT AND USA TODAY BESTSELLING AUTHOR

L. WILDER

CHAPTER 1

GUS

1994

Club life isn't for everyone, but for me—it was everything. I started prospecting for Satan's Fury MC when I was twenty-one years old, and right from the start, I knew there was no other place for me. I dedicated my life to the brothers of the Washington Chapter—my family. Through the years, they taught me everything I needed to know—not just about MC life, but about the kind of man I wanted to be: a man who'd demonstrate loyalty, pride, and grit. I wanted my brothers and those around me to know that I was someone they could trust, that I would always hold true to my word, and that I'd never waiver or show signs of weakness when it came to my commitment to the club and its prosperity. I'd felt honored that my brothers had seen those very qualities in me when they voted me in as their sergeant-at-arms. I thought I'd end out my days there with them in Washington, but Saul, the club's president, had other plans for me.

We'd just dismissed from church when Saul asked me to join him in the bar for a beer. I followed him over to the counter, grabbed us each a cold one, and sat down next to him. He took a quick pull, then said, "Butch called last night. He was just checking in, and we got to talking. We both think it's about time for us to start gaining some territory down south."

Butch was the president of the original Satan's Fury chapter in Utah. At the time, their chapter was twice the size of ours, and it was steadily growing with at least six prospects ready to patch in. Butch and Saul created Fury in their vision, and I was curious to hear what they had planned. "Sounds like a good idea. What do you have in mind?"

"Right now, we have chapters in Washington, Utah, Colorado, Oklahoma, and as of recently, Kansas, so it makes sense to keep moving further south." He pulled out his pack of smokes, lit a cigarette, and continued, "I'm thinking it'll probably be Memphis, but there's always Little Rock or Birmingham."

"Memphis is thriving, and it's sitting right on the Mississippi River."

"That's what I was thinking. We looked into some local chapters there but aren't sure they're worthy of the Fury name. Butch and I both agreed that it would be smarter to send some of our own down to get things started. Check out surrounding clubs and see if any might be worth patching over. We just need someone we all can trust to make it happen."

"Okay, so what does any of this have to do with me?"

"Everything." He took a drag off his cigarette and smoke billowed around him as he continued, "We think you're that person, Gus. You've proven your loyalty to the club. You've got a good head on your shoulders, and you're a born leader. We both think you have what it takes to get things rolling down there. That is … if you're up for it."

"I'm up for whatever you need me to do. You know that." While I was flattered that Saul asked me to take on such a vital task, I didn't let it go to my head. I knew a lot was taken into consideration when they chose me, like the fact that I was not only experienced but also single with no strong ties to outside family. Regardless, I was grateful that the two decided on me to lead the new chapter, and I'd do everything in my power to make it a success. "I'm just going to need a little direction here. What exactly is it that you're wanting me to do?"

"We'd want you there as president of the new chapter and get things started: Find a location for the clubhouse, check out other clubs and look for potential patch overs, and draw in some new prospects. You'll need to establish some work fronts. The whole nine yards." When Saul saw the look of concern on my face, he smiled and said, "Don't worry. We won't be shipping you out there alone. Along with a few members and prospects from both chapters, Butch will be sending one of his best to be there at your side."

"I'd be honored, Prez." I couldn't hide my enthusiasm when I answered him.

"I was hoping you'd say that."

"You have any idea on when you want this to go down?"

"The sooner the better." He put out his cigarette and continued, "I'll get back with Butch later tonight and let him know you're on board. We'll talk it over, and once we have more of the details sorted, we'll discuss it with the others during church."

"Thank you for this opportunity, Prez. I won't let you down."

"I know you won't. That's why you were chosen." Saul finished off his beer, then stood to leave. "Best get your things in order."

He patted my shoulder and walked out of the bar, leaving me alone with my thoughts. It was hard not to feel pumped about the opportunity I'd been given, but as I sat there thinking about all the things that would need to be done, I started to question whether or not I was prepared to take on such an overwhelming endeavor.

By the following morning, Gus confirmed that Memphis would be the location for the new chapter. At the end of the week, the brothers threw us a kick-ass farewell celebration, wanting to wish us well and congratulate me on my new position as president of the Memphis chapter. Once I'd recovered from the festivities, I packed up the rest of my belongings and headed south.

My mind was racing as I drove down the interstate. While I was eager to move to Memphis and get things started, I was feeling a little apprehensive. There was a lot weighing on the success of this new chapter, and I didn't want to let Saul or my brothers down. Luckily, I wouldn't have to take on such a huge responsibility alone. Moose, along with his old lady, Louise, their two-year-old daughter, Rayne, and Cyrus from the Utah chapter, as well as Bane, Widow, Half-Pint, and T-Bone from ours were following close behind me as I continued towards Memphis. Once we got to Tennessee, they would be right there at my side to help get things rolling.

As soon as we hit the city limits, we found a place to stay and set to work. I'd like to say that everything went exactly as planned, that we didn't have a single hiccup, but I'd be lying. We ran into one obstacle after the next, but thankfully, it wasn't anything that couldn't be handled. We kept pushing forward and, after a few weeks' time, had started to make some real progress. We'd purchased an old train depot that was located on the east end of downtown, right on the banks of the Mississippi River. The place needed some work, but it was the perfect size and the location couldn't have been better for our clubhouse.

After spending the entire day busting our asses on some of the renovations, we all met up at one of the local pizza places to grab dinner.

The waitress had just brought over our drinks when Moose turned to me and asked, "You got any thoughts on what you want to do about the exterior fence?"

"It's gotta be at least ten feet with electric gates at the front and the back."

Moose was in his early thirties, and big as a fucking ox with bulging biceps and tattoos from head to toe. He was the Utah chapter's enforcer, and I'd learned early on that he wasn't a man who was afraid to speak his mind. I wasn't at all surprised when he argued, "You sure we're gonna need all that? Back in Utah, we only have a six-and-a-half-foot fence, and with the additional barbed-wire, it's been more than enough."

"Yeah, and it's located on the outskirts of Davis County in a fairly safe neighborhood. That's not the case here. Memphis has gangs at every corner." My voice grew more forceful as I told him, "As soon as they realize that we're encroaching on their territory, they're gonna be out for fucking blood, so if that means we have to put in a ten-foot security fence with barbed-wire, install a high-tech security system, and have guards posted around the clock, then that's what we're gonna fucking do."

With an almost defeated expression, he nodded and answered, "Understood."

"We're getting close." Trying to ease the tension, I told him, "It won't be long before we're out of that fucking hotel and into the clubhouse."

"Can't happen soon enough," he grumbled. "I can barely breathe in that tiny box of a room and having Louise and Rayne in such close quarters isn't helping."

"At least she doesn't fucking snore like T-Bone," Cyrus complained from across the table. He was Louise's brother, and while he was barely twenty-one and the youngest of the mix, he wasn't the least bit intimidated by anyone sitting at that table. Cyrus spoke his mind and didn't give a damn who he pissed off. "It's like I'm sleeping next to a fucking bear."

"Who said she doesn't snore?" Moose chuckled. "Hell, your sister's been sawing timbers since the first night."

"Yeah, well, the snoring's one thing, but the gas he's been letting out all week is another. It's like something died in his fucking gut." Cyrus yawned before he added, "I haven't slept worth a damn since we got here."

"It's not that bad." T-Bone, the jokester of the group, actually sounded a little bothered by Cyrus's comment. He'd only been prospecting for a couple of months, but in the short time he'd been with us, T-Bone had proven himself worthy as a brother, never failing to make himself available when we needed him. His eyes narrowed as he continued, "And just so you know, you're not exactly easy to live with either, brother. Your clothes and shit are all over the floor, and there's never any clean towels. I don't get it. What the hell are you doing with them? Do you take three fucking showers a day or what?"

Before Cyrus could respond, our waitress came over and placed our pizzas down on the table. As everyone started to fill their plates with food, Cyrus turned to me and asked, "So, what's going on with the diner?"

We'd bought a small place right on the corner of Beale Street, but we hadn't started working on any renovations. "Nothing right now. We need to make a final decision on what we're going to do."

"Louise says simple is always better." Moose added, "I'm telling ya, brother, she knows her shit. Give her a few months, and with Cyrus's help, she can make a real go of it. Daisy Mae's will be the talk of the city."

I looked at the others and asked, "You guys good with Daisy Mae's Cafe?"

"An all-American-style café with checkered tablecloths and pictures of all the great legends of Memphis plastered on the walls: Elvis, B.B. King, Aretha Franklin, Morgan Freeman, Cybil Shepherd, and Isaac Hayes. Hell, yeah. No one would ever suspect that it's a front," Bane agreed.

When the others nodded in agreement, I said, "Then, it's settled. Daisy Mae's it is. Tell Louise to get the ball rolling."

"Consider it done."

"Before she gets started, we'll need to make sure the electrical and plumbing is up to code," Half-pint warned. Over the past few weeks, his experience with all the ins and outs of construction had been invaluable. For a prospect, he'd saved us a lot of headaches. "And once we get a construction plan together, we'll need to get the necessary permits."

"Agreed. I already checked all the zoning codes, so we should be able to get the permits without any issue. It looks like it will pass inspection, but we all know that doesn't mean a damn thing." I leaned back in my chair and crossed my arms. "I'll go by there tonight and check things out. If all looks well, we'll get the city inspector to come down to see if he'll give us the go ahead."

"While you're doing that, we'll head back over to the clubhouse and finish up some painting," Moose offered.

"It's been a long day, brother. You boys go back to the hotel and get some rest." As I stood up, I placed enough money on the table to cover the bill and the tip, then told them, "We'll get things finished up in the morning."

"You got it."

After I said my goodbyes, I walked out of the restaurant and headed towards my bike in the parking lot. Every muscle in my body ached as I swung my leg over the seat and started the engine. I was so tempted to put off checking the pipes until morning, but knowing I'd just end up regretting it, I pushed myself forward. Thankfully, as soon as I pulled out onto the main road, the cool night air started working its magic on me, and it wasn't long before the tension I'd been carrying with me all day started to fade. I'd always liked riding in the city, seeing all the bright lights and the people wandering along the streets, but there was something about Memphis that took that feeling to a whole new level. Cruising around in the birthplace of rock & roll, seeing the Arkansas bridge with all its lights, and hearing the blues down on Beale Street got to me like no other city ever had. By the time I made it to the diner my spirits had lifted, and I was feeling optimistic about our club's future.

I checked inside and was pleased to see that I was right about the plumbing and electric. They both seemed to be in good condition, and I didn't see any reason why we wouldn't pass inspection. Relieved, I locked everything up and headed back out to my bike. I was just about to start the engine when my attention was drawn to a man and woman who were arguing across the street. Something didn't seem right, so I got off my bike and started towards them.

As I got closer, I was able to see them both better. The woman was young, maybe in her mid-twenties, with long blonde hair that was pulled back in a high ponytail, and she was wearing a black knee-length skirt with a black suit jacket. Even in the dark I could tell she was beautiful. The guy standing next to her was twice her size and looked like he'd just crawled out of a fucking dumpster, so I couldn't exactly blame her for being scared. I was just about to approach them when the guy reached out, jerked her purse out of her hand, and took off running. Without thinking, I started chasing after him. He was fast, *really fast*. I raced behind him, worried that I might not be able to catch up to him, especially since I was exhausted. But as soon as my adrenaline kicked in, I got close enough to lunge towards him. With a hard *thud*, I tackled him to the ground and used my weight to keep him in place. Once he'd recovered from the impact, he started thrashing around, trying with all his might to free himself from my grasp. Unfortunately for him, there was no way in hell I was gonna let him go. I yanked his arm behind his back, pinning him to the ground, then said, "Knock it off before I put a fucking bullet in you."

"What the hell are you doing?" he barked as he tried to buck me off him. "Get the fuck off me!"

Careful to keep it out of sight, I took my gun from the holster and shoved it into his side. "Not going to say it again, asshole."

"Whoa, man!" He stilled then said, "I wasn't gonna hurt 'er. I just needed a few bucks. I'm jonesing something awful and need a fix."

"So, you just figured you'd steal a lady's purse? Damn." My patience was wearing thin. "You're a real piece of shit," I growled.

"Done told you. I wasn't gonna hurt 'er," he whined. "Just let me go and I'll get gone."

"I'm thinking that's not a good idea." I pulled his arm back even further, causing him to cry out. "I'm thinking you'll just do this shit again, and that doesn't work for me."

"No, man. I learned my lesson. I ain't gonna do it again. I swear it."

"You better mean that." I jabbed the barrel of my pistol into his side. "Cause if you do … I'll find out and I'll come for you."

I picked up the woman's purse, then eased off him, making sure to grind my knee into his back. He got up as soon as he was able, and after giving me the once over, he scurried off. Once he was out of sight, I turned and headed back towards the young woman. I handed her the purse and asked, "You okay?"

Her voice trembled as she replied, "Yes, I think so."

"Good. I was worried he might've hurt you." I expected her to say something more, but she just stood there staring at me with a stunned look. "You sure you're okay?"

"I'm a little shaken up, that's all."

"I imagine you are."

"I don't know what I was thinking." She dropped her head into her hands and groaned. "I should've known Haley wouldn't show."

"Haley?"

"She's one of the pharmaceutical sales reps at MBC Pharmaceuticals. We were supposed to meet at Morgan's for dinner, but she didn't show." She motioned her hand over to the back lot and continued, "Since I parked close by, I thought I'd be okay, but then that guy came out of nowhere."

"It's not your fault. Just need to be a little more careful at this time of night."

"I know. It was a stupid move. I don't know what I would've done if you hadn't come along." She looked up at me with those beautiful eyes, and I was done. "Thank you so much for helping me like you did."

"No need to thank me. Happy to help."

"Well, I really appreciate it." A light blush crossed her face as she asked, "If it's not too much to ask, would you mind walking me over to my car?"

"I'd be glad to."

As we started towards her car, she turned to me and said, "By the way, my name is Samantha Travers."

Samantha Travers. I repeated her name in my head, committing it to memory.

"Nice to meet you, Samantha. I'm Gus." When we reached her car, I waited for her to unlock the door and get inside. "Be careful heading home."

"I will. Thanks again." I nodded and turned to leave. I'd only taken a few steps when I heard her call out to me. "Gus?"

There was something about the way she said my name that made my chest tighten. "Yeah?"

"Will I see you again?"

"You can count on it."

A smile crossed her face as she closed her door and started the engine. It was the kind of smile that let me know she was interested, and I couldn't deny that I felt the same way.

CHAPTER 2

SAMANTHA

"I JUST FEEL TERRIBLE," HALEY COMPLAINED. "I MEANT TO CALL YOU TO LET you know that I couldn't make it, but it must've slipped my mind."

She'd called me into her office to apologize for being a no-show the night before. After hearing about what had happened with me, she was even more regretful. I'd been interning under Haley for the past couple of months, and things had been going really well. I didn't want anything to jeopardize my chance to land a job there, so I decided not to make a big deal of it. "It's okay. Things happen."

"It's not okay. You could've been hurt."

"Yes, but I'm perfectly fine."

She leaned forward and placed her elbows on her desk as she continued, "You watch the news. It seems like every night someone has been shot or raped. To think that could've happened to you and it would've been all my fault!"

"Don't be silly. It wouldn't have been your fault." Haley had a flare for the dramatic, and today was no different. I tried to settle her down by saying, "Besides, this man, Gus, was there to make sure nothing happened."

"Yes. Thank goodness for that!" A mischievous smile crossed Haley's face as she said, "Sooo … Tell me more about this Gus fella. Was he hot?"

"Umm … Yeah, he was very hot. He was tall and muscular with dark hair and dark eyes."

"Oooh … Tall, dark, and handsome." She smiled. "I like it."

"I did too." I could feel the warmth rush to my face as I thought back to the way he took charge of the situation and tackled that awful man to the ground like it was nothing. With his tattoos and thick beard, I should've thought I'd simply traded one bad guy for another, but that wasn't the case. There was something about him that made me feel safe and protected, something more than the fact that he'd rescued me. "He was a little rough around the edges, but in a good way … a very good way. I'd never met anyone like him before. Gus had this confidence that just radiated off him."

"And he just appeared out of nowhere?"

"Pretty much."

"Maybe he's some kind of superhero or something." She teased.

"I highly doubt that, but he definitely saved the day."

As she looked towards the doorway, her eyes grew wide. "You said the guy had dark hair and dark eyes … Did he, uh, have a beard?"

"*Yes.*"

"Was he wearing one of those motorcycle vests and boots?"

"Umm … Yeah, I think so."

Haley was still looking over at the doorway as she continued with the questions, "And did he have tattoos?"

"Yes?" Curious to see what had her so enthralled, I turned to look behind me. "How did—?"

I didn't finish the question. I couldn't. My mind went completely blank when I noticed Gus walking in our direction, wearing jeans and a leather vest. He sure didn't look like the other men in our office—and I liked it. *Different* looked good on him. So good, that I couldn't take my eyes off of him as he approached the doorway. "Hey."

"Hey." His eyes met mine. "I thought I'd stop by to make sure you were okay."

"That's so sweet of you." I smiled as I stood up and walked over to him. "But you didn't have to. I'm fine."

"I know I didn't *have to.*" A sexy smirk crossed Gus's face. "I wanted to."

Haley came up beside us and batted her long eyelashes as she purred, "Sam was just telling me how you came to her rescue last night. You're quite the hero."

"I'm far from a hero," he scoffed. "Just doing what I could to help."

"I'm Haley, by the way." She was practically drooling as she added, "Samantha and I work together."

He glanced over in her direction just long enough to say, "Nice to meet you. You mind if I have a moment with Samantha?"

"Oh, uh … sure," she stammered from the rejection. "I'll just go grab myself a cup of coffee."

Once she'd left the room, he looked back over to me and asked, "You got plans for tonight?"

"Um … No, not that I can think of."

"You wanna grab a burger or something after work?"

Trying not to act too eager, I forced myself to take a breath before I answered, "Sure. I could do that."

"What time do you get off?"

"Five o'clock."

"Great. I'll be here at five to pick you up."

I was dressed in a pair of slacks and a white blouse, not the kind of thing I would normally wear on a date, so I asked, "Umm … could we make it five thirty or six, and you pick me up at my place?"

"Absolutely. Just need your address."

"Okay." I grabbed a post-it note off of Haley's desk and wrote it down. "Here ya go."

As Gus took the paper from my hand, he said, "Gonna be on my Harley, so wear jeans and boots if you have them."

"Your Harley? You mean a Harley motorcycle?"

His lips curled into the sexiest smile I'd ever seen. "You gonna be all right with that?"

"I've never ridden a motorcycle before."

Still smiling, he replied, "That wasn't the answer to my question, Ms. Travers."

"Yes, I'm good with it."

"Great. I'll see you at six."

And just like that, he was gone. I probably would've spiraled into a fit of uncertainty about my impending date, but I had four appointments scheduled before noon and three after. I was already running late, so I rushed to my office and grabbed my things and then raced to my car before I made myself even further behind. I spent the entire day bouncing from one doctor's office to the next, so I didn't have time to dwell on my doubts about going on a date with a complete stranger and riding a motorcycle for the first time. That freak-out came five minutes before he was supposed to arrive at my apartment. My heart was pounding in my chest and my palms were sweating as I looked at myself in the mirror. I took a couple of deep cleansing breaths, but just as my nerves were starting to settle, I heard a knock at the door. I wiped my palms on my jeans, then made my way over to the door and slowly eased it open. When I saw Gus standing there and looking all kinds of sexy in his jeans and leather jacket, my nerves kicked into high gear. Trying to pull it together, I forced a smile and said, "Hey, come on in. I just need to grab my things."

"Take your time." Gus stepped inside my apartment and took a quick look around. "You've got a nice place."

"Thanks." I grabbed my purse and jacket off the sofa, then walked back over to him. "I'm ready when you are."

His expression grew soft as he said, "You look beautiful."

"Thank you. You look really nice too."

Once we were downstairs and I spotted his shiny, big, black motorcycle parked next to the curb, I started to feel a little apprehensive. Sensing my unease, Gus stepped towards me and smiled. "Don't worry. There's nothing to it."

Minutes later, my arms were wrapped tightly around his waist, and we were weaving in and out of traffic. To my surprise, I actually loved being on the back of his bike, feeling the wind in my face and hearing the sounds of the city roaring in my ears. It didn't hurt that it gave me an excuse to be close to Gus. I loved his scent—a hint of cologne mixed with leather and smoke, and he appeared to be so confident and self-assured. It made me feel safe, like he was in complete control, and I was just there to enjoy the ride.

Just as we were leaving the city limits, Gus started driving down an old side road that led up to a small, crowded café. As we got off the bike and started inside, he smiled and said, "I know it doesn't look like much, but they have incredible burgers."

"Great. I can't wait to try one." He opened the front door and waited as I walked in ahead of him. As soon as I smelled the delectable scent of home-cooking, I immediately understood why the place was so packed. Gus reached for my hand and led me over to one of the empty booths in the back. Once we were seated, I told him, "It smells incredible."

"It tastes even better." He took a quick glance around, studying the old rustic farm equipment and photographs on the walls. "The club's going to open up a diner like this close to Beale Street, but instead of the Old South, ours will have a Memphis blues theme to it."

I was about to ask what he was talking about when the waitress came over to take our order. After handing it in to the kitchen, she returned with our tea and placed them on the table. I said to Gus, "I'm not sure I know what you mean by 'the club.'"

"Yeah. I guess I should take a minute to explain that." For the next half hour, he explained how the club was much more than a group of men who rode motorcycles and worked together, and that they were a family who lived and died for each other. I'd heard of clubs like his and knew some were decent, while others were bad, *really bad,* but I'd never actually met anyone who belonged to one, much less ran one. I didn't know what it meant to be a president of an MC, but it was clear that Gus took great pride in his position. He practically beamed as he told me how he'd been sent to Memphis to start up this new chapter of Satan's Fury, describing all the progress they'd made. "The clubhouse is almost done, so now we can start moving in there and focus on getting the restaurant up and going."

"That sounds like a lot of work."

"It is, but it'll be worth it when we're finished." He took a sip of his drink before asking, "What about you? What's your story?"

"My story isn't nearly as exciting as yours," I admitted. "I grew up here in Memphis. I recently graduated from U of M, and now I'm interning at MBC Pharmaceuticals. I'm hoping to start working for them full time this summer."

"And your family?"

"I have one older brother, Thomas. He lives in South Carolina now, so I don't get to see him very often. And my parents ... they can be a little much at times."

"How so?"

I didn't want to bore Gus with all the petty details of my controlled life, so I simply said, "Let's just say, my father is in politics, and my mother does her best to portray herself as the perfect, doting wife. She's quite the little socialite. Always doing community service projects and rubbing noses with the city's finest. You know how it is."

"No, I'm afraid I don't." He smiled as he used my own words against me. "But it sounds like a lot of work."

"Yes, it is." I rolled my eyes, then continued, "Life under the microscope is definitely not for the faint of heart. It's one of the reasons why I decided to go into a completely different line of work."

"Can't say I blame you there." He paused for a moment, then asked, "Since you grew up in the area, maybe you could give me some insight to a few things?"

"Such as?"

"Okay. What's with all the bottles in the trees?"

"Oh, that's an old southern tradition. My grandmother once told me that people used to hang them to ward off evil spirits. They'd say that the spirits would be attracted to the sound of the bottles clinking together and end up getting trapped inside."

"Hmm. Not at all what I thought." He paused for a minute, then said, "I think I'm getting the hang of some of the southern phrases, like 'fixin', over yonder, and blowin' up a storm,' but there's one I'm still not sure about."

"Which one?"

"When women say 'bless your heart.' That has more than one meaning, right?"

I couldn't help but laugh as I answered, "Yes. It has all kinds of meanings. It just depends on the situation."

"Not sure I'm following ya."

"Okay. It can be used to show genuine concern, like 'I'm so sorry to hear you aren't feeling well, and you have a fever too? *Oh, bless your heart.*' And it can also be used to soften the blow of an insult, like 'that poor fella doesn't have the sense God gave a goose. *Bless his heart.*'" I smiled and told him, "You just pay attention to the tone."

He chuckled at that. "Now, that's just not right."

We talked nonstop through dinner, sharing stories about our pasts and hopes for the future. It seemed strange that two people from two completely different worlds could have so much to talk about. I was having a great time being there with him and was disappointed when he glanced around the empty restaurant and said, "I guess we better get going before they run us out of here."

I followed him out to the parking lot, and we were both silent as he helped me on the bike. Before I had a chance to say something cute or flirty, he started the engine and we were on our way back to my place. It seemed like we'd only been riding for a few minutes when Gus pulled up to the curb at my apartment and parked. Once I got off the motorcycle, I unbuckled his extra helmet and handed it to him. "I had a really good time tonight. Maybe we can do it again sometime."

He swung his leg across the seat of his bike and eased over to me. "You got plans for the weekend?"

Gus stood just inches away, and the way he looked at me made every nerve in my body tingle with desire so intense that I almost forgot to answer his question. "Um … No, I don't have any plans."

"You do now." Before I had time to think, he placed his hands on my waist and pulled me against his chest. My heart started to race with anticipation as he lowered his mouth to mine and kissed me. His lips were soft and warm, and suddenly I was leaning right into him. It was clear that he was no Prince Charming. There was no white horse. No castle on the hill. He was rough, tough, and sexy as hell—and the man could kiss like no other. His arms tightened around me, inching me even closer as his tongue found its way into my mouth. I was holding on by a thread, and just as I was becoming completely lost in his touch, he pulled back, quickly breaking our embrace. His dark eyes danced with lust as they locked on mine. As he handed me his card, he said, "Friday night at seven. If something comes up, just call me at that number."

"Okay."

He leaned in for one last brief kiss. "Good night, Samantha."

"Good night, Gus." I started up the front steps of my building, but just before I went inside, I turned around and waved. "I'll see you Friday night."

"Looking forward to it."

As I opened the door, I couldn't help but smile. I knew it was just one date, one simple dinner, and yet I knew it was so much more.

It was the beginning—*our beginning*.

CHAPTER 3

GUS

ON THE DAY OF DAISY MAE'S GRAND OPENING ONLY A HANDFUL OF customers had shown up, and the weeks that followed weren't much better. I was beginning to think that opening the diner was a mistake, but then things took an impressive turn. For one reason or another, customers started streaming in, and it wasn't long before we were packed from open to close. Our hard work was finally starting to pay off. The renovations to the clubhouse were complete, the diner was thriving, and we'd even taken on a handful of new prospects and were looking at the Lost Knights MC as a possible patch-over club. They were a small club with only twenty members, but they showed great potential—the kind of potential they'd need in order to be patched in as members of Fury. I was feeling pretty good about things, so I decided to take Samantha somewhere special to celebrate. I wanted it to be a surprise, so I didn't give her much to go on—other than the time I'd come by to pick her up and to wear something comfortable. Of course, that didn't set well with her. She was one of those women who liked to be prepared, so when I knocked on her door, I wasn't surprised when she came out of her apartment with a large duffle bag in her hand.

"You planning on moving in?" I cocked my eyebrow as I teased her. "We've only been seeing each other for a few weeks, but I'm good with it. It would be nice to wake up with you next to me every morning."

"Umm … No." Samantha gave me one of her looks as she answered, "I brought this bag because *somebody* wouldn't tell me what we were doing tonight."

I didn't understand her concern. She looked absolutely stunning in her jean-shorts and sandals. "Did you or did you not hear me say to wear something comfortable?"

"Yes, but that's all you would tell me. *Comfortable* could mean flip-flops and shorts or a t-shirt and pajama pants ... or jeans and—"

"Okay. Okay," I interrupted. "I get it. I'll try to be more specific next time."

A satisfied smirk crossed her face. "Does that mean you're going to tell me where we're going tonight?"

"Nope." I took a hold of her duffle-bag and started walking towards the elevator. "Come on, beautiful. The clock's a ticking. We don't want to be late."

"Late for what?" She tried again.

"You'll see." As soon as the elevator doors closed, I reached for her waist and pulled her close, then whispered, "You know, it never fails."

"What?"

"Just seeing you makes my day."

Samantha's expression softened as she wrapped her arms around my neck. "Well, in case you didn't know, you do the same thing to me."

"You gotta stop doing that."

"Doing what?"

"Stealing my compliments." I teased her.

"I don't steal your compliments!" She paused for a moment, then added, "Well, I do, but only if I mean it."

"Um-hmm." I placed my hands on her hips and inched her even closer. "I know something you could do to make it up to me."

"Oh, really?" She smiled. "And what's that?"

I leaned towards her, pressing my mouth against hers, and kissed her long and hard. Like so many times before, her body melted into mine, making me ache for more. I didn't understand how one woman could turn me inside out the way she did. Her touch, her scent ... everything about Samantha made me lose all sense of control. She shifted her stance, causing the rigid length of my erection to press against her. A light moan rippled through her chest, and I was suddenly torn between taking her right there in the elevator or carrying her back upstairs and throwing her on the bed. Sadly, neither was an option—at least not for the time being. I had special plans for Samantha tonight, so before we got any more carried away, I took a step back and released her from our embrace. "Damn, woman. You keep kissing me like that, and we'll never make it out of this elevator."

A mischievous look danced in her eyes. "I'd be okay with that."

"I would be, too, but if we don't get moving, we're going to be late." I leaned forward and kissed her on the temple. "But … I have every intention of picking up from here when we get back later tonight."

Before she could respond, the elevator doors opened and I led her out to the SUV. I put her duffle-bag in the backseat, and we hopped inside, then I drove us over to the Shelby Farms Park. By the time we arrived at the park it was well after dark, and people had already started to claim their spots on the lawn. As soon as we got out of the SUV, I went straight to the back and grabbed a blanket and the picnic basket of food that Louise had fixed for us. Samantha came over to me with a surprised look and asked, "What's all this?"

"You'll see."

While we made our way towards the crowd, Samantha noticed the large movie screen tucked in the corner by the trees and smiled. "A movie night at the park?"

"Yeah. I heard some folks talking about it down at the diner. I thought it might be something cool to try."

"It's very cool." She followed me over to an open area towards the back and helped me spread out the blanket. As we sat down, she gave me a sly smirk. "Look at you being all romantic."

"I'm just gettin' started, darlin'," I told her, using my best fake southern accent.

After we finished eating, Samantha curled up next to me, and just as I hoped, she loved the movie. I, on the other hand, had no idea what it was even about. I was too busy watching her to keep up with what was going on. I couldn't seem to help myself. With every moment I spent with Samantha, I found another reason to fall for her—the sound of her laugh and the way her nose crinkled every time she did, or the softness of her lips when they were pressed against mine. I never imagined that I'd ever find someone who got to me the way she did, but damn, Samantha was everything I'd always wanted and more. She had me thinking about having a future together, and the more I thought about it, the more I liked the idea.

When the movie was over, we collected our things and headed back to the truck. Samantha was practically beaming. "I can't remember enjoying a movie as much as I did tonight."

"Good. I'm glad you liked it."

As she got inside the truck, she asked, "So, where to now?"

"That's up to you. We could head over to the clubhouse and have a couple of drinks, or we could go back to your place and pick up where we left off in the elevator."

"Hmmm." A smirk crossed her face. "I guess if I have to decide … I'd have to go with … picking up where we left off in the elevator."

"I was hoping you'd say that."

Not wanting to waste another second, I pressed my foot against the accelerator and sped towards her apartment. The second we were inside her apartment complex, Samantha rushed over to the elevator and she glanced over to me with lust-filled eyes as she pressed the button. Anticipation crackled around us as we waited there together, and a relieved smile crossed her face when the doors finally opened. She stepped inside and watched with bated breath as I took a charging step forward, pinning her back against the wall. I looked down at Samantha and watched the rise and fall of her chest as she panted with need. Her eyes darkened as her gaze drifted to my lips. When she couldn't stand it a moment longer, Samantha's fingers dove into my hair, and she pulled me towards her, crashing her mouth against mine in a hungry kiss. The kiss quickly became heated, making my cock throb.

"Dammit, woman. You're killing me," I told her as my hand dropped to her shorts. With a quick twist, I undid the first couple of buttons, then slipped my hand down her shorts. A light hiss escaped her lungs when I eased the lining of her lace panties to the side and grazed her center with the tips of my fingers—my already-hard cock pulsed against my zipper when I found she was soaked. "Damn. You're so fuckin' wet for me."

She gasped as I used my free hand to lower her shirt just enough to reveal her perfectly round breasts. With her eyes on mine, I lowered my mouth and began swirling my tongue around her nipple. Her head fell back as she moaned, "Oh God."

I nipped and sucked, relishing the sounds of her little moans and whimpers as I teased her with my tongue and my teeth. I cursed when the elevator doors opened. After I removed my hand from her shorts and she adjusted her tank top, I followed her inside the apartment. As soon as Samantha closed the door and tossed her things on the counter, she unbuttoned her shorts and let them fall to the floor. When I started towards her, she took several steps back, watching me like I was a starved predator as she bumped into the kitchen table. "You have any idea how bad I want you right now?"

"Um-hmm." She purred. "Just as much as I want you."

I lowered my hands to her hips and reached for her lace panties, sliding them down her long, lean legs. Desire flashed through her eyes as I lifted her up, then guided her to lay back on the table. I was so thirsty for her that I could barely think as I eased her legs over my shoulders and lowered my mouth between her thighs. She inhaled a deep breath when the bristles of my beard brushed against her soft skin, her back arching off the table as my tongue skimmed across her smooth center. I spread her trembling legs wider, and a needful moan echoed through the room as I slid my tongue between her folds. "Damn, baby. You taste like fucking heaven."

Samantha's breath became uneven and hitched as I slipped my finger deep inside her. Focused and unrelenting, I teased her g-spot with a slow and steady rhythm. Her hips inched forward as she tensed around me and goosebumps prickled across her skin. Loving how her beautiful body responded to my touch, I continued grazing and teasing her clit with my tongue, tormenting her as she writhed beneath me. Overcome by her impending release, Samantha's hips lifted up from the table, begging me to give her more. I instantly drove another finger deep inside her while I played with her clit using the pad of my thumb until she got exactly what she needed.

Her head thrashed back as she gasped, "Yes!"

"That's it, baby."

I slid my tongue over her as I continued moving my fingers inside her, tormenting that spot that was driving her to the edge. Adding more pressure, I demanded, "Come for me."

That's all it took. While muttering my name incoherently, she submitted to her release and clamped down around my fingers. Damn. Nothing turned me on more than watching her come undone. I couldn't wait a moment longer. I had to be inside her. She was still in the throes of her release when I got undressed and rolled on a condom. Her eyes locked on mine as I slipped my hands under her ass and pulled her to the edge of the table. *Fuck.* She looked so damn beautiful sprawled out on that table, bare and waiting for me with that wanton look in her eyes. I couldn't imagine wanting her more.

I brushed my throbbing cock against her slick center and nearly lost it. Inhaling a full breath, I tried to calm the storm raging inside me, but my woman was eager for more. She wrapped her legs around me and forced me deep inside. I froze. She felt too fucking good. As I slowly withdrew, I looked down at her and asked, "You like having my cock inside you?"

Samantha managed a slight nod and muttered, "God, yes."

A slight hiss slipped through her teeth as I drove into her again and again—each time a bit faster and unforgiving. Her heels dug into my back and she shouted, "Oh my God!"

As much as I loved having her this way, I wanted more. I needed to feel her, touch every inch of her gorgeous body, so I lowered her legs to my waist and carefully lifted her from the table. With my cock still buried deep inside her, I carried her over to the sofa and lowered us down onto the cushions, letting Samantha's knees saddle me. I dropped my hands to her waist and started guiding her over my cock in an unforgiving rhythm.

She placed her hands on my shoulders, trying to steady herself as she shouted, "Gus!"

There was something about hearing her call out my name that sent an intense heat coursing through my body. I burned for her, every fucking inch of me was consumed by my need for this woman, and I knew I'd never feel this way for anyone else. Samantha would be mine—*all mine*—heart and soul. Shifting her hips upward, she continued to gyrate against me, grinding her warm, wet pussy over my cock. When I rocked against her, I could feel her muscles contracting all around me as her second orgasm started to take hold. My body grew rigid as my release inched its way through me. Her head fell back as she cried out, "Oh my God, Gus! *I'm coming!*"

I fisted my hand in her long hair, giving it a gentle tug, as I thrust forward, driving inside her once again. She was so fucking hot, so tight, and it was all too much. Damn. I couldn't imagine a better feeling. I drew back and slammed into her again, taking her harder and deeper.

"*Fuckkk!*" I shouted out as my throbbing cock demanded its release. My fingers dug into her hips as I guided her forward in a feverish rhythm until I came deep inside of her. We both stilled, fighting to catch our breaths, and after several moments, our heartbeats began to slow.

"Woman, you're gonna be the death of me."

"Oh, really?" Looking slightly dazed and completely sated, a sexy smile spread across her gorgeous face. "You complaining?"

"Umm … *Hell, no.*" I glanced down at my cock still buried deep inside her. "I can't think of a better way to go."

"Neither can I." She placed the palms of her hands on my face as she said, "I love you."

"Good thing you do, cause you're stuck with me."

"I'm good with that." She pressed her lips to mine, then added, "I kind of like having you around."

"Kinda?" Before I could continue, my cell started to ring. Knowing the boys wouldn't call unless there was a problem, I lifted her off of me and said, "Sorry, baby. I gotta get that."

Once I'd lowered her to the sofa, I got up and grabbed my phone out of my jeans. "Yeah?" I answered while I pulled the condom off and tossed it in the trash.

"The Ravens made their move," T-Bone announced. "Gonna need you to get back to the clubhouse."

The Ravens were a small local gang who'd been making their presence known over the past couple of weeks. At first it was just idle threats and graffiti, but they were steadily stepping up their game. It was to be expected. The more it got out that a new MC was in town—especially one with the kind of reputation Satan's Fury carried—there would be those who'd try to take us down. It was up to me to make sure that shit didn't happen. The Ravens had no idea who they were fucking with. Even though we were still building our numbers, they were no match for us. "I'll be there in ten."

As much as I didn't want to leave Samantha, there wasn't a choice, so I threw on my clothes, kissed her goodbye, and headed out to my bike. When I got to the clubhouse, T-Bone was waiting for me at the front door. "What happened?"

"Widow was coming through town with a couple of the prospects when two black Audis came racing up beside them and started shooting. They shot Widow and Sprocket ..." His voice trailed off for a moment. "They didn't make it, Gus."

"Fuck!" I spat. "You sure it was the Ravens?"

"Yeah," he growled. "The motherfuckers were sporting their colors."

"We end this shit, now."

"I'm with you, brother. Got any idea on how we're gonna make that happen?"

"It's time to see if the Lost Knights really have what it takes to wear the Fury name." As I reached into my pocket for my phone, I continued, "If they're half the club they claim to be, then we'll have all the manpower we need to take those motherfuckers down."

Rage surged through me as I dialed Brewer's number, the Lost Knight's president. I'd barely gotten out all the details of what had happened when he said, "We're on our way."

Fifteen minutes later, the Lost Knights came rolling into our parking lot, ready and eager to prove themselves. I headed over to Brewer and clapped the back of his shoulder. "Appreciate you boys coming to give us a hand."

"Don't mention it." He shook his head, as he said, "The Ravens fucked up tonight.

"That, they did." I couldn't hold back my anger. "They came looking for trouble and they fucking found it. We're going to burn those motherfuckers to the ground."

"We're here for you, brother. Just tell me what you need us to do."

Knowing we'd already lost two brothers, I warned, "We need to be smart about this. Gotta get in and get out."

"Understood."

After laying out a plan, we loaded our ammunition in the back of my SUV and headed over towards the Raven's warehouse. Under the circumstances, we had to act fast and catch them off-guard, so we didn't have the luxury of setting up surveillance and monitoring them for weeks on end.

Once we got close to their warehouse, we drove up into an abandoned lot and got out, quickly surrounding their compound. Armed and ready, we searched for the best entry point. When we found a backdoor open, Brewer and two of his men, Grinder and Rivet, followed Moose and me inside while T-Bone and Bane monitored the front. As I'd hoped, the Ravens were a bunch of fucking dumbasses with no fucking security and had no idea that we'd just entered the room. Six guys were sitting around a table playing cards, three were on a sofa just shooting the shit, and others were huddled around a couple of cars they'd been working on. As soon as they saw us, they started scampering for their weapons, but it was too late. Gunfire rang out throughout the warehouse, and one by one, their lifeless bodies fell to the floor. Once we'd taken them all out, we burned their warehouse to the ground, and there was nothing left of the Ravens.

While the war over the territory was far from over, we'd won our battle over the Ravens. I was grateful that the Lost Knights had come through for us, and I had no doubt that Saul and the others would agree that they'd proven themselves worthy of being patched over. The city of Memphis would soon learn that Satan's Fury MC was here to stay, and if I had anything to say about it, the territory would be ours to rein supreme above all others.

CHAPTER 4

SAMANTHA

"LAUREN AND I ARE GONNA HEAD DOWN TO MORGAN'S AFTER WORK TO GRAB a few drinks," Haley announced as she stepped into my office. "You should come along. Help us shake off the horrendous week."

"I wish I could, but …"

"Let me guess." She smiled. "You've got plans with Mr. Wonderful tonight."

"That, I do." Over the past few months we'd been spending a lot of time together, especially on the weekends, but since the night he'd rushed out of my apartment, I'd only seen him once and that was only for a couple of hours. Something was going on with the club—something he couldn't tell me about. Over the past few weeks, I'd gotten a chance to meet the brothers, along with Louise and Rayne, and I enjoyed the time I'd spent with them. They were good people, so it shouldn't have been a surprise that I was concerned about their wellbeing. Whenever I asked him about it, he'd tell me that he was doing everything in his power to resolve it before things got out of hand. I wanted desperately to know more, but he'd made it clear that there were aspects of the club that I simply wasn't privy to. I tried not to let it hurt my feelings, but it hadn't been easy. I wanted to help, or at the very least be there for him, but he simply wouldn't allow it. I did my best to hide my concern as I feigned a smile and said, "The guys are having a birthday party for Rayne tonight, and Gus asked me to come."

"So, things are going good with you two?"

"Yeah. Things are better than good." I could feel myself smiling as I added, "We're still figuring things out and all that."

"I totally understand." Then, Haley's tone changed. "Have you thought about what you'll do if you get transferred to the Nashville office?"

"Yes and no. I was waiting to see if I actually got the position before I started worrying about how it would affect things with us."

"So, you haven't even mentioned it to him?"

"No, not really."

"Sam, if things are going as well as you say they are, then you need to talk to him. It's only fair."

"You're right." A nervous feeling washed over me. "I will tonight."

"Good." As Haley turned to leave, she gave me a half-smile and said, "If you get done with the party early, give me a call. Maybe you can meet up with us after."

"Sounds good. I'll definitely do that."

"Great." With a quick wave, she walked out of my office. "Catch ya later, alligator."

Once she was gone, I turned my attention back to my weekly reports so I could leave on time. Gus was expecting me at the clubhouse at six, and I still needed to run by the apartment to change and grab Rayne's birthday gift. As soon as I finished my report, I emailed it to my advisor, then shut down my computer and gathered my things. When I got out to my car, I was relieved to see that I was actually ahead of schedule. If I played it right, I could be there well before the party started, and I might even get a few minutes alone with Gus.

Unfortunately, everything usually took me longer than I planned, so by the time I arrived at the clubhouse, everyone was already gathered in the family room. Balloons were strung in every corner, presents were piled high on the front table, and Rayne couldn't have looked more excited as she sat perched on Louise's hip. As I walked over to place my gift with the others, I smiled at Rayne and said, "Happy birthday, sweet girl."

"I'm t'ree," she boasted as she tried to hold up three fingers. "I'm dis many."

"I know you are! You're such a big girl now."

"She likes to think so," Louise scoffed.

Rayne leaned forward and tried to grab one of the presents. "Mine."

"Not yet, Rayne."

"Mine, Momma."

"I know they're yours, baby, but it's not time to open presents yet." Louise looked over to me and sighed. "I blame her father for this. He spoils her like crazy."

I really liked Louise. She was beautiful, with shoulder length hair and a killer figure, but she never used her looks to get what she wanted. Louise was too smart, too strong-willed for that. When she set her mind to something, she made it happen, and everyone who knew her respected her for it. I smiled as I told her, "Daddy's have a way of spoiling their little girls. I know my father always did me."

"Mine spoiled me, too, but Moose is going to make her absolutely rotten." She motioned her hand towards the table of gifts. "Most of these are from him, and all she'll care about are the boxes and the balloons."

When Rayne reached for one of the balloons and fisted it in her little hand, I chuckled. "You might be right about that."

We were both laughing when Gus came up behind me and wrapped his arms around my waist, easing me back against his chest as he whispered, "Hey there, beautiful."

The sound of his voice sent a delicious chill down my spine, causing my knees to tremble as I leaned against him. "Hey, I'm sorry I was late."

"You're right on time." He lowered his mouth to my neck, softly kissing me before turning me around to face him. "Glad you could make it."

"I wouldn't miss it." I took a quick glance around the room, and I was surprised by how many brothers were gathered in the family room. When Gus first brought me to the clubhouse, there were only six brothers and two prospects. But now they were making plans to patch over the members of the Lost Knights, and they'd also enlisted four new prospects; one of whom wasn't in the family room and neither was Widow. "Looks like you have a couple who are even later than I was. Are Widow and Reeves working at the diner?"

"No. They aren't working at the diner." There was no hiding the anguish in his eyes as he continued, "They ran into a little trouble. I'll tell you about it later."

"Oh, okay." That left me a bit curious and concerned, but I knew better than to push. I noticed several men in the back corner wearing Satan's Fury cuts, but I'd never seen them before. I looked over in their direction. "Who are the new guys?"

"Oh, that's Saul. He's the president of the Washington chapter, and the other two are a couple of brothers he brought along with him."

"They're from your old club?"

"Yeah. Same club. Different state." I could tell he was holding something back when he added, "They came down to help me get a few things sorted, but they'll be heading back in the morning."

After hearing that there had been some trouble with Widow and Reeves, I couldn't help but wonder if that's why they'd come to Memphis. I knew I was pushing it, but I had to ask, "Is everything okay?"

"It is now." He reached for my hand. "Let's go grab a beer, and then I'll take you over and introduce you."

"Okay."

I was a little nervous about meeting people who'd had such an important impact in his life, but I quickly learned I had nothing to worry about. They were just as kind and loyal as Gus's other brothers, and they treated me like they'd known me for years. It was easy to see why Gus loved being with them like he did. Even though they weren't blood relatives, they truly were like his family, and I found myself wondering if they could be mine as well.

Dinner was almost ready, so we all moved into the family room to watch Rayne open her presents. By the time she was done, it looked like a toy store had exploded. I couldn't help but laugh when I glanced over at Rayne and watched her play. She was building a tower with all the empty boxes, and I leaned over to Louise and whispered, "You were right about the boxes."

Nodding, she replied, "At least, now I know what to get her for Christmas!"

"That, you do!"

By the time dinner was ready Rayne was starting to tucker out, so Louise had one of the girls carry her back to Gus's room and put her down for bed. Once we'd brought all the food out from the kitchen, we gathered around the table and made our plates. We all started eating, and it wasn't long before the guys began goofing around, poking fun at one another. When the topic of conversation turned to old flames, Bane looked at T-Bone and asked, "What about that chick who wanted to marry your sorry ass? She was hot as fuck. I can't believe you passed that up."

"She might've been hot, but that chick was three shades of fucked up." T-Bone looked horrified as he continued, "She had a list of rules for me on the refrigerator … and she smelled my clothes, especially my underwear." He cocked his eyebrow and nodded. "Yeah … my *fucking underwear,* and she followed me around like some kind of goddamn stalker … calling at all times of the damn night, over and over. But worst of all, she refused to give head. Said it wasn't hygienic."

When the laughter finally died down, Half-pint looked over to him and said, "My ex used to take pictures of me when I was sleeping. Used to creep me the fuck out."

"One of my exes used to spray her perfume in my bed. Guess she thought other chicks might smell it and hit the ground running, but it just ended up making me smell like a fucking pussy," Bane complained.

"Oh, hell. That's nothing. I was with this one girl who had a thing for feet, and … Damn." Cyrus's face turned an odd shade of green as he told us, "Some of the shit she wanted to do. It just wasn't right."

The room exploded in laughter, but Cyrus was too lost in his thoughts to even care. The guys continued to tell stories and carry on until everyone had finished eating. We cleaned up the dishes, and everyone was talking amongst themselves in the kitchen when Gus leaned over to me and said, "I need to have a quick word with Saul, and then I'll run you home."

"But I drove here."

"In that case, I'll follow you home." He placed his hands on my hips and pulled me towards him. "Unless you have a problem with me spending some time with my woman."

"No, I don't have a problem with that." I inched a little closer. "In fact, I was going to be a little disappointed if I didn't get a little alone time with you."

He leaned forward and kissed me on the forehead. As he turned to leave, he said, "Give me a minute … five at the most."

When he turned to leave, I headed over to the others to say my good-byes. Louise and Moose thanked me for the gift I'd given Rayne, and then T-Bone and the others each took a moment to speak before they wandered over to the bar. I was about to head out to the parking lot when I saw Gus walking in my direction. Just the sight of him got to me like no other man had before. He was just so damn handsome, so confident and self-assured, and the way he looked at me, like I was the most beautiful woman on the planet, made every nerve in my body long to be touched by him. As he made his way over to me, I smiled and said, "That was fast."

Gus wrapped his arms around me and lifted me in the air. "Told ya I just needed a minute."

"That, you did."

Then he gave me a brief kiss and lowered my feet to the floor. Wasting no time, he took my hand and started for the door. "Let's get out of here."

Once he'd walked me over to my car and got me settled inside, he hopped on his bike and followed me over to my apartment. We parked and headed inside and got in the elevator. The second the doors closed, we were on each other like two sex-starved teenagers, kissing and pawing like there was no tomorrow. When the doors opened, Gus lifted me into his arms and carried me to my apartment door. Fumbling with the key, I finally unlocked it, and while he carried me inside, I was surprised to find that my lights were on. Gus was about to lean in for another kiss when I scooted out of his arms and stepped into the living room. As soon as I saw her and noticed the expression on her face, my heart dropped to the pit of my stomach.

"Hello, Samantha Grace."

"Mom … Uh, what are you doing here?"

Her eyebrow was raised high in annoyance as she said, "If you had checked your cell phone, you'd know that I was coming."

"I'm sorry." Gus walked up next to me as I told her, "We were at a birthday party, and I—"

I'd never told her anything about who I'd been seeing, so I was surprised when she stood up and interrupted me by saying, "You must be Gus."

"I am."

"Well, it's nice to finally meet you." She extended her hand. "I'm Elizabeth Travers. Samantha's mother."

As he shook her hand, he replied, "It's nice to meet you, too, Mrs. Travers. Samantha has told me a lot about you and your family."

"Umm … well, that's nice to hear. Wish I could say the same about you." She was wearing one of her fitted blouses and a string of pearls along with black slacks and heels, but it wasn't *what* she was wearing that made her seem pretentious. It was the way she looked at him and the tone she used when she spoke. Mom didn't have to say the words. She'd already made it clear that she didn't approve of Gus, and to top it off, she glanced over at me with one of her looks. I knew then I was in for it. Her focus was still on me while she told Gus, "Maybe we can rectify that in a bit when Samantha and I are *alone*. I'm sure we will have lots to talk about."

"I'm sure you will," he answered and seemed completely unfazed by her rude behavior.

"Mom," I warned.

Before I could say anything more, Gus looked over to me and said, "I'm gonna get going."

"Wait. You don't have to leave." I glared over at my mother, adding, "She won't be staying long."

"You need to spend some time with your mother, Sam." He leaned towards me and kissed my cheek. "I'll check in with you tomorrow."

"Are you sure?"

"Positive. I wasn't able to stay long anyway."

"Okay." Disappointment washed over me as I followed him to the door. Before he walked out, I whispered, "I'm sorry about this."

"Don't be." Gus kissed me one more time, then stepped into the hall. Before I closed the door, he called out to my mother, "It was nice meeting you, Mrs. Travers."

She didn't respond, which only aggravated me even more. Once he was gone, I stormed back into the living room. "What the hell was that?"

"I was about to ask you the same," she snapped. "And watch your tone, young lady. I don't care how old you get; I am still your mother and I will not be disrespected."

"I'm not trying to be disrespectful, Mother." I took in a deep breath and crossed my arms. "I just want to know what you're doing here?"

"I came because I heard that my daughter had gotten herself a new boyfriend."

"And where did you hear that?"

"From Evan. Everyone informed us that he was the best campaign manager in the country, but when he alerted me that my daughter had gotten herself mixed up with some delinquent, I thought he'd made a terrible mistake. Lo and behold, I arrive only to find you here with him." She walked over to the window and watched Gus get on his motorcycle, then grumbled, "A biker, Samantha? How could you delve so low?"

"You're wrong about him, Mom. He's not a delinquent. He's a good man, and he's been wonderful to me." Her back was still turned away from me when I said, "I love him. I don't care if you approve of him or not."

"And your father? What about him? Do you care about him at all?"

"You know I do."

"Well, you certainly aren't acting like it." She turned to face me as she continued, "You know what becoming governor means to him. He's spent his entire life working for this chance, and how do you think he's going to feel when you're the one who takes it away from him."

"What are you talking about? I'm not taking anything away from him."

"Of course, you are! When the media learns that their lead candidate—the man who has an impeccable record with not one single skeleton in his closet—has a daughter who is tangled up with some miscreant who belongs to one of the most dangerous biker clubs in the country, then your father's political career is over!" Her face flushed red as she continued her rant. "He's supposed to turn this state around and make it a safe, thriving place for the rich and the poor. How's he's supposed to do that when his own daughter is running around with criminals?"

"Just because he's in a motorcycle club doesn't mean he's a criminal, Mother."

"No, but he is." With a huff, she stormed over to my coffee table and picked up a folder. As she thrust it in my direction, she spat, "See for yourself."

I opened the file and quickly scanned the first page. It was a record for an Augustus Peterson, born in Piedmont, Washington, in 1966. At first, I was thrown by the name, but when I got to the bottom of the page, I noticed a black and white photograph of Gus. I looked up at my mother with pure disgust. "What is this?"

"It's everything he could find on your new boyfriend. From the looks of it, he's been a very busy man."

"You had no right to do that!" I tossed the folder down on the coffee table.

"Of course, I did! Your father's career is at stake!" She walked over to me and sighed. "You father has moved heaven and earth for you, Samantha ... giving you everything you could have ever wanted, including this apartment and that internship at MBC. Now, it's time for you to return the favor. End this thing with the biker before it's too late."

"I'm not ending things with him."

"I know you think you love him, but he's simply not the right man for you." She placed her hand on my face as she continued, "He can't give you the kind of life you deserve."

"He can and he will."

"I wish that were true, but it's not. You'll see that for yourself soon enough." She lowered her hand and let out a deep breath. "Your father had a meeting with a nice young man last week. His name is Dennis Rayburn. He's a lawyer in Nashville, comes from a good family, and everyone thinks highly of him. We were thinking of having him come for dinner in a couple of weeks. You should come, especially considering your new position at work. You two would be in the same city."

"That's not going to happen."

"Just think about it." She picked up her purse and coat from the sofa, then added, "In fact, I want you to think about everything I've said tonight. Your family is counting on you to do the right thing."

With that, she turned and walked out. As soon as the door closed, I broke down in tears. I wasn't sure why I was crying. Maybe it was my anger at all the things she'd said about Gus, or maybe because I knew she was right.

CHAPTER 5

GUS

SAMANTHA'S BODY GREW RIGID AS I BEGAN TO THRUST DEEPER, HARDER. HER snug pussy throbbed against me, weakening all of my restraint. When she showed up tonight in that tight, little black dress and those fuck-me heels, I knew exactly what she was up to. My little temptress wanted my attention, and by God, she fucking got it. I was done the second she walked into the room and I saw that spark of lust in her eyes. I tossed Samantha over my shoulder and carried her straight back to my room. I watched with bated breath as she slowly undressed and revealed her perfect curves, then I led her over to the bed. After I shed my clothes, I lowered myself down between her thighs and explored every inch of her body, making her come undone over and over again. Once I was inside her, I intended to go slow … wanting to savor every damn second, but she was so tight, so warm and wet. I couldn't hold back. I tightened my grip in her hair as I quickened my pace to a demanding rhythm. Her nails skated up my spine as her hips bucked against mine, meeting my every thrust with more force … more intensity. I could feel the pressure building in my cock as she constricted around me.

Her head reared back as she shouted, "Oh god, Gus!"

"Fuck," I groaned as she clamped down on me like a fucking vice. She panted wildly, moaning and clawing at my back as I plunged deeper. I knew she was close, unable to stop the inevitable bliss of her impending release. I looked down at her, and my chest literally ached with emotion. This woman had a hold on me like I never thought possible. I lowered my mouth to her neck and whispered, "Mine."

"Yes!" she cried out in pleasure. The muscles in her body grew taut, then stilled as her orgasm took hold. I continued to drive into her, the sound of my body pounding against hers echoed throughout the room and pushed me over the edge. My hands reached under and lifted her ass off the bed as I drove into her one last time, submitting to my own release.

Samantha's body fell limp under mine. I remained deeply seated inside her, not ready for the moment to end. I would miss nights like these if she decided to take that job in Nashville. I was surprised when she'd mentioned it earlier in the week, but knowing what it meant to her, I assured her that we'd make it work. That didn't mean I was happy about the idea of her being away from me. I rested my head on her chest and listened to her rapid heartbeat begin to steady. Samantha's breathing began to slow to a point that I thought she'd actually fallen asleep. I looked up at her and was surprised to see a sexy smile on her face. Settling myself alongside her, she slowly began to wiggle her way into the crook of my arm and rested her head down on my chest. I leaned over and kissed her on the temple. "You are really something, Samantha Travers."

"You are too."

"There you go again … stealing my compliments." I joked.

"Well, they're good compliments. I can't seem to help myself." She giggled, and my heart nearly leapt out of my chest. "But I have one you haven't used yet."

"Oh, really? What's that?"

She trailed the tips of her fingers across my chest as she whispered, "I love you more every minute of every day."

"You're right. I haven't used that one." I hadn't said those three little words to her yet. She knew I loved her. I showed her in every way I could, but clearly, she needed to hear me say it. "But that doesn't mean I don't love you, because I do. I think you know that."

"I do." She smiled and said, "Seems strange."

"What?"

"That we might not have met if that guy hadn't tried to steal my purse."

"It might've taken me a little longer, but I would've found you, Samantha. You were meant to be mine. I have no doubt about that."

The room fell silent for a moment, and then she glanced up at me and said, "I think we missed our dinner reservations."

"Yeah. I'd say I'm sorry, but that's on you."

"On me? How so?"

"You knew what would happen when I saw you in that dress."

"Are you saying I had ulterior motives for wearing that dress tonight?" she asked, feigning innocence.

"That's exactly what I'm saying." I looked down at her beautiful face. "You thinkin' I'm wrong?"

"Nope." She giggled. "Not at all."

"That's what I thought. You knew exactly what you were doing, so now, you have to decide what we're gonna do for dinner."

"How about a night in? We can order a pizza and watch a movie."

"Sounds like a plan."

Once our pizza arrived, we made a make-shift picnic on the edge of the bed and started a movie. As Samantha took a bite of her pizza, she asked, "Do you think you'll ever get a place of your own like Moose and Louise?"

"Eventually. Right now, I need to be here so I can keep an eye on things."

"So ... in a couple of months or a couple of years?"

"A year ... maybe a little less." I took a drink of my beer, then added, "It just depends on how things play out."

"And what about kids?"

"What about 'em?"

She rolled her eyes. "Do you want any?"

"Yeah, sure. Just not right now." As I reached for another slice of pizza, I went on to say, "I've got too much on my plate to even consider taking on more. Maybe in a few years."

"Oh ... Okay."

When her eyes skirted over to the floor, I knew something was up. "You got something on your mind?"

"I'm just trying to see where you stand, I guess." Trying to play it off, she took another bite of her pizza, then said, "It's important to be in the know."

"Samantha." I waited until her eyes met mine and then said, "As long as you are with me, I'll do everything in my power to make you happy. You want to take that job in Nashville, then take it. We'll find a way to make it work until you can get something here. You want a house? I'll buy you a house—the biggest, nicest house you've ever seen. You want some fancy apartment by the river? I'll make it happen. You want kids? I'll give you as many as you want, and love and protect them until the day I take my last breath."

Tears filled her eyes as she muttered, "Gus."

"I mean it, Sam. I take care of the people who are important to me, and you're on the top of that list. I'm just asking for a little time. Can you give me that?"

"Yes." She nodded as she leaned towards me and wrapped her arms around my neck, hugging me tightly. "I can give you that."

"Good. Now, finish your pizza, 'cause as soon as this movie is over, I'm gonna be wanting another go." I kissed her on the cheek. "I still can't get that fucking dress out of my head."

As she eased back on the bed and smiled. "I think I'm gonna have to get me a few more of those little black dresses."

"If you do, you better be ready to suffer the consequences."

"I'm more than ready."

When we finished eating, Samantha curled up next to me, and we turned our attention back to the movie we'd been watching. As soon as it was over, we made love again, and by the time I was done with her, she was completely spent and had fallen asleep in my arms.

After the club's encounter with the Ravens, we all struggled to come to terms with the loss of one of our brothers and a prospect—especially me. It was my job to keep my boys out of harm's way, and it gutted me that I'd failed them. Samantha knew something wasn't right, but she didn't push. While she was still learning the ins and outs of the club life, she understood that there were things I simply couldn't, and wouldn't, share with her.

Things were just starting to get settled down with the club when Sam mentioned a possible job transfer to Nashville. I'd barely had a chance to wrap my head around the news when her mother had shown up for an unexpected visit. I knew from the moment we'd met that she wasn't happy about us being together. It wasn't like she tried to hide the fact, and even though Samantha tried to deny it, I knew it got to her. I wasn't blind. I could see the worry in her eyes, the wheels turning in her head whenever she was at the clubhouse. Even though Samantha and I were from two different worlds, traveling on two completely different paths, I could also feel the love she felt for me whenever she was in my arms.

But as I lay there watching her sleep a thought crossed my mind, causing a knot to twist in my gut. I was a man who had it all. I had my club, my brothers—my family, and I had a woman who I loved like no other. This realization should've made me fucking ecstatic, but I knew how things worked. No man could have it all forever, and the same would hold true for me. I didn't know how and I didn't know when, but the tides of change were coming.

THE END

Gunner: Satan's Fury MC- Memphis will release late July or early August.

L. Wilder's Author's Note

For those readers who've read *Satan's Fury - Memphis Chapter*, you know that there's more to this story. To find out what becomes of Gus and Samantha, be sure to check out Gunner's book, which will be releasing late July or early August.

FACEBOOK: https://www.facebook.com/AuthorLeslieWilder/
BOOKBUB: https://www.bookbub.com/authors/l-wilder
NEWSLETTER: http://eepurl.com/dvSpW5

AT YOUR SERVICE BY LARAMIE BRISCOE

A Heaven Hill Generations Novella

INTRODUCTION

Author's Note: If you don't want to be spoiled, you should read this book following "Wild" book two in the Heaven Hill Generations Series. The next generation of the original Heaven Hill MC Series.

In case you're going in blind, I'll do my best to make it easy for you!

Cast of Character

Drew: Adopted son of Liam Walker (ex-president of the Heaven Hill MC). Biological son of Denise Walker. Twin brother to Mandy. Half-brother to Tatum. Married to Charity, and father to twin girls Harley and Justice. He is now the president of the Heaven Hill MC.

Charity: Wife to Drew, mother to Harley and Justice. An attorney in their hometown of Bowling Green, KY.

Dalton: Best friend to Drew, husband to Mandy, father of Walker. He is now the VP of the Heaven Hill MC.

Mandy: Twin sister to Drew, half-sister to Tatum, adopted daughter of Liam, daughter to Denise, wife of Dalton, mother of Walker. She also works alongside Charity in her law firm.

Remy: Member of the Heaven Hill MC. Boyfriend to Tatum, the daughter of Liam and Denise.

Blurb: When Drew Walker takes over the Heaven Hill MC, it means lots of changes for his family. It's hard to make it all work, but he'll stop at nothing to be the man who can do everything.

CHAPTER 1

DREW

"Looks good on you."

The rough, southern-tinged accent flows through my veins like Jim Beam and University of Kentucky blue, it's home. Looking up in the mirror, my eyes meet the ones of the man who adopted me as a mouthy teenager. Liam Walker is my dad in every single way that counts. He's the one who taught me how to ride, helped me purchase my first bike, caught me and Charity in the most compromising of situations, but at the same time didn't embarrass me. Earning his respect has always been one of the biggest goals of my life. Wearing this president patch on this cut? It's right up there with them.

"Still can't believe you stepped down," I move my arms within the brand-new piece of leather, stretching it this way and that. A gift from him after I publicly accepted the new position yesterday. In the next few months, the cut will soften, will mold to my body like butter, and eventually I'll feel naked without it on.

"Nobody else I'd rather have as leader than you, my man," he answers, smoothing it over my shoulders. Reminiscing of him checking to make sure my tie was done correctly right before my wedding. He and I, we've gone through just about every rite of passage a man can, together.

Turning to face him, I stand straight, slightly taller than he is. "It's a lot of pressure."

He nods, knowing what he's gifting me is the oldest club in the area, the one to come to when things go to hell, one of the pillars of our Bowling Green community. "If anyone can handle it, it's you."

My dad has always had more confidence in me than I've ever had in myself. Typically, I brush it off, act like it's no big deal; today I take it all in, let it permeate my bones. Hope like hell I can be the leader he thinks I can be.

"You really think so?"

He nods, putting his hand out for me to shake. "I still remember you,that almost-teenager standing up for your mom. You weren't scared, or if you were, you didn't show it. Then taking up for your twin sister – you've always been a man."

I wince as I think back to my early-twenties. There was some shit I did, I wasn't proud of. "Maybe not always a good man."

The look he gives me is one of understanding. "You had your heart broken. The woman you wanted to spend the rest of your life with left here and went to college without you. We lived that pain with you, Drew."

"And you rejoiced when she came back," I remind him, my chest cavity filling with contentment as I think about my wife.

"We did," he nods, with a grin. "Then the two of you gave us the cutest granddaughters to ever walk the face of the Earth."

"You're biased. They are holy terrors," I argue. "They keep me and Charity up at night. Ya know, not thinking about what's gonna happen when they hit their teenage years. They legit keep us up. We've got to get them out of the same bedroom. They giggle, play games, and whisper for hours. I've tried to get Charity to stop putting the baby monitor in there, but she's scared to. So all night I have to listen to the giggling, when all I really want is to go to sleep," I complain, running a hand through my hair.

"Welcome to parenthood, son. You think I wasn't worried about you every time you left the house? Especially when you got your first bike, you were so much wilder than I ever was."

Running a hand down my face, I give my dad a look of honesty. "How am I going to live up to the man you are? You've been the leader of this club for years. People respect you, they come to you when they have a problem, they don't question when you lay down an order, you're so well-respected."

"So are you," he speaks the words softly. "Those guys have watched you. They've seen you go from a hot-headed young man to a level-headed father and husband."

"I'm still hot-headed," I remind him. "I haven't ever been able to shake it all off."

"But for the most part you're fair and you don't get too far ahead of yourself. As long as you respect these men, they will respect you. It's as simple as that."

It's not as simple as that, but I do get what he's saying. "Thank you for trusting me with the job. I know it wasn't easy to step down."

"Easiest thing I've ever done, giving the reins over to you. I don't even think I was this sure about marrying your mom," he grins.

"Don't let her hear you say that, she'll cut your dick off."

"Of that I'm sure," he lights another cigarette. "If you need help I'm always here. The door will always be open, and you will never be alone."

"I know, Dalton will be with me," I mention the name of my brother-in-law. Never in a million years could I have picked a better man to marry my sister. He and I have been best friends for the biggest part of our lives, and to know he's the one taking care of my twin means the absolute world to me.

"And I'll be a phone call away, as will Tyler."

Squaring my shoulders, I nod. My eyes take in the cut one more time. I have a feeling seeing that president patch will throw me for a little while, but I will rule the Heaven Hill MC the best way I know how. My heart thuds against my chest, all at once causing me to feel the weight of the gift I've been given.

There were other men who deserved this more than me, but it will always mean the world to me that my dad thought I was the one who should have it.

"I'll make you proud," the promise is in my voice.

"I have no doubt about that, Drew. Don't ever think I worry about you making me proud. You've done it many times over. That's not even a blip on my radar."

It's hard to hold onto the emotion his words invoke. For so many years I grew up without a father, my mom doing double-duty and me worrying. Fucking worried about everything. Would we have enough food to eat, would we have money to make bills, would I hear my mom crying at night when she thought no one could hear? The worrying has followed me into my adulthood, but for the most part, I've been able to push it down and live my life. I have a suspicion I'm about to start again.

"Did you know he was gonna do it?"

Glancing over at my best friend and now VP, Dalton, I shake my head. "No fuckin' idea he'd name me or you, didn't even know he was thinking about it."

"I think he did it the way he wanted to. Kind of how he's lived his whole life to this point."

Those words truly sum up the man who adopted me and my twin after he fell in love with my mom. I hope like hell I can be half the man he is, but I know it'll take time. For a long time our club has been on a good path, no one has tried to bother us, we've been straight. However, me and everyone else know that won't happen forever. There's always someone in the shadows ready to pounce, ready to take away what's ours, and turn the tranquility we've experienced for the past few years into a time of violence and panic. That time is coming. We all know nothing good lasts forever, and it looks like I'm going to be the one to lead us into whatever battle we're going to be facing.

"You're right about that," I take a drag off my cigarette. "Just hope like hell I'm the right man for the job."

"Brother trust me, there's no other man who could do this job. When push comes to shove you're gonna push right the fuck back. I will follow you into the depths of hell and I will stand beside you through whatever gets thrown at us. Liam is a goddamn amazing leader, you learned from him. Give yourself some credit."

I let his words roll around in my head until they settle. There they take root, holding tight as they start to grow. "C'mon, let's go make some plans."

"That's the man I know."

The two of us leave the garage, heading to the clubhouse with the wind whistling against our ears and the sun beating down on our backs. Free as a bird, with nothing to cage us in sight.

CHAPTER 2

CHARITY

A few days later

"How have things been going at your house?"

I glance up at my paralegal who also happens to be my sister-in-law, squinting my eyes at her. I get the feeling she asked me a question, but damn if I heard it. "What? Did you say something?"

She giggles, rolling her eyes. She's used to me by now, but this is even a little bit more absent minded then I normally am. "You look like you slept here last night and you're paying attention like you did too."

Sighing deeply, I pull a mirror over to me, gasping as I get a good look at myself. My hair is every which way, at some point I put it in a bun, and pieces have fallen out haphazardly. Any make up I had on is gone, and the dark circles under my eyes can have their own zip code at this point. "I did kind of sleep here last night. I have to get this brief over to the courthouse in less than three hours," I explain, taking a huge chug of the coffee on my desk.

As soon as it hits my tongue, I lean over the trashcan, spitting it out. "I don't know how old that is, but it's cold," I shiver with grossness.

"Why didn't you tell me last night?" She shrieks. "I would have stayed here to help you. I wouldn't have gone gallivanting off with my husband and left you here to do all the work. We took a two-hour ride while Dad watched Walker."

"You need to gallivant with your husband," I argue. This is my business, I'm the one who started it, and I feel as if it's my job to make sure it does well. That's not up to her; I make the hard decisions. Last night just so happened to be one that sucked for me. "Now that he and Drew have taken the lead for the club, I have a feeling we're going to be seeing less and less of them."

Mandy gets up, going to the bathroom where I hear her rummaging under the sink, then running water, before she comes back out, handing me a wet washcloth. With a sigh, I accept it from her, running it over my face. It feels good to wash some of the grit from my eyes, wakes me up slightly, and gives me the renewed energy I need to power through.

"So, what about you?" She asks, holding her hand out to take the washrag back.

"What about me?" It may be the fact I haven't slept in over twenty-four hours, but I'm not entirely sure what she's talking about.

"If I'm going to be seeing less of my husband, you're going to not be seeing yours at all. Why didn't you go home last night?" She presses, raising an eyebrow in my direction.

Letting out a deep breath, I push the laptop away from me, and lean back in my chair. "I love my family, don't get me wrong. My girls are my life, Drew is the only man in the world I can see myself with, but they require a lot of work and attention."

Mandy laughs, an unladylike snort working its way from her nose. "Yeah babe, that's what they do. They expect us to take care of them."

"Which is fine," I run my hand through my hair. "When I don't have a deadline like this beating down on me. This case means a lot to me," I bite my lip, hoping I'm explaining it in a way she can understand. "It means a lot to the community, and I don't want to let any of them down."

"Your children mean a lot to you too."

"They do," I agree. "But I can't be in two places at once and burning the candle at both ends has been killing me. I asked Drew if he could take over last night. Ya know, get the baths done, make sure they got in bed on time, I'm sure he got them pizza and they loved him for it. All the cool things Mom never does," I wrinkle my nose, thinking of how much grease they probably ate.

"What did you tell him you were doing?" She puts a hand on her hip, jutting it out further than she needs to. When she knows she's right, she gets sassy.

"A little extra research, he may have thought I had to drive up to Bardstown," I give her a shrug. "Too long of a trip to make it back home in one night after leaving late in the afternoon."

"So, he thinks you stayed the night out of town and got a good night's sleep?" She finishes it up for me, her tone more accusatory than I would like for it to be, but right now I can't force myself to give a shit.

"He may think that."

She taps her nails on the desk in front of her. "He's gonna be pissed when he finds out what you did."

Fuck my life. Those two don't keep shit from each other. Given the fact that they're twins, and for the longest time the only people they could trust were themselves. "Please don't tell him," I beg. I'm not beyond begging. I just want to get this damn brief over to the courthouse and go on with my life. "He'll never get it, and I don't want to waste time trying to explain it to him."

"That's not fair," she answers. "He will get it, you can't assume your job and your life aren't as important as his. That will piss him off more than anything will."

"I made a choice, maybe it was wrong, but it was my choice."

"I can't keep this from him," she folds her arms across her chest, shaking her head. "If you do it once, it'll become a habit."

"He has his bad habits too," I point out. Drew Walker isn't perfect and never has been, so I'll be damned if I'm the only one getting drug across the carpet right now. "Which more than likely will double now that he's president."

"Don't turn this around on him, honey, this is about you."

My gaze peers into hers, hoping she'll cut me a break, hoping this is the one time she won't have to tell her brother, but I know their bond, and I know I'll need to be strong. "Do what you need to do Mandy, and I'll do what I need to do."

Quickly my fingers type the remaining words, I quickly save the document and send this over to our printer. Slamming my laptop shut, I gather up my things, not bothering to say anything to her. Out of habit I automatically put my highlighters, white out, and pens back in their place. I make sure the picture of Drew and I on our wedding day is just slightly left of the newest picture of us and our girls. There are many times a day I look to it for strength. Right now I feel like it's taunting me.

"I take it you got done."

Her tone is annoying.

I'm pissed and slightly petty, I don't even acknowledge she's speaking to me. Silently I give myself a pat on the back for remaining strong. I hate when people are mad at me, but today I'm angrier at her.

"I'm gonna let Drew know what happened here, he won't be happy. You know he hates when you keep things from him, and he automatically assumes the worst. Is that really how you want to start out your day?"

Walking over to the coat rack, I grab my purse and briefcase, slinging the purse over my shoulder, I tighten my grip on the briefcase. It takes a lot, but I breathe in deeply, breathe out, slowly and steadily, forcing my racing heart to return to normal speed. When I've calmed down enough, I glance at her. "Go ahead and tell him, I'm going to pick this up, swing it by the courthouse, and then I'm going home. Whether or not he shows up early will let me know what you've done, but the fact of the matter is we all have to live with our choices. Can you live with yours?"

Her laughter follows me as I step into the mid-afternoon daylight. Wincing, I feel like a vampire who has just woken up and is seeing the sun for the first time. Placing sunglasses over my sensitive eyes, I hope like hell the fight I might possibly have with my husband isn't going to take a long time. I desperately need to sleep.

CHAPTER 3

DREW

My phone vibrates in my pocket as I bend over the car I'm working on. Half the time I ignore it, but fuck I'm feeling old today and my back hurts like a son of a bitch. Taking the moment to straighten up and work out some of the kinks, I reach in, grab it out, and take a look at who's texted me. Fuck, my twin sister. I've got a shit ton of stuff to do today, and messing with her isn't on my list. Still though, I go ahead and read what she's sent me.

M: Do you know where your wife was last night?

The fuck? What's that supposed to mean. "Can you finish this up?" I ask one of the other members of our club, Remy. "I need to go take care of this."

"No problem," he rushes over to take my spot. I know part of that has to do with the fact he's in love with my little sister, Tatum, and he wants to make a good impression. The other part though? He's just a good kid, he's going to grow up to be an asset, not only to the club, but to our community.

D: Yeah, she had shit to do in Bardstown for some case she was working on. She stayed at a hotel and should be back today.

• • •

M: Wrong.

IMMEDIATELY I'M SEEING RED. Did Charity do something I never imagined in a million years she would do? I thought our marriage was strong, I love this woman with every breath I take.

D: You better explain right fucking now.

THIS TIME MY PHONE RINGS. Seeing it's Mandy, I answer before it rings again. "Speak."

"I understand you've got shit going on. Totally get it that you've got a lot of pressure on you thanks to Dad handing over the title of president to you," she rushes out in one full breath. "But did you ever stop to think maybe Charity's got a ton of shit going on too? She didn't go to Bardstown last night. She lied to you so you wouldn't worry, she slept in the office to get some paperwork done for a brief that had to be delivered to the court today."

"Shit," I feel like my formally bright world is now dark and gray.

"Yeah, while you've been trying to get things going with the club, I think you forgot that the mother of your children is doing all she can to keep her own business running smoothly. She's been doing double-duty, and she's tired, Drew," Mandy is just getting started, I know this from experience. If I let her keep on, I'll be listening to her until the sun sets.

"So what do you propose I do?" I cut her off. "Is she still at the office."

"No, she went home."

Silence. Complete silence. I'm waiting, trying to patiently let her make her point. When she doesn't and I get sick of waiting, I growl instead of form my next words as a question. "What am I supposed to do."

I can almost hear her smile through the phone. She knows she's got me, and she's going to embrace it, bring it up for years to come, and hold it over my head like a goddamn rain cloud whenever she can.

"I'm gonna pick up the girls and they'll be staying with me and Dalton tonight. She headed home about an hour ago, so she should be done with what absolutely had to be taken care of. Now it's your job to go home and pamper her. Take her mind off all this shit, and show her what an amazing husband you are."

There are times when I loathe my sister, many other times I love her. "I suppose you want a thank you."

"I mean it wouldn't kill you to give me a little credit for keeping your marriage on track."

I laugh loudly. "Thank you. Thank you for pulling my head out of my ass, thank you for taking care of Harley and Justice, and I appreciate you always being the person who isn't scared to get in my shit when it's needed."

"Love you, bro. Have a good night!"

"I plan on it."

Disconnecting the call, I shove my phone back into the pocket of my worn jeans, directing my guys to what I want them to do for the rest of the day. Dalton catches my eye as I'm barking out orders.

"Got a text from Mandy, see you tomorrow," he hitches his chin up with a grin.

The wave I give him is hopefully nonchalant, but the truth is I can't wait to be alone with my wife. It's been too long, and fuck if I'm not excited.

CHAPTER 4

CHARITY

My eyes open before I see him. The two of us, we've loved each other so long, I can *feel* him. He's a part of my DNA. Since I came back into town and the two of us got married, we've rarely spent any time apart from one another, and staying away from him last night was harder than I care to admit.

I can hear him now, on the last step of our stairs. This is the one that squeaks since the house settled. Leather creaks as he moves, his boots make no sound, but his scent wafts ahead of him. Leather, motor oil, the sunshine of outside, along with the shampoo he uses. Musky, masculine, and everything that I like to curl up with at night in bed. My husband comes through the doorway of our bathroom, filling up the space with his tall frame and big shoulders.

"Babe, why'd you lie to me?" The whiskers on his face move along with the bottom lip he pulls between his teeth.

Sitting up in the tub, I let the bubbles fall away, there's no modesty between the two of us. "I didn't mean to lie to you," I argue.

"Pretty sure ya did," his hands had been bracing against the doorframe, but now he folds his arms over his chest. His wedding ring glints in the light coming through the window across from us.

Sighing, I put my hands up before bringing them back down. "I just don't want to be another problem you have to fix."

To my embarrassment, tears come to my eyes and my chin wobbles with restrained tension and sadness. I've been keeping all this pressure in, and now it's hit it's breaking point. The bottle is about to be uncorked.

He walks over to the tub, kneeling before reaching in and steadying my chin. "If you think you're a problem, then we have more going on here than I thought. Fuck Charity, you're the reason I get up every morning, what's going on in that head of yours," he runs his other hand through my hair, cupping the back of my skull.

"I don't want you to get hurt," I rub my finger under my nose. "Now that you have that patch," I point to the new one on his cut. "You're the one people will come after now."

"So you want to make sure I don't worry about anything, right?"

I nod, hearing how stupid it sounds as he says it. His grip on my hair tightens, forcing my chin to lift, my eyes to meet his.

"Don't you know I worry about you every day?" I can see the storm of emotions sweep through his eyes, can feel the intensity of his gaze. "No matter what you're doing, no matter who you're with, if you're not with me, I worry about you. You're my heart, babe, and if something were to ever happen to you..." he lets his words drop off. "There wouldn't be a me."

"I've just been so stressed," I breathe deeply.

"That's my fault, and we're about to correct it right now," his voice is low, dangerous, and full of promise I haven't heard in months.

"What do you mean? Oh shit," I moan as he bends halfway into the tub, capturing my wet nipple in between his lips. His tongue rubs against the puckered skin, his teeth nibble biting down with enough force to make me squirm. His cheeks hollow as he sucks on the abused flesh.

Leaning my head back against the tub, I spread myself wide open for him, give him free reign over my entire body. His hand cups the underside of my tit, holding it up for his mouth to worship. His other hand cuts through the water, two fingers slide into me, causing me to moan and thrash. When his mouth lets go and his fingers withdraw, I'm dizzy, hazy about where I am, and drunk on the feeling of wanting his cock to cure the ache inside me.

He's taking his clothes off, throwing them on the vanity, cursing loudly as his jeans get caught on his boots. "Son of a fucking bitch," I giggle as he takes his pocket knife, cutting the laces off, throwing the boots in the corner.

When he comes back over to where I am, he reaches in, clasping his fingers around my wrists, pulling me up. I'm not sure what he's going to do, but I've learned not to question him when he's in this kind of mood. His cock bobs in front of him, and I want desperately to reach out and touch it, but with my wrists bound by his strength, that's not possible.

My question is answered as he has a seat in the tub, then pulls me into his lap, my back to his front. Immediately, his lips go to my neck and shoulder, kissing me, mouthing me, biting at my ear as his hand goes down the middle of my body. His palm cups my pussy as I rock against him, wanting nothing more than for him to slip his thick fingers inside.

"Please," I beg.

"How bad do you want it?" His voice is dark, slurred, and just the way I like it.

"So bad, please either fuck me, or get me off."

He bites my earlobe. "You're so dirty when you know the kids aren't home."

I let out a slow breath, shifting my thighs apart further so he has more room to work, then I grab his free hand, pushing my fingers around his wrist, before bringing it up to my throat.

"You want it a little rough today, baby? Do you need to let go, need to let me do all the work and you just let me play your body?"

When his fingers – one by one – tighten slowly around my neck, I let out a slightly muffled, "mmm hmmm."

"Then that's what you'll get," his words are a promise and I know I can only hang on for the ride.

As his fingers move in and out of my core, his other fingers tighten and then loosen against my neck. When I'm able I take a breath. The feeling of not being in charge sends me in a whirlwind up as I begin rocking against his fingers, cupping my own breasts, twisting my own nipples. His mouth at my neck is sucking, biting, marking me for anyone who wants to see. He loves to do this right before I have court, and I can't help but love it too.

"You close?"

I nod, not able to speak, I'm so overwhelmed with all of the feelings coursing through my body. I'm moving, rubbing my ass against his cock as he works me harder, faster, rougher, all the things I love about him.

"Come for me," he whispers in my ear as I fly high.

When I start to come down, he separates my thighs, pushing his cock into me as I reach for the lip of the tub in front of me, still unsteady from my orgasm.

"Won't take long," he grits out.

I'm still spasming as he plunges into me. The strokes are fierce. One, two, three, and then a fourth when I feel him let go. Another smaller orgasm rolls through my body as he pulls me back against him.

"So tired," I whisper and that's the last thing I remember.

CHAPTER 5

DREW

I'M BREATHING EASIER AS I HOLD HER IN MY ARMS. MY NOSE IS BURIED IN HER hair, loving the smell of her shampoo. This right here, is home to me. Wherever she is. Nothing is more important to me than the three females who live under my roof, but this one in my arms? I can't live without her. She makes me better, makes me soft in ways others can't even see, makes me hard too, and together, we've built a life.

"What are you thinking about so hard?"

She's turned in my arms. Reaching up, she smooths the skin between my two eyebrows. As she does, the sheet moves, exposing her nakedness to my gaze. "Thinking about how much I love you," I grin.

"Promise me," she whispers as she wraps her arms around my neck. "Promise me that the club isn't going to come between us. We'll make time for each other, and we won't do this again."

"You're my number one, babe, you always have been, always will be. Nothing will ever take your place in my life."

My wife, she looks at me, but I can see it in her eyes. She's scared. This new position worries her, but more than that, I think it intimidates her. Wrapping my arms around her waist, I pull her smaller body closer to me. "I will always do whatever I can to make sure you're safe."

Her head moves up and down. "I know, but I feel it, Drew. There's a storm coming in, and I have a feeling it's going to stall out right over Bowling Green. We can't be this happy and expect that it'll always be like this."

"We can be as happy as we want to be," I argue, reaching down to capture her lips with mine. But as I pin her to the bed, mouthing at her neck, I admit something to myself.

I feel it too.

Dark and angry. The fury of a gathering storm. One that feels like it's about to unleash on every single one of us.

Connect With Laramie

Website: http://www.laramiebriscoe.net
Facebook: https://www.facebook.com/AuthorLaramieBriscoe
Twitter: https://twitter.com/LaramieBriscoe
Pinterest: http://www.pinterest.com/laramiebriscoe/
Instagram: http://instagram.com/laramie_briscoe
Mailing List: http://sitel.ink/LBList
Email: http://Laramie@laramiebriscoe.com

RIDE DEEP BY LAURA KAYE

A Raven Riders Novella

CHAPTER 1

YOU'D THINK HE'D FEEL BETTER NOW THAT HE WAS OUT OF PRISON. BUT THE ugly truth was, Jagger Locke really fucking didn't.

Seven months had passed since he'd been exonerated and released, and he'd only served four months. It should've been no big deal. But it fucking was. Because their enemies had set him up. Because even though those who'd wronged him had been taken care of, he hadn't had a hand in getting that vengeance. Because while he'd been behind bars, he hadn't been there to help protect the club when they'd needed him most.

All of it had him coming apart at the seams with a rage like he'd never felt in his entire goddamn life.

Jagger pulled his truck into Frederick Auto Body which, as of a few months ago, now belonged to his Ravens brother Sam "Slider" Evans, one of the two lucky fuckers who'd found a woman to settle down with while Jag had been incarcerated. He parked right next to the truck of the other lucky fucker, Maverick Rylan, and killed the engine.

Jagger blew out a breath like he carried the weight of the world on his shoulders.

Because the worst part of all that rage? He couldn't hear the music anymore.

As far back as he could remember—all the way back to even before his father had walked out on him, his kid sister, and their mom—Jagger had heard music in his head. Sometimes when he met someone for the first time, or ran into an old friend who was going through a tough time, or he went someplace new, notes and riffs would take shape in his mind as if his brain translated what his eyes saw and his hands felt into song.

At least, that was the only way he could describe it. It was fucking weird, he got that much. But it was why, if Jagger wasn't playing one of his guitars, he was humming or singing to himself or, without realizing it, playing guitar chords with his fingers against this palm.

But the rage had crowded it all the fuck out, leaving his head quiet when the last thing he wanted was to be alone with himself.

Jagger heaved himself out of the truck, cast a glance at the dark clouds hanging in the late May sky, and went inside where he found Slider and Maverick studying a set of blueprints.

"How go the plans for world domination?" Jagger asked, managing a smile.

His brothers looked up at the same time. Slider and Maverick were opposites in so many ways. Slider had dark hair and odd pale green eyes and was more reserved by nature, whereas Maverick had sandy blond hair and the bluest eyes you ever saw and was absolutely fluent in sarcasm. Their smiles were genuine, and it made him feel like a morose motherfucker to be carrying this baggage around all the damn time. Of course, both men had plenty to be happy about—Maverick had gotten married in April and Slider was expecting a baby any day now.

Slider braced his hands on the counter, then peered over at the still-empty space of the new two-bay addition to his shop. "Man, I'm itching for this to be done."

"It's gonna be fucking sweet," Maverick said. "And now it's all about picking out which toys you want."

Slider chuffed out a laugh. "Sometimes I think you're even more excited about this than I am."

"I think it's called jealousy." Jagger smirked and joined them at the counter.

"Jealous as fuck," Maverick said, quirking a grin and giving Slider a look. "Jealous enough that your damn reno is gonna cost me fucking money because it has me thinking about what I want to change at my shop." Slider was adding customization services—painting, complete car builds, and classic car restorations—to his shop under the new name Frederick Auto Body & Customs. Tricking out Slider's new business was why Maverick and Jagger were there. Mav, because he did similar work—he owned a custom bike-building business was so highly regarded that people came from other states to hire him. And Jagger because he was the Ravens' Race Captain, which meant he oversaw all operations related to Green Mountain Speedway, the club's racetrack that generated the Raven Riders' primary source of income.

In other words, they were both fluent in all things fast.

Slider chuckled, but before he could reply, the door to the second bay eased open, rolling upward until they could just see the rear end of a car one of Slider's guys had towed in. "That's Jake. Gimme a few." He went to guide the car inside the bay, an older-model Camry with damage to the front bumper, the front passenger-side quarter panel, and the tire beneath, which was torqued in a way that suggested a broken axle. Damn, that bill wasn't gonna be pretty on a car that old.

Maverick spoke in a hushed tone. "Never thought I'd see Slider this happy again."

Jagger met his brother's gaze and nodded. Several years ago, Slider's wife had died of cancer and it'd been like the man had died along with her in every way except for one—taking care of their two young sons. But all that had changed last fall when Slider hired a nanny to take care of the kids. Now he and Cora were expecting a baby of their own and it was like Slider was a whole new man. "Me either. It's damn good to see, though."

"It is. And how about you?"

Mav's words hung there while Jagger's brain scrambled. He'd been home almost eight months and not a soul had called him out in all this time. So he went for the bluff. "What about me?"

Bluff called, apparently, if he was reading Maverick's don't-bullshit-a-bullshitter expression right. "You're probably the smartest motherfucker I know, Jagger. I don't really think I need to explain what I mean."

Yeah. No. He wasn't doing this. He gave a shrug. "I'm getting by."

Just then, Slider disconnected the wreck from the tow truck, which rumbled back outside again, leaving quiet to hang heavy in the air. Jagger turned towards the Camry, looking for absolutely anything to redirect the focus off him.

And then he had it.

Because a woman followed Jake into the shop. A beautiful woman with nearly waist-long black curls. A woman with a guitar case strapped to her back and...was that a puppy tucked in her arm?

She looked up, her gaze going from Jake to her car to Slider before passing over Jagger. She did a double take. And so did he.

A familiarity he couldn't place. But he knew he'd seen those nearly teal-blue eyes before. And then he clocked where he knew her from. It was the hair that'd thrown him off. He'd never realized how long it was because she'd always worn it up in these soft, intricate hairdos that'd made him think of the flamenco chord progressions of the Spanish guitar. "Hey, Teach," he said.

Her expression went from puzzlement to realization. "Jackson?" She used his given name rather than his nickname, because that was how she'd known him. In prison. When he'd taken her literature class—one he hadn't yet finished when he'd been released. "What are you doing here?"

Andi Everly hadn't thought her day could get any worse—and then she'd run off the road and into a ditch. Now, here she stood, wet, bedraggled, and with dirty paw prints covering her damp white T-shirt as she ran into a man she hadn't seen in seven months.

Jackson quirked a grin as he shrugged one big shoulder—a shoulder covered in a denim and leather cut-off jacket with a name patch that read *Jagger*. The man was as tall and broad-shouldered as she'd remembered. His brown hair was longer than it'd been before, and he had a bit of a five o'clock shadow along his jaw despite the fact that it was only eleven in the morning. In a pair of worn jeans, a black T-shirt, and that motorcycle-club vest—a vest that a blond-haired man leaning against a counter was also wearing, Jackson was ruggedly handsome—a thought that caught her off guard. "One of my best friends own the place. What are you doing here?"

To distract herself from ogling her one-time student, she glanced over at the mangled frame of the car. "Oh, uh, rain plus puppy unexpectedly in the road equaled my car in a ditch. Apparently…"

As if he knew she'd been talking about him, the puppy squirmed in her arms, and she peered down at the little ball of gray and white fur that looked too thin and dirty to have an owner. Most likely he'd been dumped. He'd trundled out onto the road when she'd been so close that she couldn't stop in time. It was like her tires had started to hydroplane, and then she'd had no other way to avoid hitting him than to veer off the road. Except there wasn't much to the side of that particular road except for a thin strip of gravel bordering a ditch. The car had slid into it and slammed to a halt. Her chest still hurt from the quick restraint of the seat belt.

Jackson stepped closer, a smile on his face as he looked at the puppy. "Looks like you've got your hands full there."

"Yeah. I don't know what I'm going to do with him—"

"My fiancé might be able to help." A man with dark hair and a close-cropped beard joined them. He wore a shirt with the shop's name and a tag that read, *Sam*. "She works at the animal shelter. I'm Sam Evans, the owner. Would you come out to the reception area with me so I can get some information?"

Andi gave Jackson a little smile as she stepped away. Just as she passed through the doorway, she heard the blond man asked, "You two know each other?" She was curious to hear how Jackson would answer, but Sam distracted her with forms and signatures and the realization that she was going to be without a vehicle for a few days. That it was Friday afternoon was her only saving grace—she didn't have to be to work until Monday morning.

When he finished checking her in, Sam asked, "You need a ride somewhere?"

She stroked her hand over the silky hair of the puppy's head. "I can probably call an Uber or something."

"Suit yourself," Sam said. "We can help if you change your mind."

She nodded, and the man left her alone in the waiting room. "I'm gonna put you down for a second. Okay, buddy?" Crouching, she put the pit bull—if she had to guess at the breed—down beside her and fished her cell phone from her purse. She hit the home button. Then again. The screen remained dark. "Just perfect." Her battery had been draining quicker and quicker lately, but she'd been putting off the expense of replacing it. And now the car…

On a sigh, Andi eyed the phone behind the counter.

Not sure what else to do, she went back into the shop, the puppy following behind. "I'm sorry, can I use your phone? Mine's out of battery."

Sam, Jackson, and the other man looked up from some paperwork spread out on a counter. "No problem," Sam said, coming back into the office. He grabbed the phone and hauled it onto the customer service counter so she could reach it.

Except then she realized she wasn't sure who she could call. Without her cell, she couldn't call an Uber. A taxi, maybe?

"You want some help, Teach? Slider's gonna reschedule our meeting so he can focus on your car, so I'm free to play taxi driver."

Andi turned to find Jackson leaning against the door jamb, the puppy in his big hands, holding him so that he and the puppy were looking at each other. The dog pawed Jackson's nose and the man laughed.

Her brain shorted out for a minute—because she was having a whole day just then, because Jackson looked equal parts cute and hot holding that puppy up to his face and talking to it, because of his offer to help. All of which was maybe why her only reply was, "Slider?"

Jackson chuckled. "Oh, I mean Sam. Sorry, using club names is a force of habit."

Her gaze ran over his vest again. She'd heard of the Raven Riders—their races at the Green Valley Speedway; their brushes with the law; and, interestingly, the fact that they provided protective and even relocation assistance to vulnerable women and children. You couldn't live in the area and not have seen or heard about them.

"This guy is cute. His lip curl makes it look like he's doing an Elvis impersonation."

Hugging herself, she moved closer. "I think he has a little cleft lip.

Someone must've dumped him, though I don't know how anyone could do that to an animal."

Something dark flashed across Jackson's expression for just a moment. "Nothing surprises me these days." He glanced up at her. His brown-eyed gaze ran over her face much more directly than he'd ever dared when he was in her class. Then again, that was a whole different environment. Now, he was free. And she was on *his* turf. "Can I run you somewhere?"

"I don't want to put you out."

"I'm offering, so you won't. But I'll understand if being alone with me makes you comfortable."

Andi blinked, an awkward guilt settling into her stomach. He'd been an inmate, yes. But she also knew that he'd been exonerated. A lot of prisoners professed their innocence; Jackson Locke actually had been.

Teaching college courses via the correctional education program, she saw the men she taught as *students*, not inmates. And share cared about them the same way she'd cared about all the other college students she'd worked with. Jackson had been one of the students who'd most made her wonder about him and what his life had been before prison. In class, his comments had been thoughtful, and his analysis of the readings always seemed to go a level deeper than anyone else. On his papers, his writing was well organized and effective, and his prose sometimes bordered on the lyrical. It wasn't unusual for her students to impress her, and Jackson was one who definitely had.

And then he'd been released. Exonerated. And it'd made her wonder about him even more.

Now, here he was, offering to help her.

"Oh, no, it's not that. I..." She shrugged, which reminded her that she still bore her guitar on her back. She slid it off and rested it against the wall. "I've just had such a bad day that I'm a little at a loss."

"Then let me help make it better."

CHAPTER 2

Jagger wasn't sure why he was pushing, but it was the right thing to do and Professor Everly clearly needed help. Professor Everly. None of them had called her that. They'd all called her "Teach" because that's what she'd done for them. She was one of the best in the whole correctional education program. Everyone had said so, which was why Jagger had signed up to take a class from her in the first place. She'd been the kind of teacher who truly cared. Who saw them as students, not criminals. She'd valued their life experiences and encouraged them to come at the books and stories they read through the lens of their own lives.

"Okay, thank you," she said. "Um, I guess the first thing is maybe taking him to the shelter?"

Jagger looked at the little runt in his hands. Dogs were so damn pure that you couldn't help but feel a little better after petting one. "Let's get you some help, Elvis. What do you say?"

"Elvis?"

He grinned at her and shrugged. "Gotta call him something."

Chuckling, Teach nodded. "Guess so." She pulled a little band out of her pocket and whipped her hair into a quick, messy bun on top of her head, exposing a distracting sliver of her stomach as her shirt rode up above her jeans. Damn. Jagger swallowed hard and reached for her guitar—at the same time she did.

He got to the strap first. "I got it."

Their faces close from how they'd both leaned down, something sparked in her blue eyes. Surprise? Challenge? Interest? He couldn't say.

And probably shouldn't even wonder about it, given who she was and who he'd recently been. "Okay," she said.

Outside, the rain was coming down steadily, so he opened the door for her and slid her guitar to lean against the middle of the big bench seat. When she was in, he ran around to the driver's side until they were shut up in the truck's cab together. Rain drummed against the roof as Jagger pulled out his phone. "Cora—that's Slider's fiancé—is at the shelter today. I'll let her know we're coming in." When he was done, he put the truck in reverse.

"It's nice to know there's someone there I can trust to take care of Elvis." She petted him where he lay almost asleep on her lap.

Jagger grinned at her use of the name, and then pulled out onto the road. A few minutes passed in relative quiet, and he was trying to think of something to say—or whether to say anything at all. It wasn't like she was here for a social call. And he still wasn't convinced that she didn't feel uncomfortable being alone with him.

"A little light reading?" she said, peering down at the backpack on the floor which the guitar case had tilted toward her.

He followed her gaze to the backpack. "Something like that."

She reached for the top book, but then froze and peered over at him. "May I?"

He shrugged as he came to a stop at a traffic light. "Help yourself." For a long moment, the rhythmic beat of the windshield wipers filled the car.

One by one, she pulled books out and made a little stack by her leg. Vonnegut's *Slaughterhouse Five,* Huxley's *Brave New World,* Ginsberg's *Howl,* Morrison's *Beloved,* and Nabokov's *Lolita* sat in a pile together. She held *To Kill a Mockingbird* and *The Autobiography of Malcolm X* in her hands. "You have some great books here."

Jagger cleared his throat. "You inspired everything in that bag."

Her gaze whipped toward him just as the light turned green. "I didn't assign all of these."

No, but it was due to her that he'd sought all these books out. Her course had been based around banned books, and he'd been fascinated. But he'd gotten out of prison before the semester had ended. It'd been the only thing he'd missed about that hell hole. And he had missed it. So he'd decided to continue reading on his own, guided by lists of banned books he'd found online. "You inspired them, though. I didn't have you, but I had everything you'd taught me about how to identify the values put forward and challenged by books that've been banned, about what they say about the society that bans them, and about the role of provocative books in shaping how we understand ourselves and the world."

Teach blinked at him. Then again. And then she shook her head as if confused. "Wow, Jackson. Can I ask why you've never gone to college before my class?"

"It wasn't for lack of wanting, but when your father splits when you're fifteen and it falls to you to provide for your mom and sister, schooling sorta takes a back seat. By the time I started working at the speedway and connected up with the Raven Riders, it felt more important to save money to put my sister through school. So that's what I did. She's a geologist." Thinking of Cassia made him smile, especially because she was doing so good these days. An accident a few years back had nearly brought her whole life crashing down on her—literally, but it seemed like she was getting more and more over what'd happened every time he saw her. He guessed her new boyfriend, Quinton, had something to do with that.

Her expression went soft and appraising as she looked at him. "You're proud of her."

Hooking a left onto the animal shelter's street, Jackson smiled and nodded. "Damn proud."

Teach pulled out another book. *The Catcher in the Rye*. "What did you think of this one?"

"Dude would *not* stop complaining."

She laughed. "You're not wrong."

He eased the truck into the shelter's lot and took the spot closest to the door. "We're here, Teach."

"You can use my name, you know."

Killing the engine, he looked over to her and tried not to feel sucker punched by how pretty she was. But, damn, she really was. Those soft black waves that'd fallen loose from her updo. The brilliant contrast of her eyes. How freely she smiled. "Professor Everly?"

She smirked. "Miranda. Or even Andi."

"Miranda." The name had a soft sweetness to it, whereas the nickname was tougher, no-nonsense, and sexy, as if there were two sides of her. He liked both. "Andi. Okay."

"Do you prefer Jagger?" she asked.

He tilted his head as he looked at her. She had no reason to care what he preferred one way or the other, which made him respect her even more for the fact that she did. "I'm probably more used to it at this point, but I don't mind either way."

"Jagger it is, then." He liked the way his name sounded when she said it. The puppy whimpered and squirmed in Andi's lap, drawing their attention to him. "Hey, little man, let's get you checked out."

Inside, they found Cora at the reception desk. With shoulder-length wavy blond hair and an out-going personality, she was Slider's total opposite, but they worked together like they'd been meant to be—something that seemed all the more true when you saw Cora with Slider's two sons and witnessed how much they adored her, too.

"Should you be on your feet?" Jagger asked by way of a greeting.

"Hi, Jagger. Please don't tell Slider. Having a belly this big makes it nearly impossible to get on and off the stool. It's just easier." Wearing a pale blue dress, she came around the reception desk, one hand on her rounded stomach. "So where did this guy come from?"

Jagger gestured to Andi. "Cora, this is Miranda Everly. Miranda, Cora." The women shook hands and say hellos.

"He ran out into the road and I nearly hit him earlier today," Andi said. "I thought he should get checked out. He doesn't have a collar or anything."

Cora petted the puppy's head. From somewhere in the back of the building, a chorus of barking dogs sounded out.

"She's being modest," Jagger said, knowing Cora of all people would respect what this woman had done to protect this dog. "She drove off the road to avoid hitting him. She totally saved him." Andi's appreciative gaze landed on him and he met it head on. Because he liked her looking at him. And he liked looking in return. Unlike when they'd first met in her classroom, they were both free to look.

"Wow," Cora said, seemingly unaware of the tension bubbling between them. "I hope you're okay."

Andi pressed a hand above her heart. "I drove my car into a ditch, so I don't know whether my ego or my chest is more bruised."

Jagger frowned. He hadn't thought about her being hurt, but of course the seat belt would've done a number on her. Hell, the air bag, too. "You sure you're okay?"

"Yeah. It's not a big deal." She gave him a small smile, her gaze less direct this time.

"Can you put him on the scale for me so we can get a weight?" Cora pointed to the big silver floor unit against the wall.

Andi plopped him down. "Twelve and a half pounds."

"He's just a baby," Cora said. "Did you give him a name, or do I get the pleasure? We have to call him something."

Jagger held out a hand and grinned at Andi. "See?"

She laughed, and he loved the sound of it. "Yeah, yeah. Jagger thinks his name should be Elvis."

Cora beamed as she typed some information into the computer. "Elvis is an amazing name. He's got the lip curl and everything." When she was done checking him in and taking down Miranda's information, she looked up from the computer. "Well, say good-bye to your saviors for now, Elvis. We'll get him checked out. Are you wanting to adopt him? If not, puppies are always great candidates for our foster program."

"Oh." Andi's expression was wistful as she peered down at the pup. "Can I have some time to think about it? I hadn't really set out today to adopt a pet, but I'm also a little attached to him."

"Man, do I understand that," Cora said, reaching out for Elvis. "Of course. I'll call you as soon as the doctor has had a chance to evaluate him and we know if he needs anything." Andi nodded.

"Should you be carrying him?" Jagger asked.

Cora rolled her eyes. "You're as bad as Slider."

The words were too filled with affection for Jagger to buy her annoyance. "He's my brother. I'll take that as a compliment."

"I guess you should," Cora said, coming around the counter to him. She leaned up onto tiptoes and kissed his cheek.

"What was that for?" Jagger asked, looking down into her bright green eyes.

"Because you're good people, Jagger Locke." It was a nice fucking compliment, even if it slinked around uncomfortably inside his chest. He hadn't felt like a good person—or even like himself—in way too long. Cora smiled at Andi. "It was nice to meet you."

"You, too." That wistful look became more pronounced as Elvis disappeared into the back. "I guess it's kinda silly to get attached to something you've known for so little time."

Jagger nailed her with a stare. Part of him almost wanted to imagine she was talking about him, about *them*, even though he knew she wasn't. "Some situations forge a connection fast and deep. There's no logic to it. Just feeling and truth."

Her lips parted as that blue-eyed gaze collided with his. "Is that right?"

His gaze skated over the dark pink of her lips and he was suddenly ravenous—for a taste, for a connection, for something to make him feel good again. "I think it is."

She licked her lips, and it felt like fucking victory when her cheeks went flush because it meant he wasn't the only one feeling the slow burn kindling between them. He didn't know what that meant or where it might go—if anywhere—but he liked it. He liked it a fucking lot. "Sometimes the way you say things is almost lyrical. Do you know that? It was true of your writing, too."

The words brought them back onto safer ground. Books and class, that was what they'd had. That was what they knew of each other. But maybe he wanted more than that. So he pushed, just a little. "So where to next, Miranda? Tell me what you want or need, and I'll make it happen."

Staring at her, he let the words hang there for her to do with what she pleased. And he hoped like hell that she might be interested in taking the bait.

CHAPTER 3

Heat slinked through Andi's blood, and she had absolutely no idea what to do with the fact that she was attracted to one of her students.

Former student, her brain helpfully supplied.

True. Former inmate, too. Even though, that wasn't really fair, was it? Not when he'd been set up to take the fall for something he hadn't done. And yet, despite that, nothing about him came off as embittered or combative.

"Um, honestly, I…" She shook her head. "I guess. I don't know, actually."

Her stomach growled, loudly. Like, embarrassingly loud.

A slow grin grew on Jagger's face. "I think maybe you do know, woman. What do you want to eat?"

She chuckled and rubbed her head. "I'm too filthy to go anywhere."

"I can fix that. Wait here." He disappeared out into the parking lot, and Andi…appreciated watching him walk away. A lot. The man was sexy and fit, muscled without being bulky, and he did all kinds of justice to a pair of jeans.

What in the world had happened to her today? She'd gone out to run some errands and pick up her guitar from being repaired. She'd gotten a later start than she'd intended after receiving a call from one of the social workers at the prison informing her that a former student, a man who'd been paroled about a year ago, had died in a car accident. Learning that Antoine had gotten his life back on track only to lose it in such a senseless way had left her shell shocked and gutted. And then she'd had an accident herself—and had run into another one of her students who seemed intent on…what? Helping her? Yes, for sure. Taking care of her?

Jagger jogged back through the door, his brown hair and Ravens jacket spotted with rain. From underneath the jacket at his waist, he pulled a bundle of clothing, like he'd tucked it there to keep it dry. "I have a shirt and a sweatshirt. They're clean. Take your pick or wear both if you want."

Wow. So, clearly, taking care of her was a check, too. "Thank you, Jagger. That's really sweet of you." She accepted the worn-soft cotton into her hands.

"Yeah, well, don't tell anyone. I've got a reputation to uphold."

The self-deprecation was sweet, too. "Your secret is safe with me." Although, Andi suspected she wasn't the only one who knew he was sweet judging by what Cora had said to him a few minutes before.

As if the thought summoned the woman, Cora returned from the clinical area. "I didn't know you guys were still here."

"I was just giving Miranda a clean shirt since Elvis got her all muddy. Can she use the bathroom in the back?" Jagger asked.

"No problem. Through the door and to your right," Cora said.

Andi gave them a nod and ducked her chin as she scurried out of the room. She closed herself inside the restroom and braced her hands on the sink. What was she doing? Considering adopting a puppy she'd just met? Considering going to lunch with a man she barely knew?

That's not the only thing you're thinking about the man…

She whipped off the dirty T-shirt to find that some light splotchy bruises now marked her sternum and shoulder. They were a little tender to the touch, but not so much that she was concerned. Sighing, she punched her arms through the shirt Jagger had given her. It was way too big, so she knotted it at the waist. The once-black tee was faded to nearly a dark gray and had a washed out outline of an electric guitar with words that read: *Fender: An American Original. Established '46.*

"Wait," she said to herself. Did this shirt mean he might play, too?

Jagger. The man's nickname or motorcycle name or whatever. It was Jagger. Was there any chance that wasn't a reference to one of the founders of the Rolling Stones who was still going strong as a musician after five decades? That seemed unlikely.

Andi smoothed her hands over the mess of her hair, then washed them. Then dug to the bottom of her purse for some lip gloss. She halted with the little wand half way to her mouth. Why was she putting on lip gloss? Or worrying about her hair?

Because hot, sweet, smart man?

She avoided meeting her own gaze in the mirror as she smoothed the glossy mauve over her lips. After that, she scooped up her dirty shirt and Jagger's sweatshirt and went back out.

"I just want you to be happy." Andi heard Cora say those words just as she'd been about to push through the door. She wasn't trying to eavesdrop, but she also felt awkward about interrupting their conversation. And she had to admit at least a little that she was curious about how Jagger would answer.

And then he did. "I'm mostly okay. Don't worry about me. Worry about all those Evans males and this new little one about to pop out any day."

Cora chuckled, and Andi took the opportunity to return before she overheard anything else that hadn't been intended for her ears. Like the fact that Jagger maybe wasn't happy.

I'm mostly okay...

Her gut squeezed over that sentiment, but then he smiled when she walked back into the room. "Hey, thanks again. This works."

"Have you heard Jagger play yet?" Cora asked.

Andi blinked at the change of topic, and then realized she was talking about his Fender T-shirt. "No, I didn't know you played."

"Just for fun." So, suspicion confirmed then.

Cora rolled her eyes. "He has an entire wall filled with guitars. It could be more than just for fun if he wasn't, you know, almost single-handedly running the entirety of the Ravens' business as the speedway."

Andi's eyes went wide. She wasn't sure which part of that to react to first. "Wow, how many guitars do you own?"

"Eleven, a mix of electric and acoustic. A few Gibsons, a few Martins, a couple Fenders." He shrugged with one big shoulder.

Wow. With each new thing she learned about this him, he became more and more interesting to her. Talk about still waters running deep. You wouldn't necessarily look at this man and expect lyrical literary analyses of books or a significant passion and talent for playing music, but Jagger Locke was all of that. And it made her want to peel back more layers, to go deeper, and see what else she might learn—and like. "That's impressive. I bet that's quite a display."

"It's so cool," Cora said. "You should show her some time." The phone rang. "Oh, excuse me."

Jagger tucked his hands into his jeans pockets. "Consider that a standing invitation. Ready to go?"

Andi nodded, grateful that he'd given her a graceful way out of answering. She *was* curious about and interested in his guitar collection. Given Cora's praise, she'd love to hear him play some time. But following on the heels of her bathroom what-the-hell-am-I-doing semi-freak-out, she couldn't think about actually going to his house just then.

Waving quietly to Cora, who was still on the phone, they left. Once again, Jagger opened the truck door for Andi. "Thanks."

He got in and started up the truck. "Where are we headed?"

"There's a diner-type place downtown. Dutch's. Do you know it?" she asked.

Jagger chuckled as he backed out. "I know it."

"What? We don't have to go there if you don't like it."

"I love that place." He pulled out of the lot.

She stared at him for a long moment, trying to figure out what his reaction had been about. His face in profile was rugged, handsome in a man's man kinda way. Freaking hot. "Then what's funny?"

"It's one of my favorite places in town. Cora's best friend, Haven, works there. And since Haven is engaged to the Ravens' president, you can usually find a few of us there on any given day."

"Tell me about the Ravens," Andi said. "A few of you were at the repair shop helping Sam. Cora and her best friend are both engaged to members of the club and Cora obviously holds you in pretty high esteem. Why does it sorta feel like a big family?"

"Because it is," he said, maneuvering them through town. "I've been a part of them since I was seventeen. They gave me a good job, a home, a brotherhood."

She shifted so that she was angled toward him. "Is it true that the club offers protective services?"

He nodded. "That's why I love what I do at the speedway. It funds a lot of what we do for people."

"You mean people don't have to pay?" Because damn if that wasn't another interesting layer.

"We occasionally hire out, but when it comes to helping a woman or child out of a bad situation, standing guard so they can't be intimidated out of testifying in court, or helping them start fresh somewhere, we don't ask for money to do the right thing. Sometimes people don't want charity, and they'll give us what they can, but it's never expected." He glanced over at her.

That was...seriously impressive. "Is that a normal kind of thing for a motorcycle club to be into?" She'd lived in the area her whole life, so while she knew of the Raven Riders' existence, she didn't know much about them. Really, most of what Andi knew about motorcycle clubs was what she'd seen on television shows, and she had no idea how realistic that was.

"It's normal for us. And it's important to all of us, for one personal reason or another." He eased the truck into a street space about a half block from Dutch's.

She really wanted to ask him what *his* personal reason was, but it felt like a line she maybe shouldn't cross. They hopped out and walked side by side down the street, something that emphasized their height difference. She wasn't particularly short at 5'6", but Jagger still had another half foot on her. She peaked up at him, and of course he caught her looking. Heat filtered into her cheeks, and the satisfied expression he wore on that handsome face might've been irritating if it also wasn't so freaking hot.

Damn him.

The rain had stopped, though dark clouds still hung heavy and ominous in the afternoon sky. They crossed the intersection to the corner where Dutch's sat. It was one of those been-there-forever holes-in-the-wall with a long Formica counter, spinning stools, red-and-white booths, mini-jukeboxes on the walls over each, and a huge dessert case filled with everything sweet you could ever want.

Inside, a pretty woman with long hair in a brown-to-blond hombre stood behind the counter, her smile immediate when she laid eyes on Jagger. "Hey, Jagger. I'm so glad to see you. You just missed Dare. How are you?" Her tone was filled with an affection that spoke of a close friendship.

"I'm good. You know I can't stay away from your cakes, Haven." Smiling, he turned to Andi. "This is my friend Miranda." They exchanged hellos.

"Whoa," Andi said, glancing between Haven and the dessert case and back again. "Am I understanding right that you bake all of this?"

Haven chuckled. "Guilty as charged."

"Just wait. You have to save room for dessert," Jagger said, then he nodded toward the booths. "Matter which one?"

The younger woman shook her head. "Sit anywhere." Despite it being a little late for lunch, the diner was still pretty busy, so they picked a booth toward the back.

Lunch was a fun—and delicious—affair, wherein their booth turned out to be the busiest corner of the whole joint. Haven came to chat, then a few Ravens came in, saw Jagger, and stopped by to say hi—which happened twice, and then the owner of Dutch's—Dutch himself—stopped to talk awhile, too.

Andi had a few close friends, but not as many as she'd once had. A lot of her friends from academia had fallen away since she'd stopped pursuing a more traditional academic path and instead had gone into correctional education. She loved having a career devoted to teaching, reading, and writing, but she wasn't the biggest fan of all the hierarchy that came along with being a professor. And she really didn't give a rat's ass if some people thought she'd thrown her "promising career" away. She loved what she did.

So seeing all these people stopping by to talk to Jagger—and seeing how many friends he had and how much everyone liked and respected the man—it really struck her. She didn't have as much of that in her own life. Andi was happy that he had such a great community around him, especially after everything he'd been through.

Then came dessert time.

"Tell me you saved room," Jagger said.

She held her stomach. "I shouldn't have eaten all of my fries. Though they were really good fries."

He arched a brow. "Tell me."

"We could split something?" His whole expression went skeptical, and it made her laugh. "Come on, those pieces of cake are huge."

"And your point?"

Andi chuckled. "You should be nice and give me a taste."

He tilted his head and nailed her with a stare, both humor and heat in those dark eyes. "A taste, huh?"

Her belly went on a loop-the-loop. Flirtatious Jagger was damn sexy. "Yes, that's what I want," she said, completely aware that both of them were slinging innuendo. "I want a taste. And you said that you'd make happen whatever I wanted or needed." Now she arched a brow.

His mouth slid into a slow grin and his eyes crinkled at the corners. "Yeah, I did. So, tell me, Miranda, what else do you want or need?"

Maddeningly revealing heat spread over her cheeks, but Haven saved her when she arrived to take their dessert order. "What would you all like?"

Jagger smiled up at her. "The usual. Two forks."

Haven blinked. She looked at Jagger, then Andi. "You're sharing your cake?" He nodded, and now Haven was smiling, and Andi's cheeks were getting hotter. "Well, okay then."

When they were alone, Jagger reached across the table and stroked his knuckles along her cheekbone. It was the first time that he'd touched in such a direct, purposeful way, and she felt that soft brush of skin on skin *everywhere*. At least, she certainly wanted to feel it everywhere. "What's this for?"

Andi chuffed out a little laugh. She was so busted. Still, she brazened it out. "Nothing."

Haven settled a plate with a head-sized piece of cake onto their table. That was only a slight exaggeration.

"You couldn't have eaten all this by yourself anyway," Andi exclaimed when Haven moved on to the next table.

Jagger's expression was full of mock outrage, and it had her grinning again. When was the last time she'd had so much fun? "I have a second stomach reserved for Haven's desserts."

"Is that so?" Andi sliced into the chocolate cake with her fork.

"Mmhmm." He watched expectantly as she took a bite, and then the amazingly rich and decadent flavors burst on her tongue.

She moaned. "Omigod," she said around the bite.

"See what I mean?" He took a forkful for himself.

"This might be better than sex." She took a second bite and looked across the table at him.

He had the smuggest, sexiest expression she'd ever seen on any man's face. "This cake—" He pointed at it with his fork. "—is the best I've ever had. But I think you've been having the wrong kind of sex if you think this is better than that."

Andi was really freaking glad her mouth was full just then, because the cake was so good that she was tempted to tell him to prove it. Still, she couldn't stop from grinning like an idiot.

He chuckled, and the deep rumble of it was as appealing as though laugh lines around his eyes. This man was funny and kind and thoughtful and obviously well-liked by a lot of people. Those laugh lines revealed a man who laughed a lot. And yet, *I'm mostly okay...*

It made her want to keep him laughing. "If you say so."

He winked. "Oh, I do, Miranda."

Her belly flipped, but she let the words fly anyway. "You seem very sure of this, Mr. Locke."

His gaze narrowed and scanned over her face. Lower. And she felt it like it'd been a physical caress. "You really wanna tease me, Teach?" She was just about to reply when his cell phone went off. He glanced at it where it lay besides his drink cup on the table. "Oh, that's Slider. Mind if I take it?"

"No, of course not." Maybe the man would have some news about her car. Like how many thousands of dollars it was going to cost her to repair it.

"Hey, man," Jagger said. And then, as Andi watched, Jagger's expression made a slow slide from easy-going to concerned to angry. It was like watching a storm roll in across the horizon, and for some reason it made Andi's stomach sink. Those dark eyes flashed at her from across the table. "I'm sorry, Andi. Gimme a sec?"

"Sure," she said, watching as he slid out of the booth and stalked through the place and out the front door.

Andi set down her fork, her appetite suddenly gone. She had no reason to think that call had anything to do with her, except her gut seemed a hundred percent sure it did.

CHAPTER 4

"There's no doubt about it, Miranda's brake lines were cut." Slider's voice came down the line, repeating the news that was currently whipping up the rage Jagger had been carrying around all these months until he felt like a bomb waiting to explode.

"So that's why she couldn't stop in time. It didn't have anything to do with the damn rain." Jagger looked both ways down the street in front of Dutch's, his instincts suddenly on high alert.

"Agree. How do you want to handle this?"

Jagger raked a hand through his hair. "Fuck. I should probably bring her back over there so she can see what's going on. And maybe we called Martin? She should file a report."

"Sounds right. See you soon, then?"

"Yeah." They disconnected, and Jagger heaved a deep breath. He regretted like hell that he had to give her this news—and he really fucking hated what it meant.

Miranda was in danger.

Forcing another breath that didn't quite manage to calm him, he went back inside and laid his credit card on the counter. "Can I go ahead and pay, Haven?" With one look at him, Haven clocked that something was wrong, so Jagger worked harder to school his expression. Andi needed to know, but he didn't need to go out of his way to scare her when she found out.

After he'd paid, he slid back into their booth.

Andi was so fucking gorgeous—he'd always thought so. But now here she was, spending the day with him, smiling at him, flirting with him, and wearing one of his favorite fucking shirts.

"Are you okay?" she asked, those big blue eyes so filled with concern. For him. When she was the one in trouble.

"I'm fine, but I have some, uh, troubling news." He glanced around at the nearby tables of other diners. "I'm sorry to cut our meal off early, but I'd prefer to tell you outside if that's okay with you?"

"Uh, sure. Of course." He followed her out of the restaurant and down the street to his truck. He stuck close to her side, his central nervous system primed to react to the smallest threat. When they were in the truck again, she turned to him. "It's about my car, isn't it? How expensive is it going to be?"

Fuck, if it was just about money, that would be good news compared to this. "It is about your car, Andi. The accident…it didn't happen because of the rain. Somebody cut your brake lines."

Her whole face screwed up in confusion, and then her eyes went wide. "What?"

"Yeah," he said, his gut knotted up for her. "I'd like to take you back over to Slider's shop so he can show us what's going on, and then I think you need to file a police report."

"Why would someone…*Who* would even…?" She shook her head, her hand lightly rubbing against her chest. "I'm stunned."

"Those questions are why we need Sergeant Martin. Is it okay with you if I have one of the Frederick sheriffs meet us over there?"

"Of course, yeah, that makes sense." The expression on the pretty face was filled with equal parts worry and confusion. "Thank you."

The gratitude was like a knife to the gut. Because he hadn't yet done anything to make this situation better for her. But he was going to. Whatever it took.

Jagger made the call, and the sheriff who was most friendly toward the Ravens agreed to meet them in thirty. Tension filled the truck's cab on the short ride back across town, and Jagger couldn't resist offering her at least a little comfort. He reached across the bench seat and took her hand. "We'll figure this out, okay?"

She blinked at him. "We'll?"

"Damn straight."

"Okay," she whispered, glancing down to where his hand lay atop hers. He thought maybe he'd overstepped in touching her, but then she flipped her hand over and laced her fingers with his. Her thumb played with the black band he wore on his. "Thank you."

"Don't thank me until I've made sure you're safe. And I will, Miranda. I fucking promise."

She swallowed hard, then looked over at him again. "Why? Why would you want to go out of your way for me?"

He took the turn into Slider's garage a little faster than he should've, but he needed her to know. Once he'd killed the engine, he turned to her and looked her eye to eye. "Because it's the right thing to do. Because you go out of your way for people like me all the time. And because I think it's pretty damn obvious that I like you."

"I…I like you, too." She gave him the sweetest little smile.

Intense masculine satisfaction flowed through his veins, escalating the protectiveness he already felt toward her. "Whatever you need, remember?" She nodded. "Okay, then."

He came around to find her climbing out, so he gave her a hand—and she used it to step down and come right into his arms. 'I know you said not to thank you, but I would be freaking all the way out if you weren't here."

Jagger wrapped his arms around her and reveled in the feel of her against him. Her face against his chest, her hands clutching his back, all of her soft curves against all of his rough edges. That moment right there might've been the best he'd felt in almost the entire past year, but he couldn't take any satisfaction in it when it'd come about because she was in harm's way.

Who the fuck would want to hurt her?

Just the question had his hackles way the hell up.

"I got you," he whispered against her hair.

She nodded and then looked up at him, her eyes an absolutely brilliant blue. Their faces close, the world seemed to narrow down around them. Until it was just the two of them. In a place where this problem and the way they'd first met and even the rain didn't exist. It was just them and the fucking intense desire suddenly lancing through his blood.

Her gaze dropped to his mouth, and that was all the invitation he needed.

Jagger kissed her. A soft claiming that quickly flashed hot. One hand around the small of her back and the other in her hair, he drew her closer as he deepened the kiss. She met him kiss for kiss, her tongue intertwining with his as he took his first sweet taste of her. The little moans she unleashed went right to his dick. Fuck, he wished this was happening amid different circumstances. For her sake.

He took her face in his hands and withdrew, swallowing hard as he reined himself in. "Let's get you in out of the rain."

He searched for regret or discomfort in her eyes, but he didn't find either. Instead, her gaze was steady and warm as she looked at him. "Okay."

Jagger took her hand and led her in, satisfied as hell when she smiled at him for doing it. He hadn't even debated it, though. Touching her felt right way down deep.

Slider's expression was as serious as a heart attack when he saw them. "Really damn sorry about this." He nodded to Andi and clasped hands with Jagger.

"It's better to know, I guess," Andi said. "Are you sure they were cut and not just damaged?"

Jagger could read the answer on his brother's face before he said a word. "I'm sure." He walked them over to where the car was up on the hydraulic lift. Sure enough, the cut to the front brake line was too clean—and too fresh—to be the result of a crack or a leak. And the rear brake line appeared punctured, which might've allowed her some braking ability when she'd first started out or at slower speeds, but that would've released all the pressure in the system so that when she hit higher speeds, they'd fail, too. "And it wasn't just the regular brakes either. The cable to the emergency brake has been cut, too."

"Sonofabitch," Jagger bit out.

Andi's face went pale. "Holy shit. Who would do this? And why? I'm nobody."

Jagger's gut clenched at her characterization. She wasn't nobody. Not to him and not to a lot of other people, too. The thought raised goosebumps all down his neck. "You're not nobody, Andi. Not by a long shot. But you do work in a prison, which means you interact with people every day who might think they have a reason to be upset with you. A bad grade or getting thrown out of class or feeling like you dissed them somehow." For as well-liked as she was, no one was going to be liked by everyone. Add to that reality the fact that she was fucking beautiful, and who knew what kinds of reasons someone would concoct to do something like this to her.

Her jaw dropped. "You really think it's because of my job?"

"I think it's a possibility. That's all." He put his arm around her shoulders. "Come here."

She turned into his embrace. Jagger felt Slider's surprised gaze on them, but he ignored it for the time being.

A jingling bell out in the waiting room indicated someone had arrived. Jagger turned to find Sergeant Henry Martin take off his sheriff's hat and lean into the service bay. "Hey, can I come in?"

Jagger nodded. "Thanks for coming, Martin." After learning that another of the Frederick sheriffs had been a part of the scheme that'd sent Jagger away, he hated having to have anything to do with any of them. But that feeling wasn't entirely fair to Martin, who'd believed in Jagger's innocence from the beginning and had worked with the Raven Riders to find out who was behind the whole thing. So he trusted this man, even if he had major issues with the rest of his department.

"Of course, Jagger. Happy to help. And you must be Miranda." Martin introduced himself to Andi, his easy-going demeanor helping to put her at ease—or as close as she was going to get in this situation.

Andi recounted exactly what'd happened, and then Slider followed by showing Martin what he'd found. Martin turned to Andi. "Can you think of anyone who would have a grudge against you or want to hurt you?"

The question parked a boulder of regret and anger in Jagger's gut.

She shook her head. "No, not really. I mean, even if it was a disgruntled student, most of them are still in prison."

Martin frowned. "What do you mean?"

"I teach in the correctional education program at the Central Maryland Correctional Facility. Inmates can earn college credits through a collaborative program with Granger College."

Slider's eyes went wide as he realized how Jagger and Miranda knew each other, because of course the man knew where he'd served his time. But Jagger kept his attention on Miranda, especially when a frown settled onto Martin's face.

"You think it's related to that somehow?" Jagger asked him.

"It's hard to say for sure," the man hedged. "But it's definitely an angle to work." He sighed. "The real problem is, figuring out when this happened. And then obtaining proof of who did it. That would require the vandalism to have occurred in a place with security cameras." The sheriff turned to Slider. "How much time do you think might've lapsed between the time of the vandalism and the time her brakes were completely out of commission."

"It happened today," Slider said. No hesitation, no reservation. "When a car brakes, most of its weight is distributed to the front brakes. So even if the puncture in the rear brake line was a natural occurrence and unrelated to this, she wouldn't have been able to drive long or very fast before she would've noticed that it was taking longer to stop or that she didn't have as much control of the car when she hit the brakes." His brother looked at Andi. "Did you notice anything like that?"

"This morning, all my driving was in town, so it was all at lower speeds." Her gaze went distant. "But now that I think about it, I did feel like I had to hit the brakes harder to stop at a light. I remember that now. Last night when I left work, though, I don't remember having any of those problems. And I took Interstate 70 home, so if it'd been cut before then, I wouldn't have been able to stop when I exited the highway, right?"

Slider nodded, and Martin made notes on his pad. "So that establishes a time frame, then. Can you give me a list of the places you went after you left your house this morning along with approximate times of arrival and departure?"

She reconstructed her morning for him, narrowing the possibilities down to a coffee shop, a dry cleaner, the post office, and a guitar store. Jagger was already mentally picturing each of the locations and thinking through the likelihood and location of potential security cameras at each. But then it occurred to him—there was a fifth possible location. Her house.

What if this had been done at her house while she slept?

The possibility sent white-hot ice through Jagger's veins. Until they knew about any possible film evidence, her house wasn't safe. Fuck.

Martin flipped his note pad closed. "I have enough to file a report and open an investigation." He shook his head. "Frederick is small enough that you wouldn't expect this kind of behavior. I'm sorry you're in this situation, Ms. Everly."

"Thanks," she said. "What now? I mean, I know you'll open an investigation, but how long will that take? And what should I do in the meantime?"

"I can't say how long just now," Martin said, "particularly with tomorrow being a Sunday. But I can promise to make it a priority." He nailed Jagger with a stare. A silent promise between the two of them.

Jagger nodded, appreciating the seriousness with which the man was handling this.

Martin turned to Andi again. "In the meantime—"

"We'll keep you safe." Meeting Andi's gaze, Jagger made a promise of his own. One he intended to keep, no matter what.

CHAPTER 5

AND ANDI THOUGHT SHE'D HAD A BAD MORNING...

That was nothing compared with the reality that someone had tried to hurt her. Or even kill her. God, what if she'd hit another car? She could've hurt someone else, too. The thought made her queasy, and she wrapped an arm around her stomach.

Jagger was right by her side, those dark eyes burning with so much concern and determination that it was almost possible to believe that he could keep his promise. Except... "I don't doubt that you'll try, but it's not like you can be with me every minute of the day."

He grasped her gently by the arms and leaned down until he was looking her eye to eye. "That's exactly what I mean. And if there's ever a moment that I can't be there, or you don't want me there, my brothers will be. This is what we do, remember? You have my word."

She rested her forehead against his, seeking out his heat and his comfort and his strength. "I want you there."

"Good," he said. She didn't think she was imagining the satisfaction on his face even if she didn't fully understand why he cared so much. She couldn't deny that she was glad for it, though. Because this was quite possibly the scariest thing that'd ever happened to her.

Still, it was way, way above and beyond. "If you're really sure," she said, not quite able to let go of her doubts. "This is a lot to take on for a stranger, Jagger." Her brain rejected the characterization even as the more rational side of her knew that it was true.

He cupped her face in his hand, and it was a gesture that was as sweet as it was reassuring. He'd said he had her, and in this moment, it felt like he really did. "You don't feel like a stranger to me, Andi. Whatever you need, remember?"

A pang set off inside her chest to hear him say it. Because, somehow, he didn't feel like a stranger to her, either. Not really. And with everything he was doing for her, he deserved to know. "You don't to me, either."

He kissed her. "Good. Hang in there. I need to make a few calls, okay?"

"Okay." She gave him a small smile, and watched as he turned and crossed the shop, his cell phone already at his ear.

The sheriff turned to Slider. "You know you guys can call me any time. Day or night." The men shook hands. "And that goes for you, too, Ms. Everly." He handed her a card.

"Andi, please."

He nodded. "Okay, Andi. You're in good hands here with the Ravens."

"Thanks," she said. The sheriff didn't have to say that, but she was really glad that he did. Especially when she and Jagger arrived at her house and found eight motorcycles in her driveway. A group of Raven Riders stood in a circle chatting and waiting, all of them wearing their club jackets. The insignia on the back of the them depicted a raven sitting on a dagger that went through the eye socket of a skull. If that didn't intimate her anonymous enemy, she didn't know what would. A few of them waved as they pulled in.

Jagger squeezed her hand. "I know this situation isn't okay right now, but it will be okay. And these guys are gonna help." She nodded.

Andi was really glad these men were on her side, because they were a badass wall of muscle and leather with a long tradition of standing up for people who couldn't stand up for themselves. Or at least standing at their side, just as they were doing now for her.

"These are my brothers," Jagger said. "They're up to speed. Everyone, this is Andi."

"Hi," she said, hugging herself. "I can't thank you all enough for being here. This is such a crazy situation."

"Crazy situations are our specialty," said a man with dark hair, a playful grin, and a jagged scar that ran from his eye to his ear. "I'm Phoenix."

"Good to know," she said, appreciating his humor.

"Crazy is *your* specialty, anyway," the blond man next to Phoenix said. She recognized him from being at the garage earlier. "Hey again, Andi. I'm Maverick."

She enjoyed their camaraderie, seeing now why Jagger had described them as a family. Hell, they seemed more like a family than her own since her parents and older brother disapproved of her work so much that it was almost painful to visit them. And God if what'd happened today wouldn't just affirm their views of what she did.

A man with dark hair, ice blue eyes, and tattoos on his throat gave her a nod. He didn't joke around the way the other two had; he just gave her his name. "I'm Caine." She wasn't sure she was going to be able to remember all these names, but she'd definitely remember those unusual and world-weary eyes.

The next man stepped forward. He was tall with longish dark hair and a face that was almost harsh, but his words were kind when he spoke. "I'm Dare. You need anything, don't hesitate to ask. We'll get you through this." His patch indicated that he was the club's president.

"Oh, Haven's Dare?" she asked, remembering Haven that mentioned the name earlier. A few of the men immediately started laughing and hassling him, and Andi felt terrible for saying the wrong thing. Dare flipped them all off, unleashing another round of laughter. "I'm sorry."

He shook his head. "Don't be. I am one hundred percent Haven's, and these guys are all assholes."

She grinned, and the rest of them introduced themselves in turn. Ike, Meat, Bandit, and Tank, whose size matched his name. Andi felt like she'd maybe fallen through a rabbit hole into a new world.

"Pretty much just say 'hey you' and any of them will answer," Jagger said at her side.

Andi chuckled, and it didn't escape her notice that the other guys seemed interested in how attentive Jagger was being towards her. She was interested in it, too. And liking it. At least not everything in this new reality was bad. Not bad at all.

"So, what's the plan?" she asked Jagger.

Caine was the one who spoke. "We'll do a sweep of the house, set up some security systems for you, and keep a few guys here at all times until this is resolved."

Wow. Andi didn't know what to say, so she simply handed over her keys and let the Ravens do their thing.

Inside, she showed everyone around, and then she went to the kitchen and got drinks and snacks to set out. Food never hurt anything, she figured, and anyway, keeping herself busy would give her something else to think about. And the guys seemed to appreciate her efforts as they grabbed handfuls of pretzels or chips and cans of soda as they did what they had to do.

Which included reinforcing the locks on the basement door of her little rancher, adding window sensors, and installing motion-triggered lights in the front and rear of her house.

"Cameras focused on all the exterior doors?" Phoenix asked Caine.

The man nodded. "I also want one pointed down at the street. Let's see if we have anyone driving by with any sort of regularity."

The thought raced shivers down Andi's neck.

But all the while, Jagger stayed at her side. "They're pros at this. You're in good hands," he said, echoing Sergeant Martin and coming up behind her as she stood at the kitchen counter refilling one of the snack bowls. His hands settled on her hips, and somehow in the midst of the whirlwind of activity and despite some unnamed threat, arousal flooded through Andi's body.

"I know I am," she said, peering over her shoulder at him. Those dark eyes blazed at her. This time, she was the one to initiate the kiss. She turned in his arms, and he pinned her against the counter. And suddenly she wanted nothing more than to lose herself in this man. In any way. In every way. The rest of the world be damned.

Jagger's fingers raked into her hair as his tongue tasted her. She felt the penetration as if it'd happened elsewhere on her body, which explained why she got wet from his kiss alone. "Jagger," she rasped.

He pulled back from the kiss and nailed her with a stare. "What, baby?"

This whole day had her coming apart at the seams. The accident, the puppy, the flirting, the fear, the feeling that being with this man was so damn right. Maybe it didn't make sense, but that didn't make it any less true. "I need you."

"Fuck." He claimed her mouth again, his cock hardening against her belly, driving her need harder, hotter. "You can have me. Any way you want."

She was a wound-up mess by the time the Ravens cleared out another half an hour later. Outside, motorcycles revved like thunder in the night, so loud that her windows vibrated. And then they all rolled out.

Jagger closed the front door and turned to her. "Caine's gonna surveil the house from a distance so nothing seems out of the ordinary if someone comes by who's been keeping an eye on the place. He pulled my truck into your garage."

Andi nodded. "But you're staying?"

He looked her up and down, his dark-eyed gaze absolutely on fire. "I'm staying." And then he was stalking across the room to her and getting right up in her space. Right where she wanted him to be. "You still need me?"

Her breath was shaky when she released it—not from nerves, but from anticipation. "More than I've ever needed anything in my life."

She wasn't sure whether he moved first or she did, but they were suddenly all over each other. His mouth claiming hers. Her hands shoving off his jacket while his hands went to the button on her jeans. She went for his shirt next, forcing them to break the kiss as he helped work it over his head. And holy wow, Jagger was lean and hard-bodied, rugged and masculine, and inked in too many ways and places for her to track just then. They stumbled backward toward the hall kissing and touching and moaning, and leaving a trail of clothing in their wake.

By the time they stumbled into her bedroom, they were both bare to the waist, both of their jeans hanging open. Jagger only parted from her long enough to close the blinds, which was the first time she saw the enormous tattoo of the Raven Riders' insignia on his back. It moved with his muscles, as if the raven was alive and watching her. And then Jagger paused and looked at her from across the room. "God, you're fucking beautiful."

She pushed her jeans over her hips and stepped out of them, leaving her in a pair of black boy shorts and nothing else. "You make me feel beautiful when you look at me like that."

"Like what?" He closed the distance between them slowly, purposefully, like he was the predator and she was the prey.

A thrill raced over her skin. "Like you want to devour me."

And then he was right there, running his lips up her neck as his palms settled on her ass. "And what if I do?" he rasped into her ear.

"It would be exactly what I want, too."

"Jesus, woman, you're like a dream," he said before his mouth slanted over hers again. His fingers slipped under her boy shorts until he was pushing them down her thighs. And then he went to his knees and peered up at her. "I want my mouth on you."

Nodding, Andi gasped as this big strong man grabbed her by the hips and buried his face against the juncture of her thighs. The first stroke of his tongue against her clit made her cry out his name, but he didn't give her a second to get used to the feel of him. Pushing her stance wider, he ate her like he was *starving*. His fingers dug into her hips and ass. His tongue licked and penetrated. His mouth sucked until the room spun around her. Andi was moaning and gasping and trembling as sensation gathered and tightened low in her belly. She braced a hand in his hair, and when he groaned his approval, she tightened her grip and urged him on, pressing his head more firmly against her. Understanding what she needed, he went at her hard, sucking and flicking at her clit as if commanding her to come.

She did. God help her, she hadn't ever come so hard in her entire life. Andi screamed his name until the orgasm stole her breath, and then her whole body trembled under the force of her release. Her knees went soft, but Jagger caught her. Of course, he did. Just like he'd been doing all day.

He lowered her into his lap and kissed her like his mouth hadn't yet had its fill. And Andi wasn't complaining. Not one damn bit.

"So fucking beautiful, baby. You come for me so good."

"I want you to come for me," she said, her voice breathy and soft.

"Yeah? Don't you worry about that. Because we're just getting started."

JAGGER LOOKED at this gorgeous woman in his lap, cheeks flush from the orgasm he'd wrung out of her with his mouth, smiling at him like he was somehow worthy of everything she was giving him. Maybe he could be worthy if he kept his promise to her. And, damnit, he would do everything he could.

And what he was going to do right now was give her the pleasure she needed to make it through the rest of this day and forget that something was looming somewhere out there in the darkness.

He lifted the both of them to their feet and held her until she was steady, and then he toed out of his boots. Fishing a condom out of his wallet, he winked at her before he dropped his jeans and bared himself.

Andi's gaze was heavy lidded and hot as she drank him in, and it made his cock even harder. "Fuck, baby, the way you're looking at me."

"I want you inside me, Jagger."

Her words drew him to her again. "How do you want me?"

"There's no way I don't want you," she said with a sexy smile.

But he wanted her to say what she wanted from him, what she *needed* from him. "How do you want me *now*?"

She licked her lips and let the words fly. "Bend me over the bed."

"Yeah? Fuck, yeah." He kissed her and walked her to the bed, and then bent her over the bottom corner of it. The position spread her legs for him, laying her out so fucking perfectly. He made quick work of the condom, and then he was lining himself up with her opening and sinking deep.

Both of them groaned at the sweet fucking intensity of it.

"Christ, you're perfect," he rasped as he got deeper and deeper until she'd taken him all. "Jesus, baby, feel that."

"God, Jagger, it's so good." Her words were filled with a desperation that went right to his balls.

He started to move in her then, his body exploring hers, his senses hyper-focused on her sounds and movements and reactions. He wanted to ring every ounce of pleasure out of this moment for her. Coming down on top of her, he braced a hand by her shoulder and kissed her neck. "What do you need to come again?" he asked, his hips working on a slow grind in and out of her.

"Harder," she whispered. "Harder everywhere."

The words turned his blood molten as he gave her what she needed. His hips slapped against her ass on deep, punctuated thrusts. His hand went to her hair and gathered up a thick fistful that he used to pull her head up so he could kiss her. Just once. His thrusts were too fast now for them to hold the kiss, so he released her hair and braced his weight against her lower back, holding her down right where he wanted her.

"Harder?" he growled.

"Yes," she cried. "Yes."

"Put your hand between your legs for me."

When she did, he gave her what she asked for. The force of his thrust moved the bed, but he couldn't care when she moaned his name in that pleasure-drenched way. So he gave her his hardness again. And again. Until she was babbling and moaning and rocking her hips against her hand and his dick. His orgasm was barreling down on him, a freight train he wasn't going to outrun, but he wanted her to get there first. He wanted to feel her coming all over his cock.

On the next stroke, he brought his hand down on her ass.

Andi's whole body arched up off the bed and her body clamped down on his. "Jagger! Oh God!"

"There it fucking is," he gritted out as her muscles fisted around his dick so tight he nearly saw stars. And then there was no holding back his own orgasm, especially when she scissored her fingers around where he was gliding in and out of her. "Jesus fuck, Miranda, I'm coming in you, baby. I'm coming so fucking hard." His whole body jerked as the orgasm wracked through him, leaving him wrecked and boneless and more goddamned sated than he'd ever felt in his life.

Their panting breaths were the only sounds in the room—

Except that wasn't true, was it?

Because for the first time in nearly a year, he heard music in his head. The rhythm was set to the beat of Andi's heart that he could near where his head rested against her back. Runs were inspired by the wild curls of her hair spilling all down her arm. Something in a major chord with a fucking hopeful feeling to it.

But even though she'd given him back the miraculous gift of his music, his hands didn't itch for a guitar like they usually did when his mind filled with inspiration. Because he had the flesh-and-blood inspiration in his hands. And she'd given him every reason to hope that he'd get his music back after all. Back for good.

"You're fucking amazing, Miranda," he said as he eased off of her. "Are you okay?"

She crawled further onto the bed and rolled onto her side. "That was... wow...way better than that cake."

Jagger laughed. He threw his head back and laughed like he hadn't done for *months*. Andi laughed, too, and fuck if the music of it didn't light him up inside.

He disposed of the condom in the trash can and then he came to her and crouched down at the side of her bed. "Hi."

"Hi." She grasped one of his hands and played with his rings. He wore matte black bands on his thumb and middle finger on his left hand, and on his pointer and ring finger on his right. Each one had a slightly different shape. "These are sexy," she said. He'd worn them so long he barely paid them any mind anymore, but now he was never fucking taking them off.

Jagger grinned. "Yeah? Not half so sexy as you laying there looking so damn satisfied."

Andi smiled. "Your fault."

"Baby, I'll take the blame for that any damn time."

"Stay with me," she whispered, those blue eyes filling with a different kind of need now.

The words and that need grabbed ahold of his heart. Just reached right on into his chest and grabbed on tight. "Just try to get rid of me." He winked.

And it made her smile again. Fuck, that was happiness right there, knowing something he did could make a woman like Andi light up.

They made quick work of turning off the lights and using the bathroom, and then they crawled into bed together still naked. Jagger opened his arm and Andi pressed up against him, her face against his neck, her arm over his chest, her thigh across both of his. And fuck if Jagger didn't feel claimed by the way she held him. She might not have meant it that way, but it was clear his body wanted her to.

Fuck.

There was so much to figure out, and not just between them. There was this faceless threat out there somewhere, coming for what was his. And nothing was certain as long as that was true. But, goddamnit, it was possible they'd never find out who tried to hurt her. And what then?

"I'm so grateful for today, Jagger," she whispered against his neck.

His gut clenched. No, he had to find the sonofabitch. He had to keep Andi safe. "I told you, don't thank me until we know you're safe."

She shook her head. "I don't mean that. I mean I'm grateful for *you*. For getting to know you, for getting to be with you like this."

He pulled her tighter against him, like something might take away this incredible thing they'd somehow found. Just let them fucking try. "Aw, baby. I'm in deep in this with you. And I feel the same damn way."

Andi peered up at him. "The rest we'll figure out?" she asked.

He kissed her, hoping like hell he wasn't making a promise he couldn't keep. Because, Christ, he'd die trying. "Yeah, baby, you better fucking believe it."

Read the Raven Riders Series:

Hard As Steel
Ride Hard
Ride Rough
Ride Wild
Ride Dirty
Ride Deep

Connect With Laura

WEBSITE: http://www.LauraKayeAuthor.com

CREED AND Mia

USA TODAY BESTSELLING AUTHOR
M. ROBINSON

CHAPTER 1

MIA

"YOUR HUSBAND IS SUCH A BARBARIAN," CAMILA, DR. AIDEN PIERCE'S WIFE, who became a part of the family, teased over the phone.

"Yeah… he's always been that way. It's actually one of the things I love the most about him. Creed doesn't care who you are or what you think about him, he's going to be an asshole to you regardless."

She laughed on the other end as I finished up cooking dinner. Mixing in the enchilada sauce the way she'd advised.

"Harley Jameson never stood a chance," I added, shaking my head. Thinking about all the times my husband guarded our fifteen-year-old daughter, like it was his sole purpose to ruin her life.

Just last week they were going back and forth about her wanting to wear a pink bikini.

"But, Daddy… every girl is wearin' two-piece bathin' suits."

He took one look at the bikini in her hands before he snatched it away.

"That's just a fuckin' string!"

"You're ruinin' my life!"

"Creed, come on she's—"

With one look, he rendered me speechless, but that didn't stop Harley.

"It's called a string bikini for a reason!"

"Which is why you ain't fuckin' wearin' it!"

To think, how I thought my father and brothers were bad when I was growing up. They weren't anywhere near the level of overprotective Creed was with our only daughter.

"Does he know Harley has Cash over?"

"Umm… not exactly."

"So, you lied?"

"Of course not."

"So, Creed knows?"

"Hell no!"

She busted out laughing.

Creed had left me no choice. Harley would be turning sixteen soon, and as soon as she started socializing with other kids, he turned into a rabid dog.

Cash McGraw was the son of one of the Good Ol' Boys. Detective Dylan McGraw's son to be exact. They'd known each other since the day they were born, but of course, Creed didn't give two shits about that. Let's be real, the kid could have been the Pope's son, and it still wouldn't have mattered to Mr. Overprotective.

No one was good enough for his baby girl.

Not one single boy.

We had to hide her boyfriends, her guy friends, her study partners, exactly how we were doing right now. Anything or anyone that pertained to the opposite sex was hidden from her father, or else he'd threaten to "break his fuckin' legs." His words not mine.

The sad thing was…

I wasn't exaggerating.

Creed may no longer have been a 1% biker, but that didn't detour who he was raised to be.

His nature.

His blood.

It ran deep in his veins.

He was all outlaw.

Not to mention, her Uncle Noah Jameson, Creed's younger brother. Together, they were a force to be reckoned with. Never allowing boys to come near Harley.

Ever.

"Where are Harley and Cash now?"

"In the living room, on the couch studying."

"That's probably safe if Creed comes home. As opposed to her bedroom."

"He never comes home before the sun goes down. His shop is his second woman," I half-joked, referring to his motorcycle business located in downtown South Port. He owned and ran it along with his brother and a few other MC boys. Business was booming to say the least.

Creed's knowledge of motorcycles had him booked out for months. He prided himself on providing for his family. Our kids—Harley, Luke, and Owen—didn't want for anything. Creed made sure of it.

He was the best daddy. Nothing like his old man was.

Between the shop, home life, and his End of the Road MC, Creed never had a moment of rest. He preferred it that way though, staying busy kept him out of trouble.

"How's Jackson?" I asked, referring to her oldest stepson, Jackson Pierce.

Otherwise known as Harley's arch nemesis.

They'd hated each other since the first time they laid eyes on one another. Who could out prank the other was a running theme between the two of them. Through the years, they'd put us through the ringer.

From Jackson putting gum in Harley's hair, to Harley kicking him in the nuts, to God knows what else. They had no limits. There were no boundaries between them. Constantly battling each other any way they could think of.

I still remember Skyler showing me the surveillance from the nanny cam at the Pierce residence of when he'd put gum in her hair a few years back.

"Hey, Harley, you have something in your hair," Jackson told her.

"I do?"

"Mmm hmm."

"Where?"

"Right here."

Seconds later, an ear-piercing shriek vibrated off the speakers of her phone.

"Jackson Pierce! You put gum in my hair!"

"No, that's what was in your hair."

"You're such a liar!"

"Relax, it's just gum."

"I'm going to have to cut my hair now!"

"Maybe it will make your face look better."

She gasped. "There is nothing wrong with my face!"

"Yeah, if you're into ugly girls."

"I am not ugly!"

"Says who, your parents? They're supposed to say stuff like that."

Harley gasped again before screaming, "I hate you!"

"Yeah, well, it's mutual. Here, I'll help you cut your hair."

"Get away from me!"

It took me hours to get the gum out of her hair with peanut butter. That wasn't even the worst of it. I couldn't begin to tell you how many times we'd grounded Harley up to this point, but it never mattered. I swear it just gave her more time to come up with her next retaliation on him.

Although, it always fell upon me to discipline her when it came to Jackson, Creed didn't bat an eye. If anything…

He was proud as fuck of her.

Where do you think she learned how to kick him in the balls?

My husband was like having a fourth child. However, I loved him with every last part of my soul. He was mine.

Past.

Present.

Forever.

Before she could reply, Harley hollered, "Mom!"

"Give me a second, honey!"

"But, Mom I need ya now!"

"Alright, Camila, I gotta go."

"Me too. The boys just got home. Talk soon."

"Bye." I hung up.

"MOM!"

"Oh my God, Harley!" I shouted in response, walking down the hall toward the living room. "Why all the screaming?"

"Cuz you said dad wasn't comin' home till later tonight! We'd be safe from him, so we could study!"

I rounded the corner, coming into the living room, "He isn't, honey. You're safe from your dad," I expressed, stopping dead in my tracks when I saw him sitting there.

Cocky.

Pissed.

Looking all Creed like with his cut on, Glock showing, with a snide grin and intoxicating eyes…

Glaring directly at me.

Our intense stares locked. He didn't hesitate, speaking with conviction, calling me by his nickname for me since I was nine years old.

"You ain't, Pippin."

CHAPTER 2

CREED

Mia Jameson.

Mia 'fuckin' Jameson.

Even after all these years, she was still a pain in my fuckin' ass.

Except now, I had two fuckin' hurricanes destroying everything in their fuckin' path in the form of my old lady and my baby girl.

Mia's eyes went wide, looking fuckin' beautiful. "Oh, shit," she muttered.

"My thoughts exactly," I snarled, shifting my glare over to the teenage motherfucker sitting next to my baby.

"Dad…" Harley coaxed in an uneasy tone. "Be nice…"

"I'm always nice."

"Daddy, we're just studyin'. Look." She held up her Advanced Geometry book.

I didn't waver, eyeing only Cash McGraw with my hand over my gun. "Even your old man's badge won't protect you from me, boy."

"Creed!" Mia reprimanded.

"Sir, I'd never hurt Harley," Cash contended for what felt like the hundredth time. "She's my best friend."

"Her momma was my best friend too, but that didn't stop me from makin' her mine. Did it?"

"It ain't like that between us."

"Better stay that way, boy. Your dick goes near her, I'll shoot it the fuck off."

"Dad!"

Mia grabbed ahold of Harley and Cash's arms. "Why don't you guys head to the library on your bikes? Here's some money."

"But, Mom—"

"Do you see your father's face? Go, now."

She grumbled, "Cash, let's go before my daddy chops your balls off."

"Harley!"

"What?" She shrugged, pointing to me. "That's what he says. I'm just repeatin' Daddy's words."

Damn fuckin' straight she was.

Mia shook her head, but I didn't pay her any mind. I was too busy plotting McGraw's boy's death.

For some reason that I couldn't fuckin' fathom, the Good Ol' Boys thought their kids were fair game for my baby girl. Like they could all be friends, and without consequences if they so much as looked at her in the wrong way.

Don't get me wrong, we were all on good terms, so long as their boys kept their dick in their pants. Cash could see it in my eyes, I wasn't fuckin' around. I wouldn't think twice about putting him to ground.

As soon as Mia walked back into the room, after shoving them out the door, I stated, "My cock ain't gonna suck itself, sweetheart."

Her mouth dropped open.

"Now get on your knees and show me how sorry you are."

"You arrogant asshole!"

"Not gonna say it again, Pippin. You're up to no good, yeah?"

"No," she sternly stated, looking me straight in the eyes.

"Think ya can lie to me? Think I wouldn't have fuckin' found out? Walk me through your thought process, babe. Please, fuckin' enlighten me."

"I'm not talking to you when you're like this," she replied, shaking her head. Crossing her arms over her chest, causing her tits to pop out at the seams of her yellow summer dress.

My cock twitched at the sight of her.

"I didn't lie to you."

"Ya didn't exactly tell me the truth either. Not gonna ask again, Mia. Did you think I wouldn't have found out?"

She sighed, knowing I wasn't going to let up until I got a straight answer.

"What am I supposed to do? You remember how I was raised, right? Of course, you do. You're the guy my parents tried to keep me away from, remember?"

"You of all people can understand my protection over Harley. I don't want her fallin' in love wit' a motherfucker like me. Ya feel me?"

"Creed, the more you shelter her, the more she's going to want to rebel. *Ya feel me?"*

"No, but I will."

"What's that supposed to mean?"

Before the last word even left her mouth, I was in her face. Gripping onto her ass, hard.

"Ow! Creed!"

In two seconds flat, I was lifting her up my body, wrapping her legs around my waist.

"Now, do ya feel me?" I patronized, rocking her hips against my bulge. "Don't got anythin' to sass at me, do ya? Not when your pussy is dry fuckin' my cock."

She swallowed hard, waiting for my next move.

"Yeah... that's what I fuckin' thought," I added, backing her into the wall.

I was over this fuckin' bullshit. These little punk ass kids trying to piss on my territory. I needed to shut that shit down really fucking quick. Ain't gonna happen.

Not now.

Not ever.

"I protect Harley's guy friends from you."

"Is that right?"

"Yeah, that's right."

"Then who's gonna protect you from me?"

"I don't need protection from you, Creed Jameson."

"Is that right?" I repeated, mirroring her loving stare.

"Yeah, I'm your girl. Been your girl for as long as I can remember."

"No, sweetheart, you're my old lady. Who's bein' a pain in my fuckin' ass. Let me handle my business, Mia."

"Stop bossing me around."

"Stop fussin' like you don't want me to. We both know how wet this is makin' your silk fuckin' panties," I mocked, smacking her ass for good measure.

"You're such an asshole!" She tried to push me away, but I didn't move an inch.

"Babe, we both know... if I want in, I'm gettin' in."

I smiled, cocking my head to the side. Getting closer to her face, I started kissing my way from the corner of her lips, down to her chin and neck. Working my way toward her tits that were just as eager for my touch.

She unconsciously moaned, unable to help it. It's what I always did to her.

Made her wet.

Come.

Love me.

"I should spank your ass raw for this stunt you pulled," I growled. Never once letting up on my sweet torture of rocking my hard cock against her pussy. "Who do ya think you're fuckin' wit', Pippin? I know everythin', especially when it comes to my property."

"Your property, huh?"

Hiking her a little higher, I unzipped my jeans and stroked my cock.

I always loved her this way…

At my mercy.

Since the first time I claimed her on my motorcycle when she was Harley's age.

I straddled my bike with Mia now on my lap, yanking her closer, molding us into one person and kissing her as if my life depended on it. She moaned into my mouth. I groaned into hers as I fisted her hair by the nook of her neck. My other hand glided down the side of her breast to the seam of her panties.

"Please," she begged against my lips.

I roughly jerked her hair back to look into my eyes. Fighting an internal battle, she wanted to win so fucking bad.

She rocked her hips, pleading with me through her lust-filled glare.

Baiting me.

Tempting me.

Doing whatever she could for me to touch her. When she felt my fingers slide her panties over, gliding them into her pussy.

She swallowed hard.

"Fuck, you're so wet. I did this to you. Me," I growled, continuing to work her clit.

She leaned into kiss me again, but I pulled her hair back harder, wanting her to stay right where I wanted her, spread wide open for me.

"Feels good, yeah?" I raspingly taunted.

"Yes…"

"Here?" I provoked, pushing harder against her g-spot. "Come on my fingers, Mia. Wanna feel your tight, sweet fuckin' pussy."

Her body erupted in a fit of spasms, her eyes rolled to the back of her head and her breathing hitched. Panting out my fuckin' name. I pulled her close, kissing her.

"Eyes on me," I demanded.

She opened her hooded gaze, trying to catch her bearings.

I took a long, hard look at her and spoke with conviction, "Only I can make you fuckin' come like that. And now I'm gonna make you come on my cock. No more bullshit between us. You want to be kissed, touched, fucked," I groaned against her lips. "Then I fuck you. I'm claimin' you, Pippin. You're fuckin' mine."

"You remember the first time I made you mine?"

"I've always been yours."

And she was.

She always had been.

"I know," I stated, grinning like a fuckin' fool. "Nothin's changed since then… always doin' what you want, never fuckin' listenin' to a word I say. No matter how many damn times I fuckin' tell you, it's always done in Mia's way."

She giggled. "At least I'm consistent."

She pushed me too far over the edge this time. I was going to have my way with her, exactly how I wanted to.

Gliding her panties to the side, I slid the tip of my cock into her warm, welcoming heat.

"Creed, I love you."

"I bet you do, sweetheart."

"Please…"

"Please, what?"

"Forgive me for being a bad girl."

In one hard thrust, I slammed my cock into her pussy. "Fuck…" I groaned in a low, rumbling tone. "How you always feel this fuckin' good?"

Seconds later, I was thrusting in and out of her in a slow, tortuous rhythm that had her coming undone. Making it much easier to fuck her the way I wanted. The slapping sound of my balls against her ass cheeks with each hard thrust echoed off the walls.

I leaned forward, brushing her hair to the side of her neck. Giving me access to kiss and lick her overly heated, sensitive skin.

I knew what she liked.

What she loved.

What she craved.

I fuckin' taught her.

"Please…" she shamelessly begged, pleading with me to give her what she wanted.

"Please, yeah? What do ya want? Want me to touch you, here?" I taunted, my fingers rubbing her clit. Leaving nothing but desire in my wake. Purposely trying to drive her fuckin' insane.

"Oh God," she panted, her legs trembling while her cunt gripped onto my dick like a goddamn vice.

"Please… please… don't stop… please…"

And right when she was about to explode like a fuckin' volcano, I pulled out.

Dropping her ass down to the ground.

My balls throbbed and my cock ached to be back inside her, but that wasn't the point in this sudden lesson.

I grinned, gazing down at her while she peered up at me through dark, hooded eyes.

"This is bullshit!"

"No, what's bullshit is you lyin' to me 'bout my baby girl."

"*Our* baby girl."

"If you ever wanna come again, don't fuckin' try me. Ya feel me?"

MEANING EVERY LAST WORD.

Connect with M. Robinson

WEBSITE: http://Www.authormrobinson.com

No Man's LAND

MARIALISA DEMORA

INTRODUCTION

Members of the Incoherent MC are no strangers to the pull and tug of disagreements with other clubs in their territory. But waking awash in the bloody aftermath of war's opening salvo wasn't typical.

After the slaughter of Hitch's brothers, he has two goals.

One, keep breathing long enough to avenge them.

Two, learn all there is to know about the angel who saved his life.

Talia had successfully wedged her way into the fringes of her brother Ewell's motorcycle club despite his attempts to keep her out. Her EMT skills come into play more often than she'd like, and when the IMC, a friendly rival club, asks the Jailbreakers MC for a favor, Ewell—and Talia—can't turn them down. Even if the aftermath means Talia could be drawn into the maelstrom of war between clubs.

CHAPTER 1

I BLINKED UP AT A FLAT SURFACE HOVERING OVERHEAD. IT TOOK A MINUTE, BUT I decided it was a ceiling, dotted with tiny flecks of crimson. I watched in idle fascination as a fly crept closer and closer to one of the largest spots. Clearing my throat, I tried to swallow, not finding enough spit in my mouth. A painfully dry click echoed through my head, sounding frighteningly close to the slide of a gun cocking. I squinted as the fly broached the edge of that circle of red, no doubt drinking his buggy fill of my life's blood.

Another attempt to clear my throat was no more successful than the first, but the resulting pain in my middle was new. My eyes squeezed shut when I choked, having to brutally smother an urge to cough, already dreading whatever my next move needed to be.

My lungs ached with the longing to suck in a big ole breath, but every attempt fell short, slashed into shreds and leaving me panting. That pain slipped away, like the backwash of a wave, and I relaxed into the easy numbness it left behind, forgetting there was always another wave.

It came roaring back with a vengeance, tightening my muscles until I was sure my bones would break. Rolling over me, churning me into pieces, wedging itself between all the bits of me, the pain separated my mind from my body, and I groaned at the release. The echoing sound did more to map my surroundings than my eyes had done.

It was a large and open space. Flat out on the floor, I tried to lift my arm. Heavier than anything I expected, it twitched, a promising movement accompanied by an odd rustling. I tried again and managed to lift my hand from where it had been sprawled next to my body. My palm landed on my belly, and I had a frozen instant of terror when all I felt was fabric, but then I slid my fingers farther across and encountered that familiar stiff resistance that could only be leather.

No matter what else happened, this discovery left me giddy, because if I died right here and now, it'd be in my goddamned cut.

An attempt to lift my head sent me soaring, so dizzy and lightheaded I was floating without a tether. The clunk of my skull hitting the hard floor drove me back into myself, the pain taking up so much room it wasn't clear how I'd keep it company in my skin. The next try was more successful. Eventually, I had my chin buried against my chest, gaze roaming what I could see of the room.

Alone.

Door open.

Everywhere I looked was draped in plastic, and on that plastic were drying splashes and sheets of red.

Something jutted from my side, and I spider-walked my hand across my body until I could grip whatever it was, wanting to fling it away. That proved impossible, and just the attempt woke the pain monster, so I struggled to simply pull it free. Extending my arm to its limit finally gained my objective, and I stared at the foot-long blade in disbelief before my hand spasmed and the dagger clattered to the floor.

Motors roaring outside abruptly expanded my awareness, and I listened intently, hearing the barest hint of voices over the rumbling of exhaust and engines. Gradually all sounds diminished, moving off into the distance in staggered groups of noise until silence reigned.

I looked at the ceiling, noticing the fly had been joined by dozens of its family and friends.

The muscles in my neck gave way in fits and jerks until my head rested on the cold plastic again.

My eyes closed, and in that comforting darkness, I finally found relief.

THE BUZZING WAS LOUDER when I gained consciousness again. Hundreds of clusters of those damn flies were everywhere. Since I was still breathing and determined to vacate this hellhole, I wedged my elbows underneath me and pushed up, gravity nearly winning the battle when my head swung loosely on my neck, dipping backwards towards the floor for long enough to give me an upside-down view of something I hadn't expected and never wanted to see. Three bodies lay behind me, stacked neatly into a row next to the wall, each rolled in a shroud of clear plastic, faces distorted and gray.

Still I knew them.

My brothers.

Trammer, who'd grown up at my mom's table, seated side by side with me for most meals. His father was a waste of space, and his mother'd gotten hooked on dope our junior year.

Graceless, the man who'd taught me the full meaning of the saying that accidents wait for audiences. I'd helped him pick his bike up more than anyone else I knew.

Had known. *Fuck.*

Pizzaboy, who'd so wanted to be called Donatello—and us being the fucktards we were, we hadn't given him that moniker. Instead, we'd labeled him after his favorite food.

Such was the nature of our lives where names were given, not taken, and being a brother meant so much more than blood.

I flipped to the side, or attempted to, managing a slow roll. My blood-saturated clothing unstuck from the plastic with an obscene sucking sound. My side ached like a bitch, but the crippling pain seemed to have packed its bags and vamoosed. *Thank God.* If I could just get to my feet, I'd be set.

There was no noise other than the flies and crinkling of the plastic. No voices. No traffic near or in the distance. Just me, and three bodies wrapped for a delivery I was gonna do my damnedest to derail.

I surveyed the room, baffled why I wasn't in the same shape as them. This much blood meant I lay in what my brothers had spilled, along with what had seeped out of me from that pigsticker.

On hands and knees, I wobbled for a moment, swaying backwards and forwards like a windblown tube man in front of a pop-up pawn store. If anyone came through the door, any fighting I tried would be about as effective as those arm-waving freaks. Finally overbalancing in the direction where I aimed, I rocked back onto my heels, pushing upright. I looked down my torso at the blood and rips in my shirt and realized I'd be lucky if I found only the one hole in me.

With the hilt of the blade in my hand, I considered the length and heft of it, finally taking a moment to slide the tip between the leather of my belt and my jeans, seating the handle snug against my hip. As long as I didn't fall down and stab myself on it, it'd be good to have a weapon. I could already tell the holster at my back was empty, as was the one under my arm, and my boots were too light to still be hiding my knives. Running bare had never suited me, not since I found the truth behind club wars and desperate assholes unconcerned with family or innocent victims.

I studied the plastic-wrapped bodies, a chill pebbling my skin as I realized they'd been similarly stripped, but while I still wore my vest, theirs were gone.

Music played abruptly, as if it had woken up midsong and was determined to see the tune to its end. I jerked so hard I nearly fell over. It cycled through the few notes again, then fell silent. Somewhere close by was a phone, and if I could find it and it was one of ours, I could make a call that would start the wheels of rescue, recovery, and revenge. Club officers were keyed to all authorized devices, and with the tap of a finger, I'd reach salvation.

The phone helpfully played that damn song again; it was coming through the open door. I hadn't made it to my feet before the sound died away, and perched wavering on one knee, I could have screamed at the damned silence. Finally vertical, I staggered to the doorway and clung to the wood like a leech, trying to remain upright while the world swung in wide circuits.

The same do-do do-do-do-do music ricocheted through my head, and I zeroed in on the location before turning loose of the doorframe. A saddlebag lay on the floor, propped next to a battered dining room table in the center of the room. Black leather poked out of it. After a year of staggering through the open space between me and it, I stumbled to a stop next to the table. I kept my hand flat on the wooden surface in an attempt to stay upright, unsure I'd make it back on my feet if I went down again. Digging through the vests, I did my best to ignore the patches and names, titles and regions—each a memory shared with one of the bodies growing cold in the other room—until I found the device.

The music started again. The screen said *Kate Calling,* and my eyes closed. That was Trammer's ole lady. I declined the call, used my thumbprint to unlock the phone, and dialed from memory.

Until Rampage answered, I hadn't realized the pounding in my head was from holding my breath. "Tram," he said, his voice free and easy, ready to joke and shoot the shit with a brother. "What the fuck you need, man? I got a case'a suds and a screen, and there's a damn game on, which means I got my feet up while I swear at the TV."

"Ram." I startled, pain blooming in my side. I didn't recognize my own voice, rough and hoarse, like death had camped out in my throat. "Ram."

"The fuck?" Background sound on his end of the call muted, and he asked, "Tram? What's up, brother?" I didn't answer him. Couldn't while the eagerness—the raw need in his voice to help, however it was needed, throttled my words. "Trammer, where the fuck are you, man?"

"Tram—" I swallowed and tried again. "Trammer's dead. Graceless and Pizzaboy, too. Ram, I been stabbed. I don't—" The room swung in a slow circle, and when I closed my eyes, it sped up, with me as a focal point while it whirled. "I'm not—"

"Where?" He was begging, and I knew all I had to do was give him a direction, tell him a location, suss out an address, and he'd be here. No questions asked. That's what true brothers did. When I stayed silent, he tried again. "What's happened?" I struggled to answer, my mouth dry as dust, tongue stuck to the back of my teeth. "Who's this? Who's got Tram's phone?"

"Hitch." I finally named myself, and that settled me in a weird way. If I could say my own name, if I could speak that truth, I could do the rest that he needed. "Hitch. Ram, we're... I don't know. It's a house or something. In the—" I was about to say woods, but I didn't know anything other than the room where I'd woken and this table. I stared at the windows across the front of the building, seeing green globes of trees, but not woods. "In a grove. I can't hear anything."

"Where's Tram?"

I wished my voice would fail again. Wished my words would dry up and drift away, because to speak it aloud would make it true. "Dead."

"Fuck."

Even if he couldn't see me, I nodded in agreement, gagging when the movement set the room to swaying again.

"Look at the map on Tram's phone, see if you can figure out where you are." The sound quality had grown an echo. "You're on speaker, my old lady's walking out now. You can say what you need. I'm gonna rally the boys, and we'll come, Hitch. Swear on my grave, we'll come."

With that inauspicious phrasing ringing in my ears, I fumbled the device, fingers determined to send it plunging to the hard floor until I wrestled them into submission, dropping it only an inch onto the table. The clatter must have been louder to Rampage, and he yelled, "What's happening?"

"Nothing," I tried to say, but the absurdity rolled over me, and I chunked out a laugh, carving it into pieces until it fell apart on the air. "Dropped the phone. I'm—" I poked the screen with a fingertip, putting Rampage on speaker and then opening the correct app on only the second try. A big green dot pulsed in the center of a swath of darker green, and I maneuvered the map until it pulled back, showing more green, finally broken on the north edge by a red line. "Highway...uh. State highway. A road. Meridian. I'm—" I made the map slide from side to side until I found a wide blue line. "I'm west of the interstate, just south of Meridian." Frustrated, I poked around until the map finally gave up the most useful information. "I'm here. We're here at Stone McCauley Groves." The place was smack in the middle of unclaimed territory, and we'd always called it "No Man's Land."

"On our way." Rampage must have realized how reluctant I was to sever this lifeline. "I got the boys, and we're comin', Hitch. We're comin'."

"Hurry." Voice roughened with anger and pain, I tried to urge him, only I was speaking to dead air.

I'D FIRST BECOME aware of the Incoherent Motorcycle Club when Trammer and I were in high school. We'd been hanging around the local drive-in, ogling the flirty waitresses flitting around on roller skates, when the ground under our feet literally began to shake. Within moments, it was as if a mob of motorcycles had swarmed the parking lot, unmitigated chaos to my eyes. The men had parked their bikes, dismounted, and slung arms around the women who'd ridden in with them. While my mind had insisted there'd been hundreds of bikes, only ten men sauntered underneath the overhang and claimed two of the picnic tables.

Trammer, named after a suburb in faraway Michigan where he'd lived as a child, leaned across our table, only three down from the black-leather-clad bikers, and hissed excitedly. "Did you see?" He rolled his eyes towards the bikers, then back to me. "So cool, man."

I lifted my chin and grunted, my disinterest entirely affected. Someone sat heavily beside me, and I turned to see Karen crowding close, her long legs folded awkwardly underneath the table. A girl who I sometimes dated, she rolled the wheels on her skates back and forth, and nervously laughed.

"Mikey, would you take their order for me?"

Michael Hitchcock was me, Mike to my friends, Mikey to Karen and only allowed because I'd boned her. I'd not yet earned Hitch as a nickname but had tried it out on mirror-me once or twice. I liked it so far.

"Mr. Thomas said I've got to wait on them 'cause it was my turn when they came in."

"Why don't you?" Trammer curled his lip at Karen. "Too good for 'em?"

"No." She huffed. "I just… They scare me, okay?"

I cut a glance over to the tables and caught the eye of one of the men. He nodded at me, and smiled, then turned back to give the red-headed woman perched on his knee a different kind of smile.

"Sure, I'll do it." I pushed up from the table and snagged her ticket book. "You sit here and try not to kill anybody."

Trammer and Karen weren't each other's biggest fans, Trammer certain she was trying to get between us and being all "bros before hos" about it. Karen said

Trammer wanted in her pants, which was certainly true. He'd fuck anything standing still. "Be right back."

As I neared the tables, I became acutely aware of the differences between me—high school cool in my half-laced sneaks and tight, ripped jeans, a faded graphic-tee sagging around my too-thin shoulders—and the men seated on the table and benches. Each wore what was undoubtedly a uniform of sorts. They were dressed in dark jeans made of thick fabric for hard use, scuffed black leather boots, shirts of varying colors, most with a distinctive shield proclaiming their devotion to a brand of motorcycle, and a black leather vest. Whether snapped in the front, held together with swinging chains, or draping along their sides, each proudly bore a fabric patch in the center of their back.

"Hey," I offered, coming to a stop about three feet away. "Do you know what you want?"

One man at the far table—the only one without a woman on his knee—scoffed far back in his throat. "Wanted that pretty chickie to come be my sidepiece for the day." The men around him laughed, women ducking their chins and tittering. Others took up the idea, and I heard other, more indecent suggestions about how Karen could service them.

The third time I heard, "She could suck my cock, too," Karen's ticket book crumpled in my fist.

The man seated nearest where I stood never took his eyes off me as he barked out, "Shut it." I tried to hold his gaze, but the weight of it was massive, as if there was a repellant force causing my eyes to dip. "Boy, she means something to you, ain't no shame in steppin' up and dealin' with assholes disrespecting your girl." The other men had stopped talking when he ordered them, and silence was thick around the tables now. "She don't, and you're just painfully unaware of the ways of men and women, that's a different kind of lesson I ain't up for teachin' today."

I cut my eyes up and found his face. Not smiling, not scowling, he looked open and somehow confused.

"She's my girlfriend." I shrugged. "I'm here because you scared her, without her even talking to you. Now…" I tried to mimic the scoff the other man made, the sound coming out weak and frightened. I winced. "Now I understand why."

"She suck your cock?" The original speaker opened his mouth wide, waggling his tongue obscenely. "I could teach her if she don't."

The leader—I took him to be that with how they'd quieted a moment ago—looked at me with a "what now" expression. Tearing my gaze from him, I fixed the other one with a stare I hoped could pierce through his ignorance, and told him clearly, "Shut up. What happens between me and her isn't your business. Now, do you want food or not?"

"Oh, boy's got some nads, Twisted." The instigator hadn't taken offense at my declaration and seemed somehow pleased. "Might wanna get his name, see if he grows into 'em over the next couple of years."

Twisted, evidently the leader, grinned broadly. "Might do that, Catfish. Might do." He angled his body and looked at the men around him, getting a nod from each before he turned back to face me. "What's your name, boy?"

I stared at him, my brain considering and discarding all options before I told him the truth. "I'm Hitch."

That had been ten years ago. I'd been a member of the Incoherent MC for eight, an officer for four.

ENGINES AND VOICES startled me awake, and I grunted as my back arched against the hard surface I was lying on. I was immediately convinced that whoever had started this tango was back to end the dance. I'd pulled the sticker from my belt when I'd assumed this position on the table, and the handle was clasped in my grip as I fought through the pain to sit.

Facing the door, I stayed where I was, mostly because I wasn't certain my legs would bear my weight. Those half breaths had my ribs gnawing at my sides, begging to be stretched and strained, promising to make me buckle with pain. Woozy, I pulled my hand from around my middle where it was holding me together and thudded it against the table to keep from falling on my face.

Words and sounds buzzed as unintelligibly as the flies until I heard one voice clearly and knew who spoke.

"If Hitch said Trammer was dead, same for Graceless and Pizzaboy, and he's alive to make a call, I'm not standing around here with my thumb up my ass while you decide what you want to do." Catfish was our VP, and even after everything that had gone down the first time I met him, had been my sponsor to get my chance to prospect for the club. I trusted him as much as I did Trammer, which meant with my life.

"Here." The intended shout was weaker than I expected, so I pulled in another half breath that burned all the way down and pushed it back out on a yell. "I'm here."

Bootheels thudded against packed dirt, then cement, and then they were bursting through the door. Rampage came straight to me. Hands on my shoulders, he swept me up and down, then spoke over his shoulder, "Wave Dyno in, then call and tell him no need to dispatch the second van." He shook his head when he looked at me, brows pulling down in a dark scowl. "He's ambulatory, at least."

"You gonna poke me with that, brother?" When Catfish took the blade, I realized I'd been pointing it towards the door, and unintentionally directly at him. "Lemme have it a minute, yeah? I'll just hold it for ya."

"No, man. They left that in me." I tried for humor as I gestured towards my side, even knowing it'd fall flat. "I'm attached to it now."

Catfish plucked my shirt free from where it'd dried stuck to my skin, and I heard a rip followed by cool air that raised the hair on my arms. "Fuck, man. There's definitely a hole ain't supposed to be there."

My chuckle turned into a cough that threatened to rip my guts out.

Rampage asked, "Anything else, Hitch?"

I shook my head, more an "I don't know" than a "nope," and he understood, giving me a quick going-over. His fingers discovered two tender places on my head, one with a knot big enough to make him *tsk* far back in his throat. Another hole in one arm, something he deemed a through-and-through shot, so I guessed at least a fair amount of the blood I wore was my own.

The other men had fanned out through the structure, and I knew when they found the abattoir, the shouts and curses louder before dying off as the gravity of what had happened here struck each of my brothers.

"Where's Rags?" My words came out in fits and starts, syllables strung together by threads of pain as Rampage and Catfish braced me, my arms over their shoulders. They lifted and let me find my balance, feet flat on the floor instead of toes dragging behind. *I'll thank them later.*

Rags, or Ragman, was our president, a leader like no other. A man who'd been through enough shitty times between drug cartel invasions and club wars to know how best to avoid them in today's club climate. Until he wasn't present, I didn't know how much I'd hoped to see him. If Ragman was here—or Twisted, our national president, and the first man in my life to tell it like it was—I'd know in my bloody gut everything'd be okay.

"Workin' the horn." Catfish dipped to the side, and when he came back up, I saw he'd grabbed the bag with our brothers' vests. "We got nothin' in the air on this shit goin' down, and once we had a lock on your location, Dyno activated the drones and saw the locale, including the lack of company." He angled his neck, face turned to me. "Thought we'd have to handcuff Rags or some shit. Finally convinced him to call national." That was his way of tellin' me Ragman's absence wasn't anything to do with me. "Three of our own dead, our enforcer bleedin' out—he's got to sort this shit now."

Multiple exhausts sounded in the distance, and I swallowed. If my brothers were in here with me, there was only one truth of who could be headed in. "Think you can give me back the sticker? Or better yet, dig through there"—I dipped my head toward the bag in Catfish's hand—"and find my iron?"

Strangely calm, he tightened his arm around my shoulders and steadied me against his side. "Nah, brother," he said with a twist of his lips. "Listen."

I did.

Ride of the Valkyries.

"Fuck me."

He nodded. "Dyno. We made him stay back at the highway with half the men. He's got the eyes in the sky on his phone, so we waved him in a few minutes ago."

Dyno was our tech guru, and he had a thing for some Coppola war movie made in the previous century. The flick had featured Wagner's epic song in a crucial scene, and he was prone to blasting it when we rode to war.

Within a minute, the room was filled with a wall of flesh willing to stand between me and whatever might come. Men who followed the code of brotherhood, believing a man was only as good as his word and wrongs were best righted with might. My brothers, members of the Big Bend chapter of the Incoherent MC. Our clubhouse was outside Tallahassee, and our territory stretched for miles along the Gulf Coast. Men I trusted, could count on, and all of which were, at this moment, pissed as fuck about what had happened to me, Trammer, Graceless, and Pizzaboy.

DYNO CAME DIRECTLY TO ME, brows drawn into a deep frown. He held a tablet aimed in my direction and spoke to the air, either recording or streaming. "Fucking hell, Hitch might be on his feet, but our boy ain't lookin' good."

I closed my eyes when I heard the voices of two men who weren't present, telling me Dyno was facilitating a video conference with the leaders of our club.

Ragman's hissed, "Jesus," was overridden by Twisted's demand, "Tell me what the fuck went down, Hitch."

Since I'd woken the first time, coming to surrounded by blood and death, I'd been piecing everything together, knowing the first chance I had to tell it would need to be accurate and as articulate as possible.

"We were at Hot Lips."

A bar owned by the wife of a retired biker from the frozen north, Hot Lips was the local hangout for our club. Houlihan was her official name, but her old man, Hawk, still called her Hot Lips often. He'd been president of the North Chicago chapter of the Rebel Wayfarers MC, moving to Florida when it was time to fly the icy coop. He wore support patches for the RWMC, us, and the Jailbreakers. No conflict there, since our clubs were tightly twined together these days with both blood ties and patchovers.

"Graceless got a call someone broke into his ole lady's car."

We'd been seated at a booth, discussing an upcoming poker run, when his phone rang. I'd heard every shrill word and had winced on his behalf at how scared she'd sounded. I'd exchanged a glance with Trammer, dug out my wallet, and dropped bills on the table, ready to roll at my brother's back in an instant. That's just what we did.

"She works at that place out on Pommel, the booze warehouse."

We'd rolled up loud and proud, no hiding who we were or why we were there. Our bikes had surrounded her car, which had been pushed up close to the back of the building. It had been turned sideways between two columns and wasn't just broken into—it had been trashed, windows shattered and hood caved in.

"We thought we heard her call out from inside the loading docks."

We'd dismounted, listening to Graceless cussing and shouting at the cost, the waste, the ignorance of it all. The pain in her voice had taken us off guard, and the three of them had rushed inside without utilizing any caution, no matter how I shouted. My role in the club meant I knew better, and my inability to control my brothers had led directly to their deaths.

Dyno stared at me over the tablet, understanding dawning in his expression.

"It happened fast. I didn't really see anything. Darkness and blurs. When I came to, I was here. From there to then, nothin'." I stiffened my spine, pushing upright and taking my weight off Catfish's and Rampage's shoulders. I wished I could see Twisted and Ragman's faces, wished I could know if they blamed me like I did myself. Wished for clear knowledge of what had happened. "I take responsibility." A jerk of my head woke the pain in my middle, and it coiled like a snake about to strike. "It's on me."

"Unless you held the blade and gun, our brothers' deaths ain't on you. Ambush like that? Wouldn't have mattered what you said or did once you were in their noose. Do not take that shit on, brother." Twisted's voice was flat, filled with certainty, and told me he'd brook no argument. "I got a lead on some shit. Ragman, I'ma be rollin' that way in five. Catfish, you and Ram get Hitch to the Jailbreakers house in Adkins, man. They're gonna help get him patched up. If at all possible, I want him ready to rock and roll when Rags and I get there, you get me?" Ram grunted his agreement. His outline was wavering, the edges of his face blurring.

Twisted's voice echoed through the room, a surreal soundtrack to my loss. "We got you, brother. Be there soon."

After a final look at the room where I should have died, I turned my back on the shack and leaned heavily on my brothers as we walked into the hot Florida sunshine.

The van ride lasted for at least a hundred excruciating days. Not only was the suspension way past needing work, and jounced around at the least provocation, but the cargo laid out in front of me meant I spent the time in dark contemplation. Side by side, shoulder to shoulder, my brothers were stretched across the width of the vehicle, heels towards the back doors. We'd left them in the plastic shrouds, figuring it was the cleanest way to transport them.

We weren't preserving evidence for the officials. No need. I didn't worry about how the details would be sorted out; we had enough cops in our pocket that it'd happen however Twisted and Rags wanted it.

What we were damned sure doing was preserving their dignity, same as we'd do for any fallen brother.

I couldn't tear my gaze away from Trammer. I tortured myself imagining his last minutes. Picturing what my mother's face would look like when I told her he was dead. He had a woman and a little girl, and their coming life's weight of grief bore down on me.

Pickle, one of the men who'd ridden in the van, spoke from over my head, "We'll get 'em."

"Yeah," I gritted out, fingers sliding as I pressed against the bleeding wound in my side. "Yeah, we will."

IMC was a club used to violence. We didn't deal it in regularly, but we wouldn't shy away when necessary. From the looks on my brothers' faces back at the grove shack, I wouldn't be running alone when I tracked down the bastards who'd spilled my blood and taken the breath from our brothers.

The next bouncing jar nearly shattered my control. The pain was like a fishhook lodged deep inside my chest, anchored in the bedrock of agony and rage. I'd already decided I'd try to not let them sideline me, no matter the consensus on my injuries. Rampage had bandaged my arm before I'd loaded myself into the van, but I hadn't let him take my cut off to do more. Call me superstitious, but it seemed like retaining it and the breath in my body had to be connected. In my own mind, I'd vowed to not remove it until everything was done and whoever had killed my brothers shared their fate.

As the van slowed, Dyno called out from behind the wheel, "Bump, brother." I gritted my teeth through the series of suspension-yawing potholes with only a muffled grunt. "Sorry, man," Dyno muttered as Pickle's hand landed on my shoulder. His fingers wrapped in the leather and helped keep me upright as the van lurched around a final corner and rocked to a stop.

The back doors opened, and Rampage stood there with Catfish, lines of grief etching their features. Unfamiliar faces crowded behind them, men's gazes cataloging the contents of the van with muttered curses. One man pushed up beside Catfish. Gaze fixed on the bodies, he thrust out his hand towards Catfish and offered us welcome. "Be welcome, IMC. Ain't gonna lie and say it's good to see you guys. Sucks the reason." His nameplate declared him Sparks, and under that, an officer's plate titled him President, obviously of the Jailbreakers. I hadn't much contact with them officially, just a few members here and there. Seemed like good men. They were all about the brotherhood and making life better for their members. From what I heard, they followed protocol, and that went a long way to keeping a club from straying too far from its stated mission or motto.

Catfish took his wrist and gripped, their shake going up and down twice before releasing. "Appreciated, man."

"Twisted done called and gave me the rundown. We got a couple of rooms set up with what we thought you'd need." He lifted his chin to me, and I returned the gesture. "If you wanna climb out that side door, we got an EMT ready for you. You're Hitch, right?" I dipped my head in a brief nod. "Yeah, let's get you situated. Then we'll give honor to your men."

The door beside me opened, and Rampage was there. Determined to not show weakness in front of strangers, I took a moment to convince my body to move, and after I slung my legs over the edge, it was an easy transition to standing. Not so easy to keep that position, but thankfully Ram was there to keep me from taking a header. *Fuck.* A swath of blood smeared from where I'd been propped against the back of the front seat to the door—could have only come from me.

"Ram," I said on a grunt. I waited for his muttered response and acknowledged, "I might need some help."

"No shit, Sherlock." His arm slipped under mine, shoulder wedging me upright.

Pickle was on the other side, and it took everything in me to manage it, but I put one foot in front of the other until we got to the back of the van. They paused when I did, and I turned my head to stare at Sparks.

"All respect." That was as close to thanks as I would get when talking to an officer of another club, not wanting any chance of obligating my brothers for anything.

He lifted his chin again and responded, "No worries."

The pain was so bad my head hung low by the time Ram and Pickle got me to the door of the Jailbreakers clubhouse, a single-story ranch-style building that had been added to on both sides, creating wide wings. There were dozens of bikes in the front lot, and from the cooling ticks coming from the engines, I deduced most were ours, which meant Jailbreakers probably had a parking lot out back for their own bikes.

Together, Ram and Pickle lifted me over the threshold and into cool dimness. Walls had been taken out in places, making the space stretch across a good length of the building. It was furnished with couches and chairs, a small bar in one corner, and three TVs mounted to the walls. It was also filled with men and women and children, which told me the Jailbreakers had gone on lockdown, and the fact they still took us in meant a lot. We'd probably be stretching their hospitality thin.

If the Jailbreakers were on lockdown with families in play, that meant — "Graceless. His ole lady? Is Dottie—"

Pickle's head went side to side, and Rampage made a pained sound. "Fuck."

I'd sat at their table for many a meal, her softly scolding Roger, Graceless' government name, about his manners. Dottie was a sweet woman who worked hard and loved the club nearly as much as her ole man had.

"Where'd they leave her?" I hadn't seen her at the shack. Only two rooms and both mapped easily even in my state. No way I would have missed seeing her if she were there.

"Tow driver called it in about thirty minutes ago. He was picking up an abandoned car and found her in the back seat. No doubt they did her after they got what they really wanted." I couldn't tear my gaze away from Pickle's clear pain. "From what was said, it was quick at least."

Sometimes a body had to take comfort in the small things.

Rampage asked the room, "Know where the EMT's at?"

Two men pointed towards a hallway, and one said, "Second door on the left."

That short pause had settled into my bones, and it turned out starting walking a second time was so much harder than the first. My heavy head dragged at my neck, and I watched my boots stumbling and twisting underneath me until I was walking on air, leather of my soles never striking the floor as my brothers took my weight, lifting me up.

The room swirled, corners coming close and receding in turn until I was disoriented. A high bed stood central to the space, and along the walls were cabinets with sinks and drawers. It looked like a clinic, and that struck me funny.

I heard Pickle's muttered question, "What's he laughing at?"

"No idea. He's been in and out of it since we got there." Ears buzzing, I nearly missed his next words as the bed came up to meet my back. "It's a goddamned miracle he made it."

My gaze stuck on a dark spot on the faraway ceiling, a fleck, a speck, a tiny dot of something that grew until it swallowed me whole.

CHAPTER 2

TALIA

WHEN TALIA'S BROTHER HAD FIRST CALLED, SHE'D BEEN ANNOYED AT BEING woken in the middle of the afternoon. Working third shift on the ambulance meant her days only held the most restless of slumber, and she had been chasing a sweet dream before the jangle of his ringtone dragged her back to consciousness. They had a texting relationship, and she knew he wouldn't dial unless it was dire, so she'd shoved that irritation down and answered.

Three minutes later, she'd dashed water in her face and shoved her feet into utility boots on her way out the door.

Ewell had launched his MC years ago, needing to surround himself with strong men with morals. Their neighborhood growing up hadn't been the best, and he'd wandered down a bleak path for a very long time, finally dragging his life out of the darkness by strength of will. The club provided the framework to be the man he should have always been, and he saw it as a chance to give others the same opportunity.

They were the Jailbreakers, and their name didn't refer to any bent towards busting brothers out of jail but focused on tearing down the prisons men made for themselves. The learned behaviors that conspired to send them behind bars again and again. If Ewell, known as Sparks to his men, could put a stop to the cycle, he could keep more men free—like him.

As a male-dominated club, they'd had their fair share of altercations. When she'd gained enough knowledge from her studies to be useful, Ewell started calling her for help as needed. For a long time, she had gotten more practice stitching up his men than the pig feet the medical school issued. She gained her EMT license, ready to work the rest of her way through school. With the club's frequent need for assistance, she'd been doubly glad for the breadth of knowledge since.

As the club had grown, so had the scope of the altercations, until they no longer had one-on-one fights but club versus club. Ewell and his men knew outing her as their medical professional would scrap her license and ruin her professional plans, so they were careful to keep Talia hidden from all but the most trusted of their friends. Seeing how Ewell had developed into a mentor for his men, maturing in ways she hadn't thought possible, she'd do anything for the club.

After arriving at the clubhouse today, she'd laid out supplies based on threadbare information. Male victim—*duh, it's always the men*—gunshot and stabbed. Talia'd been making coffee when the unmistakable sound of women and children trickled in from the front rooms. Having family at the compound wasn't unheard of since the Jailbreakers were family oriented, but with her being called in too, this was unusual enough to note.

When a mass of motorcycles had roared up, she'd watched through the window as a van had driven into view and immediately been surrounded by Ewell and his men. More men in black leather vests crowded around, all bearing the patch of the Incoherent MC, another club with roots in the area. *What in the world?* The back doors opened, and she'd gasped. There were six boots in view, three pair, toes up, all unmoving.

Ewell greeted one of the men, and there was a muted mumble through the glass of the window as they briefly discussed something; then the van shifted and moved. A moment later, three men came around the side. The two on either side of the one who was clearly her patient held him upright, and he seemed barely conscious until he stopped next to Ewell. His head lifted and he said something.

He was gorgeous. Dark brown hair hung down either side of his face, and the apparent pain he was in made his brows gather together. With widely spaced dark eyes framed by cut cheekbones, and the added enhancement of a trimmed beard a shade darker than his hair, this man was everything any woman could want. His surge of energy faded as the moment ended, and his helpers started towards the front of the house.

When she rounded the corner to the hallway by the treatment room, she pushed past the men crowded around the door to the place she thought of as hers, shoving between them without apology. They were between her and the patient, and all she could think of was what she'd already heard and seen.

Women and children in the clubhouse unexpectedly.

Three dead men.

For some unknown reason, a friendly but rival club had brought those men here to her brother.

One of theirs was walking wounded, a man who, despite his clear pain and exhaustion, paused to pay respects to Ewell.

It all added up to something very bad going down, and she and her brother's club were right in the middle of it.

Talia

INSIDE THE TREATMENT ROOM, the men positioned the injured man on the table as she pulled on gloves. *My patient.* He was out, which she decided to count as a boon. From the amount of blood soaking his clothing, she wanted him as calm and peaceful as possible.

"What happened?" Prepared for the need to cut his clothes off for treatment, Talia approached the table with scissors in hand and was surprised to find them plucked from her grip. Whirling to glare at the man who held them overhead, she snapped, "What the hell do you think you're doing?"

"His cut stays on." He gave her nothing more than that, and she let her gaze drop to the man's nameplate.

"Pickle?" He nodded. Without looking, she pointed at the man on the table behind her. "You want me to help him?" Pickle's mouth pulled to the side, but he nodded. "Then you got to trust me."

"His cut stays on." Now the other man in the room chimed in, and she tossed a dark glare his direction. "Sister."

Breaking the stare, she lifted a hand and tried to hide her surprise, thumbnail scratching her eyebrow. She knew from Ewell what this man had just called her was as much an honorific as ma'am. Pulling in a deep breath, she rolled her lips and shook her head, huffing air out her nose.

"You're already on my last nerve." There was a chuckle from the doorway, where Ewell parted the crowd and walked in. Ignoring the men who were frustrating her, she barked out, "They won't let me treat him. Why did you call me here if I'm not going to be allowed to do my job?"

"Sparks." Pickle addressed her brother, and she knew she'd lost any ground she might have gained. *Men.* "His cut stays on."

"Then his cut stays on." Ewell slipped an arm around Talia's waist and tugged her sideways for a hug. "But you get the fuck out of my sister's way and let her do her goddamned job."

Pickle shoved the scissors her direction, and she yanked them from his hand with her own version of a biker's scowl. Turning back to the table,

Talia was once again struck by how handsome the man lying there was. But he was also pale, tinged with gray, and she knew she had to get to work.

One arm of his shirt had been ripped wide, with a makeshift bandage placed around the bicep. The hidden wound seemed to be the source of much of the blood soaking his clothing. Upon closer visual inspection, she saw a smaller tear in the fabric along his side, also surrounded by a decent amount of blood.

The second IMC member crowded close, and Talia flicked her hair back with a huff, glaring at him. This man, Rampage by his nameplate, gave her a concise rundown she didn't expect, ratcheting up her opinion of him by about a dozen notches.

"Upper arm is a GSW, through and through. He's got a stab wound in the abdominal upper-left quadrant by what appeared to be a ten-inch double-edged blade, removed before we arrived on scene. He's presenting with tenderness on that side, but there's also significant contusions indicative of blunt force trauma. Closed head injury with one distinct subdural hematoma and a secondary smaller one, both without palpable skull fractures. Respiration, pulse, both within normal range. Nominal confusion, but he's been in and out. Pupils normal and reactive, when he's got his peepers open." Rampage paused a beat then said, "If you'll pass me the scissors, I'll get his shirt off under his cut so you can look at his side."

Wordlessly, Talia handed them over, then ignored him working on the other side of the patient while she untangled the knots holding the strips of fabric in place on his arm. They worked together like that as she cleaned the hole bored through the flesh of the patient's arm before using tidy stitches to close the wound.

She had just finished bandaging the arm, about ready to move to the stab wound, when the man groaned and his eyes flickered, lashes fluttering against his cheeks. She bent over him with her hand on his other shoulder, prepared to hold him in place if he woke up combative. His eyes opened halfway, sleepy and unfocused, and so dark blue it was as if a piece of the evening sky had fallen there. Up this close, the dark hair at his temples was springy, curling in Florida's ever-present humidity. His gaze latched onto her, and Talia forgot to breathe. Even in this state, his stare was powerful. One corner of his mouth curved up, and he blinked languidly, as if nothing was going on, as if he hadn't been beaten, shot, and stabbed and wasn't still bleeding on her table.

"An angel," he murmured, and a weight landed on the back of her neck. His hand curved around and pulled down, down, down, until her lips brushed his. Gentle and soft, more a yearning caress than a kiss—still the electricity that sizzled through her was raw and powerful. Then he relaxed, losing consciousness again, eyes drifting closed as his hand fell away.

"God damn you, Hitch," Rampage muttered as she straightened. Talia turned to look at him, startled. He offered a wink, mouth twisted in a fake pout. "Even half dead as he is, he finds the prettiest woman in the room to hit on."

She rolled her eyes. "Whatever." *Men.*

He ducked his head, and she turned back to Hitch—her patient.

Hitch

VOICES FADED IN AND OUT. Whispers and murmurs, rough rumbling conversations that hovered on the edges of my mind. I was dreaming, but it felt so real, and I knew in my gut I was safe.

"Without imaging, I can't know for sure what kind of internal damage has been done." The woman's words were stark and spare, no discernable accent, but that was the norm for this stretch of Florida with such an influx of people from all over. Finding a true Floridian was rare.

There was the tiniest catch in her voice when she said, "The trajectory means it's likely low enough to have missed his kidney, spleen, pancreas, and stomach, but unless you let me take him to the hospital, we can't rule out bowel involvement."

Uh, nope. Not happening. They couldn't take me to a hospital, not without causing a whole lot of trouble. Even if I went on my own, given who I was and the club I claimed as my home, there'd be questions, an investigation, and the last thing any man like me wanted to do was invite the po-po all up in our shit.

My eyes wouldn't behave, staying stubbornly closed against all my attempts to pry them open. Same with my lips, those damned traitorous bastards.

A touch against the side of my face jolted me, the cool glide of a hand up and over my brow, then down along my cheek. The contact felt so good I wanted to lean into it, make it stay. There was a dusting of a caress across my lips that stroked my memory.

There'd been a woman. So goddamned beautiful, leaning over me. Dark hair twisted into a ponytail over one shoulder, she'd stared into me with her gorgeous brown eyes, sinking so deep I knew she'd seen the dark stains on my soul.

I'd kissed her. Kissed her and felt a connection that yet pulled at a space in my chest I'd thought forever empty.

The sounds became a mumbled buzz before thinning out to nothing.

My last memory was something I held tight to as I slid back into the darkness.

She'd kissed me back.

CHAPTER 3

TALIA

SHE STARED AT EWELL, WORRYING THE EDGE OF HER LIP WITH HER TEETH. HE knew enough to give her a little space so she could think through his request to stay at the clubhouse for the foreseeable future. He'd backed off a couple of steps to have a quiet conversation with two more IMC patch wearers who'd shown up not long ago. One was nondescript, a man who looked like he'd had a hard life but wasn't bitter about it. The other practically oozed danger. It flashed from his eyes when he'd stalked in, owning the room, no matter it belonged to her brother and his club. Bearded, long dark hair tied back into a thick braid, and even clubbed at the end it hung to the middle of his back.

She angled her gaze to where Hit—her *patient* was resting. It had become harder to keep a distance since he'd kissed her, but Talia was determined to be as professional as possible. He grimaced, muttering something unintelligible, and she pressed a hand to his forehead again. Still cool, thank God. Not only had Rampage opposed calling an ambulance—*oh, the irony, since we're both EMTs*—but so had her brother.

"Talia?" Ewell called her name, and three pairs of eyes locked on her. "We need someone to look at the bodies." He glanced at the two men, then back to her. "Please. Twisted"—he gestured towards the dark-haired man, and she stiffened. That name was one everyone who lived on the coast recognized. "He has a guy, but he can't be here for a few hours."

"Yeah." She sighed and was pulling away from the table when a hand grabbed her wrist. With a gasp, she looked down to see Hitch was awake and staring straight at her. It had been hours since she'd finished patching him up, and this was the first attentiveness he'd shown. "Hey—"

He cut her off with a brief shake of his head. His lips moved, but there was no sound.

"What?"

He mouthed something again, and she bent closer only to find she'd been duped when his other hand wrapped around the back of her neck, tugging her down. Bristly cheek pressed to hers, his mouth was beside her ear as he whispered, "Be careful, angel." There was a gentle glide against her cheek that could only be his lips as she pulled away. This time, instead of lapsing directly into unconsciousness, he stared right at her as he struggled to get an arm underneath him. Rampage helped pull him upright, taking the strain off Hitch's arm.

"Twisted." Hitch's voice was clear if raspy, and his gaze left her to go to where Ewell stood with Twisted and the other biker. "Ragman." He swallowed hard and winced. "What do we know?"

"Not here, brother." Hair raised all along her arms. Twisted's intonation was smooth and dark, the sound a deadly ocean undertow would make if given voice. "Not with citizens."

She shook her head. "Sparks." His nose wrinkled when she called his club name, knowing how she disliked using it. With her brother, with their family, there was a story behind everything, and this one could have ended in a different, deadly way. "Where are they?" She couldn't bring herself to say anything else.

Hitch's grip on her wrist tightened, and she flinched, surprised he held her with such strength. His voice was a harsh growl when he said, "I'll go with you." She turned to argue, but he was still staring across the room. "Brothers." Disappointment crossed his face, and he dipped his chin. "Much as I want to be in whatever comes next, I'm a liability right now and know it. Don't delay on me to do what you need to do."

"So noted, my brother. But we got a bit of waitin' to do," Twisted said. "Mayhap you will, mayhap you won't. We'll see when it's time."

"Talia." Ewell's tone was cautioning, but when Hitch pulled on her arm, she didn't resist, stepping closer to where he sat.

Something about the man was intriguing, beyond his looks and that surprising warning. The hours spent at his bedside hadn't been enough. She needed to know more about him. *Moth to a flame.*

"I'm good, Sparks." She let the half smile she'd given her brother slip from her lips before looking at Hitch. "Can you even stand? I'm not going to carry you." She knew her opinion was no threat for whatever he wanted to do and was unsurprised when he didn't answer.

Instead, he flashed her a smile and restated more firmly, "I'm going with you."

She fixed him with the sternest look she could muster. "If you rip my stitches out, I'll be testy."

Her scold earned another grin. Hitch's lips pulled sideways like he wanted to say something but was holding back. *Whatever.*

Her brother would have insisted on the same if it were his friends lying dead. *No use arguing with him.*

The bruising on Hitch's torso was extensive, but he didn't give any indication of pain when he shifted to dangle his legs over the side of the table. Rampage came to his side as Hitch's feet slipped to the floor. He wavered, gripped Ram's shoulder, and grunted once he looked like he was steady on his feet.

Talia found a strange expression of resignation on Ewell's face. She studied him, trying unsuccessfully to determine what it meant.

"Ready." Hitch curled his arm around hers, sandwiching Talia's elbow against his side as they passed the trio standing by the door. Twisted stared at her with a puzzled look, broken when he caught her gaze on him. A brilliant smile split his thick beard. So at odds to the anger and rage still in his eyes, it made Talia press closer to Hitch.

In the hallway, Ram led them deeper into the warren that made up the Jailbreakers clubhouse. Talia had been here often enough to know her way around. She knew where family and non-members were allowed and the places off-limits to anyone but officers. The direction they were headed was one of the latter, and she hemmed and hawed internally before quietly asking, "Are you sure this is where..."

Ram nodded. "Yeah, our men are back here. Earlier, Sparks told me how to find them."

Well then.

"What's your name, angel?" That was Hitch, and Talia found his gaze fixed on her, not where they were walking. "Sparks, the president here, he called you Talia? Is that your name?" She nodded. Something flashed in his eyes, and his jaw tightened as if with pain before he asked, "What's he to you?"

"Are you hurting? This was a bad idea." She tried to stop him, but the stubborn man wouldn't be swayed. "Hitch."

"What is he to you?" His words came out with tiny spaces between, a breath, no more, and it made her look at his face. What she'd taken for pain was anger, which surprised her.

"Sparks?" He nodded, and she tipped her head, unsure what he was truly asking. She decided to give him the truth. "He's... Ewell's my brother."

"Your brother?" His voice was laced with disbelief, so strong she was compelled to reassure him.

"Yeah, Sparks is my big brother." He chuckled, and she echoed it with a nervous laugh. "Why?"

"We're here." Rampage interrupted them as he paused before a wide set of doors.

She'd never noticed before, but the hallways and doors on this side of the clubhouse were all wider than normal for a house. Rampage had walked ahead of them, but if he'd needed to stay beside Hitch, he could have, with ease. Same for the door in front of them. Given she was pretty sure they'd had to carry Hitch inside when they arrived, she understood the reasoning. She didn't like it, but she understood.

Hitch's grip on her arm tightened as Rampage opened the doors.

The smell hit her first.

While the air conditioning had been turned full-blast in a clear effort to delay the inevitable process of death, it couldn't be halted, not in a crude morgue like this. Hitch made a guttural sound, and she sympathized with his distress. The three bodies rested on folding tables in the middle of the room. Talia was glad to see enough space had been left between the tables so she wouldn't have trouble moving around them to conduct her examinations.

She twisted her arm, intent on releasing herself, but found the strength of Hitch's grip unbreakable. He gazed at one of the dead men, expression distant while he stared fixedly at the body.

"Hitch?" His head jerked at her soft call, and his eyes swung to look at her. Wet with unshed tears, they were focused and pained. "I need to—" She didn't finish her explanation before he'd released her, flinging her wrist from him as if the connection burned him. "Are you okay?"

"No, I'm not." The muscles in his throat flexed and bunched as he swallowed hard. "I fuckin' am not. Never be again. Trammer's my brother, see? Those are my brothers, and it hurts like God's fist in my chest. But you got a job to do, and mine is to stay outta your way." He thumbed over his shoulder to the wall where chairs were drawn in a line. "I'll be over there. You need anything..." Hitch hesitated before he reached out and ran the backs of his knuckles down her cheek in a touch that was electric against her skin. "Just say the word, angel."

He made his way to a chair, unsteady on his feet. Hitch sat slowly, the movements carefully guarding his side, and she glanced at the bandage under his cut to find it still a pristine white. He was as well as she could make him, and given the arguments he'd ignored about taking it easy, he'd be as good as he allowed himself to be.

Taking a shallow breath, she turned away and faced those three tables again.

Time to get to work.

Talia

"WHAT?" She startled and sat upright, palm scrubbing across her face as she blinked into Hitch's blue eyes. "Are you okay?"

He smiled, and that expression, plus the heat in his gaze, swirled all through her body, tingles running rampant along every inch of skin. She refused to glance down to see if her nipples were as hard as they felt, but from the attentive interest in Hitch's eyes, he'd already noted her reaction to him. *Every single time.*

"Yeah, Tee. I'm good."

Hitch had started calling her the nickname on the second day. The Jailbreakers were still on what Ewell called a lockdown, which basically meant everyone attached to the club was jammed into the limited number of available rooms. A few of the IMC members had stayed on-site too, including her uncooperative patient.

After their first joint trip up the hallway, he'd accompanied her everywhere he could between long, restful periods of sleep. His stride slow but steady, he'd trailed after her as he kept up his quiet but persistent questioning. Talia had no doubt that Hitch now possessed a full and thorough history of not only her but her family. The man was stubborn, and he was imbued with that certain breed of tough she'd only seen with Ewell and his men. She'd caught her brother watching them now and again, his expression always a mix of amusement and irritation.

Being around Hitch was no hardship, and she'd told herself it helped to keep an eye on her patient. It didn't matter what they were doing, Hitch made it better. Cutting up vegetables for dinner? He'd managed to tell a clean but suggestive story even the kids found amusing. Changing out his bandages? Depending on the audience, his stories were a lot more suggestive, and a lot less clean, but Talia found his crudeness wasn't a turnoff. *Not at all.*

"What do you need, Hitch?" She'd been curled up asleep on a big chair someone had pulled into her treatment room. Something poked her hip when she moved, and she realized it was the key her brother had given her. "How'd you get in?" *I know I locked that door.* She had meds in here, and security was second nature, even with her brother's men.

"It's dinnertime." He moved, and she saw a tray balanced on the exam table. "I brought you something to eat."

"That's sweet."

The door slammed open, rebounding against the wall. Hitch was between her and the door in a smooth movement, and she had to look around him to see Ewell in the doorframe.

"Talia." Ewell held his hand out commandingly. "Come on."

Hitch tightened his fingers around hers, and the tactile connection was the first realization Talia had that she was gripping his hand. She stepped up beside him, stopping when he applied pressure in his grip against the movement. Ewell and Hitch were locked into a staring contest.

"Hitch brought me some food." Hitch's fingers squeezed hers in response to her words. "Did you need me, Ewell?"

After another long, uncomfortable moment of silence between the two men, Ewell said, "Don't fuck up."

"Wha—"

"I won't." Hitch had cut her off with his answer.

Ewell looked at her finally, his expression fierce. "I fuckin' love you, little sis." Backing out, he slammed the door, the racket echoing in the small room.

Well if that's not the most confusing thing.

CHAPTER 4

HITCH

It had only taken two days to find out who the cowardly bastards were who'd ambushed myself and my brothers. Pissed me off it took even that long. If I'd had more than half an unmuddled second to think, I could have come up with the name myself.

Vicar's Wrath, a longtime IMC enemy. They were the cosmic cockroaches of the club world, having been put down as an organization twice now, rebounding with fake patches and a faker brotherhood.

Dyno had shoved a chair my way earlier, his muttered message of "Talia" enough of a reason for me to accept it, and I sat forwards now, elbows to my knees as I stared at the images projected onto the screen.

I'd never realized the pain of being left behind. Even if necessary given my injuries, it hurt being cut out of the action I could see going down. I'd roped Dyno into running the command center from the back room of the Jailbreakers clubhouse, since both clubs were involved in our retaliation play.

We'd also hooked up with Myron, a tech genius from a northern tier club to which we had ties, and adding the Rebel Wayfarers assets behind ours meant even if I'd been relegated to the rear guard, I still got to watch and listen. Myron and Dyno had drones positioned around the farmhouse we'd identified as the Vicar's base of operations, with twelve camera views on a giant TV mounted to the wall.

Turned out Graceless had history with one of theirs, reaching more than a decade into the past. Took a black heart to hold onto bullshit for so long. As much as we'd like to just wipe them out, it was unlikely the entirety of their membership was culpable, so our targets had been isolated and identified using security footage from the liquor store. Every one of our brothers heading in had been thoroughly briefed on what to do if one of the eight were encountered. Yeah, theirs hadn't just been a surprise attack but also eight men against four, and one woman.

None of us had stood a chance.

Coming to the realization that, except for Graceless, the rest of us had been incidental damage felt weird.

I mean, come on. If I was going to be stabbed and shot, I wanted it to at least be because of something I'd done. *Assholes.*

There was abrupt movement on half the cameras, and I stared hard at the tiny squares of dark and bright. Heat signatures of bikes were coming down the drive towards the clubhouse. The other half of the cameras came to life as red and orange blobs—our men, my brothers—boiled out of the gloom surrounding the house.

An endless twenty minutes later, it was over. Thank God the numbers were in our favor this time, which meant we had exactly the result we'd wanted. Zero injuries on our side, and eight cancerous tumors surgically excised from their fake-as-fuck organization.

I leaned back in the chair and took in the view. On screen were our brothers. Standing around, back-slapping, and no doubt hooting loudly at the win. Standing, breathing—living.

"Is it over?" Talia's voice came a moment before her hand rested on my shoulder. I nodded, not saying anything, liking her touch too much. That same connection I'd felt before resonated through me at full strength, and I fought against leaning sideways so I could press up against her. This desire sweeping through me for more than her touch was unsettling. In my life I fucked and walked—I didn't do whatever this was. Still, I knew, after only these few days, she was necessary to me. Talia soothed me in ways I didn't recognize, couldn't put a name to if I'd tried, and goddamn I wanted her.

"Is everyone okay? Sparks?" Anger and unreasonable jealousy sliced through me at her murmured questions. Of course she wasn't here to check on me, wasn't here because she felt even a small part of this immense pull. She was here to check on her cockblocking brother.

The dry click of my swallow echoed in my ears. "Yeah, everyone's good." What I didn't say—and wouldn't voice to her—was that the eight cooling bodies would soon be carted out and placed into various vehicles, headed towards their final destinations. Listening to Dyno work through the logistics of disposal had been eye-opening—I'd never realized how much of his job was spent dealing with the aftermath of a confrontation like this. The man was a master. "Sparks is just there." I pointed to the lower right camera, showing Talia the yellow and orange of where he stood next to Twisted, bright red outlines of two men kneeling in front of them. "He's good."

Her relieved sigh had me feeling like an asshole about my flare of jealousy. *The man's her brother for God's sake.*

Talia moved, and I glanced to see her looking down at me, eyes narrowed. "How are you doing, Hitch?" I started to shrug and stopped when the pain woke in my side. "What would it take to get you to go to see a real doctor?"

"I thought you were a doc?" I was teasing, trying to lighten the mood, surprised at the dark look she shot my direction. "Kidding. I know you're a damn good EMT, and in my opinion, probably better than half the docs in the county." My borrowed wardrobe was comfortable, if unfamiliar, and I rubbed my fingers lightly over the shirt camouflaging the bandage around my middle. She'd changed it out every day, making sounds about the stab wound I still hadn't seen. "You did right by me, that's for sure."

"If you won't see a doc, then could I talk you into lying down somewhere and resting? If it's over, finally over, you can rest." Her palm pressed to my forehead was cool and glided like silk against my skin as she laid a soft touch against my cheek, then my neck. "You're hotter than you were before."

"That's what all the girls say," I teased, and her expressive face molded into a mask. "Hey," I said, reaching up to trap her hand against my face, "I kid." I flicked a gaze at the views from the cameras Dyno still had on the house and called out, "We're done here, right, Dyno?" He lifted a middle finger I took as my permission to withdraw. I studied Talia carefully as I bargained with her. "I'll go lie down if you rest with me. I heard from everyone how you've been working to take care of my ass. I'm a gentleman—" She snorted, and I faked shock at her reaction, happy to see her pretty mouth twist in an effort to keep from smiling. "I *am* a gentleman, and my health is important to me. As far as I'm concerned, it's still in your hands. I think it's only right you keep watch over me while I rest. I mean—" I forgot and tried again to shrug, wincing as the pain shot through me like a return of the blade. "*Dammit.*" After a careful breath in, I continued, "I mean, it's only right you make sure I'm going to be okay, right?"

Talia stared at me for a long minute, flicked her gaze to the screen where four men were now on their feet, signaling the beginning of the true end of the conflict, and looked back to me. She wavered visibly, tipped her head back as she rolled the muscles of her shoulders, and nodded. "Okay." Nose scrunched up, she shyly admitted, "I don't stay here, ever. I know a lot of the guys have rooms, but I don't. That's not me."

My chest swelled at her admission. In one fell swoop, she'd told me she didn't hook up with the club members and wasn't part of their day-to-day but was willing to change her ways. *For me.* "I got us covered." I reached up, and she took my hand, surprising me with her strength as she pulled me to my feet. I pretended to sway, and as I'd hoped, she stepped closer and wrapped one of those wiry arms around my waist. The heat of her blazed through me, burning away the last vestiges of my caution.

As we strolled up the hallway, I watched the expression on her face flicker from concern to uncertainty, and then inexplicably to sadness.

"Whatcha thinkin'?" My question made her glance up, a flash of her beautiful eyes before they were again downcast. "There's something goin' on in that smart noggin of yours. Share?" I steered us into the room where I'd been staying. Without releasing my arm from around her shoulders, I thumbed the lock after I closed it. "Spill, Talia. Confession is good for the soul."

Rolling her eyes at my lame attempt at humor, she tipped her head up and locked her gaze on me. "I envy Ewell…Sparks. He's got this whole big family to lean on, something he built out of nothing."

"He's your family." I adjusted my hold so she stood in front of me. Arms around her waist, I gave her a squeeze. "You make it sound like you're alone. You're not. If there's anything I've learned about the man, it's that he'd do anything for you."

"Yeah." She gave me a half smile shaded by a hint of melancholy. "He's good like that."

"Nobody else around? No one waitin' on you to hie yourself home?" I was fishing and knew it, but she bit in a big way.

"Nope. I don't work again for another night, so no one to miss me." She blinked slowly and scoffed far back in her throat. "And doesn't that just sound like I'm whining? Sorry." My rigid grasp kept her from backing away, and her eyes lifted, our gazes meeting with an almost physical snap. "Hitch, let me go. I don't want to hurt you."

"You're not going to hurt me, Tee." I bent closer, moving slowly, giving her time to protest, willing to talk more if she needed. "You never could." Our faces were close enough that her every exhalation was a warm gust across my lips. "And there'll never be a time when I'll hurt you." Her hands rested against my chest, fingers fisting around the edges of my vest. "I never would."

Our lips met in the kind of soft caress we'd shared earlier, the sweetest glide of flesh on flesh as her chin tipped exactly as it should. She was the first to make a sound, a desperate moan of desire that set me on fire. I cradled her face in my hands, pulling her closer so I could devour her mouth, spearing my tongue between her lips to press deep. The decadent taste of her was the perfect mix of sweet and savory, instantly addictive as my tongue dueled with hers. She sucked hard, and I groaned down her throat, hips thrusting against her belly as my cock sought friction.

"Hitch." Her voice was scarcely louder than a breath, but I read all the need held inside her. That moan made a return as my hand fell to her breast, cupping and lifting, molding it to fit my hand as if she were made for me. "Tell me you feel this." I tweaked her nipple to make her gasp, that cool draw of air music to my ears. "Please, tell me I'm not alone," she begged, and I gave her my thigh to ride, fingers curled around her hip urging the primal movement she seemed to need.

"Fuck no, Tee. I'm right here with you. I've never wanted like this." I pulled back just enough to see her eyes. Pupils blown wide and black, the soft expression made her appear more vulnerable, and a swell of protectiveness rose within me. I needed her, full stop. "I wanna be in you, gotta watch you come apart, see what you look like when you come all over me. Gimme that, yeah? Let me have you." My dick throbbed, reminding me he was still locked behind my zipper. "We gotta hit the bed, baby. Clothes off, yeah?"

A flush rose from her chest through her throat and into her cheeks, turning her sun-kissed skin a deep rose as she nodded slowly. I kept hold of her with one hand while I tried my damnedest to work the fastening of my jeans with the other. Talia tsked softly and brushed my fingers away, dealing with it for me, the dance of her fingers so close to my cock the sweetest torture. There was one other critical thing to deal with before I could be truly comfortable.

Jeans hanging from my hips, I shrugged out of my vest, twitching it away from her when she would have taken it from me. Matching seams carefully, I smoothed and folded the leather before I set it aside. My brothers were avenged, and I'd been released from my vow. Talia seemed to understand this meant something and stood at my elbow until I finished.

She walked backwards towards the bed as she managed her own jeans, leading me with every step, showing me with each movement that this was her decision, too.

Clothing discarded on the floor, I made to follow her onto the bed and had to stifle a groan as the pain in my ribs woke. She must have seen it in my face, and her expression softened and shifted to concern. "I'm fine," I lied, then decided to offer up a morsel of truth when I told her, "but, things might go better if you're willin' to do all the work."

Talia stared at me, then dropped her head with a soft laugh. "This? All of this is against medical advice," she teased, then curled up on my good side as I lay on my back, a welcome presence I could get used to having. "But...I could be persuaded."

"Fuck yeah, I'll persuade the hell outta you," I muttered against the side of her head, shoving my arm underneath her neck to pull her closer. "Kiss me, gorgeous."

Intoxicated by the taste of her mouth, I kissed her while I stroked every inch of skin I could, memorizing each heady sound she made. Her hot palm wrapped around my cock, and the simple contact was overwhelming. I broke the kiss as I arched my neck, pushing my head into the cushioning pillow. "God damn, Tee."

She stroked down, then up, and the pad of her thumb swept across my piss slit, leaving pulses of heat behind. We set up a rhythm where on each tight and twisting downstroke, I thrust up into her grip until I was riding the edge of no return. With everything going on in the past few days, I wasn't sure I'd have any recovery if I blew my load now, so I had to stop her.

"Tee, get a condom, baby. My wallet." Fuck me if she didn't dip her head and bite my nipple, a place I hadn't realized was sensitive until that moment, the heat and pressure from her mouth making my hips jerk and chase her touch again. "Jee-sus," I drawled when she sucked hard. "Stop havin' fun like that, baby. Gonna get me off too soon."

"I wanna taste you," she told me, and good as her offer sounded, being inside her would be way better.

"No, baby. My Tee's goin' ridin' tonight." My shot and stitched arm protested as I wrapped my hand around hers, stopping her slow drag against my shaft. She tightened harder, and I grunted, then promised, "I can't do everything I want to you. Not right now. Not yet." Fighting my hold, she slipped down in the bed, mouth skipping over the bandage splitting me in two. "Dammit, baby." My good hand tangled in her hair and I stopped her mouth a bare breath from enveloping the head of my raging hard-on. "You're gonna ride me."

Faster than I expected, she caved, her agreement coming out in a softly drawn out, "Yeah," like she'd finally realized what I'd been saying.

I told her again, "Get a condom." Pointing towards my jeans with a tip of my head, I reminded her, "I got one in my wallet."

She scrambled off the bed, and fuck me if I didn't miss her heat immediately. Watching her move was nearly worth the loss, the sway of her back and arch of that fuckin' gorgeous ass definitely something I could get used to seeing. When she bent at the waist to fish the wallet from my jeans, I was presented with the prettiest hole shot I've ever seen, framed by her heart-shaped ass, with the soft curve of her plump pussy lips peeking out below. My mouth watered at the thought of getting my tongue and fingers into her everywhere. I must have made a noise, because her eyes found mine from around her legs and she grinned, telling me without words she'd posed just for me.

Talia straightened and turned to face me, fist pressed between her breasts. She said something, but I'd focused in on her tan nips, peaked and ready for my mouth. When she broke my field of view and covered those beauties with her arm, I looked into her face and muttered, "What?"

"Gah," she laughed. "*Men*. I said you have one."

She'd already lost me again, my gaze trailing down to where her bush hid the top of her pussy. Trimmed and tamed, but there, something I didn't know I liked until I saw hers done up like that. Club whores had been my only outlet for years, and they all shaved for ease of what-the-fuck-ever they did after the members partied with them. I could see her pink lips glistening between her legs and knew her sweet nectar would glide like silk against my tongue. *I want her so fuckin' bad*. Now my mouth was watering for sure, and I mentally revised the planned schedule of events for this encounter.

"Hitch." There was a tiny bite in her tone, and I brought my eyes back up to see she'd plastered a deep frown across her face. "Is your head worse? Are you with me?"

"Baby." I let my lips curl into a smirk. She stood naked, her body reacting to mine exactly like I wanted it to, but she was losing her happy place to worry about my damned head. The wrong one, I might add. "I'm good. It's just you're so fuckin' gorgeous I can't get my fill even starin' at you. Everything I see, I wanna touch and lick and bite, and your fuckin' pussy is callin' to me. I gotta taste you or I'm gonna go crazy. You're gonna ride my tongue before I get my dick in you. I wanna eat you out until you can't remember your own name."

Her smile was like a beam directed my way, bright and brilliant, and so fucking *there* it was all I could do to stay in that borrowed bed. I wanted to feel Talia's smile against my lips, wanted to ravish her mouth, wanted to kiss my woman until she could only think of me. I wanted to own that smile for myself, so she'd never give it to another man, ever again. *Just me*.

"Come here," I growled, stretching out my hand with a flick of my fingers. "Come right the fuck here."

She did, talking. "You've got one condom."

"Yeah?" Disappointing, but at least there'd been a rubber present. "Out of date?"

"Not quite" came with a partial beam, a tease of the full version, and my heart leaped at provoking even that from her. "It does look like it's been there a while."

"Yeah, I don't fuck around much." I wouldn't say never. It'd be a lie and one she'd sniff out in an instant. "Generally comes with drama and I ain't a fan." Climbing into the bed on her knees, she made her way back to my side. "So there's one. Is that a disappointment?"

"If this is the only time I get you, I guess I was hoping for a twofer at least." Talia's lips curled crookedly, and I lifted my chin in silent demand. She leaned close and brushed against my mouth, the heat and softness of her naked body draped across my shoulder making my dick take even more notice. "Then I remembered you're hurt."

"The condom's good for the main event." I watched as her beautiful eyes blinked open, pupils blown and dark again from our soft kiss. "I got lots of tricks up my sleeves to get you off without needin' more." Then I pushed. "This time." When her brow furrowed, I cut out the bullshit. "Ain't nothin' says this is it for us, Talia. I like you. There's just somethin' about you. Makes me a hella sap, because I've got all these things I want. I wanna fuck you, sure, but I wanna get to know you, too. I wanna make you happy, and not just in bed tonight. You feel like home, Talia, and I am gonna be back to explore that with you. Ain't a one-time thing for me, not in this bed, not with you. Even if I wanted to stay away, I doubt I'd manage. That's how strong whatever this is feels."

"After only a couple of days?" When she cupped my cheek, her fingers trembled, an endearingly unsteady touch against my skin.

"Yeah, Talia. After just the short time I've had with you, it's enough to know I want more." Arm curled around her waist, I gave her ass a squeeze, pulling her harder against my side. "What that more becomes, I don't know and won't lie to you just to get into your pants. Maybe outside of stressful events we're not compatible." Her lips pursed into a tiny moue, and I lifted my head to kiss the disappointment off her mouth. "I'm not expecting that as an outcome, darlin', just sayin'."

The glide of her fingers against my beard and skin was enough to fan the flames, and I glanced down to see my cock arching over my belly, a thread of shining fluid stretching down to where a pool was already gathered.

"You were basically unconscious the first time you kissed me."

"That wasn't a dream?" I knew it wasn't, and I remembered every moment of the kiss, but I wanted to see her smile. She didn't disappoint. "Damn, baby. Thought you were an angel come from on high to bring me back to life. Had to have me some of that."

"You surprised me." She laid her hand on my chest and traced a restless design there before pressing flat over my heart. I recognized it as an unconscious protective gesture, more evidence of our connection. "Covered in blood, and then you kissed me."

"And you—" I tipped her chin up as I raised my head, pressing my lips to hers, "—kissed me back."

"I..." She huffed a laugh at whatever was on her mind, then shared. "I wanted to know more about you from the instant I saw you get out of that van. You were obviously hurt, but something about you felt so vital. So alive. I guess I'm like you. I just wanted a little of that for myself."

"You got me, Tee." I tried to steer us out of the deep end and back to the fun I had planned. "Kiss me." Less a demand than I wanted, still it was the right direction. "Kiss me 'til we're both so fuckin' horny we can't wait another minute. Then you're gonna ride my tongue." Her hips moved, and her bush was bristly against my thigh. "You're gonna plant that pretty pussy on my face and go to town and I'm gonna eat you out so good, baby. And then we'll put the single rubber to use. When your legs are jelly and my tongue's wore out, we'll ride some more."

The next little bit passed too fast for me. A blur of teeth and tongues, lips and groans, hands sweeping across bare flesh. Even from the bottom I battled for dominion, and she gave it to me, somehow gifting her submission while chasing my mouth. Soft and sweet, hard and fierce, every kiss rolled into another and lifted us higher. Fingers wound through her hair, I brought her mouth back to mine again and again, until I pulled harder, arching her neck to see her face, finding the love-drunk expression I'd been working for.

"Get up here," I ordered, and her eyes widened before she moved, scrambling up the bed to plant a knee on either side of my head, tucking her toes under my shoulders. I watched the show as she positioned herself, naked body arching backwards as she steadied herself with a hand on her knee. The expression on her face was excited and turned on, but still a tiny bit hesitant. "You're not gonna break me, baby." Waggling my tongue at the promise of her only inches above my mouth. "Gimme." My demand made her smile. "Hold yourself open with one hand, Tee. Use the other to show me what you want. Don't be afraid to pull me closer. I wanna know what you need."

Mouth open, panting, she did just that. Two fingers separated her pussy lips to show me the bounty I was looking forward to, and her other hand curled behind my head, nails scratching gently at my scalp. My one arm wasn't good for anything in this position, but I grabbed her ass with the other and yanked her down the final distance separating us until I had my mouth on her. Slick and wet, and so fucking sweet I couldn't believe how she tasted.

Diddling her pearl had her humping my face with a cry, gliding those wet lips so my tongue could circle her entrance before plunging in. And the sounds she made. Damn, I didn't know that'd be a turn-on for me, but my rock-hard cock throbbed painfully with every sigh, jerked with each stifled moan, and slapped my belly when I found a particularly good angle so she whimpered. Her voice dipped low to say my name, then found a higher register as she called me a god.

I wrapped my fingers around the top of her thigh, playing until I found her clit with a fingertip and thrummed it side to side while I fucked her deep with my tongue and got her off for what might have been the third time. Her legs stiffened and lifted, and I chased her pussy with help, the hand she had gripping the back of my head holding my mouth tight against her. The rising wail of her orgasm filled the room, and I couldn't wait anymore, didn't want to, didn't give a shit if she was still coming, I needed her on my dick now.

"Slide down, baby." My words didn't pierce the veil of her pleasure, so I lapped at her another dozen times. "Talia." That got me her eyes, hooded and dark in her flushed and sweaty face.

She licked her lips, and asked, "Yeah?"

"Ride my cock."

Another glide of her pink tongue across those bitten-red lips and she nodded.

I gave her clit a final fierce suck as she bucked her sleek sweetness against my face, then gently bit the inside of her thigh. "Now, baby. I need you."

She was positioned over my dick before I remembered. "Condom. Where'd it go?"

"I don't know." Her breathy answer was nearly a sob and she wrapped her fingers around my cock, stroking up as she slid to straddle my thighs. "Where?"

The flash of the wrapper caught my eye, and I jerked my chin in that direction. Problem solved, she smoothed the raincoat down my shaft with a gentle touch, pinching the top like a good girl.

We'd been playing so long that when she seated herself on my cock, I lost it. It was so unbelievably good to be inside her heat, to feel her pussy clasping my shaft, force her open, that slick channel parting before my thrusts, I became wild. My words, my breath, even the thoughts in my head had slipped away. Everything was fucking gone, and the only thing remaining was a man desperate to fuck his woman.

Pain be damned, my hands were in a tight hold around her waist as I dug my heels into the mattress and yanked her down so the sweet curves of her ass rested against my thighs, and I was finally—fucking finally—balls deep. I froze there, surfacing from the mania, searching her face, afraid to see pain and anger there. Instead, what I saw was the sultry expression of a woman who liked what she'd gotten so far and was waiting and ready for what came next.

Pumping experimentally, I found a range of movement that worked for the wound and bruising in my side. Nothing would be completely comfortable, but God damn, this woman was worth any pain. *Anything.* Talia's fingers curled around the back of my neck as she brought her titty to my mouth, letting me tongue and play with the beaded beauty of her lush nipple before I sucked hard, making her moan softly. Another slow thrust and her head rolled backwards, exposing the delicate column of her throat, marked by my mouth from earlier. The satisfaction and possession that swept over me was surprising, and I tucked those thoughts aside, giving my dick full rein.

I held a rigid position as I swatted her ass, an encouragement to keep her moving on top of me. The long muscles in her thighs tightened and bunched as she rose and fell, using my hips as her launching point. We both worked up a sweat, turning the glide of her skin across mine into a delicious treat, nearly as mind-blowing as the way her sweet pussy clamped down on my cock, pulling and sucking me deeper. Talia's ass slapped my thighs, and I grabbed a handful on each side, tugging in time with her rhythm of taking me deep, encouraging more of that delicious slide and glide.

She leaned over me, ass moving in a pattern only she understood. Her mouth latched onto my pec again, teeth digging deep, and the unexpected burst of erotic pain had me groaning her name. She lifted and stared at me, mouth wet and swollen, her damned beautiful eyes dark and lust-filled. I wrapped my fingers in her hair and brought her in for a kiss broken only by our panting breaths. It ended with her forehead pressed to mine, and I watched as she came apart. Her pussy walls clutched me, drawing me deep as I hammered up into her, balls tight against my body. Muscles tensed with the electric spasms racking her she cried out once, then again, and then it was me who was gone, fucking gone, driving towards my own orgasm. Tight and wet, her pussy took every thrust, magnifying the sensation of being inside someone to another level.

It wasn't just someone taking my cock. It was Talia. And knowing, feeling, believing she'd wanted this as badly as I did sent me over the moon.

Talia

HITCH CRIED out as his body arched up and Talia gripped his shoulder to keep from being dislodged. She'd scarcely come down from her orgasm, the climax seeming to last forever with the thick shaft of Hitch's cock drilling into her. He'd angled his hips perfectly to glide his dick in ways that'd roused a burning fire in her belly, catching hold and setting her ablaze. Now she got to see him in the throes of his own ecstasy, and he was gorgeous as he unraveled underneath her.

Mouth open, his jaw moved, lips forming her name over and over, tongue dipping out to glide across his bottom lip. He righted his head, eyes opening and focusing immediately on her face, an expression of satisfaction coming over him at whatever he saw there.

"Kiss me, beautiful." He pursed his lips in an example of what he wanted, and she obliged, dipping low to press her mouth to his. "Goddamn," he muttered, the movement of his lips sexy as hell before he distracted her by gliding his tongue in a slow dance against hers. "Fuckin' me like that. Takin' my cock. Lettin' me have you." Each phrase was punctuated with another deep kiss as they caught their breath. "Gonna hafta—" He growled and kissed her hard, the biting edges of his teeth and brutal thrust of his tongue making her gasp into his mouth. "Keep you."

His hand slipped up her back and cradled the back of her neck, a hold he used to bring her down so she was lying on top of him, head tucked underneath his chin while his other arm wrapped around her waist. "I should move," she told him, surprised when her protest stirred another slow thrust of his scarcely softened cock into her. "Stop," she scolded, but knew it held no heat when he chuckled, the rumbling movement of his chest comforting.

"Like you right where you're at, woman. You try to move now, I'ma smack that ass." His arm gave her a squeeze she welcomed, granting silent permission to relax in place. "Lemme bliss out for another couple of minutes, Tee. This right here? This is fuckin' worth everything."

She rested on him while he stroked and petted her back and side, the movements coming slower with each pass.

"It's nearly the best part of everything." She spoke quietly, listening to his unhurried, even breaths in and out. Regular and steady, the sound was as comforting as those of waves against a beach. His grip on her waist eased, his hand coming to rest on her bent knee at his hip. "Just being." The heaviness of his breathing deepened, sound coarsening as he drifted to sleep.

Once he was well and truly at rest, she slipped off him, careful to hold the condom in place on his soft cock until she'd disengaged. Rooting around in the adjoining bathroom, she uncovered a washcloth and soap, using them to clean herself before going back to stand next to the bed. Hitch lay on his back, head angled so one cheek was against the pillowcase. His good arm had wrapped across his chest, hand tucked on top of the bandages she was glad to see unstained with blood. At least their ill-advised activities hadn't broken open his wound.

She thoroughly wiped him down, impersonally holding his penis as she did so, lifting his scrotum to gently swipe at the sweat she knew would have collected on his perineum. When he groaned and arched into her touch, she glanced up to see a tortured expression on his face, tiny lines fanning from the corners of his tightly closed eyes. His lip lifted, and she prepared for a shout or expletive, but what ground from his mouth wasn't that. Just her name, spoken in a broken plea, "Talia."

Discarding the cloth in the bathroom, she studied herself in the mirror. Tousled hair, lips red and roughened from his beard, love bites dotting her dusky skin—she looked well fucked. Then she remembered how she had felt in his arms, nestled against his chest. Cherished by a proud man willing to take a more passive role than he was clearly accustomed to if it meant they could be together for another minute.

She flipped off the light, padding through the darkness to climb back into bed with Hitch.

Her heart leaped when he reached for her without fully waking, curling around her protectively, ever the bossy man, ordering her to "Sleep" with a gruff word before he relaxed into her.

She complied, dozing off with his welcome weight pinning her to the mattress.

CHAPTER 5

HITCH

I WOKE SLOWLY, DRIFTING UP FROM THE DEEP SLEEP THAT HAD HELD ME IN ITS grip for hours. There was this immense sense of peace in my chest. Not something I was accustomed to, and I spent a few brain cells trying to sort it out before the heat of a body next to mine registered. *Talia*. I'd know her scent or the feel of her anywhere. She was not beside me. I'd sprawled out over her until the woman lay plastered to the bed.

Thoughts of the previous night swept through my head. They provided a vivid stop-action film of our activities that had my cock soaking up the memories like a sponge, fattening and uncoiling from where it rested against the small of Talia's back.

When I tried to shift to the side, the aftermath of the other events came crashing back in, reminding me I'd very nearly been dead at one point in the past couple of days.

Still, it was worth it to hear my angel's voice. "Hitch?" Soft and sleepy, she asked, "You okay?"

"Yeah, baby." I rested against her, teasing flawless skin with my teeth, then pressed a kiss there. "With you here? I'm fuckin' great. Tip-top." My chest aborted a cough before it made it to a full-fledged hack, while the resulting sharp movements made me hiss and groan. "Fuck, Jesus. What the hell?"

"You were shot," Talia helpfully reminded me, rolling out from underneath me. Hair in a tangle around her head, clasped fists curled beneath her chin, she offered a wry look. "And stabbed."

"And beaten." I couldn't argue with her assessment. "Still sucks. I woke up with plans for ya. All the plans." The stitches in my arm pulled when I lifted my hand, and I ignored the pinch of pain, counting it necessary if it meant I got to touch her.

"So many plans?" Lips lifting unevenly, she gave me a twisted grin as she pressed into the caress. "All the plans?"

"Yeah, baby, all those motherfuckin' plans." The apple of her cheek fit my hand, just like her body had fit mine last night. We were matched in every way, and my resolve from the preceding day returned. "I'm keepin' you. You know that, right?"

Talia rolled her lips between her teeth, biting down for a moment. "I live here in Adkins."

"So? That's not some magical barrier to me keepin' you, babe. That's a tiny wrinkle, not a shut and locked door. You like livin' here? Grew up here? Wanna stay here where you're close to your brother?" She gave the tiniest of nods to each question, answering each individually. "You wanna 'xplore this with me?" Another nod, larger than the others. "Wanna keep me around?" I got a grin and a solid dip of her chin to her neck, lashes fluttering to hide her eyes. "Then I'll sort my shit and figure out what it means for me."

Her gaze darted to my face, dancing between my eyes as I gave her a minute to consider what it all meant. It didn't take long before she was rolling her lips again, biting them nervously.

"What, Talia?" I shoved my other hand underneath her head, cradling her face between my palms as I drew her closer. Our noses brushed, and the heat of her breath swept over me as I asked again, "What's goin' on in that noggin, beautiful? I'm not a man to wait around. When I want something, I take it. I want you. Means a change in my life, I'm down with it. It'd be worth anything to wake up to you like this every fuckin' day. Bottom of my heart, I mean that."

Trembling lips parted, and the flash of her tongue peeked out. Then she rocked my world.

"I could love you."

"Oh, baby," I ground out, pressing her face to my throat while I buried myself in her hair. After a moment, I shoved up on an elbow and stared down at her. "If you're gonna give me all that beauty inside you all at once, I'm gonna overdose on the sweet. You could love me?" She nodded, and I busted her lips free from her teeth, taking her mouth in a deep, wet slide, drinking my fill from her. When I broke the kiss, she blinked up at me with an expression fast becoming my favorite. Love-drunk and aroused looked gorgeous on her.

"Every day I'll work to be worthy." Her lashes drifted to touch her cheeks, and I saw the muscles in her throat tighten as she swallowed hard. What I was saying meant something to her, a deep and profound emotion playing across her features when she opened her eyes to stare up into my face. "I wanna be worthy. Wanna be everything for you."

Talia lifted to meet my mouth, and I chased her lips until she was panting and writhing and my dick was hard enough to pound nails.

A knock at the door had me groaning as I whipped my head around to glare at the blameless surface.

"Yeah?"

"You still alive in there, Hitch?" Twisted's voice came through the wood, concern and amusement constant bedfellows in his tone. "Brother, it's time we hit the road. Gonna hafta say goodbye to the pretty chickie."

Another voice joined his. "Talia Rosalie, are you in there?"

Talia groaned and covered her face with both hands.

"Jesus, Sparks," I called out, pulling Talia closer, puffing up when she buried her face against my chest. *I'll protect her against anything comin' our way.* "Wanna back the fuck off my woman?"

There was silence, and when Talia drew back, I found myself smiling down at her shocked expression. "You misplace the knowledge that I'm keepin' you?" She shook her head in a slow side-to-side arc. "By definition that makes you my woman."

"That's my brother."

"So? Right now, him and my national president are both"—I raised my voice to project to our visitors—"unwelcome as fuck, pullin' this shit." Laughter from the hallway told me my words weren't taken the wrong way, giving me freedom to push a little more. In the sternest voice I could muster from around my grin, I ordered them, "Go. Away."

"Talk in fifteen," Twisted insisted, and I had to grunt in annoyance at the proof my president and friend was an asshole determined to cockblock me this morning. "You get me, Hitch?"

"Oh yeah. I fuckin' get you, boss." Ignoring the sounds of leave-taking from behind the door, I dragged my thumb across Talia's lips, reiterating the important part of what he'd said. "Fifteen."

Adjusting my position along her side, I held her in place when Talia would have pulled away. "Hitch, we've got to get up."

"I've got—" I kissed her, softly in the beginning, ramping up into a scorching joining of lips and breath, pushing until she had that dazed expression on her face again. "Fifteen minutes to teach you what's going to happen every morning from here on out." Forehead fitted against hers, I brushed the tips of our noses together.

No longer banished to no man's land, I'd somehow found myself in a paradise I could hold on to.

"Keepin' you," I reminded her.

"Lettin' you," she rejoined, and I smiled against her lips.

"Fuck yeah."

Connect with MariaLisa deMora

Website: https://www.mldemora.com

Social media & purchase links: https://linktr.ee/mldemora

ABOUT THE AUTHOR

Raised in the south, MariaLisa learned about the magic of books at an early age. Every summer, she would spend hours in the local library, devouring books of every genre. Self-described as a book-a-holic, she says "I've always loved to read, but then I discovered writing, and found I adored that, too. For reading...if nothing else is available, I've been known to read the back of the cereal box."

Her MC series include Rebel Wayfarers MC, Neither This Nor That MC, and Mayhan Bucklers MC.

KILLING TIME BY MARY MARTEL

Kings of Torment Motorcycle Club

CHAPTER 1

LANCE

Bored, I ignored the chick on her knees in front of me unfastening my belt and took in my surroundings. Night had fallen, and we were between two of the craft tents, hidden from view of the people strolling by.

The girl before me managed to unhook my belt, unbutton my jeans, and lower my zipper in record time. And I wasn't into it in the slightest.

I held my hands out at my sides, not wanting to touch her and give her the wrong idea about what was going on here. Hell, the only time I'd actually touched her tonight had been when she'd confidently walked up to me, grabbed ahold of my hand and dragged me back here. She'd whispered seductively in my ear, purring about all the dirty things she wanted to do to me.

I hadn't protested, but now I was seeing the error of my ways.

I leaned back against the pole of the tent behind me and tipped my head to the side, watching the people as they passed by the tents, rather than watching the chick on her knees before me as she slides my jeans down my thighs.

"Lance," she whined in a high voice, making me flinch.

Of course she knows my name. Everyone does.

I'm about to look down at her, even though I don't want to, when a slight, rail thin female with long locks of dirty blonde hair flowing all around her pauses in the entrance of the space we're occupying.

The chick on her knees whines my name again, demanding my attention, and the other woman must hear it because she turns her head to the side and stares straight at me.

Wide grey eyes meet my brown ones, growing wider by the second.

The sight of her standing in front of me, a woman I haven't seen for years, not since she fled town the day of her high school graduation, sends a sharp pain through my chest. I'd been fantasizing about her since freshman year of high school. The girl I always wanted but knew I was too dirty to touch. To touch her would be to taint her. She was poison to me and would be my ruin. A woman like that would get drunk and take a taste of me, then in the morning she'd run. She'd tell no one, and I'd become her dirty little secret. Something shameful but delicious, but she'd never come back for more. I'd want her to, and the poison she'd infect me with would take over my soul.

Her eyes trailed down my body, only to stop once they reached my hips. A look of disgust filled her pretty face right before she turns, dismissing me, and continues on her way.

"Shit," I hissed.

I shoved at the woman on her knees, knocking her away from me. Her arms wheeled out at her sides, uselessly, as she lands hard on her ass on the trampled grass. The short jean skirt she had on rode high up her thighs, flashing the fact she had nothing on underneath, making me sneer down at her.

I know I'm no better than she is, but I'd always wanted better for myself. I'm not sure who the sneer's really for, her or me.

Her mouth forms a pout, dark purple lipstick making her look angrier than she really is, as she stares up at me with wide eyes. Easy things weren't used to being told no, not with the crew I ran with.

"We're done here," I tell her as my hands drop to my pants and I drag them back up my thighs. I do up the zipper, fasten the button, and hook my belt back in place.

Even though I knew it was the wrong thing to do, we were done. I'd set my sights on something better. *Someone* better.

"But, Lance," she whines, "I'm just getting started. We haven't even gotten to the good part yet."

I hated how my name sounded coming out of her mouth. Nobody called me Lance, and this chick doing it now only served to deteriorate my mood even more. Being the president of a motorcycle club in a small town meant everybody and their fucking mother knew my name, but nobody used it.

"Lance, where are you going?"

She latched onto my arm in a desperate attempt to keep me from walking away from her.

"Get the fuck off me," I growled, peeling her hand off of my arm and tossing it away from me. The more she dragged this on the farther Maggie got away from me, taking the chance to rub up against something clean with her.

"But-"

Turning around, I locked eyes with her. I let the disgust I felt for her, and the rage building inside me by the second fill my eyes and show on my face. She scrambled back away from me as her eyes started leaking. She swiped at her face, chasing her tears and smearing her lipstick.

"Do not put your hands on me, ever." I ground out between clenched teeth.

She scrambled up to her feet and took a step towards me. "I-"

"Am desperate. Pathetic. Not even wearing any fucking underwear so I know you came here looking for an easy ride. Shoulda picked somebody else, babe, and not set your sights on me." She jerked back as if I'd struck her, and more wet leaked out of her eyes. "What did you think was going to happen? You'd drop to your knees, suck me off, and I'd what? Want to marry you?" I shook my head in disgust. "Sorry, but I was over it before your knees even hit the grass."

"But, you came back here with me." Another tear leaked out. I watched the trail it made on it's journey down her cheek and felt absolutely nothing but disdain.

I shrugged carelessly. "I was bored and didn't have anything better to do. Now I have something better to do, so we're done."

"Asshole," she hissed as she spat at my feet.

She had that right, but she was wrong if she thought I cared.

"Yeah," I muttered as I turned on my boot and walked away.

CHAPTER 2

MAGGIE

I DIDN'T RUN, BUT I WANTED TO.

The way Hawk had looked at me, there was something in his eyes that terrified me. Or, maybe it was just the man himself that terrified me. But I didn't run. I forced myself to walk at a normal pace, putting one foot in front of the other and not looking back. As much as Hawk terrified me I wasn't a coward anymore, and I would not run away from anyone, especially him.

I'd left this town ten years ago getting as far away from this toxic place, and the Kings of Torment Motorcycle Club who ran it, as I could get. I'd watched my mother throw her life down the toilet chasing after men on motorcycles, all the while forgetting she had two little girls at home waiting for her to come back and take care of them. Half the time she was too high to remember we even existed and, for the better part of my childhood, my sister had raised me.

It had hurt me to leave my sister behind when I ran away from this place, but she understood why I had to leave and let me go. She didn't go though, oh no, not my beautiful Franny. She stayed to take care of the woman who'd given birth to us and it had slowly worn her down as it would have anyone.

Eventually it destroyed her and now I was back to make things right for her. For my sweet Franny who hadn't deserved anything she'd gotten out of this life. But life wasn't fair and sometimes it fucked over the best of us, and we were just supposed to hold on and go along for the ride.

I wasn't interested in getting fucked unless I wanted it.

Franny'd been too sweet for her own good. I wasn't sweet, though, not anymore.

I was going to take care of my sister, even though she was dead and would never know about it. I would know, and that was the only thing that mattered anymore.

I passed by a tent with open flaps and peeked in.

Long tables were set up in rows, cheap red and white checkered tablecloths covered them. Metal folding chairs lined up alongside the tables, and a long makeshift bar had been set up along one side of the tent.

It was littered with bottles of booze, plastic cups and shot glasses. Two kegs were on the grass in front of the bar.

Two women stood behind the bar, pouring drinks. They looked just like my mother had. Big hair, lots of makeup, and not a whole lot of clothing. They were older than me, and if I'd seen them before I didn't remember it.

I wouldn't forget their faces now. I'd memorize them, just like I would with everything else about the Kings of Torment MC.

Two men stood in front of one of the kegs. They had red plastic cups in their hands and one of them held his cup under the nozzle while the other one pushed down on the pump. From their clothes I could tell they were locals and not associated with the MC.

One of the tables had been taken over by men wearing cuts, proclaiming them proud members of their club, and motorcycle boots. There were other people, random people, sitting around tables, drinking and having a good time. There was an air around anyone in a cut, a vibe they gave out, and everyone else kept their distance.

A man turned and caught my eye. He was older, with hair turning white at his temples, laugh lines shooting out around his eyes, and a ginormous beard.

I recognized him immediately. He'd been one of my mother's favorites, he'd liked her just the same in return. I know because he'd been one of the few who'd actually come to our house to see her.

His eyes flashed with recognition and he stumbled to his feet.

Damn, that'd been the second time tonight and I wasn't ready for it.

I looked away and kept on moving, this time putting extra hustle in my step.

"Hey," he shouted from behind me, his voice slurring just a little. "Aren't you JoJo's girl? Maggie? Hey, get back here, girl. I'm talking to you."

Actually, he was yelling. I didn't stick around to argue with him about it though.

I moved through people, losing myself in the crowd and, thankfully, losing my follower. I walked for a good hour, passing booths and tents alike. Vendors kept yelling out at me, trying to get me to play their games or eat their food. I didn't stop at any of them. Instead, I was stuck in my head, remembering a time ten years ago when I had last come here with Franny. Only then, I'd thrown darts at balloons, winning my sister a cute, pink teddy bear. We'd laughed as we linked arms and practically danced our way from booth to booth. We'd eaten elephant ears and laughed while we whirled around in a giant tea cup with our hair flying out all around us.

She'd been happy that night. I left her a week later, and even though I talked to her on the phone and we texted daily, I never came back. Not even when she had to bury our mom. I'd sent flowers then; they hadn't been for our mother but for my grieving sister whose heart was far too big.

I stopped in front of the ferris wheel, my neck craning back at an angle that was almost painful so I could see all the way up to the top. It lit up the dark sky with bright yellow and red lights.

This would be my one exception tonight, my one indulgence.

I got in line behind everyone else and waited. The wheel went around once, twice, three times before stopping to let people off. The line moved forward each time someone got off, and I moved closer to where I wanted to be. Eventually the line thinned out and I was the first in line,

standing in front of the little gate, waiting for the attendant to take my ticket and escort me to my seat and strap me in.

A touch, light as a feather, ghosted across my bare shoulders and had me whipping around.

Hawk stood there, tall and imposing, *right* behind me.

He wasn't looking at me though, instead he stared up at the ferris wheel, a thoughtful look on his face.

"Uhh... Hawk?" I mumbled in a quiet tone and his gaze snapped down to mine. "Can I help you with something?"

He gestured towards the ferris wheel. "Are you planning on going on this all by yourself?"

"Yeah," I said in a tight voice. That was all I had now, myself. And wasn't that the sad fucking truth.

"I'll go up with you," he said and his words were final, like he was used to telling people what was going to go down, and they were just supposed to go along with it.

I shifted uncomfortably on my feet. He'd followed me, that much was obvious. What I wasn't sure of was why.

The last I'd heard Hawk was in prison. He was a year or two older than me, but younger by a few years than my sister, yet that hadn't stopped her from having a serious crush on him. She'd said he had that bad boy hottie thing going about him when he'd been in high school and over the phone she'd shared with me that it had only gotten better with age, more intense even. Then he'd gone to prison for something having to do with his Club, and she'd never said a word about him after that.

She'd been right though, about him getting better with age and it being even more intense. The intensity was not a good thing, I could feel it; it was raw, primal, and almost tangible.

I wanted to tell him there was no way in *hell* he was getting on this ride with me but I thought better of it. The patch on the front of his leather cut read *President.* Something had changed, when I'd left that patch had belonged to his father. Death was the only acceptable reason for that patch changing hands.

Reaching up, I flicked my fingers against it and asked, "Is he dead, your dad?" It was a rude thing to ask, especially since we were virtual strangers and I couldn't remember a time when we'd ever actually had a conversation before.

He grabbed ahold of my hand before I could lower it and gave a little tug. I stumbled forward, moving right into his space, exactly where I figured he wanted me.

His brown eyes were dark and filled with something I didn't want to think about. He didn't answer my question. "You two are up next," the man on the other side of the little gate said as he swung the door open. He held his hand out to us and Hawk dropped several tickets into his outstretched hand.

I didn't protest this. He was invading my space and taking over, he could pay for the ride. That just meant I had more tickets for myself if I wanted to ride it again without him.

Hawk's hand went to the small of my back and he gently urged me forward. My skin burned through the thin material of my dress where his hand sat. The urge to move away from him and his touch was strong, but I held my ground as I walked forward with him at my side.

Silently, we climbed into the seat side by side and the man swung the bar around, locking it in place. Our thighs brushed up against each other, and this time, I did move away from him. I scooted over until I pressed up against my side of the seat.

"You don't have to be afraid of me," he muttered irately as the wheel hummed and we moved forward.

I nodded, as if I believed him, which I absolutely did not.

The thing was though, it was him who should have been worried about me hurting him. I didn't care he'd been in prison most of the time I'd been gone and in all likelihood had had nothing to do with my sisters ultimate destruction. None of that mattered because of the cut on his back, and the patch he'd now had sewn into the front of it.

The wheel moved until we were at the top where it stopped to let more people off and on. The seat rocked as he leaned forward, looking straight down.

"Tell me, Poison," he said in a voice full of gravel, "what brought you back to this shit hole place?"

Poison? He had to be joking, right?

"My sister's dead," I whispered, and I don't know why I said it. "Shouldn't you already know that though?"

I figured they all knew it since she'd died at their stupid clubhouse. Shot up, her beautiful body filled with holes because of their Club bullshit. And she hadn't been the only one to die.

He sat back in his seat and turned to look at me. I stared out at the town below us, refusing to acknowledge him looking at me.

"Shit," he said in a soft voice. A voice full of compassion. "I didn't know. I thought..." he cleared his throat. "Well, I didn't think she was that kind of girl."

Whore, he meant, and he'd be right. Franny *hadn't* been that kind of girl. But, that stupidly big heart of hers made it so she couldn't just look the other way when other people were hurting and she thought she could help them.

"If it helps, it's been taken care of."

Dead, he meant the people who were responsible were dead.

It didn't help and wouldn't until the *other* people responsible, *his* people, were taken care of as well.

"Nothing's ever going to help me," I whispered into the night, so soft I was hoping he didn't hear it.

No such luck.

Long, calloused fingers came to my chin, turning my head to the side, forcing me to look back at him.

"You shouldn't stay here in this town, Poison." he said. "It's rotten and will only ruin a girl like you. You're too good for a place like this and if you stay I can't promise I won't..."

His voice trailed off and I blinked at him, stupidly. That was not what I'd expected to hear him say.

"You don't want me in your town?" I asked in surprise, a hint of anger in my voice that I couldn't hide.

"No," he said. "That's the thing, I do want you in my town. But, you ran once and what's to stop you from running again? I don't need any more damage right now and, like I said, you're Poison."

I leaned in until we were mere inches apart and hissed, "Excuse me? Did you just fucking call me poison? Like you're better than me?"

He leaned in, closing the distance between us, and pressed his forehead to mine. His eyes closed tightly and he whispered in a hoarse voice, "You're Poison because that's what you are to me, dangerous and fucking toxic. I had my eye on you before but never made my approach because I knew better, you're too good for the likes of me. Now, I'm even dirtier than I was before. If you stick around I'm going to get what I want from you and you're going to ruin me when you run again."

I jerked back away from him and he grunted in frustration. His hands went to the metal safety bar and he gripped it so tight his knuckles turned white.

His words ran through my mind and left me conflicted inside.

I could use him, make him mine before I made them pay. I was biding time here. Killing time until I could strike, taking all the King's men down with me.

Hawk was giving me the opening I needed, I just had to reach out and take it.

The seat jerked to a stop and the man running the ride stepped into view. He unlocked the safety bar and pulled it to the side.

Hawk jumped out immediately and I was surprised when he turned around and reached for me. I put my hand in his and allowed him to help me down. He let go of me as if my skin burned and I followed him out the gate.

He stopped to look down at me and I braced at the look on his face. He leaned down and put his face in mine.

"Run, little Maggie," he said in a harsh voice. "Run and don't ever look back. This is the only chance I'm going to give you."

And with that he turned on his scuffed motorcycle boots and stormed away. The crowd parted for him, watching him uneasily before he was swallowed up amongst the people who were clearly afraid of him, and gone from my sight.

I wanted to think *good riddance.* Instead, a thrill of excitement shot through me.

I told myself it had everything to do with the possibility of being able to actually avenge my sister. I also told myself I wasn't a filthy liar, but I was pretty sure I missed the mark on that one.

CHAPTER 3

MAGGIE

I'D NEVER BEEN MORE THANKFUL FOR SUNGLASSES IN MY LIFE. I'D PICKED OUT A black, oversized pair that covered up half my face. They kept my eyes hidden from the people standing across the gravesite from me. The only emotion they got to see from me were the tears that trailed silently down my face. I couldn't help those, no matter how hard I tried.

I stood alone on my side. No family, no friends to my name, and I was more than okay with that. No one by your side meant there would be no one to betray you later.

I stared out across my sisters' casket, taking in the sea of men and women who stood across from me, and I couldn't even be mad that they were here. Franny would have loved that they were here for her funeral, and she'd have insisted they were mostly here for me. I could hear her sweet voice inside my head, chiding me, telling me to be grateful they were here and to look at the bright side of things.

That just made the tears come faster.

The preacher droned on, talking about my sister like he'd actually known who she was before last week. I wanted to grab that black book he held clutched into his hands like it was the only thing on this planet that was worth a damn, and beat him mercilessly upside the head with it.

I hadn't wanted this. I'd wanted to have her cremated then have some small ceremony for her by myself where I could say goodbye without people staring at me, and other people pretending like they loved her just because she was dead. However, Franny had other plans and she'd left explicit instructions as to how she wanted her funeral planned. Because I loved her, even though she was dead and wouldn't know the difference either way, I followed her instructions to a T.

Underneath that closed lid to the casket my sister lay dressed in exactly what she'd asked for. She had on a sweet dress covered in sunflowers. A red bandana had been folded over and tied around her blonde hair in a makeshift headband. And, on her feet, black scuffed up Chucks. I had wanted to protest this but couldn't help but smile, thinking it was so like her to not want to be dressed up in some fancy thing that would have made her incredibly uncomfortable to wear while she'd been alive. She'd asked for no jewelry so I'd left her wrists and neck bare. The only other thing in the fancy, expensive box with her was the pink teddy bear I'd won for her playing darts all those years ago.

That one had almost killed me and made me curse the stupid letter I'd found tucked away in the top drawer of her dresser. It'd been addressed to me and I'd found it on my second day back, after I'd gone looking for something of hers to wear so I could breathe in her scent. I'd clutched that stupid fucking pink teddy bear to my chest while I'd read her letter and an important piece of my heart had shriveled up and died with each word.

So, even though I hadn't wanted to part with it, the pink bear went in the casket with her. And that had been the only thing she'd asked for.

Why she'd had such a letter hidden away in the first place bothered me. Maybe she had known things with the club were going to shit?

My shoulders shook with emotion as I tried to hold the sobs at bay, not willing to give into them until I was alone and no longer on display.

Arms wrapped around me from behind and I was turned into a hard body that was way bigger than mine.

I looked up through my sunglasses at a sharp jaw. His shoulder length hair that was just slightly darker than mine hung down and free around his face. I expected to be greeted with his beautiful dark eyes and was stupidly disappointed to see them aimed across the casket, roaming over the crowd of people he'd come here with.

His strong arms wrapped around my shoulders as he pulled me into his side. His hand slid up the back of my neck. He gave a gentle squeeze as he pulled my face into his throat his rough hands grazing my skin. It was oddly sweet and incredibly intimate for two people who barely knew each other and were virtual strangers two days before. Not that we hadn't known who the other was, just that we'd never actually had a real conversation before our insane ride on the ferris wheel.

His chin rested against the top of my head and he muttered under his breath, "I don't like the thought of you standing over here all by yourself crying your eyes out. It's not right."

I wondered if he even really knew the difference between right and wrong and figured I wouldn't like the answer.

Still, something about being wrapped up in the warmth of his embrace settled something inside me and the tears stopped flowing. My shoulders stopped shaking and my body slumped into his in a show of defeat. I'd take what he was offering for now, because he and his stupid club were partially to blame for me being here in the first place.

I turned my head away from him, staring back out across the mass of people. This time, they stared right back at me. More like me with Hawk wrapped all around me. Without thought, my hands went to Hawk's middle and I grabbed fistfuls of his leather jacket, holding on for dear life.

His arms around me tightened, almost to the point of pain.

"They're not staring at you, Poison." he muttered under his breath. "They're staring at me."

He wasn't entirely truthful, and I figured he'd lied to try and make me feel better about being the sideshow freak on display at my sister's funeral. All these people knew exactly who I was and that my mother had made it so Franny and I had been off limits to them before she'd died. Then, I'd been gone and there had been no one to stand in the space between them and my sister. It had been the only good, decent thing my mother had done with her life.

Now, JoJo was dead, Franny was dead, and I was all that was left of the Mayson girls. The barrier was gone and this time I was thankful for it.

The preacher finished speaking and gestured towards me. Hawk gave me one last reassuring squeeze before letting me go. His arms dropped down to his sides, but he didn't move away from me.

I shook my head at the holy man, having nothing I wished to say about my sister in front of these people. I'd say my words later, whisper them to the wind like a vow I hoped carried all the way to wherever she was now.

I stepped up to the casket, bent down and picked up a handful of dirt. Without a word, I sprinkled the dirt on top of her casket.

Ashes to ashes.

Dust to dust.

The space around my heart constricted as bile climbed it's way up my throat.

Without a backward glance, I turned and walked away.

I felt their eyes burning into my back the whole way to my car.

No one followed me.

CHAPTER 4

MAGGIE

I WAS DRUNK. THERE WAS NO OTHER WAY TO DESCRIBE IT.

It had been four days since my sister's body had been put into the ground. Four miserable days where I'd laid around crying my eyes out and eating everything in sight. It had been absolutely pathetic, *I* was being pathetic. And I was getting absolutely nowhere in my plans to avenge my sister, which was really the only thing I had going for me at the moment.

Since I had decided I sucked at everything and I might as well make it worse for myself than it already was, I drove into town and bought myself a bottle of vodka and a carton of orange juice and went back home to drink myself into oblivion.

I'd found no oblivion, but I had stopped crying for a few hours. At least there was that. Hysterically, I wondered if Franny would see that as looking on the bright side.

Pounding on the front door made me jump. I spilled my drink on the carpet and slid off the couch, landing on the wet spot in a heap.

I laughed loudly as I rubbed my cheek against the carpet, thankfully I'd found a dry spot my drink had missed to rub my face up against.

The pounding on the door grew louder, more insistent.

"Damn it," I slurred.

I set my cup on the floor beside the couch and was proud of myself when it remained upright. Tomorrow I'd scrub out the orange stain I'd left on the floor. Tonight, I didn't have it in me to care.

I stumbled towards the front door and crashed into it.

"Shit," I muttered under my breath as my hand went out to the wall beside the door to steady myself.

With hands that didn't seem to want to work properly, my fingers fumbled but I managed to get the door unlocked and flung it open. And immediately slammed it shut again, slamming it in Hawks face.

If I was forced to interact with him in a drunken state, something unfortunate was bound to come out of my mouth.

Hawk was having none of it and he shoved the door right back at me before it could click shut.

I stumbled back away from the door and him. Tripping over my own feet, I stumbled back and slammed into the wall.

"What are you doing here?" I slurred at him.

His eyes narrowed on me and he snapped, "Are you drunk? Who sits at home all by themselves and gets fucking blotto? I thought you were at least better than that."

His words stung, and I acted out on impulse, the rage and unfairness of it all exploding out of me. I brought my hand up and I slapped him across the face. Being drunk made my movements slow and sloppy. He had time to stop me but he didn't. He just stood there unmoving and took it.

He stood there as I let out all my pain, all my hatred of his club and what they'd taken from me, and he took it all.

I slapped at his chest, over and over again, screaming incoherent words, just angry sounds coming out of my mouth. Primal noises like a wounded animal.

When there was no energy left to raise my hand to hit him again I fell to my knees, sobbing. My chest hurt so bad, it was like someone had reached inside and torn out something vital, something that had made it easy to breathe, easy to exist. Now that it was missing I had no idea how to repair the damage to my soul, or if I could ever get it back.

"I hate you," I whispered and I had no idea if the words were meant for him or for me.

Hawk knelt down on the carpet beside me, looming over me. His hands came up, catching my hair and he swept it back, away from my face.

"You don't know me well enough to hate me," he said in a quiet voice. "You're upset, hurt and lashing out because of Franny. I get that. But, babe, before a couple of days ago I'd had no idea she'd been mixed up in that mess."

How could he not know? It had happened at his clubhouse, that's what the police had told me. Police, I might add, who'd done not one fucking thing to look for the person who'd shot her.

I hadn't realized I'd spoken my thoughts out loud until it was too late.

Hawk pulled on my hair, dragging my face until we were almost nose to nose. His eyes darkened and I think I saw sorrow flash through them momentarily before he shut it down and emptiness filled its place.

"When was the last time you saw your sister?" He asked.

Confusion swam through my foggy brain, that hadn't been what I was expecting to come from him.

"Hmm... Ten years ago. I haven't been back since I left." I'd thought he knew that I hadn't been back to visit so maybe he figured she'd gone to visit me instead.

Hawk nodded as he let my hair go and stood up. I swayed back at the sudden loss of his hold on me and almost toppled over. All that talking had made me forget about the vodka I'd consumed earlier.

Hawk grabbed onto my arm and pulled me up to my feet. I stumbled into him and he bent at the waist, his hands went to the backs of my knees and he easily lifted me up in his arms.

"What are you doing?" I whispered in shock.

"Let's get you to bed," he said. "In the morning I'll tell you all I know about what your sister's been doing while you've been away."

"How would you know what she'd been doing?" I asked in a nasty voice. "Did you get reports on her while you were enjoying life behind bars?"

The arms around me tensed and he let out an unhappy growl. It had been a low blow, I knew it, I also knew he didn't deserve it. Hawk had been nothing but decent to me even though I'd been rude to him at every turn. He should call me out for being an asshole and toss me down to the floor, that's what I'd do. He didn't though. His big body relaxed and he continued to carry me through my house as if he knew exactly where he was going and I hadn't just been unnecessarily cruel to him.

I felt bad so I did what my sister had taught me to do when I'd wronged someone. I apologized.

"I'm sorry, Hawk. I shouldn't have said that. I shouldn't have attacked you like that either. I'm so sorry. I'm not a violent person, usually. I don't know what came over me and I'm so damn sorry, you'll never know."

Sorry for a lot of things I wasn't stupid enough to tell him about.

Hawk used his shoulder to push open the door to the master bedroom. The room still smelled faintly of must and I knew my sister hadn't used it since our mom passed. That was the only reason I'd taken up this room as my own. My bedroom had been turned into an office and being in Franny's room often led me to tears.

Those stupid fucking tears that I couldn't seem to shake. They found me every day and threatened my sanity.

"I don't want to cry anymore," I sighed sleepily as Hawk sat me down on the bed. He pulled the covers back and gestured for me to climb under them. I was so damn tired that it would be easy for me to slide in between those soft sheets, close my eyes and allow the peaceful oblivion of sleep to take me away.

Apparently, all the fight hadn't left me when I'd disgustingly crumpled into a sobbing mess at Hawk's feet because I wasn't going to comply, I needed to hear what he'd implied about my sister. If he knew something about Franny then I wanted to know it. She was my sister, not his. I deserved to know.

"I'll go to sleep," I said. "Sure. But I'm going to need you to give me two things first."

I glared up at him in challenge, suddenly feeling a lot more sober than I had five minutes before.

Crossing his arms over his chest, he eyed me with what looked strongly like distrust. I couldn't argue with the look, maybe I even deserved it, but it wasn't me standing in his house, uninvited.

"What do you want from me?" He asked.

For him to walk away from me and never look back, I wanted to say, but something stopped me and I had a strong suspicion it was because it'd all be a lie. Every word of it. Since he'd been decent to me, the only decent person I'd come in contact with since coming back here, it seemed so wrong to use him, to potentially hurt him. Some part of me revolted against it. I was in serious trouble now.

"Why are you here, at my house?" I asked.

He frowned. "You're here," he said slowly, like he thought I needed him to go slow in order to understand his words. "I told you, if you stuck around I wouldn't be able to stop myself."

He waved his hand down at me. "You're here so I'm here. Eventually, you'll get used to me being around and, I'm hoping, we won't have to cover this again."

"You're crazy," I informed him. This, I felt, was the absolute truth. How could you be so obsessed with someone you didn't really know, just because you thought they were pretty? That wasn't crazy, more like psycho.

I flopped back on the bed, bouncing a little upon landing. My hands went to my stomach and I laced my fingers together.

"What were you getting at earlier about my sister?" I asked in a soft voice. I was proud, there was no slur to my words this time.

"I think it's best I wait until the morning to have that conversation," he murmured. "In the state you're in now there's a chance you won't remember it in the morning and you might freak out on me if I tell you tonight."

That had me widening my eyes and sitting up.

"First," I said as I held up my hand and stuck out a finger, "I will admit to having freaked out on you. You forgave me and we've since moved on from it."

The sound of his quiet laughter, dark and rich, filled the room. It made something flutter to life inside of me.

"I forgave you, did I?"

Ignoring him, I stuck out a second finger. "Second, I drank almost an entire bottle of vodka by myself, there's not a snowball's chance in hell I will be dragging my raggedy, hungover ass out of bed any time near what one would refer to as *morning*."

His laughter got louder.

I chose to ignore it again, and stuck out my third finger. "And last, if you don't tell me tonight then I won't be able to sleep and I'm being serious Hawk, I'm so fucking exhausted that I cannot afford to go another night without sleep. At least with all the vodka I know I'll pass out and be dead to the world for a few hours instead of crying half the night and waking up every two seconds for the rest of it." I snapped my mouth shut, realizing I'd said too much way too late. The more time I spent around him the more shit just kept pouring out of my stupid mouth. It was almost like I treated him as if we were friends or something. Which was stupid because we absolutely *were not.*

"Fine," he said as he sighed in defeat. "But I'm sleeping here, and no, before you freak out for a whole different reason, I don't mean for sex. Believe it or not, babe, but you're not the only person in this room who's exhausted and needs to catch some sleep. I'll sleep here with you and maybe we'll both get in a few good hours that way. We'll talk first then sleep. In the morning, if you want to reconsider the sex thing, we can fuck before I make you breakfast. Now, get pajamas on and whatever other shit you need to do before you go to sleep. I've got to make a few phone calls, I'll just be right in the other room. When I'm done, we'll talk."

I watched with wide eyes and a mouth I feared was hanging open as he stormed out of my bedroom. He looked angry, and I couldn't understand out of everything I'd put him through since he'd shoved his way into my house why he'd choose now to be angry with me.

I had smacked him around and all was copasetic with him. But, wanting to talk was what had him looking pissed off and angry?

Yeah, he really was a psycho.

I hopped up off the bed and ran for the adjourning bathroom. I needed to wipe off my makeup and change into my pj's before he came back.

CHAPTER 5

LANCE

I SLID MY PHONE INTO THE BACK POCKET OF MY JEANS AS I MOVED FOR THE front door. My bike was already in the driveway beside Maggie's SUV so I didn't need to go outside to move it.

After flicking the locks on the door, I moved to the front window. I shifted the flimsy curtain aside and scanned the street. All seemed quiet and peaceful. I wasn't fooled though, I never took anything at face value. The shit my dad had sunk my club into while I'd been locked up, the shit I was busting my ass trying to shovel us out from under, just kept piling on, and I never knew when more of it would land at my feet.

Maggie, my sweet Poison, was right to hate me. It was shit my club was involved in that *had* gotten her sister dead. But, it was shit she'd happily gone along with, so my boys had informed me when I'd questioned them after the fair. I hadn't been around for her demise but, given what my boys had shared, it had been a long time coming, and she'd worked really fucking hard at it.

I did not want to have to share this shit with Maggie, it would only serve to hurt her and that, I feared, would fuck with my head.

I shrugged my cut off and draped it over the back of a chair in the kitchen. I sat down in the chair and removed my boots and socks, tucking my socks inside the boots. I stood and tucked the chair in and toed my boots under the seat.

I checked the back door to make sure it was locked before checking out the kitchen window, scanning the backyard. All was quiet and peaceful back there as well, as it should be seeing as it was the middle of the night and this was generally a quiet neighborhood.

A quiet knock on the front door had me moving towards it as I pulled my gun out of my shoulder holster. I held my gun down by my thigh as I looked through the peephole. Two of my men, both I was certain were loyal, stood on the front stoop waiting for me.

Ronin and Trip. We'd grown up together, and despite my going down, we'd all remained tight over the years. They were two of my biggest supporters when it came to backing my club out of the shit my father had sucked us into.

They'd followed me here and waited up the road for me to come out. They'd remained out of sight of the house because I didn't want Maggie to know they were here and think she was being watched or give her a reason to hate us even more. They'd come with me because I wasn't allowed to ride alone. With bitches getting shot up and our enemies closing in, it wasn't safe for any of us to ride alone.

I opened the door and waved them in.

"I'm crashing here tonight," I told them. "You boys should head on home. I'll call before I leave here tomorrow."

Ronin glared at me. "You know we aren't going anywhere. If you're staying then so are we. There's no reason for you to be an asshole and pretend like we'd abandon you."

Against my will, my lips twitched in amusement. The fucker didn't have to stay and he knew it. Neither of them did. They were staying to assuage their curiosity. They both knew I'd had a hard on for Maggie when she was in high school, my recent obsession with her hadn't gone unnoticed by anyone. I'd made it blatantly obvious when I'd crossed that line at Franny's funeral and wrapped her up in my arms. Her tears had made it impossible not to.

"What's going on?" Maggie called softly and all eyes went to the mouth of the hallway. Her hair had been pulled up into a messy bun on top of her head. Her clothes had been switched for a short, green tank top that ended high above her belly button. He shorts were barely existent and rode low on her hips. Black ink curved around her right hip, words I couldn't make out from here. I'd have to take a closer look when she was within touching distance again.

She tipped her head towards the couch Ronin and Trip now occupied. "Why are they here, in my house?"

The words were clear, no telltale slur to them announcing she was drunk. She looked steady on her feet and I didn't think that meant good things for me.

"They go where I go," I said in a careful voice, hesitant even. She was going to kick my ass out for sure now and I'd be forced to go because I wouldn't fight with her in front of my boys. Not that they'd give a shit, but it might embarrass her, and who knew what would set her off running again. I would chase after her, there was no doubt in my mind about that now. I was obsessed, and my fixation on her grew stronger by the day, by the hour. I'd lose my fucking mind if she left.

I hadn't been like this before prison, I'd like to think I had been a slightly normal outlaw who had loose morals and a knack for violence. Something about my time inside had changed me. I'd come out a different man but had somehow still looked the same on the outside. My looks fooled a lot of people into thinking I was still that same man. It worked in my favor a lot of time. Until it didn't, mistakes were made and messes needed to be cleaned up.

"They can stay then," Maggie murmured. "But only because you promised to tell me what I want to know. If you fall back on your promise then I'm going to kick all of your asses out of here. And," she pointed a finger towards the men on the couch, "none of you assholes better drink my vodka or eat my food. I don't care if you're starving, that is not my problem."

They both looked at her with amused faces but were smart enough to keep their mouths shut. At getting no reaction out of them she shot me a dirty look and turned, sauntering back down the hallway where she'd come from. The extra sway to her hips missed the mark when she stumbled and had to catch herself against the wall to keep from falling over.

Ronin started to chuckle. Maggie flipped him off behind her back and disappeared down the hall.

"She's drunk," I informed them unnecessarily.

"That much was obvious, brother." Trip said in a quiet voice that held a hint of concern. "I always thought she was different, untouchable, not like her ma at all, ya know?"

"She is different," I said. "She's been through a lot recently though and she's taking the death of her sister really hard."

"How well do you really know her, brother?" Ronin asked in a careful voice. Careful because he didn't want to offend me. They were my boys, loyal to a fault, but I feared I hadn't hidden the depths of my changes from them. "She's been back in town, what, a week and a half? How long have you been seeing her for?"

I counted back in my head from the moment I'd laid eyes on her at the fair. "Five days," I said in a sure voice. "Though, I'm sure she would argue that we're not actually seeing each other but she would be wrong. I've decided she's mine and she'll eventually have to come to terms with it and get on board."

They both looked at me as if I'd lost my damn mind, and maybe they were right to look at me that way.

"Man," Trip said in a careful voice, "you can't just decide some chick is yours then say it's so and expect it to all work out that way. That's not exactly how shit works in the real world."

"Shut the fuck up, Trip," Ronin muttered irately. "It's not up to you what he, or anybody else for that matter, chooses to do with their love life. Fuck. Maybe we really should get out of here tonight and come back in the morning."

"I'm not going anywhere," Trip snapped back at him.

Ignoring them, I went back to the front door and locked it. This was familiar territory for the both of them and something I remembered all too well. They could argue like this for hours and eventually it could get heated to where one of them was throwing a punch at the other one.

"I'll see you idiots in the morning," I said as I passed through the living room and headed towards the hallway. "If you eat her shit or drink her booze just be sure to replace it before she gets up tomorrow."

They both grunted in agreement before quietly starting to argue over who got control of the television remote.

Maggie was sitting up in her bed with her back against the headboard. The comforter pooled at her waist and her arms were folded ever her chest.

"What have you done that requires you go everywhere with body-guards?" She asked.

Ignoring her question, though I had to admit it was a smart one to ask on her part, I pulled down the straps on my shoulder rig, sliding them down my arms. Unceremoniously, I dropped both gun and holster on top of the nightstand. She watched me do this with a curious look on her face. I'd take curious over angry any day.

I pulled my phone out of my back pocket and dropped it down beside my gun. I unhooked my belt buckle and pulled my belt free of my jeans, rolling it up and setting it down beside the rest of my pile of shit. Grabbing ahold of the hem of my t-shirt I yanked on it and pulled it up my body, over my shoulders and off entirely. Before I'd gone down I would have tossed my shit to the floor and left it there, expecting someone else to come along and clean it up after me. Times had changed, and I'd changed with them. I folded my tee up nicely and laid it beside my growing pile.

I kept my jeans on even though sleeping in them was the last thing I wanted to do. She'd been complacent since I'd walked in here. I'd like to keep it that way.

I clicked off the lamp and pulled back the covers. She didn't protest as I slid in between the smooth sheets. A sigh of happiness escaped me as I laid back on the bed, my head landing on one of her pillows. She had the softest sheets I'd ever felt against my skin.

"Hawk," she whispered. "You promised."

I sighed as I covered my eyes with my arm.

"She was dancing," I said, and her sharp intake of breath filled the room. "At a club owned facility that my old man had used as a cover for one of his other lucrative businesses. Nobody had forced her to work there, she went looking all on her own. Ronin told me that it wasn't long after your ma died that she showed up at the clubhouse one day looking for company. And no, I don't mean the kind of company you're thinking about. She had no one, no job, was already living off of club money she'd received when your mom passed, the money she'd left both you girls that apparently you wanted nothing to do with. She showed up asking for a job and they offered her one waiting tables but she shot it down, choosing dancing instead. Out of respect for your mom and, from what I've been told, because she had been good at it, they gave her what she wanted. She excelled but apparently picked up an unfortunate habit from being around drugs all the time. She got in deep and when something my old man had set up backfired after I tried to pull my club out of it, they retaliated and shot up the entire bar where the drugs had been stored. Your sister had been working at the time and had gone down with the rest of the dancers. I have no fucking idea why you were told the clubhouse had been hit and she'd been there, and I'm trying to get down to the bottom of it but that's a lie. Still, it doesn't change the fact she got dead at a club owned place of business, and because of club bullshit."

I removed my arm from my face and chanced a glance at Maggie. She'd been silent through my entire speech and I wasn't sure if that meant she was plotting my murder or about to smack me again. I'd take both if that's what she wanted to give me. I'd take whatever she wanted to give me, violence suited me just fine.

Silent tears poured down her face and her body shook almost violently. This was worse than what she'd looked like earlier, worse than how she'd been during Franny's funeral.

"Come here, Maggie," I urged in a gentle voice as I opened up my arms to her.

"I hate you," she choked out.

"You can hate me," I murmured quietly. "That's okay. But, just so long as you know I had not one thing to do with your sister dying. I've been working my ass off since I got out to turn things around and make them better. My old man, I had to-"

I snapped my mouth shut, realizing I'd said far more than I had intended to. There were some things she never needed to know. Things no one outside of Ronin and Trip needed to know, and even them knowing set me on edge.

"You killed him, didn't you?" She whispered in a hoarse voice full of accusation.

I looked her dead in the eyes and told her the honest truth, "I was still in prison when he died." She'd get no more out of me.

"That doesn't mean-"

I cut her off. "Shut up, Poison. You know all you need to know. I told you about your sister, like I promised. Now, a deals a deal and that means it's time for us to go to sleep. Stop crying and get your ass over here. Or, you know what, I don't care if you keep on crying, just get over here, you can cry while I sleep."

She made an angry noise in the back of her throat as she wiped her cheeks with the back of her hand.

She slid down the bed and turned her back to me. Her head landed on the pillow and she tucked her hands up in a prayer under her cheek. The line of her back remained taunt, rigid and I knew it was because she worried I'd touch her or say something else to fuck up her world.

I rolled over onto my side and scooted back until we were back to back, barely touching but we were both more than aware of the heat between our bodies.

"Sleep, Maggie. Your problems will still be here when you wake up in the morning."

"First I'm Poison, then I'm Maggie." Her breath came out in a shudder that shook her thin frame. "I don't get it, and I don't think I should have to tell you again that it's you who's the poison, not me. I'm a nice person, dammit. At least I was until I got that phone call telling me the only person I loved in this whole world was dead. I've been thinking really bad, bad thoughts ever since then."

I had no doubt a woman who was capable of loving someone as much as she loved her sister was at this very moment plotting her revenge against those she'd thought had been responsible for her death. I know I should have been worried about her coming after my club, but in all honesty, it just made me want her more. I wanted that kind of love for myself even if I knew I'd never do anything to deserve it. I wanted it more than I had ever wanted anything in my whole miserable existence. I wanted it worse than my longing after being locked up to have nothing but my bike, the open road ahead of me and the wind whipping past me as I roared down the road. The ultimate freedom, and I wanted Maggie more than I had wanted even that.

Now I had a shot at both, and I was going to get everything I wanted. Even if it meant I would have to kill people for Maggie in order to avenge her sister, so that she didn't ever have to get her own hands dirty. The fact it would be some of my own people who'd die meant next to nothing to me.

Prison changed a man's priorities, especially when you found out it was your own father who'd put you there.

It took less than twenty minutes for her body to stop shaking, and her quiet sobs to die off. When she lay limp in bed beside me I knew she'd finally lost herself to sleep.

Fucking finally.

It had almost hurt trying to hold myself still and stop myself from turning around and pulling her into my arms. I couldn't remember when the last time I'd held a woman in my arms while she slept was, if I'd ever done it. Before prison, women had held an entirely different purpose for me. After prison, I'd fucked my way through a whole slew of club whores before becoming bored and entirely desensitized to it.

Gently, I rolled Maggie over onto her back and then I pulled her body into me. I slid my arm underneath her and very carefully drug her body on top of mine. Her legs fell to the mattress surrounding mine, her arms doing the same.

Brushing the hair off her face, I tangled my fingers in her hair as I slid my hand back around to the back of her skull. I held her close to me, pressing her check into my chest, above my heart.

My entire world shrank down to this moment as her dead weight settled on top of me. She could be pissed about my manhandling her when she woke up in the morning, I didn't care. It was worth every second of it.

It took me longer to fall asleep than it had her. When I did sleep, for the first time in years, I slept like the dead and didn't wake up with a nightmare once.

My boys had my back and my girl was on top of me.

The rest would eventually work itself out or end up dead. Either one worked for me.

CHAPTER 6

MAGGIE

THE HARD, INCREDIBLY WARM BODY BENEATH MY OWN HAD ME SUCKING IN A sharp breath as I slowly blinked my eyes open.

Sometime during the night Hawk must have hauled my body on top of his. It was a gross invasion of my personal space, and I wanted very much to hate him for it. Since I felt like I'd actually gotten a full night's sleep for the first time in almost two weeks, I couldn't be upset or even hold it against him.

My eyes roamed over his face, taking in the subtle differences from when he was awake. There was a slight softness to him around his mouth and eyes. He looked less angry, less likely to pull out his gun and shoot someone just for looking at him funny. It was a horrible thing to stereotype him like that, but he looked like the outlaw biker slash felon that he was.

Guilt ate at me.

He'd been kind to me on so many different levels. He'd taken my abuse, be it the physical *and* verbal kind and not said shit about it to me. He'd stood at my side when everyone else had stood before me, and then he'd held me while I'd cried my eyes out at my sister's funeral. I had a feeling that last night he'd shown up here to check on me because he hadn't seen me in a few days and wanted to make sure I was okay.

I was starting to think that Hawk, despite now being president of the Kings of Torment Motorcycle Club, was a decent, even kind man.

And didn't that just fuck with me on a whole different level.

I was all about taking the Kings of Torment men down. Laying in bed beside Hawk? Yeah, there was one man I really hoped I wouldn't drag down with the rest of them. I think I would lose another vital part of myself were that to happen, and I didn't think I could afford to lose much else before becoming a person I didn't think I could live with being.

I could live with destroying people I thought had ruined my sister. I couldn't live with harming Hawk, I was starting to think.

He was growing on me, like some sort of disgusting boil. I could pop it and clean up the mess afterwards but would it leave me with a permanent scar?

"I know you're awake," he rumbled in a deep voice that sent a happy little shiver down my spine, my body betraying me.

His eyes opened lazily, and I ended up staring down into his deep, dark depths.

"I didn't mean to wake you," I murmured.

"I was up before you woke," he whispered back and heat filled the darkness of his eyes. "Your sweet body pressed up against mine has had my dick hard and ready to go for a while now. You're driving me crazy."

I narrowed my eyes at him. "I didn't get here on my own. In fact, I'm betting I had not one thing to do with it."

He grinned at me, unrepentant, and he looked a whole lot less scary in that moment too.

"You definitely didn't get here on your own," he murmured, and my body tensed as his eyes dropped down to my mouth.

"Don't look at me like that," I whispered as our eyes locked. His hardened as they filled with determination. For whatever reason, Hawk had decided he wanted me, and that determination in his eyes solidified it.

That guilt I had talked about earlier dug its way in a little deeper, carving up my insides. It was more than that though. The more he came around, the more he pushed his way in, the more I feared he dug his way under my skin.

I crawled off his body and slid off the side of the bed. My feet hit the floor with a soft thud and I quickly turned around. With my back to him I was hoping he wouldn't be able to read the emotions crossing my face.

Sheets rustled, then feet thudded on the floor. His heat hit my back before strong arms wrapped around my middle. His palm pressed against the exposed skin above my belly button and below the hem of my top. His thumb roamed around my skin in small circles, caressing. I shivered at the contact.

He pulled me back into his body and his mouth went to my ear. His lips brushed against my ear as he whispered, "What are your plans today, baby?"

Baby?

I think I preferred Poison when it came down to it. Poison was less dangerous to me than *baby.*

"I need to get back to work," I muttered. "I've fallen behind schedule and need to make up the lost time."

He hummed into my neck. "What is it that you do for a living?"

"I'm a writer."

"Like books and that shit?" He asked.

I rolled my eyes. "Yes, Hawk, like books and that *shit."*

"That's cool," he said as he ran his palm up and down against my bare skin before letting me go. "You gotta go anywhere to do that, like a coffee shop or anything? Or, can you do that from home?"

I whirled around to face him, not at all liking where this was going. I crossed my arms over my chest while I watched him pick up his cellphone off the bedside table and start to go through his messages.

"I prefer to work from home, by myself. Otherwise I get distracted. Why do you ask?"

Please don't say what I think you're going to say. Please don't say what I think you're going to say.

He blew out a heavy breath that stirred the long hair hanging around his face. His shoulders tensed, and the fingers wrapped around his phone tightened.

Without looking at me, he spoke. "The shit with my club is only just getting started, I'm afraid. I could be wrong, and I'd be damn happy to admit it if I am, but I'm not willing to take any chances with you. I made a bold move at the funeral and all eyes were on us. Then with me spending the night here, I'm sure there are plenty of people out there who already know exactly what that means. When I leave here today I'm going to leave one of my boys here with you, and I am going to ask that you please be smart and not argue with me about it. If you don't want someone hanging out with you in your house that's cool, just tell them to get out and they'll wait outside. No big deal, no hurt feelings, just that simple."

I dropped my head, staring down at my feet.

Playing my game, biding my time, this, having his boys stay with me when he wasn't around was the golden opportunity and it had fallen right into my lap. I hadn't even had to work for it. Hawk just handed it right over.

"Okay," I said in a small voice as I squeezed my eyes shut painfully. I drew in a shuddering breath and released it in a rush.

Knuckles went to my chin, gently lifting my face. The pad of his thumb on his other hand came up and brushed across my bottom lip.

"I'll be back later," he said. "I'm pretty sure you know what I want from you but I want to make myself clear. I want you. I want you in my life, on my bike, and under my body with my dick buried inside you. And I want that in a way I've never wanted anything. You did the stupid thing and you stuck around, now you're stuck with me and I'm spending the night tonight. I'm going to let you off easy though and let you get to know me a little better before you give yourself to me because you just put your sister in the ground. But, make no mistake, Poison, you're going to give yourself to me and I'm going to love every fucking second of it."

His hand fell away, and my heart beat in overtime as I stumbled back, his words washing over me.

He spared me not a glance as he pulled his shirt from yesterday back on, slid his belt into place, pulled his arms through his shoulder holster and stuffed his phone into the back pocket of his jeans.

"If you need anything let Ronin know and he'll have someone take care of it for you."

Then he was gone, and I was left feeling like a prisoner in my own home with a guard and a whole slew of mixed feelings.

Nothing was going to plan.

Good thing I had time to figure it all out.

CHAPTER 7

LANCE

Looking over my shoulder one last time, I walked around the side of the old, half rotten, crumpled mess of a farm house and strode quickly to the back of it. Nobody had followed me, of that I was certain. But, you never knew with my father's men who were still to this day loyal to the man even though they thought him dead. I wouldn't put it past them to be hanging out around here for some fucked up reason.

The farm house and all the land belonged to my father, it had been passed down generation by generation, father to son. One day it would be mine, I already considered it as such, even if I didn't want it and hadn't asked for it.

The doors to the cellar were locked with a padlock only I had the key for. I slid the key in and turned, unlocking it. I twisted the lock free and stuck it in my back pocket. I didn't leave it hanging off the door because I didn't trust someone not coming along and locking me in down there. Paranoia was my friend and had yet to steer me wrong.

I pulled a flashlight out of my back pocket and clicked the button. Light shined down the cement steps, and I strode down them. Cobwebs brushed against my hair and I swatted at them in an attempt to get the sticky shit out of my hair.

I swept the flashlight around the room in a circle, making sure there were no surprises waiting for me. The room was empty save for a few damp, mold covered boxes sitting in a corner and a door directly across from the stairs. Ignoring the boxes and the garbage inside them, I strolled across the cracked floor to the door that was locked with yet another padlock only I had the key to.

Using my key, I unlocked this padlock too and stuffed the lock into my back pocket beside the other one. The door swung open with a noisy creak, and I pushed my way inside.

Outside of the beam of light the flashlight I held in my hand spewed across the tiny, dank room, there was no other source of light.

He had been stuck down here for weeks now, chained to the floor like a rabid dog, in the dark. The only food he'd eaten had been brought by me. The only water he'd drank had been given to him by me. Outside of that, he had a bucket to piss and shit in and you could tell it'd been a few days since I'd last visited to dump the waste out and hose the bucket off. The smell gave my absence away.

Snarling at me in angry words I couldn't understand, my father lunged forward in an attempt to attack me. The chain around his neck pulled tight when he reached the end of its length, jerking him back and off his feet. His back slammed into the dirty floor, and he grunted in pain.

I'd been smart enough to stand just out of reach of him every time I'd come here for our father son visits. These had gone a whole lot better for both of us when it had been me who'd essentially been chained up like a fucking animal.

Leaning a shoulder against the dusty wall, I sneered down at him. "Now, now, old man, you would think you'd be smarter than this by now. Yet, here you are, doing the same thing over and over again, week after week, like that brain of yours is no longer in proper working order."

"Fuck you, *son,*" he spat. "The club will figure out soon enough what you've done."

I shrugged carelessly. "I plan on telling them what it is that you've done first. Framed your own son for a crime you committed and had him sent down to do time before anyone could figure out what it was you actually did. Then there's all the attempts on my life while I was inside, attempts orchestrated by you. All because you're a greedy fuck and knew if the club had something, someone, else to choose they'd side against you, so you tried to take out your only competition. Me. Jokes on you, old man, I'm still standing."

He lunged for me again, charging like an angry bull, but once again, the chain stopped him, jerking him back.

He fell backwards and hit the floor with a sick sounding *plop* that echoed around the small room. He never did seem to learn, and here I had always idolized him growing up. Until, I'd learned the sad truth about him, that is.

"I'm not here for that, not today."

He eyed me suspiciously, and my lip curled in disgust. Like he had any choice in what went on here. He was going to give me exactly what I wanted, or I was going to end him once and for all.

"I'm not telling you a fucking thing," he snarled, and this time he actually spit at me. Nothing but spittle flew from past his lips, landing a foot before my boots.

My lips curved in a dark, sadistic smile.

He was going to give me everything I wanted to know, no matter how long it took me to beat it out of him.

I needed to know how to shut down his drug ring for good because my tentative relationship with Maggie depended on it. I'd seen the frantic, almost desperate looks that filled her eyes constantly.

Maggie, my sweet Poison, wasn't cut out for revenge.

But I was.

And I had a feeling I'd be damn good at it.

The End.

Connect with Mary:
FACEBOOK: http://www.facebook.com/Mary-Martel-Author
FACE BOOK GROUP:
http://www.facebook.com/groups/marymartelthedollhouse

MAMA BY NICOLE JACQUELYN

An Aces' Sons Short Story

CHAPTER 1

LILY

"You have to be quiet," Leo chastised, chuckling as my mouth snapped shut. "We're on borrowed time as it is."

His arms flexed as he held himself above me, and I let out a sigh as he rolled his hips. For a man that refused to dance under any circumstance, my Leo sure could move. Wrapping my legs around his, I scored my fingernails up his back.

"Oh, that ain't fair," he said, shaking his head. Just as I started to giggle, the baby monitor by our bed lit up and the sound of movement came through the speaker.

"Shit," I whispered.

"Hang on tight, Dandelion," he replied. His hand slid between us, and as his fingers found my clit his pace quickened. "I'll get you there."

"You always do." Pulling my legs further up his hips, I gasped. Yeah, that was the angle I needed. It didn't take long before I felt the beginning of my orgasm wash over me. Leo wasn't far behind.

"We're getting really good at quickies," I said as Leo rolled away with a huff.

"We've always been good at quickies," he argued, shooting me a smile. "But they're gettin' old."

"Hey," I said, mildly offended.

He rolled his eyes. "You know I'll take ya any way I can get ya." He leaned up on his elbow. "At some point, I'd like to take my time, though."

"Ooh," I whispered, rolling toward him. "I'm listening."

Leo laughed and leaned toward me, but before he could speak, Gray's voice came through the monitor.

"Daddy," he rasped groggily. "Get me."

I snorted. "The little prince has spoken."

Leo flopped onto his back. "Is it just me," he said with a groan, "or did he sleep a lot later when he was in here with us?"

"Of course he did," I replied, sitting up. I climbed off the bed and pulled on my nightshirt. "It was nice and cozy in here."

"He's doin' good in his own room, though," he said, pulling on a pair of shorts. "Better than I thought he would."

"Thank God," I joked. "It's nice to have sex in a bed again."

"I fuck you in a bed all the time."

"Your room at the clubhouse doesn't count," I shot back. "It's tiny, and hard as a rock."

"Never heard you complainin'," he mumbled.

"You know I'll take ya anyway I can get ya," I mimicked him, slapping him on the ass as I passed him. "I'll get Gray."

As soon as I stepped into the hallway, I found Gray standing in the doorway to his room, his little hands curled around the top of the baby gate that kept him from roaming the house while we slept.

"Hey, mister," I said, lifting him up as soon as his arms reached for me. "Did you sleep good?"

He nodded and laid his head against my shoulder.

"Let's change your Pull-Up," I said softly, rubbing his back as I stepped over the gate into his room. "You're feeling pretty soggy."

I set him back on his bed with a kiss, then crossed the room to his dresser. If I was going to change his Pull-Up, I figured I might as well just get him dressed for the day. As I pulled out some sweats and a t-shirt, Gray started chattering behind me. I wasn't really paying attention because it didn't sound like he was talking to me, but I froze with my hand on a tiny pair of socks when I realized what he was saying.

"Mama." I didn't respond.

"Mama, yuck." Oh, crap. I spun just in time to see him pull off the sopping wet Pull-Up and drop it nasty side down on the bed.

"Dude," I groaned, hurrying to pick it up. "I just washed your sheets."

"Ew," he said, standing in the middle of the bed in nothing but a t-shirt.

"Yeah, ew," I agreed. Scooping him up, I carried him and the dirty Pull-Up into the kitchen so I could throw it away. "Don't take your Pull-Up off, okay? I'll help you."

"I do it," he argued, sticking his thumb in his mouth.

"I'd rather you didn't," I said dryly as we made our way back down the hall.

We found Leo back in bed, one arm behind his head and the other scrolling through something on his phone.

"Merry Christmas!" I teased, dropping Gray onto the bed. "It's a bouncing baby boy!"

"And he's Porky Pig'n it," Leo said with a laugh.

"He's what?"

"Porky Pig'n it," Leo said again. "You know—wearin' a shirt and no pants."

I laughed. "I'll go grab his clothes."

The boys laughed and wrestled as I stripped Gray's sheet and blanket off his mattress, crossing my fingers that Gray wouldn't pee in our bed. He was doing awesome with potty training, but any tickling and it was game over.

"I've got clothes," I announced as I walked back into our room. "Put them on before you get peed on."

"Me no pee," Gray said, shaking his head. "Me no pee, Mama."

I stopped suddenly, stunned, but thankfully, Leo took the words in stride.

"Silly Mama," he said softly, his eyes on me. "Gray's not gonna pee."

"Right," I said, my voice scratchy and weird. "What was I thinking?"

I tossed the clothes on the bed with a smile, then spun on my heel and hurried to the bathroom so I could cry in private. I should have known that Leo wouldn't let me get away with it, though. Within a couple minutes, two fists, one big and one small, were banging on the bathroom door.

"We're hungry," Leo called as I blew my nose.

"Hungy," Gray mimicked.

"You know how to cook," I said, swinging open the door so fast it made Gray burst out laughing.

"But you do it so much better," Leo lied. The innocent look on his face didn't fool me for a second.

"I'll do the waffles if you fry the eggs," I said, poking Gray in the belly as we made our way to the kitchen.

My mind wandered as I started pulling out ingredients and Leo set Gray up in his booster at the table. I guess I shouldn't have been as surprised as I was that Gray had called me mama. Most of the other kids he spent time with had moms, so he heard the word all the time. And I did fill that role for him. I took care of him and comforted him, and he'd slept next to me more nights than I could count. I'd considered him my son since me and Leo got together.

But he'd always called me Lily, and I was perfectly okay with that.

"Hey, Mama," Leo said quietly as he reached around me for the butter.

"Did that seriously just happen?" I asked, glancing over my shoulder.

Gray was playing with his little dirt bikes, making all kinds of engine noises and completely unconcerned with us, but I still didn't want him to hear me making a big deal about it.

"Yep," Leo said easily.

"Where did it come from?" I wondered out loud. Leo laughed.

"Why are you so surprised?" he asked, cracking eggs one-handed into the skillet. "You're his mom in every way that matters."

"It doesn't bother you?" I asked tentatively.

Gray's mom had died in a car accident right before me and Leo got together, and I knew that it broke Leo's heart that Gray couldn't remember Ashley. It was something that we'd talked about a lot and I'd always been super aware of. Neither of us ever wanted Ashley to disappear completely from Gray's life. It was why we had photos of her around the house, and Leo made a point to tell Gray about his mom's favorite things and all the ways they were alike.

"Of course it doesn't bother me," Leo said, giving me a sweet smile. "There's nothin' wrong with Gray callin' you *mama*."

"But Ashley—"

Leo laughed. "Baby, Ashley would be grateful as fuck that Gray had someone that loves him like you do. Jealous? Hell, yeah. But grateful, too."

"I doubt it," I muttered.

"I know it," he said firmly. "'Cause I'd be grateful, and jealous as hell, too, if I was gone and he had a good man that stepped into my shoes."

I didn't reply, because honest to God, I couldn't imagine being grateful if Gray called someone else mom.

"You okay with it?" Leo asked as he turned off the burner and slid the eggs onto a plate. "You seem freaked."

"Not freaked," I replied, peeling a waffle carefully off the iron. "Overwhelmed."

"Doesn't change anythin'," he said, squeezing my hip as he moved around me. "You've been his mom for a while now."

"I know."

"Get outta your head, Dandelion," he teased as he moved away. "You're overthinkin' it."

AFTER DROPPING Gray off to sleep at Ashley's mom's house that night, I met Leo at the clubhouse. I was happy to have the time kid-free, but I had to admit that I wished we were spending the night at home instead of attending yet another club party. Don't get me wrong, the parties were fun.

We always had a good time, and usually made a point to spend some time one-on-one, but I was exhausted. Between finishing my degree and doing the books for a couple of small business owners my dad had introduced me to, I was stretched thin as hell.

"Good, you're here," my sister-in-law Trix said, pulling me toward the bar before I'd even taken my coat off. "Tell your brother that I'm right and he's wrong."

"She's right and you're wrong," I parroted.

"You don't even know what we were talkin' about," Cam protested.

"Let's be real," I said with a laugh. "Trix is usually the one who's right."

"Not this time," Cam shot back.

I smiled as I felt muscular arms wrap around my waist from behind.

"Gray all set?" Leo asked, kissing my neck.

"Yep," I replied, spinning to face him. "And Kathy was in fine form."

"She give you shit?" he asked darkly.

"Not any more than usual," I said, shaking my head. Ashley's mom glowered at me any time I dropped Gray off, and a few times, I'd thought she wasn't going to let him leave when I'd gone there to pick him up. She was a huge pain in the ass, but I couldn't help but give her some slack. Gray was the only connection she had to the daughter she'd lost, and it had to be really hard for her to see me taking care of him when her daughter couldn't.

"I'll have a talk with her," Leo said.

"Don't," I replied, kissing his chin. "You'll only make it worse. I can handle Kathy."

"She shouldn't be actin' like that in front of Gray," he argued. "She shouldn't be doin' it, period."

"She's grieving."

"She can grieve without bein' a bitch to you."

"Who's being a bitch to you?" my cousin Rose butt in, wrapping her arms around both of us. "I'll take care of it."

"Kathy," I said, grimacing.

"Oh, never mind," she replied. "I draw the line at old people."

"I didn't know you had a line," Leo said dryly.

"It's faint," she said, grinning. "But it's there."

"Hey," I said, elbowing her in the side. "I thought you were working tonight?"

"I am." She let go of us and took a step back. "But your little sister borrowed my coat the other day, so I dropped by to grab it from your mom."

"You were with Charlie the other day and you didn't invite me?"

"You were in class and I needed wing-women at the mall," she said, shrugging as she walked backward. "I took all the girls."

"They still love me more," I called after her as she walked away.

"Keep dreaming," she called back with a wave.

Leo's chest rumbled with laughter, and I turned back around to see my brother scowling and Trix smiling triumphantly.

"You can't just keep askin' people to say you're right," Cam bitched, "when they don't even know what you're talkin' about."

"You just said I had to get someone to agree with me," she said, pointing at him. "And I got multiple someones."

"This is bullshit," he muttered. Then he raised his voice. "Bartender!" He shot Trix an irritated look. "I'd like a Sex on the Beach."

The people around us turned to look, and when he spoke again, there were no voices to drown him out.

"With a little umbrella, please."

Trix laughed, clutching her waist as she bent forward.

"I hope you pee yourself," Cam said, making her laugh even harder.

"One for me, too," Leo called out. "Make my umbrella pink."

He raised his fist so my brother could bump it with his. "Solidarity, brother."

"Appreciate it," Cam replied, his lips twitching.

"Aw," I said, my voice teasing. "Do you guys need a second alone?"

"Real funny," Leo said, reaching for the beer that the prospect brought him.

"You were kiddin' about the Sex on the Beach, right?" the kid asked nervously.

"Yeah, man," Leo said with a laugh. "Thanks."

We left the bar and worked our way through the room, saying hi to people that we saw almost every damn day. If I hadn't grown up in the club and known what I was getting into when I got with Leo, it probably would have driven me crazy. We practically lived in each others' pockets.

"You're coming for lunch tomorrow, right?" my mom asked. She was sitting on one of the couches with her feet in my dad's lap.

"Yep," I said with a nod, sitting on the arm of the couch while Leo made his way to the pool tables. "I told Kathy we'd pick Gray up at ten, so he'd have time for a nap before we come over."

"Good call," she said. "He's going to need the energy to keep up with the big kids."

"And he'd be a monster without a nap," I said ruefully.

"Don't call my grandson a monster," she scolded, leaning against me. "He's an angel."

"Cool, I'll bring him to your house next time he won't nap," I joked.

"Perfect," she said, grinning.

"You're nuts."

"Seems like you'd be used to it by now."

"Hey, Casper," my Uncle Grease called from across the room. "Your oldest nephew thinks he can beat your ass at pool."

"I didn't say that," my cousin Will said, glaring at my uncle as my dad patted my mom's feet and stood up from the couch.

"Care to make a wager?" my dad asked as he walked toward them.

"Sit," my mom ordered, lifting her feet in the air.

"I hope Will doesn't think he actually has a chance," I said as I took the spot my dad left.

"He doesn't," my mom said easily. "Grease is just stirring the pot."

I watched as Leo laughed hard at something one of the guys said, and I couldn't help but grin. Jesus, my man was hot.

"Things are still going good there, I see," my mom said, nudging me with her foot.

"Yep," I sighed happily and turned, curling one of my legs under me. "Gray called me *mama* this morning."

"Aw," my mom cooed. "Did you cry?"

"Why would you think I cried?" I asked with a huff.

"Because you're a crybaby," she joked, jerking her feet away when I went to pinch one. "I'm kidding!"

"I only cried a little," I admitted.

"I totally choked up when Cam called me *ma* the first time," she said with a soft smile, glancing over her shoulder at my brother. "He was a lot older, though. He'd said it a bunch of times when we were trying to teach CeeCee to talk, but the first time he just called me *ma*, like it was no big deal? Hit me right in the gut."

"He's such a mama's boy," I muttered, chuckling as Cam threw Trix over his shoulder across the room.

"It's not like Leo's any better," my mom replied. "He adores Brenna."

"Good point."

"And Gray adores you," she said simply. "Girls are awesome, but boys are in a whole different league."

"Gee, thanks."

Mom laughed. "You know I love you guys the same," she said, rolling her eyes. "But a boy's relationship with his mama is an entirely different animal. Once you and Leo have a girl, you'll know what I'm talking about."

"If we have a girl," I replied. "I don't know if we'll have *any*."

"Really?" she said, lifting her eyebrows in surprise.

"We haven't talked about it much," I said with a shrug. "But anytime it comes up, Leo says he wants to wait."

"That makes sense," she replied. "You've got a pretty full plate at the moment."

"I know, it just feels like he's putting it off because he doesn't want to tell me that he doesn't want any more," I confessed.

"Nah," my mom said easily. "Leo's always wanted you to have everything you want, and if more babies are something you want, I can't see him saying no."

"Maybe."

"Just ask him," she ordered. "I swear to God, ninety percent of the problems people have are from misunderstandings, because no one actually communicates with their partner anymore."

"You're one to talk," I shot back.

Mom laughed. "I," she said, drawing the word out, "like to keep a bit of mystery."

"You just like to drive Dad crazy," I argued.

"Oh, yeah, I do," she said, smiling. I wrinkled my nose at the insinuation in her voice.

"That is *not* how I meant it."

"Hey," she said as I got up from my seat. "That's an important part of a healthy relationship!"

"*Lalalalala,*" I sang loudly, covering my ears as I strode toward Leo.

"Hey, baby," he murmured as I reached him, pulling me against his side. "You good?"

"My mom has no filter whatsoever," I griped.

Leo laughed. "Neither do you."

"Yes, I do," I argued.

"You've got the mouth of a sailor, and no topic is off limits. I'd say you're almost exactly like Farrah."

"You shut your mouth when you're talking to me," I gasped in mock horror, pulling against his hold on my waist.

"How many times has Rose given me shit about somethin' I said to you in bed?" Leo asked with a laugh.

"That's different," I protested, my lips twitching. "That's just Rose."

"What about the time you thought that chick was checkin' me out, and you started spoutin' off loud enough for the entire bar to hear you about how my favorite position was reverse cowgirl because I love to watch your ass jiggle?"

"Was I lying?"

"Not the point, Dandelion," Leo chuckled.

"She needed to know you belonged to me," I grumbled.

"Think you made that pretty clear," he teased. He leaned down and kissed me hard.

"Wait," I said, pulling away. "That's still your favorite position, right?"

"Nah," he said, shaking his head slowly as he grinned at me. "I like seein' your face when you come."

Later that night, I made all his dirty dreams come true.

"You sure you don't want me to grab him?" Leo asked the next morning, his words garbled by the toothbrush in his mouth.

"No," I replied, pulling on my underwear. "I'll get him. I'm going to bring him home for a nap before we head to my parents.'"

"Remind me why I told Will I'd help him this morning?"

"Because you were drunk," I called over my shoulder as I grabbed my bra off the bed. "You always volunteer for shit when you're drunk."

"I do not," he said, cupping his hand under his chin to catch the dripping toothpaste.

"Go spit," I ordered, laughing. I finished dressing while he was in the bathroom and by the time he got back, I was sliding on my boots.

"Lunch is at noon, right?" he asked as he went to the dresser.

"Yeah." I sat on the bed and enjoyed the show. I loved watching him undress, but the opposite was almost as sexy. I'd never get tired of watching Leo, it didn't really matter what he was doing.

"I'll try to get over there earlier than that," he told me, stuffing his wallet into his back pocket.

"Just don't be late," I said, tipping my head back as he stepped between my knees. "My mom will make everyone wait on you, and it'll turn into a *thing*."

"I'll be on time," he said, his hands coming up to rest on the sides of my neck. "Gives me a reason to bail at Will's."

"Do you think it'll take very long to build a swing set? I thought they came with directions."

"Tommy'll be helpin'," Leo replied. "Gotta make allowances for that."

"True," I said with a laugh.

"Wish we had some more time," he said, his thumbs rubbing along the underside of my jaw. "I didn't get enough last night."

"Any more *time* and I wouldn't be able to walk today," I joked, everything inside me going warm.

"We need to take an entire weekend soon." One of his thumbs traced a line down my neck, and I swear I felt it in my nipples. "Spend the entire time in bed."

"I like that idea," I murmured, reaching out to run my hand down the front of his jeans. He was already hard. My mouth watered.

"Damn," he groaned. He glanced over his shoulder at the alarm clock on the bedside table and I followed his gaze.

"Shit," I said, "I need to leave. I told Kathy I'd be there at ten."

"Alright," he said with a sigh. He stepped back far enough that I could stand up, then leaned down to kiss me.

We left the house at the same time, and I climbed into my car as he opened the garage door to pull his bike out.

"Drive safe, baby," he called.

"Always," I replied with a wave.

Kathy's place wasn't very far from ours, so it didn't take long to get there, and when I pulled into the driveway, I was still ten minutes early.

"Shit," I muttered as I parked.

I shut the car off and leaned my head back against the headrest. If I tried to get Gray before ten, I knew she'd pitch a fit. I made an effort to keep the peace, because I knew Leo already had a really hard time with Kathy, but Jesus, the woman was a pain in the ass. I understood why she was possessive of Gray, but it didn't make her any easier to deal with. The sooner she realized that we all wanted what was best for her grandson and that included time with her, the better off everyone would be.

I killed time switching through radio stations and cleaning out the center console, and at exactly ten o'clock on the dot, I climbed out of the car. It was beginning to rain, so I pulled up my hood and jogged to the front porch. The overhang wasn't very big, so I had to crowd the door as I knocked.

"Come on," I murmured when she didn't answer the door. I could feel the rain seeping through the back of my sweatshirt. I knocked again.

After a few minutes of knocking, I rang the doorbell. Still no answer. I took a few steps back and tried to look in the front window. The curtains were pulled shut, but I couldn't see any light coming from inside the house.

"Kathy?" I yelled, my nose almost pressed to the glass.

"What are you doing?" a voice yelled behind me. "Get outta here before I call the cops."

I jerked and spun to find an older man staring at me from his front door.

"No," I said, laughing nervously as I lifted my hands palm out in front of me. "I'm just here to pick up my son." His expression didn't change. "Gray?"

"Kathy's not home, and you need to get outta here," he said with a little shooing motion.

"She's not home?" I said in surprise. "Do you know where she went?"

He turned and went back inside without answering.

"Yeah, thanks, asshole," I said, flipping off his house.

I jogged back to my car and once inside, I pulled up Kathy's number in my contacts. It didn't even ring before going straight to voicemail. What the fuck? I called Leo.

"Hey, Dandelion," he answered. "Remind me why we're buildin' this shit in the rain?"

"Babe, did Kathy try to call you?" I asked, ignoring his question.

"What?" he asked. "No, she hasn't called me. Is she givin' you shit? I knew I shoulda went with you to pick him up."

"They're not here," I said, staring out the front windshield.

"Say what?"

"They're not here," I repeated. "I'm sitting in front of the house, and no one is here."

"Did you try to call her?"

"It went straight to voicemail."

"Why does that woman insist on bein' such a fuckin' cunt all the time?" Leo barked. "I'll try her from my phone. Sit tight, yeah?"

"I'm not going anywhere," I replied.

I sat in my car, soaking wet and fuming, as Leo tried to get ahold of Gray's grandmother, and the longer I waited, the more worried I got. Kathy made snide remarks and acted like she didn't hear us when we asked her not to give Gray a bunch of sweets or to have him dressed when we picked him up, but she'd never just not been home when we came to get him. My stomach rumbled with anxiety. Something was wrong.

My phone barely rang before I answered it.

"I can't get ahold of her, either," Leo said. "I'm gonna keep tryin.' Come over to Will's and pick me up."

"Okay," I said, my voice a little shaky as I started the car.

"Careful drivin'," Leo ordered. "Roads are gonna be slick."

"I know how to drive in the rain," I replied as I backed out of the driveway.

"Be careful, anyway."

The drive to Will's house seemed twice as long as usual, and by the time I got there, my stomach was in knots.

"Did you get ahold of her?" I asked as Leo met me at the door.

"Think her phone's off," he replied, running his fingers through his hair. "What the fuck is she doin'?"

"Maybe she just ran to the store or something," I said peeling off my sweatshirt. I paused. "Should we go back and wait for her?"

"Fuck," Leo snapped in frustration. "Hell if I know."

"Everything okay?" Molly asked, peeking her head around the wall between the kitchen and the living room. "Where's Gray?"

"We have no fucking clue," I replied. I felt tears sting the back of my eyes and clenched my jaw, trying to hold them back.

"What's going on?" she asked, coming into the room.

"Supposed to pick him up from Ashley's mom's place, and when Lil showed up, no one was there," Leo replied.

"Did she get the time mixed up?" Molly asked reasonably.

"No." I shook my head. "She knew exactly what time I'd be there."

"She's probably just being an ass," Molly said with a huff. "Isn't this the woman that makes nasty comments every time you see her?"

"Yeah."

Molly wrinkled her nose. "She's probably just trying to exert some control."

"She has no control," Leo said. "She's got what I give her, and after this bullshit, she'll be lucky to have anything at all."

"Maybe we should go back and see if she's home," I said, anxious to do something.

"Alright," Leo replied. He looked at Molly. "I'm gonna leave my bike in your garage if that's cool? I can come get it later."

"No problem," Molly said as Leo helped me put my sweatshirt back on. "Let me know when you hear something."

I let Leo drive and I tried to call Kathy again as we headed to her place.

"Her phone's still turned off," I said, tossing my phone on the dash. "Why the fuck would she worry us like this?"

"Because she's a cunt," Leo said flatly. "And she doesn't give a shit if we're worried."

A few minutes later, we pulled into the driveway and Leo cursed. The lights were still off, and no one was home.

"Maybe she's taking Gray to our house," I said, a little glimmer of hope sparking in my chest. "Maybe we got our wires crossed or something."

"We can check," Leo said as he turned around and drove toward our place. "But I doubt it."

"Maybe her phone's dead and she's been sitting there waiting for us." The scenario seemed so plausible that I felt really silly for getting so worked up. It wasn't unheard of for Kathy to drop Gray off after a visit. It didn't happen often, but it did happen.

I was feeling so relieved as we drove home that I relaxed into my seat with a sigh. It was going to be really embarrassing if I'd worried Leo for nothing, and Gray had been sitting in front of our house for the last forty-five minutes while I'd been freaking out.

I'd convinced myself so thoroughly that Kathy must have driven Gray home, that when we pulled up in front of our little house and she wasn't there waiting, I couldn't believe it.

"Where is she?" I asked Leo in confusion.

"Come on, Dandelion," he said, climbing out of the car. "Might as well wait inside."

I followed him into the house, but I couldn't sit still. While Leo sat at a kitchen chair, staring at his phone, I paced back and forth, from the kitchen to the living room. Then I pulled some laundry out of the dryer and folded it. Threw some dirty clothes in the washer. Scrubbed the kitchen sink. Threw some expired food in the fridge away. Swept the floor. Organized the pictures and drawings on the front of the fridge so that everything was visible. Watered the plant in the kitchen window. Went through the pile of mail on the counter.

"Lily," Leo finally said. "Sit, baby."

"I can't," I replied, crossing my arms over my chest as I leaned my hips against the cupboards. My phone vibrated in my pocket, and I pulled it out as quick as I could.

"Dammit," I said before lifting it to my ear. "Hey, Mom."

"Where are you?" she asked. "I thought you were going to help me with lunch."

"Sorry," I replied. "I went to get Gray, and he wasn't there."

"What?"

"Yeah, so me and Leo have been waiting at the house, hoping Kathy would call." I paused. "I'm sure it's just a misunderstanding."

Leo scoffed.

"How late is she?" my mom asked.

I glanced at the clock and swallowed hard. "Two hours."

"Oh, fuck no," mom muttered. "Me and your dad will be there in a bit."

"No, Mom—" I stopped talking when she hung up on me.

"I'm not doin' this again," Leo said, his fingers tapping on the table. "If I can't trust her to have Gray where he's supposed to be, these visits are fuckin' over."

"You should probably call your mom," I said quietly. "My mom and dad are on their way over."

"Christ."

"I couldn't stop her," I said in apology.

"It's fine," he said, reaching his hand out so I'd come to him. He wrapped his arm around my back and dropped his forehead against my sternum. "Kathy doesn't show up soon, I was gonna have to call them, anyway."

She didn't call. My parents showed up. Leo's parents showed up. Cam and Trix showed up. We all waited, pretending like we weren't getting more and more worried as each hour passed. By three o'clock, though, Leo had hit his limit.

"We need to fuckin' find her," he said, getting up from his seat. "How do we do that?" He looked at my dad. "Track her phone or somethin'?"

"I can ask my contact to track it, yeah, but it's gonna take some time."

"How much time?" Leo asked.

"Could be a few hours."

"Shit," Leo snarled.

"I'll see what I can do," my dad said, clapping Leo on the shoulder as he pulled out his phone.

"Why the hell would she do this?" Leo's mom Brenna asked no one in particular. "She must know she's completely screwing herself."

"I doubt she's playing the long game, Mom," Trix answered. "She's probably pissed about something, and decided to make a point."

"What could she possibly be that pissed about?" I asked, using my fingertips to rub at my eyes.

"Who knows?" Trix replied. "She's not exactly smart."

"Hey, Rose," my mom called across the room, her eyes on her phone. "Doesn't Gray have a tablet?"

"Yeah, why?"

"It says here that if you have a certain app, you can use your phone to locate it."

"We have the app, but it only works if the tablet is connected to wi-fi," I replied dismissively. It took longer than I'd like to admit before I pulled out my phone and opened up the app.

"Might as well try," Trix said quietly.

My mouth dropped open in surprise when a little blinking dot appeared.

"I'll be damned," Trix muttered. "Bingo."

"Leo," I called, zooming out on the little map. "I found him."

"You what?" Leo asked, striding toward me.

"His tablet is connected to the internet," I said, trying to make sense of the map. "I tracked him."

"You're a fuckin' genius," he said, kissing the side of my head as he looked over my shoulder.

"Technically, I'm the genius," my mom announced. We ignored her as we stared at the map.

"What's the word?" Dragon asked, crossing his arms over his chest.

I didn't reply. I didn't recognize any of the streets on the map.

"She took him to Portland," Leo said, holding out his hand so I'd pass him the phone.

I watched as he carried it over to where his dad and Cam were standing. Why the hell would she take Gray all the way to Portland? It didn't make any sense.

My dad came back in the room and joined the men as they huddled around the phone.

"They're right next to the airport," my dad said quietly. The air in the room went electric. "Look, there's 82nd Street," he pointed, "and Airport Way."

"Son of a bitch," Leo said. His eyes met mine, and my stomach tightened. He looked afraid.

"Can you zoom in?" Dragon asked. After a few moments, he nodded. "I'll call Nix and have him head over there."

"She'll freak if he shows up there," Leo replied.

"I'll tell him not to do anything unless she tries to leave," Dragon assured him, pulling out his phone. "But it's gonna take us hours to get there."

The men started making calls and moving around the house, but I was paralyzed in my seat. The airport? What the hell was Kathy doing?

"I'll get him," Leo said, crouching in front of me. "Don't worry, Dandelion."

His words snapped me out of my daze.

"I'm going with you," I said, getting to my feet.

"No," he replied instantly. "Don't know what we're walkin' into."

"I don't care." I stepped around him and went straight for my coat.

"Lily, it'll be faster if you stay here."

"Bullshit," I said. "You can't ride up there, anyway, or you'll have no way to bring Gray back home."

"My Uncle Nix can—"

"I'm going with you to get our son," I said flatly, cutting him off. "You can leave without me if you want, but I'll be right behind you."

Leo stared at me while I put my coat on.

"Fine," he finally said. "But you'll stay back."

"Of course."

"I'm serious, Lily."

"So am I," I replied, grabbing my purse. "Do what you have to do."

"I'll drive," Brenna said, coming up beside me. She rubbed my back lightly. "You shouldn't be driving."

"Thanks, Ma," Leo said.

After a quick stop at my brother's so Leo could grab his bike, we were on our way to Portland in Brenna's SUV, following a group of Aces that grew larger as we drove through town. By the time we reached the highway, there were at least ten bikes ahead of us.

"Make sure you stick with them," I told Brenna, shivering. "I wouldn't put it past Leo to try and lose us."

"I've been doing this a long time, baby girl," Brenna said confidently. "I'll keep up."

"I can't believe that bitch," my mom exclaimed from the back seat. She and Trix hadn't been willing to stay behind, and they were crammed in next to Gray's spare car seat. "What in God's name is she thinking?"

"I just hope Leo keeps his cool," I replied, my knee bouncing with suppressed energy.

"My dad will keep him reined in," Trix said, reaching up to squeeze my shoulder. "Don't worry."

"I just keep thinking that if we hadn't tracked the tablet—" I bit the inside of my cheek, my heart thumping hard in my chest. "We waited for *hours* thinking she'd show up."

"You gave her the benefit of the doubt," Brenna said, glancing at me. "All of us did."

"She could have completely disappeared with him while we sat around waiting for her to fucking call," I bit out, my eyes watering. "Jesus."

"But she didn't," my mom said. "You know exactly where she is. Stop going down that road."

I nodded and looked down at my phone, watching the little dot blinking, blinking, blinking. That drive was the longest two hours of my life.

"You stay here," Dragon ordered, standing at Brenna's window. We were parked in the lot of a crappy motel, and I could see Kathy's car less than fifty yards away. "We'll bring Gray out to you."

"We got it, baby," Brenna said. "Go get our grandson."

From our vantage point, we could see everything that was happening. I watched as my dad went into the front office and came out a few minutes later, lifting a keycard up and waving it a little from side to side. He met Leo and Dragon in the middle of the walkway, and they strode toward a room on the bottom floor almost directly in front of where we were parked. The rest of the boys hung back, talking to Leo's uncle, who'd been waiting for us when we got there in a parking spot at the side of the lot.

Leo used the card and pushed into the hotel room.

Then, nothing. I waited and waited and waited, and he still didn't come out.

"Fuck this," I said, throwing open my door.

"Lily, stay here," Brenna called.

I ignored her, running across the parking lot. My dad and Dragon were still standing outside the room, and they turned in surprise when they saw me coming.

"Dammit, Lil," my dad bitched as I reached them.

Thankfully, he didn't try to stop me.

Everything inside me quieted when I saw Leo holding Gray against his chest, our little boy sucking his thumb tiredly.

"Bitch, I should fuckin' end you," Leo said, drawing my attention to the woman across the room. Kathy was sitting on the bed furthest from the door, so pale that she looked ghostly.

"Mama," Gray said, picking his head up off of Leo's shoulder. I couldn't move fast enough when he reached for me.

"Hey, bud," I said, holding him tight against me. "Did you go on an adventure?"

"Told you to stay in the car," Leo barked.

I just stared at him.

"Gray belongs with me," Kathy said, making both of us turn to look at her. "Not with some hoodlum and his teenage girlfriend."

"Who says hoodlum?" I asked, grimacing.

"You're seriously fuckin' crazy," Leo said at the same time.

"My daughter would be rolling in her grave if she knew—"

"Your daughter don't have a grave because you fuckin' cremated her without even havin' a goddamn funeral," Leo roared.

"Mama," Gray said, pressing his face against my neck. I needed to get him out of there.

"You're not his mother," Kathy hissed, coming off the bed like she was going to stop me.

"Take one more step," Leo warned, pointing at her.

"How could you allow that?" Kathy asked in disgust.

"Allow it?" Leo said incredulously. "Who you think gives Gray a bath? Cooks his meals? Brushes his teeth and reads him stories before bed? Woman, she's his mother, no *allow* about it."

"He has a mother," Kathy snapped.

"No, he *had* a mother," Leo replied as I reached the doorway with Gray. "But she's been gone so long, he don't even remember her."

"You're just replacing her—"

I stepped out of the room and took a deep breath of the cold, clean air. Thank God, we'd found him. Thank God he was okay. I pressed my lips against his dark hair and held them there, my body trembling with relief.

"Cold out here," my dad said, coming up behind me. "Better get Gray to the car."

I nodded, glancing back over my shoulder. "Make sure he doesn't do anything stupid."

"I will," he assured me. "Go."

By the time I had Gray buckled into his seat, he was asleep, and Leo was crossing the parking lot. I met him outside and let out a huge sigh of relief as he wrapped his arms around me.

"Do you ever fuckin' do what you're told?" he asked.

"Only in bed," I replied immediately.

He chuckled tiredly. "Jesus Christ, what a nightmare."

"Did she say what her plan was? Why would she do this?"

"Takin' off," he said with a shake of his head. "Fuckin' nutcase. She lost it when she heard Gray callin' you mama."

"I didn't even think about that," I confessed. Kathy was a complete cunt, but I couldn't help but imagine how hard that must've been for her.

"Don't," Leo said. "She could feel bad about it all she wanted, but takin' off with my son was fuckin' crazy. She doesn't get an ounce of sympathy from you."

"I know," I mumbled.

Leo let out a huff of laughter. "You've got the softest fuckin' heart of anyone I've ever met."

I smiled against his chest. The relief in his voice matched my own.

"We better get Gray home," he said, tipping my head back so he could kiss me softly.

"I wish you could ride with us," I said, blinking against the sprinkling of rain.

"Hell, me, too," he said, glancing up in disgust. "Gonna be a long ride."

He walked me around to the other side of the car and opened the back door.

"We figured you'd want to sit back here," Trix said, crawling out of the car. "You get to ride bitch."

"I'll see you at home," Leo said, smacking my ass lightly.

"Love you," I said over my shoulder as I climbed in the warm car.

"Love you, too."

My hip pressed painfully against the side of Gray's car seat, but I didn't mind. I held his hand the entire ride home.

"We should have had him sleep in here tonight," I said the minute Leo stepped into our bedroom. He had a towel wrapped around his waist and his hair was still soaking wet from the shower, but I couldn't even enjoy the view. I'd been sitting in the middle of our bed waiting for him to finish so I could argue with him.

"And we'd be startin' at square one, tryin' to get him back in his own bed tomorrow night," Leo replied, dropping the towel in the middle of the floor.

"So?" I said, watching as he moved around the room, turning off the light. "It's a special circumstance."

"It ain't to Gray," he said, pulling back the blankets. "To him, it's just a regular day."

"Well, it wasn't for me," I shot back, my eyes watering. I'd already been in Gray's room to check on him four times since we'd gotten home thirty minutes ago, and the thought of going to sleep with him in another room made my stomach hurt.

"Dandelion," Leo said softly, climbing into bed beside me. "It's all good, baby. It's over."

"I just want him next to me," I said, unable to keep the pleading out of my voice. I knew it was irrational, but I couldn't help it. My nerves were shot.

"I do, too," Leo said pulling me down to lay with him. "But I don't wanna give this day more importance to him than I have to. He ain't gonna remember this shit as anythin' other than goin' on a ride with his Granny, and his mom and dad pickin' him up."

"I was so scared," I whispered, my chin quivering.

"So was I," Leo whispered back, gently brushing my hair away from my face. "But we got him back."

"What's going to happen with Kathy?" I asked, wrapping my arm around his chest.

"Told her I wouldn't press charges if she took that flight she was plannin' on," he said, his jaw clenched tight. "Maybe, in a couple years, she wants to make contact again, we can make that happen."

"I don't ever want her alone with him."

"Oh, fuck no," he agreed. "She can write him a fuckin' letter."

Leo reached out and shut off the bedside lamp, and we laid there in the darkness for a long time.

"If we have more kids," I said, tipping my head back to look at him, "it's just going to multiply this godawful fear."

"Multiply the love, too," he replied.

"I know."

"You thinkin' about more kids?" he asked, his hand sliding underneath my tank to softly rub my back.

"Yeah," I breathed. "But I wasn't sure if you wanted any more."

"'Course I do," he said, his eyebrows shooting up in surprise. "Why'd you think that?"

"You just keep saying *later*," I replied. "I thought you were just trying to put me off."

Leo chuckled. "When I said later, I meant later, not never," he said with a smile. "You got your hands full now."

"I guess we could at least wait until I graduate," I grumbled, making him laugh again.

"Probably a good idea," he agreed.

I sighed and glanced at the quiet baby monitor.

"You wanna check on him again?" he asked quietly.

"I really do," I replied, throwing back the blankets.

I tiptoed across the hall and stopped in the doorway of Gray's room. Our boy was sleeping in the middle of his bed with his thumb in his mouth, his knees tucked under him and his butt in the air. He didn't even stir when Leo spoke.

"I wanna marry you," he said, sliding his hand around my waist until it rested low on my stomach. "And I want you to legally adopt Gray, so if somethin' happens to me—"

"Don't say that," I whispered.

"I want you to adopt him," he continued, kissing the side of my neck. "And I want to knock you up and watch you get round with our kid."

"Is that a proposal?" I asked, putting my hands over his.

"Yeah, Dandelion, it's a proposal," he said. "You wanna marry me?"

"I've been waiting for that question since I was ten years old," I replied, giggling as he bit my neck. "Of course I want to marry you."

"Good," he said. I could feel his smile against my neck. "Now, wave goodnight to our son so we can go back to bed."

I waved at Gray and barely stifled my laughter as Leo swung me up into his arms.

"I hope you don't plan on sleepin'," he said as he carried me back to our room. "Because I'm gonna fuck you until that monitor lights up in the mornin'."

Connect with Nicole Jacquelyn:
Facebook: https://www.facebook.com/authornicolejacquelyn/

MY BROTHER'S OLD LADY
BY NICOLE JAMES

CHAPTER 1

She stands across the room totally unaware of me; instantly, my lust for her flares to life as if it hadn't been put out two years ago. No, that's not right, it was never extinguished, just biding its time—smoldering embers waiting for that one poke, that one blast of air to re-ignite it. And now it's roaring like an out-of-control bonfire.

She licks her lips, perhaps out of nerves, but all I can think of is how I want her on her knees before me. I want to see those pretty lips part with that half-innocent, half-knowing expression on her face as she stares up at me. I want to bury my fingers in her silky hair, pull her head toward my crotch and sink my cock into her wet, waiting mouth. I want to control her every motion and feel the nails of her dainty, trembling fingers slide up my jean-covered thighs and dig into my flesh. I want to hear her moaning around me as I pump into her cherry lips, and see those blue orbs looking up at me, pleading silently to keep going, to give her more …

"Settle down!"

My president calls the room to order, breaking into my thoughts. I look across the space of our New Orleans clubhouse from where I stand by the bar and down my drink, trying to wash away the dirty images in my head.

"Paige, honey, could you come up here," Undertaker asks.

She stands and my eyes sweep over her. A short floral skirt flows around her slender thighs, and a white tank top hugs her breasts. Her blonde hair is short, but cut in a Marilyn Monroe style that has always done it for me. Paige moves toward Undertaker, and I watch that cute skirt sway with her hips. My eyes latch on to her ass as she steps up onto the small raised dais in the corner, the one with the stripper pole. Not that it's being used tonight; this meeting is more of a solemn occasion, and every brother in the room knows the significance of this anniversary even before Prez reminds us all.

Undertaker wraps his arm around Paige's shoulders and pulls her close. "Two years ago we lost a brother. Ransack was a special member of this club."

There's a round of "Hear, hear" as beer bottles are lifted across the crowded room.

Undertaker nods. "His old lady has always been dedicated and loyal to the club and his memory." He meets her eyes. "And even though she's been away the last two years, we welcome her back into the fold tonight." There's another round of cheers as Prez pulls Paige close and kisses her forehead.

She looks almost uncomfortable with the gesture, and if I know Paige —and I do—she hates to be the center of attention. Being up there with the eyes of every brother in the club on her is not her cup of tea.

Ransack was my sponsor when I prospected years ago, and then somehow after I'd earned my full patch, we'd continued to be close, riding together everywhere. I'd been in his home on a regular basis and saw the love those two shared. They were everything to each other.

I'd also been there the night he'd met Paige and had watched them fall in love. Hell, I had a front row seat. I'd even watched them struggle with trying and failing to have a baby the last few years before his death. She'd been crushed. Ransack had been less than thrilled about the pressure she'd put on him to go and get checked out. He'd even bitched to me about not wanting to *"wiz in a cup"* for some doctor.

I knew how much motherhood meant to Paige. I thought he was being a whiny little shit and had told him so straight to his damn face right here in the clubhouse one night. Ransack hadn't wanted to hear it, but it was the damn truth, and he knew it. He'd slammed me against the wall next to the pool table and told me to mind my own damn business. I'd lifted my hands and told him he was right, it wasn't my place.

Later, after he'd cooled down, he'd run a ragged hand through his hair and apologized, admitting I was right. Said he wanted to make Paige happy, and if giving her a kid would do it, then he'd make the appointment Monday morning. But by then, it hadn't mattered, it was too late; Ransack had been hit by a pickup truck the next night—a night I'll never forget.

I was riding with Ransack that night on the outskirts of town. I watched him pull away from a stoplight, giving me a wild-eyed, waggle-tongued look, yelling "Yee-haw" as he hit the throttle and dropped through the gears. He roared down the two-lane road with its cotton fields on the left and new subdivision on the right.

It had always been a great road to really get out on and burn rubber and drag race. At least it had until they'd begun building that damn subdivision.

That moonless night, a late-shift construction worker pulled out in front of Ransack's motorcycle, crossing the lanes to make a left. Ransack locked his brakes and skidded into a power slide, dropping the bike onto its side moments before he slammed into the rear axle of the truck bed. His bike literally split in two pieces around the axle, and his body smashed into the side, before he vaulted up over the truck and was thrown thirty yards beyond and into the ditch between the pavement and the neat rows of cotton.

He was still alive when I got to him, but as I cradled his head and watched him struggle to breath through the blood and shattered, broken bones in his face, I almost wished he'd been killed on impact.

Ransack clutched my arm as his terrified eyes stared up at me. But he hung on like I told him to as I fought back my tears. He hung on until the state troopers arrived on the scene, and he hung on until the Life Flight helicopter landed on the road. But by the time I made it to the hospital, arriving just before Paige and my brothers, he'd taken his last breath.

I held her as she collapsed in my arms in the trauma bay, her wailing sobs tearing my heart out. Somehow I felt I'd failed her; somehow I felt I was to blame for all of it. If only I hadn't egged him on at that stoplight ... If only I hadn't rolled my eyes when he'd shouted over the revving of my Harley Super Glide that his bike would bury mine at the drag races coming up that weekend.

I still remember that grin he gave me just before he twisted the throttle and roared away.

Now I'm watching Ransack's widow on stage, who's totally uneasy with the proceedings and probably regretting the day she decided to return to New Orleans.

Undertaker's going on about how the club would always be here for her, for whatever she needs. It was something I'd seen him do in the past. He'd done it years ago when Skeeter, our previous president, had died. And as I recall that instance, I suddenly know what's coming. It would have happened long ago if Paige hadn't left town to return to Macon where her family lives.

He's about to assign a man to watch over her, and most likely it'll be a prospect. I know she has no clue, but I do. I see his eyes shift to the left, where the prospect stands behind the bar with his arms folded, totally clueless.

I feel my stomach drop; no way in hell am I letting that little Lothario within ten feet of her.

"Paige, I'm going to make sure you're looked after by one of the club. Your vehicle breaks down? You call him. Need help moving something? You call him. Your lawn needs mowing? You call him. Get the idea?"

She stares in shock at him. "Oh, I'm sure that's not necessary, I—"

But Undertaker ignores her protests; he's already glancing toward the prospect. Before he can name a name, my arm shoots in the air to volunteer my services and condemn us both to a living hell. "I'll do it, Prez."

His eyes connect with mine. Every brother in the club knows how close Ransack and I had been and how much his death had crushed me as well as Paige. Perhaps—as I watch his eyes narrow on me while he considers my offer and finally receive his nod of approval—my president knows too.

But it's Paige's reaction that I focus on. Her mouth opens a barely perceptible sliver and her eyes widen. We haven't seen each other since the month after the funeral when I helped her load her stuff into Ransack's old truck and head off for Macon. I'd given her a hug and she'd climbed behind the wheel, looking so out of place and small in Ransack's seat. She hadn't driven the pickup since the accident, and I'd watched painfully as she'd closed her eyes to steel her features and hold back yet another crying jag before she'd adjusted the seat and mirrors, almost hesitant to move them from the position he'd left them in. My chest had tightened in anguish when her hand had paused over the rearview mirror, then slowly tilted it down. As she'd pulled out onto the street, I'd just stood there and stared until long after the taillights had disappeared around the bend.

Ransack's death had been a huge loss for me, but watching Paige drive out of my life as well had ripped my heart out.

I've carried unspoken feelings for her since the night we all met at a downtown nightclub.

And now I've just condemned us both to the torture of being around each other for the foreseeable future. But then again, maybe I've got it all wrong. Maybe I'm the only one with these feelings, feelings that have me standing here lusting after my dead brother's old lady. *Fuck!* This feels so wrong and disloyal. I'm sure if he knew, he'd come back from the dead and beat the shit outta me.

Perhaps Paige doesn't have those feelings for me. Even still, will being around me—one of her husband's closest brothers—be nothing but a painful reminder of the man she'd lost? Is it fair of me to put her through this? Maybe I should tell Undertaker to give the job to the prospect instead.

I'm a selfish bastard because that's the last thing I'm going to do. I'm an asshole, who will probably rot in hell for the licentious, wicked, and immoral thoughts I have for this woman. And I don't give a damn.

My brothers call me Wicked—and I'm about to live up to the name.

CHAPTER 2

"WHY THE HELL DID YOU DO THAT?" PAIGE STANDS IN MY ROOM AT THE clubhouse with her hands on her hips. She's just slammed the door behind her after following me up the stairs and down the hall.

I turn back toward her and dip my head to drill my eyes into hers. "You know why."

Paige's hands drop from her hips, and she raises her chin. "I don't know what you're talking about."

I take a step forward and she backs up. "Yeah, you do."

Her eyes skitter to the bed behind me before flashing back. She turns her head, unable to hold my gaze and says nothing.

I nod. She knows; she damn well knows why I did what I did. And there's no fucking way I'm going to stand here and let her hide from me. Taking Paige's chin in my hand, I bring her face back to mine. Her eyelids flutter down, so I demand, "Look at me, Paige."

She sucks in a breath, drawing my eyes to her cleavage. Not much is revealed in the scoop-neck tank she wears. Her style is much more conservative these days it seems. But I still imagine what it would be like to take those beautiful tits in my big hands and squeeze them. She could dress like a nun and I'd still fantasize about her sexy little body.

Paige looks up and I lift my gaze, but not before she notices where I was ogling. I stare into her beautiful blue eyes surrounded by the dark liner that gives her those trademark cat eyes. It's a look I find sexy as hell. I only get a split second before she knocks my hand away and moves back, her spine stiffening ramrod straight. I grin because that's how hard my cock has just gotten.

"Quit! I don't need you looking out for me. Tell Undertaker this is nonsense."

"Tell him yourself," I challenge her. She's a spitfire with me, but I seriously doubt she's got the courage to take on our president.

She looks away, and I know she doubts it too. But still, she murmurs, "Maybe I will."

"Fine."

"Fine."

I huff out a breath, feeling like a ten-year-old child, and run a hand down my face and beard. "Look, would it really be so bad? I mean, Christ, Paige, it's what any friend would do for you. Aren't we at least *that*?"

"Of course we're friends. That's not the point."

"Then, what is?" I prod her, knowing she won't have the guts to go there. Neither of us, it seems, is brave enough right now.

"Never mind. Do what you want. I don't care." She spins for the door, and I let her go, knowing it won't be the last encounter we have. That much I'm certain of. And right now, having her in my room at the clubhouse is just too goddamn tempting, especially with that bed behind me.

The door slams shut, and I back up until my legs hit the mattress and I'm sitting down. Leaning forward with my elbows on my knees, I rub both palms down my face and blow out a slow breath. Extending my hands out, I'm shocked to see the slight tremble in them. Fuck, I need a smoke. I huff out a short laugh. I'm kidding myself if I think for one minute it's just nicotine withdrawal that has my hands shaking. That woman knocks me on my ass without even realizing she does it.

What the hell have I done? What was I thinking committing myself to this task?

I wait a few minutes, making sure to give Paige plenty of time to get out of the clubhouse and off the property before heading back downstairs. I don't stop until I'm out the front door myself, where a few of my brothers are standing around, smoking.

I reach my hand inside the front of my cut and dig out a pack of smokes from the inside chest pocket. I shake one out and dip my head to light up. Tilting my head up, I blow out the smoke.

Blood and Sandman are standing not ten feet away from me. Sandman says something low to Blood that I don't catch, then he chuckles and shakes his head. I try to ignore them. I just want to stand here and mainline the nicotine until it floods my veins and calms my shit down.

Blood cuts his eyes to mine as he exhales a long stream of smoke toward the sky. Then he growls, "What the hell was that in there?"

"What do you mean?" I ask like a dumbass. I know damn well what he's talking about. In case I don't, Sandman doesn't miss the opportunity to clarify.

"You and cutie pie, that's what."

"Don't call her that, bro." The words are out of my mouth before I can think, and they're so damn revealing. The corner of Blood's mouth pulls up, and the look in his eyes says he's onto me and he wants me to know it. Shit.

All these years I thought I'd been discreet. I thought none of my brothers knew of the way I felt about Paige. Christ, was I kidding myself? Have they known all along? Did Ransack know? Not possible. The guys might have stayed the fuck out of it, but there's no way Ransack would have let it slide. He would have confronted me. Hell, he would have beaten the fuck outta me.

"You know, we've got prospects for that kind of shit," Sandman informs me helpfully. I just glare at him.

He lets out a roar of laughter, and I can feel my blood boiling.

"You got something to say to me, Sandman?" I bark. If he wants to volunteer to be my punching bag, I'm not gonna stop him. I even take a step toward him, disregarding the fact that he outweighs me by a good fifty pounds. I may stand six-two, but he's got me by an inch or so in that department as well. I don't give a fuck. I'll give it my best shot. I may be lean, but it's all muscle.

Sandman's smile disappears, and he looks like he's gonna take me up on it before Blood puts his arm out and stops him. "Quit!"

"I'll quit when his arm's broken," Sandman snaps, but makes no move toward me.

Blood ignores him since I've got his full attention now. Lucky me. "I've only got one question. You know what the fuck you're doin'?"

"About to bust Sandman's teeth out," I say sarcastically. Blood doesn't appreciate my joke.

"Don't be a fucking smartass, Wicked."

"It's what I do." I can't seem to keep my mouth shut, and fuck if I care. "You don't like it, go back to smoking your Marlboro and leave me the fuck alone."

Not many people speak to Blood this way, not if they want to live to tell about it. I'm one of the few.

Sandman lets out a huff. "What's the bug up your ass? Oh, wait. I already know. *Cutie Pie.*"

He taunts me with the nickname he's given her—the one I hate, the one I told him not to use. I lunge at him. "You fucker!"

Before I get to him, Blood slams my chest with both fists, knocking me back on my ass. It's like I've been hit with two sledgehammers. Fuck, it hurts. I roll to my back and try to draw in a breath but can't. I think he's knocked the wind out of me.

I deserve it for acting like an idiot and fighting with my brothers over this shit. When I finally get my breath back, I let out a huff of laughter.

Sandman moves over me and peers down, but his words are for Blood. "He's loosin' it, man. You think he's on drugs?"

The only drug I'm on wears a flirty little skirt and dark eyeliner and, fuck, am I addicted.

CHAPTER 3

EIGHT OF US ROLL UP TO THE CLUBHOUSE AND THROUGH THE STOCKADE GATES. Tires crunch on the gravel as one after another we back into spots by the door. I hit my kickstand with my boot, resting the weight of my Super Glide down on it, and climb off.

It's been a long, tiring two days making the run up to Shreveport and back, and I, like the rest of the crew, could use a cold beer. I pause to stretch and crack my spine, trying to relieve the tightness that has formed in my lower back, when I feel my cell phone vibrate in my hip pocket. Pulling it out, I glance at the screen.

Paige.

She's had my number for years, and it hasn't changed. But this is the first time she's used it since she hit town two weeks ago. I swipe my thumb across the screen and put it to my ear. "Yeah?"

"Wicked, um, I hate to bother you ..."

I hate the timid tone in her voice, and that she thinks she's bothering me. That's not the old Paige I used to know. "What do you need, babe?"

"I broke down on the side of the road."

My eyes focus on the sun sliding down the western sky. It'll be dark in a couple hours. "Where are you?"

"US 190 ... across from Fontainebleau State Park. I just passed that Nature Center. Do you know the one?"

"On Bayou Castine?" Hell, she was almost to Mandeville.

"Yes, I just crossed the stone bridge, actually."

"All right. Stay in the truck. I'll be there as fast as I can." It's a good twenty-minute ride, but I plan to make it in half that time.

"Wicked?"

"Yeah?"

"Thank you."

I disconnect and shove the phone in my pocket, wishing she'd go back to calling me by my given name like she used to in the old days. It sounds so much sweeter on her lips than Wicked. If I ever get her in bed, I swear that's the only name I'll let her use. I swing my leg back over the bike and lift it off the kickstand.

Blood pauses with one hand on the door that Sandman, Joker, So-Cal, and the rest of the crew just went through. "You comin'?"

I shake my head. "Paige broke down on the side of the road."

He lifts his chin. "You need help, let me know."

I nod, already firing up the bike and popping it in gear. With a twist of the throttle, I roar off.

Ten minutes later, I roll up next to Ransack's old pickup. Paige is standing beside it, and my eyes sweep over her as I drop my kickstand. She's wearing a pretty little yellow sundress that matches the color of her hair and reveals her tanned legs to mid thigh. That has me taking a second to think about them wrapped around my body. I swing my leg over the seat and stand, unbuckling my skullcap helmet to drop it on the seat.

"It just quit running," she explains as I walk toward her.

Her eyes are hidden behind a pair of dark sunglasses. I long to pull them off and see her eyes, but I resist, moving past her to the driver's door. I open it and reach down to release the hood latch. Straightening, I see a cellophane-wrapped bouquet laying on the old-style bench seat that Ford stopped making years ago. It was why Ransack bought the used F150. He'd wanted that bench seat so Paige could sit right next to him.

The flowers throw me, and I stare at them a moment. They're already wilting in the steamy New Orleans heat. I move around and lift the hood, knowing what I'm looking for; occasionally, Ransack used to have problems with the wiring harness and the engine control module.

As I'm bent over the engine, checking the wiring and connections, I ask the question that I suddenly can't get out of my fucking head, and I know I won't be able to let it go until I have the answer. "Who gave you the flowers?" I turn, my gaze hitting her shades. I wish she'd pull them off so I could see her eyes; they always give her away.

"No one."

I stare at her until she elaborates.

"I was on my way to Mandeville Cemetery."

Trying not to let my reaction show, I turn back to the engine. *Mandeville*. Now it all makes sense why she's way out here. I should have put it together earlier. That's where the MC has its plot, and where

Ransack is buried. She's bringing the flowers to put on his grave. Here I am, jealousy flaring inside me thinking some dude gave her the flowers. I feel like such an asshole. But as I think about her paying tribute to her husband, my club brother, I'm jealous all over again. *Jealous of a dead man.* Ain't that a fucking joke? And ain't I a fucking douchebag for feeling this way?

I pull my head out from under the hood and slam it shut. "Wires are corroded. I'll have to get them replaced."

She stares at the truck. "Oh."

I pull a black bandana from my back pocket and wipe the grease off my hands. "I'll need to go to the parts store and come back and fix it."

She nods, digging into her purse and pulling out her wallet.

"What are you doing?"

"Giving you money." She pulls out a credit card and attempts to hand it to me.

"Put that back," I snap. "I don't want your money."

"It's my truck. I'm grateful enough you're helping me. Of course I'm paying for the parts."

I stride toward Paige and stare down at her. "You want my help, you don't ever flash money at me again. We clear?"

When she stands there uncertainly, I lift my brows, challenging her to argue with me.

Travis," she says my given name softly. She's the only one I'll allow to call me by that name.

"Put the card away, Paige. Now."

"Okay, fine." She shoves it back in her purse and turns to reach for the door.

"What are you doing?"

"I'm going to wait for you, I guess."

"I'm not leaving you in this heat, and I sure as hell wouldn't leave you on the side of the road. You're coming with me. Grab the flowers."

She frowns. "You're taking me to the cemetery?"

"It's on the way." I move to the bike while she grabs the bouquet and follows me. I sit on the seat and fire it up. Paige doesn't even hesitate to climb on the back in her dress. She slides the strap of her purse over her head and tucks the flowers in between us. I pass her my helmet and wait while she straps it on. Glancing down, I see her wedge sandal take its place on the foot peg and feel her thighs press against my hips. God, I'm in heaven and I can't resist reaching back and laying my palm on her bare leg just above her knee and giving it a squeeze. "You ready?"

She leans forward to reply in my ear over the rumble of the bike, and I feel her breasts press against my back. I like them there. It's where they belong, so I grab her wrist and pull it around my waist. "Hang on."

I want her to hold me tight, and I don't give a damn if that bouquet is crushed when we get to the cemetery. I pull off the dirt shoulder onto the black pavement and roar off. The cemetery is less than two miles away, but I go slow and drag out a two-minute ride to five. Finally, I coast up Montgomery Street and turn under the ornate iron archway.

There's a mix of above-ground tombs, walled vaults, and in-ground sites. There's also a rich side and a poor side, the elegant plots and the ones that look forgotten. The section of the cemetery where all my MC brothers are buried is in the back. I roll to a stop on the drive. The club's black granite stone marker reflects the setting sun.

We dismount and walk to the plot. She lays the flowers down, and we both stand quietly for a long time. I look over at her and ask softly, "The pain is still very fresh for you, isn't it?"

She nods and admits, "Something happened today that brought it all back."

"What was that?"

"I was driving and without even realizing it, I found myself riding past the spot where he wrecked. The cross is still there. Did you know that?"

I nod. I do know that because I ride down that road a lot. Not because I need to, I don't. I guess I do it to torture myself. Penance I feel I owe. And every time I do, my eyes go to that white cross—the one I helped Paige put up before she left town. The rosary wrapped around it still hangs from it, swaying in the breeze.

I stare down at the grave and ask softly, "How do you comprehend death or make any sense of it? The answer is, you don't." I pause, but I know I need to go on; there's more that I need to say. "When I was holding him in that ditch, waiting for the paramedics ... I never felt so helpless."

A sob catches in her throat at my words.

I look over at her, but with the dark glasses she's wearing, I can't read her expression. "The question is, Paige, can you find a way to go on?—because you have to—because there's so much life ahead of you, baby."

She sucks in a long, calming breath and finally nods. "You're right. I know you're right. It's just hard."

It's so quiet in the cemetery. I glance around and murmur, "The dead never really leave us down here, do they?"

"The cemeteries in Macon, like where my Paw-Paw is buried, are different than this. They look different, they feel different," Paige muses, her eyes drifting around.

I understand what she's saying as I gaze over at her. "Walk through any cemetery down here in South Louisiana and you can feel it—you're literally surrounded by the deceased. They're in the walls," I nod toward the columbarium in the distance and then the crypts and graves. "They're housed all around, and I find no comfort coming here. The life I lead, I'll be on the other side soon enough."

"Don't say that. Don't even think it."

"How can I not?"

She shakes her head, pushing the dark glasses up, and I see a tear rolling down her cheek. Is it for Ransack or me?

I nod to the MC plot. "And when I die, I'll lie here with my eternal brothers." I put on a fake smile, trying to lighten the mood. "Will you bring me flowers, too, Paige?"

She breaks down in tears, covering her face, and I pull her into my arms. I'm an asshole again for making her cry. It's not what I want. I guess I'm just jealous of the love she still feels for Ransack.

"I'm sorry," I whisper into the hair on the top of her head. Breathing in the floral scent of her shampoo, I close my eyes and clutch her tighter, letting her expend all the tears she's probably been bottling up for two years.

Finally, her sobs cease and she pulls back, brushing the wetness from her cheeks. "I'm sorry. I didn't mean to break down like that. That wasn't what coming here today was about."

I frown, looking into her eyes and can't help but ask. "What was it about then?"

She pulls away and folds her arms, hugging herself, her gaze on the stone. "Letting go."

I swallow. I know what I want those two words to mean, but I'm not sure they do, so I ask, "Letting go and moving on?"

She lifts a shoulder in a small shrug, not ready to commit to that.

"You've got your whole life ahead of you, Paige. You're young—"

"I'm thirty-one."

"And I'm forty. So what?" For some reason her answer irks me. It's all the more reason she should let Ransack go and move on. "Ransack was my brother and I loved him, and I'm sorry he's dead. I wish that night never happened. I wish I'd never talked him into going out that night. I wish—"

"It's not your fault, Wicked." She cuts me off.

"Isn't it?" I turn and ask, knowing the pain I carry in my soul must show in my eyes. And for some reason, I don't care if she sees it.

Paige shakes her head and whispers, "No."

"Maybe I wanted him dead." The words are out of my mouth before I can stop them.

"What?" she whispers.

I can see my admission shocks her. That doesn't stop me. Something inside me needs to get these words out because I fear they're true. "Maybe subconsciously I wished it all along. Maybe I wished it into being."

"Stop! Don't say that! Don't think it! Why would you say that to me?" She looks devastated, like I've just crushed whatever thread of a relationship we had left, and maybe I have. But standing here in this cemetery, ironically, seems like the perfect place for my confession. Ransack needs to hear this, too. And maybe in this place, he can.

"I've wanted you, Paige. I've always wanted you. From that very first night when I first laid eyes on you, I'd wished it had been you and me. I wonder all the time what would have happened if I'd met you first." I spin and shout to the sky. "You hear that, Ransack? I wanted your ol' lady! And God help me, I still do!"

She stares at me in shock.

Can I blame her? I've turned into a two-headed monster right before her eyes. "Don't look at me like you expect me to take it all back. I'm not sorry, Paige. I'm not fucking sorry, and I'm not going to deny it anymore. It's wrong and I'll probably go to hell, but there it is, the God's honest truth."

"I don't want to hear this," she says, shaking her head in denial.

"I'll bet you don't. Guess what, I don't give a fuck."

She turns away, marching toward the bike, but yells over her shoulder, "Take me home. Now."

I blow out a long breath, suddenly tired beyond belief. I look back at the gravestone. "I'm sorry, Ransack. Sorry about all of it. Maybe I'll see you soon. You'll probably be waiting for me on the other side with a baseball bat in your hands." I stare off at the setting sun. "And I won't blame you one bit."

I turn and head back to the bike where the woman I've lusted over for the better part of a decade stands waiting.

CHAPTER 4

I PULL UP AT PAIGE'S PLACE AND CUT THE ENGINE. SHE'S OFF THE BIKE SO FAST I barely have time to drop the kickstand. She snatches off the helmet, practically throwing it at me, and heads for the house she's renting, but not before she snaps back over her shoulder, "Don't bother with my pickup. I'll call a tow truck and handle it myself."

"Paige!" I protest, but she's already stormed inside and slammed the door. "Goddamn it."

I've got two options: I bust inside and we get back into it again, or I leave and let her calm down. I stare down the street, trying to decide.

First things first, I need to take care of her pickup, so I pull my phone out and call the clubhouse. I arrange for a prospect to bring me the tools I'll need and meet me back where we left her truck.

Next, I call the auto-parts store and hold while they check if they've got stock in what I need. Nothing I hate more than waiting on hold, but I also don't want to run all over town. Finally, they come back on the line and tell me they've got the parts.

I disconnect and am about to pull off when a car turns in her drive. I'm parked at the curb and the driver gives me a once-over as he pulls in. I rest the bike back on its kickstand. No way in hell I'm leaving now.

I light a cigarette while I watch him go to the door and knock, then straighten his tie. He's young and good-looking. Paige comes to the door and smiles at him, then lets the motherfucker in.

What the hell?

Tossing my smoke aside, I'm off the bike and just about to bust in there when they come back out the door, Paige with a little white sweater over her arm and carrying her purse. It's eighty degrees out, so if she thinks she needs a sweater, she must be planning on staying out late. I'm no Sherlock, but even I can put that much together. This is a goddamn date!

They're chuckling over something, and I suddenly want to smash my fist into his pearly white teeth.

Paige gives me a smug smile as she sashays toward his car. He opens her door like a gentleman, but manners can be deceiving. More than one serial killer has been a charming, good-looking guy. Nope, Ted Bundy here isn't fooling anyone, least of all, me.

He helps her in, then goes around to the driver's side and gets behind the wheel.

I climb back on my bike and fire it up. The prospect will have to wait, because I've suddenly got somewhere else I need to be, namely, tailing this guy and Paige. No way in hell am I letting her out of my sight.

I pull out right behind him. Paige turns around and looks through the rear window. Even from fifteen feet back, I see her roll her eyes and shake her head. She turns back around and faces the front with a dramatic flounce I'm sure is meant for me. I grin. I love that I'm getting to her. It's me she'll be thinking of this whole evening, not her date. And, damn, if that doesn't make me happy—well, as happy as I can be with Paige out on a date with another man. Oh, she's going to pay for this little stunt, that I swear to myself. If she's trying to jerk my chain, she's succeeding. I don't give a fuck how wrong it is, Paige Logan is going to be mine.

I trail behind them for several miles, idling at each stoplight and making sure to rev the throttle so that loud, thundering rumble blasts through my pipes. It gets their attention. Ted's watching me from his side mirror.

I grin, contemplating how I'm going to dispose of his body. Who'll be laughing then, Ted?

I continue to follow for another two miles when he slows and puts on his blinker. There's a steak place on the right. Typical. Dude has no clue Paige is a vegetarian. She'll eat fish occasionally, but that's about it. Yeah, I know her well.

But he rolls past the driveway and I frown. He keeps coasting and turns into the next business. I glance at the sign and the car lot.

Oh, she got me good with this little ruse. They've turned into the lot of a car rental place, one famous for their motto "We'll pick you up!"

I can see Paige through the window. She's laughing her ass off at me. I park in a spot away from them and can't help but smile. Yeah, I'm an idiot. Doesn't mean she still won't pay for this, the little minx.

I sit there and smoke a cigarette while she goes inside and fills out paperwork. She finally comes out and gets in the car she's rented. I don't approach her; instead, I wait and watch her pull past me. She lifts her hand and waggles her fingers at me in a cute little wave.

I just grin and let her go. When she turns out of the lot, back toward her house, I pull out in the opposite direction. I've got a pickup to fix, and then, little lady, I'll be coming back to settle up with you.

CHAPTER 5

I PULL UP AT PAIGE'S HOUSE AT JUST AFTER 10 P.M. THERE ARE VERY FEW lights on inside, but I know she hears the bike rumble up; my pipes are loud enough. A moment later, the porch light flicks on, proving me right as I walk toward her door.

It swings open and she's standing there in a short, gauzy white nightie with pearl buttons down the front, looking like an angel. I'm so stunned that I pause at the bottom of the porch steps, my boot on the bottom rung, letting my eyes sweep over her.

"What are you doing here?" she asks, frowning.

I trudge up the steps, my boots thudding heavily on the wood, and my eyes lock with hers. She steps back and I walk in, closing the door behind me. I don't answer her question. I just take her face in my hands and walk her backwards until she's pressed against the nearest wall. My mouth settles over hers as she sucks in a startled breath. It only takes a second for her lips to soften under mine before my tongue sweeps inside.

It's the first kiss we've ever shared, but one I've thought about for years. Paige's plump lips are cushiony soft, inviting, and seductive as they move under mine. Her head tilts back to give me more access as I step in closer and bring my body flush against her soft curves. There's nothing covering her but the thin fabric of her nightshirt, and feeling her bare breasts press against my chest is heaven. I can't wait to touch them, to suck her nipples, to see what size and color they are.

She pushes back, breaking the kiss. "We need to talk—"

"No," I growl. "Not tonight. For this one night, no words, no talking. Please, can you give me that?"

She stares up at me, considering my offer. "One night. That's all this can be."

I don't agree to that. I never will. But I don't tell her that, I just lower my mouth over hers and pull her flush against me again.

Her arms go around my neck, and I have her answer.

I've waited so long for this … dreamed about it, fantasized about it, and I don't want to rush it, but I need to get her to a bed. Now. Because if I don't, we may end up fucking right here against the wall, and that's not what I want for her, for us. Yeah, it would be erotic as hell, but Paige deserves more than that. She deserves everything.

Her kiss is hesitant, timid, but at least she's letting me in, taking what I'm giving.

I briefly wonder if she's had sex since Ransack passed away over two years ago. There may have been someone back in Georgia. I don't know and I'm not sure I want to know the answer. It's a question I'm sure as hell not asking. Maybe I will some day, but not now. Still, it reminds me I need to go slow and take care with her.

I lift her up and her legs go around me. I have no clue where the bedroom is because I've never been in this house, but I'll damn sure find it. I told her no talking, and I meant it.

We're in a small living room. There's a kitchen through an archway to the left and a hallway that leads toward the back of the house. I head that way, kissing her as I move until I find her bedroom in the back. A small light burns next to the bed.

Paige's room is not what I expect as I set her on her feet. It's not as girly as I'd imagined, but more contemporary with neutral tones. The only color comes from the artwork on the walls. They're really the only girly things in the room—that artwork.

There's a framed print of female guitarist Samantha Fish. It's a sexy shot, one taken from the New Orleans Cigar Box Guitar Festival a couple years before Ransack died. Paige has admired her since she first learned to play guitar, a hobby she took up years ago, so I'm not surprised to find her red Fender Stratocaster resting on a stand in the corner. My eyes continue around the room, revealing so much about her that I never knew.

There's a large print of a *Vogue* magazine cover. I don't know anything about *Vogue* other than it's a chick's fashion magazine. It's sexy as hell, though. It's a shot of a woman from the back, waist down and dressed in a pouf skirt made of netting, like a chick would wear under a wedding dress. It's super short, exposing the back of the woman's legs and just barely covers her ass. She's wearing dark stockings with garters and high heels. It's all in a muted, out-of-focus pink. Somehow that sexy shot speaks volumes to the power of womanhood. I suddenly realize that's exactly who Paige is: a woman who knows her power. Yes, she's grief-stricken and damaged, but underneath, she's always been a strong woman.

Another print catches my eye. It's a graphic abstract in muted pinks, blues, and yellows of Marilyn Monroe—another woman who knew her power.

I look down at my Paige, and that's who she is, who she's about to be here in this room—*my* Paige. *Mine.* At last.

I glance to the dresser and nightstands, thankful that I don't see any framed photos of Ransack.

Paige starts to say something but I cover her lips with two fingers and shake my head. "No talking. No questions. No explanations. No doubts. Not tonight."

She nods and opens her mouth, closing her lips around the tips of my fingers. It's erotic as hell and my cock goes rock hard. I've fantasized about her lips sucking on more than my fingers—too many nights than I'll ever admit.

I back her up to the bed. When her legs hit the edge, she sits down. Paige's big eyes stare up at me, and her chest lifts and falls with each quickening breath.

I lift a hand and thread my fingers through her soft curls. Her eyes slide closed and she turns into the touch, rubbing her cheek against my palm. Her hand reaches up and circles my wrist, then she presses an open-mouthed, wet kiss to my palm.

The urge to jerk the nightshirt over her head—or, hell, just rip it to shreds then push her back and take her is strong, but I fight it down. I've waited way too long for this moment. I'm going to take my time.

I drop to my knees before her and my hands go to the row of buttons down the front of her nightie. Our eyes lock for a moment before she drops her gaze to watch my fingers undo the tiny pearls.

Paige's chest rises and falls, drawing my eyes. The material is so thin I can see her nipples pebble beneath the delicate fabric.

After undoing a half dozen buttons, the plackets fall open a couple of inches to expose the sides of her breasts. Now that I'm down to her navel, there's a surprise waiting for me.

Little Paige has her bellybutton pierced. Sparkling rhinestones dangle over her tan, flat skin.

My fingers pause, but just for a moment. Then they work those buttons even faster. I'm three from the bottom when her panties come into view: sexy pale blue satin and lace with a bow in the center. They match her eyes, and suddenly it's my new favorite color.

Reaching the last button, I pull the nightie open and push it over her shoulders to reveal her naked breasts, ones I've waited so fucking long to see. And they do not disappoint. They're full and round with large pink nipples that stand out and beg for attention.

I stare and she trembles.

As I squeeze them, testing their weight and the way they feel so fucking soft, Paige moans, her head dropping back. Blood rushes to my dick and it stands at attention. My big, calloused hands close over her nipples, and when my thumbs brush over them, her mouth drops open. I lean forward and nuzzle her ear, shushing her as I pinch and tug at them.

Her breath quickens and she thrusts her breasts forward, silently begging for more. Trailing a hot, wet path down her throat, my lips pause over the fluttering pulse beating just above her collarbone. I can't resist sucking on it, hard, as I pinch down with my fingertips.

She moans louder and it's such a fucking hot and sexy sound, I could listen to it all night. I vow to make that happen, but right now, all I can think of is getting my mouth around those sweet nipples. I move down over the swell of those gorgeous breasts—breasts that fit perfectly in my big hands like I knew they would, exactly how I've fantasized, night after night.

My mouth latches on to one nipple and circles it with my tongue, learning its texture and shape, instantly committing it to memory for life.

She whimpers, her hands threading into my hair, pulling and clutching me closer to her.

I lick and suck and toy with it using my teeth until I'm ready to move to the other and give it all the attention that has it sitting up so pretty.

"Oh, Travis," she moans, and I want to reprimand her for speaking since I'd told her "No talking," but my name from her lips in that sexy purr gets my dick bobbing.

I close my big hands around Paige's tiny waist and ease her down onto the bed, my mouth trailing over her belly to her navel. My tongue traces around it to play with the piece of jewelry as her stomach trembles beneath my mouth.

Paige tries to reach for me, attempting to wrap her arms around my shoulders, but her elbows are caught in the sleeves of the nightshirt and she's trapped. I like it that way and pin her wrists to the mattress.

My lips travel slowly, pressing soft kisses down her silken skin to that little bow on her panties. I close my teeth over the fabric and bite, pulling and releasing, as it snaps back against her.

She jerks under the surprise of it.

I release her wrists and curl my fingers around the lace at her hips, dragging the panties slowly down her legs and tossing them aside.

Palming the inside of her thighs just above her knees, I push them slowly apart, taking in the prettiest pussy I've ever seen.

She's dripping wet, and I can smell the musky scent of her arousal as my eyes travel upward over her quivering abdomen, to the rise and fall of her breasts, then landing on those sexy blue eyes with the heavy dark liner peering down at me—watching and waiting.

I press kiss after kiss up her thighs, slowly alternating from one side to the other, dragging out the anticipation while rubbing my beard along her skin, teasing and tickling her.

Paige curls her fingers, fisting the sheets tight.

I like how I'm getting to her; I like how her thighs quiver, her breathing accelerates, her hips writhe, and that pretty pussy lifts off the mattress, seeking that first touch.

She'll have to wait just like I've waited years for this.

I slide my palms up that soft skin until my thumbs hover over her pussy lips.

Paige whimpers as I brush the pads over her, a barely there touch, but she jumps in response.

I make a long, low hushing sound. "Shhhh."

She swallows and stares at the ceiling, letting me have my fill of looking at her. I stroke her slowly, over and over with my thumbs, and watch her flood in response. Drawing small circles with my thumbs, I continually bring those plump lips together and apart until she's soaked and rolling her hips from my caresses.

I break my own rule and speak. "So beautiful, Paige. Prettiest thing I've ever seen. You're so wet, so fucking wet for me, baby."

"Travis—" she moans.

"Shh. No talking, Paige. You promised me."

"Travis, please—"

"Shh, baby. You do it again, I'll flip you over and spank that pretty ass of yours."

She stutters in a ragged breath and writhes, but stays quiet.

"Good girl," I say in a low growl. "Good girls get a reward." I dip my head and press the flat of my tongue in a long, slow swipe along her clit.

Paige moans and her thighs clamp tight around my shoulders. God, I love that. But I want her open to me. I move my hands to the crease behind both knees and push up and back, pinning her and spreading her wide—so open for me; so vulnerable. That's how I want her.

I dip my head again and lap, my tongue laving her clit again and again, stroke after stroke, then delving inside her pussy and taking that wetness and coating her clit with it. It glistens and stands out so pretty from her already swollen pussy lips. I like it wet like that, and I plan to keep that way all night.

I brush my beard over her and she moans.

I still haven't slid my fingers inside and decide I've waited long enough. I release Paige's legs, lean down over her, then sink two fingers into her pussy. She's tight and wet and hot as fuck. While brushing my thumb over her clit again and again, I search for her g-spot with those two fingers.

I find it and her back arches off the bed. Damn, if that doesn't fire me up.

Leaning my elbow near her head, I trace her lips with the wet thumb of my free hand.

"Open," I order, and she does, instantly obeying. She sucks my thumb as I fuck her with my fingers, my other thumb not letting up on her clit. Her hips lift off the bed to meet each thrust, eager for more and I give it to her.

Paige is getting close to orgasm, and her movements become more frantic, urgent, and desperate; her breath pants in and out as she moans around my thumb, and sucks hard on it. I slow down the motion and make her wait. She thrashes harder. I ramp it up again and soon have her on the edge once more.

She's a vision beneath me, all laid out for me to play with, and I intend to do so for as long as I want, as long as my hard-as-fuck dick can hold out. I want her to come multiple times before I'm done with her.

She's so close again. Her back arches and those pretty pink nipples are just pleading for my mouth. I give it to them, dipping my head and latching on and sucking hard.

She gasps in a breath and grabs my hand between her legs and bucks against me, rubbing hard against my hand as her channel clenches down on my fingers. I give another long, hard tug on her nipple and she shudders again against my hand, moaning as she shatters, coming hard and coating my skin.

That's my girl. So fucking beautiful as she takes her pleasure.

I lick and kiss the hard nipple that I've been tormenting. Brushing it softly with my lips, I give the other the same attention, and then trail down her belly. I pull my fingers from her pussy and lick them clean as I move back off the bed.

Paige watches me; her breathing is still hard and panting from her orgasm. I pull off my cut and hang it over the back of a chair in the corner. Then I reach back between my shoulder blades, grab a fistful of T-shirt, and pull it over my head, tossing it to the floor.

Her eyes sweep over my bare chest and the tattoos that twine down both arms, across my broad shoulders, and down along my ribs.

Reaching for my belt, I unbuckle it, and she bites her full bottom lip. God, I want those plump pink lips around my cock.

I kick off my boots, undo my pants, and strip. When I'm standing there naked, I take my hard cock in my hand and stroke it, base to tip, twisting at the head. Paige's eyes follow my motion and she sits up, shrugs the shirt off her arms frantically, and scoots to the end of the bed like she wants it. Like she can't wait to have it.

I step to her, the head of my dick just inches from her sweet mouth. "Open," I order.

She does, eagerly, as her small hands move to cup the base. I let go and stroke her head as she takes me inside her mouth.

Sweet Jesus. It's better than I fantasized.

She licks and sucks and toys with me like I did her. *Payback's a bitch* those eyes of hers say as she looks up at me.

I grin, giving her that as I lace my fingers through her hair and fist it, bringing her closer. She takes me deep and I groan when she purrs around my dick, and fuck, I love it. She gets me good and wet, slick with her mouth as I tighten my grip in her hair. She moans and I can tell she likes that—me taking control. So, I do. Both hands are tight in her hair, guiding her, controlling her as I begin pumping into her mouth, thrusting my hips in a slow rhythm, going easy on her at first.

I can tell she wants to please me, and she is. I let her know.

"Good girl. Such a fucking good girl, you are, Paige. You take my dick so good."

It spurs her on and she bobs her head fervently. After a few delicious minutes, I know I'm getting close. But coming so soon is the last thing I want. There's so much more I want to do with her sweet body.

I tighten my hold and pull her head back until her mouth pops free of my dick.

Paige looks up at me uncertainly, but I just push her down to her back. I straddle her, a knee on either side of her ribs, and I take her breasts in my hands. Pushing them together, I slide my dick between them, then reach back and swirl two fingers in her wet pussy to lube up her cleavage.

I pump my dick in and out of her plump breasts, fucking them. She lifts her head and takes the head into her mouth on each upward stroke.

"Fuck, yes, baby." We go at it until I'm about to explode. "Someday, I want to give you a pearl necklace, coat your chest with my cum, would you like that, baby girl?"

She nods and moans.

I back off her to move down between her legs, then take my cock and stroke it, looking at her pussy.

"Travis, please. I need you."

I lift my gaze to her. "Baby, what'd I say I'd do if you talked?"

Her eyes get wide, disbelieving.

I quirk a brow; she really shouldn't doubt me.

Before she knows what I'm about, I back off the bed and flip her to her stomach then growl, "Up on your knees, Paige."

She looks back over her shoulder, but complies.

I rub my hand over her soft, lush ass cheek. "You've got a pretty ass, baby." Then I smack it. "But a bad girl gets her pretty ass smacked when she doesn't listen."

She yelps, but pushes her ass up higher and I smile, giving her another one.

"You like that, baby?"

She groans and nods as I smack her cheek again, watching it jiggle so pretty as that soft skin begins to pink. My eyes trail down to her pussy and it's drenched from her arousal. I sink two fingers inside and she moans as I work in and out of her, massaging her cheek with my palm. "You gonna be a good girl or bad girl?"

She looks back at me, not sure if she should speak, and I grin.

"I think you're a good girl who wants to be bad. Am I right?" I press on that g-spot. I've already memorized its exact location.

She moans and nods her head.

"Does my Paige have a vibrator?"

She won't answer.

"Tell me. I'll find it, baby. You know I will," I threaten.

She nods and points to the nightstand. I withdraw my fingers and move to pull the drawer open. I find it and bring it to the bed.

Paige is still on her hands and knees. Her eyes follow me as I move behind her. I lay my palm on the small of her back and she jumps.

"Easy, baby girl. I'm not going to hurt you." I roll the head around the entrance to her pussy, coating it with her release. I find the *on* switch and it purrs to life. She lets out a moan when I play with her clit, and her legs tremble. While I move the head back to her opening and tease it in and out just an inch, Paige's hips tilt and she pushes her ass up, wanting more.

"So greedy. Such a greedy girl I've got on my hands."

I slowly insert it, fucking her with it until she drops her head, whimpering. Once again I find her g-spot and hold the vibrator against it, and she lowers to her elbows and groans, her ass jiggling as she humps her toy. She starts to pant. "Oh, God…"

I smack her ass. "You know the rules."

Paige practically explodes and I give her mercy, dipping my fingers between her legs to play with her clit. She orgasms hard, bucking wildly.

I draw out every last shudder before I withdraw the vibrator and shut it off. She crumples to the bed, but I'm not done with her.

"Please, Travis."

"Now, see, there you go talking again. I was going to fuck you missionary, all proper and sweet, but now I'm gonna have to fuck my bad girl from behind." I drag her hips up and lift her ass high then line up the head of my dick with her opening. "Tell me you want me."

"Yes, please. Fuck me, Travis. Fuck me hard."

I plunge inside, filling her in one thrust and she gasps. She's dripping wet, sleek and hot, and tight as hell, and I growl, "Oh, fuck yeah, baby girl. So good. Such a good girl for me. You gonna take it all? Everything I'm going to give you?"

"Yes. Yes."

I begin a rhythm, driving in and out, pumping, pulling that luscious ass back against each thrust. She moans, dragging her breasts across the sheets as she arches into me.

"So pretty, Paige. So fucking beautiful." I release my grip on one hip, sure there'll be bruises the size of my fingertips tomorrow, and I smooth my palm along her spine, then down to her nape and back again to those sexy little dimples at the top of her ass. "You take me so good, baby."

She whimpers and I reach around and toy with her clit again. She rocks against my hand until she's wild. "Oh God. Oh God."

She's getting close again. I change angles, pulling back a couple of inches and find that sensitive trigger inside her that has her panting hard until she finally sucks in a breath, holds it, and goes still, coming all over my dick.

I power into her and explode, wrapping my arms around her hips and locking them tight, and holding her to me as I come long and hard. Then I sink my teeth into her shoulder, and she rocks against me again with one more jerk of sexual ecstasy.

Breathing heavily, I collapse, taking us both down to the soft sheets and relish the exquisite bliss that's humming through my veins. I pull free and move to her side, running my palms over her trembling back, down to her ass, and dipping between her legs. "This is mine, Paige."

She moans, then nods.

I slide my arm around to pull her back against my chest and kiss her shoulder tenderly where I'd bitten her. Paige lifts her head and I kiss her cheek.

"Get some sleep, sweetheart. Round two starts in about an hour."

I see the grin on her face as she wriggles her body against me.

She probably thinks I'm kidding, but I'm not. She'll find that out soon enough.

THE FIRST STREAKS of daylight are peeking around the edge of the blinds as I stand at the foot of the bed and shrug into my leather cut. I dress as quietly as I can, not wanting to wake Paige. I just got off the phone with Blood. There's a shipment of guns coming up the bayou, south of Barataria, and the boat showed up early so he needs us all there. I don't mind that the shipment is early. Hopefully, we can get it unloaded and transported before the day really heats up. But I do mind leaving Paige.

I stare down at her and shove my cell phone into my inside pocket. Luckily she didn't hear it when it rang a few minutes ago. She's lovely, lying on her stomach in the twisted sheets, naked, one hand tucked under her cheek and her leg bent, exposing the curve of her hip and ass. I long to run my hands over her one more time, but I don't want to wake her.

I step over to her dresser and pick up a pretty pink perfume bottle, bringing it to my nose and inhaling the delicate scent. It's one she's always worn, one I've longed to know the name of for years, and now I know: *Victoria's Secret – Bombshell.*

I smile and set the bottle down.

I turn to leave and my eyes catch sight of a little scrap of pale blue on the floor by the bed—her sexy little panties. I squat down and pick them up, bringing them to my nose to inhale her scent. It's erotic, intoxicating, and sexy as hell—much better than any perfume.

I stand and stuff them down into my hip pocket.

A little souvenir of last night—our first night together, but sure as hell not our last.

CHAPTER 6

WALKING THROUGH THE CLUBHOUSE DOOR AT FOUR O'CLOCK THAT afternoon, the boys and I are tired as hell. Myself, Blood, Sandman, Joker, and So-Cal pulled this job. We don't complain. It comes with being a patch.

We crowd around the bar and soon have bottles of beer in our hands. Undertaker walks over and motions the prospect bartending.

"Pour 'em all a shot, Prospect. My private bottle."

Shot glasses slide in front of us and the amber liquor flows into each one—the good stuff—Undertaker's bottle of 14-year-old single malt Scotch.

He lifts his glass and we all follow suit. "Job well done, boys."

A drink like this should be sipped and appreciated, but I'm not a big Scotch drinker, so I down mine. That's when I look across the bar and see Paige.

She's talking with Mama Ray and Sissy, two of the middle-aged old ladies. Mama Ray is a widow like Paige. She lost her old man, Jaybird, years back and has been taking care of "her boys"—as she calls us—and the clubhouse ever since.

Paige glances over and meets my eyes, then looks away. I know what she's doing here. She's been waiting for me to get back. Oh, she's making every effort at nonchalance, pretending that she's not here for me, chatting it up with the old ladies. But I know better.

I push off the bar and stroll their way, pausing at the other end of the bar to slap Mooch, our VP, on the back and wish him a happy birthday. He's got a long braid down his back and an ever-present bandana around his head. If Willie Nelson were a biker, he'd be Mooch. He passes me a joint and I take a toke and pass it back.

I make my way around the bar to Paige. Ignoring her, I lift my chin at Mama Ray and wrap my arm around her shoulders, giving her a hug. "Mama."

"Wicked." She hugs me back, every one of her fingers laden with silver rings. "Took you long enough to come over here."

She's always quick to point out the obvious and her tongue can be razor sharp, but she's family and good people. I smile down at her stone-cold face, one that never reveals much emotion. "I was working my way over here."

"Um-hmm."

I wink at her.

"Well, I kept your woman company till you got here. She's all yours now."

Paige almost chokes on the beer she's sipping, and is quick to deny the fact. "I'm not his woman!"

Mama Ray lets out a huff of laughter as she climbs off her barstool. She leans to Paige's ear before she walks away. "Doll, you seem to be the only one here that doesn't know it."

Paige's mouth drops open and she glares at me like I told everyone. I didn't.

"Let's go," I say.

She raises her eyebrows at me, and then turns back to the bar and ignores me.

"Paige."

She won't even look at me.

"Babe, come on. We need to talk."

"No. We have nothing to talk about, Wicked."

She's pissed about me leaving this morning without saying goodbye. I know that's what this is about. But her ignoring me in front of my brothers is yanking my chain, and after a day like today, I'm not in the best mood. I wrap my hand around her wrist and pull her off the barstool. With my hold on her tight, I move purposefully toward the stairs.

"What the hell are you doing?" she snaps, pulling back and drawing the attention of more than one of my brothers. She digs her heels in, but it doesn't even slow me down.

I hear Sandman's laughter echo through the room at the show we're putting on. "Cutie pie, you need some help?"

I swear to God, he tries to interfere or lay one hand on her, I'll break his arm. I connect eyes with Blood as I round the pool table.

He smirks, but looks away. "Looks like I won the pool."

Christ, now they're betting on this shit? That's how crazy this woman has me, and I don't give a damn. Let them have their fucking fun. I hate that it's at my expense, but so be it. Paige is all that matters right now.

Bam Bam looks up from his game of pool, clueless as usual. "What? What'd I miss?" He locks eyes on us. "Oh, hell. Goddamn, Paige-y, I thought you'd hold out longer than this. I had eighteen days."

"What?" she asks, stunned.

"In the pool. I picked eighteen."

"What!" Her voice comes out in a high squeak.

"Hey, don't be pissed. I only got one square in the pool. Sandman bought four."

"You bet on me? Like a fucking football pool?"

"Come on." I pull her toward the stairs. "You can come down later and give them all hell. Right now, we've got a conversation to have."

Sandman snickers. "Conversation, huh? That some new slang the kids are calling it these days?"

Paige pulls back, knocking my hand away. "I'm not going anywhere with you! I'm leaving!"

"You want to do this the hard way, we can," I threaten.

Her brows shoot up and she slams her hands down on her hips, leaning into me. "Don't you threaten me, Wicked."

Sandman laughs again. "You tell him, cutie pie."

"Stay out of this!" I snap at him.

She whirls to leave, but I grab her arm and spin her back around. Before she can utter another word, I heft her over my shoulder and head to the stairs. She kicks her feet. "Let me go!"

I smack her ass. "Settle down and behave. We're just gonna go have a talk."

She's quiet, but I know she's fuming as I trudge up the stairs with the laughter from my brothers following us.

I carry her into my room and with a hand to the door I bat it shut. Standing with my back to it, I set her down, positioning myself between her and the only way out. One look at her flushed face tells me how this is gonna go. Oh yeah, she's pissed all right.

She lifts her arm angrily toward the door. "We're a laughing stock now! Are you happy?"

"We? You, maybe, I wasn't the one with my ass in the air." She sucks in a breath, and okay, I admit that was a low blow. "Relax, Paige. The teasing will stop and they'll get used to us together."

"Oh no, they won't, and there is no *us*."

"I think last night proves you wrong."

"I told you it was only one night and that's all it could ever be."

"Like hell, baby girl. I want more. I'll always want more, and if you've got the guts to be honest, Paige, so do you." She rolls her eyes at me and that just pisses me off. "Go ahead—deny it. I dare you."

"Fine, I want you. So what?"

"So what?" Is she kidding me with this shit?

"I mean nothing to you. I'm just another fuck."

I grab her arm again and yank her to me, anger surging through me at her ridiculous words. "Stop it! You know that's not true, Paige, you know it!"

"Do I? Then why'd you leave without a word this morning? Do you know how that made me feel? Do you have any idea?"

"I got a call out from the club. You've been an ol' lady. You know how that goes. How many times did Ransack leave you naked in bed to answer the club's call?

She shoves me away. "Shut up. Don't ever talk to me about my life with Ransack again. Do you understand me?"

I exhale a long, slow breath, trying to calm my shit. If that's the way she wants to play it, I can accommodate her. I'll never mention his name again. But we've still got a conversation to have—one we never got around to last night. Not that I'm complaining. Last night was a fantasy come true and conversation would have just fucked it up. But there is something I want to know. "Fine. Then answer me one question."

"What?"

"Why'd you leave town?"

She hesitates, confused by my change of topic and then looks like she's trying to come up with a plausible answer. "There were too many memories here."

I get that. I do. But it's not the answer I'm looking for so I push for more. "That the only reason?"

"Does there have to be more than that?" she snaps back.

Damn, the girl's got grit. I clench my teeth and her eyes drop to the tick in my jaw. "That last day … when you loaded up and pulled off?"

"Yes?" Her voice is suddenly soft and unsure, like she's wondering where I'm going with this. I hope she's ready for my confession.

"Tore my heart out watching you drive away. Did you know that?"

Paige sucks her lips into her mouth; it's something she does when she's nervous. Her eyes glaze over and she whispers, "Please don't do this. Let's not complicate this anymore than we already have. We agreed this would just be one night."

"Bullshit. I never agreed to that."

"Travis," she whispers softly. Just that one word—my name on her lips—and all the anger deflates right out of me.

"I can't help it, Paige. I gotta lay it all out there. You've been in my heart for a long time, longer than you know. If I had met you first that night—"

She finishes the sentence for me. "—it would have been us."

I know her words are true. Hearing her say them out loud, *finally*, after all these years has my throat closing around a lump. Jesus Christ, when I think of all that could have been … how different our lives would have gone. Maybe we'd have children; maybe I would have given her that baby she always wanted. Maybe we would have been happy. Maybe we still can be. "Paige."

She shakes her head. "Don't."

Like that's going to stop me. Nothing is going to keep me from finishing this long overdue conversation. We're going to have this out—to the end. "Why did you leave, Paige? Why did you *really* leave? Tell me the truth. Give me that much." Goddamn, I sound like I'm pleading, and I suppose I am. Christ, this woman could put me down on my knees, and that's a scary thought for a badass like me. Thankfully, she has mercy on me and gives me what I want, *what I need* more desperately than air.

"Because I had feelings for you, Wicked, and I was afraid," she says the words quietly, not meeting my eyes, and reverting back to my club name. She's throwing up walls, putting distance between us, or trying to at least, but I won't let her. Still, her words throw me.

"Afraid?" I frown. "Afraid of what? Of me?" My voice is gruff, as I demand an answer.

She shakes her head, and finally looks deep into my eyes and into my goddamn soul as I watch a tear slowly roll down her cheek, and she admits, "I was afraid I might act on those feelings."

I blow out a long breath as the iron chains that have been contracting around my chest for weeks now finally begin to loosen, and suddenly I can breathe again. That's what her confession does for me. But it's not enough. I want more, and I realize I'll always want more with this woman. I'm a greedy son-of-a-bitch when it comes to Paige.

"I have to go," she murmurs, her eyes already on the door behind me.

Oh, like hell. She's not walking out on me now. Not after that. She moves to brush past me, but I grab her by the upper arm and pull her back around. "You're not leaving. Not yet."

"What do you want from me?" she pleads, her tear-streaked face staring up at me.

"I want to know the answer to the questions I've always wondered. I want to know if the look I see in your eyes is a lie … if the way your mouth goes soft and you tremble at my touch is a lie. I want to know if every signal you've ever given me has all been a lie." I hesitate because saying the words seems so final. But I call up the guts to lay it all out there for her. "I want to know if you want me like I want you … if it's more than just sex you want from me."

"Yes," she breathes, so softly I'm not sure I hear it.

"Yes, what?" I demand, my voice rough, like I just choked down gravel. I feel like I have. I feel like if I don't get the answer I want—the answer I *need*—my throat will close up and I won't be able to speak. Hell, I won't be able to breathe. "Yes, *what,* Paige?"

"Yes, I want you. I've always wanted you," she whispers, and then shakes her head like she wants to take it all back. But I'll be damned if I'll let her, not when I've waited so fucking long to hear those words.

My hands close over her upper arms and I drag her against me. "Say it again. Say it like you really mean it."

"I mean it, Travis." She gasps out a sob. "It's so wrong, but it's true. And I hate myself for it."

Fucking hell, those words gut me. "Don't say that," I growl and cup her cheek.

"Don't you see?" she cries. "I shouldn't feel this way. I shouldn't want you to hold me. I shouldn't want you to kiss me. I shouldn't want you to make love to me. It's all so wrong."

"No, it's not. Don't you say that. Don't you ever say that again. Don't even think it, Paige. You deserve to be happy. Ransack wouldn't want you to spend the rest of your life pining for him, bringing flowers to his fucking grave every week, and crying for a man that won't ever be here for you again. Hell, he wasn't here for you when he was alive."

Her palm cracks across my cheek so fast, I'm stunned, my head's reeling from the blow. I feel the sharp sting and I see her pull her hand back, covering her mouth like she's just as shocked as I am by the violence that exploded out of her. My jaw clenches, but I can't be angry with her. I deserve that, that and much more.

"I'm sorry," she whispers.

I shake my head. "No, I'm the one who should be sorry. I overstepped."

"Travis—"

I hold my hand up, cutting her off and stepping back. "It's all up to you, Paige. You want me to leave you alone, I will.

She stares at me for a long moment, and I'm surprised she's not already heading for the door, escaping this confrontation. But she stands still, so still, as she looks at me with an unguarded expression, letting me see the emotion welling up inside her, letting all her walls down. Finally she whispers, "You're the reason."

I frown, pausing, not sure what she's talking about. I ask gently, "I'm the reason for *what*, Paige?"

Her eyes hold mine. They don't drop away or shift nervously around the room. They stay locked on mine. "The reason I came back."

I feel like all the air in the room was just sucked out, and I have to inhale a shaky breath. That's how powerful her admission is.

"I loved Ransack. I did."

"I know you did."

"I betrayed him—every time I looked at you." She dips her head, tears falling down her cheeks. "I'm so ashamed."

Her sobs wrench at my heart. "Look at me, Paige."

She shakes her head, sobbing harder. "I can't. It hurts too much."

I take her chin and make her look at me. "You never betrayed Ransack. We never did a thing while you were married. And I never would have. He was my brother."

"I thought about it, though. That's just as bad."

It was my turn to shake my head. "No, babe. It's not. You were a good ol' lady to him. He never doubted your love for him. Never. Not for one minute."

Her hands reach for my ribs and she buries the crown of her head against my chest. I press my lips to her hair, breathe in her scent, and wonder how I can take this pain away from her. My words seem to have no effect. Hell, I'd always been better at action, and that's what I fall back on now. I heft her up and her legs wrap naturally around my waist. In two steps I'm at the bed, taking her down to the mattress as I stretch out on top of her.

She looks up at me, and I want to drown in the depths of those wide blue eyes as I brush the tears from her face. I've never been very good at tenderness, but with her, it comes naturally. That's how connected I feel to Paige. Can she see it in my eyes? Can she feel it in my touch? My kiss?

I glance down at her lips and can't resist. I press my mouth to hers, gently, coaxing the response I know will come. I know because that's how good we are together. With her it's like no other woman I've ever been with, everything just settles into place inside me. Everything feels right in the world. Everything and anything seems possible with Paige.

But I know she's got to let go of Ransack before she can truly let me in. And I want in, more than anything I've ever wanted in my life. Maybe even more than I wanted the club. I hate admitting that, but I'm beyond lying to myself. I'm done with that. I'm done with pretending I don't feel.

If I learned anything from Ransack's death, it's that life is short. You have to grab all the happiness you can and hold on to it. And that's what I plan to do.

I pull back to stare into her eyes, then press my lips to her forehead. I feel her hands slip under my cut and grab my T-shirt, clenching and pulling me closer. I can't get closer, but I know how she's feeling. I feel the same—that I can't get close enough. "I love you, Paige. I have for a long time."

"I love you too, Travis."

I brush my thumb along her cheek, stroking softly. "Let him go, baby. Let him go and make room for me in your heart. Can you do that?"

Her eyes search mine and I hang on her answer, waiting, hoping, and yes, praying.

Finally, she nods. "It's time. I know it is."

I nod back at her. "It's our time now. And I'm going to spend the rest of my life making you happy if you'll let me."

Finally I see the smile I've waited a lifetime to see, and it's radiant, full of love, and shining up at *me*. At long last, that smile is all *mine*, and I know I'll do anything to keep it there.

Paige owns me heart and soul, and I know there's no line I won't cross to keep her.

If you enjoyed *My Brother's Old Lady*—please check out my books.
Website: http://www.nicolejames.net
Nicole James' Evil Dead MC Reader Clubhouse:
https://www.facebook.com/groups/763490467147322/

HEART & SOUL BY NINA LEVINE

INTRODUCTION

To love, loyalty, and a little mayhem.

And women with grit.

"Here's to strong women.
May we know them.
May we be them.
May we raise them."

A NOTE FROM THE AUTHOR

Dear Reader,

If you've read my Sydney Storm MC series, you've met Tatum. She's my favourite female character I've written in this series. Possibly my favourite out of all my books I've written.

This short story is focused more on her than Nitro, because I wanted to explore the love and loyalty she has for all the people who mean something to her. If you've read her story, you'll know she'd given up on people before she met Nitro. I love how he and his family helped breathe life back into her, in the same way she did for them. And I love seeing how far she's come.

I hope you enjoy this short as much as I enjoyed writing it. And if you've not met Tatum yet, you can read her story in my book, Nitro's Torment.

Nina x

CHAPTER 1

TATUM

"I'M NOT LETTING YOU OUT OF MY SIGHT TODAY," NITRO SAID AS HE SPOONED me, sliding his hand over my hip and reaching for my pussy. "Seven days straight of you chasing after Billy's shit is six days too many."

My lips curved into a smile. What he wanted to say was seven days of me chasing Billy's shit was *seven* days too many. But that was only because he still wasn't a fan of my boss. I wasn't sure he ever would be. Nitro was a man who didn't let shit go easily. Not shit that affected his family, and since he still held a grudge over the way Billy handled his relationship with Nitro's sister, I didn't see a change coming soon.

Pressing my ass against his rock-hard cock, I said, "You know I'm a fan of lazy Sundays spent at home, so I'm good with your plan, but you might wanna share it with Dustin."

He pushed two fingers inside me. "Why the fuck would I need to share that with my brother?"

I gripped his arm as the pleasure he delivered raced through my veins. God how I didn't want him to stop, but if I knew his brother well, we wouldn't have a choice soon. "Because I'm pretty sure I just heard him outside. I would say I'm surprised *you* didn't hear him, but you clearly had other things taking up your attention."

"Fuck," he muttered, dropping his head to rest against my shoulder.

"Nitro!" Dustin called out as he banged on the front door. "I brought your favourite breakfast. And I'll make porridge for Tatum."

Laughing, I pushed Nitro away and rolled over to face him. "Looks like your plans have been changed, champ."

His eyes darkened. "We do breakfast. We spend some time with

Dustin. And then your cunt is wrapped around my dick while I fuck you for as many hours as it takes to get my fill. Billy fucking Jones has consumed your attention this week; today, you're mine."

He left the bed and strode into the en suite he'd recently built for us. My eyes remained glued to his firm ass the entire time, just like they always were when Nitro was naked. That ass would always be my downfall; Nitro could convince me to do almost anything when it was on display.

A couple of minutes later, Dustin banged on the door again. "Nitro! Tatum! Wake up! It's hot out here."

Nitro exited the en suite at the same time I left the bed. "I'll let him in. You take your time," he said.

I grabbed his hand and pulled him to me before he left. Then, after standing on my toes, I curled a hand around his neck and angled his face down so I could kiss him. It wasn't a rushed kiss—Dustin could wait—but rather a long, deep kiss filled with promises. When I finally let him go, I said, "We do breakfast and we spend time with Dustin, but we do that shit as fast as we can. I need that fury of yours today."

"Fuck," he hissed. And then he was gone.

Fuck was right. Billy had worked me hard all week, and then some. I'd left early for work every day and come home late and exhausted each night, collapsing into bed unable to even entertain the thought of sex. Nitro wasn't the kind of man to go a day without sex, and I wasn't the kind of woman to do that either. We didn't need it to connect, but touch and intimacy were key parts of our relationship. We'd taken what we could this week, but what we both needed was an entire day alone, skin-to-skin.

I listened to him and Dustin for a few moments, smiling like I always did when the two of them were together, and then headed into the en suite for a shower. I didn't take my time like Nitro had said; I wanted to hurry breakfast along.

After I dressed in the tiny denim shorts and fitted white tank that Nitro loved, I padded out to the kitchen, doing my best to ignore the heat. It had become unbearable this week, and since it was already stifling, I knew today was going to be another scorcher.

Dustin's smile blasted my way as I sat on the stool next to Nitro at the breakfast bar. "I'm making you porridge, Tatum."

I returned his smile as Nitro slid a coffee across the counter to me. "You're way too alive for this time on a Sunday morning, Dustin. What's going on?"

His eyes lit up more than they already were. "I had a good night at work last night. And it's not *that* early."

Nitro took a gulp of coffee before saying, "It's eight in the fucking morning, Dustin."

Nitro was still fixated on the early drop-by, but I'd moved on from that. I was more interested in what had happened at work last night. Dustin worked a cleaning job at *Billy's*, the club my boss owned, and while I knew he liked his job, it didn't usually make him this happy.

"What happened last night? Did you talk to Stasia?" I asked. Dustin had a crush on one of the girls and had spent the last week trying to get up the courage to talk to her.

He reached for some plates in the cupboard. "No, she wasn't there last night." He looked ready to burst with pride as he said, "I did a job for Earl and he paid me two hundred dollars."

The second the words 'I did a job for Earl' left Dustin's lips, I placed my hand on Nitro's thigh, trying to steady his response. This was bad and I needed to attempt to intervene before my man lost his shit.

He ignored me, though, as I figured he would. "What kind of job?" His voice was low and edged with a dark demand. Nitro knew what kind of jobs Earl ran, and they weren't the kind of jobs Dustin should have been getting himself tied up with. But Dustin's naivety and faith in people got him into trouble all over the place, as did his desire to make friends everywhere he went.

"All I had to do was drop off some medicine to one of his friends. Easy."

"Fucking hell." Nitro moved off the stool, his body tense, his desire for blood evident with each purposeful stride he took towards our bedroom.

Shit.

I looked at Dustin. "Was Billy there?"

He opened the bag of food he'd brought with him and laid pancakes on the plates. "No. It was just Earl last night."

Earl was one of Billy's managers at the club; the only one I didn't like or trust. I'd told Billy he was bad news, but my boss had a way of only listening to some of the stuff I advised him on. He'd told me Earl had increased revenue dramatically, so he wasn't going anywhere. That had been three months ago, and I'd kept my eye on Earl since, waiting for him to fuck up. He was smarter than most, and sly; so far I hadn't discovered anything damning.

I slid off my stool. "I'll be back in a minute. You keep making breakfast."

He nodded, still smiling big, completely unaware of the storm brewing.

I hurried into the bedroom and found Nitro with his phone to his ear. His eyes came to mine, full of fury and the expression he wore when he was communicating 'Don't argue with me, Vegas'.

"Billy wasn't there. I doubt he even knows about this." I never was good at not arguing with him.

"I don't give a fuck, Tatum. It's his club; he's where the buck stops. No fucking way should Dustin have been dragged into Earl's fucking side hustle." His nostrils flared. "I swear to fuck, if this shit happens again, and if Dustin ends up on the cops radar, I will fucking spill blood."

"I agree, but—"

I was cut off when Nitro snapped into his phone. "Billy, we need to talk."

Silence then while he listened to whatever Billy had to say.

Then—"No, I'm coming to you. This shit needs to be face-to-face. Where are you?"

Fuck.

Billy must have given him the information he wanted because after listening to him for a few moments, Nitro said, "I'll be there in a couple of hours," and then stabbed at his phone to disconnect the call.

"Nitro—"

His nostrils flared again. "No, Vegas, I'm done playing nice with Billy for you. This overstepped my limit and I'll be making that crystal fucking clear to him."

I reached for his arm as he took the few steps to exit the room. "Nitro. Wait. You're being unreasonable."

He stopped and gave me his attention but I knew by the hard set of his jaw that he didn't want to.

"Let me talk to Billy," I suggested, "I'll make it crystal fucking clear that this should not have happened and should never happen again. If you go see him in the mood you're in, fuck knows where it will all end up. And you causing problems with Billy isn't something Storm needs."

He worked his jaw. He knew I was right. "Fuck," he muttered.

Before we sorted it out, my phone rung.

Billy.

I placed my phone to my ear while holding Nitro's gaze. "What's up, Billy?"

"I need you in here to take care of something."

"At work?"

"Yeah."

"I was looking forward to a day off." I tried to ignore the way Nitro worked his jaw again.

"Yeah well we all were, Tatum, but turns out some fucker has caused me a shitstorm that I need you to take care of."

I exhaled my frustration. "After this, I'm taking two days off. You won't call. You won't text. You won't even breathe in my direction."

"Fucking hell you bust my fucking balls some days. Just get your ass in here and handle this shit. If I have to sort this out, you'll be working overtime for weeks to get me free of the consequences."

I ended the call and waited for Nitro to speak. He would absolutely have something to say about me going into work today.

But he didn't. Instead, he shook his head and said, "Go take care of whatever he needs and sort this mess out with Dustin. And make it clearer than fuck that if something like this happens again, he won't have the good fucking fortune of not dealing with me."

I moved into him, scrunching a handful of his shirt. "Thank you," I said softly.

He placed his hand on my ass, pressing my body hard to his. "What for?"

"For trusting I can take care of this when I know the last thing you wanna do is let anyone fight your battles." I pulled his lips down to mine and brushed them with a kiss before adding, "I love you."

He gripped the back of my neck and dragged my mouth back to his. After his lips crashed down on mine and he kissed me like a starved man, he growled, "Get your ass back here as fast as you can. I have plans for it."

CHAPTER 2

TATUM

THE FUCKING AIR CON IN MY CAR DIED ON THE WAY TO *BILLY'S*. WORST TIMING—it was shaping up to be the hottest day on record in Sydney. By the time I arrived, any feelings of dislike I already had towards Earl were magnified, because heat and me did not go well together. I was hot, sweaty, and cranky. And most of that crankiness was directed towards Earl, with the rest aimed at Billy. So when I ran into Earl on the way to Billy's office, I stopped and gave him a piece of my mind.

His shifty eyes met my gaze before instantly roaming my body. Nothing unusual for Earl. He was a piece of shit as far as I was concerned. I managed Billy's girls at the club, and they all thought he was a vile human because of the way he treated women.

I didn't even bother calling him out on his behaviour; Earl was the sort of man who didn't care about anyone but himself. Instead, I cut straight to the point. "You paid Dustin to deliver your drugs last night."

He took his time finishing up with my body before looking me in the eyes again. "Yeah. And?"

Fucking asshole.

"And that will never happen again."

Amusement crept over his face. "Really, Tatum? You think you have any say over what *I* do? Sweetheart, you're just here to keep the bitches in line; don't kid yourself that anyone but them listens to you."

Fucking small dick energy. I stepped closer to him, crowding him, noting the flare of surprise in his eyes. "You should take more care with what you say, Earl. Those bitches pay your fucking wage. Also, if you actually knew what my real job is here and what I do for Billy, I guarantee you, you'd watch your words more closely."

He tried to throw off more bullshit masculine dominance. "I know what you do for Billy, and I'm not impressed. Like I said, I'm not here to listen to you, so if I want Dustin to do a job for me, I'll fucking ask him to do a job for me."

"No. You. Fucking. Won't. Dustin cleans. That's it. You go anywhere near him again, you won't just have me to answer to." I took a step away from him. "And get your fucking eyes off my body. I'm yet to meet a woman who wants your disgusting eyes on them."

As I stalked away from him, he called out some derogatory remark about my vagina, which I ignored. Fuck him; I was done letting Billy off the hook where he was concerned. If I had my way, Earl would be gone by the end of the day. I didn't always get my way, though, and sometimes I had to work really fucking hard for it. I figured on this occasion, I'd be working hard for it, so I suited the fuck up as I made my way to Billy.

"Tatum," he barked as I entered his office. "Shut the door." Something had him worked up. Billy was an asshole a lot of the time, but he was especially agitated today.

I closed the door and said, "What's going on?"

He shoved his fingers through his hair. His face was alive with anger. "That motherfucker, Parker, fucked with Savannah last night. I need you to deal with him, because if I do, he won't ever step foot in my club again, and un-fucking-fortunately I need him to."

Parker was one of our whales. His fortune was in the millions and he spent most of his nights here, sharing that fortune. This news of him fucking with Savannah surprised me; I'd never known Parker to cross any lines with the girls. However, Billy didn't get on with him, so I doubted he was thinking about this as rationally as I was.

"What did he do?"

"He put his fucking hands where he shouldn't have."

"Where?"

"I don't fucking know where; all I know is that Savannah is refusing to come in for her shift tonight if he's here, so clearly some filthy shit went down."

Savannah was one of Billy's golden girls—his loyalty to her was absolute. She was also one of the girls who put up with a lot from our customers, so if she was upset, something had definitely happened.

"Okay, you know I'm the first one to stand by our girls, but Parker has been coming here for years, and regardless of the issues between you two, we've never had even a hint of a problem with him where the girls are concerned. So I'm going to tread carefully here and get to the bottom of exactly what happened."

Billy took a moment to think about that and then nodded. "However you tread, make sure this is sorted by this afternoon. I want Savannah on her pole tonight, and I want that smile of hers plastered across her face while she's up there."

"Will do. And now we need to discuss Earl and the fact that you need to pull your head out of your ass and get rid of him."

He leaned back in his chair and crossed his arms, settling in for a fight. "I've told you before that he brings in too much money to get rid of."

"And I'm telling you that at some point, easy money becomes hard money. There's something off about him, Billy, and I'm concerned your club is going to suffer the consequences of whatever that is. Also, Nitro's gunning for you because of something Earl pulled last night—"

He cut me off. As much as he and Nitro had their differences, Billy tried not to piss him off because if my man was pissed, I was too, and that wasn't something Billy ever wanted. "Fucking hell, *that's* what he called me about this morning? What the hell did Earl do?"

"He used Dustin to deliver his drugs. The drugs he's selling out of *your* club. Without *your* consent." We'd discussed this in the past also, but for some reason I couldn't fathom, Billy overlooked it too.

"Fuck," he muttered. Uncrossing his arms, he stood. "I'll talk to him and tell him if he ever uses Dustin again, he's gone."

I didn't respond to that, but rather, lifted my brows questioningly, letting him know I was looking for more than just that.

Billy proved me right in my assumption that I'd have to fight hard to get what I wanted. With a shake of his head, he said, "Don't push me, Tatum; you won't like where it gets you."

Suit up, Tatum.

"Right back at you, Billy."

His eyes darkened with displeasure. "What the fuck does that mean?"

"It means that if you push *me*, you won't like where it gets *you*. And not listening to what I'm telling you is pushing me. My instincts for assholes are never wrong, and right now they're screaming at me not to trust Earl. I won't stick around forever waiting for you to come to your senses."

The displeasure in his eyes deepened. "You're threatening to quit?"

"I can't work with him anymore."

"You fucking hate ultimatums."

He was right; I did. But we all did shit we hated every now and then. "I hate Earl more."

"Jesus fucking Christ, Tatum. You know I need you. But I also need the cash he brings in."

"That's a story you tell yourself. You get rid of him, and I'll make sure that cash doesn't dry up." I cocked my head. "And since when do you run on fear? Man the fuck up and start making better decisions for your girls. I'd be more worried about losing them than losing Earl."

The last thing I heard as I left his office was him muttering about how hard I was squeezing his balls. That wasn't an odd occurrence around here. I'd learned a long time ago not to give Billy an inch. I took care of all his dirty secrets and run-ins with the law; he needed me more than I needed him.

I made my way outside, but as I walked past the office the managers used, I heard Earl talking in hushed tones. When I heard him mention King, I came to a stop and listened in on his conversation.

"Can you do it tonight? I want King taken care of as soon as possible, and I don't want him knowing it's coming. He should never have crossed my brother."

Silence then, before he talked again. "My snitch says King will be at the clubhouse tonight. He's meeting someone there at six. Get it done then, and let me know as soon as he's handled. *And* if he's still breathing when I wake up tomorrow, there will be hell to fucking pay."

More silence before—"For fucks sake, Ian, if you can't do it—"

Whoever he was talking to cut him off. He listened for a moment before snapping, "Good. You get this sorted, there'll be a lot more work for you."

I'd heard enough, so I continued making my way to my car. Once I was in it, I pulled out my phone to call King. He didn't answer, so I left a voicemail. I then called Nitro, but he didn't answer either. After leaving him a message also, I pulled out of the car park and drove to Parker's place. It was far too fucking early on a Sunday morning for this. He'd likely be passed out after last night, but I was on a mission to sort Billy's problems out. And I needed Parker to help me do that.

CHAPTER 3

TATUM

"JESUS FUCK, TATUM," PARKER SAID TWENTY MINUTES LATER WHEN HE answered his door, looking like he'd barely slept. "It's fucking Sunday morning."

I entered his house without invitation, pulling my sunglasses off as I said, "Yeah, and you and I have some stuff to discuss, so maybe you'll wanna make yourself a coffee because I need you fully awake for this. And no, I don't want any."

Parker was mid-thirties and as arrogant as they came. Unless you compared him to King, that was; that man had no fucking equal. So I treated Parker in much the same way I treated King and any other arrogant asshole I did business with—with unwavering confidence that I was right. And I did my best to boss them into what I wanted. I knew they'd fight against giving me that, so I always went in asking for the world like it was mine to take. Usually they compromised enough that I was happy with the outcome. Except King. Fucking difficult man. But for all his self-importance, Parker had never given me grief over anything.

After he grumbled some more, he made coffee, and I got straight to the reason I was there.

"What happened with Savannah last night?"

He looked up from what he was doing with the coffee machine. "You're going to have to give me more than that. A lot of things happened with her last night."

I sat on the stool across from him at his kitchen counter, keeping my eyes trained on his. I needed to see the truth of whatever he said in his eyes. "Did you touch her? And when I say touch, I mean a lot more than the usual stuff we tolerate at the club."

He placed both hands to the marble countertop. "Yes." His voice was firm, honest, like he had nothing to hide. Before I could ask another question, he continued, "In answer to your next question, I've had my hands all over her for the last month, so this isn't anything new. But I'd prefer you keep that bit of information between you and me. Billy doesn't need to know that Savannah has broken his no-fraternisation-with-the-clients policy."

I frowned. "So you two are what, dating?"

"I'm not sure either of us would call it that, but I've spent every night with her here, yes."

"So what happened last night? Because she's refusing to come in to work tonight if you're there."

He held my gaze for another few moments before dropping his head and muttering, "Fuck." When he looked back at me, he said, "We had a misunderstanding, that's all. It'll be fixed today."

"What kind of misunderstanding?"

"Must we get into this?"

"Yes. I'll be visiting Savannah next, so I need to know what I'm dealing with."

He studied me silently for a beat before saying, "It's a good fucking thing I like you, Tatum, otherwise you'd be out on your ass right about now."

I arched a brow. "Start talking, Parker. I don't have all day."

He removed his hands from the counter and carried on making coffee. "One of the other girls cornered me and kissed me. Savannah caught it. As you can imagine, she wasn't happy about it. We argued and she told me we were done."

"But you're not done? Have I got that right?"

"I'm far from fucking done," he growled.

"Okay, so I'm seeing a problem here, and it's the reason why Billy has his rule about no fraternisation. You want Savannah, but you also want the other girls—"

"No, I only want Savannah."

"Yeah, well your actions don't line up with that. I've seen you with the girls over the last month and they're all over you."

He drank some of his coffee. "They're all over me because Savannah likes that. She likes to watch. I discovered last night that she gets territorial when she finds me kissing someone though. That won't happen again."

Fucking hell, this was a headache I didn't need today. Motioning at him, I said, "I changed my mind; I need coffee to deal with your shit."

He looked less than impressed at that. "I don't recall asking you to deal with my shit."

"Unfortunately, I have to. If not me, you'd have Billy banging down your door."

The scowl he hit me with was dark and dirty. "I promise you, if that asshole turns up here, he'll wish he didn't."

I nodded. "You see my dilemma here. I'm trying to keep him away." I exhaled my frustration. "Look, I don't really give a fuck what you do, but this shit Savannah is pulling today can't happen again, and it's my job to ensure that. So you and I are gonna talk some more and figure this out."

He shook his head with his own frustration before stalking to the dining table behind me. Grabbing his phone, he dialled a number. When the call was answered, he said, "Savannah, get your ass dressed and get ready for my driver. I'm sending him over to pick you up so we can fix this problem between us."

I heard her fire back at him, but couldn't make out what she said. She was pissed, though; I could hear that clear as day.

"You're being unreasonable—" he started.

She cut him off because he stopped talking abruptly.

"Savannah—"

Cut off again.

"Fuck," he muttered when she finally let him get a word in, "do you have any fucking clue how tight your hold on my dick is? Get dressed. Edward is on his way. We're sorting this out today. And you won't be leaving here until we're back on the same fucking page."

After he ended the call, texted his driver to collect Savannah, and came back to me, I said, "I'm not sure why you don't have a wife, Parker. Your way with women is smooth."

He looked anything but calm, which was a contrast to any other way I'd seen him look before. Savannah appeared to have him wrapped around her finger without even realising it. "I've never had to deal with a woman like Savannah before. She's infuriating some days."

"Okay, enough of the Savannah talk for now. We'll wait for her to arrive before we get into that again. I have something else to discuss with you."

"Jesus, Tatum, it's too early for this. Can we discuss it later?"

I ignored his request. "Am I correct in my assumption that you aren't a fan of Earl's?"

That dark scowl returned to his face. "You are correct. I have no idea why Billy keeps him around. He treats the girls like shit and he doesn't treat the rest of us much better. If it weren't for the girls and you, I would find another club to make my home."

"Good, because I'm going to need you and your money to get rid of him."

"My bank balance isn't going to like this, is it?"

I smiled. "No, but you're going to love what I give you in return for all that cash."

He drank the rest of his coffee. "I'll make coffee while you share your plans to drain my account."

"It's simple really; you'll pay a weekly fee to the club and in exchange I'll set you up with your very own private playground. It'll be the kind of access to anything and everything in the club that every other man there would kill for."

"How much are we talking?"

I reached for his phone and keyed in the amount. Saying the number out loud made it sound far worse than just showing him.

Parker didn't agree. "Fuck. I'm going to want my own private fucking pole for that. Not to mention a long list of other shit."

"Send me your list. We'll negotiate."

As he made coffee for us, he grumbled, "Whatever Billy's paying you, he needs to double it. And tell me, how does this get rid of Earl? The only reason I'd agree to this is to see the last of that piece of filth."

I gave him a quick rundown on Earl and why he was still a staff member at *Billy's*. Talking about him reminded me I needed to still get hold of King, so once I'd finished, I lifted my phone and said, "I need to make a call."

He nodded. "You do that. I'm going to take a quick shower before Savannah arrives."

I ran my eyes over the crumpled clothes he wore. "Good idea. And perhaps while you're doing that, you could figure out how to get your point across to her without ordering her around." I wasn't convinced he could fix this situation today if he continued to behave the way he had on the phone. And I really needed this fixed today.

"Anyone ever told you you're a ballbuster?"

I gave him a pointed look. "What do you think?"

He left me, grumbling about my way of dealing with things.

Once I was alone, I called King again. And again, it went to voicemail.

"King," I snapped into my phone, "Call me back. I have information you need today."

I then called Nitro again, but this call also went to voicemail, so I left him a message too while wondering why he wasn't answering. It was unlike Nitro to miss my calls.

Parker took his time upstairs, so I was still alone fifteen minutes later when Savannah arrived. The anger she radiated told me how displeased with Parker she was.

"Tatum," she said, confusion on her face, "What are you doing here?"

"Billy told me you're refusing to work tonight if Parker is there, so I came here to take care of that. Billy was under the impression Parker did something to you last night, but that's not the real story, is it?" My tone was hard. It had to be, because while I always took my girls' backs, I also had to manage them. And sometimes what they needed was some tough fucking love.

Her mouth pulled into a thin line. "Technically he *did* do something to me last night." Oh, she was pissed off all right. Parker had a lot of work ahead of him.

"Yes, but what he did had nothing to do with your work. And all this bullshit going on today is the reason why we have the don't-fuck-the-clients rule, Savannah."

She pressed her lips together harder and crossed her arms. "I've never agreed with that rule. And if Billy has a problem with the fact I slept with Parker, he no longer needs to worry about that, because Parker and I are done."

"I'm pretty sure you're not. And because I know an infatuated man when I see one, I know there's no way to stop this relationship between the two of you, so I'm going to have a conversation with Billy about it and clear the way for you to carry on."

Her anger to deflated a little. "You think he's infatuated?"

Ignoring her question, I continued, "In return for me doing that, you're going to make a commitment to me today that regardless of what happens between Parker and you, you will never pull this shit again. If he so much as looks at one of the other girls and you're not happy, I don't give a fuck; you will come to work and you will do it with a smile. You will leave your baggage at the door and collect it on your way out, but you will never bring it inside the walls of *Billy's* again. Are we understood?"

She stared at me defiantly for a few moments before backing down. Uncrossing her arms, she said, "You know, there was no need for any of this; I would have gone to work tonight. You know I would have."

"Yeah, I do, but *I* needed *you* to know I won't stand for these games. You're a fucking adult, Savannah, so act like one. You don't like what your man does? Tell him; don't use other people to send your message."

"He's not my man."

Parker's presence filled the room before he even spoke. "Yes, I am," he growled, "And we're going to spend today ensuring you never forget that fact."

Savannah's eyes flared with heat, at which point I knew it was time for me to leave. Parker would take care of this situation from here.

I met his gaze. "Send me your requests for your playroom at the club. I'll have it set up next week for you."

"And Earl will be gone by the end of next week?"

"If I have anything to do with it, yes." *If King has anything to do with it, he'll be gone by tomorrow.* I figured this would likely be the case, so my proposal to Parker had little to do with getting rid of Earl, and more to do with helping Billy's stress levels over his finances.

Parker's hand curled around the nape of Savannah's neck as he said, "Good."

I watched her react to him and wondered how the hell she thought he wasn't her man or that they were done. The way she responded to Parker was the way I responded to Nitro; he only had to be in the same room as me, and everything else disappeared except my need for him.

"I'll see myself out."

With that, I left the cool air of Parker's home and stepped into the diabolical heat of Sydney. Instantly, sweat formed on my skin, agitation gathered in my chest, and disorder claimed my thoughts.

I couldn't fucking function in this heat.

And why the fuck hasn't King or Nitro returned my calls?

Today started as a good day but was turning into a clusterfuck of irritation and frustration and too much goddam heat to think straight.

CHAPTER 4

TATUM

"Roe, is Hyde home?" I asked my cousin forty minutes later. I'd left Parker's home and driven to the clubhouse to look for King, but he wasn't there. No one who knew anything was there, so I'd called Monroe to see if Hyde could tell me where King was.

"No, he's out with King. Why?"

"I'm looking for King but can't get him to answer his bloody phone. I also can't get Nitro to answer his phone. Can you call Hyde and ask him to have King call me? Tell him to tell King I have information he needs today. Not tonight, *today*."

"You sound frazzled. You wanna come over?"

"No, I just wanna go home, have a shower, get in the air con, and be with my man. I might just stab someone if I don't get out of this heat."

"Okay, yeah, don't come here if you're in that kind of mood. No one needs to be with you when you're feeling murderous. I'll call Hyde. You go home. Maybe have some Milo."

Monroe always helped shift my shitty moods. I laughed at her Milo reference. "I'm not even sure if Milo can help me today."

"It's worth a shot. I'll check in on you later to make sure prison isn't in your future."

"Love you, Roe."

We ended the call and I left the clubhouse to drive home. By the time I arrived there half an hour later, after getting stuck in traffic, my tolerance for heat, people, anything, was at dangerously low levels. Today was a shitty day for the air con to die in my car.

Stomping inside, I came to a halt when I discovered Nitro's niece, Renee, sitting on the couch, crying. Her messy hair, mascara-stained face, and slumped shoulders drew me to wrap my arms around her. "Who's ass do I need to kick?" I asked as she clung to me and sobbed harder.

She didn't answer me for a long while. Instead, she cried it out, not letting me go. This was unusual for Renee. She was as stubbornly independent as I was, and didn't easily ask for help or share her burdens.

When she finally shed her last tear, she looked up and said, "Zed broke up with me last night."

"Oh, babe," I murmured, wiping her tears, "I'm sorry." My heart cracked right alongside hers at this news. Zed was her first love. The guy she'd trusted enough to open up to; the guy she'd given her virginity to; the guy she'd secretly dreamed of a future with.

My words set her off again, and she buried her face in my neck as more tears fell. I tightened my arms around her, vowing to do whatever it took to get her through this. I remembered how broken I was after my first love trashed my heart. And how long I'd stayed broken, especially since I didn't have a mother who'd been there for me. Renee had her mum, but Marilyn's mental state was so up and down that I wasn't sure how much support she could offer her daughter.

When Renee was able to stop her tears again, I suggested, "How about I make us a Milo and then we can talk if you want to. Or we can just sit here and think nasty thoughts about boys who break our heart."

A small smile flittered across her face. "Can we do all that? Milo, talk, think nasty thoughts about boys. I mean, do you have stuff to do today?"

I smoothed the hair off her face that had stuck to her tears and gave her the kind of smile I wished my mother had been able to give me when I was her age and heartbroken. "I have nothing to do today. Well, except at some point I really need a shower. And I need to get in touch with King. But other than that, we can do all those things all day if you want." I glanced around the living room, noting the silence in the house. "Is Nitro home?"

She shook her head. "No. He wasn't here when I got here."

I pulled out my phone and called him again. When he *again* didn't answer, I left another voicemail. "Nitro, why aren't you answering my calls? I really need to get hold of King, so maybe you could take a minute, pick up your goddam phone, and call me back?" *God. Men. Fuck.*

Renee's eyes widened. "Ah, okay, what's going on with *you*? I don't think I've ever heard you talk to Nitro like that."

I threw the phone down and raked my fingers through my hair. My sweaty fucking hair that I could cut off right fucking now I was that bothered by it. "This heat is far too fucking much. And I've been chasing King and Nitro, and they aren't fucking answering their phones." I held up my hand defensively as I heard the words coming out of my mouth. "I know I'm being demanding, but too fucking bad. I blame Earl."

"Who's that?"

"You might wish you never asked me that question," I said before launching into a fifteen-minute tirade of all the things I hated about Earl.

When I finished, she said, "Okay, go have a shower. I'll make us Milo and one-minute banana muffins. When you've cooled down, I'll tell you everything I hate about Zed."

"And then we'll make a plan for me to kick his ass?" I was only half joking. I knew where the little fucker lived; I'd maybe swing by and give him a piece of my mind.

She grinned. "I'm not sure how or why Nitro was so lucky to find you, but I'm glad he did. I love my mum, but you're like my second mum, and I love you for being you. Even when you get a little too hardcore like this."

I shrugged. "People learn how to treat us by what we allow. I've stopped allowing them to walk the fuck all over me, so now they don't. And I won't allow them to walk all over you either."

My phone rang and I quickly snatched it up.

King.

"It's about fucking time you called me back," I answered the call.

"Don't give me hell today, Tatum. I'm not in the fucking mood." King sounded as cranky as me, but then this was standard for him.

"Good, I'm glad you're in a mood, because I've got someone for you to take care of."

"Who?"

I shared what I'd heard Earl discussing today about his plans for King. After I'd done that, I added, "Also, he's a vile human who treats my girls like shit, and I know you're not a fan of men who have no respect for women."

"You got a photo of this motherfucker?"

"I can find one."

"Send it to me. I'll deal with him today."

The line went dead when he disconnected the call, and as I placed my phone down, Renee said, "Earl has no idea what's coming for him, does he?"

I turned to her with a smile. "No fucking idea." Standing, I said, "I expect Milo when I get out of the shower, and lots of girl time."

Her smile hit me fair in the chest, and as I walked to my bedroom, I thought about how much I loved having Renee in my life. Kids had never been on my list of things to do in life, but I couldn't deny the joy she brought me. I would do whatever it took to help her through this breakup, because in the short time I'd been with Nitro, his family had become my family. And I'd do anything for my family.

CHAPTER 5

NITRO

I CALLED TATUM AND PRESSED MY PHONE TO MY EAR WAITING FOR HER TO answer. She'd called me a few times this morning and I'd missed her calls while taking care of some things with King. Her last message had been pissy, which I'd thought odd for her until King informed me about what she'd discovered about Earl. We'd just pulled up at Billy's to take care of him, and to say I was more than ready to do that was a fucking understatement. He'd given Tatum hell for long enough, but she'd made me swear I wouldn't deal with him for her. Vegas was too fucking independent for her own good some days. Her fight drew me to her, but fuck, I'd prefer it if she didn't come out swinging every time I wanted to help her.

When she didn't answer, I left her a message. "King called me out to help him with some jobs after you left this morning, and we're just about to go find Earl. Don't expect me home until the morning."

"You ready?" King asked as I slid my phone in my pocket.

I jerked my chin. "Yeah."

The beat of the music pumping through *Billy's* drowned out every other noise as we made our way through the club. I'd never been here on a Sunday; it turned out to be a busy day.

A couple of the girls Tatum worked with recognised me and sent a smile my way, but other than a quick chin lift, I didn't stop for a conversation. I barely knew them, except for the times Tatum had asked me to step in and help them when they needed the kind of help I could provide.

We found Earl in Billy's office with him.

"King. Nitro." Billy glanced between us before settling his gaze on me.

"I didn't realise you'd be bringing King with you for this little talk about your brother."

"This isn't about Dustin," I said, eyeing Earl. "It's about a little problem we have with Earl."

"Fucking hell," Billy said, "If it's not Tatum with a problem, it's you assholes. What the fuck is going on?"

King took a menacing step towards Earl. "Do you want to tell him, Earl, or should I?" His question came out a snarl that matched the storm vibrating from him.

Earl was a dumb motherfucker. He squared his shoulders like he was ready to go to war with King. "This has nothing to do with Billy. This is between us, King."

"Correction," King said, his eyes blazing with crazy. "This has nothing to do with Billy *yet*." At Earl's surprise, he continued, "You think I got to where I am today without a brain? Or without having people everywhere keeping tabs on everyone?" He shook his head like he was disappointed in Earl. "This is why you would have never pulled off what you had planned."

"Okay," Billy snapped. "Would someone care to enlighten me?"

King slowly turned his attention to Billy. "I discovered Earl's plans to take over your gun business. He was coming after me tonight to settle a score he has with me, and when I heard about that, I did some digging and—"

Earl cut him off. "What the fuck are you talking about?" To Billy, he said, "You always did say King was crazy. This proves it. I'm fucking working tonight, so I'm not sure how he thinks I can be in two places at once."

Billy wasn't fucking dumb. I might not have liked the asshole, but I couldn't deny his intelligence. The way he looked at Earl now told me he didn't believe him.

"King is fucking crazy, Earl, but he's not a liar," he said, "So I'm interested to know more about your plans." Looking at King, he said, "What else have you got for me?"

"Like fuck I'm listening to this shit," Earl said, taking a step towards the door. I didn't miss the nervous flare in his eyes.

Placing my hand on his shoulder, I stopped him. Yanking out the chair in front of Billy's desk, I said, "Sit your ass down. You're not going anywhere."

While I held Earl in place, King shared everything he'd learned today. When he finished, Billy hit his manager with a filthy glare. "Tatum was fucking right about you all along. *Fuck*."

Earl finally realised Billy wasn't on his side, and attempted to escape my hold. He shot up out of the chair and took a swing at me, but I saw him coming and ducked. I then did what I'd wanted to do for a long fucking time; I punched the motherfucker and knocked him to the ground.

His grunts of pain filled the office, and he looked up at me with contempt. Spitting blood on my boots, his lips pulled into an ugly sneer. "If only you channelled some of that anger of yours towards Tatum; you could pull her into fucking line. Fuck knows how you put up with that cunt."

Red rage consumed me and I kicked his stomach hard enough to shift him. "I would have dealt with you a long fucking time ago if not for Tatum. The only reason you're still walking is because of her." Bending, I jerked him up and slammed him against the wall before punching him again. Over and fucking over, taking great fucking pleasure every time my fist connected with his body.

It wasn't until Billy pulled me off him that I stopped. By then, Earl was a bloody mess and the wall of Billy's office was painted with his blood.

King's phone rang. "How did you go?" he asked, answering it.

He'd sent Hyde and Devil to locate Earl's friend, Ian, who Tatum had overheard him talking to this morning, so I guessed it was Hyde reporting in.

After he ended the call, he crouched in front of Earl. "If I had any intention of letting you live tonight, I'd give you a tip to take better fucking care when choosing the people you align yourself with. Turns out Ian was a bad fucking choice; he squealed before we even got to his fingers." He glanced up at Billy. "And he shared every single name of who you were working with to steal Billy's gun trade." Looking back down at Earl, he continued, "Looks like you've got a long night ahead of you while the three of us take turns gutting you."

Earl, who was curled up grunting in pain, stared at King through squinted, bloody eyes. "Fuck you," he spat, "And fuck Billy for being a weak fucking man led around by a cunt who I should have put in her fucking place—"

I had one boot in front of the other before he managed to get that sentence finished, ready to fucking crush his skull, but King beat me to it. He straddled Earl, gripping his neck with both hands, and bellowed, "You say another fucking word about Tatum and I will take all fucking week to end your life rather than one night." He yanked Earl's head up and slammed it back down onto the polished cement floor, the loud crack ringing out like my favourite fucking song.

"King," I growled, "Get off him. He's mine."

The need to deliver pain rushed through my veins.

Every muscle tensed, ready to attack.

Ready to destroy the man who had threatened my woman for far too long.

I would need hours with him to sate this need.

King took his time but he finally stood. His dark eyes met mine with understanding. "He's all yours, but we don't do this here. Hyde is about ten minutes out with the van."

Fuck.

This had always been the plan, but I hadn't realised how unhinged I'd be after confronting Earl. I should have, though, because Vegas had become my fucking world since I'd made her mine, and I would go to the ends of the earth to protect her. To keep her safe from men like Earl.

I clenched my fists and moved away from him.

"I'll wait outside for Hyde," I gritted out. There was no way I could stay in the same room and not tear Earl limb from fucking limb.

King nodded and I exited the office. I'd only taken two steps down the hallway when I turned and punched the wall. "Fuck!" I roared, driving my fist into the wall over and over.

Fuck.

I should have taken care of this asshole a long time ago. I should never have allowed him all this time to fuck with Tatum. I wouldn't make this mistake again. She was mine to protect and defend, and she could argue with me all she fucking liked over it, but she wouldn't win this battle.

She. Was. Mine.

And I took care of what was mine.

CHAPTER 6

NITRO

I STEPPED OUT OF THE SHOWER AND DRIED OFF, TAKING MY TIME WHILE DOING my best to push the adrenaline coursing through my body away. I'd arrived home ten minutes ago after spending the night working my rage at Earl out of my system. I'd need Vegas to help me work the rest of the wild energy I was left with out of me. However, the fact she was currently asleep in our bed with Renee meant I'd either need to wait or find another way to get rid of it.

Wrapping the towel around me, I left the en suite to find some clean clothes. The sight of Tatum with Renee slowed me and caused my gut to tighten. The way she loved my family always caused that. Vegas had a heart the size of Australia, and I'd watched as she slowly opened it to my family after closing it off for so long. Fuck, being with her and watching how she loved had changed me too.

She stirred and her eyes came to mine. Wordlessly, she left the bed. Taking my hand, she led me out of the bedroom and into the living room.

"What time is it?" she asked softly, sleepily, her hand to my chest.

"Fuck you're beautiful like this," I murmured, smoothing her hair from her face. "It's just after four; you should go back to sleep."

"You just got home?"

"Yeah." Reading the question in her eyes, I said, "He's been dealt with."

She moved her hand from my chest to my waist and gripped me. "Good."

"This won't happen again, Vegas."

Her brows pulled together. "What?"

"Me holding back on someone because you ask me to. If they're threatening you, I'll take care of them."

"Nitro," she started, but I cut her off.

"Don't argue with me. You won't win."

Her eyes searched mine and she exhaled a long breath. Moving into me, she reached her hand up to wrap it around the back of my neck. "You're a stubborn man," she said, pulling my mouth to hers.

Tatum's lips were soft and fucking tempting, and I was a man unable to resist. But no fucking way was I doing that in the living room where my niece could stumble across us. Lifting Tatum, I carried her to a spare bedroom at the other end of the house. Kicking the door closed behind us, I threw her on the bed and straddled her.

Smiling that sexy fucking smile of hers that always got me hard, she said, "Fuck, I've missed you and your fury." Her hands went to my towel. A second later it fell to the floor and her hand wrapped around my dick.

"Fuck," I hissed, dropping my head for a moment. When I met her gaze again, I growled, "This is going to be fast and I'm not fucking apologising for that."

She increased the pressure as she moved her hand up and down the length of my cock. "You're still pissy I worked so much this week."

"Yeah," I said as I stripped her. "I'm also pissed off that I let Earl get away with his shit for as long as I did."

"So you're going to take that out on me?"

I grasped her chin roughly and rasped, "Damn fucking straight I am. You need to learn that being so fucking independent isn't always a good thing."

She picked up the pace of her hand job. "And you need to learn that being a caveman isn't always the best thing. I know my limits, Nitro, and I know when I need your help."

Fuck, I was close to coming, and I wanted to do that inside her, so I removed her hand from my dick. As I thrust inside her, I growled, "No, you fucking don't."

Her legs wrapped around me, her nails dug into my back, and her eyes held mine as she took everything I had to give.

It was as fast as I'd promised her.

And harder than I'd fucked her in a while.

I fucking brought my fury with me this time, because my brain couldn't get past the fear of what could have happened if Earl had taken his hatred out on her. He'd made it clear during the night that he'd planned some nasty shit for her if she didn't stop giving him hell. He'd also made it clear he wished he'd just 'given it to her' a long time ago.

There were too many men out there like Earl, and while I agreed with

Tatum's refusal to tolerate men like him, her inability to accept my help meant she was a target for them. And that shit fucking terrified me.

When we'd finished, we clung to each other for longer than we usually did. And when she finally let me go, she took hold of my face and said, "Something's gotten into you. What?"

"I can't fucking lose you, Vegas. And I won't allow anyone to hurt you. So I need you to understand I'm deadly serious when I say I'll step in if another Earl comes after you."

She thought about that for a beat before slowly nodding her agreement. "Okay."

I lifted a brow. "Okay, as in you're not arguing with me over this? Or okay, as in you intend to let me think I won this round?"

Pressing her lips to mine, she kissed me in a way she didn't often. Soft. Gentle. *Surrendering*. "Okay, as in I understand what this means to you, so I agree to accept your help from now on."

"Fuck me," I muttered, relief filling every cell in my body.

Her expression turned serious as she said softly, "Thank you." I knew what those two words conveyed: a helluva fucking lot that she would never say because it wasn't in her nature to get deep and mushy over shit.

It wasn't often that Tatum shed her skin like this, exposing her vulnerable side and handing me a piece of her heart, so I took it with the care needed and didn't continue to push the point. She'd given me what I wanted—what I *needed*—so we were done with this conversation.

She left me to go to the bathroom and when she returned, I spooned her, my arms wrapped tightly around her. "Is Renee okay?" I asked. Finding her asleep with Tatum led me to believe she wasn't.

"No, but she will be. Zed broke up with her."

"Why?" If she said the little asshole cheated on Renee, there would be no holding me back.

"Apparently his ex has moved back to town. He told Renee he still loves the ex, so it's not fair to Renee to continue seeing her while he's sorting through those feelings."

"Fuck, who knew teenage boys gave a shit like that."

"Yeah." She rolled in my arms to face me. Tracing my lips, she said, "I love you. I'm sorry to cause you so much worry, and while I'll try not to be so independent, I need you to know this might take me a little time to work on."

I ran a hand down to her ass, my dick hard as steel again. "Vegas, you're the fucking definition of independent, and I don't expect you to change for me. I just needed you to know to expect a lot more fucking fight from me over it."

She rubbed herself against me, causing the kind of friction that meant we weren't going to get any sleep for hours. Not that I'd intended for us to sleep. However, I'd wanted to catch up with her first, but that was off the table now. "I received your message loud and clear, champ. I like it when you fight with me. It usually means your fury isn't far away."

"Fucking hell," I growled, pushing her onto her back and reaching for her pussy. "You'll be the death of me, woman."

She wouldn't be, though.

Tatum had breathed life back into me.

She was strong, and fierce, and brave.

Full of grit.

And loyalty.

Tatum was the kind of woman who could never be the death of me when she was everything I'd ever needed in a woman. When she was my heart and soul.

THE END

Connect with Nina Levine

WEBSITE: https://ninalevinebooks.com/
FACEBOOK: https://www.facebook.com/AuthorNinaLevine/
INSTAGRAM: https://www.instagram.com/ninalevinewriter/
BOOKBUB: https://www.bookbub.com/profile/nina-levine

Ravage MC Bound Series

BOUND BY Chance

RYAN MICHELE

CHAPTER 1

MICAH

THE NEEDLE PRESSES INTO MY SKIN AT A RAPID PACE. SOUNDS FROM THE GUN echo in the tattoo shop along with the laughter and conversations from my brothers.

Brothers. Who the fuck ever thought I'd have those?

Back home in Sumner, Georgia, it was my goal in life to stay away from the club, the Ravage MC, and not become one of *them.* It had always been such a *dirty* word. *Brother.* As if it were tainted.

One I despised.

One I didn't understand.

One that I felt took my father away.

One that I blamed for years.

Until now.

Until joining the Marines.

Having two tours under by belt and another starting in a couple of days, I now understand the meaning of the word, and it no longer holds the negative connotation I'd given it only years ago.

Now, it means everything. The bond. The trust. The commitment to one another. That feeling that no matter what, these men have my back. It took me coming here to finally understand.

"Tugger, you about done?" Malcom calls from the other side of the room where he's getting his ink covered in goop and plastic put around his shoulder. Chase Malcom is a man I trust with everything. He's had my back time and time again, even pulled me out of a dangerous situation that could've easily killed him.

Looking down at my side where the tattoo artist is working, there only needs to be a bit more shading to the Marines emblem, and my ink will be complete. My third tattoo, when I always swore I'd never get a single one. This one is the eagle, globe, and anchor, the tired symbol of the Marines.

The eagle is the symbol of the United States. The globe signifies the worldwide commitment. The anchor represents the both land and water.

"About twenty."

Malcom nods and looks over to Dryerson, who is talking it up with the sexy woman behind the counter. "You comin' out with us? Or are you covered?"

There's teasing in his tone and a chuckle escapes me. Dryerson will go to the back, fuck this woman, and be ready to go to the bar and have five more, one after the other. When he's on leave, his dick doesn't dry.

"Ten," he calls out and grabs the woman's hand on cue as he leads her to the back.

"Fucker!" Malcom laughs as Camden, Samsun, and T-Boe follow suit, and Dryerson flips us all the bird.

"Alright, boys, we have sixteen hours before we're due back." Malcom rubs his hands together. Tonight is going to be one to remember.

CHAPTER 2

CYRUS

CYRUS THE VIRUS.

The words drift through my head as the amber liquid flows down my throat, burning the entire way down to my stomach. Those three little words haunt me at every turn in life. I swear my father named me Cyrus just to use the phrase to torture me.

Each time is like a slash of a blade marring my skin. If I could erase them, I wouldn't hesitate.

"Cy, cheer up!" my best friend Ari screams over the music thumping through the bar while she hip checks into me. When my body jolts pulling me from my thoughts, she laughs. "You were miles away."

She has no idea how far from a cramped bar I was. Shaking it all off, I answer sarcastically, "I am cheered."

Her eyes roll. "Whatever. You're not getting lost in your head tonight. We're here to have fun and relax."

She's right. We both needed tonight after the hell of a week. On a smile, I call over the bartender. "Two bourbon and Sprites." He nods with a wink and moves off.

"Why, are you trying to get me drunk?" Ari asks in a sing-song tone.

"Fuck yeah. You're funny as hell drunk."

We laugh as our drinks come and down them quickly. She grabs my hand. "Come on. Let's dance!" She yanks my arm, as I toss down the last of my drink. On her smile, she pulls me out to the crowded dance floor.

It takes so much energy to get those stupid little words out of my thoughts, it feels as though I've already danced the night away. Alcohol gives me a small bit of reprieve. Add in the music, my best friend and finally, I'm able to shut it down, feel the music and let my body move. My hips sway, arms in the air, and I let the music take me away.

I get lost in the moment, Ari dances up on me as we bump and grind one another. The men love to watch two women going at it with no holds barred and that's exactly what we do. While it isn't for them, it's an added perk to feel desirable.

It's the only time I actually feel free.

Freedom isn't something I take lightly. No, more like I clutch on to it with both hands and never want to let it go.

CHAPTER 3

MICAH

DRYERSON SLAPS ME ON THE SHOULDER, GRABBING MY ATTENTION. "THE redhead is mine," he says as he stares out onto the dance floor where several men and women grind and sweat. My gaze lands on *her* instantly.

Hands in the air, smile on her face, curves for days dancing like that floor was put in just for her pleasure. The fire of her hair draws every man on the floor to her. I watch as two different men from different angles try to dance up on her, but she's skilled at maneuvering herself away from them, not giving them an inch.

The woman has moves that's for damn sure.

My lips tip as men and women alike attempt to interact with her, but the only person she gives the time of day to is a blonde woman who appears to be with her. That dismissal makes her a temptation that every single person in this bar wants to conquer.

Dryerson has game, but this one isn't going to happen. For two reasons. One, she'll catch on to him right away and will dismiss him because she's not easy. She likes a challenge too. It's in her eyes. Second, she's mine tonight. There is not a single doubt in my mind about it. I fucking love a good challenge, and she's too hot to pass up.

"Go for it," I say taking a long pull off my beer as Dryerson smiles and takes off to the dance floor, weaving through the people to make it to the women.

"Fuck, they're hot," Malcom says seeing the two women as Dryerson reaches them, dancing to his own beat.

The blonde sees him immediately and a wide smile comes across her face. Dryerson has eyes locked in on the redhead, though. Unfortunately for him, the blonde steps between him and the redhead, grinding her body on Dryerson, and in a millisecond, he's not thinking of the redhead who has maneuvered, once again, away from him. His attention is swept away pretty damn quick by the blonde, and he's all in. This isn't uncommon. When it comes to women, his attention span is that of a gnat.

"Damn!" Malcom and T-Boe say at the same time through laughter, and I join them. "Fucker got burned."

"Doesn't mean he won't tap it after," Camden announces and he speaks the truth, except when it comes to this one. I feel it. It's in her presence, aura, whatever in the fuck you want to call it, but she doesn't want him. Hell, doesn't appear like anyone has caught her eye. Or she doesn't want anyone to. That will be changing.

The blonde turns her back to the redhead, and it doesn't take long before the redhead is dancing by herself. Several men try to take over where the blonde left off, but red is having none of that. She looks up to the ceiling then heads toward the bar.

"That's me," I call out, getting up from the stool and making my way through the crowd, hearing my brothers behind me. Their teasing about failing like Dryerson makes me want to laugh.

They know better. I've learned. Failure isn't an option.

CHAPTER 4

CYRUS

I'M GOING TO KILL ARI.

Once again she found a man, and he's the only thing on her radar. Just when I was starting to loosen up and have fun, she does the dick 'n ditch.

Siding up to the bar, the bartender comes up with a wide, flirtatious smile on his face. One in which I return leaning into the bar top and getting close. "Rum and diet."

The handsome man with long hair winks. "Sure thing, beautiful." He takes off as a deep breath tries to come in, but it feels shallow like the sigh was more in my head than actuality.

Even with all the noise around me, thoughts begin to invade as my drink appears, and I down it quickly needing the escape. "Another."

"You alright?" he asks me, and I want to punch him, but that would damage his pretty face. Just because a woman drinks doesn't mean a damn thing is wrong with her.

"Absolutely." His gaze lingers longer than it should before he takes off to make my drink.

A tap comes to my shoulder, and my annoyance heightens. I've been blowing off men all night. The downfall of coming to a bar. Turning my head slowly, a man on the shorter side stands next to me with a goofy as hell grin. "Go away." The order comes with an eye roll.

He's might be a good guy, but just from one glance at him, I know he's not for me. Whatever happened to the men who were strong and dominate? The ones who take what they want and make a woman feel like she isn't so alone in a world of chaos. I've yet to find one, so maybe they don't exist.

The guy starts to talk, but it's the deep baritone on the other side of me that catches my attention. Turning to him, my breath catches for a moment, and words won't form on my lips. It's as if I'm suspended in time, unable to do nothing but stare.

Pull your shit together, Cyrus! Since when do you get tongue tied when it comes to a man?

"Just ignore him," he says to me as my brow quirks, my voice coming back after clearing my throat.

"Now, why would I want to do that?"

The hunk of a man's face is very well defined with solid angles and planes, giving him an imposing look. When his lip tips in a smirk, my panties instantly dampen. It's one of those a woman will never forget in her entire life. One that makes you stop and take notice. One of those that is burned so deep in a woman's mind, it never escapes.

Of all the men today, none of them made me feel even a speck of whatever this is.

The eyes are his other weapon, deep brown with layers upon layers pulling me and captivating me completely.

"No answer?" I jab wanting to hear more from him and curious what his story is. Everyone has a story. Some aren't so pretty. While others are intriguing. I wonder which he is.

"You're the sexiest woman I've seen in years. You think I'm lettin' you go?"

To this, I throw my head back laughing. "Flattery will get you everywhere. What's your name?"

"Micah, you?"

"Cyrus."

"Beautiful name for a beautiful woman."

To this I laugh full out. "Beautiful name? No. More like a life sentence."

He leans in to my ear. "Sexy Cyrus. Yeah, I think it's damn perfect."

My belly did a small flip, and my heart rate picks up. Fuck, I'm in trouble.

CHAPTER 5

MICAH

SEXY AS FUCK.

That's exactly what Cyrus is. Every curve I want to explore, lick, touch and taste. As she leans into me, the smell of her perfume pulls me in deeper. It's floral, but not overpowering. Subtle. Nothing like the woman herself. She's a siren. One look and you're hooked. Fuck, I'm hooked.

"Let's dance," I say holding out my hand to her. She stares down at it like it's a live wire. I wait.

"You want to dance?"

Leaning in again, my lips brush her ear. "You can tell by the way a man moves on the dance floor how he'll be in bed. Trust me. You want to know."

She shivers as lust spirals around her. I can actually smell it, and it's tantalizing.

"Lead the way. See if you can keep up."

Lacing our fingers together, we move through the throngs of people and with my bulk, a spot clears. The song is upbeat and perfect. Wrapping her in my arms, I turn her so her ass is lined up with my cock, and we move.

Seeing her out here earlier is nothing compared to being side by side with her and feeling her lush body move with ease against mine. The first song turns into four, and by this time we are both a sweaty mess. My cock is aching, and she's looking at me with lust-filled eyes.

"You wanna get out of here?" I ask after spinning her around so she faces me. Her eyes are the color of bright emeralds and sear onto my brain.

"Where would that be?"

My hips press harder against her so she can feel what she's done to me. "My hotel."

She studies me for a moment, contemplating. Her eyes dart over to her blonde friend who Dryerson has completely occupied. "I'm texting my friend so you can't kill me."

"Never can be too careful."

The following moments are a blur, and the next thing I know the hotel door is slamming against the wall as we enter. Her legs are wrapped around me and lips attached to mine. My cock rubs against her heat just begging to get attention. Moans escape her as she feels the grind of my hips.

Her legs release, fall to the ground, and she kicks off her heels, lowering her a couple inches, my lips following.

Hands grip my shirt and pull it from my body, her hands trailing down my chest. Each touch makes something inside me come alive. This is beyond the physical ... there is just something about Cyrus.

Too bad we only have one night. It won't be enough to satisfy my hunger for her, but it will have to do. Time to make the most of it.

CHAPTER 6

CYRUS

MY BODY IS ON FIRE FROM THE TIPS OF MY TOES TO THE TOP OF MY HEAD, everything coming to life. My body. My head. My heart. My soul. How in the hell is that even possible?

The core, though, is my always on repeat in my thoughts. They have shut down, and all I can see, feel, and think is Micah. It's a feeling that I've never experienced to me in my life. No one has been able to take me away.

Micah picks me up, tosses me onto the bed and is in a frenzy, ripping his and my clothes off so quickly that he doesn't give me any time to appreciate his build. The man is hard in all the right places, and the ink on him is sexy as hell. The clear plastic on this side shows the Marine symbol. It must be where he gets his strength.

He's on top of me quickly, lips attacking mine and hands all over my body.

The passion between us is electric and sparking everywhere, igniting the room.

His lips trail down my neck, collarbone, then to the V of my tits. His hands grip them hard, his teeth taking turns nipping and sucking my nipples. Each movement has my core sizzling. I try to move my body, but his holds me down in so many delicious ways leaving me unable to find my friction.

Fingers enter me and my back bows off the bed. Micah moves down my body, his eyes coming up to meet mine.

"I'm eating this pussy until you can't breathe."

There is no comeback, because his tongue flicks my clit, then sucks it in deep. My entire body explodes in a crescendo of pleasure. I have zero control over my body as it bucks and bends letting the orgasm wash over me.

Micah doesn't stop as my screams take over, and my body shakes.

His lips leave mine, but I'm out of energy, and I sag into the bed.

Vaguely, I hear the sound of a foil packet tearing. "Don't give up so soon."

My head pops up at his challenge. Challenges. They've always been my downfall. It's like a dare when I was younger. I had to do them. This is no different.

"Show me what you've got," I throw down my own. Micah's sexy grin returns as he grabs my knees and pulls my ass to the edge of the bed. In one solid thrust he's deep inside me, thrusting so hard the bed shakes.

The low curl spirals up again. His cock is so long it hits my cervix repeatedly. Micah flips me over to my stomach, grabs my ass, and pushes deep inside once again.

This is even deeper, and after several thrusts this feeling comes over me. It's deep in my core clenching my abs. My fingernails dig into the bed as whatever the hell this is bursts, literally out of me.

A gush of fluid pours from me as my cries are muffled in the sheets.

What in the hell was that?

CHAPTER 7

MICAH

We lay on the bed. Our breaths are labored as we come down from the most incredible high I've ever thought of.

"You seem surprised," I ask with my arm over my eyes.

"I've never…" Her breathlessness has my cock hardening once again. I did that to her. I caused it.

"Squirted?"

I feel her head nod next to me. "Yeah. That was a first."

Rolling into her, I pull her into my arms. "Glad I was a first."

Her laugh is as beautiful as she is. It's something I store inside my head for those long nights ahead of me on tour. Add in her body and I'll have enough to get me through another year. Yes, there is something special about her.

"Don't tell me you're done for the night?" She starts, but I have her on her back once again, arms pinned over her head as I and lock our lips together. Slipping the condom on, I thrust inside her once again. She feels like heaven wrapped in silk. The only thing better would be feeling her ungloved, but that shit will not happen.

The bed bangs against the wall as her cries intensify. Her hips raise meeting mine with every movement. Fuck, she's perfect.

Each second I memorize. Each sound, touch, and taste I store deep inside me. These things I will never forget. The woman doesn't know it, but she's captured part of me that will always and forever be hers. Something I swore I'd never give another woman. Somehow, in one night, she made her way in.

Her walls tighten around me as I release in tune with her, letting everything around us fade away but us. Fuck yes.

We pass out, her head resting on my chest.

Jolting awake, the sound of my alarm rings. *Fuck.* It's time to head out.

She lays soundly, the rise and fall of her chest the only thing I feel. It was a damn good night, but that's all it was. One night together. While I'd love to have more, time is our downfall. I'm due back and will be on time.

Slipping out of the bed, she lay with the sheet around her waist, her bare skin creamy. I can still taste her on my lips each spot I kissed and licked.

I watch her as I get dressed. Feeling my phone in my back pocket, I take a quick picture of her. Maybe I'll have enough time to get it printed before we need to report. One can hope.

With one last look at the bed, I leave, this time knowing deep inside I left something with her.

CHAPTER 8

CYRUS

2 Months Later

I STARE AT THE STICK IN MY HAND WILLING IT WITH EVERYTHING INSIDE OF ME to change. Two little lines change my life forever.

And fuck, I don't even know the father's last name.

WE WERE BOUND BY CHANCE.

Now, we're Bound by Consequences...

ARE you ready for Micah's story? Get more information HERE

Connect with Ryan

Ryan's Reader Group:
https://www.facebook.com/groups/RyansSultrySinners/
Newsletter
Facebook: http://www.facebook.com/authorryanmichele
Bookbub: https://www.bookbub.com/authors/ryan-michele
Website: http://www.authorryanmichele.com

Blaze

INTERNATIONAL BESTSELLING AUTHOR

SAPPHIRE KNIGHT

CHAPTER 1

"WELL?" TORCH MUTTERS ONCE WE BOTH GET SITUATED ON THE BARSTOOLS AT the hole-in-the-wall bar. We're close to the compound at a place that a previous ol' lady owns. Her ol' man died awhile back, and we drop in from time to time to check up on her and the business. Being a biker, loyalty, and family is everything. Not necessarily blood relations, but rather our MC family—the people we choose to have in our lives.

"What?" I groan and signal for a beer as Torch glares at anyone who even attempts a glance in his direction. A new bartender is working, and she's a hot little piece of ass. She's one of a few around here I haven't had yet and wouldn't mind getting my dick wet with.

"Do you have a plan with this female principal? We've discussed her a few times, and now you've got Viking and Odin both on your back about doing something with her." Torch may be a moody fuck and Viking's oldest friend, but he's also a nosey bastard. Most wouldn't know that insignificant fact about him, but being around him through the Widow Makers and now the Oath Keepers, well, I have his ass pegged. You don't become the Death Dealer by being an idiot. He kills people and knows shit; it's just what he does.

"You heard the brothers; they don't give two shits what I do with her as long as I get her to heel." My VP and Prez have both ordered me to take care of this feisty woman who's been giving the club brats issues at school. Personally, I'm used to being judged and treated differently being associated with the club. The kids, however, don't deserve it. From what I've heard in church, this woman's a complete snot to anyone affiliated with the club—members included.

He snorts, his merciless gaze not believing I can make it happen. He runs his hand through his unruly hair and complains. "I've dealt with this bitch and believe me when I say she's a cunt. You think this is going to be easy, but me an' Nightmare know damn well she's stubborn as hell with her nose so fucking high up in the air when it comes to the club that she'll put your ass through the wringer."

Flashing him a cocky grin, I take a swig of the ice-cold beer set in front of me before responding. "I'll try to be nice, work some charm on her. Hell, maybe I'll bring her some fucking flowers and let her know that if she needs anything at all, I'll be more than obliged to offer a helping hand. Chicks can't resist when I turn up the charm."

"Not going to work." He shakes his head and requests a double American Honey, chilled. It's Wild Turkey with a hint of sweetness. Torch drums his fingers on the bar top as he speaks. "She's going to look down that sharp nose of hers and flick you off like a motherfucking flea. You don't believe me, but you'll see."

With a shrug, I wave his comment off. "Then I'll knock the bitch out and kidnap her. The choice is really up to her. I'll put the ball in her court and let her actions decide on how I treat her."

His hand goes to his forehead, his fingers massaging his temples as he swears under his breath. Torch rarely shows emotion to anyone other than our MC brothers, and even then, it's only to those of us who used to be Widow Makers alongside him. He's learned the hard way not to trust, so I can't blame him for being the cold fucker he is today. "You'll end up in jail. She's the type to press charges, and being a biker, she won't hesitate to take your ass to court. Tread easy with this one, a quick in and out," he warns, and it's my turn to scoff.

"I'm gonna mow that bitch over before she has a clue as to what's happened. I'm coming from left field, unannounced and unexpected. She's not used to real men, for that I'm certain. It's about time that she learns alphas aren't the motherfucking enemy. We're here to protect and provide for our women, not hurt them or oppress them."

Torch nods, taking a hefty swig of the smooth amber whiskey and leaves the subject to rest. As he sets his tumbler on the bar, I catch his daughter's birthday he has tattooed along his wrist. I'd asked about it when he'd had the tattoo done; I was curious why he chose that particular spot. He'd said it's a reminder, set in an area he'll see every time he makes a kill. He wants to remember the day she was born and why he eventually chose to become an Oath Keeper. He'd made the change for her—to offer her a chance at an easier life and to become a better man for her. I respect him a lot for it too; it's easy to be selfish. Doing the right thing at times can be much more difficult.

The cute bartender comes to a stop in front of me again, tipping her redhead toward the bottle sitting in front of me. "Can I get you anything else, Blaze?"

I meet her hazel gaze, taking in her overly mascaraed lashes and button nose. She blushes as I murmur, "Anything?" I flash her a grin that women always seem to fall for.

She tucks a strand of hair behind her ear and smiles, clarifying, "Anything else to drink?"

"Darlin', you wound me. You offer me anything and then go and pull the panties right out of my reach."

She giggles at my flirting and Torch groans. He's heard me say the same thing to every new bartender we come across. Why change it, if it works? Women seem to love my personality and easy smile, and when they catch a glimpse of my abs, they love me even more.

"Come on, Mr. Fucking Casanova; my little girl's about to get out of school, and it's the perfect time for you to meet this stick-up-her-ass principal."

Another thing I respect about Torch, he hardly drinks in case his daughter needs him. It has to be difficult living the life we've chosen, doing the deeds we're sometimes forced to do and not being buzzed through any of it. There are plenty of nights I've begun with dancing on the bar and then wake up the next day not remembering shit. I like to party; what can I say.

"Fine," I huff, suddenly not looking forward to the impending fight that's sure to come. I spare one last grin toward the cute bartender as she slides a piece of paper next to my beer and then moves on to help the next customer. With a glance at it, I can't help but chuckle and send her a wink. It's her number along with 'ANYTHING' written and underlined. She has no idea what she's signing up for, but I like it.

"Ridiculous," Torch drones, watching me stuff the number in my jeans pocket as we leave the bar and hop on our bikes. He could have pussy anytime he wanted if he learned to crack a smile here and there. He'd rather brood and slit throats than fuck a harem of willing chicks; personally, I prefer getting my dick wet.

An easy fifteen-minute ride later and we're pulling up at the school. The parking lot's littered with various cages as parents line up to load in their kids. I could drive a truck once in a while, but driving those damn vans or other cages would make me crazy. We walk our bikes back into a spot, parking next to each other. Torch likes to get off and head up to the building to get his daughter. He always wants the few minutes to ask about her day before the ride home where the pipes drown out her soft-spoken voice. I feel for the day she finally brings a boy home to meet him.

Her daddy will put some sort of fear in the kid if he doesn't decide to just filet him on the spot.

He garners my attention, muttering, "She's the uptight one over there." He chin-lifts toward the right, and my gaze easily follows, used to his direction.

The woman's exactly as I was expecting. Her hair's up, twisted in some sort of fancy wrap style. It reminds me of when rich bitches get dressed up for dinner in movies or whatever. Her backs held ramrod straight, with a small ass encased in an expensive pants suit. She turns around, offering me a glimpse of that perfectly straight nose Torch had previously commented on, and I draw in a stunned breath.

She's so goddamn beautiful it makes my chest ache. It's kind of like biting into a freshly-baked, flaky, golden-crusted cherry pie, only to discover it has far too much sugar. Cherry pie is supposed to be a bit sweet but also have a hint of tartness. This bitch is a full-on toothache just waiting to happen. I can already tell she's going to be a bittersweet mistake of mine in some type of way.

My steps falter, as my confidence is unexpectedly a bit shaken. I was expecting her to be a plain Jane run-of-the-mill woman. I knew she'd have the legendary stick up her ass, but after witnessing her beauty, well, it puts this on an entirely different level. I'd planned to swoop in and spread a touch of the Blaze charm onto her unsuspecting ass. But, now I know that won't work. I'm sure she's been hit on since she was sixteen years old if I had to guess.

If I go in there with flowers and flirting, she'll chew me up and spit me out. I'm guessing someone fucked her up when she was younger to make her so uptight. If I'd been around, I'd blame myself. My sixteen- and seventeen-year-old self broke hearts left and right back then. I was a cocky asshole. However, I was in the Carolinas back then, so it wasn't me. I'd damn sure like to come across the idiot that did her in though; he's the dipshit that's to blame for making this job hard on me.

"Don't think I should talk to her today," I admit with a mumble to Torch's back. He throws a glance my way and shrugs, keeping his stride toward his kid. As soon as his sweet girl sees us, she sprints in our direction.

She plows into Torch, enveloping him in a fierce hug and rambles excitedly, "Dad! I missed you today, and you brought Blaze? So cool!"

"I missed you too, angel." He holds her, pressed to his stomach as she doesn't quite hit his chest yet.

"Hey, pumpkin!" I beam a bright smile at her excited grin.

We're interrupted by a proper sounding. "Young lady! Excuse me, you can't run across the pick-up lane like that!" The principal comes to stand in front of us, and I find myself swallowing as I take her in from head to toe. She's fine as hell and more so up close.

"Excuse me, Mr...." She huffs at my brother not appearing intimidated in the slightest.

"Torch," he growls, and she rolls her eyes. I've seen people literally shake when pegged with his glare, but not her. This is going to be interesting watching her around the MC brothers; that's for certain.

"Right. I had forgotten that we'd gotten into a previous disagreement at our last meeting about legal names. Mr...Torch, your daughter can't run through traffic," she explains exasperated. "She could get injured or worse, be hit by a moving vehicle."

And if someone was stupid enough to hurt a hair on her head, they'd be dead. My brother would make sure of it. I have no doubt.

His brow does this tiny irritated twitch. "No one was moving. Your yuppie over there has the stop sign held up to those cages in line," Torch supplies and I find myself grinning. He rarely speaks so politely to anyone, and witnessing him on his best behavior is amusing.

"Regardless," she shakes her head, "it's unacceptable."

Torch growls, murder overtaking his menacing stare, and I can't hold back my laugh any longer. At my interruption, the woman trains her piercing gaze on me, watching as I flick my irises over her again. Her cheeks heat at my obvious attention, and her temper spikes.

"Do you find this amusing Mr.-mr...."

"Blaze," I reply, flashing a devious grin, dimples on full display as I saunter a step closer. Invading her personal space throws her off-kilter enough that Torch and his daughter take off for his bike. "Or...*big* daddy, Mr. sexy-as-*fuck*, hot stuff, abs of steel...any of those would work just fine, sugar." An average woman would smile, even giggle or reach out to touch my flexed bicep. I'm peacocking like a motherfucker, and it doesn't even phase this lady one bit.

Rather than giving in, she steps even closer, to the point that my steel-toed -boots and the tips of her fancy heels are touching. The top of her head barely reaches my chin, but she's got such big lady balls, it feels as if she's staring eye to eye with me. If she were taller, our noses would be brushing no doubt. "Mr. Blaze." Her voice hardens, lacing with unrelenting smugness. "I don't believe you have a student enrolled here; therefore, you're trespassing. Shall I call school security to escort you to the property line?" Her head tilts to the side, basically mocking, believing she has the upper hand.

My grin turns lethal, my irises shining with challenge. "Only if you want to witness me break rent-a-cop's hands in front of all these innocent children. I came to greet my niece with her father, but they've gone, so I'll go for now."

"Until you're on her contact card for approved visitors, it'd be in your best interest to remain off school property. It's my duty to keep these children safe."

Leaning down, my nose nearly grazes hers; I get close enough to show her she doesn't intimidate me in the slightest. "I'd be happy to contact my friend, the sheriff, if you're ever concerned about their safety." Standing back up to my full height, I send her a parting wink and stride to my bike.

Torch and his daughter are waiting on me before they leave, his engine already idling. His eyebrow rises in a silent question, but I shake my head and climb on, starting my motorcycle up with a loud rumble. I rev it a few times, knowing the principal is staring her fill. She'll be touching herself later as she remembers the sound and thinks back to all the things she could've said, but didn't. I don't doubt that for one minute.

CHAPTER 2

CHURCH

"BROTHERS," VIKING, OUR CLUB PREZ LOOKS AROUND THE TABLE AT EACH OF us. "We've spoken about the heroin coming in over the border. I have an update from the Nomads. They're in place and keeping watch at the time until we're ready to bring some heat on the cartel. Right now, we gotta focus on breaking in these new prospects and getting the other clubs on board as backup."

Nightmare sits forward, the subject instantly infuriating him. "I'm ready to ride any fucking time of the day or night. Already told my ol' lady to prepare for it. We should be with the Nomads, not breaking in a bunch of yellow-bellied fucks."

It takes everything in me not to burst out with a chuckle. This is serious, and it'll piss off my cousin and Nightmare if I laugh. I've always used humor to deal with shit though. I only got dubbed "Blaze" from smoking my share of weed when I was younger and getting the flames tatted on my arms. Besides, "giggles" isn't a hardcore biker name, and my uncle's Widow Makers MC wasn't a place for pussies. The Oath Keepers MC isn't either, but shit isn't quite as twisted in this MC as it was in the former.

"I'm ready too, Night, but we're sticking to the plan. Speaking of," Prez turns to me, "you get shit sorted out yet with the school?"

"I spoke to her," I share, not keen to tell him how it went. The brothers will be all too happy to find out that I've met a woman who's not easily bending to my charms.

His brow rises, impatiently waiting for details. The man's face is like a slab of granite, fierce in every expression. I've had to face his anger in the past, and it wasn't fun. Thought I'd die that day. It works to his advantage;

fewer people will fuck with an MC if the prez looks like he'll pop off your head with his bare hands and not flinch.

Exhaling, I meet his stare and confess, "She threatened to have me removed from school property. I need Torch to add me to his daughter's approved visitors list."

Torch and Nightmare huff; both having previous run-ins with the woman, while the other brothers either smirk or outright chuckle. *The dirty bunch of bastards.*

I've got Odin, my cousin, who's Viking's younger brother and our VP beside me, then sits Viking, who's my other cousin and Prez. After Prez is Torch, the club's death dealer and finally, Nightmare, an original member and one of Viking's closest friends. This end of the thick slab of oak is full of grouchy, broody fuckers, unlike the other half. The opposite side of the table seats Sinner and Saint the club's hell raisers; Chaos, Smokey the club treasurer, and lastly, Mercenary, our newest patched transfer from the Chicago charter up north.

Thankfully, the prospects aren't allowed in church—only the club officers or we'd really be packed in. It's hard enough to breathe in this room with everyone smoking weed or puffing on cigarettes that when we have visiting members, half are forced to stand against the walls. When Viking built this place, I don't think he was anticipating having one of the largest active charters in the Oath Keepers MC. If we keep growing like we have been, he may need to think of expanding the compound. We could move church into the bar, use this room for storage or something, and then build on a new, bigger bar for everyone to use.

Mercenary speaks up, his deep throaty rasp commanding attention. "Why don't we just have this chick replaced if she keeps causing this much shit at the school? It seems smart to me that we introduce more of our own into the fold around the compound. You've got Scot's ol' lady with the bar down the road; it's convenient to have her keeping a look out for any incoming. My ol' lady owns the local track and can store shit for us when needed." He gestures off to the side in the general direction of his wife's business. We all stare, waiting to hear where he's going with this. It seems like a good idea if it's feasible.

Glancing around, Mercenary continues. "The Oath Keepers has a doc on payroll inside the clinic, besides 2 Piece putting in his free time patching us up. Spin's got that tattoo shop which connects him to a lot of the younger people around here as well as the seasoned birds. Twist does all that bodywork and painting with Spin whenever a local has a custom car or bike. You've got Princess and Avery who help out by taking care of the compounds and the club sluts when needed. Odin's ol' lady does all that baking for the farmer's market downtown, which people can't seem to buy quick enough...why not branch out farther and have someone at the school too? If you think about it, the more we're integrated into the community, the more they accept us."

Viking relaxes back, his gaze beating down on Merc. Finally, he glances around, his expression lightening a touch, "Damn good idea. Any of you have a woman wanting work or if get one in the future; make sure she's trying to get a job at one of the places around us. Smokey, I'll get with you later to discuss our account balance and what we may be able to buy into locally. It's about time we start thinking of the future in ways we haven't already. I'm not talking about the money we bring in now, but something the club kids can have a piece of. Maybe a sandwich shop or something. I want them to have a way to be legit and not face bullshit bias harassment because they're tied to us."

I guzzle the rest of my beer then ask, "So, I give up on the principal then? We just replacing her?"

Everyone's attention falls to me again, and Viking scoffs. "Fuck no. Plan's still in place with her. We don't have the school board on speed dial to fire her ass, so get in there and get her to submit. She's been a fucking pain to the club for long enough."

Sweat breaks out across my brow at his words, but I nod regardless. They haven't seen how fucking gorgeous she is. They're like me, assuming she's some uptight, boring, rule-enforcing, cat lady. This is not the case at all; she probably turns down assholes while pumping gas or buying groceries.

"Anything else?" Prez questions, and we grunt out various no's. "Then, get the fuck out!" He slams the gavel down, and we shuffle out, headed for the bar in the next room.

Torch approaches, folding his thick, tattooed arms over his chest. "So the chat you had with her the other day was that bad, huh?" He's fucking jack diesel; we should've called him Terminator or some shit. Back then, we had no idea how huge he'd become though.

I nod. "I was gonna hit you up about it, but Princess has had me busy fixing her car. Viking's had too much shit going on to do it, and I don't like thinking of her without transportation." Vike's ol' lady has become the little sister I never had. I've protected her since the day that the Widow Makers MC and I had held her hostage. She could've had her ol' man kill me, but she saved my life instead. I vowed from that moment on that I would do whatever I could to keep her safe. The vow evolved from a protection detail to her becoming my family and someone I'd consider a best friend.

"Did you get the car finished?" He sits on the stool next to mine, our broad shoulders making up a wall of muscle.

"Yeah. There was a coolant leak. Three hoses and a water pump later, and it runs like new. Pain in the fucking ass too."

A beer is placed in front of me along with a bottle of water for Torch. I nod my thanks to Frost, the prospect working the bar today. I had to train him, so I've been around Frost more than anyone else around here. He's not too bad; he'll make a good member someday.

"We can pop smoke in a few, and I can get you added onto the approved list before I take care of some club shit. She's a ballsy bitch, giving you the boot for that shit."

"Bet," I respond and take a long pull from the ice cold beverage. I should grab some flowers or some shit and just get this over with. It's probably a good idea to make my presence known to her as much as possible. She's gotta learn real quickly that she can't get rid of me so easily. I'm going to be like a fly on her ass, hard to swat away and always buzzing to remind her I'm there.

Finishing off our drinks, we throw a quick munch on some lasagna that Princess was kind enough to make for the club's lunch and head for the parking lot. As the heavy door closes behind us, a matte black Hell Cat pulls to a stop, doors opening wide to reveal the ol' ladies from the other charter.

London gets out of the driver's seat; she's tall with big tits nearly spilling over her low-cut leopard-print top. She's so damn curvy that the woman could make a man weep with her wide hips. Her hair's black as night, tinted with blue, and the outfit she's wearing has her looking every ounce of a pin-up doll stepping from a magazine cover. She's a bad bitch, the ol' lady to the VP down the road, and she's almost always knocked up. Who can blame a brother though. I'm sure we'd all have her ass on lockdown if we were in his shoes.

Avery steps from the passenger side, her auburn hair cut perfectly in layers and shining. Her nose is peppered with freckles that have her appearing a touch more innocent than she is. She comes from a wealthy home and wears money with class. She flashes an easy smile at us while looking damn good in a silk shirt she'd refer to as a blouse no doubt. She's always in tight-as-fuck diamond-studded jean shorts that make her ass look like you could bounce a quarter off of it. Not that any of us would ever go there; she's like our Jude, claimed by two of our brothers. Surprisingly, she balances their charter prez and gun runner flawlessly. She could easily use her club status to her advantage but doesn't; she's kind, welcoming, and loyal—all traits we want in an ol' lady of the Oath Keepers.

A tiny blonde climbs out of the back seat. Her hair's so light, it's nearly white and falls to her waist. She's pushing maybe five feet at most, reminding me of a pixie; she's the Oath Keepers' very own Tinker Bell. She may seem sweet and an easy target, but she's Twist's ol' lady, Sadie. He's one of the craziest motherfuckers in the entire club—the unholy one—so Sadie must be a secret badass. Not only that, but her older brother is 2 Piece, the gun runner. She's also part of the reason why I was nearly killed trying to protect Princess and our club a while back. Her kid is the grandson to the president of the Iron Fists MC, a rival of ours. I've learned that sometimes the sweetest women are actually the most deceptively dangerous.

"Ladies," I call out in welcome, always the charmer.

Two additional cages and a street bike pull in to park next to the Hell Cat. Bethany, Nightmare's ol' lady, gets out of a car to greet Mercenary's ol' lady in the grumbling, fully-restored Nova. Chevelle owns the race track down the road, so she's always in a souped-up muscle car with enough horsepower to make you want to check the size of your balls. The crimson-haired, leather-clad female climbing off the street bike to stand beside London is Snake's ol' lady, Peppermint. This is a prime example why so many of us are single still. How can we find a chick worthy when you compare them to the bad bitches of the Oath Keepers? These females would eat the average woman alive if offered the chance.

"Fuck," Torch mutters under his breath, taking in the gorgeous group of women. "The fuck is going on?" he asks loud enough so only I can overhear him.

"Don't know, brother," I reply. "But a group of bitches this bad...in one place has me wondering if we should leave at all. Maybe we should check their cars for dynamite or some shit; they could be up to something. Viking may need us, after all."

He snorts, folding his arms across his chest, his tattooed biceps bulging as he glares at the females in front of us. "There a problem?" he asks outright. Any other group of chicks would tuck tail and get out of here, but not these troublemakers.

London saunters toward us first with a sway in her hips; the others are quick to follow. Smirking, my dimples come out to play as I tease, "Your ol' man know you stole his car again?"

She rolls her eyes, her throaty voice nearly making my cock harden as she argues. "Loretta's my car, Blaze. Besides, what's he gonna do? Spank me? Maybe you should tattle on me, after all."

"Right," I huff and shake my head. We all know she's guilty of taking off in his car for joyrides and gets the other ladies to tag along on her expeditions. If Cain weren't such a mean motherfucker, he'd never hear the end of the teasing about his ol' lady making him hunt her down when she's feeling froggy.

Chevelle grins wickedly. "You know London, I own the track down the way...you ever want to race that pretty girl, you just let me know, hun. We'll have some fun."

Torch's and my brows rise, not wanting to bear witness to their plans that'll no doubt cause their men to worry. The door opens behind us and Princess and Jude poke their heads out. "Ladies! You're here, come on!"

I catch Princess's wrist, halting her. "P, the fuck's goin' on? Should I stay?"

She beams a smile and shakes her head. "We're having margaritas. We decided to make it a weekly thing to meet up. You guys go; we have the prospects here to make us drinks."

Torch mumbles, but being around him so often, I catch his quick inhale of "Lord help us."

"Agreed, brother," I comment, giving Princess's wrist a soft squeeze. "Call if you need anything; I mean it."

She pats my cheek gratefully. "I will. Thank you." With that, she steps back, holding the door open, and the women step around us, heading inside.

"The brothers are in for a surprise," I say as we head for our bikes.

"The brothers are about to shit," Torch retorts, and we fire our engines up.

I grin until we hit the highway, 'cause that shits hella funny.

CHAPTER 3

"CAN I HELP YOU, GENTLEMEN?" THE FRONT DESK LADY STARES WIDE-EYED AT Torch and me, tapping her pen on the desk nervously. She's probably pushing sixty-five -with her perfectly coifed hairstyle, the white having a pale sheen of pink to it. Her shirt proclaims she's a proud grandma, and I like her immediately. She's got some spunk in there, I can already tell.

Plucking the biggest daisy from my flower bunch, I present it to her with a charismatic smile. "Yes, ma'am, you sure can. I'm here to get on my niece's visitor log or whatever it's called."

"The emergency contact card and approved pick-up list," Torch mutters beside me. Apparently, he already knows these things. I have no clue. Hell, his daughter's not even my real niece, but what the school doesn't know, won't hurt.

"Of course, what's the sweet girl's name? And I'll need to see some identification, please."

He digs into his back pocket, pulling his chained wallet free and hands over his driver's license. "Her name is Annabelle Teague."

The lady glances at the ID and hands it back before heading for some stacks of papers on the shelves behind her. "We have it on the computer, but you'll need to sign a form so I can add it to her file." As she's turning to bring the paper to Torch, the door off to the left side of the room opens.

I swear it's like the first time I'm seeing this woman all over again. My chest tightens, I'm short of breath, and my cock semihardens. That's just from a fucking glance at the bitch too. I think if I were to hear her say the word cock or pussy, I'd come in my pants. Swallowing down my nerves, I grit my teeth to get my bearings. She can't know that she shakes me up like this; I have to gain control. She's been top dog amongst her peers for far too long, and it's time she learns to humble herself with the Oath Keepers. Viking doesn't take kindly to folks getting in our way, whether it's the M or the club brats.

The older lady brightens. "Ah, Amelia, I was just about to order your lunch, ma'am."

"Thank you, Florence. Was there an issue here?" She gestures to Torch and me. She automatically assumes something's going on, just because we're standing here, buff, bearded, tatted up and wearing our leather cuts. She should be happy to have us in her school. It means we'd protect it if the need ever arose. God forbid they ever go on lock-down for whatever reason, but with Annabelle and Maverick around, we'd be the first to arrive to help out.

Florence sets the fresh-cut daisy down on her desk and leans in and pats my cheek as I flash her another grin. "Not with these sweet boys," she replies before taking her seat. Torch fills out the form, and I arrogantly smirk at the principal I don't have to even open my mouth, and I already drive her a bit crazy.

"Don't think we've *officially* met," I say, and she sighs, her dainty hand fluttering to rub her temple.

"Mr..."

"Blaze."

"Of course," the stunning pissed off woman mutters and gestures toward the room she just came from. "May I speak to you in my office, Mr. Blaze?"

I'm not an idiot; I know damn well it's not a question. I spent most of my days in school in trouble. They always ask you nicely before they pull you in their offices and cut you down. Newsflash for this bitch I'm not some pussy-ass beta boy nobody. I'm an Oath Keeper, and if she thinks she can rattle me, she's got another thing coming.

Closing the door behind me, she doesn't bother sitting down before she lays into me. "Do I need to remind you of our conversation yesterday? I will have you removed from school property."

Hiking my thumb toward the door, I look her over, smugly mentioning, "My boy Torch is out there right now, adding me to the approved list you mentioned, so I'm not trespassing." Stepping forward, I toss the flowers on her desk and fold my arms over my chest. "A motherfucking peace offering." I nod to them. "Now, smile and say thank you, and then I'll be on my way."

Her cheeks warm, flushing bright red. I'm not sure if she realizes it's happening or not, but I love knowing the effect my words have on her. "*Watch. Your. Mouth*!" she hisses, and I chuckle.

"You're a real stickler for the rules, aren't you, sweetheart?"

"My name is Amelia Stone—Doctor Amelia Stone. You shall address me as such."

"I'll address you as pussy lips if I see fit, especially if you continue to have that rod stuck up your ass. I think it's why your lips look so pinched, and you walk funny. I can help ya out if you'd like?" I shrug nonchalantly, and she screeches with outrage.

"Get out! Out!" Her slender finger points to the door, and I laugh, pleased to witness her lose control of her calm, cool facade.

"Already? But we've only just met—*officially*, that is."

She inhales a deep breath, attempting to gain her composure, a pacifying smile coming to rest over her lips. She thinks she's smarter than me, better than me...I can see it in her patronizing expression. "Mr. Blaze, *please* exit my office and this school for that matter. Your language is inappropriate for the children."

Dusting my nails against my shirt, I glance at them, not a care in the world when it comes to her and argue, "We're not around any children." I lean my hip against her desk, making myself comfortable.

The action further irritates her. She huffs. "I'm well aware, but you still need to leave."

"Look, Amelia, I'm not one to go around bursting bubbles, but you need to get used to me. We'll be seeing each other often."

"Oh? How do you figure?"

I step a bit closer, just enough to crowd her and smell a soft flowery scent. She thinks she's a hard bitch, but she screams woman all over. I confide, "Babe, the Oath Keepers make multiple private donations all the time. We figure this is a good stage to make sure that's well known since we have multiple club brats going here at the moment."

Her brow wrinkles as she opens her mouth to speak, but I interrupt. My hand reaches out, lightly grazing her sharp, pale jawline. "Annabelle and Maverick both speak highly of you."

I lie through my teeth. I've heard nothing but complaints about her from the club. However, you can catch more bees with honey I've come to learn over the years.

She flinches back, stunned I've gotten that close, and she either allowed it unconsciously or else she didn't see it coming. "I can't discuss students with you."

"Of course not, and you don't need to, sweetheart. We all chat about you anyhow, so we're well aware of what goes down around here."

Her fingers flutter up to her temples. She's trying not to flip her shit, and I'm loving every minute of it. Knowing I can unnerve her is all the reassurance I need at the moment. "I think it's best if you leave now." She repeats her earlier demand, and I can't help but fuck with her a touch more.

"Say please," I murmur, tilting my head, and her shocked stare meets mine.

"Ex-excuse me?"

"You want me to leave, say please."

She swallows, irises blazing. She's probably biting her tongue to keep from lashing out like I want her to. "Fine," Amelia concedes, whispering, "please leave."

"Blaze," I grin, and her mouth drops open. "Say, *please leave my office, Blaze.*"

"I swear, I'll..."

"You'll what, Principal Stone?"

"Please leave my office, Blaze," she repeats. I think her head may explode if I keep pushing her right now.

My grin turns conceited, flicking my gaze over her again. "Good girl," I say as I turn for her door. I don't have to look at her to know she wants to throw something at my back, probably her fancy paperweight. She won't do it, but the fact I got under Amelia's skin that much, is exactly what I was hoping for.

Now I need to charm Miss Stone's schedule from sweet old Florence and start showing up enough to finally break the good principal. She may not know it yet, but she'll be mine. The bitch is far too feisty to not be on the back of a bike—*my bike*.

RAGE AND KARMA GREET TORCH and me at the gate as we make it back to the compound. They're some of our newest prospects, a set of twins aching to belong in the club. "What are you two shitheads doing out here?" We pull to a stop, waiting for them to open the gate so we can get to the clubhouse.

One of them, I'm not sure which since they both look the same to me, flashes a wicked grin. "Prez thought we were flirting with the ol' ladies."

The other lookalike jumps in. "Threatened to knock our teeth out and then put us on gate duty."

The first brother finishes. "Told us to be on guard since all the ol' ladies were in one place, and their safety is the most important."

Jesus, it might be a good idea in the future to have them wear name tags, rather than their vest that only has a prospect patch. It worked in the past, but when you have the same face on two people, it gets a little confusing. Why couldn't we come across twin club whores instead? That I could get on board with.

Torch nods at the younger men; he knows them better than any of us, being they're his cousins. "We'll be more vigilant here on out. Shit's goin' down, so be prepared." With that, he rides through the now open gate, and I follow.

It's easy for me to get distracted and push this bullshit heroin business aside when I have a gutsy woman to deal with. Torch isn't lying about shit hitting the fan; our club despises heroin and sex trafficking, especially when it's coming into our state. Our club's been recruiting from all over. Mercenary came to us from Chicago, and some of us are from the Carolinas. Chaos is from Alabama or some shit. We're an oversized group of misfits who've come to love the state of Texas along with our club. The charter down the road is made up of born and bred Texans, who've taken to us like family and we protect what's ours—family, friends, homes, and state.

"You think they'll lose the prospect cuts anytime soon?" I gripe to my brother once we park and head inside.

"Doubtful, they're too new. Why?" he grumbles back.

"'Cause I can't for the life of me figure out which motherfucker is Rage and which is Karma."

He smirks. "Rage has the smoker's voice."

"They both seem raspy to me." I shrug and head for Viking's office.

"Nah, if you pay attention, you can hear it. His vocal cords were damaged."

"The fuck?" I probe, and his hands clench into fists.

"Some shit he went through as a kid. My aunt was pretty fucked in her head and put those two through hell."

I leave it alone and hit my fist against the open door to announce our presence. "Prez?"

"Mmm?" Vike grunts.

"Figured you'd be out drinking margaritas with the women," we chuckle and take a seat on the old broken-in couch adjacent to Viking's desk.

He broods. "Laugh motherfucker, but I've seen your ass drunk on those damn frou-frou drinks my ol' lady throws together." He's got braids along the crown of his head leading into a ponytail with the rest of his head shaved. It's pretty standard for the men in our family to have similar hair. We're all blond, and with us always out riding in the sun, it lightens the various pale shades.

Rolling my eyes, my legs stretch out in front, my chunky, steel-toed boots weighing my feet down as my hands go behind my neck. The couch is comfy; we've all slept on it at least once. "You gonna tell us what the next step is in this cartel bullshit that's goin' down?"

Torch folds his arms over his chest, his broad shoulders nearly encroaching on my space. "You should have me go in alone and take a good chunk of those cocksuckers out before they know what the fuck hit them."

Vike's brow raises. He shifts back in his office chair, staring the both of us down. "They fuck you up, and I have no way to get you out. They kill you, and I'm down a death dealer." It's not the answer Torch was wanting, but he shouldn't be asking to go in the first place.

I butt in. "You've got Annabelle, brother."

His glare shifts from Viking to me, and my shoulders shrug, unperturbed. I've known these two damn near my entire life. I'm well aware that they're a couple of cruel motherfuckers. Doesn't mean I'll shrink when they get irritated. "I can probably get to their boss without them ever knowing we were coming for them. I wouldn't suggest it if I thought Annabelle would be left fatherless."

Viking grumbles. "Then you're a fucking idiot, Torch. Those Mexicans are pretty fucking sly when it comes to their cartel business, and they'd find you somehow. We'll let the Nomads keep watch, and if they catch something they can't handle, they'll hit us up."

"They helping out with border patrol down there?" I ask. We rarely work with any police unless they're on our payroll. Sometimes, however, in cases like this where the assholes are affecting us all, we step up and see what we can offer.

He shakes his head and mouths 'ICE'. "You know we don't get involved," he replies louder, making me wonder if our conversation's being monitored somehow. We sweep for bugs pretty regularly and keep watch for anyone around the compound. We learned the first time our space was breached. Hell, I damn sure learned my lesson after nearly dying because of the Iron Fists. Maybe he's concerned about some of the newer people around or the ol' ladies visiting. I should've closed his door. "Torch, we get called to ride, I want you here with the prospects. Last time it was Blaze, and he got fucked up, but I think with you and the others, you'll have a better chance at protecting the compound."

My mouth falls open, "You don't want me with P?" I'm shocked; it's always been my thing to protect his ol' lady, above all else.

"I want you riding with the club, where you should be. Torch will watch out for her safety; besides, the bitch is pretty good with a Glock nowadays. We load her up, and anyone coming for her will take a hit, you know damn well."

He's right; she nearly shot his ass when she was pissed. I almost took a bullet trying to get the damn gun away from her. Those two are crazy when they lose it, especially when it comes to them as a couple. Still, I can't help but worry. Torch is ruthless, but Princess has become the sister I never had. I would filet anyone that wanted to harm a hair on her pretty little head, and Torch better do the same in my place.

"Right now, we have various brothers and whores making sure we're prepared here and for an unexpected ride. I want you concentrating on the school, namely that principal. It's time to take care of the less pressing shit so we can focus on the big issue knocking at our doors."

Torch grunts and I place my hands on my jean-clad thighs, leaning forward a bit. "I razzed her up a bit today. I'm going to start showing up every day, so she understands I'm not backing off."

"Just take the bitch and tie her up somewhere," he broodily suggests and my hands go up, placating.

"I'm going to give her a few days to see if she'll come around. If not, I'll get something from the doc...a knockout drug, so I can take her without a struggle. I'll have to keep her in my room unless you know of a place."

"Nah." He shakes his head, muttering. "Just play it safe, and bring her here. If she gets loose somehow, then someone around here will be available to catch her. When it's time, take a truck and get one of the brothers to help if you need it."

"All righty." I stand and step for the door. "I'll make it happen." I fist bump him and nod to Torch on my way out. I was planning to be sweet on her, but Viking's impatient. Now it's time to come up with a plan to kidnap her gorgeous ass.

CHAPTER 4

AMELIA

"AMELIA?"

My gaze snaps toward Florence as I leave my office. "Yes?"

Crossing the room, I step around the few extra desks behind the parent wall. We have a barrier between us and the check-in/waiting area. It's essentially one long bookshelf with a countertop, nothing fancy but helps hide the various manuals we're required to keep up front, as well as a vast selection of printed school forms and supplies.

"You have a lunch meeting scheduled today. I wanted to let you know since it was a last-minute addition. Would you like me to order you something to eat from that organic place you enjoy?" Her wrinkled hand lightly fluffs at her short, pink-tinted puffy hair. She's in another T-shirt her grandkids made for her, and the sight makes me smile. She truly loves her job and having the chance to be around so many children. I've never met someone so family oriented before.

"I'll just have a salad from the cafeteria when I have a free minute but thank you. What was the reason for the last-minute appointment?"

I was looking forward to a few minutes by myself to recharge. It's been one thing after another this week so far it seems. I've had to deal with angry parents because grades weren't updated in the online system just yet, even though they technically aren't due until Friday at four o'clock. Then there were a couple of fifth graders who thought it would be a good idea to use their fists on each other versus talking out their issues. Those parents were so upset one was threatening to sue the other child's family along with the school. It's been a huge headache, but nothing that we don't deal with often.

Her cheeks tint just a touch at my question, and I can't help but bite my lip. Florence only flushes for three reasons I've noticed: a student destined for expulsion, the Texas heat, or a handsome man, like the contractors we've had in a few times. "Annabelle Teague's uncle wanted to discuss his niece with you. He was quite adamant about speaking with you immediately. I put him down for the soonest appointment available."

"I need you to call him back and cancel it."

Her gaze widens, stunned at my reply. "Oh, dear, is everything all right?"

Releasing a heavy breath, I offer up a placating smile. "Of course, but I can't see him today."

"Would you like me to reschedule? I can look over your calendar; do you have a day in mind?" She begins to flip through the colorful planner in front of her next to her desktop computer. She has pictures of her kids and grandchildren filling the rest of the space along with a daisy. It looks suspiciously like the daisies that Annabelle Teague's uncle brought in with him. I threw my bouquet away after I kicked him out of my office.

"That's very kind of you, Florence, but I don't intend to ever speak to that infuriating man."

Her mouth drops open, lost for words. I rarely show my displeasure to her or anyone else, for that matter, when it comes to dealing with students' parents or other family members. "Excuse me for pointing this out, but he doesn't strike me as the type to be pushed aside."

"You're completely right; he's stubborn and demanding. I may have to call the police if he pushes me any further."

She quickly snaps a tissue from the box on her desk and dabs at her brow. "Well, I, ah...I thought he was quite charming," she admits, blinking a bit too quickly.

"He's pushy, domineering, and rude," I scoff and gently lay my hand on her shoulder. I've upset the poor lady, and that wasn't my intention. Clearly, the vexatious male has Florence completely fooled, but definitely not me. "I spoke to him already, and trust me when I say he doesn't have anything to say that I need to nor want to hear."

"I'll give the young man a call and let him know you're indisposed. Shall I say the same when he calls back? We both know he's going to," she assures me and sips from her lemon water.

"Yes, and that's much appreciated, Florence. Thank you."

She nods, and I carry on toward the conference room straightening my suit jacket as I walk. I always attempt to appear the utmost professional; I am in charge of everyone in the building, after all. Jimmy Robertson's parents are due here any time now to discuss their son's repeated fighting. One more strike, and I'll be forced to expel this young man. I'm afraid he just isn't changing his ways, and there's only so much we can do for him here. Looking in at an elementary school you'd never guess that fifth graders could cause any issues, but that's entirely untrue. Half of the boys are terrors. Testosterone starts to fill them up at this age, and I find myself constantly fielding off their curiosity toward the girls and their ridiculous tempers toward other boys.

I should find a girls school and transfer. I could put my energy and expertise where it really matters. I'd say goodbye to obnoxious little boys as well as pushy bikers who think they run everything. What kind of name is Blaze, anyhow? *So absurd.* I snort to myself and take a seat at the head of the conference table. That man has no idea who he's messing with. I may have given in to get him to leave, but I had to, or I was going to seriously lose myself, and he was not worth it. I won't let him gain the upper hand.

At least I don't have to worry about seeing him outside of dismissal, and if he decides to be obnoxious, I'll just call the cops on him. We'll see if he really is friends with the sheriff or if he's fibbing. My guess is he's bluffing and would freak out if the police showed up. Maybe I'll see if they can stop by a few times this week just to shake the biker up.

Blaze

FLASHING A WIDE SMILE AT FLORENCE, I lean in and place a soft peck on her hand. It works like a charm; she blushes, and her neck and cheeks flushed. "Miss Florence, it's always a pleasure to see you, ma'am." I lure her in further with my constant politeness; older ladies can never resist it.

She waves her hand, with a bright smile lighting up her face. "Oh stop with the ma'am, young man!"

"Just being respectful." I grin, flashing my dimples and move a touch closer.

She grabs a tissue from the box on her desk and uses it to lightly pat the back of her neck. "You're such a charismatic fellow, I swear. I just don't see why Amelia wouldn't want to see you."

With a shrug, I play innocent. "I don't get it, either. I'm just looking out for my dear niece; without her momma around, she needs as many good people in her life as possible."

"Such a sweetheart," she murmurs quietly, and I don't know if she means Annabelle or me. It's a dick move throwing Torch's daughter into the mix, but he said I could. He'd rather me mention her a few times versus her having issues around here since she's a club brat.

"Miss Stone still thinks you were going to cancel my appointment, right?"

She nods and leans in conspiring. "I was pretending that I couldn't get ahold of you, so if you showed up, it wasn't able to be helped. Amelia needs someone like you in her life. She doesn't realize it yet, but she will, in time."

"Smart thinking." I wink, and she giggles a bit. "Now, you remember what we discussed?"

"Of course, and after this morning, I understand much more of what you were saying. She does need a short vacation, badly, bless her soul. That dear is so tightly wound up and won't take a moment to relax."

"It's terrible." I sigh and shake my head. "She's going to work herself to death at this rate, then who would be here to help the students like she does?" I ask, and she pats my forearm, attempting to comfort me. I'm reeling her in like a gator with a bloody, raw chicken. Pretty sure I could get her to eat out my palm if I tried.

"You're a good young man, willing to take her on a surprise vacation. I can't wait to see her come back next week after having good food, sunshine, and some sleep. The dear is thin as a rail."

"It's all that health junk she eats that you were telling me about," I agree, refraining from laughing. One thing I've discovered about sweet Florence is she's a proud grandma to nine grandchildren. She's a true old-fashioned southern lady who believes food, sweet tea, and sunshine is good for the soul. I do agree with her on that, and in this case, she thinks Amelia's putting her body through hell eating all the gluten-free, organic stuff she likes. I'd bet good money in Florence's house, macaroni and cheese is a staple, as is sweet tea, red meat, and watermelon—all my favorites.

"You're exactly what she needs."

"Thank you for that vote of confidence. I'll do my best. You canceled her other appointments?"

"Yes, they're all rescheduled for next week. I'll make sure it looks like she's here the rest of the week to administration as well."

"You're a gem, Florence. I hope she appreciates you as much as you deserve." She beams at the compliment and gestures for me to glance behind her.

"That's the private entrance I was talking about when you called. Her car is parked in the first spot to the right of the door; you two can slip out there without any issues. You really think you can get her to go with you? She's a bit stubborn, I'm afraid." It's too perfect; we'll sneak out the back door and drive her own vehicle, so it looks like she left. Viking wanted me to bring a truck, but after speaking with Florence earlier, I decided this would be the best plan.

"Yes, ma'am. You leave that part up to me. We'll be quiet and not draw any unwanted attention either. In fact, I doubt you'll even hear us, maybe just the door."

If Amelia even attempts to protest, I have just the thing to make her pass out. Luckily we have a doctor on the payroll who was willing to help me out.

Her eyes light up as she stands. "Well, come on, let's get you in her office before she comes back. I don't want her putting that wall up and turning you away. She's a lucky woman. Back when I was her age, I'd have been beyond flattered to have a handsome fella like you coming to surprise me with a fancy trip."

I wink at her again and round the counter to follow her back to Amelia's office. Florence is the only other one up here with the principal's key, so this part was imperative. Lucky for me, she's a romantic who I've convinced to be on my side. She thinks I want to take her high-strung boss on a surprise vacation and woo her. She'd probably faint if she knew I had something in my pocket to knock the bossy-ass woman out so I can kidnap her. I'm a bastard for deceiving Florence, but I've never been a good guy.

Before the Oath Keepers, I was what nightmares are made of. I'd never have hesitated in the past to kidnap a woman for my old prez. This time around was done with much more finesse. Viking should appreciate it. The club, along with Princess, has changed the way I treat women immensely.

Growing up under Joker—Viking and Odin's father as our club prez—he had all of us doing shit we'll forever regret. Not that any of it could've been helped. Back then, we were doing what we had to, to survive. Joker would've killed us in a heartbeat had we faltered at his orders in any way. Thank fuck that's in the past and Viking is nothing like his father was. The Oath Keepers never would've let us patch over; that's for certain. They hold a certain level of respect amongst the clubs, and back when I was a Widow Maker, we never would've considered having morals.

"Good luck, Blaze," Florence wishes me and squeezes my bicep as I step into the over-organized office.

"Thank you," I say to the short woman, and she closes the door. First thing I do is head for the security feed and delete the entire week's footage for the front desk. Just in case someone does report Amelia Stone as missing, I need to cover my tracks and make it look like I was never here.

Now, the real decision I have to make is, do I wait behind the door to surprise her? Or, should I sit my ass on her desk and witness the fury first-hand in her beautiful irises one last time before I use the knockout drug and take her with me?

My fingers rake over the dirty blond scruff on my jaw as I think of what would be best. Her fighting me would be much more fun, but she may make too much noise. I promised we'd be quiet. With a sigh, I step behind the door and eagerly await my woman's arrival. I've got a surprise for her; one she won't ever see coming.

CHAPTER 5

AMELIA

My head's heavy and my brain groggy with an abundance of fatigue. What on earth happened? Did I pass out? The last thing I remember was my meeting at school with Jimmy's parents. I'd finished discussing punishment options and walked back to my office. At least, I think I did. I don't remember ever making it to my desk, though. Ugh, I feel like I've been sick for a week, and I'm finally beginning to make my way out of it.

Inhaling, I roll over onto my stomach, noticing multiple things all at once. First, my wrists are squished together, my hands balled up into fists under my chest. This doesn't smell like my lavender vanilla detergent either. It smells distinctly male.

I haven't had a male in my bed in God knows how long. Actually, that's not true; it's been two years since I'd invited anyone home with me. I blame it on a long day and too much wine, but even then, it was at a hotel and not my house. I was at a conference out of state...a man wasn't in my bed at home. So why do I smell one now? It's a mixture of musky male, deodorant or cologne and soap all meshed together. Inhaling again, my stomach tightens, and I groan, wanting to keep smelling it. Whatever dream I'm in, I don't want that part to end. I could cover myself in the scent and never get my fill. It's been too long since I've had sex. I've been busy and especially haven't wanted to deal with the potential of having a relationship with anyone.

The air conditioner kicks on, and the sudden brisk breeze of cold air causes my nipples to stiffen. Now that definitely isn't right. I have to be dreaming. I don't ever sleep naked. I have a collection of comfortable satin nightgowns and flannel pajamas that I snuggle up in each night. I get a full chill and my flesh covers in goosebumps. My body squirms, seeking warmth. Where are all the blankets?

A big, rough palm lands on my bicep. My body jerks in surprise as it moves up and down, chasing the goosebumps on my arm. "Shhh," a deep voice coos from behind and my muscles tighten. My back's as stiff as a board, my frame constricting further as my mind clears enough to realize that I can't move my arms. I concentrate on the movement again but get nothing in return.

I want to ask who's there and why the hell I can't move easily. I attempt to talk, to cry out, but only a whimper breaks free. Why am I so damn groggy? What's wrong with me?

"You're all right, sweetheart. Just try and relax. It'll be easier coming out of the drugs if you don't fight. Slowly wake up and pull yourself out. You were unconscious. You have to give your head time to catch up."

My eyes shoot open. There's no mistaking, that was definitely a man. I'm exposed, naked, and vulnerable. Was I in a wreck or something? I don't remember driving. Do I have amnesia?

"Ugh," I manage as his palm moves to rub my back. I want to scream at him not to touch me, but I have to get my bearings first.

"Shhh sugar," he soothes, and I refrain from jabbing my foot backward and telling him to shut up.

Glancing around, I take in the space. I'm nowhere that I recognize in the slightest. The room's pretty standard with beige walls and a charcoal, overstuffed chair. A five-drawer walnut dresser sits on the opposite wall, bare with only a flat screen TV resting on top. There are two closed doors off to the side. If I'd have to guess, maybe it's a closet and bathroom? The place is sparse though, nothing to give away the location or who lives here.

"Where am I?" I ask after working my tongue around my mouth and clear my throat.

"You're in my room," he replies and the voice registers. I know who that rich, gravelly sound belongs to.

My eyes drop to my wrists as panic blooms in my chest. This can't be happening. I have to be dreaming. I'm in denial; there's no way this can be real. Releasing a breath, I shift to my side, attempting to look at him. Maybe if I see him I'll finally wake up—at least, I hope that's the case.

"Let me help." He grabs onto my bicep again, pulling me to turn over, and I end up on my back.

The icy air hits my front, and I realize my mistake. I've presented my nakedness right out in the open. His determined imperturbable blue gaze meets mine, and I gasp at finding him completely bare lying beside me.

His mouth turns up into his signature cocky smirk, and I scream bloody murder.

His grin drops, stricken by my sudden outburst, and then he's grabbing me. He yanks me to him, and in the next second, his lips are on mine.

This isn't a dream; it's real. I'm naked and tied up in Blaze's bed. The truth hits me like a ton of bricks as I try not to lose myself in his demanding mouth. I've been kidnapped by the very man I was avoiding. He's trouble—a deceptively sexy criminal, and God help me, but I don't think he'll be letting me go anytime soon.

READ the conclusion to Blaze's story this fall! If you enjoyed this taste, look for more Oath Keepers MC books available now.

Stay up to date with International Bestselling Author Sapphire Knight:

Website: http://www.authorsapphireknight.com
Facebook: http://www.facebook.com/AuthorSapphireKnight
BookBub: http://www.bookbub.com/profile/sapphire-knight

PRELUDE TO SALVATION BY TERRI ANNE BROWNING

Angels Halo Next Gen MC Series

INTRODUCTION

Lexa Reid knows that the one thing her father won't let her have is Sheriff Ben Davis. But that doesn't stop her from wanting him…

CHAPTER 1

BEN

THE BELL OVER THE DOOR SOUNDED, AND I LIFTED MY GAZE FROM MY COFFEE on instinct. I did it every time the door opened, unable to stop myself from watching anyone who came or went from the little mom-and-pop shop that was the best place to eat in town.

Since moving back to Creswell Springs, I'd found that out fairly quick. I had almost every meal at Aggie's, much to my grandmother's dismay. I'd moved back to be closer to them now that they were getting older, and because they were my only remaining family. All Gran wanted to do was take care of me, but my own cooking would have killed me, and the hours I worked didn't allow me to eat with her and Pops as much as any of us liked.

A young couple walked in, the man carrying a car seat in one hand, while the other was entwined with the woman's at his side. They looked tired, but I put that down to being new parents. One of the waitresses moved forward, taking them straight back to a table and producing a high chair to place the car seat on.

My eyes had barely gone back to my coffee when the door opened again, and everything inside of me suddenly went still.

I'd been in Creswell Springs for six months now, and I'd never seen *her* before. I would have remembered if I had. Not just because I had a memory that could place any face—if not their name. I was so fucking bad with names sometimes it was ridiculous.

This girl—woman—walked into the place, and the entire restaurant stopped to glance her way.

There was something about her that drew every eye, had them taking a second look, and some even a third.

Her midnight-black hair fell just past her shoulders, half over her back, the other half falling into her face on the right side, but she didn't move to push it back. Her skin was flawless from what I could see with her left side facing me, a healthy peaches-and-cream shade that looked soft as hell. She was taller than any other woman I'd seen in this town, nearly six feet in her biker boots, with a body that had my cock waking up for the first time in a long, long time.

The beauty didn't wait for the waitress to return, just walked over to the counter and sat at one of the empty chairs, placing a stack of books on the countertop and opening the first one. I sat there watching her, unable to tear my eyes off her even as the bell over the door sounded again and then again moments later.

The waitress behind the counter placed a coffee cup and saucer in front of the beauty, filling it and saying something with a roll of her eyes. My beauty didn't lift her head as she spoke back, her gaze still glued to the pages before her.

What was she reading? The cover was encased in brown paper, a makeshift jacket to hide the title. From the size of the book, I knew it was a textbook, though, and it irritated me that I couldn't see what subject she was studying.

I lifted my own coffee, sipping as I took my time soaking up the sight of her. That curvy ass was encased in jeans and, with her sitting on the stool, it was on perfect display for me. As I observed her, I assumed she was a college student, but that didn't make sense. School was out for the summer, the majority of the students having gone home for the term. That made for a more peaceful town, and I had fewer frat parties to break up every weekend.

My waitress stopped at my table, refilling my coffee, asking if I wanted dessert now that my dinner had settled. I nodded. "Whatever pie you have is fine," I told Quinn, my usual waitress, without taking my gaze off the woman at the counter.

"Coming right up," she said chipperly. Quinn was nice and professional—and also a part owner of the place, from what my grandparents told me. She never tried to flirt with me like most of the others did. Never tried to touch me. After meeting her husband once, though, I understood why.

As she walked away, my beauty lifted her left hand, pushing back a few strands that fell on that side of her face, but she kept the right side obscured with the thick, glossy mass. A flash of silver caught my attention as her bracelet shifted on her wrist. The medical alert on it had me leaning forward slightly in my booth, wanting—damn it, needing—to see what it was for.

"Peanuts," Quinn said quietly, placing the slice of pie in front of me.

Reluctantly, I looked up at her. "Excuse me?"

"Lexa's bracelet." She nodded toward the woman at the counter. "She's allergic to nuts."

"I haven't seen her around before," I commented, returning my gaze back to the counter.

"That's because she's been away at college for the past nine months," Quinn said with a shrug. "But she's home for the summer, and if her parents have their way, she'll stay local next term. Having her go all the way to Oregon for school was hard on her mom."

If I had my way, she wouldn't leave for any reason. Ever.

The thought barely flirted through my mind before I was clenching my jaw. Holy shit, where did that come from?

Needing to distract myself and the crazy thoughts going through my head, I picked up my fork and stabbed at my pie. Apple, thankfully, and not the chocolatey peanut butter I normally would have had.

I won't be able to kiss her if I eat nuts now.

Quinn walked away, taking care of her other customers, and I tried to focus on my dessert. But with each bite, my gaze kept going back to the counter.

Lexa.

I liked the name. It suited her.

I wanted to breathe it in her ear as she rode my cock.

CHAPTER 2

LEXA

I FELT HIS EYES ON ME ALMOST AS SOON AS I WALKED THROUGH THE DOOR.

It wasn't unusual. When your dad was the town's most feared yet respected man, second to none, people tended to stop what they were doing when you walked into a room. And when one side of your face looked like you belonged in the freak show at the carnival, they always came back for a second glance.

My hair fell into my face, blocking prying eyes from gawking at the souvenir I'd gotten from one of my father's enemies when I was little more than five. I hated that damn scar, but every time Mom asked if I wanted to get it fixed, I always turned her down.

The scar, I could live with. Fuck anyone who didn't want to see the ugliness. No one asked them to look anyway. Why should I alter the way I looked just to please everyone else?

I dropped my books on the countertop and parked my ass, not even looking up when Tabby came over to pour me a cup of coffee.

"Want something to eat?" the waitress asked casually.

We'd gone to high school together, but she was a year ahead of me. When she graduated, she left for SoCal for a few months, claiming she was going to be some big movie star one day. I guess being the president of the drama club gave her an instant "in" within the acting world—my eyes had never rolled so hard in my life.

Months later, she came crawling back to town, and everyone was *so surprised* she hadn't become Hollywood's new it girl.

"No thanks," I told her, my eyes scanning over the reading material for my classes. They didn't start until August, three freaking months away, but I wanted to be prepared. College wasn't easy, and I'd gone into it with my eyes open, unlike most of my freshman class back in Oregon. I wasn't going to slack off just because Mom was desperate for me to stay in Creswell Springs and wanted me to go to the local college.

Something I was debating giving in to for her.

I loved my mom more than any other person on the planet. She was my best friend, my biggest cheerleader. When she looked at me, she didn't see the scar or the broken girl underneath. Her mom-goggles saw the real me, and she loved me anyway. And the crazy part, the thing that always boggled my mind, was that, biologically, I wasn't even hers.

Raven Hannigan Reid adopted me even before she married my father. She took one look at me, claimed me as her own, and that was that. I belonged to her. I was her baby. There were times I was sure she loved me even more than my brother, and not just when Max was driving her batshit crazy either.

As the feel of everyone else's eyes slowly faded, I felt *his* remain.

To my left, five booths away. I was aware of every move he made, and yet I hadn't even looked at him. I'd caught a glimpse as I walked in, just enough to know what I was dealing with as I took a quick scan of the entire diner on my way to the counter. Dark hair, wide shoulders, sexy scruff of a beard.

Cop uniform.

That uniform had kept me from taking a second look in his direction even though I'd more than liked what little I'd seen.

My dad would freak if I even blinked at a cop, let alone lusted after one.

"No," I said again when Tabby didn't move away, sure that she would try to kill me if I dared order anything to eat from her. It wasn't like we'd been besties in high school. She'd hated me, and I could honestly say the feeling was mutual. She, like everyone else who knew who I was, was aware of my nut allergy.

One little cross-contamination and I could be fighting for my life.

And she would stand over me smiling even as my tongue began to swell and I fought to breathe.

Tabby had other customers to take care of at the counter, plus to-go orders to put together. I was thankful she was kept busy so I could focus on my reading.

But instead of being able to get lost in the words, all I could think about was the feel of his gaze. It was like a physical caress as his eyes skimmed over my shoulders and down to my ass where they lingered.

I shifted on my stool, feeling a tension begin to build low in my belly.

How could someone's eyes make me feel so needy?

Yet that was exactly what I was feeling. This ache deep in my gut, burning down to my core. Making my boobs swell and throb as my nipples pressed into the material of my bra cups. I wasn't even going to think about the state of my panties, but as damp as they were, it was becoming hard not to.

Frustrated with myself, I pushed a few strands of hair back from my face and used the moment to glance at him out of the corner of my eye. Strong jaw, broad nose, lips that made me want to lick them—

Fuck, Lexa, stop it.

Chastising myself was enough to force my attention back on the book, and I turned the page—even though I hadn't even taken in a single word I'd just read.

A soft hand touched my shoulder, and I looked up to find my aunt Quinn standing behind me. She gave me a sweet smile, her blue eyes filling with amusement as she leaned in close.

"The sheriff can't take his eyes off you," she whispered. "Have you been casting spells again, Lexa?"

I refused to look his way, but something she said caught my attention. "Sheriff?" He didn't look old enough to be the sheriff, at least not any sheriff I'd ever seen before. Sheriff Hogan, who'd been sheriff since I was five, was old as hell. He'd been a good sheriff, but I heard he'd been diagnosed with prostate cancer and retired less than a year before his latest term was up.

"Sheriff Davis stepped in after Hogan announced his retirement so the town wouldn't have to hold a special election. But he's been doing a good job, and everyone is talking about voting for him in November."

"But…" I bit into the tender flesh of my cheek to force myself from speaking the words that wanted freedom. *But I don't want him to be the fucking sheriff.*

A cop was one thing.

The sheriff of the entire county? No. Fucking. Way.

Dad would freak, and not even Mom would be able to calm him down.

Blowing out a long exhale that sounded sad even to my own ears, I closed my books and stood. Pulling out a five-dollar bill, I dropped it on the counter to pay for my coffee and tip Tabby. I might hate her, but I still figured she deserved a tip.

"Where are you going?" my aunt asked. The amusement was gone now, and I could tell she was worried about me.

I made sure my hair was down over the right side of my face, not wanting Sheriff Davis to see how monstrous I looked with my scar when I left. "I just remembered I have to pick something up for Mom," I lied, grabbing my books. "See you later, Aunt Quinn."

"Lexa, honey, be careful."

I didn't comment as I practically sprinted to my car and tossed my books into the back seat. I stabbed at the push start, only to realize my foot wasn't on the brake when the thing didn't purr to life. Cursing myself, I stomped on the pedal and pushed the starter again.

But when my car came to life, I didn't move to shift it into gear immediately. Instead, I just sat there, my heart beating me to death.

And silently breaking.

CHAPTER 3

BEN

My radio was silent as I drove through the night-darkened town, my gaze on the car two vehicles ahead of my work SUV.

Lexa had rushed out of Aggie's earlier, and I'd barely had enough thought to drop a few bills on the table to cover my meal before I was running after her. By the time I got behind the wheel, she'd pulled out of the parking lot, and I'd been following her ever since.

There didn't seem to be any rhyme or reason to where she was going, though. She drove through town, then toward the outer limits of the city. Lucky for me, I had jurisdiction over the entire county, and it wouldn't be suspicious if I went all the way to the county line.

Which seemed to be exactly where my beauty was going.

The two cars between us eventually turned off, and I was no longer keeping my distance. The way her silhouette kept shifting, I knew she was watching her mirrors. Did she know it was me?

Fuck, I was following her around like some lost puppy in search of attention.

Yet, I didn't give a damn.

I wanted her attention.

I wanted to know what color her eyes were. What she looked like when she smiled.

What she sounded like when I made her come.

Two miles from the county line, she took a quick right, and I didn't even question it as I followed her down the back road that led to nowhere. She drove for miles and miles, and I was starting to get pissed.

She didn't even know it was me behind her, and yet she was leading me into the woods?

Unable to take it a minute longer, I turned on my lights and sounded the siren. She hit the brakes, stopping right in the middle of the road. Not that there was anywhere to pull over. This road was narrow as hell and overgrown with vegetation. There was no way anyone would be coming up here without a reason.

I turned off my siren and the lights as I jerked open my door and stomped up beside her, using the headlights of my cruiser to see where I was going.

"What the fuck are you doing?" I growled, glad she had her window rolled down. "Anyone could have been behind you, ready to do God knows what to you, and you don't even seem to fucking care."

Her hands tightened around the wheel, her gaze straight ahead. "Why were *you* following me?"

"Maybe I wanted to make sure you were okay," I told her, my anger slowly starting to fade from the boil it was currently in. "You took off out of Aggie's like something was wrong. My job is to serve and protect the citizens of Trinity County. You appear to be a citizen. Hence, doing my job."

A soft laugh escaped her, but her mouth didn't even have a ghost of a smile on it. "Hence," she muttered, shaking her dark head. "Who says 'hence'?"

I leaned down, putting my hands on her door to steady myself as I got close enough to smell her perfume. It was a subtle scent, something floral and sweet. Or maybe it was her shampoo. Whatever it was, I liked it, and I breathed in deeper so I could smell it again.

"What are you doing out here, Lexa?"

Her shoulders tensed at my use of her name, her fingers tightening even more around the steering wheel. "Honestly?"

"No, lie to me," I grumbled.

Another soft laugh, followed by a tired sigh. "I don't know," she admitted. "I just felt you behind me and kept driving. Maybe... Maybe I wanted to see how far you would go before you got bored."

"You felt me?" I repeated, suddenly so hard it stunned me. I couldn't remember my cock ever being this stiff.

"Yeah," she answered, her voice soft, unsure. "I don't know why I came down this road. I haven't been here since I was a kid. My brother got pissed at me and ran away, and I knew I had to find him before our parents found out. He came up here, for some reason."

I opened her door, offering her my hand to help her out. "Let's talk out here," I suggested, waiting with bated breath for her to touch me.

She turned her head slightly, and I caught my first sight of her eyes. Blue. The clearest blue I'd ever seen. They were the same color as the glaciers I'd seen in Alaska. Pure. She looked down at my hand for a long moment before turning her gaze back to the windshield. "Only if you turn off your headlights," she said after another pause.

"But then I can't see you, beautiful." And I wanted to see her. I would have been happy standing there looking at her all damn night if she would let me.

"Then, no. I'm not getting out. Lose the lights, or I'm leaving."

Swallowing a curse, I went back to my cruiser and turned off the engine, effectively killing the lights. As I walked back to her, she was already getting out of her car, having turned off her own engine. The moon barely gave off enough light to see how to get back to her.

Shutting her door, she leaned back against it, looking up at the sky, keeping half her face turned away from me. I stopped beside her, turning to look at the stars, letting my arm brush against hers.

"So, you're the sheriff," she muttered after a few minutes passed.

"Acting sheriff," I corrected.

"Same difference."

"It wasn't my plan when I came back to Creswell Springs," I admitted. "My grandfather and Sheriff Hogan are best friends. Hogan offered me a job when I got out of the marines. It was the best option open at the time, so I took it."

"How long were you in the marines?" She shifted, her arm pressing into mine a little more. As if she didn't want to touch me but ached to at the same time.

"Went in right out of high school at eighteen. Got out six months ago at the ripe old age of thirty." I caught her hand, needing to feel some part of her skin under my fingertips. Just as I thought, she was silky-soft. Tracing my thumb over her palm, I felt her shiver.

"Thank you for your service," she whispered.

I shrugged, having heard those same words of gratitude a plethora of times.

"Thirty is still pretty young to be a sheriff, even if you are just the acting sheriff," Lexa commented after a few more minutes of silence. "How did that happen?"

"Hogan got sick. When it came time to appoint his replacement until the November election, both he and Mayor Jenkins thought I had the experience to get the job done. A few of the older guys bitched and moaned for a few weeks, but in the end, they didn't want to deal with the bureaucracy that comes with being sheriff."

"And everyone wants you to run in November?"

I shrugged again, and her shoulders seemed to deflate. "What?" I demanded, not liking that she seemed disappointed.

"I can't want the sheriff," she muttered, turning her head so she was looking off into the distance. "My dad will go ballistic."

"You want me?" I grinned, wrapping my arm around her waist and pulling her back against me. Her hips shifted, rubbing over the bulge that rested along my left thigh, the tip already leaking precome.

"But I can't," she moaned, dropping her head back on my chest. "This is impossible."

"Why?" I demanded, pressing my lips to the top of her head, my fingers skimming over the skin of her belly under her shirt.

Her shoulders stiffened, and she glanced at me over her shoulder. "You know who I am, right?"

"You're Lexa. The woman I'm about to push up against this car and make mine," I informed her, lowering my head to kiss her.

Before I could reach her mouth, she jerked back, breathing hard. "Sheriff Davis—"

"Ben," I corrected her.

"Ben…I'm assuming you know who the Angel's Halo MC is." I nodded, following her as she took another step backward.

I was still on the fence about the local MC. I'd heard rumors about them, knew they weren't exactly living the letter of the law. But I hadn't had any trouble out of them. Yet. There were plenty of times I had to go to Hannigans' to break up fights, but that was usually because some college kid went in to play pool, got drunk off his ass, and ended up in over his head. I hadn't had to arrest a single MC member so far.

"My dad is the MC president," Lexa announced, still backing away from me. "I'm Bash Reid's daughter."

I kept following her. "Don't care," I assured her.

"But my dad will," she cried, and I thought her chin might have trembled, but it was too dark to tell. "We can't do this."

"Your dad will get over it." I caught her wrists, pulled her in closer. Her hair fell into her face, putting the right side in complete darkness.

I started to push it back out of my way, but she shook her head. "Please don't," she begged. "I-I want you to kiss me, but—"

Groaning, I caught her mouth. She tasted of coffee, but there was something sweet underlying it. Something addictive that made me its victim the second my tongue brushed against hers.

CHAPTER 4

LEXA

I'd never been kissed by a guy before. Not once in nineteen years has anyone wanted to. They take one look at my scar and revulsion crosses their face, and any urge to want to be kissed goes up in a cloud of smoke.

That was why I didn't want Ben to see my scar. I wanted to know how he tasted, what it would feel like to have his tongue play with my own.

It was more than I ever could have thought. His lips were firm, yet brushed over mine so damn softly, it had my breath catching. His hands gripped my ass through my jeans, pressing me into his hardness. He was so tall that my height didn't even matter. We fit against each other so perfectly, it was like someone had used a puzzle cutter to create us.

I kissed him back, hungry for more. My hands fisted in his uniform button-up, clinging to him.

With a growl that was like an electrical current strait to my core, he lifted me and sat me down on the hood of my car. I spread my legs for him, letting him closer, then locked them around his waist to keep him in place. He laughed at how hard my thighs squeezed him, and he twisted his hips in a way that made me whimper with pleasure.

"Easy, beautiful," he murmured against my neck. "I'll take care of you."

"Ben," I moaned, trying to find some small trace of rational thought, needing to stop this before it went too far. "We can't. We really, really can't."

"The only thing that's going to stop me is you saying you're married. You married, beautiful?"

I shook my head. "No, of course not. But—"

"Then we don't have a problem."

My nails bit into his arms, but instead of deterring him, it only seemed to urge him on. His hips thrust against me, and even through his work pants and my jeans, he rubbed over the perfect spot to make me see stars.

"My dad," I panted, trying to explain. "He won't let me keep you." And that was what made this so hard. Because I wanted to keep Ben.

Oh God. I'd just met this man. Knew next to nothing about him, but I wanted him for myself. Wanted him more than I'd ever wanted anything.

"Lexa, baby." He lifted his head, his hands cupping my face.

I froze, feeling his thumb grazing over my scar before the palm of his hand settled over it. I closed my eyes, waiting for him to notice it. His eyes should have adjusted to the darkness by now; he wouldn't be able to miss the outline of the scar that went from my temple down to the corner of my mouth. It wasn't puckered and red like it had been when Fontana first disfigured me, but it still wasn't pretty. Not even makeup could cover up that grotesque thing.

And for the first time, I wished I'd given in and let Mom take me to a plastic surgeon.

"I'm not letting you go," he breathed, his lips skimming over mine. "Don't ask me how I know, but you are mine. I won't let anything fuck with that. Do you hear me?"

Tears burned my throat, and I finally opened my eyes, knowing I had to do something before this turned dangerous. I wanted to be his more than I wanted to breathe, but I also knew I needed to protect him.

Bash Reid was a dangerous man.

I loved my dad dearly, but I wasn't blind to who or what he was.

And I couldn't let him hurt Ben.

I jerked my head back from his touch, allowing my hair to fall away from my face for the first time. Even in the dimness of the moon overhead, there was no way he could miss that scar now.

He jerked back, and though that was the reaction I'd been expecting, it still shattered something inside me.

"You still want me?" I asked with a cold laugh, burying my pain as I hopped down off my car.

Ben just stood there, frozen, his eyes glued to my scar and nothing else. "What happened?" he choked out.

"This is what happens to little girls who don't follow the rules," I explained. "No outsiders. Ever. Lesson learned." I pushed past him and opened my car door. "Nice meeting you, Sheriff Davis. See you around."

I turned my car around, then drove away, but I couldn't keep my eyes from lifting to my rearview mirror.

Ben just stood there, watching me drive away.

Any secret hope that he wouldn't care, that my scar wouldn't matter to him, turned to dust and blew across the road that now separated us.

CHAPTER 5

BEN

ALL I COULD THINK ABOUT WAS WHO COULD HAVE DONE THAT TO HER. HOW could they have hurt her like that?

And then the anger took hold.

I would find out.

I would finish off the person who had dared hurt my beauty.

I didn't care what I had to do, how many laws I broke to accomplish it, but I would make whoever hurt her pay.

By the time I got myself under control, she was long gone, but I didn't follow her immediately. I'd run by her house on my way home to make sure she got home safe, but I didn't trust myself to follow her yet.

I was shaking with rage and remnants of a need that had nearly brought me to my knees. Fuck, I still wanted her so bad my balls ached, but I was afraid to touch her.

All my life, I'd worked hard to control my rage. The marines had helped with that when nothing else could, but seeing her beautiful face marred by that damn scar had stirred something that had been lying dormant for years. I didn't trust myself not to hurt her unintentionally if my rage suddenly got out of hand.

I got in my cruiser, my hands clenching around the wheel as I fought the urge to decimate and hurt someone the way Lexa had so obviously been hurt.

An hour later, I drove by Bash Reid's house and parked out front. I saw Lexa's car in the driveway and looked up at the house, wondering which room was hers. But all the upstairs lights were off, and they remained off an hour later when I finally forced myself to drive home.

I'd talk to Lexa tomorrow, I assured myself. Get the story out of her, make her tell me who'd hurt her. I'd find the sonofabitch and take care of him, then I would claim the woman who was already mine.

If only it were so easy.

Will Ben be able to convince Lexa she is his *Salvation*?
Coming soon.

Connect with Terri Anne Browning:
TWITTER: http://www.twitter.com/AuthorTERRIANNE
FACEBOOK: http://www.facebook.com/terriannebrowning.author/
BOOKBUB: https://www.bookbub.com/authors/terri-anne-browning
WEBSITE: http://www.terriannebrowningauthor.com

FOREVER LO BY WINTER TRAVERS

Devil's Knights MC

CHAPTER 1

MEG

"I'M WEARING YELLOW."

"Meg."

I looked up from my bowl of cereal. "Yes?"

Lo leaned against the kitchen counter and crossed his arms over his chest. "You're kidding."

I wasn't. Not in the least. "No."

"I don't think I have ever seen you in yellow and suddenly you're going to wear a yellow dress to your only son's wedding?" He scoffed and reached for a coffee cup. "You're going to end up wearing black."

I rolled my eyes and slurped back some milk in my bowl. "I can't do that, Lo." I wiped my mouth with the back of my hand. "If I wear black everyone is going to think I don't approve of Harlyn and that's not true. Like I'm attending a funeral."

"No, everyone is going to be fine with you wearing black because they know that you only wear black. If you show up to Remy's wedding wearing a yellow dress, everyone is going to think you're either having some mid-life crisis or that you have a brain tumor that is messing with your brain."

I rolled my eyes. "Really, Lo? Those are the only reasons why people would think I'm wearing yellow? Mid-life crisis or tumor?" I slurped the last of my milk and set the bowl down with a clatter. "You really have no faith in me."

"Well, seeing as it's Saturday and Remy is getting married a week from today, yeah, I don't have much faith in you seeing as you haven't even bought a dress for the wedding yet. You get a yellow dress, and you're gonna look like a fucking canary."

I scrunched up my nose. "I have plenty of time and you sound like you don't think I'll look good in a yellow dress."

Lo pushed off the counter and pulled me up from my chair. He wrapped me up in his arms and I tipped my head back to look at him.

"Never said you wouldn't look good. Said you would look like a fucking canary." His voice was low, and a shiver ran through my body even though I was a bit upset that he had called me a canary.

I quirked an eyebrow. "So you're into fucking canaries now?"

"We really gonna get into this?" he growled.

I didn't really want to but getting Lo riled up was kind of fun. "I'm just going off what you said."

His nostrils flared. "Babe, I'm into you, and if you want to dress up like a fucking canary, then go for it. Just don't come crying to me after you see the wedding pictures and you stick out like a sore thumb."

The urge to argue with him was strong, but I knew that everything he said was right. The idea of a yellow dress seemed fun and different in theory, but I knew I would end up regretting it. "Yellow is on the top of my list, but maybe I'll check out some other colors too." I wasn't going to let him think that I was giving into his reasoning.

"Like black," he replied flatly.

I pinched his nipple through his thin, black shirt. And twisted.

"Hey, hey, woman!" He knocked my hand away and placed his hand over his now twisted nipple. "Don't damage the goods."

I rolled my eyes and pushed him away. "I need to be at Cyn's in fifteen minutes." Gwen was also coming along and we had agreed to meet at Cyn's then drive together to the dress shop.

"That means no quickie before you leave?"

I wagged my finger in his face. "You don't get to call me a canary and then think we're going to have sex." I grabbed my purse hooked over the chair. "Besides, you should have woken up earlier if you wanted that."

Lo scoffed. "Normally you wake me up with the smell of breakfast cooking, but you had cereal today. That ain't gonna wake me up."

I had cereal on purpose. I knew if I made bacon and eggs Lo would have woken up and distracted me with sweet morning kisses which would have led to the quickie he mentioned. "Forty-five years old and he expects me to wake him up every morning." I rolled my eyes and dug around in my purse for my truck keys. "What are you doing today?" I spotted my keys and pulled them out.

"Gotta clean up the clubhouse before the reception next weekend and then maybe work on the bike."

"Work on the bike? What's wrong with it?"

Lo grabbed his coffee and leaned against the counter. "Putting a new exhaust on it. Got it in last week and I finally have time to work on it."

"What's wrong with the exhaust you have on it."

He shrugged. "Nothing."

I closed one eye and pursed my lips. "You lost me on why you would order a new one then."

"Cause this one is gonna shake the neighbors windows."

Good lord. "I'm sure Larry will appreciate that."

"Fuck Larry. You would think after living here for almost ten years the guy would warm up to me a bit but nada."

"You really think Larry is going to come over and shoot the shit with you in the driveway while you wax your bike every Saturday?" Lo was crazy if he thought Larry was going to be buddies with him. I was just glad Larry kept to himself and didn't give us shit for bikes and people coming and going from the house all the time.

"No."

"Then what the hell, Lo?"

He shrugged his shoulders. "I thought about it for a second and decided I was good with the guy not talking to me."

"And you tell me I'm the crazy one." I rolled my eyes and leaned up on my tip toes. "I'll be back later. We're going for hibachi after so you might have to fend for yourself for dinner depending on how long this takes. " I pressed a kiss to his cheek.

He grabbed me around the waist. "That kiss ain't gonna do it for me, babe. Especially if you're leaving me to fend for myself for dinner." He pressed his lips to mine, and I slipped right into the Lo Daze. Though, I had to say I basically lived there permanently the past ten years. "Behave. I don't want any phone calls needing me to bail you out."

"One time that happened and you just won't let me live it down."

His hands squeezed my waist. "That one time got us banned from the furniture store for life."

"Pfft. I still say that was all Ethel's fault." You break one bed in the furniture store and bam, banned for life. "He was an angry nugget of a man, anyway."

"That was not my mother's fault at all. I'll have to let her know when I see her that you are *still* trying to blame that on her." Lo pulled me close and buried his face in my neck.

"You're such a mama's boy," I grumbled.

"Gotta love her while she's still here with us."

Ethel had another cancer scare six months ago, and I knew it had changed Lo. He realized he wasn't going to have his mom around forever.

I closed my eyes and enjoyed the feel of being in this loving man's arms. "We do have a plate of her's you could drop off to her on the way to the shop."

"Guess I could stop by," he whispered.

"Mama's boy," I taunted.

He playful pushed me out his arms. "I'm gonna have to say you have your own mama's boy due in town in a couple of days."

I shook my finger at him. "You're damn straight I have my own mama's boy. Though he could stand to call me a bit more."

Lo followed me to the front door and held it open for me. "I tell him all the time to call you, babe. I think he's afraid of the crazy stories you're gonna tell him."

I blew a raspberry. "He should be used to it by now. The boy has known my craziness for the past twenty-seven years." I pressed another quick kiss to Lo's lips. "Now I gotta drive fast to get to Cyn's on time. You're too distracting." I pushed out the screen door and glared at Lo over my shoulder. "Have fun playing with your exhaust today."

Lo shook his head and rolled his eyes.

Larry was walking past the house with his tiny fluff ball of a dog and of course heard me. "Uh, hey there, Larry."

I could hear Lo's boisterous laugh from inside the house.

"Asshole," I hiss through the screen door.

It was only ten o'clock, and I had already made a fool of myself.

Just another day living the life.

CHAPTER 2

LO

"JESUS CHRIST!" I STUMBLED BACKWARD OUT THE DOOR AND SLAMMED IT SHUT before I fell back on my ass.

"Logan Birch! Why in the hell are you walking into my house without knocking?"

I scrubbed my hand down my face and asked myself the same question. I was catapulted back to a young child walking in on their parents doing the nasty. *Full body shiver.*

"Hush, woman," Gravel grumbled through the closed door.

"Who in the hell does that in the middle of the day with the door unlocked?" I hollered.

The front door swung open and Gravel glared down at me. Shirtless. Top button of his jeans unbuttoned. "We ain't fucking dead, son. Figured everyone who would stop by would be at work or out doing shit."

"Here." I shielded my arm over my eyes and held out the pan that belonged to Mom. "Just take this." I was going to need to go to the clubhouse and rinse my eyes out with bleach.

"You think you would have learned from the last time you did this." Mom's voice joined Gravel's but I didn't want to look. God only knew if she managed to get all of her clothes back on. "Knock on the damn door, Logan."

Mom was mad. She really only called me Logan when she was pissed off or trying to be serious. "Lock the damn door," I countered.

"You think we planned this?" Gravel asked. "One thing lead to another and before I knew it I had your mother bent over-."

"Stop!" I thundered. I had seen the visual, I didn't need the play-by-play of how it went down. I scrambled to my feet and turned my back to Gravel and mom. "I, uh, I'll see you guys at the wedding." Lord knows if I was going to be able to make eye contact with either of them. "Lock your damn door." I stomped down the steps and over to my bike.

Mom cackled like a mad woman and Gravel's low rumble laugh followed me till I peeled out of the driveway.

I couldn't hear them laughing anymore, but god knew I was forever going to be haunted with the image of my mom bent over the couch and begging Gravel to go harder.

Vomit rose up my throat, and I didn't make it to the clubhouse before emptying my stomach on the side of the road.

Twice.

CHAPTER 3

MEG

"THAT'S THE ONE."

"Lord have mercy, you look *good.*"

I did. I looked amazing. "I'm not getting this one."

Cyn's jaw dropped and the bubble Gwen was blowing popped loudly. "Come again, girlfriend?" Gwen gasped.

"Unzip me, now." I turned my back to Cyn. "Did you not hear what I said earlier. I cannot buy a black dress. Get it off me, *now.*" This was not going to happen. "Do you think they have it in yellow? Maybe orange." I glanced over my shoulder at Cyn who hadn't budged from the chair she was sitting in.

"Uh, girl. You cannot rock yellow or orange." Gwen shook her head. "At least not in a mother of the bride dress. We could do some funky highlights in your hair if you want though."

"Cyn," I hissed. "Snap out of it and get me out of this dress. Pronto."

Cyn shook her head. "Only if you promise to me that you are not going to buy a yellow or orange dress. You are not a bright color person, chick. Why don't you try plum or dark blue?"

I turned to the mirror to the side. I ran my hands down the satin fabric and sighed. "I'm not doing blue cause that's your thing. I'll match Rigid's hair and that will just be awkward."

"How's it going in here?" Peg, the sales clerk, slipped into the dressing room with a platter of champagne glasses.

Yes, booze will make this better. I grabbed a glass from her and chugged it down in three gulps. I set the empty glass on the platter and grabbed another. "I'm gonna need this dress in purple, Peg."

Peg blinked at the empty champagne glass. I don't think she was used to customers like Cyn, Gwen, and I. "I, ah, let me look at the tag." She offered the tray of glasses to Cyn and Gwen then set it on the small table next to the seatette they were sitting on. She fumbled with the tag and cleared her throat. "Uh, that dress comes in the black you have on, or white."

"Oh hell no!" Cyn jumped up and yanked the zipper down. "If you're not going to get the black, then you sure as hell aren't going to get the white." She grabbed my glass from me and set it on the table.

"Well, duh," I grumbled. Black would make me look like I didn't approve of Harlyn and the white would make it look like I was trying to upstage her.

"Cover the girly bits and let's go look at the racks. There has to be something out there that is perfect." Gwen grabbed my shirt and tossed it at me.

I smirked and pulled the shirt over my head. The dress pooled at my feet and I stepped out of it. "You mean I can't go out there in my underwear?"

Peg choked and lightly patted her chest. "Uh, that would not be the best idea."

Cyn snatched my pants off the floor and handed them to me. "Put your damn clothes on, woman. You and I both know you wouldn't step foot out of here without being clothed."

"Clothed?" Gwen snickered.

"How is she tipsy after only having one glass of champagne?" I asked. I tugged my pants on and grabbed my glass of champagne. "And for the record, we always need to shop at places that offer booze."

Gwen led the way out of the dressing room and over to the four racks of mother of the bride dresses. "There has to be a dress in here that is going to be the one."

I nodded my head. "Yup. There has to be."

Cyn grabbed the hem of a lime green dress. "But it's not this one."

Agreed. "I think first we need to just look at color. Pick out the colors that will work and then whittle them down by style."

Gwen tipped her glass to me. "I think shopping and drinking booze works for you. That was a very smart idea."

I knocked the green dress from Cyn's hand. "Thank you. Now, let's get to work, ladies, and prove Lo wrong."

"And what was it again that we're proving him wrong about?" Gwen asked.

I reached to grab Gwen's glass from her but she sidestepped out of my grasp. "You are not taking my mama juice right now. I have a six and four-year-old at home and I can't remember the last time I was free for a whole afternoon."

Cyn clinked her glass against Gwen's. "A-fucking-men to that, sister. Micha just turned eleven and I swear to god it's like he's eighteen." Cyn shook her head. "You would think it would be enough for him to be able to do whatever he wants with his hair, but now he's begging Rigid to get his ear pierced *and* a tattoo."

I clicked my tongue. "Go with the earring but tell him auntie Meg says he has to wait on the tattoo. At least sixteen."

"Meg," Cyn gasped. "His ass is waiting until he is eighteen to get either."

Gwen chuckled. "I find it hilarious that you let the kid dye his hair any color he wants but you're freaking out over an earring."

Cyn rolled her eyes. "Because I can cut his hair off and it'll grow back. You think I can cut his ear off and it'll grow back?"

Gwen and I looked at each other. "Uh, can't you just take the earring out? I mean, there will be a tiny hole there, but I think cutting his ear off would be a bit drastic." Thank god Micha had me around or he would be Picasso walking around.

"It's about the principle," Cyn huffed.

"You're married to a man with blue hair, covered in tattoos, and from the stories you've told, pierced in," I cleared my throat, "places the eyes can't see."

"Like we are ones to talk," Gwen laughed. "I think we all married men like that."

We looked from one to the other. "A-fucking-men to that!" we cheered in unison.

"Now, let's find me a dress so we can get to the hibachi place." I drained my glass and tucked it under my arm. Good food was our end game. "I want black, but not black."

"Sounds easy enough," Cyn laughed.

Twenty minutes later we were back in the dressing room with a fresh bottle of champagne and fifteen dresses.

"Those five are out right off the bat." I tugged my shirt over my head. "Let's just agree these arms need sleeves, yeah?" I didn't feel like getting out on the dance floor at the wedding and having my arm fat waving at everyone. I lifted my arm and watched my loose chicken wings flap. "Ridiculous," I grumbled.

Cyn grabbed the five sleeveless dresses and hung them on the opposite wall. "So, this will be the reject wall."

Gwen grabbed a deep yellow dress. "Who in the hell grabbed this one? I thought we decided that yellow was not the color for Meg?"

Cyn grabbed it and hung it on the reject wall. "I thought we could give it a whirl seeing as it wasn't a bright ass yellow. I didn't know we hated *every* shade of yellow."

Gwen and Cyn argue back and forth about the color yellow while Peg helped me into my first dress.

"Pfft, blah, urgh, gah," I sputtered. Peg zipped the dress up in the back and I batted down the large ruffle around my shoulders. "What in the hell is this?"

Peg turned me toward the mirror and Cyn and Gwen stopped bickering. "This is a mermaid flared skirt and off the shoulder with a ruffle. The color is regency."

"Oh, uh," Cyn muttered.

Gwen searched for her words. "The, well, uh, color is nice."

"It is very mermaid esque," I muttered.

"It's awful!" Cyn blurted. "You look like a damn clown with the puffy collar around your shoulders."

"Accurate," Gwen agreed.

"So, we'll take the clown mermaid dresses out and put them on the reject wall." Peg picked through the dresses and placed two on the opposite wall along with the first offending dress.

The next six dresses went by quickly with no real winners.

"This one has to work." Cyn fingered the lacy sleeve.

"At least it's a pretty purple." Gwen grabbed the dress from the hook and slid it off the hanger.

"This is brand new. I actually haven't seen it on anyone yet." Peg grabbed the dress from Gwen and helped me into it.

It fit snugly across my bodice, the lace sleeves glided up my arms and Peg zipped up the back.

"Holy. Shit," Cyn gasped.

"Why in the hell didn't we try this one first? It would have saved us half an hour and a bottle of champagne." Gwen circled around me with her hand covering her mouth.

"A-line, chiffon and lace with a scoop neck. It's actually breathtaking on you." Peg fluffed out the bottom of the dress and I watched in amazement as it floated back around me.

"You're like a purple goddess." Cyn circled the opposite direction of Gwen. "Lo is going to blow his load when he sees you." Cyn and Gwen high fived and laughed.

"Uh, so that means this is the one?" Peg asked. She was once again a bit taken back by the open and crassness of our group.

I twirled around and knew I looked psychotic with the huge smile on my face, but I couldn't stop. "We have a winner, Peg. Wrap it up and point me in the direction of the hibachi place."

CHAPTER 4

LO

"WHEN MAL AND I GET MARRIED, YOU CAN BET YOUR ASS WE ARE NOT GOING to do it at the clubhouse."

I kicked my feet out in front of me and popped open a beer. "You think you're too good to get married here?" I asked Turtle.

He shook his head and wiped his forehead with the back of his hand. "Not that at all. I just don't want to be the one to clean this fucking place and organize a million chairs."

"You even ask her to marry you yet?" Turtle had been seeing Mal for four years and he had a three-year-old with her. How he had managed to snag the new lawyer in town was beyond me, but they seemed very much in love.

A huge smile spread across Turtle's lips. "I was gonna do it Saturday night."

"At the wedding?"

He nodded his head. "She's been dropping hints about getting married for the past year and I've been acting like I don't hear her."

"But you do."

Turtle nodded his head. "I hear her, but I'm going to need your guys help."

Rigid walked into the clubhouse from the garage. "Help? How much more fucking help do we need? All the chairs are finally set up and that arch thing is in the garage. We just gotta haul it in here Friday after the rehearsal dinner."

"No, not the wedding." Turtle plopped down on the couch next to me. "I'm gonna ask Mal to marry me here, but I booked a room at a hotel two towns over and was hoping you and Meg would be able to watch Jonas overnight for us."

Rigid snickered and turned on the TV. "You are the only ones that don't have kids under the age of ten besides Slider and Fayth."

"They're headed out of town early Sunday morning. Something about Marco needing help with his new house." Turtle sighed. "I really hate to ask but I've made Mal wait long enough for me to ask her to marry her."

I clapped Turtle on the back. "Don't worry about it, brother. You know Meg loves Jonas."

Turtle sighed. "Thank you. I didn't want to ask, but I really didn't have another choice. I don't plan on doing it till later on in the night."

I nodded my head. "I'll have to tell her to lay off the wine coolers, but she'll be fine with it."

Rigid chuckled. "Good luck with that."

"Maybe I'll be the one taking care of Jonas after you leave." I didn't want to have to tell Meg she couldn't drink at her only son's wedding. "I think we all plan on staying at the clubhouse the night of the wedding anyway so we'll all be able to keep an eye on Jonas."

The bedrooms at the clubhouse rarely got used for more than storage these days. Most of the guys had houses or apartments and just used their rooms to store shit for the clubhouse in them.

"Speaking of which," Rigid cleared his throat. "Cyn and all the girls told me we better put clean sheets on the bed or none of them are going to stay here."

"We still plan on putting all the kids in one or two rooms?" I asked. With nine kids ranging from three to eleven we had to have somewhere for them to sleep.

Rigid flipped through the channels on the TV. "Three sets of bunk beds will be here Wednesday and the mattresses for them will be here Thursday."

"Cutting it kind of fucking close, aren't you?" With all of us being in our mid-thirties and up you would think we would have our shit together a bit more.

"Figure as long as they get here before Saturday night we'll be good."

"Better fucking hope they get here before Saturday, or you'll be the one putting them together during the ceremony." I shook my head.

"Or have all the kids staying at your house." Turtle snickered.

"They'll be here," Rigid assured us.

They better be. I was fine having to watch the kids, but I drew the line to having them share my bed with me and Meg.

That had been a no kid zone for the past ten years, and there were no signs in that ever changing.

CHAPTER 5

MEG

"My shoes should be here today."

Cyn slowly raised her head. "What do you mean?"

"I mean my shoes should be delivered today." I cut off the end of the onion and started chopping it.

"Meg, the wedding is in three and a half days. You don't have shoes?"

I rolled my eyes and scoffed. "Of course I have shoes, Cyn." I dumped the diced onions into a bowl. "They're being delivered today."

Cyn blinked slowly. "Do you think procrastination this long is going to work out for you?" She slowly stirred the beans and grabbed her margarita glass.

It was Tuesday, and we had bumped our monthly Si Senor! Margaritas and Taco night to tonight because Remy and Harlyn didn't want to have it as their rehearsal dinner. I had started the meat yesterday and now Cyn and I were working on everything else.

"The shoes will be here. I checked the tracking this morning."

"Meg." Cyn's eyes connected with mine. "It's past five o'clock. The mail has ran and the UPS guy comes around ten thirty."

"Uh, come again?" And how the hell did Cyn know the times that UPS rolled through time.

"Your shoes are not coming today."

"How do you know that? Also, how do you know what time UPS runs?"

She rolled her eyes. "Uh, hello. I order shit and don't want Rigid to know because he tells me I'm spending all the money on senseless shit."

"Are you?" I had been to Cyn's house. She had some shit I wondered why she would even buy. "And I guess they're going to come tomorrow then."

"Who's side are you on, Meg? I can't help it that Morphe came out with a new pallet and then Too Faced came out with one right after. It's completely out of my hands."

"Are you talking a different language right now?"

"Makeup, Meg. I'm talking about makeup."

I scrunched up my nose. "Girl, I get my eyeshadows and eyeliner from the Walgreens. Five ninety-nine for ten eyeshadows, you can't go wrong."

Cyn pointed the spoon she was stirring with at me. "Pigment, Meg. You're lacking pigment."

"I'm really worried about you." I set the knife down and folded my hands together. "I think we need to have an intervention."

"Who needs an intervention?" Lo walked in the back door with a case of beer in one hand and three plastic bags in the other.

"Cyn. She's blowing Rigid's retirement on makeup." I popped a piece of pepper in my mouth and smiled at Lo.

"I've heard. Rigid mumbles about pigment under his breath all the time." Lo set the bags on the table and brushed a kiss against my lips. "Guys will be here in half an hour."

Cyn huffed and turned back to the stove. "The hellion is in the backyard with Diamond. Micha was wondering when Uncle Lo was going to get here."

"What's he need?" Lo asked.

Cyn shook her head. "He's trying to rally people to take his side about getting his ear pierced."

"And?"

Cyn glared at Lo over her shoulder. "He is eleven years old, Lo. He doesn't need to start piercing things this early."

"Got my ear pierced when I was ten. I think I turned out just fine."

I brushed my fingers over Lo's crotch. "I think you just helped Cyn's argument that if he gets his ears pierced now, it's just going to lead to him piercing other things."

Cyn dropped the spoon in the beans. "Jesus, Meg! Did you really need to go there? I never in a million years ever want to think about that and Micha in the same thought."

"You don't want him to be like father like son?" Lo teased.

Cyn's cheeks heated and turned red. "You're both assholes, you know? He has no clue that Rigid has, well," her eyes darted to Lo's crotch, "that. And he will *never* know."

"Right," Lo drawled. He grabbed a beer and popped open the top. "I'll go talk to him and see if I can hold him off till he's sixteen."

"Or seventy," Cyn yelled at his retreating back.

"Girl," I laughed. "You are one big contradiction."

"Don't I know it," she mumbled.

Cyn kept stirring the beans while I chopped, diced, and prepped all the toppings and sides.

"You doing my job, woman?" Rigid walked through the front door and slid his sunglasses on top of his head.

"If you would have been here, I wouldn't have had to do it." Cyn took the pan off the heat and turned off the burner. "Micha is in the backyard with Lo."

"That kid is relentless." Rigid shook his head.

"That's all you," Cyn muttered.

"Hey," Rigid protested. "I'm in agreement with you on this, baby. He can wait until he's sixteen to get his ears pierced just like I did."

Cyn wiped her hands on the dish towel. "Well then maybe you should tell him that instead of magically disappearing every time he brings it up."

Rigid held up his hands. "All right, all right. I'm on it. Cool your jets." Rigid pulled out his phone. "I'll find some pictures of infected piercings and shit. That'll deter him." Rigid typed on his phone and instantly cringed.

"Ears, Rigid. Nothing else."

Rigid looked up at Cyn. "This almost made me want to take my piercings out." He held up the phone, and I instantly ducked my head knowing he was about to show us something absolutely disgusting.

Cyn gagged and tossed the dish towel at Rigid. "You are an asshole."

Rigid walked out the back door chuckling under his breath.

"It was a dick, wasn't it?" I didn't want to see it, but I was curious about what it was.

"If you would call it that. The thing was green and pussy."

I clutched my hand to neck and closed my eyes. "Sweet Jesus. I didn't need a description."

"I should have had a girl. I know for the rest of my life it's just going to be Rigid and Micha grossing me out."

I ripped open the bag of shredded lettuce and dumped it in a bowl. "I think we're all destined to that seeing as out of nine kids running around, only two are girls." Thank god Marley and Gwen were able to overcome the strong alpha gene and give us Luna and Greta."

Cyn raised her margarita glass toward me. "Amen to that, sister."

Lo

"WHAT THE HELL IS THIS?" Slide lifted a Mounds bar up. "I thought you said you had shit for s'mores."

Meg plopped down in my lap. "That's for island s'mores."

"What in the hell is an island s'more, woman? I want a s'more *s'more.* Graham, chocolate, marshmallow, graham." Slider motioned by stacking his hands on top of each other. "S'more."

The adults were spread out around the fire and the kids were running around playing tag and trying to catch fireflies. I was stuffed from dinner, but apparently Slider had room for a little dessert.

"There is peanut butter cups there too," Meg pointed out.

Slider threw down the Mounds bar and shook his head. "This is ridiculous. It's a sad day when a guy can't even get an OG s'more."

"I think this falls under first world problems," Fayth called. "There are kids starving in Africa and you're complaining about the wrong candy for your s'more."

Slider sat down in the chair next to her. "I don't really remember asking you."

Fayth flipped him off. "We're married. My opinion is the only one that matters."

Meg laughed and laid her head on my shoulder. "Should I tell him I have a few Hershey bars in the house?"

I pressed a finger to Meg's lips. "Shh. It's always good when Fayth puts him in his place."

"Isn't that every day?" Meg laughed.

"Yeah, but I don't always get to see it."

Meg cuddled into me and sighed. "How has this been our life for ten years?"

I held her close and looked around the fire pit. Kids were running around like crazy and the best friends I could ever have were surrounding me. "Guess we're just fucking lucky, babe."

"Ain't that the truth," she murmured. "You have everything ready for the wedding?"

The guys and I had been working on shit for the wedding for the past four days. It would have been only three days, but Gambler had brought the kids with him the other day and they had managed to knock over the archway for the ceremony. That was something Meg didn't know and wouldn't know until the day of the wedding.

"Clubhouse is fucking spotless, chairs are set up, and I pick up the tuxes on Friday."

Meg sighed and laid her hand on my chest. "I still can't believe Remy asked you to be one of his groomsmen."

I had been pretty fucking shocked too. "Pretty crazy. You raised a good kid, babe."

"I sure did. Now I just hope his dad doesn't make a scene at the wedding."

I wrapped my arms around her and held her close. "Well, we all know you know how to handle Hunter. A swift kick to the nuts will make him fall in line."

"If only that were true. He's bringing his new girlfriend and Remy told me she isn't like the other girls he has dated in the past."

"What's that mean?" I had only met one of the chicks Hunter dated and I was not impressed. He had definitely downgraded from Meg.

"He actually likes her." Meg's voice was quiet and I could tell she wasn't sure what to think or feel.

"Babe," I said softly.

"I'm being dumb, Lo. I know it. Just let me be dumb for a hot second while I think Remy is going to like her more than he likes me."

"Meg, you just said what you need to hear." I adjusted her in my lap and turned her toward me more. "He likes her, but he loves you. You're his mom and he's not going to find another mom at the age of twenty-eight."

"I know," she huffed. "I told you I was being dumb."

"Well, you can be dumb for the next ten minutes and then you better snap out of it."

She sighed heavily and closed her eyes. "You're too nice to me."

"Guess that's why I married you."

"So you can be nice to me every day?"

I pressed a kiss to the side of her head. "Damn straight, babe."

CHAPTER 6

MEG

I felt Lo roll out of bed and I moved to bury my face in his pillow.

"Get your ass up, woman. It's rehearsal day."

I groaned and held up my middle finger to Lo. "No. You kept me up too late last night."

"Pretty sure I tried to get you to come to bed three times last night."

I lifted my head and rolled over onto my back. "Remy came home. With his fiancée. Can you really blame me for wanting to stay up for a bit?"

Lo lifted one eyebrow. "You came to bed at two. I'm pretty sure that's more than staying up a little."

"Do you have a point, Mr. Birch?"

Lo pulled his shirt over his head and tossed it in the clothes hamper. He dropped the sweatpants he had on and his dick stood at attention. He looked down at his dick and smirked. "There's only one point here right now and I think it needs your attention."

I licked my lips and raised up on my elbows. "Then you better come back to bed."

"Was thinking of taking a shower."

I shook my head. "As amazing as that sounds, I'm pretty sure Remy and Harlyn wouldn't appreciate being woken up on the count of us having sex."

Lo scowled. "Damn. Been so long that Remy has been in his room that I forgot that he's right next to the shower."

I nodded my head and bite my lip. "Yup. But that doesn't mean we can't have a little fun in here."

Lo planted a knee on the bed. "Put some music on."

I rolled my eyes and grabbed my phone. "Worried?" I scrolled through my downloaded songs and picked the latest Lee Brice song.

"Not worried, just wanting to cover all of my bases to make sure Remy and Harlyn don't hear us." Lo crawled up the bed and grabbed my phone. "Never heard this song before." He tossed me phone on the night stand and looked down at me.

I constantly had music playing around the house and office at work. This was a new song, but it wasn't the first time I had listened to it. "You should open your ears. I've been playing it constantly for the past week."

Lo covered my body with his. "I tend to be distracted when I'm around you and only pay attention to you. Music and everything else is secondary."

I circled my arms around my neck. "You sure are a sweet talker, Lo."

A grin spread across his lips. "Just telling you like it is. Fell in love with you ten years ago, babe, and it hasn't changed a day since. But if you would have put on some AC/DC or Metallica I totally would have known the song."

"So predictable," I muttered.

He pressed a kiss to my lips and tugged the blanket down my body. "And that's how you like it."

"I guess that makes me predictable, too."

He trailed kisses across my face and down my neck. "Only predictable thing about you, babe, is I know you'll always love me. Everything else is a crapshoot with you."

"I can't deny that," I whispered. Keeping Lo on his toes was a full-time job. I didn't want him to get bored and find a younger and more fun version of me.

His hands traveled down my side and grabbed the hem of my shirt. He tugged it over my head and tossed it on the floor. "I wouldn't let you out of this bed if you denied it."

"Hmm, never leaving this bed sounds tempting. Were you trying to threaten me?" If I could get away with spending the rest of my life in bed with Lo I would totally do it.

"Not much of a threat when I know the idea turns you on."

I ran my hands up and down his back. "You breathing turns me on, Lo."

He kissed me.

Hard.

Passionately.

Fully.

Lo's tongue slid into my mouth and my world exploded.

I couldn't get enough. I was never going to get enough of Logan Birch. President of the Devil's Knights MC and the only man in this world who could make me melt with one glance.

"Spread your legs, babe." His hand covered my mound and I spread my legs wide.

"Permission to come aboard, captain."

"Fucking nut," Lo muttered.

"But I'm *your* nut," I whispered.

Lo's fingers felt like heaven between my legs. Stroking, flicking, and gliding over my clit.

"Lo, please," I gasped.

"You know the drill, babe. First you come all over my fingers, and then you get my dick." He pressed lazy kisses over my chest and sucked my nipple into his mouth.

My hips bucked up into his hand and my eyes slammed shut.

The combination of Lo's hand and mouth was something that always drove me crazy.

Lo drove me crazy.

My orgasm crashed over me. My pussy drenched and ready for Lo.

In one swift movement Lo's hand left my pussy. He grabbed my hips and flipped me over. I got up on all fours and moaned when I felt him behind me. "My favorite," I mumbled. Any sex with Lo was good sex, but this, this was the best. Feeling him behind me. Driving into me. Lord above, it was amazing.

Lo gathered my hair in his hand and tugged my head back. "Tell me."

"I want you, Lo."

"More," he growled.

"I need you." Almost every day Lo needed to hear that I needed him.

Every day I told him. Most of the time it was when he was buried deep inside me and my body ached for him.

I reared back into him, his dick buried to the hilt and a low moan escaped his lips. "Ten years. Ten years and I still can't get enough of you."

Lo pounded inside me. Driving into me with each thrust.

"Oh my god," I panted. His hand in my hair tugged and my head arched back. "Lo," I gasped.

"Take it, babe. Fucking take it."

I took it. I had no choice when it came to Lo. I would forever take whatever he wanted to give me and love it.

With each of my gasps, Lo moaned, and I panted through my release.

Lo growled, released my hair, and both of his hands gripped my hips.

He pounded into me, my pussy milking his cock each time he pulled out and then drove back in.

There was nothing but Lo and I.

Nothing but me and the man of my dreams.

What a way to wake up every morning.

CHAPTER 7

MEG

"BABE."

I blinked rapidly.

"Meg. We need to go."

I fanned my face and prayed for my mascara to dry lightning fast. "Hold your horses. I'm almost ready."

"You planned this damn rehearsal dinner, and we're going to be late to it." Lo leaned against the bathroom door.

My eyes traveled over him, and I said a silent thank you to Ethel for creating such a fine man. "We're not going to be late. I just need to find my shoes and we can go." And also finish my eyes and find a lip gloss that wasn't gloopy.

"Really?" he chuckled. "Shoes is all you need?"

I was also standing in front of the bathroom mirror in my underwear. "And my dress." Small detail.

"I'll let Remy know we're going to be late." He pulled his phone out and typed out a message.

Lo's phone dinged almost instantly. He chuckled and shook his head.

"What did he say?" I swiped on some smoky eyeshadow then dabbed some purple to the inside corner of each eye.

"Typical."

I laughed and finished up my eyes. "He lived with me for eighteen years. He should know how I roll."

A knock sounded at the door and Lo moved to answer it. "What in the hell is Larry doing here?" he growled.

"Not a clue." I rifled through my messy makeup bag and grabbed a lip gloss.

I could hear Lo's low timber but couldn't make out what he was saying. I finished up my makeup and flipped off the bathroom light. My dress was draped over the living room couch which happened to be right where Lo was talking to Larry.

Lo mumbled his thanks and finally shut the front door.

I dashed into the living room and grabbed the white dress with large black polka dots all over it. "What did Larry want?"

Lo turned from the door and held a rectangle box in his hands. "He said this was delivered to his house Tuesday."

My eyes lit up at the sight of the box. "My shoes!"

Lo scowled. "Woman. You have plenty of shoes. What in the hell are you ordering more for?"

I dropped my dress and snatched the box out of his hand. "These are wedding shoes, Lo. I can't wear just any shoes from my closet for my only son's wedding." I walked into the kitchen and grabbed the scissors out of the drawer. I ripped open the box and held my breath. My jaw dropped at the sight of the silver 2 inch strappy heels. "They're gorgeous."

"Babe."

I looked up at Lo. "What?"

"You're standing in the kitchen with a shoe in your hand and no clothes on. Either you need to get dressed or I'm gonna fuck you on the kitchen counter."

"We literally had sex a half an hour ago." Lo had come home exactly when I had gotten out of the shower. He figured it was a perfect time to fuck me since I was naked. I didn't argue with his thinking. "Which, may I point out, is part of the reason why I'm running behind on being ready."

Lo growled and took a step toward me. "You got two minutes to get that dress on, or you're going to miss the rehearsal dinner."

"Okay, okay," I grumbled. I dropped the shoe and box on the kitchen counter and scrambled to grab my dress. "It's sexy when you go all caveman on me, but honestly tonight is not the night for that." I held the dress in front of me and stepped into it. "You think you can control yourself long enough to zip me up and not rip my dress off." I pulled the dress up, threaded my arms through the sleeves and turned my back to Lo.

He slowly pulled up the zipper and leaned close. "Four hours," he whispered.

"What?"

"You've got four hours of me controlling myself and then you're mine." He pressed a kiss to the sensitive skin behind my ear. A shiver ran up my body and leaned back into him.

"Is that a promise?"

"You know it is, babe."

I twisted around and wrapped my arms around his neck. "Then I better get my shoes on so we can get the hell out of here."

He chuckled low and pressed a kiss to me lips. "Hop to it, babe. Times running."

CHAPTER 8

LO

"How did you manage to finally get her out the door?"

I glanced at Remy. "I have my ways with your mom."

Remy cringed. "I shouldn't have asked."

I watched Meg from across the room as she threw her head back and laughed at something Harlyn had said. "You ready for tomorrow?"

Remy nodded his head. "Been ready since the day I asked Harlyn to marry me." He ran his finger around the collar of his shirt. "Asking her was more terrifying than this. Hell, getting Roc to agree to let me marry his daughter had been hell."

"But he agreed."

Remy nodded his head. "Sure fucking did. Though it was agreed upon that if I hurt Harlyn he can run me over with the race car a few times."

"So, you'll live but just a little worse for wear," I chuckled.

"More than likely dead. I've seen what one of those cars can do to a squirrel. Ain't no way that thing will run over me without ripping all of my skin off." Remy shook his head. "Low ground clearance."

"What in the hell are you talking about?" Jay, Remy's friend and best man, walked up with a heaping plate piled high.

"Roc," Remy replied simply.

Jay nodded his head. "Say no more."

Prior to eating we had ran through how tomorrow would go and then Meg had let everyone descend upon the huge buffet of food.

"You should have had Roc make his potato salad." Jay piled a forkful of corn into his mouth.

Remy shook his head. "This is mine and Harlyn's favorite foods, Jay, not yours."

"Dude," Jay mumbled around a mouthful. "That potato salad is everyone's favorite."

Remy rolled his eyes. "Just keep eating that mountain of food on your plate and stop thinking about Roc's potato salad."

"Who's talking about my potato salad?" Roc walked up with a beer in his hand.

Jay swallowed. "I was. You should have made a vat of it."

"A vat?" Roc growled. He turned to Remy. "How much has he had to drink?"

Remy shrugged. "Either none or not enough."

Roc nodded to me. "You cleaned this place up real nice, King."

I had told Roc he could call me Lo since he wasn't part of the club, but he insisted on calling me King. "Thanks."

"I still can't believe you grew up around a motorcycle club." Jay shook his head.

"I was sixteen when my mom started dating Lo, dumbass. I didn't grown up here."

"Major bummer."

Roc smacked Jay upside the head. "You're an idiot."

"Hey," Jay protested. "I'm slightly offended though I do resemble that remark."

Frankie came to stand next to Remy with her husband behind her. "Damn. Even off the track and out of the garage Roc is still smacking you."

Brooks leaned forward. "Were we the only ones who snuck into the garage and saw all the killer bikes and cars?"

Frankie elbowed him in the gut and Brooks face paled when he saw I was standing there. "Sorry Mr. King."

"Shut it," Frankie hissed.

I chuckled and nodded to the open door to the shop. "Not really sneaking when we leave the door open. Figured you guys would want to check out the garage." I knew what a gear head Remy was, and I figured his friends would be the same way.

Jay held his head above his hand and pointed to the garage. "Onward," he yelled.

Roc, Frankie, and Brooks followed and disappeared into the garage.

"You sure it's okay?" Remy asked.

I shrugged. "They probably know more about cars than I do. If they feel like tinkering with the Cutlass, I can't get the timing right on they are more than welcome to."

Remy laughed. "Leave it to Roc. He'll have it fixed by morning."

Remy took a step toward the garage and I snagged him by the arm. "One thing."

"Yeah?"

"Just..." I glanced at Meg. "Your mom was worried about you liking your dad's girlfriend. You know how she is." I knew there wasn't anything to worry about, but I wanted Remy to know that Meg was having a bit of a hard time with it.

"I know." Remy nodded his head toward his dad who was seated at one of the tables with his family. It was hard inviting the asshole into my clubhouse, but at the end of the day the guy was Remy's dad. "My dad is dealing with the same feelings since he found out I asked you to be one of my groomsmen."

"Hard pill for him to swallow?"

Remy nodded his head. "Yeah, but, you've been a part of my life for ten years. He gets it, but it's still hard for him."

"Maybe another ten years of me sticking around will help."

Remy chuckled. "I think he knows you're here to stay."

At least the guy was smart enough to realize that. "Your mom gets it too, but you know how she is. She's ruled by her emotions and forgets to take a step back sometimes before she reacts."

"She's got you, Lo." Remy clapped me on the shoulder. "I haven't worried about her for the past ten years." Remy smiled. "I'm not going to start again now." Remy headed in the direction of his friends and I sighed.

It was nice knowing I still had the kids approval after all of these years.

"There's my handsome husband." Meg was walking toward me with a huge grin on her lips.

I looked at the empty glass in her hand. "And there is my tipsy wife."

She tapped her nose. "Ding, ding, handsome. I am tipsy and extremely happy." She stood in front of me and rested her hand on my chest. "My son is marrying the perfect girl, I have my friends and family surrounding me."

I glanced over at Hunter and his family.

Meg waved her hand in their direction. "Well, not him. Though I swear his mother likes me more than she does him."

I chuckled and shook my head. "Only you could be divorced from a guy for fifteen years and still have his family like you."

She shrugged. "What can I say? I'm likeable."

I grabbed her around the waist and pulled her close. "What's say you and I sneak to my old room and I'll show you just how likeable you are."

"Has it been four hours already?" she gasped.

I pressed a kiss to her lips. "No, not even close. I guess I just can't seem to keep my hands off of you."

Meg looked around. "I suppose we could sneak off for a bit and no one will notice."

I glanced over at Hunter watching Meg and I. I moved my hand lower, over her ass, and gave her a squeeze. The asshole had never personally done anything to me, but you can bet your ass I would forever hate the douchebag for hurting Meg. Rubbing it in his face that I was the one who had ended up with the perfect woman was my small consolation to having to invite him into my clubhouse. "Think you can remember the way to my room?"

Meg laughed. She grabbed my hand and pulled me toward the hallway. "I think I can find the way."

CHAPTER 9

MEG

"They don't fit."

"Say what?"

I hopped on one foot and tried to cram the shoe on my foot. "They don't fit," I grunted.

Cyn shook her head. "Now do you understand why I was so concerned about you buying shoes off of Amazon."

I tried one last time but gave up when the circulation cut off to my pinky toe. "I'm a size ten. I ordered a size ten. I don't understand how this is not a ten." I held up the offending shoe. "This is ridiculous."

"Probably cause you ordered them from a place overseas. You know those sizes run smaller than American sizes." Gwen finished pinning Paige's hair and took a step back. "I think I have an extra pair of shoes you can wear. I'm a ten and a half but that's better than nothing, right?"

Holy crap. "Here?" I asked. Gwen was going to be lifesaver if she had a spare pair of shoes for me to wear.

The girls and I were tucked away in the back room of the clubhouse with Harlyn and Frankie. We had offered for Mave and Delaney to get dressed with us, but in the end it had been decided it would be best for Mave and Delaney to help the guys get ready.

Gwen nodded her head. "In my car. I'm notorious for wearing heels to work and halfway through my shift having to change into tennis shoes." Gwen dug through her purse and tossed her keys to Paige. "Run out to my car and see what shoes I have."

Paige rolled her eyes. "I bet you have at least ten pairs in there." She shook her head and stood up. "Any specific color you want?" Paige asked me.

"Silver or black?" Either would go with my dress. Honestly, I just needed shoes that weren't my tennis shoes.

Gwen started working on Harlyn's hair and I figured it was time for me to give her my gift.

I rummaged through my purse and pulled out a small box. I had searched high and low for the perfect gift. I had found it six months ago and then seen the price tag. I then searched high and low again and this time paid attention to prices.

"So, I really wanted to give you something that was mine, and before that my mom's, but to be honest, my mom and I really don't do that sort of thing."

Cyn snorted. "Girl, you have never said a more truer thing."

I glared at Cyn. "Zip it, woman." She was interrupting my touching spiel I had planned. "As I was saying, I wanted to get you something special." I stepped toward Harlyn and held out the box to her. "Now, they're not worth millions, but when I saw them I knew they would be perfect."

Harlyn grabbed the box and lifted off the lid. She audibly gasped and clutched her hand to her chest. "Oh my god, Meg. They're gorgeous."

"Swarovski blue pear drop earrings. They always say you need something old, something new, and something borrowed on your wedding day. I know you're wearing your mom's necklace and the hair clips in your hair are borrowed from Gwen, so it seemed fitting that I would fill in the blue void." I wanted Harlyn to know I was happy she was marrying Remy. I didn't want to be known as the evil mother-in-law or anything.

"You didn't need to do this, Meg." Harlyn gilded her finger over the large blue crystal. "These are way better than the blue underwear I was going to wear."

"Keep those. I'm sure Remy will appreciate them," Marley chuckled.

Fayth high fived Marley. "Amen to that. You know the guys are always more interested about what's beneath the dress anyway."

Harlyn put the lid back on the box and held them box to her chest. "Thank you, Meg. You didn't need to do that, but you have no idea what it means to me."

I shrugged. "Maybe you can start the tradition of giving them to your first born when they get married or something like that." It sounded lame coming out of my mouth, but I did hope Harlyn would start the tradition.

"I definitely will," she whispered. Harlyn shot up out of the chair and Gwen shouted in protest.

"What the hell, woman? I'm trying to make you pretty."

"Sorry," Harlyn laughed. "It seemed like the right time to hug my future mother in law."

Gwen threw her hands up in the air. "Well, get on with it then."

I hugged Harlyn and tried not to cry.

I tried for about five seconds before I was a blubbering idiot rambling on about having a daughter finally.

I was a nut, but I was one happy nut.

CHAPTER 10

LO

MEG WALKED WITH REMY DOWN THE AISLE WITHOUT CRYING.

She managed to only shed a few tears when he kissed Harlyn.

But when it came time for the mother/son dance, she lost it.

Remy danced slow circles with Meg while she sniffled, babbled, and stroked his cheek from time to time.

And, Remy let her.

"Hey, Lo." Turtle sat down next to me. "You're still okay with watching Jonas for us tonight?"

I nodded my head and smiled. "Sure thing, brother."

Turtle sighed. "Thank god."

I clapped him on the shoulder. "Take a deep breath. You and Mal are perfect for each other."

"I think that and so do you, but does Mal?"

"She would have left you long before now if she didn't."

"Dada!" Jonas ran across the dance flow with Mal chasing behind him. "Can we dance now?"

Jonas shouted it loud enough and just as the music faded out. Everyone laughed and Turtle scooped him up in his arms. "Yeah, twerp," Turtle laughed. "We can dance now."

The DJ announced it was time to party and the floor was swarmed with people ready to dance.

Meg fought her way through the crowd and collapsed into my lap. "I'm dying, handsome."

"No, you're beautiful, babe." I hadn't had much time with Meg alone since I had seen walk down the aisle with Remy. She may not have been in black, but she looked absolutely stunning in the dark plum dress.

She hiked up her dress and lifted her foot. "These things are what's killing me. I don't know how Gwen manages to wear them for an hour, let alone eight." She toed them off and sighed. "Freedom," she moaned. She dropped the shoes on the floor and wiggled her toes. "Torture devices," she mumbled.

She leaned back in my arms and sighed.

"Uh, I forgot to mention something to you."

"Lay it on me, handsome. I'm about to drink a six pack of wine coolers and dance my ass off. Nothing is going to phase me."

"I promised Turtle we would watch Jonas for him tonight."

Meg dropped her head back on my shoulder. "Lo," she moaned. "How am I supposed to drink a six pack of Jamaican Me Happy when I'm supposed to be an adult?"

I brushed her hair back from her face. "You don't have to worry about watching him. He'll be running around with the rest of the kids all night and crash out before you know it."

Meg rolled her eyes. "You are such a man." She sat up and turned to look down at me. "Why does Turtle need us to watch Jonas for him and Mal?"

I smiled and pointed to the side of the dance floor where Turtle and Mal were dancing with Jonas.

Meg turned and gasped when Turtle got down on one knee. She glanced back at me with tears in her eyes. "You knew this whole time he was going to ask Mal to marry him and you didn't tell me?"

I shrugged. "You had a lot of things going on. Figured you would find out about it when Mal did."

"Liar. You just didn't want me to ruin the surprise."

"That too," I drawled.

Jonas came running over with Mal and Turtle trailing behind.

"Mama Meg!" Jonas yelled. "Dada said I get to stay with you tonight!"

Meg scooped him up in her arms and hugged him close. "You do! We're gonna dance our butts off and then we're going to have a sleepover."

Jonas scrambled out of her lap and back onto the dance floor.

"Are you sure you're okay with Jonas staying with you?" Mal asked.

Meg stood up and shook out her dress. "Girl, I am more than okay with watching him. You and Turtle just got engaged!"

Mal screeched and held out her hand. A large stone gleamed on her finger and Mal's bright smile rivaled the shine of the diamond. "Finally!"

Meg and Mal hugged then gushed over the ring.

Turtle sat down next to me.

"Told you she was going to say yes. You had nothing to worry about."

Turtle nodded his head. "You always do seem to be right, brother. I guess that's why you're the president, right?"

"Been around for a while. I know the love of a good woman and I can see it when someone else has it. You've got it, Turtle. Don't let it go."

Turtle looked at Mal and smiled. "I don't plan on it."

Meg came over to hug Turtle and congratulate him. "It's about damn time," she scolded him. "Who would have thought you were going to be the last one to finally take the plunge."

"I watched all of you guys fall. Was trying to figure out the right way to do it without all the drama you guys had." Turtle reached for Mal and put his arm over her shoulders. "You guys good with us taking off now?"

I nodded my head. "All good. Meg is going to get drunk and I'll keep an eye on the kids."

Meg slapped me. "I am not going to get drunk." She turned to Mal. "Just tipsy."

Mal and Turtle managed to grab Jonas off the dance floor and give him a hug and kiss.

I pulled Meg into my arms and buried my face in her neck. "I think all of the original members of the Devil's Knights finally found their happy endings, babe."

She glanced over her shoulder at me. "You think so?"

I pressed a kiss to her lips. "I fucking hope so."

CHAPTER 11

MEG

"ALL THE KIDS ARE SLEEPING."

I lifted my head off the armrest of the couch. "It's about time. I'm way too old for kids under the age of eighteen."

Cyn cackled and patted me on the head. "You're funny. I'm the same age as you and I have a good seven years before eighteen, and I have a feeling the teen years are going to be the hardest with Micha."

"Well, I have a twenty-eight-year-old who just got married. Three is an age I can't quite keep up with anymore." I loved Jonas to death, but I was thankful we were only watching the cutie overnight. I was going to need to take a good ten hour nap to recover from the wedding and chasing after Jonas for three hours.

"We're heading home."

I peeked my head over the top of the couch and saw Gravel with his arm over Ethel's shoulders. "Did you have a good time?" I asked.

"The best," Ethel smiled. "The cake was amazing and as with any Devil's Knights party, the booze flowed like water."

That was the damn truth. "Drive safe and maybe we can meet for breakfast in the morning. We'll have Jonas with us."

"Let's plan on it." Ethel threaded her fingers through Gravel's and they strolled out the front door.

"I wanna be Ethel and Gravel when I grow up," Paige sighed. "They're so sweet together."

Suddenly I remembered what Lo had told me a couple of days ago. I jackknifed up off the couch and gasped. "Oh my god! I forgot to tell you guys. Lo totally walked in on Gravel giving it to Ethel the other day."

"No!" Cyn gasped.

Fayth, Gwen, and Paige giggled while Marley's jaw dropped. "Good god, that is awful!" She shook her head. "I do not need to think of Gravel doing... well.. Anything. As far as my mind goes him and Ethel sit at home watching *Jeopardy* and drinking tea."

"I'll take delusional for five hundred, Alex," Fayth snickered.

Marley flipped her off. "Monks. Ethel and Gravel are monks in my head."

Cyn stood up and stretched her arms over her head. "We should totally head to bed. The kids are going to be up at the butt crack of dawn even though they went to bed after their bedtime."

I made the familiar walk to Lo's room and found him already lying in bed. "Fancy meeting you here, handsome."

Lo chuckled and rested his arms behind his head. "I was wondering when you were going to come to bed."

"I was waiting to make sure none of the kids woke up." I had actually been too lazy to get my butt off the couch.

"Get ready for bed, babe. It was a long day."

I gave him a thumbs up. "Normally I'd argue with you just because I like to get you riled, but you're so right it's not even funny." I walked to the bed and turned my back to Lo. "Unzip me." My dress loosened as he slowly unzipped the zipper and it pooled at my feet.

"Babe," he growled. "Did you seriously not have underwear on all day?"

I glanced over my shoulder at him. "Maybe," I whispered coyly.

He slapped my ass. "Get ready for bed. I'm waiting." He laid back and put his hands back behind his head.

"Give me ten minutes and I'm all yours." I was tired, but I was never too tired for Lo.

I was splashing water on my face when Lo's phone rang. I grabbed the towel and patted my face. It wasn't odd for Lo's phone to ring this late, but it also wasn't normal.

"Babe," Lo called.

The tone of his voice made me freeze. Something wasn't right.

Something had happened.

I dropped the towel on the ground and dashed out of the bathroom.

Lo was pulling a shirt over his head and the lights were all on.

"What is it?" I demanded.

Lo's eyes connected with mine and every bad thing that could have happened flashed through my head.

Was it Remy? Did something happen to Ethel and Gravel?

"There was an accident."

My heart plummeted to my feet. "Who?" I whispered.

Lo's eyes dropped to the floor. "Turtle and Mal." He lifted his head. His eyes were glazed over and a lone tear streamed down his cheek. "It's bad."

THE END FOR NOW...

Connect with Winter Travers
FACEBOOK: https://www.facebook.com/wintertravers
TWITTER: https://twitter.com/wintertravers
INSTAGRAM: https://www.instagram.com/wintertraversauthor/
BOOKBUB: https://bit.ly/2HQtk7y

ACKNOWLEDGMENTS

We are so thankful for all of your help.

Thank you to the editors who looked over our work and polished it.

Thank you to Cassy Roop for the cover design.

Thank you to Golden Czermak for the image.

Thank you Jacob Wilson for this picture. I (Ryan) have wanted this photo for years and years. This was my perfect opportunity to use it. Thanks!

CPSIA information can be obtained
at www.ICGtesting.com
Printed in the USA
LVHW101100080719
623418LV00012B/1048/P

9 780998 12806